I0585800

The Tribe

Trilogy

The Tribe: A New World
The Tribe: A New Dawn
The Tribe: (R)Evolution

A. J. PENN

CUMULUS PUBLISHING LIMITED

Copyright

The Tribe Trilogy volume first published in December 2022 by
Cumulus Publishing Limited, Text Copyright © 2022 A. J. Penn

The Tribe: A New World first published in New Zealand by Cumulus
Publishing Limited 2011, Text Copyright © 2011 A. J. Penn

The Tribe: A New Dawn first published in New Zealand by Cumulus
Publishing Limited 2014, Text Copyright © 2014 A. J. Penn

The Tribe: (R)Evolution first published in New Zealand by Cumulus
Publishing Limited 2019, Text Copyright © 2019 A. J. Penn

The Tribe Copyright © 2022 Cloud 9 Screen Entertainment Group

All Rights Reserved

The moral rights of the author have been asserted

The catalogue record for this book is available from
the National Library of New Zealand

No part of this publication may be reproduced, stored in a
retrieval system, or transmitted in any form or by any means,
electronic, mechanical, photocopying, recording or otherwise, now
known or hereinafter invented, without the prior permission of the
Cloud 9 Screen Entertainment Group.

Photographs copyright and courtesy of
the Cloud 9 Screen Entertainment Group
Artwork Copyright © 2022 Cloud 9 Screen Entertainment Group
All rights reserved

ISBN: 978-1-9911936-0-5 (paperback)
ISBN: 978-1-9911936-1-2 (Epub)
ISBN: 978-1-9911936-2-9 (Kindle)
ISBN: 978-1-9911936-3-6 (Apple Books)

Visit The Tribe's website at www.tribeworld.com

Contact addresses for Cumulus Publishing Limited
and companies within the Cloud 9 Screen Entertainment group
can be found at www.entercloud9.com

Contents

A.J. PENN

A New World

THE TRIBE

The long awaited story in the continuing saga of The Tribe

Dedication

This is dedicated to you, the reader.
And to the spirit of the Mall Rats
and all those who share it.

PREFACE

Amber walked graciously down the aisle. Bray spellbound, focused on her. She looked beautiful. The crisp white wedding dress reflecting the sun that shone through the stained glass windows of the tiny church.

For a moment Bray almost forgot that there were other people gathered for the wedding. So intent had he been on his bride to be.

Sitting on either side of the aisles that Amber passed, were faces Bray knew all too well. His grandparents. His uncles and aunts. Family members. Many from other parts of the world, who had come to witness this special day.

But most important of all, Bray exchanged a look with his parents, his father nodding in understanding and support. They looked so well. Healthy again. Bray's mother dabbed a tissue to one eye, emotional and proud of the day their elder son was going to marry, setting off on a new chapter in his life.

"Nervous?" Martin whispered in Bray's ear.

Bray turned to his younger brother, looking immaculate in a black tuxedo.

"Martin! What are you doing here?!"

"I'm your best man - remember?"

"No!" Bray responded.

"Oh, yes! Brother!" Martin smiled coldly, fixing Bray's tie, adjusting it to perfection, a trace of venom in the tone of his voice.

Stunned as he was to see Martin, Bray's attention once more fell on his bride, as Martin indicated Amber approaching the altar, ever closer.

With each step she took, Bray's heart almost faltered. He was overcome by it all. His love for Amber, the monumental day of the wedding - and the fact that so many dearly loved ones, Martin included, were somehow there to experience it with him.

Behind Amber, her two bridesmaids followed, holding the long trail of the wedding gown in their hands. Their faces beaming bright smiles of their own, Patsy and Cloe were thrilled to be involved in the special day of Amber and Bray's betrothal.

And then she was beside him. Amber looked up to Bray as he lifted the thin veil off her face so she could see into the eyes of her husband to be. The delight on her expression was clear for all to see.

It was her smile which had always captivated Bray. With that one longing look she gave him, her eyes locked on his own, her expression one of contentment, peace, togetherness. If he could freeze a moment in time forever, this would be it. Her gaze, her smile spoke volumes about the love she felt for him, reassuring him that they would always be together. No matter what happened in this God forsaken world. Everything would always be alright.

"This is a day that will be long remembered," Tai San spoke up loudly to the assembly.

Bray stared absently at Tai San. Amazed also to see her there. Presiding over the ceremony. But there she was, like his brother Martin, his parents, the dearly loved friends and family who were all there around him. She was very much real. Wasn't she? Or had Bray's memory betrayed him? Was he losing his mind? He certainly began to doubt his senses. He thought so many of the people had perished. Yes, died. Was he now in Heaven?

"It's okay," Amber whispered softly, clutching Bray's hands in reassurance.

Feeling a little more at peace, Bray focused again on Amber, putting his faith in her. Like he had always done before.

"We are gathered here today for the union of Amber and Bray," Tai San continued. "Two spirits. Drawn together. Destined to be united for all eternity."

Bray cast another glance at Tai San. Beneath her smile, he noticed her eyes seemed to be cold, vacant.

"Amber - do you take Bray to be your husband?" Tai San asked.

"I do," Amber said, gazing once more longingly at Bray.

"And Bray - do you take Amber to be your loving wife?"

Amber waited for Bray's answer, the words she was obviously so desperate to hear, yearning in her heart, from the very depths of her soul.

The doubt about what was really happening resurfaced in Bray's mind. He had spotted Dal, sitting in the audience. Amber's best friend from the days before the adults were wiped off the face of the Earth. Dal, too, had met an untimely end. What was he doing - at the wedding?

"Are you alright, brother?" Martin asked quietly, so the assembled crowd could not hear.

"Do you take Amber to be your wife?" Tai San repeated once more in a monotone, her voice almost robotic. Certainly not the spiritual and emotional Tai San that Bray had known from his past.

"Answer her, Bray!" Martin shouted out, seizing Bray by the arm.

Squirming to get out of Martin's iron grasp, Bray was horrified by the realization that Martin was no longer wearing the immaculate tuxedo as before - but had turned into the visage of Zoot, complete with the leather jacket, goggles resting on his black cap, his hair long and scruffy, his eyes burning in manic intensity.

"Do you, or don't you take Amber to be your lawful and loving wife?" Tai San asked again, an element of impatience and threat in the tone.

"Let me go!" Bray shrieked out, desperate to escape from the hold of his younger yet powerful brother. Zoot clung tightly, his firm grasp restricting Bray, struggling to get away.

"You're not leaving! You're staying put - brother!" Zoot yelled contemptuously.

"Well?!" Tai San probed, trying to contain her anger.

"Do it!" Zoot shouted.

Were they going to forcibly put a wedding ring on Bray's finger?

Unable to free himself, Bray was powerless, looking on at Amber, Tai San, the assembled loved ones who gazed impassively from the aisles, ignoring his pleas for help, assistance.

Amber reached into her wedding gown - and rather than presenting a ring, she now held a long medical syringe in her hand.

"Oh, I do. I do, I do, I do," Amber repeated, carefully moving the syringe into position above Bray's arm. "Till death do us part!"

"Power and Chaos!" Zoot roared, urging Amber on, a look of complete madness in his darting eyes, fierce with energy.

"Amber - no!" Bray shouted out.

But it was no use. Amber suddenly plunged the needle into Bray's outstretched arm, Bray yelling out in intense pain as the syringe penetrated deeply into his vein.

"Please help me!! Amber!!!" Bray cried out, desperate.

Calmly, Amber pulled back the top of the syringe, the needle gradually drawing up blood.

Terrified at what he was experiencing, Bray felt his heart racing, and he was overwhelmed with nausea at seeing Amber taking the blood sample from his arm, examining it coldly as the syringe filled up.

"Amber!" Bray called out, trying to make contact, get through to her.

It was hopeless. Amber ignored his pleas, focusing on the syringe.

"Martin, help me!" Bray begged, looking now to his brother, to see if he would help get Bray out of this nightmare.

But Zoot still held onto Bray tightly, refusing to yield.

"Keep going," Zoot insisted to Amber, more blood being taken out of Bray's arm, entering into the syringe.

"Why?" Bray cried out, tears welling up in his eyes at the cold, calculating nature of it all. The unwillingness of anyone to come to his aid, the brutality being bestowed upon him by those he cared about the most, his friends and family, Amber, his loved ones who didn't feel the same way about him, tearing him apart.

Bray was feeling faint, increasingly light headed. Yet he fought to keep consciousness. To listen to his brother's explanation for the macabre turn of events.

"You are me, Bray," Zoot went on. "And I am you. We are one!"

"His pulse rate is high," Judd spoke calmly. But from his tone it was clear he was concerned at the health of his patient.

Bray was laying on an operating theatre table, a reality space visor attached to his face.

Though he was strapped down, his body convulsed, shaking, the nerve impulses causing his fingers to twitch rapidly, his head thrown from side to side by invisible forces. He was attached to a bank of monitors displaying his vital signs, pulse rate, temperature, blood pressure.

Two girls stood nearby wearing reality space visors, the shorter of the two holding a long medical syringe in her hands, removing more blood from Bray's arm.

"It's getting dangerous!" Judd insisted. Dressed in white, Judd was like some mad scientist, his eyes now gazing at the complex instrumentation all around him as he stepped away from Bray, examining the equipment readings.

"That's enough. For now," the taller of the girls, Eloise, agreed, reluctant to end proceedings but submitting to the advice of Judd.

Removing the reality space visor from her face, Eloise shook her head, readjusting to being back in reality. Her cold blue eyes surveyed Bray. That had been an intense session. They had really gotten through to Bray that time. Pleased with her efforts, Eloise smiled, stroking Bray's hair reverently.

Taking the reality space visor off her own head, the shorter girl holding the syringe filled with blood, carefully passed it to Eloise, bowing in respect to her leader - and to the deep red contents of the syringe.

Judd began to unfasten Bray's own reality space visor, Bray murmuring in pain and confusion.

"Brothers and sisters!" Eloise called out suddenly to the viewing gallery.

The operating table on which Bray lay was in the middle of a surgery theatre, bright lights shining down in the centre, illuminating the patient for all to see.

In the gallery - which was more like a sealed chamber divided by glass - there were about twenty observers, most about the same age as Bray. They had one thing in common, however, that united them. Every single one of them wore Zoot style hats, complete with goggles. And they gazed at Eloise in excitement, an air of collective tension and anticipation as Eloise held the syringe in her hand up to the light.

"The blood of Bray. And of Zoot!" Eloise uttered in awe, as if she was holding an artefact of immense value.

Judd had unfastened Bray now from the bed. Bray was barely conscious.

With the shorter girl assisting, the two of them supported Bray, his arms draped over their shoulders, and they began to drag him away towards the exit doors.

"Martin... Amber..." Bray quietly murmured in distress to himself, ravaged, tears streaming down his face.

Eloise turned from Bray to face the gallery of observers.

"We have communed with the Mighty One," she said. "Visited his realm, the plane of other existence."

"Zoot will lead us, we will obey," the gallery chanted in unison, in reply.

Eloise emptied the blood into a glass vial, which she held up for all to see.

"The blood of the brother. The blood of Zoot!" Eloise intoned, staring at the vial with fascination, her blue eyes intense.

"We are of one blood. We are one with Zoot," the gallery chanted in unison, in response. All were now staring in reverence.

"He will lead - and we will follow!" Eloise shrieked.

Approaching the exit door, Bray was drifting in and out of consciousness. His body was weak, his spirits low, his mind confused, all a scramble.

Repelled by the bizarre goings on, Bray just about had the energy to turn his head to one side to look behind him.

To his horror, he saw Eloise sip from the vial, blood overspilling around her lips.

The gallery erupted into loud, rhythmical chants which resonated in the medical theatre, as if shaking the very foundations of the building itself.

The last thing Bray was aware of was the continuing chanting of his brother's name from the gallery before he lost consciousness...

"Zoot! Zoot!! Zoot!!!!"

On the opposite side of the gallery in a private viewing platform, a figure stood in the shadows surrounded by his fellow council members.

They were all wearing blue flowing robes.

One, The Guardian, gazed intently at the proceedings. And slowly broke out into a manic smile.

CHAPTER ONE

The little trawler pitched up and down as the ocean waves carried it ever onwards. But to where, Amber wondered, the spray from the side of the boat drifting into her face.

She was standing at the stern, staring out to the endless horizon of water surrounding them in all directions. She had always loved the sea. Her Dad had taken her to the beach many times when she was a little girl, and she had an appreciation of the beauty of nature, a respect for its awesome power. Nature had a way of putting things in perspective.

If this was any other occasion, Amber would have been soaking up the experience, enjoying every moment of it. The sound of the waves. The sun beaming down, bathing her in its warmth. The ocean, Amber reflected, wouldn't have changed for thousands of years. Despite the loss of the old world, the demise of the adults, this was one constant. And Amber took comfort from that. From the notion that there was one thing unchanging in this completely changed world.

Amber's thoughts turned to the plight she and the others now found themselves in. She needed some time away from them. A moment alone to consider everything that had happened since they fled the city that had been their salvation.

How many days had they been at sea? And where were they, Amber wondered. It must have been several weeks, with land now being a distant memory. Jack had tried to keep track of the number of days of their voyage but as time passed, gave up.

Their close confines had led to frayed nerves. Nineteen of them, cramped together in a little fishing trawler designed for a crew of eight.

Amber knew the situation was dire but she and Jay tried to keep everyone else's spirits up. Which was easier said than done. A feeling of unease had taken over the vessel. Of pointlessness. Despair. Arguments erupted over the most petty issues. Everyone got on each other's nerves. With all the bickering, it hadn't been easy for Jack to concentrate and despite his best efforts, he hadn't made any progress in trying to work out exactly where they might be.

The original plan was to head for the outer islands in Zone 4, which they calculated would be about a thousand miles from their previous home in the city. Jack had charted a guideline course. Even at three miles per hour then they should have hopefully approached land within ten to fifteen days.

But now their very survival was at stake. How ironic. To be on a fishing boat, but to have no fish, and hardly any food. The trawler had long ago been looted of nets. And other equipment. Salene, Jack and Ram had tried to fashion together makeshift fishing lines but with no bait, there hadn't been any bites so far.

The only food they had was that stored on the boat by Zak, the trader who the boat belonged to back in the city. Zak had been one of May's contacts. Someone she could go to if she needed any kind of supplies. And it was thanks to Zak's boat that Amber and the others had a means to embark upon their voyage.

The key to the food locker had been given to Amber, voted the leader - or the 'Captain' of the vessel by the others, and she had been carefully rationing the small amounts of food and stored bottled water accumulated by Zak. But supplies were running dangerously low.

Jack had tried to fix the fresh water issue by rigging together a rain water collection device using a tatty plastic tarpaulin. But he had been unable to test the ability of his invention to collect water since it hadn't rained.

Water, water, everywhere - and not a drop to drink. Amber recalled the line from Coleridge's famous poem about a doomed ship, shaking her head at how cruel fate could be, putting them in such a predicament.

Their physical health was further endangered because the one toilet the boat had was blocked and no longer working. A terrible noxious odour had begun to fill the air in the cramped cabins below. Most of the Tribe had started to sleep on the outer decks.

The issue of where they were going had caused many a fierce argument. When they had first escaped, Ram wanted to head out to open sea to get away from the pandemic which they thought had infected the city. To sit it out. But Amber and the others knew that their only hope for survival was to try and settle in a new land.

A couple of days into the voyage, it became apparent that Zak wouldn't be any help to them in practical terms of navigating. He had admitted, bashfully, that he knew nothing about the ocean or how to sail. It wasn't even his boat originally. As always, Zak had an ability of 'acquiring' things. Items, even people. It was only by a miracle that there had been a small amount of fuel in the engines, that it hadn't been siphoned off by the Locos or some other tribe in the city. Zak was a trader, not a sailor, and though the boat had been his home, he wouldn't be of any use in the Mall Rats finding their way.

Ram gloated at this. Sure his plan had been the better. If they had anchored a safe distance off shore, then they could have assessed matters. Perhaps even explored the land along the coast. He had explained his worry that out in the ocean, they could get caught in currents and end up lost.

The others agreed with Amber that staying in the region was tantamount to committing suicide.

Besides, she didn't quite trust Ram. And was never too sure exactly where he was coming from.

Some in the party - especially Lex - blamed Ram in the first place. Had he not devised the computer program which had connected to Mega's chemical arsenal, then the Mall Rat tribe - along with other tribes in the area - had a chance, however slim, of building a new world.

Now they had no choice but to look for somewhere else to settle.

As it became apparent that the little boat was lost, Ram had been all too eager to say "I told you so" and had rubbed up the others, irritating them deliberately. And clearly hoped he could persuade them to return. Without a compass, no GPS, nobody able to navigate by the stars (though Jack was trying to teach himself how)... they were directionless, drifting. The only question was - to where?

Amber's mantra had been to keep heading north. Her resolution was that they use the sun as it rose each day as their compass. It's how Amber had learned to keep her bearings when she was in the Eco-Tribe, living in the forest, gauging where east or west was to identify the time of day, reliant on the position of the sun.

The helm still worked. So they were able to at least steer the boat. Jack had thought it wise to preserve what little fuel they had. Amber agreed, the power to the engines had been cut a few days out into their voyage.

The others looked to her as a leader because so often she had the right idea at the right time, a solution for every problem that confronted them in this world of no adults. But now, Amber realized that she had no solution. She was as scared as everyone else. Here they were, stuck in the middle of nowhere, supplies and morale running out. But they had no choice. And she was determined that they would survive. Somehow. Somewhere.

"Amber?" Jay asked, wrapping an arm lovingly around Amber's shoulders, having just emerged from the cabin to the outer deck at the back of the trawler. "Are you okay?"

"Yeah, I'm fine. I just needed a bit of space."

"Whatever happens, we will get through all this. I promise," Jay encouraged her, giving her a tender kiss on the side of her face.

But he sounded more convinced than he looked. The two of them stood hugging for a moment, staring out at the endless expanse of ocean all around, confronting it, as if they would never back down from any challenge it presented.

* * *

At the bow of the boat, May patted Zak's back. He was leaning over the side of the trawler, coughing and spluttering, throwing up into the sea. Again. And again. He had been ill for days now.

"That's it, get it all out," May encouraged, trying to help Zak, though being in such close proximity to someone vomiting was hugely unpleasant to her, her face scrunched up in disgust at the awful smell and heaving sounds coming from Zak.

May had known Zak back in the city and respected him for his survivor skills. He was a rogue. From the streets. Like she was in many ways. A resourceful and persuasive type who somehow was able to make deals with others and come up with food, batteries or other worthwhile items. He was a tough negotiator. And might sell his soul if he could benefit. But May liked him. She couldn't help herself. Except for Pride, she had always been attracted to guys who weren't exactly squeaky clean. And she knew that somewhere within Zak's flawed psyche, he wasn't devoid of any feelings. He clearly liked her.

"Has he got the virus?" Gel shouted loudly, staring at Zak and May from within the front of the cabin interior.

"He better not, or else he's outta here," Lex threatened, trying to ignore the proximity of Zak and his seasickness.

Gel was sitting on the sculpted carbon fibre interior bench with Lex laying down, his head resting on Gel's lap as a makeshift pillow.

"I guess the good thing about not eating is you get to lose weight," Gel said out of the blue, prompted by the rumbling of her stomach. She, like the rest of them, was always hungry, trying to get by on the small amount rationed by Amber. "At least I've got a slimmer figure," she added, glancing down in admiration of her more slender than ever frame.

"Yeah, well the bad thing about not eating - is you die," Lex scoffed.

Sammy, along with the others, also watched May try and comfort Zak.

It made Sammy heave. And he threw up all over the floor.

"Man - that's gross!" Darryl said, looking as if he might also vomit. "If you're going be sick, get out there with them. Don't do it in here!"

Trudy stared intently at the pool of sickness, spreading across the deck. And suddenly lunged, scooping some up, forcing it inside her own mouth, savouring the taste as if it was a welcome feast.

Ram blurted out in uncontrollable laughter. While the others stared in a mixture of disbelief and disgust.

"What the hell are you doing!?" Lex asked.

"Trying to survive. And I don't care how I do it. This is mine! All of it! I saw it first," Trudy spluttered, mouth full, the vomit overspilling from her mouth and drooling across her face. She forced it back in, licking her fingers.

"You're welcome to it," Lex said, gazing at Zak, who was vomiting again. "Hey - save some of that for Trudy! She's hungry."

"Shove it!" May yelled.

"No, you shove it!" Ram shouted impatiently to May. "Why don't you tell your loverboy that if he owns technology... even a boat... he should have at least figured out how to use it!"

"Cut it out, Ram," May countered. "If it wasn't for Zak and his boat, where would we be right now?"

"Anywhere would be better than being stuck here. On a boat full of idiots," Ram sighed to himself.

"That can be solved easily, Ram," Lex replied. "If we throw you overboard, then at least there'd be one less mouth to feed."

Ram considered Lex, realizing he was quite capable of carrying out the threat.

"If you're bored, Ram," May admonished him, "go and troll somewhere else. I'm sure the sharks would appreciate you annoying them!"

"Ram winding people up? Well there's a surprise," Jay joked, trying to lift everyone's spirits as he moved inside through the cabin, with Amber beside him.

She glanced at Trudy, now licking the floor.

"Trudy - what on earth are you doing?"

"Having some 'seconds'. Of vomit," Gel said, disgustedly.

Amber helped Trudy up and sat her back on the bench.

"I know how you must feel, Trudy. But that's not the way. Come on, now. Everything's gonna be alright. There'll be enough food and water for everyone. As long as we keep rationing it."

"If not... we'll just have to look for other 'things' on the menu," Lex suggested, casting a threatening glance at Ram, who ignored it, but felt deep within that he wouldn't put it past Lex to resort to cannibalism.

With dry lips, a thumping headache, but an iron will not to give up, Amber had called the Tribe for a meeting. Every few days the group met to go over their plight, see if anyone had any ideas to improve their situation. Amber was above all concerned that with Ram's dissent she could have a mutiny on her hands. She wanted to keep everyone focused. And calm. Especially Trudy. She was never the type that needed much encouragement to panic, with her histrionics.

Sammy was asked to join Lottie, who had already taken Trudy's daughter, Brady, and Amber's baby to the cabin below so the rest of the Tribe could meet, despite his protestations at being a baby sitter.

"Sorry I'm late," Ebony said, reaching the top of the stairs leading into the main cabin area. She was followed by Slade. There was a cool and tense air between them.

"Make yourself - comfortable," Jack said, a hint of humour in his voice. They were all so cramped, squished together in the cabin that there was little room for them all.

"Mind if I sit here?" Ebony asked Slade, settling next to him.

"Do what you want. What do I care," Slade replied coldly.

The others could see that their relationship was still strained and that they must have been arguing.

The meeting went ahead. And once again, Ram stated strongly that they should turn the boat around and head back in the direction they had come from, intent as ever to return to their old home in the city.

Ram was outvoted. The overwhelming majority chose to keep following Amber's recommendation, sure they were bound to reach land eventually.

"We might be dead by then," Ram cautioned.

"You have such a way with words," Salene admonished him, while discretely indicating Trudy, who was staring vacantly into the distance, tears welling up in her eyes.

"I don't feel so good," she said, her voice a fragile, hoarse whisper.

Salene sat beside her, trying to provide some emotional support. Trudy had been on a rollercoaster ride of emotions of late. Amber and the others were always aware of her vulnerable state and moodswings, even at the best of times. Amber suspected that she probably suffered from clinical depression. She had been through so many traumatic experiences in her young life. And always found it difficult to cope.

"She needs a drink," Ellie suggested.

"We all need a drink," Lex said. "I could sure do with a shot of Jack Daniels."

"Same here, Lexy-boy," Ram quipped, eager to ingratiate himself to Lex. "And Trudy here looks like she needs - a psychiatrist."

"That's enough, Ram," said Amber, steeping forward, offering Trudy Amber's meagre water ration.

Salene held the bottle to Trudy's lips but Trudy didn't seem to notice it there. She was lost as if in a vision, in another world. Her eyes transfixed.

"What's up with her?" Gel asked no one in particular as Trudy suddenly began to sob uncontrollably, her shoulders heaving.

"We should get her downstairs," Amber said, concerned for Trudy's wellbeing, thinking she might feel better if she rested for a while.

Salene tried to encourage Trudy to stand up, Ellie going to the other side of Trudy to support her.

"Get your hands off me!" Trudy wailed hysterically.

"Trudy, it's gonna be okay," Salene whispered.

"Come on, Trudy. Try and keep it together," Amber said. "Everything's going to be fine."

"No. It's not! You know it. And I know it!" Trudy screamed. "We are doomed! All of us! We're all going to die!"

CHAPTER TWO

His eyes closed tightly, Bray imagined himself in another place. A different time. It was the only refuge he had right now, his imagination. The only way he could escape from the predicament he had ended up in.

His thoughts drifted back to Amber. To their life together back in the city. He loved her with every fibre of his being and the pain of their separation ached deeply to his very core. He could picture her, looking back at him with love in her eyes. She was the kindest, most gentle, sincere person he had ever met. He thought they were destined to be together, starcrossed lovers in a fairy tale ending, living happy ever after.

Yet were those many precious memories of Amber - themselves real? Had his life of the past with her even happened at all? Or was it all some part of a virtual reality program? Was he even sitting, in solitary confinement in his cell, like he perceived he was?

Bray had been subjected to so many simulations that he was beginning to doubt his own mind, losing sight of what was real and what was illusion.

He was even in danger of losing himself, his sense of self-identity, his very being. All the barrage of information he had suffered, the sensory stimulation, the virtual worlds he had been trapped in, the experiments he had endured. It was now taking its toll. He felt as if his spirit had been drained. And that he wouldn't be able to keep going on for much longer.

But he had to try. What little dignity and essence he still had, Bray now consciously clung on to. He wouldn't give in, or give up. Somehow, if he could only find the time to think, separating the real from the illusionary, he hoped he could discover some way of getting through this living nightmare that fate had thrust upon him.

So immersed in his thoughts, Bray didn't notice the guards entering his cell, the iron door creaking with rust as it was unlocked, swung open.

They surveyed their prisoner. Bray lay on the ground, covered in dirt, his brown hair matted in mud. He hadn't been washed for some time.

One of the guards tried to suppress the body stench as he carefully approached, placing a tray on the ground beside the prisoner.

"Breakfast," the guard whispered caustically, staring at Bray with contempt.

Bray snapped out of his reverie and returned to the stark realization of the hell he was in. He looked at the 'breakfast' plate. A bowl of cold gruel, flies crawling and buzzing on the foul rotting food.

Bray met the guard's stare with his own, his eyes full of resistance.

"Eat!" the guard ordered, keen to watch Bray consume the disgusting meal.

"I'm not hungry," Bray lied. He was starving. But he realized this was almost a power struggle between him and his captors and he was determined to not give his jailors any satisfaction.

Suddenly the guard lifted the bowl and rubbed Bray's face in the contents. Bray struggled to resist but with his feet and hands bound, there was little he could do. He found himself choking, inadvertently inhaling the oats, the flies up into his nostrils and mouth.

"That's enough!" barked the all too familiar voice as a tall girl entered the cell, the guards bowing their heads in respect. She was about the same age as Bray. And he recognized the voice. It had haunted him since the first time he had arrived at the compound. Now he felt an involuntary shudder as she strode purposefully towards him, her piercing blue eyes studying him.

Tall, with flowing black hair down over her shoulders, Eloise was an imposing sight, a commanding figure who exuded natural authority and charisma. Her black uniform clung to her body and she swayed seductively while surveying her most important prisoner, the burly guard nearby stepping away to allow her some space. She was aware of her good looks and in a camp full of many male guards as well as prisoners, she was always happy to use her natural attributes to get her way. But being firmly in control of the compound, didn't need to rely on anything other than her status. And power.

"Leave us!" Eloise ordered the guards.

Nodding in deference to his leader, the huge jailor ushered his fellow guards out of the cell, the thick iron door shutting behind them.

Every day was full of many ordeals, Bray wondered what had been planned for him this time.

Eloise smiled, her impeccable white teeth leering as she leaned over him and began to stroke his hair gently, wiping flecks of spilt oats away, scoffing her displeasure at seeing Bray this way.

"How are you feeling?" she asked out of care, but Bray picked up her tone was obviously not as sincere or genuine as she was making out.

"What do you think?" Bray spat out an oat of gruel which landed on Eloise's shoulder.

Casually, Eloise brushed off the gruel. "I think you are a stubborn human being. But you will learn - that you are not as stubborn as I. So why don't you and I become allies? We could do great things together," she pouted seductively.

Bray stared back at her. Eloise was clearly an intelligent individual who took delight in mindgames, Bray reasoned. But he wasn't about to play. Not now. Not ever. He wasn't about to give in.

"Come on," Eloise encouraged, casting a coy glance at Bray, playing the temptress. "Give a girl a break. Surely I'm not that bad in your eyes? You must find me... even a little bit attractive?"

Bray appreciated Eloise's obvious external beauty, her blue eyes staring into his own. She was certainly attractive. Yet he was repulsed by her. Who she was as a person. He fully knew she was in charge of his imprisonment and would have been the one to order the guards to act so mercilessly, let alone subjecting him to so many reality space experiments.

"Leave me alone," Bray demanded.

"My dear Bray, surely you don't mean that," Eloise said in mock-hurt at his words. "I mean, look at you and me here. Together. We're one with Zoot. Aren't we?"

"What do you want with me?" Bray snapped, angered at the mention of Zoot. He never agreed with the path of his brother. But still felt outraged by anyone manipulating Zoot's name and reputation, distorting his brother's life and legacy.

"I want you. For one night. That's all. You and I to spend one night together," Eloise smiled disarmingly.

"You're crazy!" Bray scoffed.

"Crazy for you, you mean. Praise Zoot!" Eloise added, playfully mentioning Zoot's name once more.

"I'd rather die! Than spend one night with you, Eloise!"

"Both can be arranged," Eloise cautioned. "If you're nice to me, I can be nice to you. But if not..."

Out of nowhere, Eloise slapped Bray hard, in the face.

"You think I really care about you? Or your stupid brother, Zoot? The 'Zootists'? Any of that? If so, you're very much mistaken. You're nothing more than a very valuable commodity, Bray. Worth more to me alive than dead. As long as you father a child. My child, that is. Either willingly. Or maybe... in our next trip into reality space!"

"You're mad!" Bray protested.

Eloise seized Bray by his jaw, pressing down on both sides of his face with her hands, digging her nails into his cheeks, her blue eyes intense, inches away from Bray's face.

"One night, Bray. And one child, that's all. Don't let down all those who put their faith in 'Zoot'. Let's give them something real to worship! My baby... Our child!"

And with that, Eloise kissed Bray passionately, Bray squirming to avoid her but unable due to being tied down.

"Think about THAT," Eloise said, pulling herself away from Bray and scrambling to her feet.

Snapping her fingers to her guards, the iron door creaked open and Bray braced himself as the guards entered.

"I'm patient but you don't have forever, Bray!" Eloise said.

Spinning on her heel, Eloise headed out of the cell, a guard closing the door behind her.

"Show him what happens. When I run out of patience," she called back to the guards who remained in the cell.

Defiant to the last, Bray gritted his teeth as the guards descended on him quickly, their fists flailing.

CHAPTER THREE

Despite thinking the situation couldn't get any worse, Amber realized that they were now moving into a more difficult state than before.

That morning, the last of the food supplies had run out. Amber carefully rationing a small tin of rice pudding, giving most of the share to the youngest, Brady and baby Bray. She had done her best to stretch the rations as far as she could during their voyage but there were too many mouths to feed, not enough food - and now, there was no food.

The final bottles of drinking water had also been used up first thing that day but thankfully the boat had passed through a rain squall during the night. Jack's improvised water collection had done its job well, a little pool from the rain being held in the tarpaulin, which Jack was trying to carefully drip feed into the empty bottles.

Amber's lips were sore. They kept cracking open, resulting in a number of little cuts which bled from time to time. Her physical condition was deteriorating, as it was with the others, and she wondered if they had the onset of scurvy or God knows, what other kind of illnesses. This is how sailors in the old days must have felt, Amber considered. She had studied elements of the European voyages of 'discovery' at school in history and in a way felt an affinity with the explorers, a connection. After all, she too was on her own epic adventure. Except at least the sailors knew what they were doing, whereas Amber and her Tribe had limited nautical skills. And now were hopelessly lost. Running out of hope.

Baby Bray was fast asleep in Amber's arms. She cradled him protectively and tried to keep calm. She knew that panic was the last thing they needed right now. But it was hard to keep a level head with the constant tension in the air and anxiety of all the others. The stress of their dire situation was getting to everybody.

Amber focused on her baby. He was so beautiful. Pure and innocent. But hungry. And without any more food... Amber dreaded to think.

Most of the Tribe sat on the outer decks. It had been too hot and humid to be down below lately. There was no air circulation and it was more comfortable, relatively speaking.

Various people reacted in different ways to the situation. Their only routine was that they had no routine. Each day was just like the day before. With the boat drifting. A collective delirium was almost setting in. Some were bored, others tried to find ways to pass the time. But all were worried about what the future lay in store for them.

"I spy with my little eye - something beginning with S," Gel said to Lottie and Sammy playfully, for the umpteenth time.

"Sea," Lottie blurted out unenthusiastically.

"You could at least try to enjoy it," Gel complained.

"I spy something beginning with I - Idiot," Ram scoffed disdainfully at Gel, as he paced back and forth.

Lex immediately sprang to his feet, pinning Ram by the throat to the wall.

"And I spy something beginning with L. Loser about to go overboard!" Lex glared menacingly.

"Let him go, Lex," Amber demanded, crossing to them. "Come on. Let's not make matters worse."

Slade and Jay moved to Ram and Lex, separating them.

"Back off, Lex. Now's not the time," Jay said.

Lex released his grip but glared as Jay and Slade led Ram away.

"Just don't turn your back on me, pal. I mean it," Lex threatened. "You're not even a Mall Rat. And after all you've done in the past - you have no right to even speak!"

"We're all in the same boat now though, Lex," Salene said gently. "And we've got to look out for each other."

"Or how about we all leap over the side? End it now!" Trudy suggested.

"Don't give up hope, Trudy," Amber said encouragingly, while casting a knowing glance at Salene.

Amber had mentioned earlier to all of them that they especially needed to keep an eye on Trudy. If she lost hope, then with her precarious state of mind, who knows what would happen. She might try and harm herself. Amber hoped that her suspicions would prove to be inaccurate. But deep down thought it was wise to implement a suicide watch.

At the bow, May and Zak sat next to each other, talking. Holding hands. They had been chatting the whole morning. For all that they had known each other back in the city - they were bonding more throughout the voyage.

May had never been lucky in love. Those she had lost her heart to before had either fallen for someone else, like Pride with Salene, or something had gotten in the way of May having a close relationship. Maybe this time it could be different? If they all survived, of course.

On the upper deck, Ebony had been trying to find some shade and get some fresh air. She stared at Ruby and Slade nearby, who were themselves engrossed in conversation, reminiscing about people and adventures shared in the past in the town of Liberty, where both had spent some considerable time.

Earlier that day, Ebony had tried to make up with Slade again after their previous arguments. Slade wouldn't accept Ebony's apologies, however, instead wanting her to stay away from him. As far as possible within the limited confines of the tiny trawler.

He couldn't forgive the things she had said about his brother, Mega, the insensitivity she had displayed at his death. Yes, it was true that Mega had been responsible for many terrible things as a leading member of The Techno tribe and was instrumental in releasing the 'virus' causing them to flee the city. Slade was still trying to come to terms with it all and had difficulty reconciling Mega's actions with the emotional sense of loss he felt as a result of his brother's death.

But what really got to Slade was the fact that Ebony seemed to have selective moral standards. She was the last person to criticize anyone. He was sure that she was no angel, being a past leader of the Loco tribe. And her hypocrisy repulsed Slade. He needed time to go over it all in his mind. But primarily, space away from Ebony.

In her mind, it seemed like Slade was spending too much time with Ruby, rather than time alone mourning his brother and thinking over things. Including their fractured relationship. Maybe she was being paranoid though and wondered if Ruby and Slade were just idly talking? Or was he deliberately being with Ruby - in front of Ebony - to teach her some kind of a lesson? Make a point?

Whatever was going on, Ebony felt pangs of bitter jealousy. She was angry at Slade and resentful toward Ruby. Ruby was a survivor who made the most of her opportunities. Ebony didn't trust her. Her mind calculating, Ebony wondered the best way how to win back her man.

After the altercation between Lex and Ram, Salene moved along the deck to dangle an improvised fishing line in the water. Her Dad had taken her fishing many times as a young girl but so far she had caught nothing. It was almost as if the ocean was empty of fish.

"You really think you're going to catch something?" Darryl asked as he sat beside Salene, looking out over the side of the boat.

"If I don't try, I'll never know - will I?" Salene responded, concentrating on the fishing line. A little piece of dried rice pudding had been tied to the other end of the line. Salene hoped something would take a bite, though the notion of a fish eating rice pudding was quite ludicrous to her. What would her Dad have thought of using that as bait?

Darryl inched closer to Salene and smiled suavely.

"There's plenty of fish in the sea."

"What's that supposed to mean?" Salene asked but suspected Darryl wasn't just interested in her fishing.

"Oh, you know. I'm single. You're single. Everyone else round here pretty much are couples. There's Jack and Ellie. Amber and Jay. Ruby - or Ebony - and Slade. May and Zak seem to be getting on okay. Gel thinks she and Lex are an item. And, well, it's just a pity to be alone. I dunno. How about you and I...?"

Salene, flustered, unsure how to respond, sighed.

"That's lovely, Darryl. And you're sweet..."

"So are you," Darryl quickly beamed.

"But the answer's no. No offence. But... it's not the time for this. And you're not my type."

"Oh, come on. A good looking girl like you. A good looking guy like me," Darryl insisted.

"Right now, I would rather kiss a good looking fish. I'm sorry but no, Darryl!"

The line tugged in her hand. "I've got one! I've got one!"

Suddenly she stumbled as the trawler engines roared into life and the little boat arched dangerously, spinning about 180 degrees.

"What the hell?" Jay shouted, trying to steady himself along with Amber, nearby.

"Where's Ram?" she snapped, realizing Ram was no longer there.

Jay and Amber rushed to the upper deck bridge to the helm where Ram stood like a man possessed, turning the wheel, his teeth gritted in determination.

"Ram! What are you doing?" Jay shouted.

"Saving us!" Ram called out. "We're going back!"

"Turn the engines off!" Amber roared, aware that the precious little fuel they had was being used up. She reached out for the ignition key but Ram pushed her away and continued clutching the wheel tightly.

The trawler banked on a steeper angle, causing all the others on board to scream in mounting panic, wondering just what was going on, the horizon tilting, Ram spinning the wheel, cackling crazily.

Jay and Amber grabbed Ram, forcibly removing his hands from the wheel, yanking him away.

Amber corrected the helm, the trawler boat gradually righting itself level.

"Witch!" Ram hissed at Amber. "Don't you see? A few more days of this and we'll all be hanging out with the angels."

"In your case, Ram - I think you have an appointment with the devil!" Amber said.

Ram glared defiantly at her.

"We should have gone back to the city when I said. Now, we're doomed. We're all going to die. And you know something, Amber? It's all your fault!"

* * *

Amber stood at the front of the little trawler, staring up in wonder at the stars that twinkled above her. It was a magical night. There was a sense of peace. Even the ocean was calm, as smooth as glass, barely a ripple all around as the waves gently lapped the side of the boat, the crescent moon shining down brightly, reflecting on the water's surface.

They had come so far, Amber reflected. Back in the city, in the days after the 'virus', Amber and the others had fought so hard to bring order, to create a new society and to overcome many challenging obstacles from Zoot and his Locos to the religious fanatics of The Chosen, to the invasion of the Technos. And now, stuck out here, stranded on the boat, it just didn't seem fair. They had all given so much effort. They had tried so hard. But life wasn't always fair, Amber knew. Were they drifting to their doom, like Ram said? And if so, was she responsible?

"Can't sleep?" Jay spoke quietly as he walked up and stood beside Amber.

"No."

"Lex's snoring?"

"I wish. I thought it was bad when we lived in the mall," Amber reflected, thinking of Lex's snoring, which was indeed very loud and the source of many a sleepless night for the others. "I was thinking more of Ram."

"That was quite a day, wasn't it," Jay sighed in marvel as he took in the breathtaking starlit sky.

Amber nodded. "Four fish caught. Thank goodness for Salene's fishing skills... and let's see, six arguments... one potential nervous breakdown with Trudy... one near capsize due to Ram... one major mutiny," Amber counted on her fingers.

"At least Ram's quietened down. Must have been in the sun too long. Something's gotten to him."

"You mean... me?"

"I wouldn't pay any attention to what he said, Amber. All of this... it's not your fault."

"I just don't understand why he's so intent on trying to get back. It doesn't make any sense. Surely he knows we didn't have a choice. You know him better than anyone. Any ideas?"

"Nothing. If he's got a hidden agenda, he's hardly the type to reveal it. The only thing anyone can ever know about Ram, Amber - is he's a person of extremes. A true enigma."

"As if I needed any reminding," Amber replied bitterly.

Ram had been a scourge to Amber, all of the Tribe, in the past. The entire city. He had caused so many problems, heartache. Though he claimed innocence, not knowing what had happened to explain Bray's disappearance, Amber couldn't help but doubt him. She felt distrust.

Thrown by circumstances into working together to try and defeat Mega's tyranny, Ram and Amber had never been friends or gotten close. They had been allies of convenience. And now there was no common enemy, Amber felt an unease that of all the people she would be stuck with, drifting on a boat in the middle of nowhere, one of them was Ram.

A moment passed as Amber and Jay stood, the only noise the sound of the water lapping the boat as the two of them searched the stars.

"It's beautiful, isn't it?" Amber breathlessly said, in wonder at the view. "Makes you think. Here we are. A tiny boat on a vast ocean. Itself on a little planet. We're just a dot in the universe, aren't we? I mean, what's it all about?"

"Who knows?" Jay responded. "I guess that's the mystery of life. What makes it interesting. We don't know."

"Do you think there's something greater out there?"

"Like God or something?"

"Mmm," Amber assented. "My Mom... she was religious. But I couldn't understand if there is a God - then why was there so much pain and suffering in the world? How could that be? How could what happened to the adults - be allowed to happen?"

"There were certainly enough problems in the world when the adults were around. And now it's up to us, isn't it? How do you think we've done so far? Is the world a better place?" Jay asked.

"Not for us, so far it isn't. But we've got to try, don't we?" Amber replied, with complete conviction. "If we don't try to make it a better world, who will? How can we expect anyone else to? We've just got to do our best."

"In the past, our ancestors would look for answers in the night sky," Jay suggested. "That what you're doing?"

"I guess so. I've got enough questions. Such as why are we on this boat? What's going to happen to us... Are we ever going to get out of this thing alive? What about my son? What future do we have? So far, it's not as if any answers or solutions are jumping out at me."

"You've been amazing, Amber. And you're doing great. If it wasn't for you trying to help everyone else, we might not even have got this far."

Amber smiled bashfully, touched by Jay's words.

"I don't know if we decide our own fate," Jay went on. "Or if destiny is set out for us already, and what will be, will be. But what I do know is, I love you, Amber. And whatever happens the rest of today, tomorrow - I couldn't be happier right now than being here with you. There's no other place, and nobody else, where I'd rather be."

Tears welled up in Amber's eyes. She certainly hadn't expected that tonight when she stepped out to gaze at the sky. She was so touched by Jay's words, the honesty of them. The magic of the moment, there under the night sky.

Was there anyone else she would rather be with? Once, she thought it would have been Bray. But after he disappeared - and presumably died - Amber was happy to have met and then fallen for Jay. She hadn't chosen Bray to vanish - and had he lived, she would have always been faithful to him. But there they were, her and Jay, under the Heavens. Perhaps it was fate after all, outside their control.

Unsure what words to say, she leant forward, tenderly kissing Jay, wrapping her arms around him, hugging him tightly, the two of them together but alone as the millions of stars shone, glimmering above.

Whatever their destiny, in her heart Amber was glad Jay was a part of her life - however much time she had left to live, whatever the future had in store.

CHAPTER FOUR

"For what you've been through, you seem in remarkably good health," Judd said, feeling Bray's pulse.

They were in the medical theatre and Judd had been checking the condition of his prized patient to make sure Bray's body would be up to the stresses and rigours of another reality space interface that Eloise had planned.

"Your pulse rate is steady, your blood pressure's good. I just wish there was something more I could do for you," Judd said, looking sympathetically at Bray, who sat on the bed in the medical theatre. He was dazed, staring lost.

"Thanks for looking out for me. You're the only one who has round here," Bray replied, his voice quiet, weak.

"If you want to know the truth - I don't entirely agree with all that goes on around here," Judd stated. "Science and medical advancements are one thing. Human experiments are not something I can ever sanction."

"Then do something about it, Judd."

"Like what? I'm a scientist. Not a fighter, Bray. I'm not a warrior like you."

"My dear Bray," Eloise called out, striding into the medical theatre, in an air of eager anticipation. "Our guest will be ready for tonight's initiation, Judd?"

"His body's ready. Whether his mind is in order, that's another matter entirely."

"Such a pity he wasn't being more co-operative," Eloise said, caressing her fingers gently down the side of Bray's face.

"I'll be on my way then," Judd suggested.

Nodding out of respect to Eloise, Judd walked away, guards flanking the entrance to the medical theatre opening the door for the scientist to exit.

Bray cautiously glanced at Eloise, her blue eyes examining his own tired, beaten features. He wondered how she would react to what he was going to say.

He hoped Amber wouldn't be disappointed in him. He hadn't had many relationships in his life. And was close at once with Danni. But Amber was different. His one true soulmate. He would never willingly be unfaithful to her. Dishonour her. But he was out of options. Running out of time. Hope. He had no other choice. At least that's what he wanted Eloise to believe.

"You win, Eloise," Bray said, his voice a whisper.

"Say that again?"

Eloise's eyes narrowed, concentrating on him. Had he really just said what she thought he had?

"I'm beaten. I'll do whatever you want of me. Everything you ask..."

"Everything I want of you?"

"Everything," Bray admitted reluctantly, turning with shame to look at his conqueror before him.

Eloise grinned. She couldn't suppress the delight welling up inside. If Bray was serious - if he would give her what she wished for - this would elevate her to a whole new level. Her hold on the 'Zootists', her influence as the Mother continuing Zoot's bloodline, would put her into a great position to powerbroke. With those in authority. After so much stubborn resistence from Bray, she was finally going to be victorious. And it felt delicious.

"You've made the right choice, Bray. I will be - honoured - to carry your child. Together, we can achieve so much. Perhaps more than either of us can possibly imagine."

Eloise's eyes were lively, dancing with energy, excited at the promise of what that night would bring as she looked over Bray's body in anticipation. At last. He was completely her's.

She called out to the guards.

"Wash him. Clean him up. Then bring Bray to my quarters. Tonight - he and I will... make history!"

* * *

Two guards, flanked either side of Bray, escorted him from the cells to the living quarters of the compound, their heavy boots echoing on the metallic floor.

Bray hoped he knew what he was doing.

His wounds from his beatings had been tended to. And he had been showered. Some guards had even dressed Bray in a dinner suit, and he almost felt like he was going on a date to some high school ball. It was very surreal and for a moment he wondered if this was another reality space program.

Now clean, smartly presented, Bray almost felt human again on the outside. But inside he felt empty, used, exploited. Like a walking piece of meat. A possession. No longer in charge of himself. Or his life.

They reached a double doorway. One of the guards politely knocked.

"Send him in - and then leave us be!" Eloise's voice rang out from the other side of the doors.

The door was opened. Bray was pushed inside, the door quickly clicking shut behind him.

Eloise's quarters were lavish. A huge log fire burned, providing an ambient light. There was a buffet of food on the table. Bowls of fresh fruit. Blood red wine in decanters. At least Bray thought it was wine. A thick fur rug lay on the floor. And the air was punctuated by a rich perfume.

It was strange to see such comfort, after all the deprived conditions he had been exposed to for so long in his cell. Bray expected Eloise to live well - but not this well.

And there, gazing at her reflection in the mirror, stood Eloise.

She was squirting herself around her neck with scent, but she didn't really need to embellish her allure.

Bray was taken aback by her. She looked beautiful. There was no doubt about it. Her long black hair brushed carefully over her shoulders. Just the right make up. She wore a silk gown but in the light, Bray couldn't help make out the naked contours of her body, the enticing natural silhouette revealed through the thin silk.

She was Aphrodite. A goddess.

She was his. And he was her's.

"It is finally time," Eloise whispered, putting down the perfume and extending her hand as she walked towards Bray.

"You look stunning," Bray admitted, dry mouthed.

"So do you," Eloise smiled seductively.

Bray's hands had been firmly bound but Eloise began working on the ropes, untying him, her long nails clattering away as they worked on his restraints.

She was so close to him now, Bray couldn't deny the natural physical attraction he felt to Eloise.

"There - that's better now, isn't it?" she whispered.

With the last of the knots untied, the ropes around Bray's wrists fell to the ground.

"And there..."

Eloise dropped her dressing gown, the light silk collapsing to the floor revealing Eloise's natural form.

She led Bray by his hands to the large bed nearby in the centre of her quarters and began undressing him. His jacket. Undoing the tie.

Her expression one of longing, to her delight Bray began gently kissing the side of her neck, Eloise closing her eyes in complete bliss at what was transpiring.

"Oh this will be such a pleasure," Eloise murmured appreciatively.

"Absolutely. A real pleasure," Bray said, seizing her arms forcibly.

Eloise recoiled in shock as she realized Bray was using the rope from his bounds to tie Eloise's hands together behind her back.

She struggled to free herself but it was no use as Bray fastened the ropes tightly around her arms.

"Sorry about tonight. But I'm already spoken for," Bray said matter of factly, placing the dressing gown over Eloise's otherwise exposed naked body, covering her to protect her dignity. Despite all the wrongs she had given him, he was ever the gentleman.

"Guards!" Eloise screamed out, enraged at Bray's deceit.

The double doors burst open.

Two guards swept into Eloise's quarters.

Initially, they were surprised at seeing Eloise sprawled on the bed. They were not used to seeing her in anything but her usual uniform. But suppressed their urge, aware of the consequences.

The distraction she unwillingly provided them was just the opportunity Bray needed.

He sprung into action, striking one of the guards with a powerful punch. The huge guard fell to the ground, knocked flat out cold.

The other guard leapt at Bray.

Bray moved to kick the guard, who raised his arm to block, before Bray suddenly spun on his heel in a feint, unleashing a rapid blow into the groin, the guard collapsing to the ground in agony.

Out of the corner of his eye, Bray noticed Eloise rushing toward a control panel, and backing to the wall, she adjusted her bonds to press an array of buttons.

Suddenly a pulsing and piercing alarm echoed as Bray rushed through the doors and into the metallic corridor outside the quarters.

He now had a chance. However slight. He just had to take it.

* * *

In the maternity wing, female disciples in the midst of giving birth and groaning in pain at the height of their labour, gazed panic-stricken as did the white gowned medical team, looking around in concern at the sound of the alarm and the pulsing lights.

Guards immediately sprung into action on high alert, rushing out of the ward.

In the manufacturing infant wing, hundreds of new born babies started crying, awoken by the alarm. Their attendants exchanged concerned glances in confusion, watching other guards reacting, rushing away.

The complex he had been imprisoned in was huge, Bray considered, as he raced down the metallic corridors. And once again he wondered if this was real or if he was trapped in some virtual world. Amidst the noise of the alarms, he was sure he could hear the distant sound of babies crying, their anguish echoing throughout the cavernous compound.

He had no knowledge of the geography. Or what other gruesome events ever took place in the complex. All he had seen were the medical theatre, the cell he was kept in, the virtual reality space simulator rooms.

With no idea where he was going, Bray was running on pure instinct, hoping to find the fire exit. He had noted it earlier en route from his cell to Eloise's quarters. But there were so many corridors and he was unsure of just exactly how to retrace his steps.

He knew from talk amongst the other slaves and disciples that no prisoner had ever escaped the compound. Or even tried to.

Rushing around a corner, he almost collided with Judd.

"I thought that alarm might have something to do with you!" Judd said, indicating. "That way to the very bottom, you'll find another corridor veering off to the right. And some emergency exit doors. You'd better move. In a few seconds this area will be overrun by the militia."

"You've got a chance as well, Judd. If you want to take it!"

Suddenly two guards approached.

Judd pointed to Bray.

"Seize him!"

The guards confronted Bray, who exchanged blows.

Judd removed a hypodermic from his white lab coat pocket and plunged the needle into the back of one of the guard's necks. Within seconds the guard slumped unconscious to the ground, while Bray unleashed a blow into the gut of the other guard, doubling him.

"Follow me!" Judd yelled.

They ran in full flight as more guards converged from other corridors, pursuing Bray and Judd, who disappeared through the emergency exit fire doors.

* * *

Bray gratefully breathed in the cold night mountain air. He was thrilled to be outside once more. With Judd beside him, the pair ran on in full flight towards the lush forest environment surrounding the compound.

Behind them, the sounds of guard dogs barking and yelping suddenly accompanied the pulsing distant alarm. Bray could hear guards shouting and was now aware of spotlights arcing, sweeping all around, illuminating the area.

For a split second, Bray still wondered if this was all really happening. If he was once more in a reality space program of Eloise's - without even knowing it.

"This is real - isn't it?" Bray questioned Judd, the two of them scrambling towards the dense foliage.

"You think reality space air smells this good?" Judd replied, panting as he ran. "This is real, Bray. Believe it. You've made it back out to the real world. And so have I. Thanks. I owe you one."

The bright glare of a spotlight suddenly outlined Bray and Judd's silhouettes, their shadows momentarily trapped by the beam of light.

Pushing themselves on from the pursuers gathering behind, and fuelled by adrenalin, Bray and Judd quickly avoided the spotlight glare, racing away, disappearing deeper into the forest. Into the night.

CHAPTER FIVE

There hadn't been a breeze for days. The little boat was motionless. With no noticeable current pushing it along. All around, the ocean itself was now lifeless. There were no waves. None of the movement of the boat, pitching and rolling, that had been so much a part of their voyage so far. There was an eerie silence. Not a sound. Even from the calm water all around them. Except for the noise of static.

Inside the trawler, Jack leant over the radio in the wheelhouse, twisting its dials, concentrating as he listened intently. Each day Jack had turned on the radio for a few minutes at a time, hoping to preserve its battery for as long as possible. But today, just like all the other times he had tried - all he had gotten back so far was the sound of radio silence.

"What are you hoping to get? The top ten best selling songs? The weather forecast? There's nothing, Jack," Ellie said as she sat beside Jack wearily, her voice hoarse and dry.

"There has to be something out there. Someone still transmitting. A ship?..." Jack insisted, though he seemed less convinced as each frequency he tried resulted in squealing static. "Someone else... Some land, somewhere."

"You don't give up, do you?" Ellie said admiringly, kissing Jack on the side of his face through her cracked, dehydrated lips.

They were in the doldrums. The heat from the blazing midday sun overhead glared down onto the boat. The rest of the Tribe took as best shelter as they could, lounging in the shade to conserve their energy.

Apart from Jack and Ellie in the wheelhouse, the others were all taking refuge around the upper deck.

Darryl was trying to entertain Lottie, Sammy and Brady, doing impressions of famous adults from the old days, who Darryl had hero-worshiped in his dreams of becoming an actor. Though neither Lottie, Sammy or Brady knew who Darryl was impersonating, being too young to remember the adult celebrities of the past, they were entertained by the odd voices he was making, the strange expressions on his face. They had difficulty focusing in their state. And there was no enthusiasm in Darryl's performance. He just didn't seem to have the strength. And his twisted facial expressions took on a surreal haunted element, his eyes drained of hope, almost life.

May and Zak were half asleep, leaning on each other for support. May had felt elated, suspecting she might have found a soulmate at last, though she wished this had happened in another place, another time, where she might have had more time to enjoy their growing relationship.

Slade rested his arm on Ruby, her head on his chest as she slept. Stroking her hair tenderly, Slade had enjoyed the renewal of his friendship with Ruby since they embarked on the boat.

He and Ebony still hadn't spoken further about their fallout over Mega's death. Neither had the energy or desire, not wanting to risk conflict with one another - especially in front of the other Tribe members. And not now, when their very survival was at stake. All were intent on conserving their precious life force.

Ruby had kept Slade company the past day or so. Not saying much, just being there, with him. That's what friends were for, wasn't it? It was just that, friendship? Nothing else? Slade couldn't help but feel there might be something more than friendship though on his part. But his thoughts were dominated by the recent loss of his brother. And whether he was also about to confront his own mortality.

Gel seemed to be drifting in and out of semi-consciousness.

Lex was keeping an eye on Ram, who was preoccupied, lost in some secret thought.

Ebony was fast asleep.

But as Trudy stared at her, she wondered if Ebony was actually dead.

Trembling with anxiety, Trudy wiped away tears filling her eyes. She was deeply concerned about Brady but she tried to keep herself calm, holding her emotions in check. She didn't want Brady to see her so upset. The others had tried to keep Trudy's spirits uplifted. To support her. But she knew, there was nothing anyone could do to help. It was just like the days when the adults were wiped out, Trudy worried. Though this time, she was sure it was their turn to face their doom.

Part of her hoped she would succumb before Brady. But another part of her couldn't bear to think of Brady left on her own. Perhaps it would be better for Brady's end to occur first. In Trudy's fragile state of mind, she was beginning to consider if it was her duty as a mother to take back the life she had given her child. To end her suffering.

On the outer deck, Salene once again dangled the fishing line out of the water. They hadn't caught any fish for a couple of days, with none visible in the silent ocean, it felt like even the fish had abandoned them, leaving them to their isolation. Except for a few sharks trailing the little boat. Salene seemed too weak to have noticed the fins protruding on the surface.

It hadn't rained for a while. The last of the water collected by Jack's tarpaulin invention draped on the roof of the boat had been used up earlier that morning.

With no food, no water, it was the hardest part of their voyage since they had left the shore. Everyone was starving... sunburned... dehydrated. It was just a matter of time. Surely they just had a few days left.

Everyone knew it. Though nobody voiced it. But it was like all of the Tribe were mentally preparing for it. Coming to terms with the possibility that they might be experiencing what could be the last few days of their lives. None of them wanted to give up. They weren't ready for the end. But so much of what they faced was out of their hands. If they didn't get food or water soon, they knew deep down they would all perish.

They were all in the same situation, united in adversity. Their fates bound together. The quarrels and disagreements that had so characterised the voyage had now ceased. They had lost energy even for that. Whatever conversations they did have, brief as they were, were ones of encouragement. Not conflict. Support. The stark situation they faced was bringing them all together closely. They may have not had much hope. But they still had each other.

Ram was still a source of irritation to all, however, which he brought about himself. He could never relate to the Mall Rats. His was a different ideology.

Amber glanced at baby Bray fast asleep with Jay cradling Amber's child in his arms, Jay himself deep in sleep on the deck of the trawler. Like Trudy, Amber worried greatly about the future for her own child. As parents themselves, Trudy and Amber had a perspective nobody else could fully appreciate. But where Trudy was a single mother, Amber was glad to have Jay in her life.

With her own survival in jeopardy and that of her son, Amber's thoughts turned once more to Bray. The father of her child. Was he really dead? Or was he out there, somewhere, and had survived? Maybe he had met someone else, like she had with Jay, and began a new life? Whatever the situation, he would always remain precious in her thoughts, her entire being. She would always care for his memory, but Jay was Amber's present life. And her future. If they would only live to see it.

Ram began cackling quietly to himself. He was trying to restrain his giggling but in spite of his efforts, he couldn't help but erupt into manic laughter.

"What's so funny?" Amber asked.

"I was just thinking... Dead men tell no tales," Ram said.

"What the hell's that supposed to mean?" Lex snapped.

"Don't know about you, Lexy-boy, but it looks as if all my secrets will be going with me to my grave. Along with everyone else around here."

"You're pathetic!" Amber exclaimed.

Something suddenly caught Amber's attention out of the corner of her eye.

She turned to look at the ocean - and for a moment thought she was seeing things. Perhaps it was a vision brought on by her weakened physical state.

Amber stared, open eyed, making sure what she saw was real.

"Oh my God!" Amber yelled excitedly, her mouth dry.

"What is it?" Jay awoke with a start, carefully standing up with Amber's child in his arms.

"Everyone! Look!" Amber screamed, delirious, pointing out to the ocean.

And there in the distance, on the horizon, the outline of a massive ship loomed.

CHAPTER SIX

Bray ran for his life, terrified. Panic-driven. He was racing through the thick undergrowth of the forest, trying to keep his balance as he sprinted, stumbling over the twisting tangle of branches and tree roots he sped through.

In the distance he could hear the pursuing group of Eloise's forces. They were shouting out for him. Hunting him down.

Bray and Judd had parted ways soon after they left the compound, thinking that they had more chance to escape by splitting off, hoping to divide the guards tracking them. Bray wondered how Judd was getting on, ducking below a thick tree branch, nearly scraping his head as he hurled past.

Eloise would be furious at his escape, Bray realized. In the time he had gotten to know her, he had been totally unsettled by her vindictiveness and brutality.

How one human being could treat another so cruelly, exploit them, he just didn't understand. If he was caught, he didn't expect any mercy. Which only added an extra dimension to the adrenalin pumping through Bray's body as he fought to overcome the fatigue and breathlessness threatening to stop him running on, ever onwards.

Bray had experienced being chased in the city many a time. Be it from Locos, Demon Dogs, The Chosen, or a host of dangerous tribes.

But here, in the forest, Bray was on unknown ground. He had no knowledge of where geographically Eloise's mountain complex was located. Sprinting as fast as he could, he also had no idea of what dangers lay ahead. Whatever it was, Bray only hoped it was a better prospect than the threat posed by Eloise and her guards relentlessly pursuing him.

* * *

On her orders, the guards had themselves split up into several groups and they would catch their prey, Eloise knew. There was nothing Bray or Judd - the traitor - could do to escape their fate.

Eloise and some of the guards were on quad-bikes, daring to hit the thick undergrowth at speed as they tore through the terrain, searching for any sign of Bray or Judd.

Ahead of Eloise another group of security guards used sniffer dogs, following the trail.

And all around, the Zootist' initiates sprawled out through the forest searching for Bray, their 'demi-God'. They were all capable warriors. Manufactured in the image of their master. All chosen for their fighting skills. The sight of so many seemingly cloned figures of Zoot joining the hunt was a chilling and sobering reminder of the 'research' being conducted at the compound.

With the help of the extra personnel scouring the terrain in the shape of the 'Zootists', obsessed with Bray and the legend of his brother, it was just a matter of time, Eloise promised. They would find him. And she would make Bray pay for his deception of her.

In the event they were unsuccessful, Eloise, ever calculating, had already devised an extravagant excuse to give to her superiors. Judd was certainly to blame. But she would embellish that she was attacked by him and Bray during the escape. But at least she could still manufacture the bloodline and DNA of Bray, even if it meant her becoming impregnated by someone else. How could anyone ever know?

* * *

Up ahead, Bray realized a group of guards were gaining on him. He could hear the tree branches and vines snapping as his pursuers closed in. And he could hear the sound of the 'Zootists' chanting his name, then the name of his brother, Zoot.

Bray was all consumed with adrenalin. Fear. This was madness. Crazy.

The sound of sniffer dogs howling and barking excitedly, getting closer, ever nearer, meant Bray didn't have long before his scent gave him away.

Bray had only one chance...

* * *

Judd was exhausted. He felt as if his legs couldn't carry him any further. But he had to go on. He knew helping Bray escape wouldn't be tolerated. His betrayal would be punished. He pushed himself. Don't give up, don't stop.

Behind, the revving of the quadbike engines grew louder and Judd knew he needed a miracle to avoid being captured.

Making an instant decision, he began to climb a tall tree, hoping it would offer a form of protection, a place to hide. Perhaps the pursuers would be so busy looking around, they wouldn't think to look up.

* * *

In another part of the forest, the guards with the tracking dogs smiled leeringly. The dogs were on the trail, tails wagging enthusiastically as the pursuit went on, surely now nearing its end.

"We've got him!" one of the guards called out as a sniffer dog barked out at a tree, altering its master.

The hunting party swarmed around the base of the trunk.

"Got you!" the main guard shouted, the dogs yelping, teeth snarled.

Another guard pointing, noticed something up in the bough of the branch.

The main guard stared in the direction indicated, looking forward to seeing Bray - or Judd's fearful expression.

He bellowed in frustration.

Instead of either, all the main guard could see was Bray's shirt, tied to a branch, blowing in the breeze.

* * *

Bray was close enough to hear the guards' shouts and curses of disappointment. He was glad he had the quick thinking to leave a trace of his scent behind as a decoy for the sniffer dogs.

Onwards he raced, wondering how long the forest would continue, what lay ahead. At least the forest offered some form of visual protection, the thick foliage obfuscating Bray, keeping him hidden from his pursuers.

Bray nearly lost his footing again, tripping over a thick fallen branch.

He had to keep going. The guards wouldn't catch him, he vowed, as the sniffer dogs resumed their pursuit.

* * *

Eloise screeched her vehicle to a halt, a cloud of dust and twigs flying as the tires skidded across the ground.

"One of them's around here somewhere!" she shouted, her icy blue eyes manic, obsessed with revenge, realizing the howling dogs were onto something.

Eloise smiled. She had him. Question was, which one?

In the tree above, Judd looked down on Eloise. He dared not breathe, make a sound, his chest heaving after his exertion. He closed his eyes, clutching the branch that he sat on, hoping to blend into the tree itself, becoming invisible, his heart racing with fear.

Casting her gaze upwards to the huge tree, Eloise was thrilled by what she saw.

"Well, well well...," she giggled jubilantly.

Judd felt as if he was staring into the personification of all his nightmarish fears, now come true.

"You did well to escape, Judd," Eloise shouted, congratulating him, the guards around her dismounting their quad-bikes, getting ready to reel in their prey.

Eloise indicated. A guard tossed an AK-47 to her, which she caught.

"I surrender!" Judd yelled in growing panic.

"Oh, I don't think so, Judd. No can do!"

Eloise took the safety latch off, aiming the weapon in Judd's direction like she was targeting a shooting game with an electronic gun she used to play as a girl in the arcades.

She grinned, taking careful aim.

"Noooooooooo!" Judd screamed.

"Yes! This bullet has your name on it. Game over, Judd!"

* * *

Bray stopped running, distracted as he heard the explosive sound of gunfire suddenly crack and Judd's agonized screams in the distance.

The forest erupted as flocks of birds quickly took flight, their wings beating rapidly as they soared to the sky, squawking in protest at being disturbed.

Bray said a silent prayer for Judd. He hoped the ending had been quick, that he hadn't suffered. That Judd was now at peace.

But hearing engines being revved ominously, signalled that the hunt was far from over.

He didn't have long, Bray knew all too well, and he sprinted off, a renewed sense of urgency in his stride. He had to keep running - but to where?

CHAPTER SEVEN

Ellie looked up. It was huge. The massive bulk of the cargo ship Amber had first noticed cast its shadow over the little boat that had been their home for so long, while Jack carefully did his best to manoeuvre the trawler, drawing it alongside the giant vessel.

"I love you!" Ellie cried out to Jack, giving him one more look before she took her turn. If these were the last words she would ever say, they seemed appropriate, giving her comfort as well as courage.

Jack dared to look away from the cargo ship for a fleeting second, nodding to Ellie, giving her an encouraging smile.

"I'll see you there!" he called out from the trawler's wheelhouse.

Given a renewed surge of confidence from Jack's assurance, Ellie prepared herself, Jack carefully steering the trawler a few inches closer, the gap between her and the container ship closing. Ellie climbed onto the roof of the wheelhouse where Darryl was crouched, balancing himself with the motion. He had volunteered to remain to steady everyone. The elevation of the wheelhouse providing a better 'launchpad' to bridge the difference in height between the roof of the trawler and the open deck of the cargo vessel.

Ellie took a deep breath, then leaped.

The Tribe had decided to head towards the cargo ship to see if anyone might be able to help them, using the last of their fuel, the engines of the little trawler coughing and spluttering as Jack had earlier steered the boat towards the mysterious vessel. Yet despite calling out for help as the two boats see-sawed side by side, it seemed as if the cargo ship was deserted. Nobody had responded to their shouts.

Realizing they couldn't stay on the trawler forever, now it was out of food and water supplies - and very likely was to run out of fuel - the Tribe quickly resolved that they had to take their chances on the container ship. Hopefully, they would stand more likelihood of survival on it than the trawler.

Ellie gripped at the safety railing of the mammoth container vessel.

Slade and Lex pulled Ellie up by her arms, hauling her onto the open deck.

"Well, look what we've caught here," Lex joked.

"Thanks," Ellie smiled appreciatively.

So far, most of the Tribe had made it. Jay had been the first to make the leap of faith and had rigged some ropes, bound as an extra safety for the others to cling to in case they missed the railing.

Amber was so relieved that destiny had played an opportune card. She dreaded to think of the Tribe trying to cross the gap from the trawler boat to the cargo ship if the waves had been rougher. Thankfully, although the wind was picking up, it hadn't affected the evacuation from the trawler so far.

It was hard enough as it was for Jack to manoeuvre the tiny ship alongside the mammoth vessel. They didn't have any ladders for the transition. It was just their tired and exhausted bodies they had to rely upon to physically traverse the distance between the trawler and the container ship. Boarding at the open deck level. The prospect of leaving the trawler had given them all a renewed sense of hope, a surge of energy. They were nearly all safe, Amber thought, with two more to go.

"See you on the other side," Darryl shouted to Jack, struggling to keep the two vessels close enough, doing his utmost to minimize the distance between them. Jack wondered if Darryl was referring to the afterlife rather than the huge vessel.

Darryl jumped - and just made it. Slade and Lex's arms ached as they pulled Darryl up over the safety railings, onto the deck, massive metal containers stacked all around them.

One more to go, Amber thought nervously, her stomach churning with tension.

So far it had been a miracle they had all made it across, Amber felt. The most difficult challenge had involved Brady and baby Bray. Trudy had been hysterical when she had lifted up Brady, pushing her with all her might, to the safe arms of the others who had already made it, reaching out toward the child from the deck of the cargo ship.

And Amber had felt the intense stress of the moment when she made her own leap, her little son clutching to her. They had coiled a safety rope around each of the youngsters as an extra precaution if they fell. Baby Bray had been also tied to Amber in a makeshift harness made from the tarpaulin that served as Jack's improvised rain collector. They were all safe, so far. But now it was Jack's turn. And Ellie couldn't bear to look, comforted by Sammy who noticed a shadowy shape in the water of what he knew was a shark and turned Ellie away, hoping she wouldn't catch a glimpse.

Inside the little trawler, Jack only had a few moments, aware as he cast his eyes towards the back of the trawler, its engines coughing and heaving, that the precious fuel was running out. Jack had volunteered to be the last to go, feeling he was the best helmsman of them all, given his innate technical skills. He just hoped he had made the right choice. But all the tribe had confidence in him. He had always been the tribe's 'Mister Fixit', able to turn his hand to all things mechanical.

One last time, Jack thought, idling the engine of the trawler, getting one final spurt of power to help him steer the little boat, inching it closer, closer, to the cargo ship, the two vessels almost touching.

"Come on, you little boat," Jack urged, getting in 'tune' with the trawler. Mechanical objects, as well as computers, almost had their own personality to Jack and he exhorted the trawler not to let him down, not now, when they'd been through so much together.

Judging the trawler was as close as he could make it without causing a collision, Jack let go of the wheel and climbed onto the roof.

From the cargo ship, Ellie jumped up and down nervously, hardly bearing to watch for signs of her loved one. And the others all watched breathlessly.

Now the trawler began to inch away from the cargo ship, with nobody left to steer it, to keep it level.

Jack gritted his teeth. He was going to have to give it all he had. He stepped back a few paces, then sprinted, leaping, taking flight across the divide, soaring from the little trawler towards the mammoth cargo vessel. It felt like everything was in slow motion, as if he was flying. He was all too aware of the growing gap that had now opened up, his arms flailing to reach out to the vessel, sensing the distance widening, like an invisible force was trying to pull him down into the unforgiving ocean below.

Ellie screamed. Jack wasn't going to make it.

Jack felt himself descending, sure he'd mistimed his jump. As he desperately reached out, extending his arm, in that split second, he knew he had got it all wrong, it was too late.

And then it was over.

Jack's arm nearly snapped as he felt the strong grip on him, quickly reversing his momentum. Jack clattered into the side of the ship, pain searing through his body as all his weight concentrated on his shoulder, his feet dangling, gravity trying to pull him into the watery abyss.

Slade called out a primal yell of fury, urging himself to hang on as he leaned over the side of the railing, every tendon in his body aching, struggling to grip Jack's arm.

Lex and Jay held onto Slade's legs to stop Slade from himself falling over the edge of the vessel.

Tears streamed down Ellie's face. She couldn't take the anguish, and the others around her could also hardly bear to watch either.

Jack managed to get a foothold into the safety ropes Jay had rigged, propelling him upwards.

With a mighty heave, Lex and Jay pulled Slade towards them, Slade continuing to bellow in determination.

And there, in Slade's strong arms, Ellie and the others could see that Slade had saved Jack, who was now on the deck, shaking in fear, Ellie racing over to give him a hug.

"You always... been this good at catch?" Jack quipped to Slade, trying to make light of things, though he was visibly shocked by his close escape.

"Oh, Jack, thank God you're okay," Ellie said in relief.

"Thank Slade, you mean," Jack replied, looking at Slade in all sincerity, cradling his arm Slade had been holding, hoping it hadn't been dislocated.

"We all owe you, Jack. If it hadn't been for you steering the trawler - none of us would have made it onto here," Slade responded.

Jack looked around at the Tribe, gazing at him with a mixture of concern, gratitude and relief.

"So I'm a hero," Jack smiled, in mock self-adoration.

"My hero," Ellie beamed through tears, kissing Jack lovingly on the lips.

Amber was so grateful they had all made it. Just. But made it to where? What exactly was this ship?

She watched the little trawler boat drifting away on the current, taking all the memories of what they had experienced. Now there were many questions that needed to be answered.

* * *

The Tribe decided to split up into two groups to explore the massive ship that fate had put in their way. They had boarded roughly in the middle of the vessel, with several hundred feet of hull going each direction either side.

Amber suggested that one group go to the bow to examine the open deck and metal containers stacked high, while the second group headed to the towering structure at the aft of the ship which Amber suspected was the crew living quarters, and where the bridge would no doubt be located at the very top, beneath the satellite dishes and golf ball-shaped radar visible on the roof.

Just what was this vessel doing here, out in the middle of nowhere? Was there anybody onboard? And if so, were they friendly or hostile? Was there any food? Any useful supplies they could use?

The wind had begun to pick up and it roared at the front of the ship, howling like a banshee, as the first group picked its way cautiously through the gaps in the containers piled high all around them.

"It's like being in a big maze," May whispered, giving voice to her thoughts, peering up at the containers.

"Wonder what's inside them?" Zak questioned, patting the outside of one.

Some had United Nations logos displayed on them. Just what was the cargo being carried inside?

Slade was on edge, treading carefully in case they bumped into anyone. Surely the crew of the ship, if there were any, wouldn't take kindly to the Mall Rats inviting themselves aboard.

"Relax, Slade," Ruby insisted, putting her hand on Slade's strong arm. "I think the only people here are us."

"Better to be safe," Slade countered, his eyes vigilant for any movement, any sign of life.

Slade and Ruby rounded a corner, peering ahead, the wind whistling between the metal containers.

"Wait!" Ram said in an undertone, putting his finger to his mouth to signal the others to be quiet. "I can hear something," he continued, a look of panic on his face.

* * *

At the back of the cargo ship, Amber and Jay led the other group as they carefully made their way towards the main accommodation structure, treading cautiously through the walkway between the metal containers stacked highly each side.

"Think anyone's here?" Salene asked, looking around nervously, the wind increasing in strength, making her shiver in cold, as well as fear.

"We'll find out - one way or the other," Jay answered.

The ship's hull groaned and creaked as it rode through the waves, the ocean gathering strength, pitching the ship up and down like a massive pendulum.

"So far so good," Ebony said, studying the tall accommodation structure they had now reached. It must have been four or five stories tall above the outer deck.

"Hellooo?" Gel called out, as she, too, looked up at the crew quarters.

"Shut it, Gel!" Ebony ordered. "We don't know who's in there! Duh!"

"We don't know if anyone's in there," Lex retorted. "And nobody tells Gel to shut up - except me."

"Pig!" Gel blurted to Lex, sticking her tongue out, making a face at Lex.

"Please, cut it out!" Amber implored, hoping to focus the others.

"Look... up there," Trudy said, squinting, distracted by the sun reflecting from the windows of the accommodation structure looming above. "I think... I can see someone."

* * *

At the front of the vessel Ram was absolutely terrified. He stood, trying his best to hide against the side of one of the stacks of metal containers. The others froze, eyes wide open, wondering what - or who - Ram had noticed.

Slade tensed, anticipating someone to leap out from behind one of the containers at any moment. If there was going to be a fight, he'd be ready.

The wind shrieked, the creaking steel of the cargo ship hull reverberated as the waves struck the bow. Adrenalin coursed through the group's veins, all gripped by anxiety, their senses heightened.

"Boooooo!!!" Ram suddenly shouted, leaping forward, causing the others to nearly jump out of their skins in fright.

"Ram, you idiot, what the hell are you doing?!" Ruby shouted, gasping for breath.

"You nearly gave me a heart attack!" May protested.

Ram burst out laughing, enjoying his little trick. "I got ya! All of ya! You should have seen the look on your faces!"

"Is he always like this?" Zak stared disdainfully at Ram, cracking up manically at his practical joke.

"On a good day. On a bad day he can only get worse. A lot worse," May shook her head in disapproval.

"Was that really necessary?" Slade asked, clearly irritated as much as all the others.

"Oh, come on, Slade-y boy. You gotta admit. That was funny!" Ram grinned gleefully.

Slade stared Ram in the eye.

"Well done, Ram. If there is anyone else on board, you'd better hope they think so. Because your little joke might have just alerted them to our presence!"

Ram's chuckling faded as he appreciated Slade's words and realized he might just have made a grave mistake.

* * *

About fifty feet up above the outer deck, Amber held tightly onto the rails of the fire escape they had climbed, taking them to the top floor of the accommodation structure tower. With the ship now heaving in the waves, she felt dizzy, engulfed by a sense of vertigo as she looked down at Darryl and Salene far below, the two of them looking after the little ones as Amber and the others reached the top of the emergency outside stairwell.

They were now at the bridge. It was difficult to see inside due to the angle of the sun shining brightly, a white reflection of light dazzling off the windows, though that didn't stop Trudy in particular from staring at the bridge, sure someone was inside.

Jay tried the doorway to the bridge leading in from the outside fire escape. It wouldn't budge.

"It's locked," he pointed out, trying the handle again.

"Leave it to me," Lex suggested, taking a step back down the fire escape. "I always travel with my - 'keys'."

Suddenly Lex charged forth like a bull, bashing into the door with all his force, shouldering it open. Then he collapsed in a heap to the floor from his own momentum.

Jay took a combat stance and jumped through the doorway.

Amber followed Trudy in.

Trudy stopped as soon as she stepped through the doorway, her eyes wide with deep fear. And screamed, petrified.

* * *

Slade and the rest of his group heard Trudy's cries and raced towards the back of the boat as fast as they could. The others were in trouble - and they needed help.

"Up there," Salene pointed to the top of the accommodation tower structure as Slade raced past, clambering up the fire escape stairs. Salene and Darryl stayed put on the outside deck with Amber's son and Trudy's daughter. They had promised Amber they wouldn't move, in case Amber and the others encountered danger up in the bridge. Salene's face was contorted in worry. She wondered what was going on up there but did her best to comfort Brady, who was weeping into her shoulder, worried at hearing her mother's distraught scream.

Slade raced through the doorway into the bridge, with Jack and the others not far behind him.

Skidding to a halt, he first noticed Trudy passed out, laying on the floor of the bridge.

Anxiously looking around, Slade saw Amber, Jay and Lex, startled and unsure, recoiling from what Trudy had noticed.

There, in front of them all, sat the adult crew of the cargo ship. Or at least what was left of their rotting, skeletal remains.

CHAPTER EIGHT

Bray's feet and legs ached as they pounded the ground, his heart beating rapidly. His entire body felt like it was going to give up due to exhaustion but Bray's sheer power of will kept him going, running further, pushing him on. And on.

He wondered if Eloise was still after him. He hadn't been aware of any guards in pursuit or heard the quad-bikes, the sound of the sniffer tracking dogs, the 'Zootists', for some time now.

The forest he had been fleeing through was vast, the undergrowth thick. Who knew what lay around the corner, past the next group of trees. He was constantly vigilant, ever attentive to the slightest sound or visual clue signifying if danger was approaching.

Bray hadn't slept for a couple of nights. He believed the worst thing to do was to stop running and make a camp somewhere. If he fell asleep, he was so tired he worried he wouldn't wake up, wouldn't notice Eloise's guards moving in on him, if indeed they still were hunting him down. He couldn't risk that. Stopping wasn't an option.

Filthy, Bray had earlier covered himself in dirt, rubbing plants and mud all over him. He hoped the conflicting smells would be a way of distracting the sniffer dogs from his scent.

Tired and hungry, Bray survived - just - on nothing more than handfuls of berries grabbed from plants. He looked around, hoping to find something he could eat.

Suddenly, the forest began to clear. There were fewer trees, and Bray stopped running as he reached the boundary.

The terrain was opening up. Ahead lay nothing but barren wilderness, a bleak looking landscape - with no cover, nowhere to hide.

Had the area been subject to a natural phenomenon? Some kind of disaster? It certainly looked as if it had, with only charred tree stumps remaining. Had there been a fire? Or was it due to a clearance of the vast area by man at some point in time? And if so - why?

Confronted by the choice of heading back or taking his chances in the wilderness that lay ahead, Bray decided the best thing he could do to further his escape was to put as much distance as he could between him and the forest.

After taking a few precious seconds to catch his breath, Bray sprinted forward towards the open barren land, covering the ground much quicker than before, no forest and myriad of trees to slow his progress this time.

He wondered just exactly where he was. What lay ahead. And if the danger from Eloise and her forces was still lurking behind. Fighting overwhelming fatigue, Bray just hoped he could keep going long enough not to find out.

* * *

Back in the forest, Eloise examined Bray in the crosshairs of her binocular lenses. She could see that he was stumbling. He looked weak, in a terrible state.

"Should we go after him?" one of the guards asked, almost afraid to question Eloise or pre-empt her orders - but was also clearly afraid and uneasy to continue with the pursuit.

"No need. He's in the 'wasteland zone'," Eloise replied.

The 'Zootists' and guards gathered around her, gazing intently, as she lowered the binoculars from her eyes.

She was preoccupied, deep in thought, her blue eyes sparkling in the sun.

"It seems our master, Bray, has gone to join his brother, Zoot - in the afterlife!" Eloise cried out.

"Zoot, Zoot, Zoot!" The Zootists erupted into a frenzy of chanting at the news, circling around Eloise, some bowing to offer their allegiance, displaying their loyalty.

Basking in the adulation, Eloise lifted the binoculars to her eyes again for one last look at her former prisoner, racing off into the wilderness. He must be at least two or three hours away.

"So long, my dear Bray," Eloise spoke to herself smugly.

Perhaps revenge came in different shapes, she considered, and this is how it was meant to be. Out there in the 'wastelands', Eloise knew Bray didn't stand a chance. Not if he became contaminated. Bray's suffering would be slow, drawn out. Delicious. There were some punishments worse than even she could devise. And the best thing of all, she reasoned, was that Bray didn't even know what he was getting himself into. He had no chance whatsoever of survival.

CHAPTER NINE

The Mall Rats stood on the open deck of the cargo ship, the vast stacks of metal containers all around them, their contents still a mystery - as was what had happened to the ship's crew, causing their demise.

The crew had been laid out on the deck. Their remains covered in blankets and linen found in the cupboards and cabins of the accommodation tower structure.

Amber thought of Bray suddenly. She wished he was here. He was so wise, philosophical. He would have known what to say in this situation. But now it was up to Amber. To preside over the funeral of the ship's crew.

Following the gruesome discovery in the bridge, the rest of the accommodation quarters had been explored and Amber and the others were convinced that there was no one else alive on board the ship except themselves.

A few more bodies had been found, lying in beds inside cabins, another in the kitchen galley. The bodies couldn't be left there forever so it was partly a practical decision to bury the dead. More than that though, Amber felt they owed it to the crew, whoever they were, to give them a dignified send-off, and to pay their respects.

Some of the others looked at Amber, waiting for her to speak, while the rest stared at the shrouded bodies before them, contemplating their thoughts.

Salene had her arm around Trudy in an encouraging hug. Trudy fought back tears. She had been freaked out by the discovery of the dead. Really spooked. It reminded her so much of the old times, when the adults first passed away. Many memories, painful to her core, flooded back as she looked at the covered remains of the crew, images of her parents and family flashing before her eyes. Though she was showing the most visible signs of emotional distress, she was not alone - everyone was feeling much the same as her, thinking similar thoughts, encountering the ghosts of the past.

"We stand here to pay our respects to those who have gone before," Amber began. "We do not know who they were. Where they were from. But one thing was for sure. They would have been someone's son... or daughter. Perhaps parents themselves. Brothers. Sisters. Whatever happened to them - we hope that they are now at peace and I would ask you to all join me in a moment's silence before committing their souls..."

The wind drifting in from the ocean began to pick up, howling in gusts through the gaps in the metal containers stacked throughout the mammoth vessel. It was as if the ship was haunted by an unknown presence, causing Trudy to steal uneasy looks around. And she wasn't the only one. Some of the others, including even Lex, were just as uneasy.

This was such an unusual place for a funeral, Amber thought, waiting for the wind to subside so she could continue. They had all endured loss, said their goodbyes to loved ones, in many different places back on land. And now they were doing so again. Amber hadn't expected to ever encounter adults. Now in a way they had to bury the past all over once more.

"Everything has its beginnings and endings," Amber went on. "Life is no different. We are all born. And we all, one day, will meet our end. But we live on forever, in memory. And though we didn't know the crew of this ship... they have touched us and reminded us never to forget the adults. All those from our past, who were special to us. Who will always be a part of us. Out of the ruins of the old, we will create a new future. We owe it to them, to those who have gone before. But most of all, we owe it to ourselves..."

Amber looked at her son, a symbol of hope for the future, being cradled in Jay's strong arms.

"Life will continue. It will endure. There will be challenges to meet. But we'll face them. Head on. We promise you this - whoever you were," Amber addressed the covered crew members. "Your passing will not have been in vain. The old times, the adults - none of it will be forgotten. We'll pass down the stories of the past to our children. We will ensure there is a future. Somehow. Humanity will survive. May God bless you. And I'm sure I speak for everyone when I say our only hope now is that you all rest in peace."

Amber nodded to the others. One by one, the covered corpses were carefully lowered over the side of the ship and dropped into the ocean below.

Stepping forward, Amber helped lift the last of the crew members, grabbing hold of the linen shroud. She thought of the others from the past she had buried. Her parents. Her best friend, Dal. And her heart ached for those she had lost. Her lover, Bray.

Life was so precious, beautiful. As the final crew member was released overboard, Amber vowed that somehow, for the sake of her son, for the others, for her, they would get through this. They would survive. She would do everything to make sure of that, give all that she had so that they wouldn't end up suffering the same fate of the crew. Their destiny wouldn't be to end their days on the vast cargo ship.

Or so she had hoped.

* * *

It would take several days for the Tribe to explore every inch of the container ship. It was that massive in scale. They had checked every cabin, store room and most compartments on all the decks but would need to assess all the containers and contents, to confirm that there was indeed nobody else on the ship. Just them.

Then they would need to identify some kind of a plan. And to see if Jack and perhaps even Ram could work out a way to navigate the vessel to a destination, whatever that destination might be.

The issue now was to settle in to daily life in their new home. It felt strange at first. The living quarters, in the five story accommodation tower structure, still had the personal remnants of the crew, with everything left in the same state since each item was last touched. It was like the Marie Celeste, seeing the chairs, the cutlery, dishes left in the kitchen galley... and clothes hung in cupboards, almost like time had been frozen since the adult days, with everything unchanged.

Compared to the little trawler that the Tribe had survived in for so many weeks, the enormous cargo ship was like being in a floating palace. Now, everybody had their own bed. There were more than enough cabins to go around. Just so much space.

Settling inside their cabin, May and Zak were putting their own personal touches to their temporary new home. Zak was making the beds while May was inside the en suite bathroom.

It was no secret what their priority was. Being alone. They were now a couple. So rather than having their own individual cabins, they were going to share one.

She looked a mess, May thought, examining her reflection in the bathroom mirror. No one had washed for weeks. They all stank, filth all over them, their hair mottled. May could hardly bear to look at herself. But she took comfort that she aroused something in Zak. Not just sexually. It was clear that he was also interested in her as a person.

Twisting the tap on the shower, May hoped that by some miracle, the ship would have some running water. She heard the pipes connected to the bathroom creaking and grinding. Nothing. Not a drop came out of the shower.

"Is that normal - you making so many noises going to the bathroom?" Zak quipped, calling out from the bedroom as he made the beds.

"Ha, ha. It isn't me," May smiled, twisting the tap on the shower further clockwise, disappointment showing on her face as her hopes were dashed.

Suddenly, water exploded out of the shower head, hitting May in the face. She yelped out.

Zak rushed in to see May leaping up and down for joy in the shower, as cold, clear water flowed all over.

"You never told me you wear your clothes in the shower either," Zak beamed as he cast an admiring glance at the wet garments clinging to her shapely body.

* * *

The morale of the Tribe soared with the discovery that the massive ship still had running water. Everybody felt so much better having taken a bath, washing their clothes.

And it wasn't just the water. In the kitchen galley, they discovered that the storage cupboards were stacked with tins of preserved food.

"This feels like Christmas!" Ellie said elated, opening a tin excitedly. Most of the tins had Chinese writing on their labels so nobody knew exactly what was inside. Ellie squealed in delight as she realized she had a can of peaches. "Fruit! Oh my God! Fruit!"

"At least we won't go hungry," Ebony sighed gratefully, holding up a tin to the others. "Anyone like fish?"

"How'd you know that?" Darryl asked in admiration. "I didn't know you could speak Chinese."

"There's a lot you don't know about me, Darryl," Ebony said, her demeanour cool, pointing to a large picture of a fish on the can in her hand, tapping it. "What do you think would be in there? A banana?"

"There's no need to be sarcastic," Darryl shrugged, his pride wounded.

"I hear there's some food around here," Slade said, entering the kitchen galley, with Ruby not far behind. Ruby and Slade had obviously just both had showers in their respective cabins and got cleaned up, Ruby fiddling with her hair, the two of them arriving by coincidence at more or less the same time from different parts of the ship.

Ebony wondered if they had both had anything as an 'aperitif' before arriving for their main meal.

She and Slade still hadn't had a chance to reconcile with each other over their falling out about the death of Slade's brother.

"We've got piles of food," Lottie spluttered between mouthfuls of tinned spaghetti, tomato sauce all over her face.

"You wouldn't believe how hungry I am," Ruby smiled.

"I'll bet," Ebony scoffed, giving a disdainful look.

"This is delicious!" Sammy said, cramming chocolate liquid into his mouth.

But Ebony ignored them all. She was far too knowing in the male female game not to pick up the soupçon of flirtation between Ruby and Slade, who was feeding Ruby a mouthful of the chocolate dessert.

Throwing the can of fish at Darryl, Ebony snarled.

"Suddenly, I've lost my appetite!"

And she stormed out of the galley.

* * *

Out on the open decks, Salene was assisting Amber, Lex, Gel and Jay, trying to solve the mystery of what cargo the ship was carrying. They had found some crowbars and were using them to wedge loose the doors to the metal containers.

Earlier, they had discovered a few of the containers housed medical supplies inside, with untold amounts of bandages, wound dressings, antiseptic, paracetamol and other pain killers.

It was like providence had provided them with a bounty, something to help them in their time of need, Amber thought. She was also touched by the irony that the medical supplies hadn't been enough to help the adult crew originally on board.

Gel was ecstatic. She had personally discovered a container stacked full of toiletries, with thousands of bottles of shampoo, liquid soap and shower wash.

"I think I've died and gone to Heaven!" Gel said.

"Stand back - or you just might if this door smashes into that pretty little body of yours," Lex commanded as he braced himself, with the crowbar stuck in a gap in the metal container, Gel giddily ambling around him.

"How do you think I should have my hair?" Gel asked dreamily, imagining all the ways she could impress Lex and look good.

"It might be an idea to try and keep it on your head," Lex replied, prying the container door open.

Inside, it was full to the brim of more preserved food, with boxes stacked, hardly room to spare. There had to be thousands of tins of food in that one container alone.

"There's just one problem... deciding what to have for dinner," Lex said.

"Have you always got nothing but food on your mind?" Gel teased.

"Oh I don't know. I can think of something else I might be interested in tonight," Lex winked to Gel.

"Then I'll go and make myself look prettier," Gel beamed, scampering off toward the accommodation tower structure where the cabins were, her arms laden with toiletries.

Lex watched her go. She was sure scatty, he smiled. But he found her attractive enough. And she might help him pass the time rather than face a long, lonely night.

Right now though he was thinking about the mysteries of the cargo ship. So far they had discovered a lifetime of food and supplies on it. But why? Where had it been going? Where were they now? And what had killed the crew?

Amber and Jay shared the same concerns. There were so many questions. And they just hoped they would come up with some answers.

* * *

An hour later up in the bridge, Jay entered, carrying a tray full of processed tinned meat, cold beans and canned vegetables, laid out on three plates.

"I've brought you lunch, one plate each," Jay said, putting the tray down on one of the empty swivel chairs. "It's not much but it's the best I can come up with."

"Not much? It's a feast," Amber smiled, tucking into the meal appreciatively.

She had gone to the bridge to meet up with Jack and Ram, who were examining the controls and instrumentation.

"Did you wash your hands?" Ram asked warily.

"For you, Ram, always," Jay replied, well aware of Ram's germ fetish.

"Thanks," Jack said, putting up a spoonful of cold creamed corn up to his mouth - which dribbled down his shirt, to his bemusement.

"So how's it all going?" Jay asked.

"Everything seems so complicated," Jack answered between mouthfuls. "It's like being on the bridge of an alien spaceship. We're still trying to work out what each symbol means - none of it is in English."

"I have utmost faith in you, Jack," Amber said.

"What about me?" Ram cut in, clearly offended.

"That all depends. On the results. What you can contribute."

Every dial and control panel in the bridge was written in Chinese. And compared to the little trawler with its simple helm and gear to throttle the engines up or down, this was far more complex, Jack explained. There were so many dials and symbols and he didn't know exactly what they all did.

"But you still think you'll be able to figure it out?" Amber asked, the tone of doubt obvious.

"I don't know about Jack. But arr, me hearty. Shiver me timbers. Ram'll succeed alright. And we'll be back home again before ye know it!" Ram said.

"Maybe we don't want to return, Ram - remember?" Amber pointed out.

"How could I forget," Ram scoffed. "But I'm warning you, I'm not used to taking orders from anyone, let alone landlubbers forcing me to live on the high seas."

"Please, Ram - no more pirate speak," Jack pleaded. Ram knew it irritated others and he was always more than happy to indulge his mischievous side.

"Then let's try some - geek speak," he considered Jack, as if throwing down the gauntlet.

"You're something else, Ram. You really are," Amber said. "There's no time for power struggles - or competition."

"With my brain," Ram replied, supreme confidence in his manner as he pointed at his head, "my special brain - and Jack's help, we'll work it out eventually. We just have to be careful. We don't want to press the wrong button and lower the anchor or something. Or we could be in the same position as we were on the trawler. Stuck in the middle of a vast ocean with nowhere to go."

The last sentence was a clear dig at Amber.

She didn't take the bait. But decided that it might be to everyone's advantage to further nourish the competitive spirit between Jack and Ram. She was fully aware of Jack's natural abilities. And as much as she loathed Ram, she was aware that where Jack had an aptitude for all things mechanical, as well as computers, Ram was an experienced and talented programmer. Surely between them they could work out all the systems on the bridge.

"I could steer the trawler but this," Jack pointed all around him. "I mean, look at the size of it. It's on a completely different scale."

Jay and Amber appreciated the difficulty of the task, with the mammoth length of the container ship stretching out the front windows of the bridge for several hundred feet ahead of them.

"That has to be the dial showing the wind speed, shipmate," Ram said, pointing at one of the control panels.

"I don't think it's just the wind speed. I think it's something more to do with the strength of the currents," Jack said.

"Don't doubt my intelligence," Ram snapped.

"Oh - and it's alright for you to doubt mine, I suppose. I never thought you could be so stupid," Jack replied.

Jay glanced at Amber and cast a slight smile. The logic in her trying to pit Jack and Ram together in a technical battle might have motivated them both to get a quick result in understanding all the charts, maps and instrumentation on the bridge but if they weren't careful, it might just fuel a bitter argument and them falling out.

"Settle down guys," Jay said. "You've got to try and work together - right, Amber?"

Amber didn't reply. She was focused on a journal she had discovered and was now flipping through the pages. It was written in English - and what it had to say was mind blowing.

"Did you call me stupid?" Ram bellowed to Jack.

"Yes. Right now you're being stupid," Jack argued.

"Amber - can you tell Jack to stop calling me names?" Ram asked. But Amber ignored him, preoccupied by the journal. "Amber!?" Ram called out, insisting he would be heard. "The only name I will accept is - brilliant!"

"Come on, guys. Let it go, will you?" Jay said, crossing to Amber.

"What is it?" he asked her.

Amber snapped out of her reverie, her eyes wide open in wonder. She shook her head as if dazed, trying to take it all in, absorbing what she had read.

"Is everything alright?" Jay questioned, noting Amber's uneasy demeanour.

"I'm not sure," Amber replied, indicating the journal in her hand.

* * *

"My name is Doctor Jane Gideon..." Amber began, reading aloud from the journal she had found. The others had been summoned to the bridge and were now listening intently, desperate to know what Amber had discovered, except for Lottie and Sammy, who were in one of the cabins babysitting Trudy's daughter and Amber's son.

"Aren't you gonna start with Once Upon a Time?" Lex chirped up, chuckling at his own sense of humour, the others hushing him in response, telling him to be quiet.

Amber gave Lex a look that said all that she thought about his joke.

She cleared her throat, and continued.

"... I'm a Lieutenant, one of the medical personnel on the USS Theodore Roosevelt, part of the United Nations Emergency Task Force, Pacific Fleet. I have been helicoptered in to the Chinese merchant vessel, Jzhao Li, and will be recording my notes on my investigation in this journal in case I need to refer to my findings. The Captain of the Jzhao Li had radioed for immediate medical help. So my team and I have been deployed to assist. The Jzhao Li is carrying invaluable supplies which will be crucial to the success of the rendezvous and it is imperative the ship proceed.

So far I have examined all the crew. The engineers have shown symptoms of the pandemic sweeping the world but none of the other crew are infected. Yet. I have recommended the engineers be quarantined. Also that the results of our findings be marked classified."

"Classified?" Salene asked. "That's odd."

It wasn't exactly a secret that the 'virus' had spread as an ominous pandemic around the entire world.

"Assuming she is referring to the virus," Amber replied.

"What do you mean - there was something else?" Lex asked, as confused and concerned as were all the others.

"Could be. I don't exactly know. What follows next seems to be measuring the health of each of the crew, recording their medical records," Amber said, flicking through some of the pages in the journal. "Here we go," Amber said to herself, finding the spot she had been looking for. "This is another entry a few days later."

She continued reading aloud.

"Sadly the engineers have passed away. Predictably succumbing to R18SYT. Which is accelerating within its mutation. So ends my observations of them in this journal. May they rest in peace. I will request evacuation for post mortem study back at Base 12."

"Base 12? Wonder where that was?" Slade pondered.

"Probably near Base 11," Gel said, causing the others to exchange frustrated glances at her.

Jay couldn't help but notice Ram's expression clouding.

"Any idea?" he asked.

"Not a clue," Ram responded.

"Go on, Amber. Keep reading," Ram urged.

"As for the rest of the crew, they are now displaying symptoms and we are all suffering. Myself included. The main mystery to me is how this is spreading when the engineers had been isolated 180 degrees north, 27 degrees south. I am referring, of course, to the survival grid identified through the global initiative rather than any nautical bearing.

The pattern emerging seems to illustrate the diagnosis and treatment originally identified to be inadequate. And our separation from the rest of the Task Force continues. We are isolated, as with the other ships that have now been infected. So many questions, but so little time. God knows how much longer we have left before we, too, succumb..."

"Suddenly I don't think it was such a good idea coming on board this ship," Gel said, gripped by fear.

"Shut up, and listen!" Ebony chided.

"This is a couple of days later," Amber went on...

"I am finding it hard to record my thoughts. The pain in my head is intense.

Over half the bridge crew are now dead.

The tissue samples I have taken show a foreign origination. Coupled with the broadcasts received from the other ships of the Task Force, this proves conclusively that the beta serum now being tested will not work as it was originally intended, and outlined in our briefing papers provided to the military authorities. As a consequence, we are all suffering here on this very ship. And I am at a loss what to do!"

Amber skipped forward a few more pages. There was utter silence in the bridge, the only sound that of the churning ocean waves outside as the cargo ship, the Jzhao Li, they now knew it was called thanks to the journal, continued drifting, the sea wind rattling the windows of the bridge.

"I don't understand why the requests for evacuation have been denied to the isolation sectors of the Task Force. Protocol clearly states that all those quarantined should not be ignored. Yet radio contact has been lost. And we are seemingly left alone to die. I sit here, in the bridge, my pen and journal my only companions, as I look out at the ocean. And the occupants of the Jzhao Li are passing away.

My fingers ache. My body has convulsions. I, too, am not for this world much longer.

The survival of our civilization is at stake. It is ironic how this curse upon our planet, something we cannot see... can reek so much devastation, pain and suffering. But this pales in comparison to a feeling of being misled. If the governments of the world were truly aware - as I suspect they might - hopefully history will discover and record this act of utter sacrifice and betrayal.

I have lived my life well. I have tried to help others. But I now know that help will not reach me. In time."

Amber squinted her eyes. The handwriting of Dr Jane Gideon was increasingly hard to read, no doubt due to the difficulties the Doctor was encountering at the time.

"This seems to have been written less than a day later," Amber explained...

"This will surely be my final entry. To my family, I love you. If you have survived this catastrophe, then I hope my words bring you comfort, if they ever reach you. If not, if you too are subject to the plague of our age, then I will see you again, if the good Lord is willing. Nothing can separate us, not even death will keep us apart.

I sense the call and I am ready. I pray our humanity will survive. And that whoever is responsible will be held to account. I leave this world as I came into it - Jane Gideon."

"And that's it," Amber said quietly, taking it all in as she put the journal down. The others around her were quiet as they also tried to assimilate what they had heard.

It had been an eerie experience, reading Doctor Gideon's words, holding the very same journal that she, too, had once held, hearing the account of her last days on the face of the earth. It was all unsettling, tragic, though Amber took some comfort from Doctor Jane Gideon's obvious kindness and humanity to others.

"We're going to be okay - aren't we?" Trudy asked hopefully, breaking the silence in the bridge, the anxiety in her voice obvious.

"I dunno about that," Lex replied. "All that stuff that Doctor wrote... it sure as hell doesn't give me much hope."

"We all have a resistance, don't we?" Salene added. "That's why we survived the virus in the first place."

"Who knows?" Jack said, muttering his thoughts aloud as he tried to make sense of it all in his mind. "That doesn't sound to me that she was just referring to any kind of 'virus'."

Trudy broke up, sobbing, as Salene comforted her.

"Well done, Jack," Ellie said, giving him a dirty look.

"What did I do? I'm just trying to help."

"I think we should all calm down and try and go over it all together later," Amber suggested. "Rather than jumping to any kind of conclusions."

"Oh really?" Ebony said coldly. "Well, I'll tell you this for nothing. I've already arrived at my conclusion. And we're in it. Deep. Right over our heads. Just like those crew we buried. This isn't a ship. It's a floating tomb."

CHAPTER TEN

Bray trudged through the barren, charred wilderness, every muscle in his tired body aching, urged on by sheer willpower alone. Fatigue threatened his progress, tempting him to give in.

Losing his footing, Bray tumbled and just managed to catch his fall, scratching his hands as he tried to land in a controlled manner, his fingers hitting some gorse plants, their bristles cutting into him.

Bray winced, cursing his luck that out here, wherever 'here' was, in the middle of nowhere, he should trip and fall onto one of the few plants that did manage to survive in this forbidden wasteland. The only question was, could he survive too?

Once more, doubt entered his conscience. Give up, give in. What's the point in going on?

Fighting back, dismissing the notion of surrender, Bray pushed himself up, regaining his footing. His right leg searing with pain, Bray yelled out in agony.

He had cut himself in an earlier fall the day before, on a jagged rock. Feeling his gashed thigh gently, Bray guessed he had probably got an infection by now. He had tried to fashion a makeshift bandage out of his clothing, wrapping the ripped material on his wound. But there was little more he could do. Every so often, his wound resumed bleeding, his improvised bandage covered in red.

"With the bloodline of Bray, we are one with Zoot!"

Bray shook his head, dismissing Eloise's voice, the image of her cruel expression, embedded deep within the recesses of his imagination. He hoped more than ever he had finally got away from her, would never see her again - or her crazed 'Zootist' followers.

Her experiments, the invasion of his very mind, through the many forays into reality space, sharing a virtual fantasy - they had all been insufferable. And even now, had an effect. Bray once again had difficulty deciphering if his current predicament was real or if he had been caught and was now trapped in a virtual reality simulation.

What Bray had found even worse, harder to stomach, was the distortion of how he viewed his brother's legacy and life.   Compared to how others he had encountered throughout his imprisonment seemed to think of Martin. Was Zoot a God? What had he done to deserve such worship? He was certainly troubled, disturbed. Extolling his mantra of 'Power and Chaos'. But Bray knew he was no monster. Deep down inside, 'Zoot' was still 'Martin', Bray's brother. He had good in him. And they enjoyed a close relationship growing up. Surely the deep bonds of two brothers could never disappear? For all of the confusion, having been subjected to all the simulation programs, Bray was sure he was close to Martin once. Wasn't he? Or had that all been programmed, a fantasy?

To Bray, Martin would always be the quiet, shy young boy who loved his family and idolised his older brother. Martin would have been disgusted at the world that was taking shape after the adults had perished. With people like Eloise, manipulating, pursuing selfish agendas, all too happy to trample on others to get their way.

A warm breeze blew in Bray's face. Dry as he was, dehydrated, it only intensified his discomfort. As did the intense sun, beating down. So used to being inside, the bright outdoor light hurt his eyes, the sun burning his skin. There was no shade or protection.

There had been trees here in a different time, no doubt a continuation of the forest that must have grown there once before. Now, only endless tree stumps remained, the ground charred in places. Ashen. The topography was truly post-apocalyptic. Bray noticed what he perceived to be a huge, deep crater and bypassed it, for many hours, rather than risk scaling down and crossing the mammoth divide. It was as if some thermonuclear explosion had occurred. Or a meteor strike. Something had happened.

Parts of the soil were crystalizing. Swirling circular shapes rippled as if fossilized by an ominous shockwave.

Bray felt in a way he was the only person left in the world.

Though he had regained his freedom and was overjoyed to be away from Eloise, the isolation he now felt, his painful solitude, the awful predicament, was difficult to bear.

There was nothing in this wilderness. Just the great likelihood of a slow, painful death. Either starving. Or succumbing to his infection.

Continuing onwards with a limp, dragging his infected leg and trying to put most of his body weight on his other side, Bray's thoughts of his own mortality... and his brother... led him to recalling the funeral of Zoot. The memory was so clear to Bray - like he was there, remembering every detail, even though he knew it was all in his mind. Was he going to join his brother soon? Would anyone mourn his likely passing - or even know of it?

What had happened to Amber, Bray wondered as he trudged on. She had been such comfort to Bray then, at Zoot's funeral. And not long afterwards, throughout their time together as a couple, when they were very much in love. Had she survived the Techno invasion? What of the baby?

Last he saw, going through it in his mind, Amber had gone into labour, before the Technos captured him. He had left her in the barn, hearing the sounds of the Technos' planes as they flew over the city, beginning their invasion.

Recognized by Techno forces, Bray had been dragged, kicking and screaming. Taken from Amber. Away from the life he knew. The life he cherished.

Bray had encountered many other fellow prisoners. He met up with KC and Alice in a slave camp prior to them being shipped to various locations for laboured servitude. And he heard tales from them that the Guardian had resurfaced. Somewhere. Even that Ryan was still alive and had been transported somewhere overseas, where he had met up with Paul. In one of Bray's own camps, he was sure Tai San had been there previously - the description Bray's fellow slave gave, certainly matched Tai San.

News of Bray's tribe, the Mall Rats, had also spread to so many other areas and he was proud of their reputation and primarily, aspiration of building a new world order out of the ashes of the old.

Bray himself had been passed from one group of oppressors to another, traded as a slave, exchanged like he was a piece of merchandise, not a fellow human being.

He didn't know how long he had been under Eloise's sway at the compound in the mountains. His mind, his memories cluttered. Conflicting images, sounds, assaulting his senses, creating almost a new reality. With the only constant being he was unsure if he could rely on his recollections.

But Amber had been real. Their love. He wouldn't forget her, even with the mental and emotional turmoils he had been subjected to under Eloise.

He never knew what happened. There were rumours, word that Amber had perished, as well as lived, passed on from other prisoners he had encountered in his incarcerations. Alice and KC had heard talk that Bray had a daughter. In another camp as Bray desperately pressed for more information, other prisoners remembered hearing something about the leader of the Mall Rats having a son. Twins. Others said the baby hadn't made it. Some told him Amber had died in childbirth. Bray would only know for sure what had happened to Amber and the baby if he saw them for himself. And he was determined, for them, to do so, to make it out of this hell he now found himself in.

He couldn't yield, he had to survive.

"Come on!" Bray urged himself through cracked lips, his voice dry and hoarse. He was so thirsty. His last drink had been when it had rained the day before - he had walked around with his mouth open, catching the drops. He must have looked so stupid doing that, Bray laughed. How Amber would have laughed as well, he felt. But there was desperation in the tone, a manic intensity.

As he pushed himself on he gazed up at the Heavens and screamed angrily, amidst his almost hysterical laughter.

"Thank you for the rain! I couldn't have survived without it! But it'll probably kill me now!"

In his confused state, there was an element of truth. He had slipped and stumbled onto the rocks trying for even a drop of moisture, causing the very gash now painful in his leg.

His skin agitated and sore, blistering in the dry sun... if only there was somewhere to get out of the baking heat. A tree to provide shade. A shelter.

"You gonna help me with the tent?"

Bray suddenly smiled fondly, recalling Martin's voice, his question that was asked frequently in the times he and his brother had struggled putting up the family tent, often in the pouring rain, on their camping vacations. He could almost imagine Martin in front of him now, in the wilderness, looking for a place to set up camp, Bray ready to help out.

He had loved the outdoors when he was younger. The family would go away on vacation and he would have many adventures, exploring all that the great outdoors had to offer with his brother, Martin.

Bray recalled how back in the city he had longed for the natural world. How he had missed it. As a Mall Rat, his life had been a fight for survival in the urban jungle and he had always felt an affinity with nature. The purity of our mother Earth. The purity of his relationship with his brother. Once. In a different time. Now he felt as if he was almost in a different world, almost on another planet.

How he missed him. He felt the pangs of separation still to this day. A sense of loss. Not just at Martin's tragic passing. But what Martin had done to his own life, reinventing himself as the city tyrant, Zoot.

Could Bray have done more to stop the transformation of Martin into 'Zoot', the frightening and unpredictable force that had terrified so many?

Was it something he had done? Had he contributed to Martin's fall? Heaven knew Bray had done all he could, given everything in his power to bring the real Martin back, to get rid of Zoot. And Martin had been close to coming round. The humanity in him returning, before his sudden death prevented any chance of Bray saving him. He would never forget his younger brother, he would carry his memories of the good times with him for the rest of his days. Even as he was perplexed and saddened by the many bad times and experiences with Martin... the tragedy of Zoot, his love for him remained.

Was Bray now being punished? For having the same bloodline? Was he now in purgatory?

Suddenly Bray heard a noise behind him, a rustling, and froze in his tracks, his body coursing with tension.

Was it Eloise? The 'Zootists'? Some other threat? The devil?

Spinning around, Bray spotted some gulls, waddling around on the ground, pecking for bugs with their beaks.

He smiled initially as the birds' heads comically bobbed up and down, curious at what they might find, their eyes searching the terrain. The only living creatures around, apart from himself. In a way they were like him, out here, in the great unknown, fighting to survive and he felt an affinity with that struggle.

But then as he focused his gaze, he wondered if they could somehow even be vultures. Just waiting. Biding their time. for when he would succumb.

In his heart, Bray knew he was dying. And through his disorientated state, wondered who he would be reunited with, if there was an afterlife. Martin? Or did Zoot live on, in Heaven?

* * *

Time went on. How many days, Bray didn't know.

"Don't give up," he muttered to himself, dragging his infected leg. Every time he moved it, the pain was excruciating. His thigh had swollen up. Felt like it would burst.

The agony of his isolation was nearly crippling. He was going mad. Out here on his own, with only fear and uncertainty as his companions.

And he wondered if what was right in front of him was even real. Or another hallucination. All in his mind. It had loomed on the horizon at first and Bray had headed towards it, fascinated by what he saw - or thought he could see.

He reached out to touch it.

There. It felt real, poking his fingers through the wire mesh.

It was a barbed wire fence. Perhaps a dozen feet tall, with wicked twists of sharp wire knotted all around it.

The fence ran the entire length of the land in front of him, as far as the eye could see. And he could see no end of it. No beginning. Just the barbed wire bisecting the entire wilderness. An impenetrable barrier.

And there, just visible through the mesh on the other side of the fence, in the middle of nowhere, was a military style truck. Half buried in the dusty dirt. With its sand coloured dessert camouflage, the vehicle looked like some ancient artefact, a relic from a bygone age, sticking out of the ground. At the back of the truck, a tattered door flap billowed in the warm wind that blew across the desolate landscape.

Perhaps the wreckage would work out as a makeshift shelter from the burning sun? Maybe there were supplies inside he could use.

Putting his hands on the mesh, gathering his strength, Bray began to slowly climb the wire fence.

He gashed his fingers on the barbed wire, crying out in pain, his dry skin bleeding profusely from the fresh cuts being inflicted. His tired, weak body urged him to let go. The agony was unbearable. Like he was being tortured.

But he kept climbing, reaching the top, where the barbs were especially tangled.

Yet as with Eloise before, Bray wouldn't yield. He had come too far. Fighting his natural urges to release his grip, he forced his fingers to keep clinging on to the wire, willing his infected leg to hold his body weight, in complete inner torment as the wire bristles sharply cut into his body again, blood now dripping to the ground.

It was then, at the top of the fence, that Bray spotted the castle, further away. And for a moment, struggling through his weakness to hold on the jagged wire, he felt that it was too late. He had surely lost a grip on his sanity and was seeing things.

But there it was. It was real. The castle stood in the distance, the sun setting on the horizon.

Bray gazed, transfixed, clutching the fence. Staring at the castle. Was it Heaven? Was this what death was like? Did he have the will to let go? Propel himself to the other side.

With the sun continuing to set on the horizon and the light growing dim, Bray was now becoming engulfed in darkness. Illuminated slightly by fading beams.

Trapped at the top of the wire and weakly balancing precariously, Bray's life force felt as if it was ebbing away, disappearing with the setting sun.

He yelled out in bitter frustration, pain. A sustained wail of anguish. Realizing he wasn't going to make it.

The vulture-like birds he saw earlier swooped, their wings fluttering in a frenzy as they began pecking at the wounds oozing blood, dripping from his leg dangling over the fence.

CHAPTER ELEVEN

Stop it, Amber thought to herself. She couldn't help it, and gazed one more time at her reflection in the outside window on the ground floor level of the accommodation tower. How did she look?

Eyeing her image in the window, the sun shining on it so it was like seeing into a mirror, Amber had a look of concern, rather than checking herself out vainly.

Since the discovery of Dr Jane Gideon's journal, Amber and the others had all been anxious about their health and the questions posed by the journal.

"I look fine," Amber said to herself. Didn't she?

She focused again, studying her appearance.

So far nobody had been showing any obvious symptoms. Of any illness. Other than being cast adrift at sea for so long.

Amber tried to tell herself to stop worrying. She knew that once you allowed fear to take a grip, it would never let go and she didn't want to allow herself to be driven by her worries, taking counsel of her anxieties. This was the approach she had always taken in the darkest days back home in the city, when the adults perished and the world fell into the abyss, looking like the survivors wouldn't be far behind with the future grim. Amber had always fought her fears, she had tried to keep calm, level headed. It wasn't easy though.

And she could see how voodoo was such a potent force. If someone was ever told they were cursed, then that's all that was needed. The torturous power of the imagination would do the rest.

"I'm okay..." Amber insisted, thinking positively, forcing herself to turn away from her mirror image. She looked - like she always looked. She felt fine. She just hoped that for the sake of her baby and the others on board that they wouldn't meet the same fate as whatever happened to the crew of the Jzhao Li.

So many questions remained unanswered. Who were they? And most importantly, what was their mission? The journal had mentioned Dr Gideon was part of a so called United Nations Task Force. The Pacific Fleet.

What exactly was the United Nations Task Force doing in this region in the first place? The Tribe had talked at some lengths about it all, wondering what Dr Gideon's journal had recorded. None of them remembered hearing about a United Nations fleet assembling anywhere in the days when the adults began to die out. There was nothing about it mentioned on the news. Had they perhaps stumbled by chance upon something that had been top secret?

Dr Gideon had indicated in her writing, Amber having studied it, re-reading it several times, that the United Nations fleet was part of an effort to combat and escape - something. Which certainly could have been the so called global 'pandemic'. But she had referred to so many elements being 'classified'. And Amber wondered if there was something more to it all than the 'virus'.

During the days in the city, the Mall Rat tribe thought they had the answers surrounding Pandorax as a result of all the investigations when Ellie spearheaded her enquiry and published her newspaper, The Amulet.

Amber had never been a particular fan of conspiracy theories, believing many of them to be far fetched, sources of unnecessary worry. The mysterious journal of Dr Gideon only fuelled a seemingly inexhaustible amount of potential reasons. Was the Task Force dealing with the pandemic or onto something else? If so, it would pose to be an almost impossible challenge trying to decipher just exactly what.

One thing for certain though. There they were, living on a vast container vessel, a remnant from the adult days, a ship that was part of a fleet intended to 'save humanity', as Dr Gideon put it in her words. Had the governments of the world, the United Nations, known more about the pandemic than they had let on to the public? Was there something more to it all than the information that had been released?

The priority was to formulate some kind of a plan. Dealing with what they knew to be fact. Opposed to any pointless speculation.

It seemed to Amber, along with all the others - except Ram - that their only option was to try and steer the ship to some kind of destination on the assumption that they were in a position to do so, of course.

Amber had every faith in Jack and Ram's technical skills, and she wondered how they were getting on up in the bridge.

Though she didn't trust Ram as an individual, suspicious of his true motives, believing his past actions had shown him to be nothing but a selfish tyrant, Amber was well aware that he was a genius after all. At least with computers. Nobody doubted that. Ram's intellect and wizardry were clearly off the scale. Jack's technical skills had always been incredible and he too had an aptitude for computers though he lacked Ram's programming flair. But if anyone could reactivate the instrumentation on the bridge, then they could.

Such a pity Ram wasn't able to channel his many gifts into something positive for humanity, Amber felt. Maybe this was a start, an opportunity for him to change, continue as he meant to go on. She hoped so. He certainly had a lot of ground to cover, amends to make from his past wrongs.

"How are they getting on?" Amber asked as Jay entered the cabin. "Any breakthroughs?"

Jay had just been in the bridge checking on Jack and Ram's progress and Amber could see that something was troubling him.

"Is everything okay?" Amber asked.

"Difficult to know. They managed to get a Sat Nav signal for just a few minutes. But the grid just doesn't make any sense, Amber. The co-ordinates show that we are somewhere near the Pacific islands. But the grid readings don't refer to any by name. Only zones. And no matter how hard Ram tries to cover it up, it seems to be freaking him out big time."

"Why?" Amber replied. "If this was part of a United Nations fleet, maybe they just used zones for their charts rather than any geographical names. The military would often do that. Wouldn't they?"

"Maybe," said Jay. "But Ram's still going on about using this ship to head back home, to the city. I could understand in a way when we were on that trawler. But on this ship, we have a real chance. And I don't get it. Why he can't see."

"You don't think he knows something - we don't?" Amber considered.

"If he did, he's not exactly the person to be very forthcoming, Amber. You know that."

"What about Lex and the others? How are they getting on?"

Apart from Sammy and Lottie, who were looking after the little ones, all the others had been deployed in shifts to check out more of the containers, crack them open, see what else they could find.

"I'll go and catch up with them for an update," Jay said. "Amber, there is one more thing though."

"What?"

Jay kissed Amber on the cheek tenderly. "I love you."

"Thanks," Amber smiled. She suddenly felt a whole lot better.

Jay left and Amber sat, re-reading Doctor Jane Gideon's journal again. Trying to fit together any piece of information which might shed light. But she was more preoccupied by Ram.

That she still so doubted him, was unable to trust him, only added to her unease at the Tribe's dependence on Ram in their time of need. He had proved in the past he could be a dangerous individual. And if he was holding some secret of any kind, then they would all have to be careful.

* * *

Slade pounded the rusty steel beneath him as he jogged on the outside deck of the cargo ship, passing Lex and his team examining the containers. He was due to take the next shift. And in his break, welcomed the opportunity to have a work out, determined to keep his fitness levels up.

But it also helped him to spend some time alone away from the others, his mind wandering as he jogged, considering all kinds of issues from the passing of his brother back in the city, his life before the 'virus' when the adults were still alive, to what the future held out for him and the others. And his relationship with Ebony.

He had calculated a circuit for his jogging, weaving in and out of the stacks of containers piled all around. Each lap must be a third of a mile.

This was some jogging track, he thought, as the massive cargo ship pitched up and down on the ocean below. He must have jogged a good three miles, Slade added in his mind, with just a few more circuits to go. He was trying to achieve a target of five miles.

Slade rounded a corner, accelerating his stride. It was time to pick up the pace over the last laps and get the cardiovascular system really pumping.

Ebony stepped out from a stack of containers on the opposite side of the ship where Lex and the team were working and Slade took a momentary fright as he nearly collided into her, stopping immediately in his tracks, his chest heaving from his exercise.

"Ebony! Always full of surprises," he said, gathering his breath.

"I've been trying to find you, Slade."

"Well, you have... what is it you wanted?"

Ebony seemed bothered. Agitated. She cast furtive glances around, making sure nobody was listening to them.

"I want to talk with you! This is a death ship! You heard what was in that journal. It isn't safe on board. There's two lifeboats, back there" Ebony indicated the two small boats hanging from the accommodation tower structure at the back of the ship. "We've got to get out of here!"

"What do you mean 'we'?" Slade asked.

"Who do you think I mean? I mean us. Me and you."

"Ebony... there is no 'us' anymore, in case you haven't noticed. And I'm going nowhere. I'm not leaving the others, getting off this ship. And neither are you."

"I thought we had something special going. That we were an item?"

"Yeah... we had something. At one point. Long ago."

"So what is it?" Ebony implored, her eyes welling up with tears.

"It's you!" Slade snapped. "You... mystify me. First I lose my heart to you. Falling head over heels in love. Then you rip it to shreds, as if you don't even know who I am. I've come to realize you're not the person I thought you were."

"If it's about Mega, once again - I'll say it, I'm sorry. What more can I do to show you - I was wrong about what I said."

"You're right about that. I remember every cruel word. "He deserved what he got," you said. You were glad. "Happy," I think was the word you said. "Happy" that he had died. That I deserved more than him for a brother."

"What did you expect me to say? That you should feel really proud of his achievements, unleashing all those chemicals into the city?" Ebony snarled.

"You don't get it. No matter what Mega did - he was still my brother! All that I had left of my family from before!"

Slade looked at her. It wasn't just hurt in his eyes. But regret, pity. And utter loathing.

"From what I've learned about some of the things you've done in your life, Ebony, especially as Queen of the Locos, you're hardly in any position to criticise anyone. At least I had feelings for my brother. Unlike you with Java and Siva. I mean you weren't exactly a loving sister now, were you?"

"It's Ruby, isn't it? She's lured you in. I've seen you both together. The way you look at her. She's always trying to impress you. Tarting herself up. Constantly fiddling with her hair. She can't take her eyes off you!"

"Is that all you've got to think of with everything we're going through?" Slade asked disdainfully.

"There is just one other thing," Ebony snarled. "Is she good? In bed?"

Suddenly Ebony sprung forward, her arm a blur as she took Slade by surprise, scratching the side of his face with her fingernails, deep scratch marks visible on his cheek.

"You keep the hell away from me from now on!" she screamed. "And you'd better tell that bitch to do the same!"

Giving Slade a filthy look, Ebony stormed off.

Slade watched her leave, feeling the cuts in his face.

And she had gone, doing her very best to put as much distance between them, getting away from all the thoughts and feelings she once felt for him, leaving Slade far behind her.

* * *

"Jack - you'll never guess what I can see?" Ram asked, peering through the binoculars he held to his face, staring out of one of the windows in the bridge.

"I dunno. The Easter bunny. The Loch Ness monster. No - let me guess. It's blue, wet and starts with the letter W?"

Jack sat on the floor with his back to Ram. The two of them had been arguing - again - about what the different instrumentation meant on all the equipment in the bridge.

"It is blue and wet but it starts with the letter O - I see nothing but Ocean," Ram said.

"Enough games, Ram," Jack replied, flicking through some print outs recovered from the engine room. "We've got work to do."

"You still sulking, Jack? Now I know how Ellie feels when you two have been arguing."

"We do not argue, thank you very much, Ram. And no, I am not sulking! Can't we just - get on and try and get all this to work?"

Ram put the binoculars down and looked at Jack. He enjoyed winding him up, really took delight from Jack's reactions to Ram's never ending practical jokes and barbs. But he realized Jack was right. They did have a lot to be getting on with, working out through a process of deduction what some of the dials and readings must mean. They knew the speed of the ship - it was drifting about 3 knots per hour. They knew the direction it was headed. North west. They had reactivated the Sat Nav signal for a minute or so. Now they were trying to engage the engines and auto-pilot system.

Ram had his view about what buttons to press to achieve a certain result, while Jack interpreted things differently. Both shared common ground that nothing should be touched or activated till they were confident what the item in question would do. They didn't want to endanger the ship, releasing ballast which might cause it to capsize or something.

Ram was in high spirits. He was lapping up every second of it. The task they faced was a difficult one. There was just so much complex equipment in the control room. But Ram found it a stimulating mission, something to challenge even him, his mental powers, his own self-declared 'genius'.

By contrast, Jack was getting frustrated not just by Ram's arrogance, but the pressure was getting to him. It was up to them to try and make some use of the ship, to figure it out, how it ran, if they could steer it. There were so many 'ifs', Jack thought, as he went over the engine room diagrams.

"Cheer up, Jack," Ram said, slumping down in one of the tall swivel chairs at a control dashboard, spinning around merrily in circles for a moment. "Enjoy it - this is fun!"

"This is not what I would describe as fun," Jack said.

"Well, I'll be..." Ram mumbled to himself, holding the binoculars up to his eyes again and staring out of another window.

"What is it now? You found Gel and the girls out sunbathing on the front deck?" Jack chirped up.

"Jack - would I do that?" Ram said in mock protest, a wicked grin on his face.

"Yes, you would. And you have."

"No, not this time, Jack. I've got my eyes on some other 'scenery'."

"What do you mean? A dolphin? A mermaid? Tell me."

"If only it was one of the girls sunbathing..." Ram pondered in disappointment at what he observed.

"Ram, you've spent far too much time on computers," Jack jested. "You've gotta get out more."

"Look who's talking. No, what I can see... How did they used to say it in the old days - that's right. Land ahoy..." Ram said casually.

Jack dropped the engine room charts and scrambled to his feet, Ram passing over the binoculars so Jack could have a look.

Ram was right. Out there, in the distance, Jack could barely contain his excitement as he saw the unmistakeable signs... the outline of land on the horizon.

And unbeknownst to Jack, rather than hope, it clearly filled Ram with an awesome dread.

CHAPTER TWELVE

He was alive. For how much longer, that was another matter, Bray thought, feeling the agony in his infected leg, the pains all over his body, ravaged from the many barbed wire cuts when he climbed the barrier that had so challenged him.

Drawing weakly on his fading strength, he had managed to scramble down the other side of the fence before finally falling to the ground.

Spending the night in the wreckage of the overturned vehicle, Bray had rested up, regaining what was left of his energy following his trek through the wilderness.

The military truck had provided a welcome though temporary refuge, nothing more. There was no food inside it. But to Bray's delight, there had been an out of date can of cola left in the front seat glove compartment, that had sustained him during the long night, the foul tasting liquid nonetheless truly appreciated by his dehydrated body.

And now with the sun beaming down overhead once more, the temperature rising, Bray was thrilled to be alive still. He had dug deep, summoning everything within his spirit, his very core, to get that far on his flight from Eloise.

He had made it to another day.

Now he would find out if it was worth it. If all the suffering, the risks he had taken, would pay off.

Heading towards the 'castle' and buildings that he had spotted the previous night, Bray discovered a long section of tarmac. It must have been a runway at one point, Bray was sure in his still confused state. It was sheer joy to walk on such a surface compared to the rugged terrain in the wastelands, though the tar had melted in places. With lots of cracks, the runway was damaged, in a state of disrepair, almost mirroring how Bray felt himself with his body so weak.

The runway stretched for some time. Approaching the 'castle', Bray noticed other buildings in the distance in the perimeters. And every quarter of a mile, parallel to the barb wire fence, there were warnings signs displaying: DANGER. BIO HAZARD.

Hours later, nearing his goal, Bray was able to identify that the buildings formed part of what had to have been a military base.

There were massive hangars, with airplanes still inside. The strange thing was, Bray considered, the planes were from different time periods. Was this a war museum? He had his doubts. The majority of aircraft were modern day fighters, their sleek aerodynamic forms resting at peace, in contrast to the high speeds they had been designed to attain.

Was there anyone else there? Or just himself?

And yes, once again Bray wondered if he was inescapably trapped in a virtual reality program.

He pushed himself on, finding stamina to examine other parts of the base.

There were several outbuildings. Construction machines sat idly, like prehistoric monsters, frozen in time. Fossils from a bygone era.

Some hangars were incomplete, obviously still being built by whoever had worked on them before they had been abandoned, presumably left part finished in haste when the 'virus' spread around the world.

Bray noticed dozens of buildings which he was sure had once been barracks. Inside were empty beds, rusting lockers with doors open, cupboards bare. There was nothing of value for Bray to use. Just the ghosts of the past. Remnants of what had once been.

Nature was now reclaiming the base. There had to be water somewhere. Perhaps under ground, Bray reasoned. Above the ground, young trees grew in random patches, bursting through concrete paths, their roots making the paving slabs uneven. Plants of all shapes and sizes dotted the dusty soil, wild vines extending up walls as if nature itself was reaching out. But Bray was aware since entering the wastelands that apart from the vultures he was sure he had seen, this entire area looked to be devoid of any other birds or animal life. Perhaps their natural instincts were keeping them away. Did they knew something Bray did not?

Having checked out several of the buildings in the outer perimeters of the base, Bray turned his sights on the mysterious 'castle' that loomed nearby.

Maybe it would have the answers Bray was looking for, as well as something inside that could aid his struggle to survive.

* * *

Bray entered the castle through its open portcullis, the jagged metal tips of it pointing down at him threateningly. His boots scrunched down on broken glass and debris which littered the floor.

This was no castle, Bray had come to realize.

It was a shop.

Treading warily, unsure of what or who would be inside, Bray continued to cautiously examine his surroundings. The 'castle' was a facade, covering the shop inside. Most of the shelves had fallen down, the building had been ransacked, but one shelf in the store still held up, a few toy dragons sitting on it, their mouths wide open angrily, breathing out little orange plastic breaths of fire.

A knight wearing a suit of armour stood in the corner, its gauntlet empty of where it had surely once held a sword. The knight had been sprayed in layers of graffiti, strange whirls and symbols that seemed like an alien language, Bray unable to decipher any of it. He stared at the knight, who wore a crown at the top of his helmet. A plaque stuck to the base of the stand the armour stood on read 'King Arthur'.

Going outdoors through the 'castle' entrance, Bray identified that he had stumbled into an amusement park. What was left of one.

All around him were decrepit, decaying rides. There was no sound, just that of his breathing and his feet as he walked around, checking out his environment. To his left was an old merry-go-round with plastic horses that no longer carried any riders, the heads of the horses smashed, missing legs and hooves. On his right was what had once been a charming fairy-tale themed restaurant, its windows broken, chairs and tables upturned, toppled over like a hurricane had tore through. And he couldn't help but notice all the buildings seemed to have been charred.

Bray tensed, the pain in his leg throbbing as he spotted a small roller coaster in the distance beyond the buildings in front of him. Its frame looked as fragile as he did, the skeleton of its wooden struts marked by burn marks where it had once been on fire, great gaps visible in the loops where its carriages had once twisted and turned.

It was a strange, haunting place. Bray could all too well imagine how it would have been in its day, a fun place, where kids of all ages would have enjoyed spending their time, being together, Mums and Dads frolicking with loved ones. If only any of them knew of the 'virus', the catastrophe that had been waiting to transform the world that once was into a nightmarish hell.

It was the first time he'd been to a theme park, Bray smiled slightly to himself, thinking how ironic it all was. His family didn't have a lot of money when he was growing up which is why most of the time they had gone camping on vacation. His brother, Martin, had always wanted to go overseas, visit one of the famous destinations he had seen only in brochures or in commercials. And now here he was. Bray had made it to an actual amusement park.

Bray cautiously hobbled around the ruins, vigilant in case those who had graffitied and damaged the place still remained. He needed to find food. Drink.

Walking through the fairy tale-themed fantasy village, the cozy storybook buildings with their plastic wooden beams and atmospheric arching roofs, Bray spotted a vending machine inside one of the houses, itself another shop.

Entering slowly in case someone was inside waiting to ambush him, Bray saw toy cuddly knights and damsels in distress inside the machine, waiting for someone to rescue them.

In another section there were some chocolate bars. Bray picked up a witches broomstick left on the floor in the shop and used it to smash through the glass. Then he grabbed the chocolate bars inside, left well past their sell by date. And ravaged, began to consume the bars, savouring the food, the sweetness, even though the chocolate was stale and tasted horrible.

Bray suddenly heard laughter. The sound of young children, giggling.

Was he imagining it? Was this whole theme park nothing but a dream?

The high pitched squeals of delight rang out again and Bray knew that he wasn't hearing things. There were definitely some children around somewhere nearby.

He stealthily stepped out into the twisting fairy tale street, taking cover as he carefully made his way toward the source of the sounds of laughter.

Skirting the sides of the buildings, Bray peered around the corner of the street, poised in case he needed to put up a fight, his body tense with adrenalin.

He noticed a young girl and boy. They had to be no more than seven or eight years old. They were sitting either side of a see-saw in the shape of a dragon, bouncing happily up and down, laughing merrily as they took turns soaring vertically. The boy wore a far too big fighter pilot's helmet on his head, the girl a tattered, filthy fairy tale princess dress.

Bray breathed out a sigh of relief, his body relaxing. They would be no danger to him, but he had to make sure there were no other threats around.

Stepping out into the street slowly, so as not to frighten them, Bray approached, his hands held up as if in surrender.

"Hello," he smiled, his lips dry and cracking open.

The two kids stopped swinging on the see-saw. Turning to see Bray before them, they screamed suddenly in fright, terrified by him.

"I mean you no harm," Bray said, hobbling toward them, his leg searing in pain.

The girl and boy took off, panicked expressions on their faces, determined to get away from the stranger in their midsts.

"Please! Wait!" Bray yelled out and began to chase after the kids. He must look threatening, he thought, having been in the wilderness for so long, his face unshaven, hair matted, his filthy clothes torn, covered in dirt, blood.

Moving as fast as he could, Bray gained on them.

"Please stop! I'm a friend, I mean no harm," Bray called out, though it did nothing to reassure the terrified kids.

The young girl and boy raced through the entrance of what must have once been the foyer of a large administrative-looking type of building and he quickly followed.

"Hello?" he called out, his voice echoing as he paced around.

"Please - is there anyone there?" Bray shouted, his eyes darting furtively, trying to catch a glimpse of the kids, of anyone.

Spotting movement, just a tiny shadow, Bray walked up to a reception desk in the large foyer, his feet scrunching on the floor, trampling broken glass and layers of dust.

Peering over the side of the reception, Bray saw the younger girl and boy huddling together, doing their best to hide.

"I am begging you, please help me," Bray implored.

They looked up at him, terrified that he had found them. Maybe they didn't speak English, Bray reasoned. They might not understand him. What could he do?

He stretched closer, his hands held out wide open, showing he meant no harm.

The kids recoiled, screaming.

And Bray noticed their eyes were looking not just at him, but at what was behind him.

Bray turned to see - but it was too late.

Struck on the back of the head from behind, Bray collapsed in a heap, losing consciousness.

CHAPTER THIRTEEN

"I can't believe it's really out there!" Salene said excitedly, peering through the binoculars at the outline of land, still several miles away.

"And it's all thanks to me - I saw it first..." Ram said distantly to himself, slumped back in his seat, deep in thought, his feet resting on another chair. But from his tone, he was hardly elated.

"I'm so happy I could nearly give you a kiss!" Salene enthused, putting down the binoculars and turning around to face Ram and the others, the group assembling in the bridge to discuss the news of land being discovered.

"If your lips are willing - my face is ready to receive," Ram grinned.

"I said 'nearly' give you a kiss," Salene backed down.

Darryl blushed. He had developed a crush on Salene and all this talk of her kissing anyone made him feel awkward.

"I don't see why everyone seems so happy round here," Trudy spoke up, agitated, indicating the bridge all around them. "Haven't you forgotten where we are? The bodies we found here? Whatever happened to that crew might happen to us! Especially if it's a mutation of the virus! And who knows what dangers could be ashore!"

"Trudy - I agree," Ram said. "You're talking a lot of sense."

"Rubbish," Lex interrupted. "It's land, Trudy," he continued. "We've been dreaming about getting back on land for who knows how long now. And finally, there it is!"

"Trudy - I know what the journal said. We all heard it," Amber replied, trying to keep Trudy calm. "But I honestly don't think that any of us are infected by whatever killed the crew. Look at us all. We all seem fine, healthy."

"Physically anyway - if not mentally," Ram said, casting a cool glance at Amber.

"Shut it, Ram," Lex ordered. "In the Mall Rats, majority rules. We've all voted to try and head ashore. And that's the way it's going to be."

"There's no chance in hell we'll get to that land, Amber," Ram scoffed.

"And why's that?" Amber asked suspiciously.

The two stared at each other, their mutual antagonism obvious.

"It's simple. How do you suppose we get there, Miss know-it-all?" Ram explained, raising his voice in hostility. "We don't know how to even control this ship yet, do we?"

Amber smiled, unflustered by Ram's outburst. "That's your and Jack's department, Ram. I guess we're just lucky to have such a 'smartypants' like you among us. Unless - you're not as smart as you keep telling everyone."

Ram glared, agitated by her deliberate provocation.

Just like she hoped he would be.

"Prove me wrong," Amber said. "That you can help Jack get this ship working. Or aren't you up to the challenge?"

* * *

Amber and the others reasoned that if they could find a way to reactivate the ship's propulsion, it would at least get them closer towards the land, with little risk of the ocean's current taking them away from their objective. Then they might have a chance to use the small lifeboats to tender ashore.

The rest of the Tribe left Jack and Ram alone so they could concentrate and work together on the bridge - but with the two of them interpreting what all the great swathes of buttons and readings before them meant, they were at odds with each other and achieved very little. It felt like they were going nowhere.

"Ram - can't you see? This must be some form of ignition," Jack said, from where he was standing. "I can't believe you can't see it."

Ram growled in frustration at Jack, thumping his fist on the outside of the control panel.

"Careful!" Jack tensed, worried Ram was going to hit some buttons without first knowing what each of them did.

Ram peered out of the window of the bridge to the outer deck below, as Jack returned his attention to understanding the myriad of buttons stretching before him.

"Jack - I think Ellie's looking for you."

"I didn't hear anything."

"I heard her shout from outside. You must have been absorbed in your work. She just waved at me. By the look on her face, she must be needing you."

"She could have at least come up here and asked. She know's how busy we are," Jack flustered, heading out of the door to go and see what she wanted.

A leering grin appeared on Ram's face, thrilled at his deception.

With Jack out the way, Ram studied all the instruments in front of him.

He would show them. Especially Amber. Ram felt she was self-righteous. Had they forgotten? He had been a Tribal leader. And not just any Tribe. But the Technos.

He had achieved so much and the others treated him like he knew nothing, Amber in particular.

For all their sakes, especially his own, Ram was determined to use the mighty Jzhao Li container ship as a means of transportation. But not to go ashore. Ram was still intent to get back to their homeland.

And away from the island that beckoned.

He resolved that once he kick-started the engines, then he would alter the auto-pilot compass to turn the immense cargo ship around and point it in the opposite direction.

Ram had the answer, like always. Everything was simply a process of elimination, deduction. He knew he could meet the challenge that now faced him.

"It's elementary, my dear Jack," Ram spoke softly, dangling his finger over a button, the Chinese lettering keeping hidden what the button did - though for no longer, Ram thought. He had worked it all out.

Pressing the button firmly, then several around it, Ram stepped back, waiting for a response from the ship.

A few seconds passed.

Then suddenly a loud grinding sound could be heard coming from the very depths of the ship, the noise of grating machinery moving, the hull vibrating as the once mammoth and dormant mechanisms of the Jzhao Li sprung to life once more.

A look of triumph was on Ram's face.

"Told you so," he said smugly. He had done it.

The rumbling noise bellowing from below continued, a whirring, the screech of metal high-pitched as it resonated.

And then Ram noticed something was wrong.

The front of the ship stretching out from the window ahead of him was not pointing straight, as it had since they first stepped aboard. Nor was it altering course.

The ship was beginning to lean, ever so slightly, on an angle.

Ram wondered if his eyes were playing tricks and he stared, fascinated, trying to understand what was happening.

There was no doubt about it, the cargo ship was tilting.

With the imminent danger, suddenly the land on the horizon seemed very far away.

Jack burst in the door of the bridge panting, out of breath from running up the stairs.

"Ram - what the hell have you done!?" Jack shouted.

Ram looked despondently at Jack, the worry on his own face all too visible.

"I don't know..."

Sammy and Lottie gazed eagerly out of the cabin window. They had been excited at the prospect of going ashore with visions of playing parts in a real life adventure, similar to some of the tales they had read in the old books. Sammy's imagination was coloured and distorted in experiencing what it might be like to be a modern day Robinson Crusoe. But now he and Lottie were deeply concerned by the angle of the ship. Behind them, Brady played with baby Bray, oblivious to the threat which was now occurring.

Trudy appeared out of the bathroom. She had just taken a shower. She stared through the window, transfixed.

"Oh, my God! What's happening?!"

* * *

"I don't like it down here," Darryl whimpered as he followed Lex, Ruby, Jay, Salene, Ellie and Amber.

"None of us do," Amber whispered, her voice echoing in the metallic corridor.

She had suggested that they examine the ballast tanks while Ram and Jack continued on investigating the bridge.

May and Zak had been sent to check on Sammy and Lottie, who were caring for the two children in the cabins - but also keeping an eye on Trudy. Amber had reinforced that May and Zak try and keep Trudy calm when they explained what Ram had done. She didn't wish to add to the danger they were clearing facing with any unnecessary histrionics, suggesting that Trudy then work with Gel, May and Zak gathering food and supplies.

As an added precaution, Amber had deployed Ebony and Slade to check out all the lifejackets and make sure there was enough for everyone in case they needed to use them quickly, along with inspecting the lifeboat stations.

Amber's group was creeping along in the engineering room section in the bowels of the ship, several decks beneath the waterline. The corridor was dark, the electric lighting that had once lit it no longer working, and Jay used a flashlight to illuminate their way in the gloomy depths.

"This is creepy!" Darryl muttered.

"Darryl, would you calm down? You're freaking me out!" Salene snapped.

"Be quiet - please!" Jay insisted, trying to concentrate.

The beam of the flashlight in his hand cut through the darkness that lay ahead, with its spotlight falling on metallic walls, illuminating signs in Chinese text.

It was very humid and there was a lot of moisture in the air, with water dripping down.

"Do you hear that?" Ruby asked.

She could hear a rushing sound. Perhaps it was the ocean outside on the other side of the hull, the waves crashing against the sides of the ship.

The group arrived at a watertight door that stood in their way.

Through the other side they could all hear the torrent flowing louder and they were soon up to their knees and ankles in water.

It was unmistakeable. The door was straining to hold the mammoth weight of the unforgiving ocean.

"I dunno about you guys - but I think it's time we got out of here," Lex said, rightly concluding that the ship was taking in water.

* * *

Ebony peered at the ocean below, the waves rolling against the side of the ship. At least it wasn't too rough, she thought.

News the Jzhao Li was taking in water had spread like wildfire among the Tribe and a mood of panic had set in. Here they were, so close to land but so far. The island was still several miles away, the jagged outlines of the terrain now visible, and who knew how much longer they would have.

Ram had accidentally tampered with the ballast of the ship, flooding it with too much water, activating the watertight doors in the process. The huge doors did their best to stem the flood of water flowing in but with the ship listing, minute by minute, the situation was clearly precarious for the entire tribe.

Amber had sent out the alert for all to be on standby to abandon ship.

Which is exactly what Ebony had in mind as she jumped onto the gantry attached to the side of the vessel, towards its stern, harnessing the lifeboats.

It was now the moment to look after number one.

Ebony expected the small lifeboat to still have some fuel in it. Surely the crew of the Jzhao Li long ago, would have left the lifeboats on standby, ready to go, with supplies of food and water, enough fuel. She was willing to take that chance.

Spotting a handle on a little panel at the edge of the gantry, Ebony shifted it and to her relief, the lifeboat began to gradually swing out, dangling high above the water. At least something worked around here still, Ebony smirked.

Hitting a green button on the control panel in front of her, the lifeboat started to lower, suspended by the ropes it was attached to and Ebony knew it was time to take a leap of faith.

Jumping onto the lifeboat as it rapidly descended, she landed on its deck with a clatter, well balanced, using the feline agility she had been born with to full effect, finding her footing quickly.

It was only now Ebony appreciated the sheer scale of the Jzhao Li, towering above the lifeboat, angling dangerously above on its tilt. If it leaned any further, Ebony worried that the massive cargo ship would capsize and suddenly come crashing down on her.

The lifeboat reached the surface of the water and bobbled up and down on the current.

Pulling out a knife she had taken from the kitchen galley, Ebony cut the ropes that dangled, tethering the lifeboat to the mother ship. With the last of the threads torn away cleanly, Ebony realized she was finally free.

"Come on!" Ebony pleaded, turning the rusty key left in the ignition of the small lifeboat that she had placed all her future in, her very life.

The engine coughed and spluttered, smoke bellowing, diesel fumes filling the air.

The propeller at the back cut into the water as Ebony shifted the throttle, steering the lifeboat away from the monstrous cargo ship leaning above her.

The lifeboat sped away. Ebony let out a shrill yell of delight. The relief of her escape, her continued survival in this crazy world, was almost fun and she was engulfed by a feeling of jubilation. Just like how she had felt in the days when she used to drive around in Zoot's police car, back in the city.

She was ready for whatever adventure lay ahead. Bring it on!

Looking back behind her at the Jzhao Li as it continued its tilt precariously to one side, the distance opening between it and the lifeboat, Ebony grinned.

"So long, suckers," she hissed, turning forward to the mysterious land that lay in the distance ahead.

* * *

"Do something!" Ellie pleaded, as Jack frantically scanned the buttons and dials in the bridge.

"Like what?!" Jack shouted, panic on his face.

"Anything!"

"I'm trying, Ellie!"

Amber burst in. "Any luck?" she asked, but already knew the answer as she watched Ellie, Ram and Jack gaze despondently.

It was getting hard to stand and move around now, with the ship badly listing.

"Looks like we're running out of time, Jack," Amber continued. "It might be an idea to get your lifejackets on and join the others. I'll alert them. We really should all be on standby. This thing feels like it could go over any second."

"Looks like Ebony's already abandoned ship, Captain," Ram said, indicating.

Amber and the others noticed Ebony in the lifeboat, speeding away and Amber sighted to herself. Typical. Ebony didn't waste much time.

"There has to be something we can do!" Jack shouted, fastening his life jacket on, along with the others.

"Oh, to hell with it!" Ram snapped, and he began pressing buttons randomly on the console in front of him.

"Ram! Haven't you learned anything?" Amber said.

"I guess you're right, Amber!" Ram replied. "I'd better go and gather a few things up if we're leaving."

He crossed to the door and exited.

Jack focused on all the dials on the bridge. Each item on the instrumentation panel had to do something, perform some function. It was just like using a computer, albeit a very big computer. One that was sinking fast.

"Just give me one more minute, Amber. I promise!"

Amber nodded and watched eagerly with Ellie as Jack took the plunge and pressed a button. He waited with baited breath, in an air of anticipation.

Nothing happened.

Plan B. Another button pressed. Nothing.

"Oh, come on," Jack uttered, looking up to the Heavens above, imploring. "Give me a break."

Jack pressed a few more buttons.

Suddenly it was like the entire ship was struck by enormous vibrations as far below, a rumbling sound swept upwards, shaking their very bones. An ominous noise, the hull shuddering, reverberating as a powerful force exerted itself.

Jack stepped back, unsure. He had certainly done something, and he looked around at the others to see if they knew just what.

Amber raced out onto the outside fire escape stairwell, leaning over to see the back of the ship.

Down below, the water was churned into a white froth of foam as the powerful back propellers spun, driving the ship forward, the Jzhao Li slowly picking up speed.

Pumping her fist triumphantly, Amber ran back into the bridge.

"You've done it, Jack! You've done it!" she grinned.

Jack leaned back and gave a huge sigh of relief, Ellie hugging him, whooping for joy, and all three exchanged hi-fives.

The remaining members of the Tribe, assembled on deck, looked up at the bridge and also whooped it up, relieved as the ship was now gathering speed, which was also helping stabilise the mammoth vessel.

* * *

Ebony cursed her luck, the engines of the lifeboat spluttering in protest as they misfired, the boat slowing down, like its very life force was fading.

Ebony urged the lifeboat on, gripping its wheel with one hand while the other struggled with the gear, trying to coax the last remnants of power from its engines.

It was so typical, Ebony thought, her teeth clenched in a mixture of frustration and determination.

"Come on!" Ebony shouted, desperate. "Don't run out of fuel on me! Not now!"

The unknown land was still some way ahead of her. Ebony could make out rows of palm trees on the horizon, some sandy beaches. Just where was she?

Behind her, the Jzhao Li was quite a distance away but powering through the ocean towards the land, heading away at an angle on a different course.

Ebony wondered how on earth the others had managed to get the ship going again. She resented their success while she struggled, the lifeboat failing her in her time of need.

She thought about swimming to shore, calculating how far away it was, if she would make it. She had never been an expert swimmer. And who knew if there were sharks, rocks or other menaces lurking beneath the surface. Besides, with the powerful currents, she might be swept further out to sea while struggling to reach land. Swimming to the shore would be a last option, only if she had to.

The small lifeboat might have abandoned her, but she wasn't about to abandon it.

* * *

"The good news, I can see some sandy beaches - the bad news, there seem to be reefs surrounding the entire coast. And cliffs," Salene commented, staring through binoculars at the land straight ahead.

"That's just what we need," Jay said sardonically.

The Jzhao Li was moving at some speed now. It had been hurtling through the water at about 20 knots per hour and at that rate they would reach landfall in about 12 minutes, Jack contemplated. He had suspected that it was increasing speed, set by the auto-pilot. Problem was, Jack didn't know how to disengage the system. And consequently had no idea how the vessel could ever slow down.

If they couldn't find a way to steer the ship, the huge cargo vessel that had been their refuge would be their doom as the Jzhao Li, speeding towards the landmass, was clearly on a collision course, out of control.

Amber stood transfixed, the ship rapidly approaching the land which was looming closer. Closer.

"Jack - you've done well. But that's enough!" Amber said.

"I can do it, Amber! I'm sure I can!" he protested.

"No!" Amber replied emphatically. "Our only hope is with the lifeboat."

Unwilling for a moment to give up his efforts, Jack looked out the window of the bridge at the landmass stretching beyond them. He knew Amber was right, there was no other option. They only had a matter of minutes before the ship would run aground. Or worse still, hurl ashore.

* * *

"Is everyone here?" Jay asked, looking around, doing a headcount.

"Everyone except Ebony - bitch!" Lex answered. "Talk about every man - or woman - for himself!"

"What about Ram?" Slade asked, glancing around.

Suddenly they noticed Ram in full flight approaching along the deck towards them. He had for some reason changed out of his Techno uniform and was now wearing clothes he had recovered from the Jzhao Li crew.

"Well - how do I look?" Ram asked, as he arrived.

The others stared open-mouthed. It was macabre. And Trudy was especially repulsed.

"How could you, Ram?" Trudy said. "Wearing the clothes of a dead man?"

"Never know who we might meet ashore," Ram explained. "Thought I might try and make a good impression, make myself presentable."

The Tribe were assembled at the back of the ship, clambering into the remaining lifeboat, which wasn't easy, given the angle the Jzhao Li was still tilting on.

Ahead of them, they could see the land very clearly now, countless rows of palm trees, the sandy beaches, the reefs in shallower waters bordering the coast, rocks protruding menacingly.

Jay and Slade stood either side on the gantry while the others boarded.

"Well, what are we waiting for?" Jay said, yanking the lever on the gantry control panel to lower the lifeboat. "Let's get out of here!"

Slade nodded as the lifeboat edged out, the hydraulic lift grasping it shifting position, dangling the lifeboat high above the water. Slade climbed on, joining the others huddled together.

"Green must mean go," Jay said, pushing the green button on the control panel, the wind rustling his hair as the cargo ship sped through the waves.

He leaped into the lifeboat, which descended toward the water and hoped, as they all did, that it would lower quickly enough so they could get away from the massive vessel before it struck the land.

And then without warning, the lifeboat stopped dead in its ropes, dangling in mid-air.

Trudy and Gel shrieked in fear. Everyone in the boat exchanged panicked looks, wondering what had happened.

"What the hell?" Ram asked, looking up at the rope attaching the lifeboat to the cargo ship.

It was as they all feared. The mechanism was stuck. They were all stranded, nearly three stories above the ocean, the lifeboat swinging on the ropes, the waves beneath rushing past.

"I'll be back!" Slade shouted.

"Where are you going?" Ruby called out.

Slade didn't answer and clambered up the rope, his arms straining to haul himself upwards.

Following in Slade's trail, Zak, too, suddenly began to climb up the rope attaching the lifeboat to the Jzhao Li.

"Careful, Zak!" May shouted.

Swinging onto the gantry, Zak joined Slade, the two examining the control panel to manoeuvre the lifeboat.

Looking up at Slade and Zak on the gantry, Jay and Lex stood up, determined to lend their assistance. But the lifeboat wobbled and they lost their balance, Amber grabbing hold of Jay as the rope shifted, lowering the lifeboat a few feet nearer the water.

Slade pressed the green button again, hoping the lifeboat would resume its descent, but to no avail. The lifeboat was stuck.

"The handle!" Zak shouted, pointing, clutching the gantry as the wind bellowed, the cargo ship picking up speed.

Slade looked at what Zak had noticed, spotting the manual release handle on the other side of the control panel.

"Jay!" Amber cried out in worry, as Jay stood up again, struggling again to keep his balance. He held onto the rope, steadying the lifeboat, ensuring it remained taught in the pulley above. Lex assisted, both straining with all their might.

"We've got it!" Slade shouted to Zak, as he cranked the handle as quickly as he could.

Suddenly the taught tension in the rope was released. No longer stuck in the winding mechanism, the rope eased through the pulley it was fed through, the lifeboat descending at speed toward the water.

"Hold on!" Jack yelled.

Thinking quickly, Jack turned the key, throttling the engine of the lifeboat, which thankfully came to life, with a splutter. He knew as soon as they hit the surface, they would have to speed away from the momentum of the massive cargo vessel, with the land looming ever closer.

"Come on, boat, don't let me down!" Jack muttered.

"Slade! Zak! Jump!" the others shouted at the top of their lungs, gazing up at the gantry now five stories above them, the lifeboat striking the surface of the water, throwing its occupants with the force of the impact.

Revving the engine for all it was worth, Jack tried to keep pace with the speed of the Jzhao Li to give Slade and Zak a chance.

But they were stranded on the stricken vessel.

Having spent its life crossing the oceans of the world, the Jzhao Li was now making its final journey.

In the lifeboat racing away in the other direction, Jack struggled to steer with jagged rocks beckoning, tantalizingly close.

The others could hardly bear to watch what they knew was about to transpire. They were powerless. There was nothing they could do, though Jack tried to alter course and head closer toward the vessel.

Slade closed his eyes and jumped while Zak clutched the railings of the gantry, staring with horror into the abyss, aware that impact was inevitable.

The Jzhao Li ran aground, striking the reefs at speed, the ship screeching and shrieking as its steel hull peeled open.   Over a hundred thousand tonnes colliding with an enormous underwater landmass.   Like a lumbering leviathan, the mighty propellers at the back of the vessel kept spinning, cutting into the submerged reef while at the front of the ship, the Jzhao Li was literally torn apart.   Groaning in an agony of twisted metal, debris strewn everywhere, the stacks of containers on its outside decks tumbling, crashing into the water.   The noise was terrifying.   Like a monster of the sea meeting its end, metal rending, grinding.

"Slade!!" Ruby cried out.

May gazed around for any sign of Zak, while the others surveyed the area in mounting panic as they clung to each other desperately.

Jack cursed as the lifeboat scuffed against the side of another rock, a scraping sound revealing that though they had escaped the Jzhao Li, the lifeboat was far from safe.

A mighty explosion suddenly erupted at the back of the huge container vessel, tearing through the Jzhao Li, punching a hole in the hull, flames soaring into the sky as the fuel caught alight, roaring upwards, smoke billowing into the deep blue sky.

The shockwave sped across the surface of the water, the occupants of the lifeboat struggling for cover as the massive cargo ship met its doom before their very eyes.

CHAPTER FOURTEEN

Bray felt the cold water impact as it struck his face, awakening him with a start.   He instinctively gasped at the shock and shook his head, water flying in all directions from his wet hair, droplets dripping down his face.

His body felt weak and his mind totally groggy as if he was still fast asleep and hadn't fully woken up yet. In a stupor, Bray took a moment to try and make sense of his surroundings - and what had happened to him.

His vision was blurred and it was then he felt the throbbing pain in the back of his head where he had been struck.

Adrenalin filling his body, he blinked his eyes rapidly to try and clear his vision. He would have wiped his eyes but suddenly realized he was unable to do so - both his hands had been bound tightly behind his back. He tried to move, to get up from the prone position he found himself in - but his legs had also been bound, tethered at his ankles. So he was a prisoner once more, he thought, slumping his head back - on a very comfortable pillow. This was no ordinary prison, Bray thought. Just what exactly was it?

Though he felt like he was still in a deep sleep - and for a moment, wondered if this was all a dream - Bray finally was able to take in details of his environment, the blurred vision he had first experienced on waking up beginning to dissipate.

He was in some kind of living quarters. Laying on a bed, the mattress inviting and supportive. The ceiling above his head was missing the customary graffiti that had been so evident in the post-adult world and there weren't any obvious signs of vandalism or damage. Scanning his line of vision downwards, the walls around him were also in good condition. It felt as if he had almost gone back in time, to how living conditions used to be. But he also noticed a bank of security monitors, displaying outside images of the runways and various vantages of the barbed wire perimeter.

It was then that Bray spotted the young boy he had followed earlier... when? How long ago? The boy was staring at Bray from the other side of the room, examining him with fascination like he was an animal in a zoo.

Beside the boy stood the little girl Bray recognized from his previous encounter with them in the ruins of the theme park and administrative building. She was now holding a large bucket in her arms, watching Bray with curiosity, a hint of anxiety in her eyes. So she must have been the one to give him his wake up call, Bray figured.

"Hello," Bray began, trying to strike up a conversation, giving a friendly smile to the young boy and girl before him.

"Don't speak to them, talk to me," a warm voice spoke, determination in its tone.

Bray turned to where the voice was coming from and another girl, taller, obviously much older than the other kids, was slowly approaching him, one of her arms touching the bed as she edged nearer, using it as a guide, running her fingers along the side of the mattress. Bray couldn't make out much of her features. She was mostly in darkness, that side of the bed in shadow from the dim table lamps doing their best to illuminate the room.

"Be careful!" the young boy called out protectively.

"I'll be fine," the much older girl reassured him, moving forward towards Bray.

Stepping out into the diffused light, Bray could see that this girl was not that much younger than him. Tall, standing with good posture, her brown hair tied in a long ponytail that swung behind her back. She had a gracious air about her. A few freckles on her face, she was pretty.

It was her eyes though which were so striking. Full of expression. Yet opaque as if staring into the distance, the realms of an unknown world. Bray recognized that this girl was blind.

"Who are you?" Bray asked, looking up as the blind girl sat by the side of the bed.

"The one asking the questions," the girl replied matter of factly.

Bray winced as the girl touched his infected leg, pain shooting up his body. He wondered if he was about to be tortured, just what she meant to do with him.

"I'm sorry. I was just feeling your wound. To see if your infection is healing," the girl said, her fingers gently caressing around the wound on his leg. It had been bandaged, Bray only now appreciated, feeling the gauze fastened over his infection.

"Thanks," Bray said, the pain in his leg subsiding from her gentle touch.

"We could have left you to die. But we've cleaned you up, tended your wounds. Given you antibiotics. My younger brother has even given you a shave," the blind girl said.

Bray felt alarmed at the thought of the young boy being anywhere near a razor blade - let alone one near his neck - but it was true. He could feel the air in the room on his face, which was now smooth, the stubble he had grown during his time in the wilderness shaved clean.

"What do you want of me?" he asked.

"Answers. Like - who are you?"

"My name is Bray."

"Why were you following my younger brother and sister?"

"They were the first people I had seen in ages. I've been lost, wandering around for some time and if I hadn't found you - this place - I'm sure I wouldn't have made it."

"Where are you from?"

"That's a long story. Another land, originally. Least of all, I think. But now? I've been on my own for some time, trying to survive." Bray omitted any details about being an escaped prisoner, on the run from Eloise. He had to find out who these people were. For all he knew, they might hand him back in to Eloise's forces, or be in some sort of contact with them.

"Are you saying that you travelled over the wastelands?" the blind girl asked in disbelief.

"Just believe me. I'm a long way from home."

"That's very hard to believe. That you made it here. Some of our people climbed the barrier. Tried to head to the north. Across the wastelands. But none of them ever returned. Did you have anything to do with it?" the blind girl asked, a sense of anger now in her demeanour.

"No, I promise. I'm on my own. I haven't seen anyone else and I don't know what happened to the people you're talking about."

"Neither do we. And if you are responsible in some way...?"

Bray could only guess that whoever the blind girl referred to must have encountered Eloise's forces, if they had even made it that far through the unforgiving wilderness.

"Where are your markings?" the blind girl asked suspiciously.

"Markings? I don't know what you mean."

Without saying a word, the girl leaned forward and placed her hands on Bray's head, her fingers gently feeling his face.

"I can't identify you..." she said, reading Bray's features. "You have no markings anywhere." Then she ran her hands around his powerful arms. "No barcode?" she continued.

"He has a small tattoo on the side of his face, Emma, but I don't recognize the sign," the young boy advised.

"Well?" Emma asked Bray, who was still keen not to give too much information away.

"It's just something I got done a long while ago. Do you like it?" he smiled to the younger girl, who nodded shyly and received a kick from her brother.

"Are you really - free?" Emma asked, finishing her face reading and leaning back, dropping her hands onto the surface of the bed.

"Free? Free from what?" Bray replied.

"Nobody... owns you?" the blind girl questioned, Bray spotting a hint of surprise in her tone.

"Owns me? No, no one owns me at all."

"Then your presence here gives us much to think about."

The blind girl stood up and backed away from Bray, feeling her route with her hand, touching the bed as she moved on.

Bound and tied, unable to go anywhere, Bray began to feel a sense of injustice and the fighter in him began to emerge as he struggled with his bonds.

"Aren't you going to tell me anything?!" Bray called out, frustrated.

Emma turned to him, hearing his voice, her opaque eyes staring in his direction.

"You need to save your energy. And so do we. Get some rest. While you still can. We'll talk again. Later."

With that, Emma opened the door and exited, her brother and sister following, the younger girl flicking off the light switch by the door as she departed, extinguishing the room in darkness.

Bray struggled to keep awake but feeling tired, confused, his body weak and head still hurting from where he had been struck before, the last thing Bray heard before he fell asleep was the door to the room being locked from the outside.

CHAPTER FIFTEEN

"I claim this land for the Mall Rats!" Jack spoke in mock grandeur, standing on the beach of this unknown world, surveying his surroundings like an explorer of old.

"I still can't believe we made it!" Trudy exclaimed, looking up at the clear blue sky to thank her lucky stars, hugging Brady protectively in her arms.

"Don't speak too soon. Not until everyone is accounted for," Amber replied and instructed those who had survived to search around the beach until they had checked that everyone was okay, found. Also to see what could be salvaged. Then they would need to make some kind of shelter.

Splitting up, the survivors spread out around the beach, the waves rhythmically lapping as the tide rolled in, hitting the shore and bringing in all sorts of debris from the Jzhao Li.

All around them, the sandy beachfront was strewn with pieces of metal, plastic bottles, drenched tins of food, many of which spewed out their contents into the ocean, having been damaged, crushed when the mighty vessel ran aground.

Jay stood in the water, knee deep, wading around to see if they could find anything useful. Or if there was a sign of any bodies.

The surface of the water must have had thousands of items floating in it, bobbing around, having fallen out of the containers which had once been on the outer decks of the cargo ship.

The Jzhao Li itself was several hundred metres away, breaking up, its burned out hull creaking as the tide came in, engulfing the damaged superstructure, gradually shaking loose whole sections of the riveted hull, the occasional loud shriek of screeching metal audible from so far away. What was left of the ship lay on a severe angle, the wreck collapsing into the growing depths of the ocean, the last remaining metal containers it carried tumbling into the waters with a mighty crash, like ice falling off a glacier.

"Anything, Ellie? You okay?" Amber asked loudly so her voice could be carried from the beach to the lifeboat, still out in the water.

"There's nothing more in here, no sign," Ellie shouted back to the shore.

She and Lex had been checking out the splintered lifeboat they had escaped in, a massive dent on the front from where it had collided with a gigantic rock. A gash was visible in the side of the small vessel and it was taking in water. The lifeboat was still stuck fast, as it had been when it first struck the rock that held it pinned in its grasp, Ellie and Lex standing on the rock and leaning into the lifeboat, trying their best to keep their balance.

"Be careful, Ellie," Jack called out from down the beach, concerned, then he gazed around for signs of the others.

Satisfied that there was no sign of those unaccounted for still trapped in the lifeboat, Lex traversed, leaping from the boat to the rock, joining Ellie, and began swimming to shore.

It had been so close, such a lucky escape and they both hoped all had made it. But they were beginning to have their doubts.

Ram sat on the beach, cradling his head in his hands, lost in another world of his own.

"Ram? Are you hurt?" Amber wondered, walking among the cluttered assortment of debris, her eyes scanning the beach for any sign of absent friends.

"Leave me alone, Amber. I'm thinking," Ram grumbled.

"You can save your thinking till later, once we've found everyone. Why don't you get off your butt and help, start looking around?"

"Fine! If you insist!" Ram snapped, getting to his feet - and lashed out petulantly at a pile of shampoo bottles that had washed ashore, kicking them venomously, venting his frustration.

Just what was his problem, Amber thought to herself as Ram waded into the shallow water and began searching through the myriad of items floating around him.

Amber shook her head, mystified as always by Ram and his behaviour. But now wasn't the time to be concerned by any of Ram's histrionics. There were lives in danger, missing people to find.

May sat further down on the beach, her legs tucked up as she rocked back and forth, crying. Amber crossed to her and sat down beside her to offer some comfort, wrapping an arm around May, her shoulders heaving in emotion.

"There, everything will be okay," Amber said, doing her best to give some reassurance, to help with the hurt May was feeling.

"Really?" May blurted out doubtfully, her eyes welled up, wet with tears.

"We'll find them. Zak and the others. I promise you."

"What if he didn't make it?" May asked, dreading to ask the question. "What if he's - "

Unable to finish, May choked up and buried her head in Amber, wailing at the potential loss of her loved one she so painfully expected, Amber hugging her tightly, trying to absorb May's pain.

* * *

"Oh, my God - Darryl!" Salene called out. Far away from the others, Salene noticed a figure and ran towards it, finally reaching Darryl, his body lying inert face down on the beach.

Concerned, Salene knelt above Darryl, casting her eyes up and down at him, wondering if he was alive.

"Oh, my God, oh, my God," she repeated over and over again, hesitating, lost in her fears.

Following her instinct, Salene slowly pushed Darryl onto his back. He didn't react.

Behind her, Jay and Lex were sprinting along the sandy shore, making their way towards her to lend assistance.

"Relax, Sal, remember?" Salene urged herself, telling herself to keep calm and trying to recall the first aid lessons she had taken at school.

Leaning over Darryl, she could hear his heart beating in his chest. So he was still alive. For now.

Opening his mouth to free up the airwaves, Salene gave Darryl the kiss of life, breathing into him, willing him to live. He responded, poking his tongue into her mouth and she recoiled in amazement.

"I didn't know you cared!" Darryl said, looking up at Salene.

She was shocked by the immediate transformation in Darryl's health, then the truth dawned on her.

"You were faking it?!" she asked, in disbelief.

"I saw you heading my way, thought I'd play possum. I had to do something to get a smooch from you."

"You'll get a punch in the mouth!" Salene retorted angrily, and she began to hit Darryl, furious at his deception, as he shielded himself, yelping out.

"Easy. That's a weird form of lifesaving, Sal - it won't work. You look like you're going to kill him!" Lex said, out of breath as he and Jay arrived, the two of them stunned at seeing Salene pounding Darryl.

"He deserves it. Idiot!" Salene shrieked, and with one more hit, she stormed away, heading to another section of the beach.

"Women, eh?" Darryl sighed despondently to Lex and Jay as they helped him to his feet. "I can never figure them out."

* * *

About another hundred metres ahead, Ruby and Lottie gazed around, examining the beach for any glimpse of the missing others.

"Ruby!" Lottie shrieked, suddenly noticing someone, and pointed ahead.

Racing over, as Ruby and Lottie neared the figure, they identified Slade laying still on his side, a gash on his head, dried blood caked on the wound. Ruby and Lottie's expressions were full of concern as they crouched behind him.

"Hello, Ruby," Slade whispered casually.

Ruby grinned in delight that Slade had survived. "How'd you know it's me?"

"I can smell your perfume."

"You're alive!" Lottie shrieked, thrilled.

"Either that, or this is some afterlife."

"Are you hurt?" Ruby asked, examining Slade's body.

"I'm okay, don't worry."

"I wouldn't be too sure about that," Lottie replied.

Stepping over him to get to his other side for another look, Ruby suddenly put her hand to her mouth, gasping as she, too, noticed what Lottie had seen.

Slade's right hand was covering a gaping wound in his side, a jagged piece of metal sticking in his stomach, below his left ribcage, blood oozing through his shirt, flowing through his fingers.

Lottie could hardly bear to look at the sickening wound and turned away.

"It's that bad, huh?" Slade wondered, groaning at the pain.

Holding back the tears, Ruby's silence told Slade everything, confirming the worst fears he suspected about the extent of his injury.

* * *

"Of all the places we could have ended up, trust us to find one without any hotels," Gel complained, dropping palm leaves onto a pile, gradually getting bigger.

She had been deployed, along with Trudy and Sammy, to gather some leaves to build a makeshift shelter.

"What's the matter? You missing your hair conditioner? Shampoo?" Sammy scoffed, adding some palms of his own to the collection, Brady beside him, throwing her own small bundle on top.

"Stop thinking about yourself for once, Gel, and get your priorities straight," Trudy said.

"I was only talking," Gel mumbled.

"Exactly! Try thinking as well, for once," Trudy snapped.

Gel stuck her tongue out at Trudy, making a face behind her back.

Noticing, little Brady retaliated, poking her own tongue out at Gel, sticking up for her mother as Sammy cast a glance at Heaven.

Tempers were beginning to fray within the entire group as the reality of the situation they faced was beginning to dawn on them.

There had been no sign of Zak, who was still missing.

Slade's injuries were horrific, a source of concern to everyone, especially Ruby.

And with the day advancing on this strange land they found themselves in, Amber had realized they had best start making a shelter before it got dark or the weather turned.

As well as gathering a pile of palm leaves, branches and sticks to construct a shelter, they needed to erect some kind of cover for Slade. They felt he was too injured to be moved from his current location.

There was concern also at exactly where they were. And if this land was populated. They would need to check out their environs. All hoped, if there was any other form of life around, that the inhabitants were friendly. Not hostile.

The priority though was to consolidate their base, gather supplies, search for any sign of Zak, and tend to Slade.

After a brief catch up to identify the next stage of their plan, Darryl was to accompany Amber, who was going to join Ruby to offer what assistance they could provide to Slade, now that they had recovered medical supplies.

Lex, Salene, Lottie, Sammy, Gel and Trudy were to assist Jack erecting the makeshift shelter.

The little ones played nearby in the sand. Young Brady was having the time of her life, racing around Trudy, eagerly picking up leaves fallen from the palm trees like it was some game, and playfully kicking sand in the air. Trudy's daughter had rarely seen sand before and this new world was so different to the concrete jungle of the city that had been their home in the past.

Though upset by all that had happened to them, Trudy herself seemed overall more content than she had on the Jzhao Li, her spirits lifted as she found joy at the delight of her daughter in their new environment. But this was marred by the injury to Slade and concern at Zak being missing.

Jay was to catch up with Ram and search the opposite end of the beach in case Zak had washed ashore elsewhere.

"I've never seen so many trees," Darryl said, keeping his good humour, indicating the palm trees lining the beach, as he crossed with Amber towards Ruby, crouched by the injured Slade.

"We're certainly not in the city anymore," Amber said.

"Palm Tree Rats rather than Mall Rats? Maybe we should change the name of the Tribe. What do you think?" Darryl grinned.

"First things first. We've got more important matters to deal with," Amber replied.

For all of her concern, Amber couldn't help but notice - as had Darryl - that the landscape was beautiful. In another time, another place, she would have been thrilled to be here. In this strange land. In some ways it seemed like the perfect holiday destination, somewhere you would go on a honeymoon. The aesthetic straight out of an exotic brochure. But this was no vacation. The reality of their situation was that they all had to survive, Amber resolved. Get through their predicament, one minute, one hour at a time, then each passing day.

As Amber and Darryl approached, they could hear Slade's groans, his teeth clenched as he tried to ride out the agony he was feeling from the wound in his side.

Ruby knelt beside him, cradling his head tenderly, doing her utmost to pacify, take away the pain, her expression one of complete concern at Slade's suffering. She resolved that she would never leave him.

"How's it going?" Amber whispered to Ruby.

"Good, real good," Ruby lied, her face contorted in a grimace of worry. She was doing what she could to put a positive light on things so Slade wouldn't be any more in distress than he already was. But she needn't have bothered. He didn't hear Ruby or Amber. Slade was in a world of his own, fighting the pain he was going through.

And as Amber exchanged concerned glances with Ruby and Darryl, and Slade groaned again, Amber cringed at his discomfort, wishing there was something she could do to alleviate his suffering. She examined what medical supplies they had but realized that they really needed to come up with something more substantive. The problem was, with no apparent help around, she was at a loss what else they could do.

"Steady him - we're gonna have to remove this and bandage him," Amber said, referring to the piece of metal still embedded in Slade's side.

Ruby gently caressed Slade's hair, then glanced as Amber took a deep breath and gently, carefully, removed the piece of metal.

"Pass me those bandages, Darryl. Come on, as fast as you can!"

Darryl was rigid, his eyes gaping at the blood oozing from Slade's side. The colour drained from Darryl's face and he fainted, collapsing onto the sands.

Amber sighed. That's all she needed, though she too felt queasy as she tended to Slade's wounds, bandaging him.

* * *

"Ram, so there you are!" Jay called out as he ran up the beach. "I've been looking everywhere for you."

"Nice to have been missed," Ram said, his back to Jay as he sat on the wet sands, the tide lapping around his legs.

"We need all hands to try and search for Zak."

"You can all manage without me, I'm sure. Amber's still in charge, isn't she? You usually get by without my involvement. I may as well speak to myself half the time, nobody ever listens to me anymore."

"That's not true," Jay said, smiling slightly at Ram's sulking. Despite being such a genius, Ram could act so childish sometimes. "Come on. We need you."

"I'll wait a little longer, if you don't mind."

"Why? What are you doing?"

"Trying to catch fish."

"With just your bare hands? Now this, I've got to see."

"Let me be, Jay. Please."

"What is it? You still harping on that we should have gone back to the city? That you were right all along? If so, now's not the time to be out here throwing tantrums, making a point. What is, is. We're shipwrecked on this land and we've got to make the best of it."

Ram scoffed, unconvinced.

And it was then Jay noticed the blood in the water, the waves slowly lapping around Ram as the tide moved in.

"Are you hurt?" Jay asked in sudden concern, aware now that Ram had kept his back to Jay this whole time.

Leaning forward to check Ram out, he realized that in reality Ram was up to something. Hiding, keeping something from Jay.

"Get away from me!" Ram exploded, shifting position in the sand to keep his back to Jay.

"Enough games!" Jay shouted.

Grabbing Ram by the shoulders, Jay physically spun Ram around.

He was astonished to see blood pouring from a recent flesh wound on Ram's forehead.

"What? The wound? I tripped, bashed my head on a rock."

"You're lying" Jay said, curious and angry at Ram's strange behaviour.

For Ram's 'accidental' injury was confined to one part of his head.

"We need to talk, Ram!" Jay insisted.

To all intents, the wound looked self-inflicted. And that Ram had been trying to scratch away his 'Techno' symbol markings from his forehead.

CHAPTER SIXTEEN

Ebony was gripped by panic as the lifeboat she was in continued its inexorable drift out to the open sea.

She had given up trying to restart the engine, which had long ago spluttered out the last of its fuel in a cough of fumes. Since then, all she could do was steer the helm, trying to angle the tiny vessel back towards the land.

Ebony had never been too knowledgeable about the sea, she was a city girl. Whatever explained the changing current though, one thing was for sure, it was taking the lifeboat and Ebony with it, further and further out towards the vast emptiness of the ocean.

She had always been a survivor. From the streets.

Now, for one of the few times in her life, she was vulnerable. Exposed. Helpless. It had been agonizing being so close to the landmass, the promise of escape, after so many days at sea. The lifeboat was drifting away, as if fate was teasing her, toying with her feelings.

At one point earlier she had jumped into the water and tried to swim to shore when she realized the danger she was in. Unable to make much headway against the prevailing current, she had swam back and with all her efforts, just made it onto the lifeboat. It had been a frightening moment when she had truly felt like she was alone in this unforgiving world, worrying she was going to drown.

At least the lifeboat afforded her some sanctuary out here, in the middle of nowhere, but for how much longer, she couldn't say. Ebony had precious little in the way of food or water supplies due to her hasty escape from the Jzhao Li. Everything she tried to do now to survive seemed like it was hitting a dead end, with the tide driving her further towards the open ocean.

For a moment Ebony wondered what had happened to the others - and to Slade. Last time she saw them, the Jzhao Li had been hurtling towards the land on a different course to her's. She had been drifting for several hours since then. The Jzhao Li was now far away, out of sight.

Had they survived? What did she care, Ebony felt. Slade had made his choice. And she couldn't help but hope that Ruby was suffering, pinning the blame on her for Ebony's break up with Slade. If Ruby had been dealt a cruel blow of fate, then it served her right. Bitch.

As far as her own fate was concerned, Ebony started to sob. She wept for herself, her plight, the cruel and unfair way that her destiny was unfolding. She wondered if this was a punishment for all the bad things she had done in her life, if what was happening to her was some form of divine retribution, God paying her back in kind, causing her to suffer. With the expectation that all that lay ahead for her was a long, lingering, painful death, Ebony struggled to come to terms with it, sure she would end her days on this floating tomb.

But Ebony didn't believe in karma, she thought, through teary eyes. She had got away with a lot in her life and surely she would make it, somehow. Maybe the tide would change and her lifeboat would drift back towards shore once more. It wasn't over till it was over, she thought, trying to raise her fading spirits.

She was alive, for now, and as desperate as the situation she faced, Ebony tried to dismiss her fears, clinging to her instinct for survival. She'd been through hell before, when the adults first perished and she had been forced to use everything in her considerable arsenal of tricks, cunning, guile to endure in the city. She had to keep going, she urged herself. Somehow she would survive.

For all that she was trying to provide herself with some form of hope, she felt utter despair, misery welling up inside. And she wailed at the injustice of life and the situation she was in.

Tears flooding her eyes, overwhelmed and exhausted, Ebony cried herself to sleep.

* * *

Hours later, it was the sound of the approaching engine that woke Ebony up with a start.

Reacting quickly, she poked her head above the side of the lifeboat to find out what was going on, doing her best to keep herself hidden.

All she could see, all around her, was the ocean. The land was barely visible on the distant horizon. She calculated that the current must have obviously taken her miles out to sea while she had slept.

Suddenly she noticed a white cruiser approaching at high speed. It was still some distance away. Ebony shook her head in disbelief. It was unbelievable. Out here, in the middle of nowhere. Who were they? What the hell were they doing?

More importantly, what should she do? Try and attract their attention? But clearly she already had their attention and she felt like a sitting duck, exposed. She had no idea who was in the cruiser, where they were from, and what reason they had to move towards Ebony's lifeboat. Maybe they would be friendly and were simply going to rescue her. Or worse, the occupants of the boat could be hostile.

Ebony always looked to cover the worst case but now had no option, being stranded, other than to pull one of the blankets that had been stored in the lifeboat over her head. Maybe it would turn out there was one person on the cruiser and she could take them out, whoever they might be, overpower them and take the cruiser for herself. She just didn't know. For now, it seemed like the best idea was to hide, assess her options until she knew what she was dealing with.

Peeking through the blanket, Ebony tried to catch a better glimpse of the cruiser as it approached, closer, closer. Then it circled like an animal viewing its prey, before striking.

Adrenalin pumped through Ebony's body, her mind racing to decide what she should do. Stay hidden or show herself?

The engines of the cruiser were deafening now.

Ebony risked another look, poking her fingers through the blanket, lifting it up so she could try and check out just exactly what was happening.

The cruiser idled its engines, mooring itself at the front of the lifeboat. From her angle, Ebony still couldn't see how many people were involved.

She hid again at the sound of someone jumping aboard, heavy-footed, telling Ebony it was obviously at least one person. But then her heart sank as she heard more people bounding on deck.

Suddenly the blanket covering Ebony was whipped away, exposing her.

She noticed four powerfully built-guys. About the same age as her. They were dressed all in black, wearing balaclavas rolled up into berets which covered their heads, their hair close shaven as if they belonged to some kind of military. Their leader indicated his subordinates in a ruthlessly cold and efficient manner.

"Check the identification plates. Commander Blake will want details of where the Jzhao Li was registered!"

"Yes, sir!" the subordinate said, then scoured the lifeboat, punching in details of the brass plaque on the instrumentation panel into a small mobile device he was holding.

The others yanked Ebony to her feet.

"Identify yourself," the leader ordered her.

"I'm a mermaid, lost at sea," Ebony replied seductively.

She knew she was attractive and could turn it on and off when needed. She had never been afraid to use her allure to get her way with guys in the past. And thought she'd try this time. But it wasn't working. The leader considered Ebony, then turned to his team, with more important matters on his mind.

"Any other stowaways?"

His companions were methodically checking to see if anyone was hiding under the other seats or blankets.

"Doesn't seem like it, Sir," one said.

The leader indicated and two of his men assisted Ebony to her feet.

"Keep away from me!" she yelled, striking out, punching one in the face, kicking the other with all her might into his groin.

It seemed to have no effect whatsoever.

They were impassive and didn't react to her attack other than grabbing Ebony by the arm, which they forced up behind her back to restrain her so she couldn't move.

These guys knew what they were doing, Ebony thought, and quickly realized that she'd better back down and go along with them. For now. They were obviously well trained in the art of combat, unlike some of the tribes she had encountered in any battles on the streets.

Her oppressors led her onto the deck of the lifeboat where they transferred her to the cruiser. It was much bigger than Ebony had envisaged and could hold several passengers.

Ebony noticed a girl, again about her age, also dressed the same way as the boarding party. She had hideous scars across one side of her face and must have been in a bad accident at some point, Ebony thought. After the first wave of revulsion, Ebony even managed to garner a degree of sympathy. Since the darkness descended in the post adult world, life was hard enough without having to face it behind a disfigured mask like that.

"Welcome aboard!" the hideous girl said contemptuously.

Ebony gazed around in growing fear. Members of the boarding party were securing the lifeboat with ropes, presumably to tow the tiny vessel somewhere.

The hideous girl tossed a fishing net over Ebony, then extended one leg, pushing Ebony to the floor with ease like the martial arts expert she clearly was, before yanking the net, tightening it and leaving Ebony unable to move her limbs, her movement totally restricted by the bonds.

She braced herself, petrified, wondering just what lay in store for her as the cruiser was revved and sped away, hurtling through the ocean, towing the lifeboat in its wake. But to where?

CHAPTER SEVENTEEN

The Mall Rats decided to call their new home "Camp Phoenix," naming it after "Phoenix Mall," the shopping mall that had been their home back in the city.

It was an appropriate name, given the hope everyone shared that like the mythical bird, they too would rise up and survive, life would go on, from facing doom at being shipwrecked in this strange new world. The image of a phoenix conjured up flames and that too was applicable, Amber felt, given the intense searing heat that seemed to cook the very air around them.

Amber was like a bee, buzzing from one place to the other, as she tried to encourage everyone and bring some semblance of order to Camp Phoenix, which was still more a name only than a proper camp.

Her thoughts drifted to Jay. And Ram. They had been gone now for what must have been a few hours, though Amber had no way of exactly telling the time, relying only on judging the position of the sun in the sky.

Jay had left with Ram to explore the perimeters.

Before they departed, Jay informed Amber what he had discovered, with Ram trying to remove his Techno markings.

Ram had maintained to Amber and the others he had accidentally hurt his head and there was nothing more to it than that.

But Amber's constant distrust of Ram prevailed. To Amber, he had always proven from his actions in the past he was capable of being up to something, usually no good.

Throughout their entire time on first the trawler, then the Jzhao Li, Amber had been unsettled by Ram and his insistence on going back to the city. It just defied all sense, wanting to return to a city gripped by pandemic.

Was there some connection between his extreme moods, changing out of his uniform and trying to dismiss any sign of his markings, and desire to go back home? Or did he know something about this strange land that the others didn't know?

If anyone could find out the answers, it would be Jay. He'd coax the truth out of Ram, somehow, and Jay told Amber he had been quietly hopeful that if he could talk with Ram in a one-to-one conversation, away from Amber and the others, he would discover what it was that had so troubled Ram since the moment the Tribe had fled - and why he was so eager to get back to their doomed home city.

Ram was a dangerous individual though. As much as Jay was skilled in combat, able to handle himself, Amber hoped he would still be safe going off into the unknown undergrowth with Ram. You could never be too safe with the former leader of the Technos. Amber tried to dismiss such thinking, instead looking forward to Jay's return, with Ram - and hopefully the unearthing of any secrets Ram had been trying to keep from them.

Jack and Lex had been deployed to search another area and agreed not to venture too far. All were just keen to gain more insight into the perimeters of their environs.

As the oldest male left behind while Lex, Jack, Ram and Jay were away, Darryl had sincerely tried to 'man up' to his responsibilities and was pouring sweat as he sorted through great piles of palm fronds, branches and sticks to use in the construction of their shelter, Lottie, Gel and Sammy helping him out.

Amber was somewhat surprised and displeased by Gel, however, who Amber spotted laying in the sun like she was lounging on the beach in a luxury resort on holiday.

"Gel - what do you think you're doing?" Amber asked, walking up to her.

"What do you think I'm doing?" Gel replied, as if it was all so obvious.

Amber shrugged, her confused expression showing Gel she didn't know what she was talking about.

"I'm sunbathing - duh!" Gel petulantly explained, deliberately ignoring Amber, and went on with improving her suntan.

"Gel - if you stay there one more minute, I swear I'll-"

"Amber - give me a break!" Gel called back. "You're not my mother!"

"Thank goodness. This isn't some kind of break away, Gel. You either get up and pull your weight or you get out of here and have nothing to do with our camp. It's up to you."

Amber stormed off, pacing down the burning sands and behind her, sighing like a spoilt child, Gel reluctantly went to help Darryl, Sammy and Lottie in constructing the shelter.

Slade was asleep now, Amber could see as she approached, his dreams a refuge from the pain he felt in his side when he was awake.

Like before, Ruby was steadfastly by his side, watching over him.

"You should try and get some rest yourself," Amber whispered to Ruby, so as not to disturb Slade.

"I can't leave him," Ruby replied. She looked like an emotional wreck, which she was, her make up smeared over her face from the tears she had shed.

"I'll stay with him, make sure he's okay," Amber insisted. "You've been here for hours. What would Slade say? He'd want you to take care of yourself. Go and take some time out, gather yourself together."

Understanding the sense behind Amber's suggestion, Ruby smiled, appreciating the help, leaving Amber in charge of Slade.

Salene and Ellie were continuing to assist May in the ongoing search for Zak, his disappearance causing all great concern.

In another area of the beach, Trudy had lit a fire with some fallen branches and was carefully holding improvised skewers of tinned meat over the flames as Ruby arrived and sat down to join her.

"Hungry?" Trudy asked. "This should be ready in a minute."

Ruby nodded gratefully.

Some of the canned food from the Jzhao Li had been gathered into a pile of stores. There had been no can opener so Trudy had to bash the tins open with a coconut.

It had been ironic using food to open food, she thought. Brady was crawling on the sand, pushing one of the coconuts like a toy while Amber's baby lay asleep under the shade of some palms.

"This is kinda fun, isn't it?" Trudy said.

"I wouldn't call this fun," Ruby protested, "with Slade injured!"

"We're all worried about Slade," Trudy explained. "I just mean, in a way, this is an adventure. Cooking on the open fire. Sitting here on the beach. The kids are certainly having fun."

Ruby obviously didn't share Trudy's enthusiasm for their surroundings, their 'adventure'. In fact, she took offence at Trudy's apparent lack of concern or worry for Slade. Trudy was being overly happy, Ruby felt, unnaturally so.

"Come on, Ruby. Can't we just take our mind off things, just for a minute?"

"What? And stick our head in the sand, pretending that everything's alright? Because it isn't!" Ruby replied disdainfully.

Then she felt guilty, knowing that Trudy was trying as hard as she could to keep her emotions in control and spirits up. They were all struggling in their own ways, she realized. But Ruby felt there was nothing to gain by pretending that things weren't as bad as they really were.

"Mister Claw Claw!" Brady shrieked, thrilled at noticing a crab moving across the sand.

"Be careful with that 'thing'," Trudy shouted, "I don't want you to get hurt."

"You're pathetic, Trudy, you really are! Talk about being selective with your concern." Ruby couldn't help herself. She felt Trudy was being insensitive, not seemingly showing any care for Slade.

"How dare you speak to me like that!" Trudy snarled at Ruby. "Who do you think you are?!"

"Hey - you two going to cook up some seafood?" Darryl called, trying to diffuse the argument between Ruby and Trudy. He was still working on the shelter nearby and put his fingers to his lips in anticipation at his imagined meal. "Crab thermidor - magnifique!"

Sammy appeared from the undergrowth looking a bit sheepish.

"Well? You look to me like someone who feels... 'relieved'." Darryl said.

"Shhhh. No need to broadcast it, Darryl!" Sammy snapped.

"And there's no need for you to be embarrassed, Sammy boy. When someone's gotta go, they gotta go. Least with all that jungle back there, there's no chance of the toilet overspilling like it did on the boat."

"I wouldn't bet on it," Sammy groaned, rubbing his stomach.

Gel suddenly shrieked out, dropping a pile of branches she had cradled in her arms.

"I chipped a nail!" she bellowed.

Lottie let go of the ropes she was holding to secure the shelter Darryl was putting together and crossed to Gel nearby.

"And I've got calluses and blisters all over my hands - look!" Lottie said.

"Oh, poor you!" Ruby mocked. "Not as bad as some others around here if you'd only take the time to notice!" She cast an angry glance at Trudy.

Darryl focused on the shelter, its frame slowly taking shape, carefully tying on a palm leaf, wrapping it around the flimsy branches. But now, with Lottie no longer holding the base in place with the rope, Darryl froze. In one swift motion, the shelter they had worked on for hours collapsed like a house of cards around him.

He turned and glared at Lottie and Gel, who both sighed.

"It's not our fault!" Gel said helplessly.

* * *

Jay and Ram wound their way through the dense jungle, the air humid and moist. It was incredible just how thick the undergrowth was, the shade from the massive trees overhanging providing some relief from the otherwise almost impossible heat.

The jungle was alive with the sound of insects, the buzzing almost deafening, piercing the ear.

Ram waved at his face for the umpteenth time as more mosquitos swarmed around his exposed features.

"They obviously like you," Jay said, leading the two of them.

"Doesn't everybody?" Ram said, swatting at more bugs biting into his neck.

Jay also had many bites but he was trying to ignore the irritation, knowing that once you started, it was nearly impossible to stop scratching.

"I just hope they don't have malaria or some other - diseases," Ram grimaced, itching an ear with his finger.

"Think yourself lucky we haven't seen any snakes. Yet. They've probably seen us though."

"Can we go back now?" Ram pleaded, nervously looking at the jungle all around. "Doesn't seem to be any sign of anyone."

"Yeah, we'll head back. But not until you've talked."

"I told you - there's nothing to talk about!"

"And I told you - I don't believe you. I know you better than you think I do. And I can tell when you're keeping secrets."

"What do you want? A medal? A promotion, Jay?"

He had once, long ago. When the two had worked closely together in the Technos, Jay as Ram's general, Ram making an allusion to their past. But that was in a different life, Jay thought. It was all history.

"I want the truth, Ram. About why you were so keen to change your clothes, get out of your uniform, scratch away your Techno markings..."

"That's my business," Ram insisted.

"Oh, I don't think so. And you'd better tell me why it's been so important to you to want to go back to the city we fled. Why? Is there something out here - that you know about? Come on, Ram. Your behaviour's been extreme from the moment we arrived in this God forsaken place!"

Ram sighed, staring at Jay. Frustrated by his continued suspicions. His probing and persistence.

Ram gulped nervously, looking around the mysterious jungle environment, his eyes darting. Scared. There was definitely something about this place that was getting to him.

"Let's go back, Jay. We've come far enough."

"Not until you're finally ready to talk."

Ram bit his lip in growing unease.

And before Jay knew it, Ram was off, sprinting, finally tripping over the thick tumble of plants and branches on the jungle floor, struggling to keep his footing.

Like a panther chasing down its prey, Jay grit his teeth, moving in on Ram at top speed, determined not to let him get away.

Ram was panic-driven as he picked himself up and continued running quickly, desperate to escape.

But with Jay's longer stride and athletic prowess, it didn't take him long to close the gap and he launched himself at Ram's legs, rugby-tackling him to the ground, Ram shouting in disappointment, frustration at being caught.

"Get off me!" Ram struggled.

"Think I need any more proof!?" Jay grabbed Ram by the scruff of the neck, dragging him to his feet. "Something's going on, Ram! And it's about time you explain exactly what it is!"

Powerless, Ram began to laugh. Was he just trolling? Doing it to annoy Jay? Or had he lost it completely, going mad? Jay would find out, he promised, soon enough.

"So? What is it!?" Jay demanded.

"Don't look at me," Ram said, a manic glint in his eyes as he laughed uncontrollably. "I think you'd better look up, Jay. There's something in the trees. And it ain't no bird!"

Unsure exactly what Ram meant, Jay kept his grip on Ram so he couldn't escape, then cast his eyes upwards.

There, perhaps thirty feet off the jungle floor, visible through the thick undergrowth, he could see the wreck of a huge grey-coloured military cargo plane, stuck in the mighty boughs, covered slightly by the massive trees and vines. It looked like a Hercules or Tupolev, its enormous wings spanning across, blocking out the sun. The titanic-sized trees and density of foliage supported the bulk of the aircraft, which lay on an angle, as it must have done when it crash landed.

"What the hell?" Jay said, in awe of what he was seeing.

"So what about it, Jay? I reckon you should forget about me," Ram said, cackling to himself. "Don't you? Because I'm not your mystery. This land is."

Jay suddenly felt uneasy about leaving Amber and the others behind at the camp. But he couldn't head back now. He had promised Amber he would return with answers from Ram. And Ram was right, the plane added another mystery to the equation.

There was so much they didn't know. And maybe Ram knew more than he was letting on.

"You'd better start talking, Ram, if you know what's good for you. I mean it," Jay threatened, tightening his hold on Ram.

Ram considered Jay for a long moment. His laughter gradually subsided, then he nodded.

* * *

The waves pounded all around, surging across the rocks, exploding in a mist of spray.

Heads down, Salene, Ellie and May continued to scan the beach, as they had done for several hours now.

It was like finding a needle in a haystack. There were so many pieces of debris, bits of metal, broken objects of all sizes, from the wreck of the Jzhao Li, edged between the rocks, caught up in the gaps between.

Ellie was carrying a plastic drinks cooler that had been washed ashore. As well as searching for Zak, she was gathering up any other potentially useful medical supplies the girls had found throughout their search.

The drinks cooler was getting increasingly heavy as additional items were thrown into it. They had accumulated a good many packets of paracetamol, some bandages, bottles of disinfectant, cans of food.

But there had still been no sign of Zak. Only the girls, alone in this section of the beach, and in the distance, a good way off, Camp Phoenix.

Out in the ocean, the immense hull of the container ship lay on its side like a prehistoric monster from the deep, stranded on the reef from where it had run aground.

The sound of the surf was accompanied by the occasional noise of metal creaking, grinding and twisting from above and below the waterline, the Jzhao Li groaning as it slowly continued to be broken up by the pounding of the changing tide.

The girls had considered at one point diving underwater, to swim into the wreck to see if they could find some additional medical supplies. Or any sign of

Zak. But they had abandoned such notions as being too dangerous, fearing that they might get stuck in the wreck and risk drowning.

"We should probably head back," Ellie called out.

"I'm not going anywhere!" May shouted. "You can go if you want."

"But we can't leave you here alone," Salene spoke loudly over the roar of the waves striking the rocks. "We don't know who - or what - is out here."

"I've got to find him, Sal!" May replied, the determination in her tone clear.

Seagulls squawked as they flew by, floating on the breeze, angling their wings, scavenging for any food.

Salene let out a scream. A piercing cry.

Ellie and May followed her gaze, and then they too, recoiled.

Caught between two rocks, Zak's body twisted in the movement of the water, like a lifeless doll. The colour had drained from his skin, his eyes shut, his features bloated.

"Oh, my God!" May screamed and began running towards the shallows, followed by Salene and Ellie.

* * *

The jungle seemed to be alive with the noise of so many insects as Jack followed Lex, weaving their way through the thick green undergrowth, with nothing else visible but the countless plants above them, under them and all around. They were engulfed and Jack shuddered to think of all the millions of tiny insect eyes staring at him that very moment.

A wild whooping sound rang out from some of the massive trees above, startling Jack even more.

"What do you think that is? A monkey?" Lex asked.

"Either that or maybe Trudy's having a panic attack," Jack smirked, trying to find the humour in the situation, like he always did, and to settle his nerves with a joke.

"Ha, ha, very funny," Lex replied. "But it sounds a bit too calm for Trudy. Man, I've been bitten so many times I'm surprised there's any blood left in me. I feel I've been attacked by a vampire."

"Well, let's just hope that's the extent of it. And we don't get attacked by anything else."

"Doesn't seem to be anyone around but the two of us," Lex said.

"And a bazillion insects," Jack mumbled.

"Some closer than you think," Lex said, putting his finger to his lips, indicating Jack to be quiet.

Wondering what Lex meant, Jack looked down to where Lex was gazing - towards one of his legs. Crawling on Jack's shin was a gigantic spider, slowly making it's way up Jack's leg.

Jack mouthed a silent scream, a look of anguish on his face.

Snapping a branch from a plant, Lex knocked the spider to the ground.

"You are such a wuss, Jack. I wonder what Ellie would say if she saw you now. Don't faint on me."

Relieved to be spider free - for now - Jack thought he heard noises around them, a branch swishing, the sounds of movement, and he spun around, nervously scanning the trees.

"Jack, would you please relax?" Lex said, then continuing on, suggested, "How about we take a break for a while? Have something to eat."

They stopped and opened a bag that they had placed their food rations in and snacked on some asparagus and tinned vegetables which they had opened earlier, before they left.

"This is the life, eh, Jack? Out here in the wide open spaces."

"Don't know about open spaces - I feel like this jungle's strangling me," Jack said wearily gazing around with a growing sense of claustrophobia and being engulfed by so much foliage.

"Chill, Jack. Calm down. We'll be alright. It's no big deal."

"Aren't you... scared?" Jack wondered.

"Nothing much scares me anymore... not these days," Lex said.

It was true. He wasn't just trying to raise Jack's failing spirits. He had experienced a lot, surviving back in the city on the streets since the adults had all perished.

"Then what is it?" Jack asked, noticing Lex gazing ahead.

He had spotted a dead bird. But all the feathers had been plucked.

"That's weird," Lex replied. "Check that out."

Lex and Jack moved towards the carcass.

Lex sniffed at it and resolved that it hadn't been dead for too long and didn't seem rotten.

"Look - there's another one over there," Jack said, gazing in growing intrigue.

"I'm sure Ellie will give you something special tonight when we arrive back with this fresh meat," Lex mocked, looking forward to a feast of something other than the canned rations which had been gathered back at base.

The other dead bird has also been plucked of feathers, which again confused Lex as he swaggered over to grab it. Then he suddenly disappeared, the ground beneath him giving way with a whoosh as he fell into a wide hole, the branches covering it imploding under Lex's feet.

"Lex!" Jack yelled out, gripped by panic.

But it was too late. Lex had gone.

CHAPTER EIGHTEEN

Bray wondered what his captors had in store for him, confused at the mixed signals he had received.

He had been kept in the room for several days now, his hands and feet bound. That he was their prisoner, was in no question. But he had also been treated well, his infected leg regularly cleaned so that now the wound had pretty much healed. He had been fed and watered several times each day. This was so different compared to his incarceration under Eloise with all the mental and physical stresses he had suffered. Yet he was still a prisoner. They were keeping him alive - but why?

Bray was genuinely baffled by the intentions of his captors. In the times that they visited him, he had managed to gradually piece together a picture of who they were. Where he was. They had been guarded with him, trying not to be too friendly, but in conversation a few clues and details had slipped through, Bray attempting to ask some subtle questions here and there, probing for information.

The young boy's name was Shannon, and the girl was called Tiffany. They were brother and sister, Bray discovered, and had been very kind to him on their visits, bringing and clearing away food, feeding Bray since he could not do so himself with his hands bound. They were so young, Bray felt a sense of protectiveness towards them. Just as he did to the other younger Mall Rats like Patsy and Cloe in the city so long before. And he considered what kind of future lay in store for them all in this dangerous world they all found themselves in after the demise of the adults.

The leader of the captors was undoubtably Emma, the blind girl, who Bray had learned was the older sister of Shannon and Tiffany. Emma had been less friendly to Bray, suspicious of him, wondering in turn what his motives were and who he was.

Bray had been able to gauge from his conversations with Emma, Shannon and Tiffany that they were all surviving in the remnants of what had once been called Arthurs Air Force Base. It had been used in World War 2 as a refuelling station and seemed to have been reactivated when the pandemic was reaching its peak, spreading globally.

All Shannon and Tiffany knew, they had told Bray, was that Arthur's Base had seen major building work and activity just before the 'virus' killed the adults. They themselves were far too young to remember much detail but it gave some kind of explanation for the construction machines and massive hangars Bray had spotted when he stumbled into the base, as well as the military aircraft left behind.

Apparently a lot of United Nations personnel from all around the world had spent time in this remote base, adding new hangars, buildings. For what reason, Shannon and Tiffany were unsure.

The small 'amusement park' itself had been introduced, Bray had been told, so the military personnel stationed there could enjoy the facilities with their families, the rides and fairy tale setting put in place as a break from whatever activity the United Nations teams had been carrying out. Also schools and accommodation blocks were built with the area being prepared as an evacuation camp to house several thousand children.

According to Tiffany and Shannon, both far more talkative and less guarded than their elder sister, they had been told that the base was also to have been used by the adults as a makeshift hospital in the days when the 'virus' struck. And nearby in the area now known as the 'wastelands', there was a huge burial ground of mass, unmarked graves. But Tiffany and Shannon didn't seem to know too much detail about that either. Emma never liked to talk about it. The younger kids were not allowed to visit the 'wastelands' because Emma said it was far too dangerous to set foot there. The whole area was off limits because it was contaminated. But they didn't know by what.

Though the amusement park had been visited by other kids and teenagers since the adults died, trashing it in the process, apparently the fact that the base had once housed a hospital now worked in its favour. Likewise, that it was located near the 'wastelands'. It had a 'taint' from the past, that it wasn't safe, perhaps even still having traces of the 'virus' or some other diseases, its reputation ironically providing a safe place to stay.

Bray couldn't decipher if Emma, Tiffany and Shannon were the only ones now living at the base. Emma and the younger kids didn't give any detail. And Bray was determined to try and discover more. Then it might shed light on what they wanted of him.

Bray felt that they weren't going to hand him in. He had been there for so many days they would have had ample time to arrange for his return to Eloise's compound, if they were somehow connected to her forces. But equally, although he was gaining Tiffany and Shannon's trust and was beginning to know more about their set up, he still didn't want to take chances or have a false sense of security with any flawed assumptions. He needed to get some more facts.

There were so many questions floating around in Bray's mind. It would soon be time, he hoped, for some answers.

Bray's thoughts were disturbed as the door to the room was unlocked and swung open - by Tiffany, the young girl stepping aside so Emma could enter the room.

"Thank you, Tiffany," Emma said, entering. She clearly knew the layout well and gradually made her way towards Bray, carrying a glass of water in one hand and an open tin of baked beans in the other, a spoon sticking out of it.

"You may go," Emma instructed Tiffany, the young girl casting a furtive uncertain glance at Bray before closing the door and locking it from the other side.

Emma sat down on the side of Bray's bed and slowly inched the glass of water to his face.

"Thirsty?" she asked Bray.

"Thanks. But I don't understand," he replied. "You feed me, clean me up, but keep me under lock and key. Why?"

"We've been wondering the same thing," Emma answered carefully, putting the glass of water down on the side table next to Bray's bed that she knew was there.

"I just don't get it, Emma. Is it your idea to show hospitality by taking hostages? You got anyone else locked up here? The three of you seem nice. You've treated me well. But still, here I am, your prisoner."

"And lucky you are, too. You should be grateful."

"I am in a way. But not totally. You going to keep me here forever? You enjoy doing this or something?

What's your plan, Emma? Please - let me know, what's going on!"

"You have no idea - about anything - have you?" Emma seemed flustered, agitated.

"All I know is, this isn't the way to treat people. What kind of world are you wanting? For Shannon and Tiffany? You giving them a crash course in kidnapping and imprisonment?"

Emma angrily threw the tin of beans, spilling their contents.

Bray sat back in his bed. Part of him worried what Emma would do to him, she was fuming. Upset. Tears began to well up in her opaque eyes.

"Do you know how hard it's been? I mean, look at me!" Emma said, pointing to her eyes, staring, unseeing at Bray. "How am I meant to look after the little ones when I can't even see?"

"What happened?" Bray asked.

"As if you care," Emma said, bitterly.

"If I didn't - why would I be asking?"

Emma wiped at her tears, breathing deeply to compose herself, trying to keep her dignity.

"It's a long story."

"Seems I'm not going anywhere," Bray ventured.

Her face scrunched up in thought, Emma blinked her tears away.

"Where to begin...."

"How about you tell me how you lost your sight?" Bray asked.

"How about you just keep quiet?" Emma replied.

"Please..." Bray asked after a moment, sensing that Emma was about to open up.

And after a long moment, she eventually did.

"When my Mum told me she was sick, my whole world caved in. I needed her. So badly. She was everything to me - and suddenly, she was gone."

"The virus?" Bray questioned.

"No. She had cancer. Not long after she died, we were evacuated here. Just before the 'virus' hit. We had no idea where we were going. We were put on a ship, like animals, and sailed for many days. My Dad... he was in the military. There were a lot of other kids, just like us. Their parents also serving their countries. We were all so scared. Missing families and friends back home. We were told we had to stick together. Safety in numbers."

"I know how that feels. I was in a tribe of my own."

"Not long after we arrived here, my Dad also died."

"How? Was it the virus?"

"I don't know exactly. All I know is that he was with other servicemen who went off. They were on high alert. All the adults at the base were. All the children... we were supposed to stay in the bunkers. But I wanted to see what was going on. And I did. Until the explosion, that is. The light was so intense. Ever since then, all I've known is darkness."

Bray considered her in growing concern.

"Explosion! So what happened exactly?" he asked.

"I don't know. My Dad never came back. Neither did any of the other adults. None of them made it."

"What about the other evacuees?" Bray carefully probed.

"You ask so many questions," Emma pointed out suspiciously.

"I need to know, Emma. Not just for my sake. I'd like to help you, and your brother and sister. If you'll let me. Along with anyone else around here."

"If you're trying to find out how many people are still left, Bray, then… there are at least a couple of hundred of us."

"That's odd. I haven't seen any sign of any of them."

"You think I'm - lying?" Emma said.

"Are you?" Bray enquired.

"I could be. Then again…" she shrugged.

"You know what I think? There are only the three of you."

"You're wise, Bray. Very wise. But maybe not wise enough," Emma said.

"Why don't you just tell me, Emma?"

"Of all the original evacuees," Emma finally revealed, "most who survived split into different gangs. Some went away to explore. Others decided to stay. In our group there were about thirty of us. We called ourselves the Roaches."

"So these Roaches still live here, in the base?"

"They've gone, Bray. You're right. It's just the three of us left now. Me, my brother and sister."

"What happened? To the other members of the Roaches?"

"I was hoping you might be able to tell me," Emma answered. "Most ended up as slaves, I think."

"I never told you I was a slave," Bray reminded her.

"You never said you weren't either," Emma replied.

Bray could see she was wistful, staring into the distance in a reverie. She was sad, mournful.

"Have you ever heard of a tribe called The Fallen?" she asked.

"The Fallen?"

"We thought that if we traded with them, that they'd leave us alone. And for a time, it worked. But after a while, they made it clear it wasn't just food they wanted from us. But people. That's when they began to take my friends. One by one. Our little group, our family that had grown so close, pulled together to look after one another, began to be picked apart. I thought I'd never lose a family again. But I did."

"These Fallen? Had they been evacuated here?"

"I don't know. For sure. I doubt it. They didn't seem to know much about the wastelands. After I told them about what it had really been used for... burying so many people... they didn't seem that interested in taking any more of my friends or visiting here. Again. Pretty soon after, they left us alone. And haven't been back since."

"What about your friends? Any more of them still around?"

Emma considered Bray, even though she couldn't see. It was as if she was searching by instinct to establish whether or not she could trust him.

"If you must know... all my friends... they died. All of them. Including my elder brother. He would have been about sixteen then. And now, like I said, it's just the three of us."

She was trembling with emotion and it made Bray feel distraught.

"I understand how you must feel," Bray said. "I also lost my brother. I know all about the pain when those close to you die. Or are taken away."

What he said struck a chord with Emma, looking deeply in Bray's direction through unseeing eyes, which streamed more tears. Perhaps Bray and she had more in common than she had thought.

Bray felt truly sorry for her. Before in their encounters, Emma had seemed confident, in control. But now so vulnerable, which endeared her to him.

"Why don't you let me help you, Emma? If you let me go. Believe me, I can help. I don't mean you any harm."

Emma shook her head. She gathered her composure and once again, the barriers were raised as fast as they had been dropped.

"No... I can't do that, Bray. Can't risk it."

"Risk what? Release me and I'll help you!"

"What would do in my situation, Bray? I might be blind but I'm not stupid. You say you stumble into our lives, as if by chance. And that might be true. But if I let you go so you can walk out the door - would you really just walk away and leave us alone?"

"I told you, Emma. I'll help you!"

"What? Help us get captured by The Fallen? Traded?"

"No. I'd never do that," Bray replied.

"I'd be worthless as a slave anyway," Emma went on. "But I've still got to try and protect Tiffany and Shannon. Whereas you, Bray. You might have a value. So maybe we should hand you over to The Fallen if they ever pay us a visit. Perhaps they'd be interested in getting their hands on someone to trade, like you."

"Emma! You can't mean that! You must know this is wrong," Bray insisted.

"You say you arrived from the north... I told you I'm not stupid, Bray. I've heard tales of what goes on up there. And to someone, you must have been of value. Once. And who knows, you could be of value again. If we ever decided to trade you, that is."

Emma stood up, crushing the tin of baked beans beneath as she accidentally stepped on it, making her way unevenly towards the door, which she knocked on, giving Tiffany on the other side a signal to open it.

"I have to do what I have to do to protect what's left of my family. To survive. I like you, Bray. But I'm sorry. You're not going anywhere."

CHAPTER NINETEEN

Lex had gotten himself out of a few holes and tough places in his life but so far he was well and truly stuck.

The pit he had fallen into was a good ten feet deep. It was obviously man-made. Lex could see it wasn't natural, due to the chips and marks in the earth where the symmetrical shaped circular hole must have been dug.

"You sure you're okay?" Jack called down from above, peering at Lex.

"For the millionth time, I don't need your help!" Lex shouted.

His pride had taken a fall when he had, and he was determined to get out of the mess he had gotten into under his own steam.

He was now clutching the sides of the earth, trying to climb up, struggling to get various foot and hand holds from the vine roots.

It was no use though. Despite his best efforts, Lex lost his grip and collapsed to the ground, landing on his backside.

Jack winced as he edged closer, at the top of the hole.

"Why don't I find some vines and try and haul you up?"

"Why don't you just shut it?" Lex replied, brushing off the dirt from his fall.

"You got nothing to prove, Lex," Jack said.

"Maybe not to you."

"It's obviously a trap. Bet it's the first time it's captured a wild 'Lex'. It must be designed to normally catch a wild pig - or something," Jack said, his voice echoing from above.

"What's that supposed to mean?" Lex called up.

"Nothing!" Jack smiled mischievously.

"Well, if it makes you feel any better - I hate to admit it, but maybe I do need your help."

"About time. That's all you had to do, was ask," Jack hollered. "I'll see what I can find. Back in a min."

Jack was just relieved that all that seemed to be hurt was Lex's feelings - he must have landed on his thick head, Jack chuckled to himself, as he scrambled away from the hole and scanned the undergrowth for something Lex could cling to.

Lex paced around the muddy floor of the hole, looking up at the darkening sky directly above, just visible through the overhanging thick jungle of trees and plants. They had been gone from Amber and the others for some time and it would be completely dark soon. He just hoped the two of them would be able to find their way through the jungle to the beach. It would have been hard enough remembering the way in the daytime, let alone at night.

Jack better not tell the others about this, Lex fumed, embarrassed at being unable to take care of himself.

Suddenly, a twisted tangle of vines dropped down from above.

"Thanks, Jack. I owe you!" Lex called up.

Lex grabbed hold, feeling the strength of the vines, and he felt sure they would be able to support his weight. He was continually impressed by Jack's practical skills, his ability to make mechanical devices out of basic items - and this improvised rope made of 'vines' seemed perfect.

Lex began to clamber up, hauling himself, his arms straining on the vine, trying to assist his ascent with a better foothold in all the vine roots.

But suddenly, to his surprise, he was making rapid progress towards the surface as if he was in an elevator.

"Whoa, Jack," Lex admired, he would never have thought Jack had it in him. "You been working out?"

As he neared the surface, the sounds of the jungle life getting louder with him getting closer, Lex was thrilled to be finally regaining his freedom.

But as he arrived at the top and out of the hole, he gazed in sudden unease.

Jack was squirming, trying to call out a warning, though his cries were muffled, a big hand clasped over his mouth. He was being held by a huge 'native' looking figure, daubs of war paint on his face and body.

"Get off him!" Lex barked, his anger rising.

Lex was going to rush to Jack's assistance but as he scrambled to his feet, he noticed other similar looking natives and was quickly overpowered.

The last thing he saw was Jack's wild, panicked eyes, before a massive hand covered Lex's eyes and another his mouth, muffling his own shouts of frustration and resistance.

CHAPTER TWENTY

It was so strange to be back on dry land, Amber thought, as she looked up at the twinkling stars above in the night sky.

It had been her routine before bed, to stare up to the Heavens, taking a moment to gather her thoughts. She had done that every night during their voyage in the ocean, when   they were first on the trawler, then the Jzhao Li. Normally Jay would accompany her, the two of them having some quiet time together to try and make sense of everything.

And now Jay had gone and Amber was worried. Jay and Ram hadn't returned back to camp yet from their excursion. There had also been no sign of Lex and Jack.

At least the girls had returned earlier, to Amber's relief, bringing back more medical supplies with them from the wreck of the Jzhao Li - and most importantly, Zak.

It was a miracle. He was alive. Just. His pulse was weak and he hadn't regained consciousness. He had obviously nearly drowned, hitting his head, a huge swelling visible on it. Amber and the others feared that they wouldn't see him again, suspecting the worst had occurred when Zak heroically lowered the lifeboat, allowing them all to escape the cargo vessel, becoming trapped on it when it ran aground.

May lay beside Zak's prone body, huddling herself against him, determined to remain by his side.

Similarly, Ruby was still keeping a close watch on Slade, inside the makeshift shelter. Slade let out an occasional murmur of pain from the wound in his side, Ruby doing her best to ease his plight. But thankfully the blood loss had been stemmed from Amber treating the wound earlier. Now they had to watch for infection.

The temperature felt as if it was dropping as the night advanced but it was due to the wind from the ocean.

"It's cold," Lottie said nevertheless, through chattering teeth, sitting as close as she dared to the heat of the fire they had made.

"First it's too hot, then it's too cold," Darryl muttered, trying to get some sleep, Lottie irritating him, not to mention the swarms of mosquitoes. Darryl waved his hand, trying to shoo away the insects that seemed to have a fondness for him. They continued to buzz in the humid night air and Darryl sighed to himself. He wouldn't call this cold. What did Lottie expect - snow? And that she would be building snowmen in this region, which was clearly sub-tropical?

"Ellie - Jack and Lex know how to look after themselves," Amber said, trying to reassure Ellie, who paced up and down the sands around camp.

"They're taking too long!" Ellie said, her anxiety all too clear.

"I'm sure they'll be back before too long," Amber insisted.

"Jack..." Ellie broke up in sobs on saying his name.

"He'll be okay, don't worry," Salene said, giving Ellie a hug.

"You hope!" Trudy said, as she gazed around uneasily at the dark jungle bordering Camp Phoenix. "You won't fall asleep on watch or anything, Amber?" Trudy continued.

"No, don't worry. I'll keep awake. So why don't you all settle down and try and get some rest."

Trudy nodded, then lay down near the little ones, already lost in slumber.

Clutching a roughly-made spear she had fashioned earlier, Amber crossed to where Sammy was sitting, also supposedly on watch. But his head was drooped forward and he was emitting a loud snore.

Amber touched the point of the spear to his neck.

Sammy awoke with a start, then sighed with relief. "Oh, it's only you, Amber."

"And a good job, too," Amber replied disdainfully. "No point in taking a shift on night watch if you sleep, Sammy. If you're really that tired, off you go."

"Sorry," he said guiltily, then scampered away nearer the fire to join the others as Amber embarked upon her own shift.

It was an eerie night, the moonbeams casting an unnatural glow, the waves rolling onto shore incessantly, the water a strange pallor of grey, illuminated from the bright moon. The wind rustled through the foliage. They were all so exposed. So alone.

What was this place, Amber wondered as she gazed around at the endless rows of palm trees bristling in the wind, the dark outline of the jungle full of mystery. Just what or who was out there?

Amber gripped the spear tighter in her hand, readying it in case she needed to spring into action at any time and tried to dismiss her growing worry for the continued absence of Lex and Jack. And Jay and Ram.

But this unknown land wouldn't get the better of them, Amber resolved, vowing that whatever was in store for them all, she would be ready to face it and reassured herself that the other four would be alright and would return soon.

* * *

"Ground control to the Technos. This is Ram. Over?"

"Earth to Ram. Just what the hell are you doing?" Jay asked.

Ram was sitting in the pilot's seat in the cockpit of the massive cargo plane, spinning the wheel and pressing buttons on the instrumentation panel like a happy child playing with an oversized toy.

"I thought you wanted to get some sleep?" Jay continued. "If not, we can always talk now."

"Maybe you're right," Ram said, slumping back in his seat. "It's getting late."

He had promised to go over a few things with Jay in the morning but Jay was beginning to have suspicions that Ram was intentionally drawing it out, avoiding matters. He apparently had a headache and reassured Jay that there was nothing of much importance which couldn't wait until morning.

Jay was eager to find out the reason for Ram's unusual behaviour but felt tired himself and thought it might be better for them both to grab a few hours sleep while they could.

The priority had been to discover the mysteries of this aircraft and then he would deal with the mysteries surrounding Ram.

The two of them had climbed up earlier to check out the interior of the downed plane, stuck high in the trees.

They had searched the cavernous hold. Which had been empty. There was no cargo. Just the aircraft, with its onboard built-in equipment still reasonably intact.

Thankfully, there hadn't been any bodies. Presumably the crew would have bailed out, Jay considered. Or escaped the wreckage when it must have crash landed, ditching in the jungle. Someone must have obviously been piloting the plane and since there was no telltale signs or any skeletal remains, Jay concluded that the occupants might have survived.

The aircraft had United Nations insignias on its tail.

What the plane had been doing and why it crashed still remained a mystery though, as did so much of the final days of the adult times.

Jay wondered if there could be some connection between the cargo plane and the Jzhao Li. Perhaps it was involved somehow in the United Nations Pacific Fleet that Dr Jane Gideon's journal had mentioned. Was it part of some last ditch effort to escape the 'virus'? Or something else?

Despite their efforts to find out by clambering into the wreckage, Jay and Ram hadn't discovered any answers, however.

There were no maps, no paperwork. The power to the onboard computers had gone. Ram was unable to reactivate them. But Jay was aware of Ram's continual eagerness to at least try, which reinforced Jay's suspicions that Ram was avoiding revealing information regarding his irrational behaviour of late.

Jay cast a glance at Ram, beginning to snore in the pilot's seat, and couldn't help but smile slightly. The former leader of the Technos had really enjoyed being in the plane, reacquainted with technology, the only sign of happiness he had shown for some time.

For all of Ram's eccentricities and manic intemperance, Jay liked him. And in many ways admired him. They had met just before the 'virus' struck when they were streamed into a boot camp during the height of the pandemic. Amidst all the panic, the authorities had began emergency evacuation for those uncontaminated and aged under 18. A survival program had been implemented. It was known as S.E.E.D, an acronym for Survival Education Endurance Development.

Basically the rational was that various segments within the demographic of young people would be streamed during the course of the evacuation so that they would spend some time in boot camps, where they would be trained in all manner of areas.

Different regions specialised in different skills.

The camp where Jay originally met Ram focused on working with those with a flair for computers. Jay had always been interested in programming but knew from the first time he encountered Ram that he was no match. Ram possessed abilities right off the scale. Though his biggest skills seem to have been dating Siva and Java at the same time, both of whom had also been evacuated to the same camp, excelling at Information Technology.

During the course of the induction, all at the boot camp were taught in the limited time available a range of matters which were thought to be crucial to aid any chance of survival. Such as programming electricity grids. Or rebooting sewage and other infrastructures.

In the aftermath of the adults dying, Jay felt drawn to Ram's vision of starting his Techno tribe - though he didn't entirely agree with his ambitions to dominate and control, resulting in invading other sectors.

Ram justified his ambitions, feeling that society could benefit from the expertise of the Technos but had a contempt for those he considered to be 'virts'. All those illiterate and uninterested in the marvels of technology. The one constant being that Ram was someone of great extremes. Cunning. And brilliance. He excelled strategically but as with his beloved computers and all inanimate technological objects, seemed to be devoid of any 'human' feelings. Other than displaying stubbornness. He was certainly a complex individual.

Jay knew something was troubling him since the time they left the city but so far Ram had avoided explaining anything.

Jay had a stubborn streak of his own and was determined that he would get Ram to open up.

A wave of fatigue washed over Jay. Before long, he fell asleep.

As soon as his eyes closed, Ram's own eyes opened widely. He knew now was the time.

Jay had tethered Ram's wrists with vines on the dashboard control panel in the cockpit in case Ram tried to run off again.

Casting a careful glance to make sure Jay was asleep, Ram began to rub the vines against the instrumentation panel.

Who was Jay to think he could keep Ram bound? Didn't anyone know by now Ram made the rules? He decided the fate of others. Not the other way around.

With a grim look of determination, Ram worked the vine, trying to not make too much noise, resolving that he would soon be free.

* * *

Jay turned, shifting positions, aware of noises in his semi-dazed slumber.

There was constant creaking as the wind blew against the hulking wreck of the Hercules aircraft, which shifted slightly, suspended high within the trees.

Somewhere, in the recesses of his mind he was also sure that Ram had stopped snoring.

Squinting a tired sleepy eye open to check on Ram, he was jolted by a sudden unexpected vision of Ram staring down at him, just inches from Jay's face.

"What the hell are you doing, Ram?!"

"Trying not to disturb you...so you didn't disturb me," Ram drawled, all too pleased with himself at showing Jay he had managed to get out of Jay's bonds. "You were sleeping soundly, Jay boy. Just like a baby."

Ram settled back into the pilot's seat, stretched and yawned before considering Jay. "And you wanna know something, Jay? You really hurt my feelings. Tying me up. What is it, don't you trust me?"

"Well, that's one way of putting it," Jay smiled, despite himself.

"I could have clambered out of here, down these trees, and escaped. Or 'attacked' you, Jay, taken you out without you even knowing it," Ram grinned.

"So why didn't you? Worried I would wake up? Catch you in the act?"

"No need to be so hostile, Jay. I didn't choose to escape. Because I don't want to. And I don't want to 'fight' you either. We're on the same side. You should know that by now. I wanted to prove you can trust me. I'm still here even though I don't need to be... I'm not gonna run from you - or myself - not any more..."

Jay sat up and was now leaning his back against the metallic wall of the plane's hold, staring at Ram with a degree of fascination.

"You do my head in, Ram, at times. You really do."

"I do my own head in, Jay, if you want to know the truth. It's not easy living with a mind like mine." Ram pointed at his head. "This brain, can you imagine how many petaFLOPS I've got swirling around, processing quadrillions of files? What might take a computer a second, might only take me a millisecond. If only we could have programmed software, eh Jay, the way God programmed humans, then maybe this world wouldn't have ended up in such a mess."

"So you admit - you are human after all?" Jay smiled affectionately.

Ram was suddenly intense and began sweeping his hand through his hair nervously. "Yeah, I'm human.

I wish I wasn't. I wish I was a computer. At least a computer doesn't have a conscience."

"Go on," Jay encouraged warily.

"You're right, Jay. I have been keeping something from you. I've even been trying to keep it from myself."

He started patting his head with the palms of his hands in growing frustration.

"These damn petaFLOPS. I can't programme them to stop what I've been thinking. And I've been thinking... a lot. You wouldn't believe what's been going through these data files these past few weeks. I thought, when I tried to get away from you earlier, I could run from my problems. Or keep them hidden somehow, pretend they didn't even exist. But I realize - now we're here, well and truly stuck on this land - I can't just trash all the files. And above all, I can't get through just by myself. I need your help, Jay. We're in this together."

"In what together?" Jay replied, intrigued.

"There's... a lot of things you need to know. I've been keeping a few 'things' from everyone. I've been doing it for everyone's good. Protecting you - as well as Amber and the others. But it's time you know the truth."

At last, Jay thought. He could hardly believe Ram was opening up to him this way. In Ram's own way. And he felt sorry for Ram because he was clearly suffering, patting his head obsessively, anguished by some inner turmoil.

"Where do I begin?" Ram yelled. "Let me try and recover a few things from limbo! Just hope I don't get caught in an infinite loop! We wouldn't want this old brain of mine to crash now, would we!? Or we might not be able to reboot!"

"Why don't you just tell me everything?" Jay said.

"In order to do that, I need to go back to the beginning. And it's one hell of a bedtime story, Jay."

Ram seemed to be hyperventilating now, his eyes flicking, his head twitching like he had a nervous tick while he processed information embedded in the deep recesses of his mind.

"Me! You! Everyone here! We're all in terrible danger!"

CHAPTER TWENTY-ONE

The cruiser towing the lifeboat ploughed through the water. Ebony, bound in the net, gazed uneasily ahead, noticing a towering silhouette in the distance. Flames poured out of the top, glowing in the dark night sky. The infrastructure stood on four legs like some colossus. It was gigantic. Ominous. And the cruiser was heading directly towards it. Ebony suspected it could be an oil rig.

The cruiser arrived just over an hour later. Ebony was in awe of the rig's size, let alone its existence. She was amazed that out here in the middle of nowhere, far from land, this behemoth stood as if defying everything Mother Nature had to throw at it. The wind had picked up, the waves increasing in size, sweeping against the massive struts that supported the immense infrastructure, like they had no impact on it at all.

She noticed that a larger vessel had already arrived and was moored on a dock surrounding the base of the rig. Prisoners were disembarking, herded by a wild, feral-looking bunch of thugs. Like most of the tribes Ebony had encountered back in the city, they all were about the same age. But few she had ever come into contact with looked as menacing as this bunch.

Ebony was as confused as she was afraid, wondering how the military-looking boarding party who had captured her were connected to these vagabonds.

It took some time for Ebony and her fellow group of captives to climb several stories of metallic stairwells of the oil rig. When they reached the summit, arriving on a helicopter deck, their ankles were bound by metal chains.

Some of the group begged to be released, others wailed in self-pity as the vagabonds marshalled all the prisoners in lines. It seemed they were being separated by gender and into different age groups.

The military-looking types watched impassively as if they were some kind of overseers, checking on the progress of whatever was being planned.

The pit of Ebony's stomach churned. She had no idea of her fate, the intentions of her abductors.

"Over there!" one of the vagabonds bellowed, kicking a boy from behind into place. The petrified child seemed as if he was about to erupt into tears, struggling to keep his composure for fear of any repercussions.

The first group was the largest. They looked to be the oldest, strongest, biggest, the most physically fit, Ebony reasoned. All were male.

The next group was quite the opposite, comprised of the smaller and younger members of the prisoners assembled. They were scrawny. Some of them didn't look well at all. They were clearly malnourished and must have been living rough for a long while to be in such a state. They were comprised of both males and females.

Ebony formed part of the last group, with only six other girls. And she wondered why they had been singled out.

Satisfied they had arranged the prisoners in the right order, one of the vagabonds crossed to the leader of the military. "We're all done," he said.

"Stand by!" the leader replied. Then he spoke into a walkie-talkie. "Ready when you are, Commander Blake."

The wind howled on the open deck.

Ebony and her fellow prisoners shivered in the cold night air but also in growing anxiety at what was to happen next as a shadowy outline appeared on the outside walls, dimly lit by flaming torches.

Tall, well built, intimidating... Ebony and the captives gazed transfixed by the shadow, which was soon revealed to belong to a young man, striding confidently across the helicopter deck.

He, like the boarding party, was dressed in black with a similar balaclava, which had been rolled on top of his head. But unlike the others, his hair wasn't close cropped. On the contrary, a mane of blonde locks tumbled across his shoulders, rippled in all directions as the wind howled. He was also unshaven with stubble on his broad jaw. But it was his eyes that Ebony noticed. And which unsettled her. They were deep blue, intense, as he paced around, surveying the prisoners as if inspecting them on a military parade ground.

There was a utility of motion and emotion in him. An undercurrent of energy and impatience. He exuded power. An ominous power. He ticked like a bomb. No doubt that he had to be the alpha male around here.

He was good looking, Ebony had to admit. Very much so. Despite her loathing of her captors, she had never been one not to ignore any male physically attractive. And this dude was hot. His magnetism and presence took her breath away. She surveyed him like a lioness, as if he was to be her prey.

He seemed to be around the same age as Ebony and the military-looking boarding party but unlike their regimented behaviour, was more relaxed, casually eating a ripe apple.

"One hundred and twenty-two intakes, Commander Blake," one of the vagabonds said in deference, proudly over the cold wind. "We exceeded our quotas."

Blake nodded, clearly impressed, and took another bite of his apple, his eyes scanning back and forth, analyzing all of the assembly.

Then he turned to the leader of the boarding party. "Axel - what have you got to report?" Blake asked.

"There was only one on board, Sir! A female. She's in the third group."

Axel indicated, then led Blake to where Ebony was standing.

Blake eyed her up and down, examining her hair, ears, teeth.

"So you're the 'blip' on the radar screen, eh?" Blake said.

Ebony smiled coyly, uneasily.

"My name's Ebony."

"I didn't ask your name!" Blake snapped in sudden anger.

Ebony's smile quickly disappeared as Blake turned to Axel.

"I was hoping for a few more. But she'll do," Blake said.

He examined the hair, eyes, teeth and ears of the others in Ebony's group.

"Have any of you ever been pregnant?" Blake asked.

"Why?" one girl replied, confused by the question, as were the others in their group, including Ebony.

But they were astounded by what was about to transpire.

Blake lifted the girl with ease over one shoulder, her arms and legs flailing as he crossed towards the railings - and casually thew her over the side.

Ebony and her fellow prisoners listened, terrified, hearing the receding wailing cries of despair as the girl fell, plunging into the ocean far below.

Blake casually took another bite of his apple, then threw the core into the ocean.

All watched intensely, petrified, as Blake returned and addressed the assembly.

"I don't ask much during your time with us. But I would strongly suggest never to answer a question - with a question. When I - or any of my team - ask anything, we expect an answer. Understood?"

A murmur spread through the prisoners.

But Ebony yelled at the top of her voice. "What's the matter with you all? Can't anyone speak? You heard the man! Tell him you understand!"

Blake cast a surprised glance at Ebony, a glint of amusement in his deep blue eyes while the other prisoners shouted out in unison, indicating that they were fully aware of his instruction.

Ebony raised her voice loudly above the chorus. "Don't forget - Sir! Let me hear you all now!"

"We understand, Sir!" the prisoners replied.

"Nice one!" Ebony said.

Blake sighed to himself, then addressed the assembly as if purposefully ignoring Ebony.

"So you must remember one thing! All of you! You obey. Or you suffer!" he bellowed to the cowering prisoners.

Then he crossed briskly to Axel, indicating impatiently. "Get them out of my sight!"

"What about the girl, sir?" Axel asked, glancing at Ebony.

"Bring her to me," Blake ordered. "I'll deal with her!"

* * *

Ebony, accompanied by guards and manacled by her leg irons, shuffled as she walked down a long corridor of the living quarters.

Axel tapped politely on the closed door before him. So strange, Ebony thought for a moment, to see mannerisms of the old world still being observed.

"Come in," a female voice replied.

Axel opened the door and Ebony was pushed inside by the guards.

Blake sat behind a huge oak desk.

The grotesque girl with the scars running down her face who Ebony had seen earlier during her initial capture, stood behind Blake, gently caressing his shoulders, giving him a massage. She glared disdainfully at Ebony, then nodded as Axel spun Ebony around like she was on display. Which she was.

Blake sipped on his glass of wine and examined Ebony. He was in the midst of eating a meal.

"Get your hands off me!" Ebony snapped, squirming in the grasp of her captors.

Axel raised a fist to strike.

"That won't be necessary!" Blake said. "I don't want any blood spilled in my quarters. Not while I'm eating. You and your men are dismissed, Axel. Thank you."

Axel nodded, then left with the other guards.

Blake continued eating, sipping on his wine, the disfigured girl still massaging his shoulders.

From what she had witnessed earlier on the helicopter deck of the rig, Ebony decided it would be wise not to be the first to speak.

The silence seemed to go on for ever, with Blake almost ignoring Ebony. She started to feel faint, standing motionless for so long.

After a while, the silence was broken.

"Why?" Blake probed, without looking up, spooning the remains of his dessert.

Ebony didn't now exactly what he was referring to, suspecting though that he was seeking details of how she ended up drifting on the lifeboat, but wasn't about to give any information. Not until she had a better idea of just who exactly these people were.

"Why not?" Ebony replied. "Philosophically speaking, that is. I'm not answering a question with a question...Sir. Just trying to engage in some friendly conversation."

"Who are you?" Blake said, topping up his glass of wine.

"Why don't you try and get to know me a little better and you might find out," Ebony said, unbuttoning her blouse.

The hideous girl cast Ebony a pathetic look.

Blake reached out for a small toothpick and started cleaning between his teeth, sucking out the remnants of food, seemingly oblivious to Ebony stripping before his very eyes.

"Why would I want to do that?" he asked.

Ebony removed her blouse and began undoing her bra.

"I can bring skills to that table of your's. Skills like you would never imagine," she said seductively.

"Can you now?" Blake replied, taking another sip of wine. "Well, isn't that interesting?"

"Why don't you release the creature of the deep - and we can discuss it? In greater detail?" Ebony said, dropping her bra to the floor.

She was desperate. She had no idea who these people were but had to make an impression and take her chances while she still could. And instinctively, this was the only way she knew how.

She was aware she was attractive and she was going to use anything and everything in her considerable arsenal she had to in order to survive.

"That sounds like a sensible suggestion. Leave us!" Blake commanded casting an appreciative glance over the upper parts of Ebony's naked body.

"You can't be serious!" the disfigured girl protested.

Blake spoke quietly, tapping the girl on the hand reassuringly. "Please."

The grotesque girl sighed to herself, then reluctantly left the room, closing the door behind her.

"Hungry?" Blake said, indicating the spoils on the table.

"Ravenous," Ebony smouldered, shuffling towards him. "I've got one hell of an appetite. And I just hope you can satisfy it."

She sat on his knee, cupped his hand on her breast and started to kiss him gently at first, then with increasing passion.

CHAPTER TWENTY-TWO

Bray slumped on the bed, wiggling his ankles and moving his wrists, trying to get the circulation flowing in his bound limbs. His tethers had been tied together well, he had to give Emma and her siblings credit. He had done everything he could to try and prise himself free but doubted if even the most flexible contortionist would be able to extricate themselves from the bonds keeping him a prisoner.

Just what was Emma going to do with him?

He felt pity for her. It couldn't have been easy with her disability, struggling to survive with her much younger brother and sister. And if Emma's story was true, they had endured their share of heartache and suffering with the gradual erosion of their tribe, the Roaches, reduced to just three members. Would they hand Bray over to The Fallen? Or ever let him go on his way?

He wouldn't stop trying to persuade Emma that he meant no harm to them, hoping she would set him free. Then Bray could formulate a plan to discover just exactly where he had been held all this time, and how he could get back to his friends and tribe in the city.

The sound of screaming from outside jolted Bray out of his reverie. It sounded like a young girl crying, calling for help, in great distress. Was it Tiffany?

Bray braced himself. There was danger out there, alright. Something was wrong. And here he was, powerless to help.

The door to the room was unlocked, then opened, revealing young Shannon entering, tears in his eyes, with his older sister Emma following.

"Is he there? Is he still there?!" Emma shrieked.

"Yes! He's here!" Shannon yelled back, panicked.

"What's happening?!" Bray called out as Emma stumbled slightly, following Shannon headed back towards the door.

Emma stopped, turned and gazed at Bray through her opaque eyes.

"I thought it was you at first!" Emma cried. "That'd you gotten out, were going to hurt Tiffany... or hold her ransom."

"What are you talking about?" Bray yelled, frustrated at Emma's continued suspicions of his character and intentions.

He could sense her very feelings of helplessness as no doubt she was sensing his despair. Emma nodded. Shannon flicked a switch. The security monitors suddenly displayed various images of a wild-looking gang moving through the base.

"The Fallen?" Bray enquired.

"Yes," Emma replied, in mounting unease. "And they seem to have Tiffany."

"You can't fight them on your own. Set me free, Emma! I'll help. I promise!"

Emma's mind was racing. She didn't have much time. Was it a ruse? Could she trust him? Would he turn against her if she let him go? Her face betrayed the tormented emotions she was feeling of doubt and agonizing uncertainty as Tiffany's cries for help outside continued, though the revolving security camera didn't pick up any images, displaying only members of the gang entering various buildings, searching.

"She needs help! I can help her!" Bray yelled out.

Reluctant, with no option, Emma nodded to Shannon. The young boy ran over to Bray, pulling out a small knife from his pocket, the blade glinting in the light.

For a moment, Bray wondered if Shannon meant to use the knife against him - but his anxiety about that was put to rest when Shannon cut the bonds securing Bray loose, the ropes falling to the ground.

Bray didn't say a further word and angered by whatever harm had happened to Tiffany, he raced past Emma and Shannon, both recoiling as he brushed past them in full flight.

Tiffany let out another piercing scream. Emma shuddered, terrified, feeling helpless, young Shannon hugging his big sister as Bray disappeared out the door.

* * *

"Where's your good-looking sister?" a member of the gang yelled. He was standing outside the accommodation block where Bray was being held, twisting little Tiffany's arm back painfully, a grimace on Tiffany's face as she did her best to resist.

"Here!" Bray shouted, gazing around for any sign of the other gang members.

"You don't look like Emma to me!" the gang member said. "Who the hell are you?"

"Your worst nightmare, if you don't let her go," Bray replied, threateningly.

"I could either do that. Or break her arm!" the gang member replied, backing away slightly, forcing Tiffany's arm up more.

He was clearly threatened by the imposing figure of Bray who looked like a guy who could take care of himself.

Other members of The Fallen appeared.

They were all dressed in black grungy clothes, with self-inflicted scar marks on both sides of their faces from where they must have at one stage cut into themselves the shape of the letter "F", indicating their tribe. They looked gothic, each with dyed black hair, red make up outlining their eyes and mouths, as if they were smeared by blood. They had chains with skull jewellery and adornments.

"What have we got here?" one asked. She was the only female member of the tribe Bray could see and must have been the leader. The others seemed in awe of her as she surveyed Bray.

"A hero, Belle," the thug holding Tiffany replied, "Least that's what he thinks he is."

Belle considered Bray and suddenly lunged forward snarling, like a wild animal.

Bray recoiled.

Belle started to laugh manically, smacking her lips as if she was savouring an imagined taste.

"Oh, I don't think so! Doesn't look to me like any hero. Besides, heroes never taste too good! I prefer my meat a little more raw!"

She and the others were now converging on Bray, circling him menacingly.

Bray suddenly noticed a red laser dot moving across the face of Tiffany's captor. Emanating from one of the windows of the living quarters. It was Shannon, using a small keychain laser, trying to help in his own way. And as the light pointed into the eyes of the captor, Bray quickly took his chance. In one lightning movement, he twirled and unleashed a powerful kick into the gang member holding Tiffany. It was enough for him to release his grip.

Tiffany took off, running as fast as she could to the living quarters.

Bray sprinted in the opposite direction, The Fallen in pursuit. Now all were snarling like wild animals, hunting prey.

Bray arrived in the amusement park area and noticed buildings on the other side beyond the roller coaster.

Roller coasters had never been his thing, and they certainly weren't now. But this was crucial to the plan Bray quickly formulated in his mind.

Clambering the rickety wooden frame, Bray could feel the fragility of the structure beneath him, fearing that it would collapse at any moment.

Soon he was a good fifty feet off the ground, clutching the outer frame at the top of a loop de loop. A piece of the wood he was clinging to ripped away from the railing, the rotten timber twisting as gravity pulled it downwards. Bray felt dizzy, glancing at the piece of wood as it plummeted to the ground far below. It was another reminder, as if he needed it, that the slightest mistake and he too would fall to his doom.

The Fallen gazed up, their eyes wild as they focused on Bray.

Belle indicated. A member of the gang rushed into the nearby control booth, pulling levers.

To Bray's surprise, carriages began to move. The ride was obviously still operative and now posed another threat as carriages gathered speed and would soon crash into him as he clung to the tracks.

Bray climbed higher, higher, hoping that at least he was providing a distraction to enable Tiffany, Shannon and Emma to escape.

The carriage was approaching closer. Closer.

Within seconds of it arriving, Bray leapt spectacularly on to the roof top of the hangar building located opposite the roller coaster infrastructure. He tumbled to one side as he landed to try and break his fall.

Then he clambered down the side of a drainpipe.

Belle and The Fallen appeared round the other side of the building and converged on him.

Once again, Bray was now a captive.

CHAPTER TWENTY-THREE

They had obviously gone back in time. Either that, or they were in a movie set.

Something had to explain it, Jack thought, peering out as best he could from the mud hut in which he and Lex were being held. Their hands were tied by thick vines, wrapped around their wrists, attached to wooden poles driven into the muddy ground, which supported the mixture of grass and leaves that formed the roof of their hut.

It was so strange. Such a bizarre sight compared to what they had been used to with their old lives in the city.

Jack could see many 'natives' wandering about the primitive camp outside, along with other huts of various shapes and sizes.

The 'natives' themselves - for that's how Jack and Lex had referred to them - were made up of males and females. Some of the oldest - and biggest - were about the same ages as Lex and Jack. They had to be the warriors of the group, Jack reasoned. They were certainly imposing physical types, the muscles on their bodies rippling, showing their strength, which had been enough to subdue Lex and Jack and bring them to this village.

Other 'natives' sat on the ground, girls singing an unusual melody in a language Jack had never heard before, as they weaved together flax and plant material. Very young kids, probably two years old, raced around the camp playing. Some stopped by to cast an occasional intrigued glance into Jack and Lex's hut, fascinated by the two strangers inside.

"It's just like being in one of those documentaries I used to see when I was a kid," Jack said. "One of those travelogues. Either that, or I'm dreaming."

"You must have some pretty weird dreams," Lex replied, pulling with all his might on the vines binding his hands to the massive wooden poles.

"What do you think they're going to do with us?"

"I dunno. But I'm not planning to stay and find out," Lex said, inching forwards toward Jack as closely as he could, leaning so he could get a better glimpse through the open door which had been cut out.

"If I could only get loose. I reckon I could take on a couple of those warriors..."

"Leaving just the rest of the village to me," Jack interrupted, the skepticism showing on his face at any notion of escaping.

Darkness had fallen. In the centre of the village, a pig was being roasted over an open fire.

"Man. I am so hungry," Lex said, the aroma of the cooking wafting through. "They might have a lousy sense of hospitality. But it sure seems they can cook!" he continued, breathing in the aroma of the roast wistfully.

Then he considered Jack, preoccupied with a sudden thought.

"I just hope we're not on the menu. You don't think they might be cannibals? Do you?"

"Well, that's food for thought," Jack joked.

Lex deadpanned. "I know."

"Don't you get it, Lex? Food? For thought?"

"Yeah, I get it. I just hope they don't get us!" Lex replied, but was in no mood for Jack's jokes. He poked his head toward the doorway as far as he could.

"Hey, you!" Lex yelled at some of the natives passing nearby. "I'm talking to you!"

The villagers ignored Lex, continuing on their way with what they had been doing.

"Answer me! Are you deaf!?" Lex bellowed in frustration. "You can't keep us here! What are you going to do to us? Who do you think you are!?"

"Um, Lex - maybe they're not answering - because they can't speak our language."

"Well, that's their problem, Jack. But lucky for us, I speak the universal language."

"Which is?" Jack questioned, wondering just what Lex had in mind.

Lex wolf-whistled at one of the native girls kneeling near the fire, turning the spit roast.

Puckering his lips, Lex's bizarre behaviour and noises attracted the attention of the girl and she looked at him out of the corner of her eye.

Achieving contact, confident he was making inroads, Lex winked roguishly, blowing her a kiss.

The girl raised an eyebrow dubiously and shifted position, turning her back on Lex.

"Well, I'm impressed. That was effective," Jack muttered sarcastically.

"Give it time." Lex protested, his pride knocked. "She's just playing hard to get. I'll rely on my charm to get us out of here. You'll see."

The clatter of an arrow thudding into the ground by the entrance to the hut startled Lex and Jack, both of them recoiling back further into the interior of their confinement.

Three huge warrior figures appeared at the entrance, staring down at their prisoners, brandishing weapons threateningly.

"Obviously don't like you hitting on the women," Jack whispered.

"Let us go - and we'll just forget about it!" Lex ordered, staring defiantly at the warriors.

The warrior in the centre replied in his native language. But from the contemptuous look on his face, it was clear whatever he was saying wasn't friendly.

"What's your problem, pal? All this because of a couple of lousy chickens? What's so special about them anyway!? They looked well and truly - plucked!!" Lex bellowed.

Jack cast Lex a glance, reacting to the innuendo, widening his eyes as if to say don't go there.

Then he gazed in unease as the main warrior who had been speaking drew an arrow back in his bow, aiming it directly at Lex - who froze submissively, finally silenced by the prospect of the arrow pointing at him.

The disdain and hostility towards Jack and Lex was clear as the warriors glared threateningly.

Jack swallowed nervously, dreading what might now occur.

But as quickly as it had started, it was over.

The main native pulled away the bow, glowering at Lex, and the warriors moved off, leaving Jack and Lex alone in their hut.

"Next time I'll do the talking!" Jack insisted, breaking the silence. "You really have a way with people - not!"

"Shut it!" Lex insisted, slumping down onto the dirty earthen floor of the hut, taking stock of what had just happened. "This is crazy!" he continued. "I mean, what have we done wrong? What did we ever do to them?"

"Apart from offending them, you mean!" Jack said.

For once, Lex was silent, staring up at the roof of the mud hut.

That had been too close for comfort.

Whatever they had done to upset the 'natives', Lex knew for sure that he and Jack were obviously in a whole heap of trouble.

CHAPTER TWENTY-FOUR

Jay felt like he wanted to either thank Ram and be grateful for what he had told him the night before - or that he was going to kill him.

They were retracing their steps through the jungle, the blazing sun burning down as they tried to find their way back to Camp Phoenix.

"You're quiet," Ram said, his eyes shifting to and fro, anxiously surveying their environment while they walked.

"After all you've told me, Ram - I've got a lot to think about," Jay replied with a degree of contempt in his tone.

"Now you know how I've been feeling... why I might have been a little 'tense' lately..."

Jay went through the story once again in his mind that Ram had explained in the Hercules aircraft the night before.

Ram had told him that before he even formed the Technos, in the days when the adults were still alive... that Ram had been a prolific geek. No surprises there, Jay had thought.

But what did surprise Jay was when Ram revealed how he had been in contact with a number of other like-minded computer-obsessed people of all ages, based around the world. They had met online, gaming, Ram forming teams that competed in professional competitions. He had boasted to Jay of the achievements of his guild and the status he had as a role player. Ram's dream was to either become a computer engineer - or a pro gamer. Jay was aware that technology was Ram's life and that he had never been able to relate to people, understanding the logic and structure of the computer, feeling like he thought like one himself.

But he was unaware that beyond gaming, Ram and his online friends kept in touch through the Internet. And that they had tried their hand at hacking. First, into school computer networks. Then, harder to crack businesses. Finally, Ram and his associates had broken into the computer systems of major corporations, taking them down, perfecting their hacking skills. There was nothing philosophical driving them, just the challenge of it all. Their next targets were government agencies. Eventually the military. They could hack into anything, they felt.

Ram's point in telling Jay all this was that he became particularly close with one online friend. Someone who hid behind their online identity of 'KaMi-1314' - or as Ram called them affectionately for short, 'Kami'.

Ram thought initially that Kami was a girl, the two of them flirting at times online - but he eventually discovered that Kami was a guy. He couldn't be exactly sure of who he was or where they lived, Kami just revealing that he and his friends were based somewhere in the Far Eastern Region. Ram used his own online identity when they communicated, calling himself infinIT-Ram, an allusion to being infinite with Information Technology, and having a memory of no limits. Ram felt that described him perfectly.

When the 'virus' descended upon the world, Ram formed the Technos Tribe. That part, Jay obviously knew. He had been recruited not long after the Technos came into existence. Ram had worked hard building the tribe under his leadership, with the assistance of his close friends, Java, Siva and Mega.

But what no one was aware of was that Ram had hacked his way through automatic security systems of the military. And obtained information on some advanced hardware and weapons.

In those initial days when the adults began to perish, Ram still kept in touch with 'KaMi-1314' through the Internet, until it eventually shut down as the pandemic spread.

He then resorted to hacking into the UNANET, along with 'Kami', to continue their online relationship. UNANET was a successor to the old ARPANET that had gone so long before, which had been developed by the military in the event of a nuclear attack. UNANET stood for 'United Nations Agency Network' and was designed to enable communications to continue around the world in the event of any catastrophe by transmitting data through old copper telephone lines - almost like a more modern version of the 19th century telegram.

What Jay also didn't know was that this Kami contact Ram befriended online, became leader of an alliance of Tribes that became known as 'The Collective'. Drawn mainly from friends initially in his guild.

Their plight had been similar to what young people were experiencing in most of the major cities throughout the world in the wake of the pandemic, with smaller 'tribes' beginning to form from the scattered survivors. Whereas the tribes in Amber's home city had been at war, with Zoot and the Locos the most dominant among them, in Kami's home city the tribes had recognized the need to co-operate under his leadership, forming a powerful coalition of several tribes.

He had been inspired when studying the historic globalisation which had occurred. Where countries had formed alliances into unions. Thousands of years before, of course, scholars were fascinated - as was Kami - with the structures of ancient Rome, which grew from a city state to become a vast empire. And no doubt Kami had ambitions in that respect, too.

The 'Collective' insidiously and ruthlessly were able to seize raw resources such as fuel, vehicles, food, medicines and any useful technology they could get their hands on. Neighbouring communities were taken over by them, the smaller fragmented tribes and strays who lived in them unable to defend themselves against the superior numbers and forces of The Collective. They had no option but to go along or they would be eliminated.

According to Ram, The Collective had discovered classified files during the time when they were hacking at the height of the pandemic, revealing that governments were implementing a repopulation program. And Kami himself was intrigued to use this as a springboard to embark upon his own 'breeding' initiative, aware that he required a critical mass in his quest to dominate and eventually rule.

Ram had told Jay that The Collective had also hacked into a United Nations system, the data files of which showed that in anticipation of trying to survive the deadly 'virus' and mitigate its effects - along with any other potential threat -governments had co-operated in a top secret plan where they established a series of military bases dotted in key strategic points around the world.

Each base contained a compound. A place where top scientists and leading members of the government, as well as talented minds from academia to the arts, could be protectively housed, hoping to outlive any danger ravaging the world, sealing them off from the outside until it was safe to re-emerge. The bases were customised from earlier designs for nuclear proof bunkers and shelters from the 'Cold War'.

The adults assigned to each base were going to continue their research on combating the pandemic, trying to find a breakthrough, a cure. Substantial resources and funds were poured into this classified project as it was vital to prevent the possible extinction of humanity.

There were other similar but ocean-based approaches undertaken, with fleets of 'Noah's Arks' brought together, carrying important cargo. Some top secret. The Jzhao Li vessel that the Tribe had so fortuitously stumbled upon, was probably part of one of these fleets, Ram suspected, under the guise of just providing medical support. But in reality, there were a lot more objectives which probably many of the crew were unaware of.

Perhaps there were even isolated groups of adults who still survived, Ram had mused, living safely to this day, in the thick protected walls of the bases, atmospherically sealed off from any apocalypse, waiting for the day they could re-enter the world outside.

The Collective also uncovered a program of propaganda designed to drip feed information as the governments saw fit, so as to minimise panic.

Jay knew enough about history to realise that in the past, previous pandemics that decimated humanity had mutated and returned many times in waves. This had been the case with the Black Death in the medieval era - it didn't happen once but was a series of outbreaks, each one slightly different than the other. Similarly with pandemics of Influenza that had destroyed significant populations around the world.

But while Ram agreed with the potential threat of the virus mutating, he advised that Kami had a lot of theories and was beginning to suspect that there was more to the 'virus'. He saw references to bacterial warfare in some documents. Also genetic engineering. Even threats from germs from outer space, which resulted in the aged NASA program being stopped, with space station activity occupying the major focus. Kami wondered if the entire planet would be evacuated at some point. And if so - why?

Ram had tried to obtain more information, feeling that Kami was holding a lot back, fully aware that knowledge was power and that he wouldn't reveal all to Ram, choosing to maintain his own series of classified information. Equally, he might have shrewdly been sending out false signals through his own propaganda to throw anyone like Ram off his scent.

Jay was always aware of Ram's germ fetish since the first time they met and reflected that his phobia must have been heightened by not only the pandemic, if indeed that was the reason for the adults being wiped off the face of the Earth. But he wondered if Ram was being totally honest with him and that he, too, had his own series of 'classified files', just as he had accused Kami, and that Ram himself was holding something back.

"Jay, look," Ram indicated as they noticed a clearing which had been carved out of the jungle.

Ahead of them was the first of many vehicles they could see stretched on a makeshift road, which had been cut through the jungle.

The wind rustled through the foliage as Ram and Jay cautiously moved to examine the wrecks.

"Where do you think they were headed, Ram?"

"I think we'd better ask the grim reaper," Ram replied.

Not the answer Jay was looking for. Ram could be so weird at times.

There were no bodies inside, Ram and Jay noticed, as they checked out each vehicle that they passed.

Both of them felt like they had emerged almost into another dimension, a glimpse of the past, like a moment had been frozen in time and they wondered what had happened to the occupants of each vehicle and the reason for this long line of traffic. Especially why the vehicles had been abandoned.

Deciding to try and head back to Camp Phoenix, Jay questioned Ram more about his online contact, Kami, and discovered that Ram had hacked into The Collective's computers, furious at being kept in the dark by his enigmatic friend.

Previously unknown to Jay or any other member of the Technos, The Collective leader had tried to recruit Ram into joining Kami's team.

Kami had proposed that if Ram and his Technos joined The Collective, they could then be an advanced force, using their technology to invade the very same city where Amber and the Mall Rats had lived, securing it for The Collective.

Ram had found in his hacking that The Collective believed the observatory at Eagle Mountain near the city was actually an underground military compound, potentially bristling with secrets and equipment kept hidden away.

Jay remembered Amber telling him how she and the Mall Rats had gone there in the past, hoping to find an antidote for 'the virus' as well as more clues which might reveal exactly what happened to kill off all the adults. At the observatory, Amber and the Mall Rats had heard adult 'voices', Jay recalled Amber saying, having made contact with some sort of satellite before an explosion went off, killing one of the Mall Rats and nearly taking Amber's life in the process.

What Jay hadn't realised was that Ram was expected to carry out other invasions but felt he couldn't trust Kami or The Collective anymore, beginning to realise that Kami was keeping information of magnitude from him.

He was anxious, Ram told Jay, that he was just being manipulated, used, and had ambitions of his own for the Technos. He wasn't satisfied for them to be just a junior partner if Ram accepted Kami's offer to form an alliance to join the other tribes in The Collective.

So Ram's response had been characteristic. He had come up with a strategy, deciding to move in first, mobilising his Techno forces for the invasion that took place that memorable day when the city fell under Ram's sway, taking all the spoils - and Eagle Mountain, with its potentially hidden military compound - for himself.

"You're not mad at me, Jay?" Ram asked suddenly.

"You've got to be joking," Jay scoffed. "I've got all kinds of feelings inside, Ram. And yes, anger is one of them. As well as betrayal, distrust. Regret. I could go on."

"I did what I had to do."

"You should have told us before. Told me," Jay said.

He had believed that the Technos invaded the city to take the next step in making the world a better place. That's what Ram told them was the motive for their invasion. They were going to force peace onto the warring tribes who lived there, help the people build a new world through harnessing technology, Ram the architect of the future. For all involved.

Jay was completely unaware of this power struggle with The Collective. He didn't even know they had existed.

"Don't blame me for Kami trying to take over the world," Ram said. "I was just making sure there was just a little piece left for ourselves. So you should thank me, Jay. Not criticise. I mean it hasn't exactly been easy for me knowing that I had a price on my head."

"Don't try and pull one of your sympathy tricks on me, Ram, because it won't work!" Jay said.

"I thought you were a friend," Ram replied, wounded. "And after all the sacrifices I've made."

"Sacrifices!" Jay scoffed.

"Yeah, sacrifices," Ram reiterated. "I could have been right up there. In a position of real power. But I turned down the offer to join The Collective. For us, Jay. You, me. All the other members of the Technos. People who wanted to join."

Jay scoffed again, knowing only full well that Ram's brazen act in invading the city was first and foremost to probably turn it into his own fortified personal kingdom.

Ram explained he actually thought Slade was a bounty hunter retained by Kami to search for him and had been so relieved to find refuge in the little town of Liberty, rather than having his head delivered on a plate to the head of The Collective. But, of course, Slade had his own reasons for using Ram, to help him get to his brother, Mega.

Ram advised that he just had to keep the fact he was persona non grata among The Collective a secret. Ram was paranoid about any one of the highest ranked figures, Jay included, and that they might start a coup against him. That they would hand him in.

Kami was fascinated with the Roman Empire. If he considered Ram to be a potential Caesar figure, then he would have loved to have seen someone acting as Brutus. Stabbing the Technos' emperor in the back. And thought if anyone else discovered The Collective existed - and that Ram was their enemy - this would prompt a call for a change in leadership and only lead to a rebellion in the ranks. In the end, it had been Siva and Java, Ram's own wives, who had conspired against him, deposing Ram from the very tribe he had founded.

"I don't feel safe out here," Ram said, gazing around at the jungle as they retracted their steps back towards Camp Phoenix. "I'm taking a huge risk. For all we know, The Collective could be crawling around."

"What - here?" Jay asked. "God - if there's anything else, Ram, you'd better let me know. I mean it!"

Ram revealed why he was worried this land could now be under the influence and control of The Collective. When he hacked into their computers, Ram had seen plans for future expansion phases, which included a string of islands, one of which Ram suspected they were now in.

Like Eagle Mountain near the city, Ram claimed that The Collective had uncovered secret military compounds in other areas. He didn't know the exact locations but was sure he recalled the co-ordinates which he had noticed displayed on the Sat Nav back on the Jzhao Li.

Ram was beginning to panic, sure that he and the Mall Rats were accidentally drifting straight into enemy territory, with Ram being the most endangered due to the bounty The Collective must have placed on him. So he was desperate to obscure his features, protect his identity, just in case he was right and encountered members of The Collective who might so otherwise easily recognize him.

"You know, this is all your fault, Ram," Jay admonished him. "If you had just said something about it, maybe we would have listened and turned back, instead of drifting on the ocean. We could have avoided coming here if you had said earlier."

"Yeah, well nothing like hindsight, is there?" Ram grumbled. "Let's imagine for a moment. Back on the trawler. I say, "Hey everybody, let's go back to the city we fled from because The Collective could be lurking on some islands in the middle of the ocean. And they're real nasty pieces of work"... If I said that, would you honestly have believed me and decided to turn round and try and head back from where we had come from?"

"I don't know if I believe you now," Jay admitted honestly. "You could be making all this up."

"Believe me, Jay, for your sake and the others, I'm telling the truth. I can't say for sure but I reckon we might have drifted straight into the lion's den. There's no shopping mall to hide behind. We're not in the city anymore. Not now. If The Collective's really out here, we're all in danger. Not only me!"

CHAPTER TWENTY-FIVE

The sun continued its climb into the clear, deep blue sky, the heat increasing. All around in the palm trees lining the beach, the birds and insect life emitted a noisy dawn chorus.

Amber sat on a huge log that must have been washed up onto the beach long ago. It made the perfect seat now for what she needed, as Amber balanced a large drinks container retrieved from the wreck of the Jzhao Li, which sat unevenly on her lap.

She was tired, having found it difficult to sleep during their first night on the mysterious land. As the night had gone on, Amber and the other's imaginations had gone into overdrive, Trudy's in particular. All the Tribe felt vulnerable, unsure of what was lurking out there, in the jungle beyond.

Amber had stayed awake most of the night, keeping watch, never far from the improvised spear she had made, vigilantly on alert for any signs of danger.

Something had to explain the continued absence of Lex and Jack, Ram and Jay. None of them had returned to Camp Phoenix.

Amber had tried to keep the morale of everyone up, reminding them to trust in the abilities of those who were missing. They were all skilled, having survived in the dangerous city that used to be their home, and Amber was sure that they would all be safe out there - wherever they were - and would come back soon.

In the same way Ellie missed Jack, her love, Amber in particular felt the pangs of separation from Jay. She hoped he was alright, with the unpredictable and untrustworthy Ram as his companion.

Trudy hadn't helped matters. And had become slightly hysterical about the disappearance of the others, sure that they were dead. And that before long, all would suffer a similar fate. Amber had managed to get her to stay rational, at least as rational as Trudy could ever hope to be. They would never survive if they gave up hope.

Zak and Slade remained critically ill. Something had to be done for them, urgently.

"Let's see what we've got in here," Amber said to herself, peering through the contents of the drinks cooler, seeing what other medical supplies they had at their disposal.

Already earlier that morning, she had worked with Ruby to replace the gauze bandages covering Slade's wound, after first cleaning it with disinfectant from the bottles Ellie, May and Salene had brought back. While being treated, Slade had roared with pain, wincing with each touch Ruby made. He was mostly unconscious. Ruby knew her efforts were better than nothing and she just hoped they would go at least some small way to help Slade. She had to at least try something, she felt.

Amber's concern, as the day before, was that infection might be setting in. She recalled her parents once had gone on vacation in the tropics and her mother had cut her foot while snorkelling in the shallow waters. The infection from the coral in the reefs had made her terribly ill for weeks. Without expert medical help, she surely would have died.

Whereas Slade's wounds were visible, Zak's situation was a lot more problematic, difficult to discern. Since he had been found trapped in the rocks near the wreckage of the Jzhao Li, Zak had spent most of the time unconscious. Salene, trying to remember her own basic first aid training from school, had felt a pulse when his body was discovered initially and given him the kiss of life, Zak spewing salty sea water from his lungs. But that was as active as he had been since they found him.

May continued to watch over him, distraught. All the colour had drained from him and they were all uncertain what exactly was wrong. Amber suspected it must be some sort of internal injuries sustained when the Jzhao Li ran aground. There were certainly few signs of any obvious external wounds to explain why Zak remained unconscious. But one thing for sure. It looked like his very life force was slowly fading from him.

Amber wondered, if due to his head injuries, that he might even have lapsed into a coma.

Treating Slade and Zak wouldn't be easy. None of them were doctors. They didn't have the expertise or knowledge, let alone a hospital and proper medical equipment, to give the care Slade and Zak so clearly required. Thankfully though, they had recovered more medical supplies that Ellie, May and Salene had brought back to the camp. At least it was something.

"We've got 14 tablets of Morphine... maybe 40 paracetamol and these look as if they're some form of antibiotics," Amber said, examining bottles and counting the contents.

"There might be something more that we missed laying around," Ellie responded, feeling bad that despite scouring the beach, that was all they had managed to recover. There had to be other medicines to be sure but most of them were either submerged in the wreck, or if they had washed ashore, were now drenched in salt water, dissolving the tablets and liquids that had once been inside.

"You did great," encouraged Amber.

"So what do we do now?" Salene asked.

"I guess - we share it out between them," Amber suggested. "They're both in a lot of pain. Let's split it up. Seven tablets of Morphine each. And we hope for the best."

"It'll be difficult getting any tablets down Zak's mouth," May thought out loud. "I guess I could crush them up, force them in. Until he gains consciousness."

"I can't believe I'm saying this. But..." Ruby interjected.

"But what?" Amber wondered.

"I don't think we should be wasting any medicines on Zak," Ruby explained, almost ashamed to admit what she was thinking.

May scoffed. "What are you talking about!?"

"I know how much you care, May, about Zak..."

"Do you?" May replied warily, looking at Ruby in anticipation of what she was alluding to.

"But... I mean, face it. He's not going to come round. We have to be real here, deal with the facts. Zak could be in some sort of coma. I wish it were otherwise but from the looks of him, he won't be for this world much longer. I'm sorry, May, I know you're going to feel angry with what I'm saying but we have to use all the medicines on Slade. He's got the best chance of making it and pulling through."

May was shocked. She was actually speechless for a moment and could hardly believe what she had heard.

"You - bitch!" May spat out, bubbling over in fury. "How dare you even think such a thing, let alone say it!? Have you forgotten? We owe Zak. He risked his life, as did Slade, to free us all. Without Zak, none of us would be here today. We would have been stuck and gone down with the ship! Maybe for some of us, that would have been the best thing!"

May stared at Ruby with venom in her eyes, like she was going to attack her.

"Cut it out you two!" Amber shouted, stepping between May and Ruby. "I hear what you are saying, Ruby. But I disagree with it."

"Amber," Ruby appealed. "We've got hardly enough medicine as it is!"

"Which is why we have to use it carefully," Amber insisted. "We can't leave either Slade or Zak just to die. And the only way we can help the two of them is by sharing the medicine we have, 50/50. That's the fair - and only - way we're going to go about it."

"What's fair about wasting medicine on Zak? Denying Slade what he needs?"

"We're not going to 'deny' Slade," Amber interrupted. "Or anyone else if they get sick. As well as the morphine to help his pain, we'll have to give Slade some of the antibiotics. He's bound to have infection setting in."

"Amber, I respect you. But can't you see how wrong you are on this?" Ruby went on. "If we don't focus all we have on Slade, we could be needlessly condemning him to die! Zak is done for - there's nothing more we can do for him!"

"That's right, Doctor Ruby," May snapped furiously. "You're real impartial about all this, aren't you?"

"I'm only suggesting what makes sense! Focus what we have on the one most likely to survive! Save Slade! It's better to risk one life, than two."

"How dare you!" May screamed.

Amber had to physically restrain May, so enraged was she.

"May, stop it!" Amber urged, slapping May's face.

The shock of it caused May to calm down but she was still clearly worked up, glaring intently, dangerously at Ruby.

"We are not going to give priority to either of them!" Amber insisted. "We're going to be absolutely fair about this. We split the medicines equally. Is that understood!?"

Ruby shook with emotion, frustrated at not getting her way.

"Do you both understand? We share what we have. And I don't want to hear anything else, Ruby, about Zak or anyone else dying around here! Alright?!" Amber emphasised her point again.

"Then you can all go to hell!" Ruby exploded into tears and stormed away down the beach back towards Slade.

"Ruby!" Salene called out after her but to no avail.

"That went well," Ellie muttered.

"Who does she think she is?" May complained, staring with bitterness at Ruby. "What a nerve!"

"I'll go and talk with her," Amber said, concerned at what had transpired. "Will you keep an eye on the medicine, Sal? Make sure nothing happens to it?"

"Is that supposed to be a dig at me?" May snapped.

"For God's sake, just settle down will you? Please!" Amber said. "I was merely suggesting that we have to make sure we don't lose any of it. It's all we've got. And we're all we've got as well, and need to look out for each other."

May exchanged glances with Amber, then nodded.

"I'd better get back to check on Zak."

Sammy was taking his shift beside Zak while Darryl had relieved Ruby, watching over Slade.

Salene closed the lid of the plastic drinks cooler to protect its contents.

Amber smiled her gratitude to Salene then headed off to Ruby, passing Trudy, who was cooking some fish on the open fire.

Brady was playing in the sand while Amber's baby was fast asleep under the shade of a palm leaf.

"This smells good," Lottie said. "But I'd prefer cornflakes for breakfast rather than crab."

"Just be careful with anything you're preparing to eat," Amber called out to Trudy. "Make sure that crab's fresh. We can't risk all of us getting sick with any shellfish that's been left lying around. Not in this heat."

"What - you think we might get poisoned or something?" Trudy replied, gazing at the skewers of crab placed in the fire.

"Calm down, Trudy," Amber called back. "None of us will get any food poisoning - as long as we're careful."

Trudy gazed at the crab she was preparing then removed the skewers, pieces of fish, and buried them in the sand.

"No need to get paranoid," Lottie said, her stomach rumbling. "Otherwise we'll all starve to death."

"Well, I'm not taking any chances," Trudy replied, frantically throwing more and more sand over the crab meat she was burying.

* * *

Ruby sat on the beach, shoulders slumped, heaving with emotion, her face buried in her hands.

Amber could hear her crying as she approached.

"Ruby..." Amber said, unsure what to say. "What happened back there? I'm on your side, you know. We all are. It's just what you were suggesting, pragmatically, might make sense but none of us can ever decide who might live. Or die."

Ruby broke down sobbing uncontrollably.

"Come on, try and not get yourself so upset," Amber said.

She put her arm around Ruby to offer comfort.

Ruby buried her head into Amber, bawling tears, Amber hugging her to try and give whatever support she could.

"This isn't like you," Amber said, rocking Ruby back and forth slowly in her embrace. "You're normally so cool and level-headed."

"Not anymore!"

"What's got into you?" Amber wondered. "If it's me, I didn't mean to get you upset. Believe me, I want Slade to get better, as well as Zak. There's no favouritism or anything."

"I know... and I'm sorry for shouting at you," Ruby explained between sobs.

"That's alright. I understand how you must feel," Amber said.

"I don't think so," Ruby replied, trying to gather her emotions. "It's just something else you said earlier, Amber, which really got to me. About deciding who lives and dies."

Amber considered Ruby, aware that there was something else troubling her. Deeply troubling her.

"Do you... want to talk about it?" Amber asked.

There was a long pause, then after a while Ruby exchanged glances with Amber.

"How does it feel? Being a mother?"

"To the tribe, you mean?" Amber smiled. "At times I feel like everyone's mother around here. And it isn't easy, believe me."

Amber's smile made Ruby smile slightly and she wiped more tears.

"No. I wasn't just meaning the tribe. But baby Bray?"

Amber thought for a moment, unsure of how she could ever begin to explain motherhood.

"That's an interesting question, Ruby. I remember someone once saying that love... well... it's like someone else's happiness and wellbeing is central to your own. So you always put yourself second. Especially being a mother."

Ruby broke down again in wracking heaving sobs, but this time convulsing her entire body.

"What is it?" Amber probed.

"Back in the city, I was pregnant once. And I didn't want to go through with it. I didn't really care for the guy. It was just a casual relationship. So I... terminated."

"That's your decision," Amber said gently. "Every woman's right."

"You don't understand," Ruby replied, trying somehow to contain her emotion. "This time I want it. I want it so badly, Amber!"

Amber considered Ruby. She recalled back in the city, days before they embarked on the fishing trawler, that Ruby thought she was expecting but the makeshift pregnancy test was negative.

"You're pregnant?!" Amber asked, delighted and surprised.

Ruby nodded.

"Are you sure this time?"

"No doubt about it," Ruby said.

"Slade?" Amber enquired.

Again Ruby nodded then gazed down at Slade and stroked his head gently.

"Does he... know?"

"Not yet. And I don't want anyone else to know either," Ruby replied. "I just couldn't keep it bottled up inside any longer. I can't take it anymore!"

"Don't worry, I won't say a thing," Amber said gently, extending one arm around Ruby. "Not until you're ready to tell everyone yourself."

"Slade's his own person. I wouldn't want to tie him down, make him feel I'm some sort of burden. That he has to be with me because of some sense of 'duty' or something."

"It's obviously up to Slade to speak for himself. But from what I've seen, he really cares for you, Ruby."

Amber watched sympathetically as Ruby gently caressed Slade's hair and wiped at tears flowing from her eyes.

"I can't let him die. He has to live. Our baby will need him! And I do, too!"

CHAPTER TWENTY-SIX

Blake wrapped one of his massive arms around Ebony as she leaned on his chest, running his fingers through her hair.

It had been quite a night. In another time, another place and situation, she could have really got into him in a big way. But this was all about survival. Her survival. She just hoped Blake had at least enjoyed himself and she had done enough to make an impression.

Blake started to get out of bed but she pulled him back.

"Do you have to go?" she said, kissing him. "I'm still hungry."

"I've got 'things' to do," Blake replied.

"Like what?" she asked, then suddenly caught herself in mock concern, a hint of melodrama in the tone. "Sorry. But sometimes it's difficult not answering a question. With a question."

"You seem to be more than capable. Of knowing what to do. Or say," Blake said, gently running a finger down the side of her cheek.

She wondered if that was a compliment or if he was letting her know that he was suspicious of her. He was unpredictable, capable of exploding at any time and she would have to tread with care, rely on her innate survival instincts. And charm. Then maybe she could find out any information and be better equipped to come up with a plan. It was essential to know more about what she had gotten herself into. She knew she was in a precarious - though where last night was concerned, not entirely unenjoyable - position, and just had to try and find out more information about who Blake and his people were. Information was power, Ebony had come to realise, during her time ruling over Zoot's Locos tribe in the city. The more knowledge the better.

He slapped her on the backside then climbed out of bed. "Come on. You've got 'things' to do as well. You've not been fully categorised as yet."

"Categorised?" Ebony replied, as she pulled herself up and watched Blake putting on a robe over his naked body. "What - are you interested in checking out how greasy my hair is or something? I mean, you and your people out here in the middle of nowhere searching for oil? Or is this rig used for something else?"

"You'll find out. All in good time."

"Why don't you tell me more about it now?"

"What business is that of your's?"

Ebony decided to back off, not wishing to push her luck. "Got you. Answering a question - with a question. But don't worry about it. You're forgiven," she beamed, trying to ingratiate herself while she climbed out of bed and placed a robe around her own nude body. "Any chance of me coming back later - for dessert?"

"You're persistent - I'll give you that. Yeah, there might be a chance for some desserts tonight. After you're categorised."

"Sounds like fun. Look forward to it," Ebony replied carefully. Then added, as if in a casual afterthought, "What does it involve?"

"Let's just say it's getting to know you a little better," Blake said, pouring himself a glass of orange juice.

"After last night, I reckon you already know me pretty well."

"Not well enough," Blake said, turning to gaze at Ebony coldly, handing her an orange juice he had also poured.

Ebony kissed him on the side of the cheek coyly. "I'm just a poor, lonely shipwrecked girl. Worried about what might happen to me, that's all."

"Sure you're not playing... some kind of game?" Blake said, eyeing her intensely, searching to read her expression.

"I could be," Ebony replied, poker-faced, deciding to change tactics, testing what buttons to press to draw a more favourable reaction, realizing the sympathy card wasn't going down well. "Maybe I even wanted to be captured. And am here by choice."

"Is that so? Well, maybe I've been expecting you."

"Really?"

She realised he was toying with her just as she was toying with him and wouldn't put it past him that he was enjoying seeing her squirm in unease at the prospect of what might lay in store for her.

He was sure one smart cookie. Shrewd. She was going to have to be very shrewd herself if she had any hope to come through this. Alive.

As much as Ebony tried to gain some kind of control, she was painfully aware that the only person fully in control of this situation was Blake. And that he wasn't giving anything away, leaving Ebony deliberately hanging in the uncertainty of her fate.

There was a knock on the door.

"Enter!" Blake said.

The door opened. The disfigured girl came in, nodding to Blake respectfully but also giving a quick glare of jealousy and distrust to Ebony.

"They're ready for you, Blake. On the helicopter deck."

"I'll be there in about half an hour. After I take a quick shower."

"What about 'her'?" the hideous creature asked in disdain.

"Why don't I just stay here? I could do with a shower myself," Ebony ventured.

"You can shower. But you can't stay here. You're a new intake. Everyone needs to be categorised. No exceptions," Blake replied firmly.

* * *

Outside, the waves had picked up, crashing into the colossal rig, its huge steel legs holding firm against all nature had to throw at it.

On the helicopter deck, the slaves were in a terrible plight, Ebony could see, as she arrived with Blake and the hideous creature.

It wasn't that they looked to have been mistreated. All seemed to have been cleaned up and Ebony wondered if they had been fed. It was more the agony in their expressions, the fear, the uncertainty about their futures. She knew exactly how they were feeling, mirroring her own concerns. She felt sympathy for their plight. It was a wretched spectacle. At least she wasn't bound and manacled, unlike all the others assembled, with the military-looking guards and vagabonds all around overseeing whatever was about to occur.

There was no way she could escape. Not yet. There was nothing she could do. Except bide her time, see what was going to unfold.

"A ship will be here in a few days!" Blake called out, addressing the assembled slaves, shouting so his voice could be heard over the wind howling across the open decks of the oil rig.

A ship? From where, Ebony wondered, as Blake continued.

"And you will all be transported. But right now we've got to categorise you. It's painful. But don't resist. Otherwise you'll know what pain really is!"

Ebony and the prisoners braced themselves in growing fear and anticipation.

A vagabond put on a glove and picked up one of several iron forks that had been sticking in an urn, bubbling away with hot tar inside boiling over.

It had a letter 'M' shaped on one end of it. Other vagabonds steadied a young boy and in one swift movement, pressed the steaming fork against the boy's face, the youngster's cheek sizzling while the fork imprinted the letter 'M'. The boy passed out from the agonizing pain and had to be dragged by two other vagabonds, steadying him, before carefully laying him in a recovery position on the deck.

Over the course of the next hour, other prisoners were branded 'M'. Ebony wondered just exactly what it signified. Until Blake addressed the segment of the group, all clutching at their cheeks and groaning in agony.

"In any roll call - remember you're all categorised 'M'. Manual workers."

He cast his gaze on another group. All female this time. But rather than just six the night before, more girls had been added. Ebony was unsure if they had not long arrived.

"All of you," Blake advised the group. "You are to be assigned to the breeding program and categorised 'B'. Remember if anyone asks your identification - it's 'B'."

Another vagabond removed a fork from the steaming cauldron and approached the group of females. Ebony watched nearby and could feel the cries of agony permeate into her very soul as the group were all branded. She couldn't stop herself watching and wondered what the hell she had gotten herself into. Sickened by the brutality of it. But equally, she admired the efficiency of it.

Overall though, the gruesome nature of it all repelled her. And she was right smack in the middle of it. She was also aware that Blake had been casting an occasional glance at her so she tried to suppress her reaction, not wishing for him to know how it affected her.

"Ebony," Blake said, crossing to her. "Now it's your turn."

"I've got just one request," Ebony said, overly casual. "If I'm going to be branded - I'd prefer it on my backside. I've always been proud of my complexion. Would hate to have it ruined."

Blake smiled slightly at the gall Ebony displayed, requesting this. But once again, Ebony was conjuring up a plan in her mind, deciding that this gruesome event might provide her with an opportunity of impressing Blake.

"Can I do her?" the hideous girl said, striding up to Blake.

"I'd prefer not," Ebony said. "If she's done herself, I'm not impressed with the result."

The disfigured girl lashed out, slapping Ebony's face.

Ebony struck back, flooring her with one punch, blood oozing from the girl's nose as she sprawled on the floor.

"Don't mess with me, sister! I mean it!" Ebony snarled before faking a slight smile to Blake. "Sorry about that. You got a thing about answering questions with questions? Well, I've got a thing about my face. So if you want me branded, I'd prefer it somewhere more interesting for you to notice."

Blake considered Ebony, clearly intrigued, as the hideous girl climbed to her feet.

"Back off, Karin," he said. "I'm sure you'll get a chance to repay our friend, Ebony, here. At some point."

The hideous girl glared at Ebony, who watched as Blake crossed to the cauldron, removing an iron fork with the letter 'L'.

"What do you think this stands for?" he asked the remaining group.

"Loser?" Ebony offered up.

Blake crossed back to her. "What did you say!" he snapped threateningly.

"If you think I meant you, then obviously... it would be 'Leader'. But they all look like a bunch of losers to me," Ebony replied, trying to defuse matters.

"And what about you?" Blake asked.

"Only one thing 'L' could stand for with me - 'Lover'."

"Could be," Blake said, sabre-rattling further. "There again, it might be labourer. Or even... liar."

"Oh, I don't think so," Ebony replied.

She exchanged glances with Blake and tried to mask her tension as he added, "in which case 'L' could also mean... liability."

"The opposite of that, is asset," Ebony tried to reassure him. "And you'd better believe it. That's what I could be to you and your team, Blake. If you'd let me."

"Prove it," Blake ordered Ebony.

"How?" Ebony was genuinely perplexed.

"I couldn't help but notice, that despite all this bravado of your's..." Blake said, eyeing Ebony coldly, "throughout the branding so far... you seem not to 'enjoy' it. What is it? As well as having a 'thing' about your face... do you have a thing about seeing people in pain?"

"Doesn't bother me," Ebony said. "Not in the slightest."

"Then maybe you'd like to assist?"

"Glad to."

Blake removed the glove from his hand and passed it to Ebony.

Now she had a chance, Ebony figured, putting the protective glove over her hand. She was so tempted to pick up the steaming fork, use it as a weapon against Blake. Perhaps she could hold him hostage, somehow make good her escape. But decided against that. For the time being. The disfigured girl and the military team were far too efficient and would no doubt spring into action. Though she reckoned she could take out some of the vagabonds. But not enough of them.

"Right, then. Who's first?" Ebony said, realizing that this could be some sort of initiation for her.

Blake led Ebony to a group of assembled prisoners who were overseen by Axel and some vagabonds.

Ebony glanced at a slave trembling in line. A girl perhaps thirteen or fourteen years old, quaking with terror, waiting to be branded. She looked straight into Ebony's face, her eyes pleading. Urging, as if hoping to make some kind of contact, beg her to either make it quick and get it over and done with, or take her away somehow from the fate inevitably unfolding.

"Close your eyes," Ebony said.

The girl did this.

Ebony pressed the fork against the girl's face, the steam singeing, and Ebony almost threw up, smelling the searing of human flesh. The girl screamed in intense agony throughout the branding process with the glowing red hot poker bearing into her cheek. Ebony tried as hard as she could to mask any sympathetic reaction, well aware that she was being watched closely by Blake and his men.

"There you go," Ebony said to the girl. "That wasn't so bad, was it?"

"Why don't you decide - when it happens to you?" Blake suggested.

"Can't wait. You know what they say. No pain, no gain. Let's get it over and done with."

She unbuckled her pants, dropping them.

Blake smiled. "Would you like me to assist?" he asked, reaching out for the poker. But Ebony yanked it back.

"No," Ebony insisted. "I'm quite capable."

She gritted her teeth, pressing the scolding poker on the side of one cheek of her backside, determined not to give Blake or any of her captors the satisfaction of hearing her groan or cry out. And managed through her gritty determination to retain a smile throughout the long, painful process. Then Ebony hurled the poker back into the cauldron, removed the glove, drew up her pants.

"That feels a lot better. Nice one. Why don't you try it? See for yourself?"

She gazed at him intensely as if she had just offered a challenge.

He returned her stare evenly.

"That won't be necessary," he finally said.

Ebony knew she got him. Finally. He backed down, not rising to her challenge.

At last she was beginning to seize some control. And recognized something else during what had occurred. For all that Blake had clearly been taken aback at her actions, Ebony was in no doubt at all that he had also been impressed.

CHAPTER TWENTY-SEVEN

Jack strained with all his might, trying to loosen the tight vines tying him to the wooden poles inside the mud hut. He had given it everything and he kept pushing, using every fibre of strength in his body.

Exhausted at his effort, Jack collapsed to the ground, panting heavily.

"It's no use. Seems we're going to be stuck here forever. There's no way out," Jack said breathlessly.

"If I can't break those vines, and I've got these babes," Lex said proudly, pumping up his biceps, showing his muscled arms, "what makes you think you could break them?"

"I had to try. At least I tried," Jack replied despondently.

"Jack, for a clever guy, you can be pretty stupid sometimes. Why don't you just leave it to me? I'll get us out of this. I promise."

Lex crawled along the muddy floor as far as his tether would allow, looking out at the natives, continuing with their activities, busy weaving, sharpening weapons, cooking, seemingly oblivious to Jack and Lex's very existence.

Lex took a deep breath.

"Hey, you!"

A native warrior cast a glance at the hut as Lex continued.

"Yeah, I'm talking to you!" Lex bellowed angrily. "If you don't get someone to release us, I swear I'm going to take those spears of yours... and stick them in a place where the sun don't shine!"

"Lex - that's probably not helping!" Jack insisted, uneasy at Lex's bluster.

"Answer me!!! What do you want from us?!" Lex hollered, then sighed as he withdrew from the door. "It's no good."

"They want you to be quiet," a female voice said.

Lex and Jack were startled as a girl, around about their own age, walked into the mud hut, ducking her head as she entered. She was tall, gangly, and wore a pair of thick glasses over her piercing green eyes, one of the lenses covered in scratches. With long curls of blond hair ruffled over her shoulders, she wore a Tribal costume similar to that of the other native girls. The one startling difference, however, was that she didn't look like the rest of the 'natives', beyond the dress she was wearing. More like a girl of European origin.

"All your noise! You sound like a big baby," the girl said, Jack noticing her accent.

"Me? A baby?" Lex protested.

"Are you the leader of this Tribe?" Jack asked, as the girl stood over Jack and Lex.

"No, not at all," the girl laughed off the idea as ludicrous.

"You're not from round here, are you?" Lex blurted out the obvious.

"So you must be the smart one," the girl teased.

"I am, actually," Lex responded in all seriousness, Jack giving him a funny look.

"I was born in Germany, if you want to be precise. But I live here now."

"Well, guten tag," Jack smiled, trying to be friendly. "It's just nice to finally meet someone who can understand us," he continued. "What are you doing here? What's going on?"

"I'm here to translate, to talk and find out the same thing from you. So... tell me. Who are you?"

"I was about to ask you the same question," Lex shot back, turning on the charm, "what's a good looking girl like you doing in a place like this?"

"My name is Lia. That's all you need to know... For now. You don't look like some of Blake's people?"

"That's because we're not. Whoever... this 'Blake' is," Jack explained.

"Really?" Lia retorted, suspicious of Jack and Lex. "You could be some type of spies."

"We're not 'spies'... secret agents or superheroes. Just prisoners. With no idea why," Lex said, casting an admiring glance down Lia's figure.

"It's true," Jack insisted. "We've done nothing wrong - Lia. Honestly. All we were doing was tying to get some help. We were shipwrecked. My friend, Lex, here - he's always thinking with his stomach..."

"That's offensive, Jack," Lex interrupted.

"He saw some poultry, couldn't resist the idea of a free meal... fell into a hole and next thing we knew, this Tribe showed up and brought us here. We don't mean anyone any harm. So if we could just be let go, then we can head back to the others."

"Others?" Lia asked. "There are others of you?"

Lex cast Jack a look to keep quiet, not to say anything more. They couldn't necessarily trust this girl, whoever she was.

"Yeah, there are others," Lex clarified. "If you don't let us go, before long they'll come and rescue us. They're armed. Dangerous," he bluffed. "So you better listen, 'Lia'. If you want to spare some bloodshed, save a few lives, the last thing you want is the others to arrive and break up this party. They'll tear this place apart. And anyone dumb enough to hurt me - or Jack, let alone touch one hair on our heads. So why don't you just have a word with whoever is in charge, will you? Let Jack and I go, and we'll say no more about it."

"Was that a threat?" Lia scoffed.

"You're obviously not such a good translator," Lex scoffed back.

"Because if it was, you haven't done anything to help your case, believe me," Lia said. "I'm to report back what I have learned. Every single word."

Lia turned her back, ducking to head out of the mud hut.

Jack gave Lex a look - then called out.

"Lia - please!"

Lia stopped in her tracks at the doorway to listen.

"Lex was just trying to 'impress' you. He's bluffing. There is no threat from any of us. We truly mean no harm. Honestly. The reality is we've got injured and sick people back where our shipwreck happened. We're a long way from home and we need help."

"I'll tell that to the Priestess. It's not my decision."

"What are we meant to have done? Why are we tied, cooped up in this hut?" Jack pleaded. "We're here by accident."

"You have trespassed on our land. That is undeniable. And for all we know, you could be spies for Blake, though you deny it. The Priestess will know what to do."

"What does that mean?" Lex asked, choosing his words carefully. He was frustrated but realised he was in no position to bully his way out. "And this Priestess... who the hell is she? What does she do around here?"

"If you are guilty of trespassing, you will be punished. Broken. You have tainted the Tribe's sacred lands."

"Then what?" Lex couldn't help butt in.

"Believe me. You don't want to know."

Lia turned on her heel and walked out of the mud hut, leaving Jack and Lex, who exchanged concerned glances.

CHAPTER TWENTY-EIGHT

After the initial joy at their safe return to Camp Phoenix, Jay and Ram wasted no time in calling the Tribe together for a meeting. Ram told Amber and the others - with a bit of prodding from Jay - about Kami. And The Collective.

"So the sooner we find a boat and get as far away from this island as we can, the better!" Ram concluded, after relaying all the information.

The Tribe were seated around the fire they had lit as the night descended. For a moment, all that could be heard was the crackling of the embers and the waves rolling onto the sands. Everyone was absorbed by what Ram just told them and were trying to assimilate it all.

"You're crazy!" Trudy broke the silence.

"Well, you should know," Ram threw it back at her.

"What are you going to tell us next?" Trudy carried on. "That you've been abducted before by little green men? Hitched a ride on Santa's sleigh? I don't believe a word of it, Ram, and I don't believe you!"

"There's a surprise," Ram said caustically.

"It does sound a little far fetched, you've got to admit," Amber pondered. "I mean - some mysterious leader... you never met. Who you used to communicate with. But only on your computer?"

It was clear Amber didn't trust Ram now, anymore than she had before. And the others seemed to share the same sentiment, though Lottie and Sammy stared wide eyed.

"This 'Collective' group... you don't think they can morph, do you, Ram?" Sammy asked. He was being serious and Ram thought about it.

"'Morphing?' Now that's an interesting concept," Ram said, considering the notion.

"What do you mean, Sammy - 'morph'?" Lottie probed.

"I mean, who knows? They could be watching us right now. In the trees. They might even BE the trees - "

"Oh, stop, Sammy. Please, for goodness sake!" Amber interrupted.

"At least someone seems to believe me around here," Ram said in disdain, but also was clearly hurt. All present were having great doubts about all he revealed.

"Sure you're not a member of the Collective yourself?" Darryl wondered. "Come to think about it, if they CAN morph - maybe they could have infiltrated any one of us!"

There was a hint of melodrama in the tone. Darryl couldn't keep a straight face and burst out laughing.

"This is no time for jokes, Darryl. Working with the Technos, and especially Ram, I'm well aware of all they could achieve. We have to take what he has to say seriously," Jay said. "If he isn't being truthful, then we've got nothing to lose. But if he is -"

"If you have been telling the truth - how dare you!" Ellie interrupted. "If this land might be under the control of this 'Collective'... that could explain why Jack isn't back yet, with Lex... They could be in danger!"

"That's true, too," Ram agreed.

"And you said nothing about it until now!? You let them go, like innocent lambs, wandering off into enemy territory?" Ellie said.

"Lex - an innocent lamb?" Ram scoffed.

"You are so selfish!" Ellie screamed. "If something's happened to Jack or Lex, I'll make you pay!!"

"The way the Collective operate, they'll consume you, for nothing. But you'll never be free," Ram shuddered at the thought.

"Where's your proof, Ram?" Salene joined in. "There must be some way you can back up what you've claimed."

"You want proof?... Let me think!"

Ram paced around the camp, running his fingers through his hair. Then he started patting his head with the palms of his hands, the others exchanging incredulous glances.

"What's he doing?" Gel asked.

"Just processing. Give me a few seconds till I examine all my files," Ram said.

After a while, he spun around, addressing them all, a manic glint in his eye.

"I've got it! What about Paradise and reality space?"

"What about it?" Amber said, watching Ram, as puzzled as all the rest.

"Kami might have tried to take credit for programming it. But it was me. I put it all together. One of my greatest accomplishments."

"I don't know if others would agree with you," Trudy muttered, well aware of the devastating effect Ram's virtual reality program had on all those back in the city. "That's nothing to be proud of!"

"I understand how you feel, Trudy," Amber said. "But why don't we just let Ram try and explain? And you'd better, Ram. I mean it. You owe it to us to tell everything you know."

"After we invaded, we checked out the observatory at Eagle Mountain and found the military complex The Collective wanted."

"What?" Salene said. "You were at Eagle Mountain?"

"That's where the virtual reality technology came from," Ram continued. "And Kami was desperate to get his hands on it. But I adapted it. Using the protons I needed, otherwise I'd never have known if what I had in mind could work."

"Are you saying The Collective were involved in the invasion?" Amber asked.

"No," Ram replied. "Just the Technos. One of our objectives was to check out Eagle Mountain and try and obtain this equipment. Without it, all we had was a theory. But Kami knew... and above all, I knew, that we needed the right technology to bring it all into existence."

"And why would it have been at Eagle Mountain?" Salene asked, sceptically.

"It's obvious, isn't it?" Ram answered. "It was being hidden. In the military base. Kept under wraps. So the adults could use it. To try and develop it themselves and presumably conduct their own simulations, eventually."

"You forget, Ram. We went to Eagle Mountain too," Amber said. "And there was no sign of any hidden military base. Just the observatory."

It brought back painful memories for Amber, remembering the tragedy when the compound erupted in an explosion which had also nearly claimed her life.

"But you obviously didn't go underground, did you?" Ram explained. "We did. We found this entrance, bypassed its security. And discovered an underground facility. Still there, beneath what's left of the observatory. Just like the information Kami had obtained when he hacked into the government computers. And to think, you didn't even know it existed. It was there, right under your feet..."

"That's not exactly proof though, is it?" Salene demanded.

The others murmured in agreement.

"Tell them about the hibernation chamber," Jay said to Ram.

"Hibernation chamber?" Trudy exclaimed, exchanging more incredulous glances with Amber and the others.

"I found one of many. Right there at the complex in Eagle Mountain," Ram continued. "So I also adapted the chambers. Who knows, I could have lived forever."

Ram had always been paranoid about his health throughout his life but no more than when was in charge of the Technos, forever obsessed with germs of all varieties, in the aftermath of the pandemic. The possibility that the 'virus' would mutate in particular. But had planned to survive whatever other threat he might also have encountered by making sure he was protected. In hibernation, Jay explained, recalling Ram's anguish at being forced back into the real world when he was showing dangerous signs of preferring reality space, along with all the other population of the city, through the use of Ram's Paradise virtual reality network. Most had become almost as addicted as Ram.

"There's another thing you should know. We found adults inside the chambers," Ram continued. "Their bodies, anyway. Don't you see? They must have tried to seal themselves away as a desperate last resort to escape the 'virus'. As much as I'd like to take credit for inventing that myself - I didn't. The military did. I just adapted what they had put in place."

"That's not exactly proof that a base was hidden away there," Amber stated.

"Tell them, will you, Jay?" Ram sighed, frustrated.

"Yes - why don't you tell us, Jay? Everything you also know about all this," Amber said, considering Jay suspiciously. "Are you saying that you also went to Eagle Mountain? If so, why on Earth didn't you say anything about it before?"

"Because I never went there," Jay replied.

"He didn't. I did" Ram clarified. "Jay was no longer a member of the Technos by then, having thrown his lot in with you. And I'm telling you, Ebony and the rebels reeled you in like a fish."

"If the Collective really wanted to take over the city and all the sectors," Amber asked, "and you and the Technos got there first - why didn't The Collective ever show up? To try and take back what they wanted? And get their own back on you?"

"Because I scared them away," Ram said.

"What - with your face!" Gel suggested.

"I sent messages. Through my computer," Ram continued, ignoring Gel's taunt. "I told Kami it wasn't safe. To come to the city. That the 'virus' had returned with a vengeance. If they arrived, there was risk they would all be wiped out. So they did stay away. It worked - for a while."

"And...?" Salene enquired, eager to know more.

"They got suspicious. Kami's so smart, believe me. I knew it wouldn't take long for him to cotton on that it was just an excuse. At that time I was trying to hack into his system and unleash a virus of my own. To get him off my trail. Once and for all. But he countered. And I've got to admit, it was brilliant."

"What was?" Amber asked.

"The Collective sabotaged the Techno computers. No doubt about it."

"What are you talking about?" Trudy probed.

"Resurrecting Zoot... Remember? It all started to get out of control. I'm telling you, it bore all the marks of the type of thing Kami would do. Pure genius. And it sure as hell got you all spooked."

"That was Mega," Trudy said.

"Was it?" Ram replied.

All were now gripped by what Ram was saying, starting to believe that there was some plausibility in it all, well aware of the disruption and confusion the virtual reality Zoot had caused throughout the city.

Then they were astounded when Ram suggested that the Collective could have been responsible for unleashing the chemical attack.

"Now that's stretching it a bit," Amber said. "You seriously expect us to believe that?"

"You really think Mega or I were so slack that our systems would go out of control? At least give us some credit, please."

"What are you saying - exactly?" Amber asked.

"Believe me, there's only one person who could have possibly made those computers fail. 'Kami'. And his Collective," Ram stated.

"But the Virus Mark II... Mega owned up to it," Salene pointed out. "He said it was him."

"He might have thought it was him. That's why it was all so brilliant. Don't get me wrong. Mega had such great potential. But he was my apprentice. I was his master. And I don't believe for one minute that he was intentionally going to wipe everyone out. Himself included."

"So what are you suggesting happened?" Trudy asked uneasily.

"I can't say for sure. All I know is after I was kicked out of the Technos, Mega was playing in a different league. When I was working with Kami, I could match him. Even better him in some areas. But you can bet when that virtual reality Zoot started to go out of control, Mega must have known something was going on. But he might have not had the skills to realise just exactly what. And you know what I think?... His systems were sabotaged..."

"What - by the Collective?" Amber enquired.

"Think about it. There's only three possible things that could have happened. One. That Mega rigged up a system to launch those chemicals into the air. Or two, that he wanted someone to at least believe that he did."

"Why?" Salene asked.

"So they'd be under the impression that the city and area was contaminated," Ram explained.

"You're not seriously suggesting that it was all a bluff?" Amber demanded.

"It might have been. Initially. Either that. Or if The Collective did breach Mega's security, option three would be that they triggered it all. Which means that it was either a real chemical attack. Or just a lot of hot air was released into the atmosphere. Not germs."

Ram was referring to the release of the deadly chemicals upon the city which forced the Tribe and everyone else to flee in the first place, with Ram and the Mall Rats escaping on Zak's trawler, beginning their drift out to sea. Leading up to that, the Techno computers, with the virtual reality Zoot, had been going out of control. The electrical grids were playing up. And throughout Zoot's apparent resurrection, there were a lot of unexplained events prior to that fateful day when everyone escaped the city.

Ram tried to explain all the technicalities, that within Mega's master control centre, he could have discovered his systems were being compromised. And might have tried to retaliate. Sending out false messages. But it was either a bluff. Or, if for some reason he did want to unleash chemicals into the region, he must have realised that his plan had backfired and that ironically, it was tantamount to committing suicide. He was clearly trying to oppress the region with some kind of threat. But why? In Ram's logic, it didn't make any sense for him to do it just for the sake of it, and that he was trying to send a clear signal to The Collective that it wouldn't be safe for them to ever come to the city or any of the sectors. Maybe he had even rigged up something so all he had to do was press the button. So that if anyone was trying to threaten him and the Technos, then they'd destroy themselves in the process. Just like in the old days when countries used to send out nuclear threats. So if The Collective did hack into Mega's system... Ram couldn't say for sure.. but he suspected that they were responsible and not Mega - for what eventually transpired.

"Just one thing I don't understand," Amber asked, considering Ram. "If what you're saying is correct, this theory of your's. Then why were you so keen to get back?"

"Like I say. Mega might have hooked up something but I got to know him really well. When I was training him. And no way he would have destroyed everything in existence, himself included. So we could have a situation where The Collective thought the city was in danger. Even if the odds were 50/50 and those chemicals unleashed were active and posed some form of threat, then it might have been only confined to a radius. Other areas might not have been contaminated."

"That's a pretty big gamble to take," Amber said. "I'm not sure I'd like those odds."

"I'd prefer them rather than encounter the Collective somewhere like here."

"What makes you think The Collective... could be here?" Trudy asked nervously.

"You just don't understand, do you?" Ram sighed, frustrated. "Just believe me. Throughout the time the adults were being wiped out and we were hacking into some of the government systems, we discovered several military bases. Just like Eagle Mountain. In strategic places. And no, I can't say for sure that there's a base here. Because I don't know the exact co-ordinates. But on that death ship we all ended up on, there's no doubt in my mind that whatever that United Nations Task Force were doing, they were clearly active in this region. Now we're marooned here."

"I know it's a lot to take in," Jay spoke up. "And Ram's been very brave to open up like this..."

"Brave?" Amber retorted. "More like deceitful!"

She and the others were still outraged. They had already so much to deal with, such as Lex and Jack's disappearance, the critical conditions of both Slade and Zak. And with Slade unconscious, they couldn't check if he knew anything about it. Amber wondered if he might have any detail regarding who he worked for when he was on the trail of Ram back in Liberty, and that might help shed some light on it all.

She felt so overwhelmed. Above all, angered why - and how - Ram chose only now to reveal all of this. Amber just couldn't understand what made him tick, why he hadn't said any of it before.

"Are there any other secrets you've been keeping away from us, Ram?" Amber demanded bitterly. "Anything else you care to tell us about?"

"Yeah, there is..." Ram glared, not liking Amber's tone. "I hate spinach - and I've got a big mole on my backside! There, you happy?"

"Spare me the sarcasm for once, Ram! That is so typical of you, isn't it? Are you sure this isn't all some kind of game to you? Like another of your precious computer games you said you used to play? Is that what you're doing? Playing with us? Are you enjoying this? Getting some kind of thrill out of others' misfortune and suffering? If not, you've got a lot of nerve to reveal all this stuff! After all this time!"

"And here we go, more moral pronouncements from the lips of Miss Sanctimonious!" Ram snapped. "You don't ever do anything wrong, do you, Amber? So squeaky clean. If only the world was as perfect as you are. Too bad not everyone can live up to your high and mighty standards!"

"High standards? You call being truthful 'high standards'? It's common decency, Ram! How dare you put your own safety ahead of others? You ask us to believe what you say - but how can we trust you now? After all, you've proven yourself to be nothing more than a selfish liar!"

"Well, that's up to you, Amber!" Ram said. "As well as the rest of you. You can either believe what I've told you or not. I'm not some moron. I was the leader of the Technos. We could have done so much if it wasn't for Kami and The Collective. And all I've been trying to do is protect all of you. Not just myself. After all, most of you... you've become like friends now."

"With friends like you, Ram..." Trudy said.

"I'm not an enemy. There's only one enemy we should be worried about. That's Kami. And The Collective."

"I wouldn't be too sure about that," Amber said, trying to contain her anger. "Sure you haven't overlooked anything else! Like what happened to Bray and the others who disappeared after you just happened to 'invade' our city?"

"I had nothing to do with anyone's disappearance. That was Mega's department. He was in charge of all the prisoners! I had more important things on my mind - than all the small details!"

"Small details? They were human beings!" Amber cried out. "You had no right to ruin innocent lives!"

Amber and Ram stood head to head, eyeballing each other.

Jay crossed to Amber, who looked as if she was ready to strike out at Ram.

"Amber, please calm down! We have to listen to Ram. Everything he's saying. You're not being reasonable right now."

That did it.

Amber slapped Jay hard, stinging him in the face, surprising herself, as much as Jay, along with the others, by her sudden outburst.

She was utterly dismayed and deeply hurt by the insensitivity of Ram, and now Jay.

"I'm not being 'reasonable', you say?" Amber repeated Jay's words, wincing as she said it.

"I didn't mean it like that!" Jay insisted.

"What? I'm wrong or something... to ask what happened to the person I once loved? The father of my child, who got snatched away!? Along with others who were special in this tribe?"

"Amber... that's not what I meant!"

"How could you?"

Amber shook her head in disbelief and began crying, as she strode away, Jay following on after her.

"Great! Just what we need, for them to fall out!" Trudy said.

"I'm so glad to have you back, Ram!" Salene added sarcastically. "Thanks for everything!"

The meeting broke up, the others dispersing from the fire in the centre of camp, going their separate ways in the wake of Amber and Jay's row.

"You'll all wish you had thanked me for telling you the truth if The Collective show up!" Ram bellowed out into the night. "Unless we come up with some kind of a plan - believe me, it's game over! For all of us!"

CHAPTER TWENTY-NINE

"It's party time!!" Belle yelled, the rest of The Fallen whooping it up at the prompting of their leader.

The crazed tribe were leaping around a swimming pool. But Bray had no way of knowing. He could only listen. Which he did in a mixture of disbelief and disgust. They were a despicable group, he felt. Sub-human. Totally unstable. And more frighteningly, unpredictable.

Not long after being captured back at the base, Bray had been beaten. The leader, Belle, took great delight in licking blood, then sucking it, like a wild animal, as it oozed from his wounds. He was then taken, blind-folded, and bundled into the back of a military vehicle along with Tiffany, Shannon and Emma. Sadly they hadn't been able to escape.

The Fallen probed if anyone else was left. Emma reassured them amidst her panic that despite Bray and her brother and sister, there was no one else around. For a moment, Bray was uneasy at the prospect that they didn't believe Emma and that she and her two younger siblings might even become victims of torture to obtain information.

"There's no one else here. I swear! I promise you! If there was, I'd tell you!" Emma had pleaded, amidst her tears.

"How would you know anyway?" Belle had teased. "Least you don't need a blindfold!" she taunted, while masking tape was wound around the eyes of the petrified

Tiffany and Shannon. The same had occurred to Bray earlier, shortly after his capture and beating.

Bray felt he had let Emma, Tiffany and Shannon down. If only he hadn't climbed up the roller coaster and had run somewhere else, maybe there would have been a better chance for him to have made good his escape. And Emma and her brother and sister might have gotten away.

He had tried to provide a distraction, luring The Fallen further from the accommodation quarters and into the amusement park area so that Emma, Shannon and Tiffany at least had a chance.

Shortly after his own capture, he realised that it had all been to no avail.

Belle didn't believe that Bray had made it across the wastelands. And pressed for detail of where he had come from. But of course, Bray didn't know much other than he had been held by Eloise's forces. And he wasn't about to reveal this, suspecting he could have a bounty on his head, preferring to take his chances, rationalizing that even if he had provided detail, there would be no guarantee that it would result in being better treated. Not from the extraordinary inhumane behaviour he had experienced so far from his new captors.

Throughout the long ensuing journey, Bray began to appreciate more what life must have been like for Emma. With his sight totally obscured by the blindfold, he had to rely solely on his hearing to gain any idea at all of what was occurring. He also tried to calculate just exactly where they might be heading and thought they must have driven in the military vehicles for at least ten hours. But again, he had no way of knowing for sure.

Emma whispered that they were probably being taken to The Mirage, a once thriving resort in the south which was now the home base of The Fallen.

Bray pondered why they should have returned to the military base. And had now taken the last of what was left of Emma's tribe, the Roaches. He hoped they weren't connected to Eloise and that he was somehow responsible for all this. Due to his escape, and inadvertently getting Emma and her siblings involved.

There was no chance of obtaining any more information. Members of The Fallen accompanied Bray, Emma, Tiffany and Shannon in the back of the vehicle, instructing them all to remain silent. But Bray managed to decipher from elements in The Fallen's conversations that they were running out of 'human' flesh to trade and were desperate to meet their quota.

Bray couldn't comprehend what they meant and shuddered to think what Belle and her Fallen tribe were involved with, primarily what they had planned for their hostages. Were they really to be traded? Or was there something more chilling in mind?

They clearly had a sadistic streak, one that would have done Top Hat and Tribe Circus or any of the other crazies Bray had encountered back in the city proud. Everything Emma had warned him about The Fallen was true. They were certainly dangerous but Bray hadn't expected them to have been so wild, almost feral.

There had to be some way out, Bray thought. Something he could do. But he realised for the time being at least that he, Emma, Tiffany and Shannon were all helpless.

His natural sense of justice was enraged at being once again held prisoner. Which was enflamed, knowing that Emma and her siblings were suffering the same fate.

Especially when he heard one member of The Fallen ask if he could 'play' a little with Emma when they arrived at their intended destination before handing them over.

"I've never had a blind girl," the tribe member had said. Bray could hear Emma struggling, heaving, and Bray's frustrations and feelings of helplessness were unbearable. He tried to prise himself loose but his hands had been tied so securely with thick packaging tape, just as taut as it had been wound around his head, covering his eyes.

It was a surreal experience to rely solely on what he was hearing as opposed to seeing what was unfolding. And Bray was unsure if it was better to leave it all to his imagination and not see. Or see, without his imagination distorting matters.

"She bit my tongue!" the tribe member cursed. "I'll kill her!"

"Back off," Belle had warned. "Remember there's one value for the living. And another for the dead."

Bray couldn't bear to even think about what they were referring to.

From the conversation, he knew that Belle must have started kissing the tribe member. The one who must have tried to kiss Emma, with her biting her assailant's tongue in the process.

What Bray found disturbing was that rather than being concerned for any injuries, The Fallen seemed thrilled that there was so much blood which must have been dripping from the tribe member's tongue. Belle had demanded that she be the lucky one to indulge herself before the wound congealed as if she was intoxicated by the taste of blood. Bray wondered if these people were really even sub-human after all, or through their struggles to survive in the post adult world had been reduced to behaviour normally exhibited by wild animals.

Now, he was one of eight other prisoners - along with Emma, Tiffany and Shannon - standing blindfolded in The Mirage resort.

Unbeknownst to them, The Fallen were circling the frightened group, snarling and yelling, taking delight, deliberately intimidating their prisoners.

Bray could hear what sounded like the ocean, with waves pounding a beach.

What he did not know, along with the other hostages, was that they were indeed being held in a resort area, as Emma had mentioned earlier. The decaying buildings of what had once been a hotel were now covered in graffiti and had been ransacked. Looted, long ago.

Flaming torches cast looming shadows across the walls. Had they all been able to see, the prisoners would have known that The Fallen were dancing merrily around them, howling like wolves.

Bray suspected some kind of insidious initiation ceremony was occurring.

"Smile!" Belle yelled over the cacophony of noise. "You don't have long here - so smile! Come on! Show how much 'fun' you're having."

Any prisoner who did not co-operate received a stinging backhand slap and tried somehow to provide weak smiles while The Fallen continued howling, but were now grinning themselves, enjoying the surreal reactions as they continued circling their captives standing helpless in the darkness.

Suddenly Belle turned and ran towards the pool, leaping off the cracked, tiled edge of the patio, and diving into the water, disappearing under the surface. The water was so disgusting, darkened with green algae.

Belle vanished from sight, traces of diluted blood visible within the pool's density.

Bray and the other prisoners recoiled, straining to use their instincts for some kind of idea of what was occurring, hearing the splash, water spraying over them.

And for the first time since escaping from Eloise's mountain compound, Bray wondered if he was once again participating in a virtual reality program. Had he really met Emma, Tiffany and Shannon? He was definitely aware that they must have been feeling great fear through the intimidating events from hearing their whimpering, sobbing. And from the sounds of the other prisoners, they, too, were clearly suffering.

Bray tried to concentrate his hearing as the howling subsided. Unbeknownst to the prisoners, The Fallen had stopped their frenzied ritualistic dance and were now staring at the pool as if they were worried at what might have happened to their leader.

Seconds passed.

Suddenly Belle exploded through the surface of the pool, a mad look of delight on her face, to the jubilation of her tribe, who began cheering her return. In her mouth she had a human ear, which she tossed to members of The Fallen, who proceeded to fight among themselves while trying to catch it.

Bray and the prisoners flinched at the frenzied noises, then braced themselves as they struggled to comprehend what could be occurring as Belle screamed over the hysteria.

"Anyone fancy a dip?! It's very refreshing!!!"

"Let me, Belle," a member of The Fallen replied. Then, encouraged by the others, with the howling continuing again, he dove into the water. Through the spreading algae after his entry, glimpses of bodies were visible, which would have repulsed Bray, as well as the other hostages, had they been able to see. The Fallen seemed to be devoid of any respect for the sanctity of human life, any and all things living.

"Well?" Belle said, drying her hair with a towel as she surveyed the prisoners, her eyes wild in expectation. "Anyone want to join him?"

"Please! I don't know what you're doing but whatever it is, have some mercy on us. I beg you! Especially for the younger ones!" Bray said, hoping to touch even a degree of humanity, which was so obviously absent from this tribe.

"Good idea!" Belle snapped. "Wouldn't want you to think we're 'inhospitable!' So what about you, Shannon, or you, Tiffany - fancy getting 'cooled off'?"

"No! Please don't harm them!" Emma said.

"Why?" Belle scoffed disdainfully.

"I can't swim!" Shannon yelled.

"Then you should have learned!" Belle snickered. "You'll find lots of other people in there. I seem to remember... they couldn't swim either! What was it with you Roaches - didn't enjoy sport or something?"

The other members of The Fallen howled, encouraged by the panic of the stricken prisoners.

Bray was desperate to think of a way he might assist, fearing that any moment The Fallen would hurl them all into what obviously was a pool, he had concluded, and that they would suffer a slow, agonising death by drowning, unable to swim with their arms and legs bound.

Then he heard another voice shouting out.

There was an abruptness in the tone. Even concern. Definitely a threat.

"That's enough! Back off! Or you'll have us to deal with. And I wouldn't recommend that, especially if we've had a wasted trip!"

Bray and the other prisoners had no way of knowing but a team of about a dozen military-looking figures dressed in black, with rolled up berets perched on their clean shaven heads, had arrived, marching briskly toward Belle.

They were about the same age as The Fallen but unlike the tribe, exuded discipline, efficiency.

"Don't mean to break up your party," one said. "But we're here to collect. How many have you got for us!?"

"You're early!" Belle replied.

"Good job we're not late," the military figure smiled slightly, gazing around, then noticing glimpses of bodies through the spreading algae of the pool. "Looks like you've had a bit of... 'collateral damage'," he added.

"What's that?" Belle asked.

Bray knew, as he listened. He was aware of the term from the old times before all the adults perished.

"The dead!" the military figure replied. "And we're only interested in the living. Not body parts this time."

CHAPTER THIRTY

Life was strange at times, Ebony thought, resting lazily on Blake's bed, caressing the soft, silk pillows and enjoying the comfort of the smooth linen underneath. Here she was in the lap of luxury whereas only weeks earlier she had been stuck with Amber and the Mall Rats on their trawler, starving and drifting. There were so many twists and turns in life, Ebony reflected - and now it was her turn for an upside, she hoped.

She was alone in Blake's quarters, a huge smile on her face, pleased with her accomplishments.

When Blake had 'tested' Ebony, she turned the tables and had utterly surprised him. As well as impressed him. Elevating herself from being a likely candidate for a slave, as when she had first been captured, to now taking the important next steps of being Blake's mistress - and who knows what else.

One scintillating night of passion, along with her gutsy display during the time all the slaves were being categorised, had revealed Ebony's character. That she was tough. Uncompromising. Like Blake. And Ebony hoped that if she could take more steps, he would begin to come to realise that there was far more to her than just a pretty face.

Ebony stretched out, reached for a glass of wine and silently raised a toast to her absent new admirer before sipping from the glass.

I could get used to this, she thought, gazing around Blake's quarters. He was living the high life, relative to what Ebony had experienced on the streets after the virus. Blake had accumulated many precious goods, his quarters full of wine, spirits, even a gymnasium. He liked to work out. She had certainly given him more than enough to challenge his physical capabilities. And it might continue to be a real pleasure. For her. As well as him.

Her instinct told her that Blake was clearly infatuated, at least enough to want to get to know more about her. Ebony was as equally intrigued by Blake. Wondering just exactly who he was. Who he worked to. Or was he solely in command? What was the story about this rig? And all her fellow prisoners who had been categorised for manual labour, breeding and God knows what else.

She hoped she was luring Blake in with her fawning displays of affection, pleasing him in every way she could think, and that this would enable Blake to believe he could trust her.

As it was, the day had progressed well. Things were moving in the right direction. If she could keep this up, perhaps Ebony could rise up the ranks. After all, she had done much the same thing before back in the city with Zoot. And knew there was no future back there. She had to carve a new life now. And if Blake was the King, Ebony was determined that before long she would not only be his mistress - but she was beginning to have aspirations of becoming his Queen, and who knows, eventually rule alone.

Any prospect was certainly a better option than being marooned in an unknown world. She was pleased that she decided to abandon the Jzhao Li, along with the Mall Rats and those stranded on the vessel.

She had managed to decipher during a meal earlier with Blake that he and his team had been stationed on the oil rig for no more than a couple of months. They were apparently a member of a tribe called 'Legion'.

Blake revealed that the name was representative of what he wanted to achieve. A legion of warriors, which is what he considered himself to be. He demanded strict discipline of his inner circle, never questioning his orders. And the vagabonds were some new recruits being inducted. When they had proven themselves, acquiring a necessary level of skill, then they could join. But not until they deserved to do so.

He mentioned that as the reputation of 'Legion' spread, he was sure they would be seen as being fearsome adversaries, with a status like some of the greatest warriors or militia from a bygone age.

Ebony could see that his inner circle were utterly loyal to their leader and his bidding. He had shrugged modestly, advising that he would expect nothing less with the rewards they received from being by his side in combat.

Blake alluded that his late father had been in the military when Ebony admired a long broadsword displayed on the wall. It was clearly a treasure to Blake. And he seemed to be genuinely touched when he revealed details. That it originally belonged to his great grandfather and had been passed down through successive generations. All had achieved high status within the military forces. No doubt the name chosen for his tribe reflected that somewhere in his psyche he was paying homage to that.

But he seemed reluctant to provide any detail when Ebony pressed for more information. She knew anyone in the military had been put on high alert at the height of the pandemic.

When Ebony tried to ingratiate herself, appealing to the obvious vanity Blake possessed by saying that he must be very proud of his father and perhaps had taken after him, Blake seemed offended. So she quickly avoided the topic.

Blake seemed reluctant to reveal much detail about his mother. But she did manage to squeeze out of Blake that he had met his inner circle at boot camp during the streaming the authorities put in place at the peak of all the panicked evacuations, when the virus struck. She discovered that Blake and his cohorts were put through the rigours of a survival course at that time and wondered if he had adapted some of the methods, 'categorising' all the slaves being held as prisoners.

Blake certainly wasn't a trader, as such. But a facilitator. Looking after the transportation, working to someone, whoever they might be. She knew at this point that there was no way he would reveal any more detail. He was far too shrewd for that. But so was she. And she felt confident that one day she'd squeeze more information out of him. She just needed to be patient. Give it time. And then she would find out more about Blake's 'superiors'. For that's how he referred to them.

There was something about the information Blake revealed so far which bothered Ebony. At least enough for her to question if he was being honest. And she wondered if he was feeding false information to put her off any kind of trail.

He said he was concerned, not fully trusting his superiors, wondering if he had been deployed to the oil rig as a 'guinea pig'. He appeared to be almost paranoid if he had been despatched to this land as nothing more than a human test subject. Exposed to an alien environment so that he would be checked on how he adapted.

He had questioned her and she explained nothing more than the fact she and some members of a tribe had fled the city on a trawler, long after the virus occurred. And had embarked upon the Jzhao Li. Which was drifting. All of which was true.

But Ebony embellished it all a bit by saying that they were looking for somewhere new to settle. There was a terrible storm and she had managed to escape on the lifeboat but didn't exactly know what had happened to the other members of her tribe.

She didn't go into any detail about any 'virus Mark II'. She'd save that. Take it one step at a time. She also didn't mention much about her past life in the city, though she knew from the impression she had made that

Blake was beginning to realise that she wasn't just a run of the mill survivor in this post adult world. And had a lot more to offer. She decided she'd reveal only bits of information. When she had fully sussed what Blake was all about. No way was she going to lay all her cards on the table and let him know what she was all about first. Not when he was also playing it all so closely to his chest.

One thing that puzzled Ebony was why Blake and the rest of Legion would willingly accept an assignment on this rig if they believed they were in any danger themselves. And were being tested. She couldn't understand what kind of danger they could ever be in. Not with the control Blake had, which was plainly evident.

"Everyone is in danger if they don't obey 'superiors'," Blake had said with a veiled threat, considering Ebony, fascinated how her reaction would be. But she didn't rise to the bait and tried to find out more about this region.

He revealed nothing more than that this region could prove to be valuable. When Ebony asked why, Blake was the one to quickly change the subject this time. It was alright for him to answer a question with a question, she thought. He was certainly adept at doing that. She was sure there was something more to it and she was determined that she'd eventually uncover the mysteries.

But was pleased that she had managed to squeeze even this amount of information out of him like the freshly-squeezed orange juice he was keen on drinking, which also intrigued Ebony. He seemed to follow a strict diet, was health conscious, keen on staying fit, keeping in shape.

Ebony was above all keen to try and obtain more information on the slaves and the ship which was due to arrive in a few days, to transport the prisoners who were being held in makeshift compounds in various decks below.

She pitied them. No doubt some would be used for agricultural work, all manner of labour. But they would have gotten off lucky, Ebony felt, compared to the weaker of the slaves who were to be used for 'medical' purposes. And had hoped that her own brand on her backside would continue to be 'L' for 'lover' when she had learned that in the end, 'L' was actually for 'laboratory'. Blake wouldn't reveal any kind of detail on what anyone destined to end up would suffer. And she had no intention of finding out. So she decided for now not to pursue questioning.

Ebony clambered off the bed and gazed at her reflection in a full length mirror. Then she applied more lipstick, flicking her hair seductively. She sure was an enchantress, she felt, gifted - with striking looks. And was experienced and cunning enough to know how to use them, resolved that she would make Blake spellbound. Draw him in. Captivate him. Without him even realizing. And even if he did realize, Ebony felt he would soon become addicted and want more and more.

Crossing to Blake's desk, Ebony refilled her wine glass, then spotted a laptop, it's 'sleep' light blinking on and off.

She sat down in the mammoth, leather office chair, opened the lid, awakening the computer from hibernation, then hesitated for a moment, wondering if she should take a look. If Blake suddenly returned, she already had an excuse and would just say she was looking for something to entertain her. But she'd be ready to entertain him with something better than any computer could ever offer.

She noticed some directories with files which had been segmented into 'the pandemic'.... 'military installations'... 'orders'... 'prisoner status'...

Ebony went through the directories in mounting intrigue, suspecting that the rig was more than just a way station for slave transportation. It was obviously a floating fortress, the perfect place for an outpost, offering a sweeping panoramic view of the ocean around it. And rather than any exploration of oil, which it had apparently been used for once according to Blake, Ebony was intent on trying to discover more detail, sure its current operation wasn't limited to housing human cargo.

When she tried to gain access into any file, she was blocked.

Suddenly a live 'feed' activated and Blake's face appeared on the screen.

"Looking for something?" he said, his cold voice audible through the small speaker.

"No," Ebony replied, swallowing nervously. "If you can hear me - I wasn't doing anything, Blake. Honest."

"Oh, I can hear you very well," Blake replied. "In fact, I've been watching you. Closely. If you wanted some wine, then you should have asked. Likewise if you wanted to access classified files. Unfortunately, I think you'll find that you don't know the password!"

The screen went blank.

Ebony stood, bracing herself uneasily, listening to the sound of brisk footsteps approaching, echoing in the outer corridors.

She backed away, noticing the door handle beginning to turn.

Then she recoiled as the door opened, revealing Blake, who once again smiled, but it was ice-cold.

"Hi, honey! I'm home!"

Ebony continued to back away as Blake advanced, enraged. Finally unable to contain his simmering anger, he seized her by the neck with one hand, almost lifting her off her feet, pinning her to the wall.

She struggled to get her breath, writhing, trying to defend herself, scratching his face with her nails.

"Get off me!" she screamed. "I promise, I wasn't doing anything wrong!! I was just passing the time!"

He ran his own nails down Ebony's face, gouging her cheek. Slowly, deliberately, his teeth gritted. Then he released his grip, lowering her back down to the ground.

"One thing you should know about me, Ebony," Blake said quietly, but there was an intensity in his voice. "If you ever strike me, then I'll strike back. If you ever cross me, then that would be very foolish. Anyone who's ever tried never took long to realize that it was at their peril. And if you ever try to disobey or deceive me... then I'll destroy you."

"I think I get the gist of what you're saying there, Blake. And I'm just the same. Be nice to me and I'll be nice to you," she said, rubbing the welts on her neck from his clutch.

He considered her and couldn't contain a slight smile. He shook his head. "You're something else. You really are. Like an alley cat."

"Somehow that doesn't sound much like a compliment."

"Well, it is. I hate to admit it... but you know... I'd probably have done the same if I was in your situation," Blake replied. "And in a way, I admire that."

"You were setting me up, eh?"

He nodded proudly. "And you took the bait. 'I was just passing the time'," he mimicked Ebony's voice.

"I wasn't trying to pry into anything."

"You disappoint me," Blake said matter of factly. "I would want to know everything about any opponent."

"I'm not an opponent!" Ebony interrupted. "And that's why I wasn't snooping or anything. I don't consider you any kind of opponent of mine. And the sooner you realize that, the better. I can be useful to you, Blake. But I can't do that... unless you let me."

"In a way," Blake replied, "you might be right. You might end up being very useful. Having a higher value. A value beyond my wildest expectations."

"Oh?" Ebony said, unsure of exactly where he was coming from, what it all meant. But she knew deep down that she had to try and defuse matters as Blake continued.

"So why don't we just see what eventual category you fit. Just let me warn you, Ebony. If I find out I can't trust you, then it is 'L' for you, for sure. Laboratory!"

"And what does that entail?"

"Just trust me. Don't go there."

"You don't have to worry about that," Ebony replied. "I think we know each other well enough by now. Why don't we just stick to 'lover'?"

She pressed her lips on his and they passionately began to undress each other, hardly able to contain their desire.

CHAPTER THIRTY-ONE

The moon was bright, shining down on the surface of the water, the gentle waves retreating on the sands as the tide drifted out. The relaxing sounds brought Ruby some comfort. She was alone, several metres away from Camp

Phoenix, needing some time and space away from the others to gather her thoughts.

"What am I going to do with you?" Ruby spoke to herself, as if asking the baby she was carrying.

When she had confided her secret to Amber previously, Amber had asked Ruby if she was sure the father was Slade - and Ruby had been emphatic. Apart from a few relationships - and one mistaken, drunken one-night stand - she didn't sleep around.

How ironic that the pregnancy test she had taken back in the city was wrong, Ruby reflected. Very wrong. She took it before the tribe had been forced to flee the 'virus Mark II' released by Mega. At least she thought it was Mega. She, like the others, was feeling a little confused by what Ram had revealed.

But there was no doubt about it in her mind that she was expecting and who the father was. During the first few days of the voyage on the trawler, Ruby thought she was being seasick. Every so often she was overcome with nausea. But it must have been morning sickness, she concluded, discovering once again that she had missed her period.

Her life had been turned upside down due to the discovery of the life she was carrying inside her. Pregnancy tests weren't 100% accurate, she knew. There had been articles, she remembered, browsing when she was younger through her mother's stack of women's magazines, revealing how some mothers were surprised to find they were pregnant after having a negative test. And Ruby was more than surprised to know she was indeed carrying a baby. She was absolutely staggered.

New emotions were beginning to surface, along with the hormones.

She would face difficult times. In this post-apocalyptic world. She knew that. But also knew that in Amber and the Mall Rats, that they would be with her every step to give her any support she needed. Amber and Trudy had been there before as mothers themselves and Ruby would no doubt be grateful for any assistance they, along with the rest of the tribe, would provide.

Her overwhelming need right now was to keep it secret. So that Slade would know. First. Then Ruby would also know if he would stand by her. She didn't want him to feel obligated in any way. And above all, needed to know that Slade shared the same feelings she had for him.

She had never fallen in love before. But was sure that it must be the real thing. She had never felt this way about anyone and couldn't bear the thought of losing Slade.

Poor Amber, Ruby pondered, thinking back to the falling out that had happened hours before when Ram revealed his own 'secret' to everyone, about The Collective. But Ruby believed Jay and Amber would make up. Eventually. They were such a close couple.

Ruby would have to take it all one step at a time, she reasoned. Whatever unfolded on the island. The pregnancy. Her relationship with Slade, which had been further complicated by the fact that Slade's heart once belonged to someone else, with Ebony being the walking proof of that. And Ruby needed to know how Slade truly felt for her without any elements of duty of being a father clouding matters.

The most important thing for Ruby was that Slade survive his injuries. Or there would be no future for them together.

Also, Ruby was still distraught at the confrontation she had with May when she suggested how best to share out the limited medical supplies.

She wondered, going over everything in her mind, if she had she been right to insist that only Slade be treated with the medicines they had. Or if May was right, and she was being unfair.

Ruby didn't want to reduce Zak's chances of pulling through by denying him any medicine but she strongly felt there was no other choice. Zak was barely breathing, his weak pulse testament to the awful condition he was in. Ruby wished she could wave a magic wand, make both him and Slade better. But there were no quick fixes, she knew. She felt Zak didn't have much time left on this earth. So what was the point in wasting the precious limited medicine supplies that they had on him?

Yes, it was better to focus on Slade, Ruby was sure. Give all the medicine to him. At least he was semi-conscious, not in some coma, and though his wound was severe, he was surely in a stronger position than Zak to pull through.

Her thoughts drifted back to the old times when she was sitting in the waiting room in the hospital. It all brought up similar emotions. She would have been about ten years old. And she remembered the day like it was yesterday. Her grandmother had been admitted after suffering a massive stroke. She was unconscious, in a coma. Ruby had cried more tears than she knew possible. Ellen was her favourite grandparent. The doctors had entered the waiting room with a solemn look on their faces and Ruby had overheard her parents discussing Grandma Ellen's plight.

There was nothing they could do, the doctors had told them. Grandma Ellen was technically alive but without being on life support, was in reality clinically dead.

Ruby's family had decided to accept the inevitable, to reluctantly agree with the doctors' recommendations - that the life support machines be switched off, resulting in Grandma Ellen drifting from this world to the next.

Ruby vowed she would never forget Grandma Ellen - and neither would she forget the manner of her passing.

That episode in her younger life brought back painful recollections. Zak was surely going to follow in Grandma Ellen's steps. Their situations were so similar. There was no point giving Zak medicine. It was too late for him. But not for Slade.

For all of her stance, Ruby couldn't help but feel pangs of guilt as she reflected on her argument with May earlier. And the look in May's eyes when she was sitting, refusing anything to eat, the light from the bonfire back at camp reflecting flickering, dancing flames in her eyes. She looked to be so lost, eager to get back to taking her shift to watch over Zak. As eager as Ruby had been to check on Slade, both still being sheltered some distance away from the main camp, being too unwell to be moved.

Ruby wondered if she had become sensitised. To death. She had experienced so much of it throughout the pandemic. With news initially of hundreds, thousands, then millions passing away as the 'virus' spread. Before long, the impact seemed to evaporate. Death became routine, just like the struggle to survive, to live, to get through another day.

Salene was now taking a shift to watch over Slade and Ruby welcomed the chance to try and gather all her thoughts together as she waded through the shallows, gazing at the wreck of the Jzhao Li, silhouetted in the distance against the dark sky.

None of them had dived inside the wreck itself during the search for more medical supplies. Ruby suggested they check it out but had been overruled by the others, feeling it would be far too dangerous.

But she was a good swimmer. During her vacations while at school, Ruby worked as a lifeguard, plucking many people from the water, having got themselves into unnecessary difficulties.

It was all about minimizing the risks, Ruby knew, finding the right spot, being sensible.

The ocean was calm tonight, the tide gentle.

Wading deeper and deeper into the waters, a part of Ruby wondered whether or not she should continue on. Then, when she was waist high, she took a deep breath, lunged forward and started to swim towards the wreck.

Kicking her feet, harder, she submerged herself, the cold water gurgling around her ears, and proceeded toward the sunken hull.

She was lucky she was still physically fit, not so far advanced in her term that she was unable to do anything. On the contrary, she was still slim, her tummy almost flat, the baby she was carrying not yet showing as a 'bump' though she knew it was there, inside her. She just knew.

Ahead of her, the accommodation tower of the Jzhao Li now came into view, laying on its side in the moonlit waters, motionless. Ruby remembered seeing in one of the cabinets in the bridge a mammoth first aid kit when they were onboard and now was determined to see if she could retrieve it, to check if there was anything salvageable.

Her legs drove her to the surface. She inhaled, desperate to obtain air, gazing around, making sure of her bearings. Then she took a huge breath, her cheeks puffed out by the air they stored, and dived under the surface again, the beam of the waterproof flashlight she had recovered during Salene's search illuminating the way ahead, guiding her further downwards, deep into the wreck of the Jzhao Li.

CHAPTER THIRTY-TWO

Lia stooped under the low roof as she entered the mud hut, a bundle of ripe fruit in her arms, which she dropped to the ground in front of Jack and Lex, the two of them pausing for a moment, staring at the fruit. They hadn't eaten for ages and it was a tantalising sight.

The sound of insects and animal life of the night reverberated through the native camp and jungle beyond.

"Go on," Lia encouraged. "It's not poisoned, if that's what you're worried about. Eat it!"

Grateful, Jack and Lex scooped up the fruit. Though still bound by the vines, they were able to hold the selection of what was on offer and gleefully started consuming it.

"Why are you doing this?" Jack asked between mouthfuls.

"I thought you'd be hungry. And thirsty."

It was true that it was sweltering in the hut and Jack and Lex were beginning to feel dehydration set in, as well as hunger.

"There's few better things in the world than a girl bringing me food," Lex said philosophically, dribbling juice down his chin.

"Lia, why are you helping us?" Jack asked, as Lia knelt down beside them.

"I might wear glasses," she said, tapping her thick lenses, her green eyes peering through, "but I can still see that both of you could never be Blake's people."

"Why's that? Cause we're good looking - and they're ugly?" Lex suggested.

"They're nothing but bad news. But you two? I think my old pet rabbit must have been tougher than either of you! You're no match for Blake's forces, that's for sure."

"Must have been some rabbit," Lex retorted, slightly offended.

Since they had first met, Lia had gotten to know Jack and Lex better. And she liked what she saw of them, believing they were two innocents who meant no harm and were telling the truth, the two of them stumbling by accident into the world of the natives.

She was determined to help. She felt sorry for them and had earlier given them an insight into the native tribe and why there had been such antagonism displayed towards Jack and Lex.

Lia had explained that the natives were survivors of the pandemic, as was anyone else who was still living and breathing since the adults perished.

As indigenous people of this land, they had a longstanding resentment against the international community who had brought many diseases. Their people had suffered for centuries, losing their independence when the settlers first arrived and took over their lands. Trampling on customs, dishonouring their culture, tainting the sacred soil. But the tribe never lost their dignity or desire to continue the way of life of their ancestors, passing down their knowledge and traditions through the generations. And this surviving generation was no exception.

Lia described how the outside world began to creep in, with roads being carved through the jungle, as well as a small airport being built many years ago, to accommodate an influx of tourists who had discovered these paradise islands. There were no cities or towns. Just a few scattered resorts for holidaymakers to fly in and spend some time marvelling at the natural world, fishing, exploring the reefs, lounging on the stunning beaches.

The village existed in its own 'pocket', isolated far from the tourists, thankfully, so that little infiltration had occurred to further affect the culture.

In a way, the camp, as well being a home, had almost been located as if it bridged two worlds. Between the traditional way the 'natives' were so desperate to preserve and the 'modern' lifestyles of the outside.

So the tribe resented the presence of outsiders long before even the 'virus' occurred. And as all the adults began to die off, tried to seal themselves away so that they could embark upon trying to carve out a new future, paying homage to the old and all their people who had gone before.

During the height of the pandemic, Lia had told Jack and Lex, there had been a sudden build up of new activity with foreigners, the military arriving. A massive oil rig had been towed into position off the coast. Construction machinery arrived on enormous ships. An old abandoned air base from World War 2 was reactivated and developed. Many more vehicles were brought to the land. Supplies. Equipment. Soldiers and defence personnel soon outnumbered the indigenous population. At one point there was more aircraft than birds flying around, the natives felt.

It seemed as if these lands were going to be overwhelmed and the indigenous tribe were fearful of their way of life disappearing forever, like a tsunami of foreigners from overseas was threatening to engulf and wipe everything away.

But the danger was far greater than even the 'natives' anticipated. When all the foreign people in their midst began to die off. And then so did the adult members of their tribe. One by one.

When they perished, the tribe believed it was due to the way the international community had treated the world as a whole. Throughout history, they had tried to extend their empires. Greedily pillaging nature's resources with their pollution, oil rigs and spills. And perhaps the 'virus' was nature's way - or God's way - of handing out its natural justice, with the old adult world being purged, paying the price for all the wrongs that had been committed. Unfortunately the native adults had been swept away as innocent victims, they all believed.

As survivors of the plague, now the answers to their future lay in their past. In the wisdom of their ancestors. In the life that was taught to them by their forbears. So they were determined to return to the old traditional ways, to their culture, to guide them through uncertain times.

"And what about this Blake?" Lex asked.

"I don't know much about him. Or his forces. Except that they raided once. Not long after they arrived, taking away many of the villagers."

"To where?" Jack probed.

"No one knows where they end up for sure. But I think they trade in slaves. And if his men ever come back, we'll be ready if he tries to set foot on the sacred lands," Lia replied.

"What about us then?" Jack asked. "I mean, if the tribe thought we did."

"That's not a matter for me," Lia replied.

"Then who?" Lex enquired, before letting out a huge, satisfied, impromptu belch, having finished his fruit, Jack also wiping his own juicy hands on the ground.

"Honestly - you are just like one big baby," Lia teased Lex, a twinkle in her eye.

She was obviously attracted to him, though she tried not to show it too much. But Jack could see that, as always, Lex seemed to have a way with any female he encountered. And this girl was no exception, falling victim to his roguish charms.

"You should see how he can get. On a bad day. Right now he's on his best behaviour," Jack added, sensing that it might help if he could play the Lex card, though Lia seemed to be as kind as she was concerned for their well being and didn't need any extra motivation. But Jack thought it couldn't hurt.

"What is this? Pick on Lex day or something?" Lex protested.

"Just a little fun, Lex," Jack replied. Then he turned back, considering Lia. "So if it isn't a matter for you - who decides? About us, Lia?"

"The Priestess will see you soon. Your fate will be decided then," she replied.

"Do you think she'll let us go?" Jack asked.

"It is up to her. But just know, the way you treated everyone since you have been here - shouting at them, calling them names. Threatening. It hasn't helped. They are suspicious of outsiders enough as it is."

Jack sighed to himself, wondering if perhaps trying to use the 'Lex charm card' was such a good idea after all.

"I still don't get it," Lex said, slumping down on the dirt like a lion after a feast. "If these people hate all things 'foreign' so much - what are you doing here? Why aren't you a prisoner? Like Jack and I?"

"I was - once," Lia replied. "My home was in Frankfurt, originally."

"Well, that explains everything," Lex scoffed sarcastically.

Jack interrupted, not wishing to inflame matters with Lex going off on a tangent. "How did you end up here?" he asked Lia.

"My Mum and Dad were both doctors. With the Red Cross. As a little girl, I was sent to boarding schools. All over the world. But when the pandemic occurred, I was with my parents. They were going to be part of a medical mission. With the United Nations Pacific Fleet."

Jack and Lex exchanged a discrete glance, recalling Doctor Gideon's journal, as Lia continued.

"We were an international force, the last effort supposedly to save humanity. By keeping people away from the land, quarantined in ships, the idea was they would be safe. Like Noah's Ark. And one day, everyone would return to the land and rebuild civilisation."

"So what happened to this ship of yours?" Lex asked Lia carefully.

"The 'virus' happened. It spread throughout the entire fleet. My Mum and Dad put me in a liferaft. Along with some of the other children, and set me adrift. I never saw my parents again."

Lia hesitated, her eyes clouding over in pain at the memories, reliving it once more.

"They devoted their lives to saving others. And made sure I would have a chance to be saved... After many days alone at sea, I was washed up. On this land. I don't know what happened to the other children. But I think some of them might have survived. Joined other tribes. Some, not indigenous to our land but made up of foreigners."

"So you were shipwrecked yourself?" Jack enquired.

Lia nodded.

"Well, at least you know how we feel," Lex said.

"Wandering around the jungle, lost, I was taken in. At first, as a prisoner. Like you. But the Priestess's younger sister was sick. I saved her life, using my Dad's old medical kit. It wasn't anything serious. I think maybe even a cold. But some of the villagers thought I had healing powers. Sure the Priestess's sister was suffering as a result of the pandemic. So I was allowed to stay. The strange thing is that I probably wasn't even responsible. They have their own cures they use. From the land. And probably saved the Priestess's sister themselves. But they gave me credit. Since then, they've been like a new family to me. I learned their language, their customs. And decided to say good bye to the ways of the old world that I had known."

"So where does that leave us?" Jack questioned, trying to gain more of an insight into what might lay in store.

"I've recommended to the Priestess she be lenient with you. But as I say, it is not my decision. Just remember everything I've told you. Show respect. If the Priestess can see the good in you that I can see, there's every chance you will be fine."

"And if she can't?" Lex asked.

Lia was silent for a moment, unsure what to say.

"Please...," Jack said. "We're grateful for everything you've done. But we need to know. Where do we stand?"

"Unless the Priestess decides otherwise, today could be the last day you are alive."

Jack blanched. Lex looked at Lia, bravely absorbing it all.

"Well, if she has so much power around here... let's just hope she's in a good mood," Lex said wryly, but could barely mask his unease.

* * *

Jack and Lex were led through the village, their feet squelching in the mud, powerfully built warriors clutching their arms either side. Flaming torches illuminated the camp.

The entire tribe had come out to witness the spectacle and were assembled, shouting at Lex and Jack in their native tongue as the two outsiders passed by. It was a language, of course. Neither Jack nor Lex understood, though from the hostility clear in the expressions and tones let alone the jeering, it was obvious they didn't think much of Jack and Lex, other than contempt.

"What you think they're saying?" Jack whispered innocently to Lex.

"I dunno. But somehow I don't think it's how handsome I am," Lex muttered back, trying to keep his humour.

They were dragged towards a massive hut in the centre of the village where a large fire crackled, spitting out hot embers, and around it a circle of younger girls and warrior boys danced, ululating wildly, their arms flailing.

It had to be a ritual, some ceremony, Jack realized. And he and Lex were the focus of it all.

He looked around for Lia, hoping she might give some indication of just exactly what was happening, but noticed she had disappeared into an impressive dwelling.

Pushed to the ground, Jack and Lex remained kneeling as a huge warrior stood near the entrance of the mud hut Lia had entered, a conch shell grasped in his burly arms.

Suddenly the warrior blew into the conch, a loud, primal bellow reverberating around the entire village. The native crowd who had gathered to watch quietened down in anticipation.

"Remind me to never go off exploring with you again," Lex whispered to Jack.

Jack didn't smile. He was terrified by the ordeal, at being on public display. It felt like some sort of show trial. "If anything happens to either of us... it's been nice knowing you, Lex," Jack said sincerely.

Lex nodded. "Sorry about all those times I used to bully you. I didn't mean anything. You've always been a good friend." Lex seemed as if he wished to redeem himself in some way, equally sincere, before sighing to himself, "Though I can't say it's a pleasure spending my last days with you."

Lex and Jack braced themselves as a figure emerged from the dark confines of the large hut, stepping into the night and drawing gasps of awe from the crowd.

She was taller than the other villagers and wore bright multi-coloured feathers in her dark hair. She moved so regally, graciously. On her face were markings, daubs of decorative lines indicating some hidden meaning, unknown to Jack and Lex. She had a commanding aura, surveying first the crowd before her, then turning her attention to the two captives kneeling under her gaze.

Lex drew a sharp intake of breath, contemplating the Priestess. She was staggeringly beautiful. Charismatic. Svelte. Sensual. She possessed an extraordinary magnetism. She was about the same age as most of the girls Lex had bedded in the Mall Rats. And right now, his dying wish was that if this was to be his last night on earth, then he would spend it with her. She took Lex's breath away. For a moment he almost forgot that she had the power over his and Jack's life, so lost was he, mesmerised by her presence.

The massive warrior put down the conch shell and in the ensuing silence the Priestess stared at Jack and Lex, sizing each one up with her determined eyes.

Lia started speaking the native tongue, a guttural sounding language with a few clicking noises here and there. What a contrast to the voice and European accent they had gotten so used to, Lex thought, wondering how Lia could have ever even learned such a language. It sounded so complicated.

Lex and Jack wondered what she was saying.

Thrusting an arm forth, the Priestess silenced Lia. She had heard enough.

Addressing the crowd of onlookers, the Priestess began speaking. She spoke in a smooth, rhythmic tone. She wasn't shouting, just speaking as if in conversation. But so quiet were her subjects, so focused on her every word and gesture, so still was the atmosphere, the Priestess's words carried over the air for all to hear.

Lia began to translate, whispering to Jack and Lex.

"She's saying that the two strangers here among us are a curse. From the foreigners. She is sure you are both demons, sent to cause destruction."

"I think I need a lawyer," Lex mumbled.

"Bow your head in respect!" Lia urged him. Lex did as she suggested as Lia went on translating. "The Priestess claims you are both people of Blake. That you are here to spy on the Tribe. Assess its strengths and weaknesses. Before capturing more of the people, committing them to a lifetime of slavery. Like your kind have done before. You exist to pillage and plunder. Nothing will stop you going about your ways... except..."

The Priestess glowered at Jack and Lex, her eyes full of venom and spite as she continued addressing the crowd of villagers.

"Except what?" Jack whispered to Lia, desperate to know what she was saying.

"The Priestess feels that there is only one way to stop you and the rest of your kind. And that is to send out a warning. To Blake. And his people. Along with anyone else who dares step uninvited into the tribal sacred lands."

The Priestess shrieked suddenly, her high pitch call piercing the air. And the villagers erupted into ululations, the energy palpable, electric.

Backing into her hut, bowing to the stars that twinkled above, saying something in her native tongue to the night sky, the Priestess disappeared from sight.

"Is that it?" Lex asked Lia.

"What - they're letting us go?" Jack questioned, hopeful at the answer. "They want us to take some kind of message with us?"

Reluctantly, Lia shook her head. The sadness in her green eyes gave it away, all the sparkle normally shown in them now gone.

"I'm so sorry," Lia began to cry, sniffing through tears. "Tomorrow morning. At sunrise. You will be sacrificed. And your remains given to Blake and his men if they ever set foot in the sacred lands again."

CHAPTER THIRTY-THREE

Amber patted her baby on the back. He had woken up minutes earlier, crying into the night, and she was trying to comfort him. Though in effect, he was giving her the comfort she needed that moment, even though he didn't know it, Amber thought, hugging her baby lovingly.

She was still upset with Jay after Ram had explained all about the information about The Collective, Jay being the only one of the Mall Rats so far who seemed to believe Ram's story. Fully.

Jay had every right to express his opinions, Amber had always felt. That wasn't the issue.

She never wanted to be cynical. To think the worst of anyone or anything. But there was something about Ram she still couldn't put her finger on. Was he being truthful now about The Collective? Or was he holding something else back?

"Amber..." Jay whispered, stepping tentatively towards her. "Can we talk?"

"You tell me. Can we?"

"I didn't mean to get you upset before."

"Well, you succeeded. Or am I overreacting? Not being 'reasonable' enough for you?"

"Amber, please," Jay pleaded. "The word just slipped out. It was the wrong thing to say. You have every right to question Ram about what happened to Bray... and anyone else in the tribe who disappeared for that matter. Just because I might believe him and his story - that doesn't mean it's a blank slate, and the past is all wiped away. Clean. Ram still has a lot to answer for."

Amber looked at Jay, studying him. She couldn't believe that she was beginning to question even his integrity. But he had been Ram's 'general' after all, the one who planned the main invasion that led to the Technos taking over the city. Jay had always denied he knew what happened to Bray and the others, why they were taken. She had believed him. Jay eventually turned against Ram's rule of tyranny once he had been exposed to all the realities and had helped Amber lead the rebels to freedom. They had so many things in common, with their ideals and principles. It was hardly surprising they entered into relationship.

But still, Jay seemed to be siding with Ram. Amber hoped it wasn't the start of a slippery slope that would end up with Amber losing him, which would certainly be the case if he was going to do Ram's bidding. Becoming his 'general' once more. Amber couldn't bear even the thought of it. That Jay would ever reunite again with Ram. And if he ever did, she knew her relationship with Jay would be over. She could never begin to forgive Ram for all the pain and hurt he had brought to the city and sectors. For all that he protested his innocence. She was always a good judge of character and could see through people. At least that's what she thought. But now was beginning to have some painful doubts if Jay was involved in any way. If so, she had been totally taken in. He wouldn't have been the man she thought he was.

Jay knew Amber well enough to realize what must have been going through her mind. And that he might have been tarred in her view with what Ram had been saying.

"When Ram first told me about The Collective, I didn't believe a word of it," Jay said. "I thought that's it - he's finally lost it, teetered over into the brink of madness, that it was all in his head... But the more I thought about it, piecing it together... it does all make sense."

"Well, I'm glad it does. To you." Amber replied.

"All I'm saying, Amber, is that I believe Ram about the existence of The Collective. Nothing more. Nothing less."

"And these 'underground adult bases', like the one at Eagle Mountain," Amber probed. "You sure you didn't know about all that? Or anything else?"

"You know all that I know, Amber. Please. Believe me. And if Ram's right, we could all be in great danger here. If The Collective are somehow involved in these islands."

Amber considered Jay, then sighed.

"I don't mean to doubt you, Jay. It's just a lot to take in."

"That's for sure," Jay agreed, then he continued, sadly. "After what happened to Ved, I know how it feels to lose someone special."

"I know," Amber said, gently stroking Jay's arm.

Then she indicated the baby, now sleeping in her arms.

"I'm just so worried about our future. My baby's future."

"That's why I wanted you to listen to Ram. I'm as concerned about the future for you, me, the baby. Everyone. I wasn't trying to shut you up, tell you what to do. And I wasn't choosing to side with Ram. The wrong words slipped out of my stupid mouth at the wrong time. I'm so sorry, Amber."

Jay ran his fingers through her hair as he continued on gently. "You don't really think I had anything to do with Bray's disappearance? Or any of the others?"

"I had to check, Jay."

"What? If I'm a liar?"

"No. I know when it comes down to it, you're not that. I'm sorry. And I'm sorry I slapped you."

"So am I. You've got quite a right hook. If The Collective are out there somewhere, they'd regret crossing you, Amber."

Amber smiled, then looked at Jay uneasily. "Do you really think they could be out there?"

"I don't know what I think anymore, Amber. But we've got to tread with care. Ram can be a bit like a loose missile at times. But for all his faults, he just had his own agenda for the Technos. Ideologically."

"Well, I don't agree with them. I never have," Amber replied firmly.

"Well, that's your opinion and you're entitled to it. But don't you see - whoever he is, it doesn't matter if you're right. Or I'm right. Ram can still be a valuable asset. He knows more about The Collective and how they operate than anyone. Now it doesn't mean to say that I'm his best friend or that I'm working for him again, by me saying that. Or even against him. It just means that, thinking strategically, if we're going to have any kind of chance and The Collective do exist - we might need Ram."

"I understand," Amber agreed, seeing the sense in what Jay was saying. "But let's keep our eye on him."

"Now that sounds 'reasonable' to me," Jay said, kissing Amber tenderly on the cheek.

Amber smiled as well and kissed him back.

"I'm so glad that nothing happened to you. Even Ram, believe it or not. And now that you're back, we'd better think about sending out a search party for Jack and Lex. They're long overdue and Ellie's really struggling."

Amber's expression clouded, as did Jay's, as they noticed Salene.

"Amber!" Salene called out, racing towards them.

"What is it, Sal?" Amber replied.

"I think something must have happened to Ruby. There's no sign of her back at camp!"

* * *

It hadn't all turned out how she had expected, Ruby thought, gasping for breath.

She was trapped inside the wreck of the Jzhao Li. The underwater flashlight she had brought with her to guide her way in the murky depths, had stopped working several minutes before. Most likely its battery had gone.

Now, all around, it was pitch black. There was nothing she could see. Just the empty darkness that was all encompassing.

And Ruby felt terrified.

Panic gripped her. As hard as she fought to push it away, it just kept coming back.

This was her worst nightmare. Drowning, alone, in the unforgiving sea. She had many recurring dreams about it when she was a little girl. It was the very reason her parents had given her swimming lessons in the first place. And her fears had subsided, having become such a proficient swimmer, eventually a lifeguard. Now all those anxieties had returned. Ironic that she had saved so many lives in her time as a guard but was unable to help herself, her unborn baby. And Slade.

Ruby had swam into the wreck through one of the broken windows in the bridge, and had managed to find what she had been searching for. The medical kit was still there, fastened to its wall hanging, and in the air pocket.

The Jzhao Li was unstable, however. While Ruby was inside the bridge section, the hull of the ship had continued creaking, its groans reverberating under the water like a whale's song, though Ruby wondered if each shift of the vessel was going to be a death knell.

The bridge window that Ruby had entered was now inaccessible, the wreck having turned on its side several degrees so that Ruby would have to find a different way out.

The ship was resting in a good thirty feet of water and Ruby knew her air pocket wouldn't last long. She was floating inside the dark confines of the bridge, her face pressed to the ceiling, feelings of claustrophobia and a fear of drowning combined, filling Ruby with an awful sense of doom.

She wouldn't give up, though. Clutching the medical kit in her hand, fighting back cramp, her legs aching from the cold salt water, Ruby was determined to give it everything she had. A deep grinding noise moved through the hull of the Jzhao Li, stuck precariously on the reef, signifying to Ruby that the wreck hadn't finished its capsizing movement yet. It was a terrifying sound, like the gates of hell were being opened for her, a foreboding screech of rending metal that permeated through the water, through the essence of Ruby's entire being.

Taking a huge gulp of air, she managed just in time to submerge under the water as the air pocket disappeared, with the wreck shifting.

Under the water, in the dark, Ruby prayed she would be able to rise up under the bridge and find another air pocket once the wreck settled.

Panic rising through every fibre of her body, Ruby struggled to keep calm. But knew she needed to find another precious intake of breath. Soon. Would this breath be her last? Was this really how it was meant to be? Had she brought this upon herself, foolishly venturing into the water alone, underestimating the risks?

Seconds passed. The awful sound of the Jzhao Li shifting in the unstable depths subsided.

Time to kick up to the surface, Ruby thought, her lungs feeling like they were going to burst. It was now or never.

Ignoring the cramp that constricted her leg muscles, her calf throbbing painfully out of control, Ruby gave it all she had, kicking, desperate to find another air pocket - or even a window so she could escape rather than be trapped in this watery grave.

But her worst fears were realized when she reached what was once a wall, and now a temporary ceiling, due to the angle of the sideways leaning bridge section of the Jzhao Li. There was no pocket of air this time. Just the cold metal wall.

Her chest feeling like it was on fire, her lungs under protest, her mouth instinctively, desperately wanting to open to breathe, her entire body was weakening, her life ebbing away.

She was terrified at the thought of her unborn baby being starved of oxygen, along with herself. She couldn't yield though and kept her mouth clamped shut. Stars appeared before her eyes. She realized that she was drowning, losing the young life she carried inside her in the process.

Twin beams of light burst through the murky darkness, like Heaven had sent down angels to welcome her.

Ruby focused weakly. Who was this? Her Mum and Dad? Her Grandma Ellen? The baby she had terminated? Friends who had perished in the apocalyptic pandemic?

The bright beams of light cut through the darkness, enveloping Ruby, losing consciousness, swallowing the salt water.

But a feeling of total tranquility, peace, replaced her panic.

There were angels, after all.

Her body fell limp. Ruby let go of her thoughts, as well as the side of the metal wall, and floated towards the bright light, a slight smile on her face, a strange feeling of calm prevailing. Somehow everything would turn out well in this new world, beckoning her.

* * *

Blinking with uncertainty, Ruby opened her eyes.

Amber's warm smile gazed down above her face.

"Thank God!" Amber shouted for joy. "Are you okay?!"

Ruby couldn't talk and coughed up more salt water.

"We were so worried about you!" May cried out, thrilled.

"I'm... alive?" Ruby questioned in uncertainty.

"Thanks to May - yes!" Amber and Jay explained.

Ruby slowly discovered, coming to her senses, that she was laying on her side on the sand in the recovery position. She was coughing and spluttering, spitting out water, illuminated by flashlights being held by other members of the Tribe gazing down in concern at Ruby being assisted to sit under the circle of light shining down on the beach.

They explained that once her absence from the camp had been noticed, Amber split everyone up so they could search the beach and undergrowth.

May was sure she had noticed Ruby wading into the water and decided to accompany Amber and Jay swimming out to the wreck. Plunging into the murky depths, she noticed that Ruby was trapped inside the Jzhao Li.

"I was so stupid!" Ruby said. "What have I done?"

But she wasn't just referring to her search for medicines to complement the precious little that they had. She was focused, in particular, on May, who nodded and smiled slightly.

"It's water under the bridge," May quipped.

"Amber!" screamed Lottie.

The others turned in the direction of the cry, noticing Lottie sprinting towards them in the distance.

"Tell Trudy and the others that they can stand down. We don't need to search anymore. We found Ruby!" Amber shouted out to Lottie.

But Lottie continued in full flight, her shoulders heaving from the exertion of the run, and sobbing uncontrollably. "He's dead!" she screamed.

CHAPTER THIRTY-FOUR

It was such a beautiful night, Jack thought, staring up at the Heavens, the stars twinkling through the gap in the entrance to the hut he and Lex were imprisoned in. What a night. Was it really going to be the last night he would ever see?

How he missed Ellie, Jack reflected. She loved the stars. The two of them used to gaze up at them in the city, considering life, talking about the meaning of existence, their hopes, dreams, futures together in the post-adult pandemic world.

And now it was just him. Contemplating what little time he had left to live, knowing that in a few hours he and Lex were to be executed.

Was this how the adults all felt when they got the virus, with the clock ticking until they succumbed?

Jack strained on the tight vines, twisted in knots, trying to free himself. Yet the harder he pulled, the closer the vines wound around his arms and legs, further constricting him.

"We could try biting them?" Lex suggested, pulling at the vines with all his might, getting nowhere.

"Why not?" Jack replied. It was worth a try. Anything was. Their situation was desperate and called for desperate measures.

Lex bit into the vines binding his arms and yelped, the prickles and spines protruding from the flaxen sinking into his tongue.

Jack noticed a shadowy figure approaching outside and whispered, panic-stricken, "Lex! Someone's coming!"

Lex froze, spitting out the tangled, twisted vines that were his bonds - before slumping to the dirt, Jack doing the same. The two pretending to be asleep so as not to arouse suspicion from whoever was approaching.

The polished stone surface of a spear end glistened in the moonlight.

Lex stole a glance out of the corner of his eye, noticing that it was Lia, and instinctively recoiled from the sharp weapon she was holding as she crouched down.

"What are you doing?" he asked.

"Ssh!" Lia hushed him. "What do you think I'm doing?"

To Jack and Lex's relief, Lia began to work on the tangled vines, the sharp spear sawing through their bonds.

"It's such an injustice!" Lia continued. "So wrong! You are both innocent!"

"I knew you liked me," Lex grinned.

"We're not out of it yet," Jack whispered, sighing in contentment, rubbing his hands together, now cut free, feeling the circulation once more flowing in his limbs.

Lia was clearly in some emotional conflict as she crossed to cut the vines securing their legs to the wooden poles. She felt caught between her loyalty to the native tribe, who had fed her, given her shelter and support for so long - and her new-found companions, Jack and Lex, who she just knew were wrongly accused of guilt, having committed no crime.

It was her principles that guided her, and where her pleas to the Priestess to release Jack and Lex had failed earlier, she reluctantly realized she had to resort now to more direct means, even if it meant endangering herself.

"There - done!" Lia whispered happily, cutting Lex free.

"If we get out of this - I won't forget," Lex promised, staring into Lia's green eyes, beams of moonlight flowing through the cut-out windows in the hut, reflecting off her glasses.

Lia wondered if Lex could see that she was blushing.

"So...what now?" Jack whispered, climbing to his feet.

"We stay here and hope all the villagers find us," Lex scoffed, casting an incredulous glance at Jack. "For a smart guy, you still got a lot to learn."

Jack faked a smile to Lex, then considered Lia. "Well...?"

"Follow me... and don't make a sound!" she urged softly.

Lia led Jack and Lex out of the hut and they moved furtively through the native village.

It was quiet. Eerily so. All the villagers must have been asleep.

Lia waved Jack and Lex on, indicating the way ahead.

Jack was petrified. One false move and he knew they could awaken the entire village, alert them to their escape. He noticed some warriors sleeping outside huts, their massive barrel chests heaving up and down as they dreamt, while at the same time Jack scanned the dirt in front of him, making sure he didn't step on anything which would cause a noise.

Tiptoeing quietly, they finally made it, miraculously, to the outskirts of the village.

Lex grinned at Lia. He liked her. A lot. She was brave and was putting herself on the line for them. And she was pretty slinky too, noticing the way she moved, cat-like.

"Which way now?" Lex asked.

"I don't think there'll be any signs to the beach," Jack said, getting his own back on Lex.

Lia held a finger over her lips as if to shush Jack and Lex, reminding them to keep quiet, to focus.

A loud, whooshing sound through the night air surprised the three of them, and a huge spear embedded itself into the ground, the end of it wobbling from the momentum of it being thrown.

Jack, Lex and Lia stared at the weapon wide-eyed, full of fear.

"I get the 'point'. That's the only sign I think we need, Jack! You as well, Lia. Run!" Lex urged.

And they took off in full flight, Lia glancing back, noticing the Priestess at the perimeter of the village, now glaring in disappointment.

Lia wondered for a moment if this spear was a warning shot or an actual attempt to injure one of them, with Lia being the closest target to where the spear had landed. Did the Priestess mean to hurt them? Lia in particular? Or just show her displeasure?

A loud banshee scream escaped from the lips of the Priestess, as if giving Lia her answer.

Jack, Lex and Lia continued to run for their lives, receding into the dark jungle, conscious behind them of light from flickering flaming torches as the villagers began their pursuit, responding to the Priestess's call.

"Split up!" Lex shouted urgently. "It's our only hope!"

Lia and Jack nodded, then took off in different directions, realizing that they might at least have a one in three chance of getting away if the villagers in pursuit were distracted.

Alone and running as fast as she could, Lia felt like a traitor.

It was the look on the Priestess's face. She had let her down. Betrayed the entire tribe.

Pushing themselves on through the dense, dark jungle, Lia, Jack and Lex continued, panicked, their pursuers slowing, gazing around, looking for any sign, sound, so they could choose a direction to take.

CHAPTER THIRTY-FIVE

Blake extended one arm, offering a chicken drumstick to Ebony.

As she reached out, he quickly withdrew it and started gorging on it himself.

They were sitting at his desk in his quarters, having a meal. But only Blake was eating. Ebony was sitting opposite, unsure of what would unfold.

There had been no sign of the disfigured girl for a while. Ebony wondered if she had perhaps answered a question with a question and had 'gone for a swim'. Or suspected that the girl might have been some kind of servant. And now Ebony had that role.

It had been a close call when he discovered her checking out his computer and she was still unsettled by Blake's volcanic temper, hoping that he was still intrigued enough by her to keep her as his mistress for more time to come.

They had certainly made mad, passionate love after his attack but she was unsure if it would still be enough to save herself.

He licked his fingers, lifted another drumstick.

"Any chance of getting something to eat?" Ebony asked, prodding to try and establish where she stood. Although she suspected he was still infatuated enough with her to want her to share his bed, an overwhelming uncertainty engulfed Ebony. Since the situation with the computer, she was aware that he was cold.

"One thing you need to realize, Ebony," Blake said, between taking bites of food. "You're in no position to ask for anything."

"If you're still mad at me about the computer - honestly, I wasn't trying to snoop around or anything."

"What were you hoping to find?"

"I was just interested in knowing if you were still connected to a network. I mean, not many people are these days. Please. Just trust me, Blake. There was nothing more to it than that."

"So... it wasn't what it seemed," Blake smiled slightly.

Ebony knew he was toying with her and being so volatile, wondered if he would erupt at any moment.

"If I'm going to be of any use to you, that's up to you to decide, Blake," Ebony said, changing tactic. "I mean, you said yourself you'd do the same thing that I did. So if you were setting me up, how do you know - that I didn't? Know. That you're giving me some kind of test. And I'm not the type who would ever want to fail."

Blake considered her and smiled. "Nice one. Like it," he said.

"I was trying to please you. Make an impression. You're the man around here. All I ask is for the chance to be your woman."

Ebony's hopes were once again being raised, feeling that if this dude was some kind of control freak, then she'd let him think he was in control. But she knew it was important to keep him on the end of the hook, feeling that she was capable of controlling matters herself. Otherwise, she would be of no use to him in his organisation.

She needed to get more of a handle on just exactly what he was up to. She was still unsettled by his earlier references that she might be destined for the 'laboratory'. She was determined the only place she'd end up was in his bed. At least for the time being, until another opportunity presented itself. Her core aspiration was to survive.

"You've got an impressive set up, Blake," she said, looking for a way in to steer the conversation to what he and his forces were involved with. She reached out for the chicken drumstick he was holding - and this time

292

he didn't withdraw it. Now she was making progress, she thought, sinking her teeth into the meat as if it was some kind of prey she had just caught. Blake's chosen the wrong one to fool with, Ebony thought to herself, devouring the chicken, viewing the mere fact she was even eating to be an important step in her seizing back a bit of control.

"I'm glad you 'approve'," Blake said, continuing eating, but still studying Ebony.

"Oh, I do," she replied. "And I'd like to be a part of it. Like I've been telling you. I can bring skills. Not that you might need them, of course. I mean, you seem to have everything working really well. But I've also had experience. Being a leader."

"So I gather," Blake replied, gazing intently at Ebony. Then he casually added, "The Locos, wasn't it?"

Ebony was floored by that revelation, wondering how he knew. She didn't recall saying anything about it at any time when he asked her what she had been up to back in the city. But maybe she had, and had simply forgotten. But if not, he clearly knew more about her than she ever thought. The question was, how? She decided to play it coolly until she found out more. If he did know anything, then she would have to tread very carefully. She didn't want to give away any unnecessary information. But equally, the consequences could be catastrophic if he knew that she wasn't revealing all... she knew.

"Yeah, the Locos. I started out as the mistress of the head of the tribe."

"Zoot - wasn't it?"

Ebony's mind raced. This guy was good and really was in control. He had all the power with whatever

293

information he had uncovered. So she would need to keep her story straight.

"That's right. Zoot. Then after he was killed, I took over. I'd never have been able to do that if Zoot was alive. And would have never wanted to either," Ebony added, not wishing Blake to ever think that she might be a threat and the type to try and seize control. Though characteristically that was certainly the case.

"How do you know all this?" she asked Blake matter of factly, trying to mask her concern.

"Just a lucky guess," he smiled, enjoying himself and waiting to see Ebony crack under the strain. Which she was determined not to do.

"Bet you're an ace in a quiz," Ebony smiled as well, making light of it all. "I'm pretty good too. Can you imagine us being on the same team? We'd be formidable."

She could see that he wasn't entirely unaware of that from the glint in his eye. She took another ravenous bite of the chicken, casting him a seductive smile. He responded with a wild bite of his chicken drumstick, as if matching her. "Anything else you'd like to know?" Ebony asked. "Or maybe we should just think of going to bed. All this food...it's making me 'hungry'. From the first time I ever saw you, Blake - I think you must know by now that you 'whet my appetite'."

"Why don't you tell me more about the Jzhao Li first?" Blake continued to probe, ignoring her suggestion.

"I don't know that much about it."

"I do," he smiled.

"Then maybe you'd better tell me," Ebony replied, enjoying the verbal sabre rattling more and more. "You obviously know a lot more than I do."

"I wouldn't be too sure about that," Blake replied.

"Honestly, Blake. What I told you earlier is true. We fled our city on a trawler, found the ship drifting, boarded it so we could try and survive. In the midst of the storm, the ship was abandoned. I got in the lifeboat. And I want you to know I'll always owe you and your guys for saving me."

"And the others? Who else was on board?"

Ebony decided she'd better come clean. This guy had one hell of an intelligence network. So it would be wise to provide all the detail she could. Including Mega's attack, which caused them to all flee in the first place.

"This Techno tribe. What else do you know about them?" Blake probed.

"I don't know where they originally came from. They just invaded the city. They were led by this guy - Ram."

Ebony realized from Blake's expression that something about the name registered in a profound way, though Blake was clearly trying to mask his reaction, not wishing to give anything away.

"Ram?" he said, as if to himself. "That's an interesting name." But his demeanour was now cold. He seemed irritated at even hearing the mere mention of the name 'Ram'.

"Have you ever known anyone...with the same name?"

"You ask too many questions!" Blake replied.

Ebony decided to back off. She was pressing the wrong buttons.

"No problem. You're the man. In control. If you ever fancy telling me, then that's up to you, Blake. If not - no skin off my nose," she said, trying to defuse the tense situation.

There was a knock at the door.

"Enter!" Blake called out.

Axel came in, nodded his head respectfully. "Sorry to disturb you, Commander Blake," he said, casting a glance at Ebony. "But I thought you'd want to know. The next intake has arrived."

"I'll be right there," Blake responded.

Understanding he was dismissed, Axel left.

"More categorising?" Ebony asked, sensing that this might be an opportunity for her to consolidate her position. "Any chance I can help? All that branding... I think I could really get into it."

***

On the helicopter deck the clear moon illuminated a fresh intake of slaves being arranged into position. The wind howled. Ebony discovered that these slaves were the last batch due to be processed before the ship arrived, which was due to take them away to wherever they were to be taken.

They were a pathetic-looking bunch, Ebony thought, as she and Blake arrived, crossing the helicopter deck towards the assembly. They all looked absolutely terrified, quaking in fear, the metal chains biting into their ankles, clanking, as they shuffled themselves into place for Blake to examine them, as if on display like pieces of meat.

Suddenly Ebony stopped and gazed in pure disbelief. Standing amidst the group of slaves, she noticed a figure next to a teenage female, and a younger boy and girl. They were all blindfolded. Ebony was stunned. He may not have been able to see her but she could see very clearly and there was no doubt in her mind that it was him. Bray.

CHAPTER THIRTY-SIX

The shipwrecked survivors were in a circle, arms linked together as they stood around the grave, a small pile of rocks stacked, marking the headstone of the deceased, buried deep under the sands of the beach.

May shed aching tears of loss as she knelt down beside the grave, placing her bracelet on the rocks.

Zak had passed away the night before, losing his battle for life.

While the Mall Rats had split up to try and find out what had happened to Ruby, Gel had stayed back at Camp Phoenix with Lottie and the little ones. Sammy was watching over Slade while Zak, who never regained consciousness, slipped away, Trudy taking her turn to keep watch over him, was with him when he died. She had felt for a pulse, feeling none, and tried to revive him, desperately beating on his chest as if to reawaken the life that had once been inside, trying to resuscitate him. But he had gone. There was nothing Trudy or anyone could do for him any more. And it left Trudy absolutely hysterical.

May had become resigned. She was expecting it, for all that she tried to convince herself otherwise. It was a painful irony though, May felt, that she had left Zak's side, going off with Amber to try and find - and then rescue - Ruby from the depths of the Jzhao Li, at around the same time in the night Zak would have departed the world.

All present knew they owed a huge debt to Zak when the Jzhao Li ran aground. He paid the ultimate sacrifice, leaving Slade also critically injured in the process, enabling all the others to have a chance on the lifeboat to survive.

United in grief, even Ram felt emotion. Bonding in adversity, all had been through so much on their long ocean voyage, first on Zak's trawler, then the Jzhao Li.

Ruby's shoulders heaved as she shed her own tears, her anguish fuelled by her sense of guilt. Zak's death may have actually vindicated Ruby's judgement, yet she still was so ashamed of how she had devoted herself on fixing Slade's injuries and wondered if she could have done more to help Zak. But it was too late now. They would never know, Ruby sobbed to herself.

Amber stood next to May, supporting her as her head slumped, resting on Amber's shoulders, her eyes cascading tears.

"Somebody should say something," Jay whispered quietly out of respect, feeling it was important for Zak to be given the send-off he so deserved.

"May?" Amber asked softly, to see what May would like to do, how she wanted to proceed.

But she couldn't contain all the pent up emotion any longer, wailing.

"I just don't understand!" May blabbed through tears. "It's not... fair! What did he do? What had he ever done to anyone?"

"It should have been Ram," Gel pointed out. "If anyone deserves to die - it's Ram."

"Excuse me? I'm actually standing right here, if you haven't noticed," Ram protested, glaring at Gel. "You really are stupid, aren't you? Think I can't hear?"

Gel glared at Ram. He was starting to really get to her. While the others had broken away to search for Ruby the night before, she had been questioning him more about The Collective during their meal at Camp Phoenix being cooked over the open fire Darryl had made.

"I still can't understand," Gel had said. "These Collective... what do they collect?"

Sammy scoffed. "Duh! It's just their name!"

Gel had poked her tongue out at Sammy before Ram interrupted, adding, "Gel's not as dumb as she looks."

"Oh - thanks," Gel had replied, clearly unsure if it was a compliment or an insult before Ram had clarified.

"They do 'collect' people in some ways. All the tribes who work to them. That's why they're called The Collective."

"And we're what... collectables?" Gel had considered.

"I don't know about you, but I sure as hell am not!"

Now at the ceremony, Ellie cut in, still deeply concerned about Jack.

"Gel's right! That should be you in there, Ram. Not Zak. For all the pain you've caused others! And if this Collective has done anything to Jack, I'm warning you. You really will pay!"

"Stop it, you two! Don't start now, of all times, please!" Amber insisted.

"Leave it, Amber. If that's how everyone feels - I'm outta here!" Ram snapped, glaring angrily at Gel and Ellie. "I'll pay my respects in my own way. I'm sorry, May, but it seems my presence here is only making things worse."

Ram stormed away back to Camp Phoenix.

"Ram!" Jay called out, encouraging him to come back. But Ram waved Jay's protests, continuing on.

"That was a terrible thing to say," Amber chastened Gel and Ellie.

"I'm just being honest," Gel replied petulantly.

"And I'm just worried about Jack," Ellie said.

"We're all worried about Jack, Ellie. But please. Try and have some consideration." Amber nodded towards

May, who was struggling, with her emotions threatening to overwhelm her.

"Zak wouldn't have wanted this. All this in-fighting! He would want us to stick together! Help each other..." May said.

"Trudy, would you?..." Amber asked Trudy, who shook her head, sure she would be unable to find any appropriate words to honour Zak.

"Why don't you, Amber? I think it's right that you say something, being the leader," Trudy suggested.

Amber stepped into the centre of their circle as Salene moved to take Amber's place, supporting May, comforting her, the others readjusting themselves to fill in the gap where Ram had been standing.

"None of us choose how we enter this world. Or how we leave it," Amber began, searching for words, the right thing to say. "But we do choose how to live our lives. And Zak chose how to live his life well. He gave so much. Without him, and Slade - their efforts back on the ship - perhaps none of us would have been here today. It is because of Zak that we continue. We live on. As a result of his heroism. His sacrifice. And we owe it to his memory, to make it his legacy, that we go on. And survive. We live our lives the best we can. Anything less... would be a stain on what Zak did for us all. As well as dishonouring all our loved ones who have gone before."

Ellie began to cry. Moved by the occasion, Amber's words. And still worried desperately about Jack.

Trudy comforted Ellie as Amber looked down at the grave. She was sure that all present were reflecting in silence, recalling all those special in their lives they had also lost when the pandemic swept across the globe.

The waves lapped onto the shore in the distance, the morning sun ascending, the hum of insects and choir of birdsong ringing out in the palm trees and jungle beyond.

With the virus bringing so much pain, suffering and death and all the anguish of all those present to honour Zak, it reinforced the sanctity of life, Amber reflected, her words giving comfort to all assembled. But to May and Ruby especially. The purity of life was so precious. But also fleeting. Amber only had to look at her son to be reminded of the wonders of life and was determined that whatever his destiny would be, she would do all she could to ensure he had a future. They all had a future. All her friends. All of her Tribe.

One life had ended, in Zak, Amber continued, stating that another had been saved - through Ruby. And Amber couldn't help but think - though she didn't say - that one more life waited patiently, being the unborn baby of Ruby and Slade, for the day when he - or she - would emerge and take the first steps of their own journey in this strange new world the young inhabited, since the adults had perished.

"Zak. Rest in peace. You will be missed. But you will not be forgotten. You will live in our hearts. In our memories. You made this world a better place. Nothing more can be asked for any of us, in our own lives. God bless you."

Jay smiled slightly to Amber. She had said what needed to, articulated for all within Camp Phoenix, providing much comfort. And hope.

Little did Jay - or any of the others know - that they were all being watched.

* * *

Fascinated by these strangers, his eyes peered out from the cover of the thick jungle undergrowth.

Hidden from sight, the watcher stared at the group gathered on the beach conducting the ceremony for Zak.

What were they doing here in this land? Who were they?

Counting the number of them, as well as those who stayed behind at their camp with the younger ones in the distance, the watcher was satisfied he had seen enough.

Like a shadow in the trees, he moved away quickly, silently. With the wind rustling the leaves that had seconds before been his cover - like a whisper in the breeze, he had gone.

CHAPTER THIRTY-SEVEN

Lex struggled, straining his body with all his might. He was strong, no doubt about it, and if there had been two, maybe three of them, Lex could have stood a chance.

As it was, he was seized by five of the huge native warriors, lifting him by his ankles and hands, while they carried Lex, squirming, over to the Priestess's hut.

Jack and Lia were already being held by other natives nearby, both of them resisting as best they could.

Lex gave everything he could to try and escape, but there was nothing he could do as the warriors snarled, restraining him.

"And people say I have no manners!" Lex bellowed to his captors.

He knew - as did Jack and Lia - that they didn't have a chance, recalling their failed escape the night before.

They had split up, running quickly through the dark jungle. But outnumbered by their pursuers, who obviously knew the area intimately, the position of every tree and plant, Jack and Lex had been caught, overwhelmed by the superior forces of the natives.

Lia had been the last of the escapees to be captured. Living with the native tribe so long, she too had a better awareness of the layout of the land. Upon hearing Jack and Lex's cries when they had been apprehended, Lia had gone back towards them, rather than carrying on to save herself. They needed her help. She alone would be able to speak with the tribe in their native tongue, she surmised, and hoped she would be able to negotiate with the Priestess on not only Jack and Lex's behalf - but make a case for her own defence as well.

All Lia's hopes were dashed, however, by the Priestess's insistence that the original sentence be carried out.

The escape attempt had hardly done Jack and Lex's cause any good, Lia recognized in hindsight. She had undermined the Priestess's authority by rebelling against her, trying to release Jack and Lex.

And now Lia was going to be forced to watch the execution of first Lex, then Jack. The Priestess would decide afterwards what punishment Lia would face for her treachery.

Determined to show her authority, that the customs and traditions of her tribe be upheld, and still sure that Lex and Jack were somehow connected to Blake and his forces who had recently arrived within the environs of their island, the Priestess stood outside her hut, the sharp polished stone of her dagger gleaming in the morning light, the sun continuing to rise up over the horizon.

"Let us go!!" Lex shouted, as he was pushed to the ground, forced into a kneeling position by the warriors.

The Priestess stepped forward, slowly, holding aloft the ceremonial stone dagger so the assembled crowd of villagers could see it clearly. It was hundreds of years old, a connection to their ancestral past, Lia explained.

"Do they think I'll be flattered!? Being wiped out by an antique?" Lex shouted.

"This is it!" Jack said to himself in disbelief. "I've got to wake up from this nightmare! Can't you do or say anything?!" he implored Lia.

Lia bit her lip nervously, wondering exactly just what she could do, then called out suddenly in the native tongue.

"This is a terrible mistake!"

Lex and Jack turned their heads, staring at Lia. What was she saying? All they could hear was the strange guttural sound of the native language flowing from her lips.

Unknown to them, Lia was begging the Priestess for mercy, insisting Jack and Lex were innocent, shipwrecked with their friends. They didn't mean any harm, had no connection whatsoever with this new foreigner who had arrived, instilling terror when he visited the islands, referring to Blake and his forces.

The Priestess shouted back, enraged at Lia's disrespect.

The two white men were criminals, the Priestess shrieked venomously to Lia, in her ancient language. All the tribe had seen what harm could befall them if they studied their history and had seen how foreigners had brought diseases for hundreds of years, just like those in the military and all the people they brought during the height of the pandemic. But even placing that aside, the Priestess felt that it was no coincidence the two strangers were there, obviously spies working with Blake's men who were probably preparing to attack and to gather up more villagers to enslave. Jack and Lex had to be made an example of. And to show that her people are brave warriors who will resist any threat to the bitter end.

Lia tried to argue her case further but the Priestess called out suddenly. One of the warriors clutching Lia thrust his hand over her face, covering her mouth, so she could speak no more, though her garbled cries showed she was continuing to try, wriggling in an effort to get free, desperate to throw herself on the mercy of the Priestess.

"Get your damned hands off her!" Lex threatened, staring at the Priestess defiantly, as the warriors around prevented any more movement from him.

"Some justice!" he spat out with disdain.

The Priestess glared back at Lex, her contempt for all things 'foreign' from the western world, for Lex and Jack, plain to see. Lex thought it was strange how such a striking-looking girl, a picture of perfection, could show so much hostility, hatred, act so violently to others. Be so imperfect, blinded by her beliefs.

Lifting the dagger higher above her head, preparing to strike, the Priestess waited a few more seconds as the sun rose higher into the sky.

Lex prepared for the inevitable blow to arrive. He had never been religious. But he found himself saying a silent prayer anyway. Maybe he was wrong and his Mum and Dad had been right about God - and that he would see them in the afterlife. Soon.

He flinched as the Priestess took aim, ready to strike.

Then she suddenly hesitated.

A native warrior ran into the village at top speed, crying out, calling for attention.

A murmur of unrest, surprise, swept through the villagers.

"What's happening?" Jack asked Lia. He could tell the mood had changed. It was subtle but he, along with Lex, instinctively felt the atmosphere was different even though they didn't understand a word of what was being spoken around them.

The native warrior raced up to the mud hut, panting, out of breath. Then he fell to his knees, bowing before the Priestess in respect, relaying some kind of information.

The Priestess lowered the stone dagger, withdrawing it away from Lex, to his relief, and looked shocked by whatever the native warrior was telling her.

Lia began to cry.

"Is it that bad?" Lex asked.

Jack pleaded. "What is it, Lia?!"

"It's good," Lia said, overjoyed. "It's so good." She could hardly believe it, trying somehow to contain her tears of joy.

* * *

The sun was high in the sky, the intense heat of the day blazing, birds calling, a myriad of other animal and insect life chattering.

Jack never thought he would have seen or heard such a thing again. And it looked, and sounded, beautiful. He had honestly expected to die, earlier. Now, he was thrilled to be alive and couldn't get the grin off his face.

Lex was strangely quiet. By his standards. He hadn't said much since the Priestess had ended the ceremony, allowing him, Jack and Lia to live.

"Thanks for everything, Lia," Lex whispered, touched by the sweet girl who had risked so much on his and Jack's behalf. He gently patted her on the shoulder in gratitude.

Lia caught Lex's admiring glance and blushed slightly.

The three of them were invited into the Priestess's hut and now stood still as the Priestess entered.

Around were ornate carvings of animals from the forest, idols of the spirit world, with which the Priestess communed for guidance.

She knelt on the floor, and compared to the outright hostility she had showed earlier that morning, was now looking serene, with a peaceful countenance. She was deep in thought, searching for answers, and began meditating.

After a while she flicked her eyes open and began to speak in the native language, Lia translating into English after a few seconds delay so Jack and Lex could understand.

"It is all different now," Lia began, explaining what the Priestess was saying. "Everything has changed. Our scout, Kalyut, returned with news that your story was true. He saw others at the beach. People like you. The ruins of a mighty ship nearby. There was a baby. A very young girl. Some people sick and injured. It was as you described. That you are who you said you are. He saw everything that you said. She is now satisfied that you are not a part of Blake's people and mean no threat."

The Priestess took a moment, gathering her thoughts.

"Now we're getting somewhere..." Lex quietly said.

"Kalyut is one of our most trusted warriors," Lia whispered. "He had been sent to check but was late in returning. So the Priestess was sure he had been abducted by enemy forces. He's the one you owe your lives to, for he ran back faster than the wind to bring the news of your innocence."

The Priestess spoke once more.

"You are allowed to go, both of you... back to your people," Lia continued, happy at what she was relaying.

"That's great!" Jack beamed.

Lia's expression began to alter, however, as the Priestess went on, telling Lia everything the animal spirits had told her, of what had to happen now.

Jack and Lex both picked up the change in Lia's demeanour. She looked concerned, worried.

"Lia? Why have you stopped?" Jack whispered.

The Priestess stood up, walking towards Lia, her voice getter louder as she neared.

She was angry now. Shouting into Lia's face.

"Hey - leave her alone!" Lex insisted protectively.

Lia listened intently, showing her respect to the Priestess, absorbing all that she was being told so audibly and at such close range. It obviously wasn't good news.

"What's going on, Lia?" Lex asked.

The Priestess glared at Lia and suddenly yanked off the shell necklace Lia wore, which had actually been made by Lia herself years ago when she was first accepted into the native tribe, and it burst into pieces now as it fell.

The Priestess unleashed a venomous backhanded slap across Lia's face. Lia recoiled, the momentum of the blow knocking her glasses off her face, which also fell onto the floor.

Jack was gobsmacked, stunned at the sudden turnaround.

Lex stepped in front of Lia, trying to defend her.

"If you touch her again, I'll -"

"No, Lex!" Lia insisted, pulling him back.

Jack picked up her glasses from the dirt, blew dust from the lenses, and handed them back to Lia. The one broken glass lens had completely shattered.

Lia began to cry, struggling to keep her composure, obviously shaken by whatever the Priestess had told her, as well as the slap across her face.

The Priestess shrieked, raising her arms as if she was going to lash out again at Lia, at all of them, if they stayed.

"We have to go - now!" Lia said, backing out of the hut, watching the Priestess carefully, her expression showing the hurt she felt not just at what the Priestess had done, hitting her - but what had been said.

"What was that all about?" Lex asked as they stepped outside, dabbing his hand gently on Lia's cheek where she had been struck, wiping away a trickle of blood from her mouth and tears from her eyes, overspilling down one cheek.

Standing outside, the three of them were being totally ignored. Shunned by the other villagers who continued with their daily activities, weaving, cooking, deliberately not paying any attention to the three while they made their way cautiously through the village. The Priestess had shouted so loudly inside, the villagers outside had heard everything.

Lia kept her dignity, fighting back more tears, nobody trying to prevent them now from leaving this time.

"What's happening, Lia?" Jack asked, desperate to know.

"I'm an outcast," Lia admitted, shamefully. "She told me I betrayed her... all of them. I've been expelled from the tribe for treason. I can never return."

"I'm sorry," Lex said, supporting Lia as she staggered now, overcome by emotion, the three of them heading into the jungle, the village receding into the distance as they walked on. Free at last.

"What about us? They're still letting us go - right?" Jack asked.

"You are to take a message back to your friends," Lia said. "The Priestess is sympathetic to your plight but won't sanction anyone being on sacred land. You will have to leave. Get far away from this territory."

"And if we don't?" Lex asked, his inner fire burning. He felt that this was another injustice. The Mall Rats didn't mean anyone any harm and couldn't help being shipwrecked on the island.

"Then you will have insulted the land, the spirits, by your continued presence."

"What does that mean? What happens if we don't leave?" Jack wondered.

"The Priestess would need to cleanse the land of your intrusion, the taint upon it. If you are still at your camp by sunrise tomorrow, or anywhere near the native land, she and the tribe will come for you. They will deal with you. Every single one of your friends."

Jack and Lex were stunned, taking in the news.

"Well, what are waiting for? - Let's go and warn the others!" Jack cried out, doubling his pace as they made their way through the jungle.

"Everything'll be okay, Lia. If we have to, we'll fight. We know how to defend ourselves," Lex promised, trying to reassure Lia.

Lex just didn't know what they would be up against though, Lia thought to herself. Far outnumbered by the native tribe, from what Jack and Lex had told her of their numbers, Lia feared that if Jack and Lex's friends tried to resist and put up a fight, it would be a massacre.

CHAPTER THIRTY-EIGHT

Ebony walked down a twisting, metallic stairwell leading into the bowels of the rig where all the prisoners were being held, pending being transported to God knows where. And for the first time in a long while she had got the bounce back in her step.

She had been absolutely stunned to see Bray earlier on the helicopter deck. There was no doubt in her mind it was him. But what was he doing here with this new intake of slaves, being paraded before Blake and their masters?

Bray's disappearance had been a source of mystery to the entire city. And it wasn't just Amber who worried about what had happened to him. Along with the other members of the Mall Rats, of course.

Despite the troubles they had shared in the past, and although they had crossed swords on a number of occasions, Ebony always had a spot in her heart for Bray. From the very early days at school.

When he went missing after the Technos invaded, Ebony expected the worst and thought he had to be dead, surely.

And yet there he was for some reason amongst all the other prisoners, returned to her like a ghost resurrected from her past.

Now by some miracle, their paths were about to cross again.

She wondered if this was another test concocted by Blake. Letting her interrogate Bray. Not only was he highly intelligent and a strategic thinker, Blake obviously had some kind of impressive intelligence network. He had to, Ebony was sure. How else would he have known so many details about Zoot and the Locos? How much did he know about Ebony?

So she thought it was better for her to come clean and mention she knew one of the new intakes from her homeland. Just in case Blake knew. She wouldn't put it past him, to have some insidious scheme planned with the arsenal of cards he seemed to hold up his sleeve. Ebony had long decided she would need to play her cards carefully and use every bit of cunning in her own arsenal if she had any hope of survival, to elevate herself up in the ranks to work alongside Blake. There was little other option available than to forge an alliance. At least it might keep her from the slave camps.

Blake had questioned her, probing for details of her long lost companion and suggested that she look after the interrogation. He wanted to discover just exactly where Bray had come from prior to being traded. Ebony agreed, promising to report back every detail.

Ebony, forever calculating, decided she would massage any facts if it suited her plight. And was intrigued herself to know just exactly what had happened to Bray since he went missing in the city after the Techno invasion. But one thing for sure. She would selectively reveal whatever she was about to uncover. If it was some kind of test, then this was her chance. To show Blake that he could trust her. Even if he did know more than he was letting on. If not, then she was in a win win situation, feeling she could manipulate matters to her own benefit. With the bonus being she would get more of a handle on this region by finding out how Bray fit into it all.

Ebony stopped at the entrance of a cell.

"I've come to interrogate one of the latest intakes," Ebony said to the two burly guards standing outside while glancing around discretely, checking if there might be a camera and if Blake was watching. Or even listening somehow. If so, it was important for her to let him know that she was on his side.

She was met with silence, the guards looking at her suspiciously.

"Well? Aren't you gonna let me in?"

"This deck is out of bounds unless authorised," one of the guards replied.

"If you know what's good for you, don't answer a question - with a question!" Ebony shouted.

She was laying it on thick in case she was being observed, sure Blake would like that, flattered that she was carving herself out of his own control freak mould.

"What - do I have to go and explain to Blake that his men don't follow orders? I am his woman, do you understand? And he's the man! He sent me to interrogate and I can't do that standing here now, can I?! Open the damn door so I can go inside. Or do I have to smash it open using your thick heads?"

The guards exchanged glances with each other and one probed cautiously. "You were sent by the Commander?"

"There you go again. I'm the one supposed to ask questions. So if you know what's good for you, just open the door, will you? Then I might put in a good word about you both with Blake, when I see him tonight," Ebony continued, reminding them of her status.

The guards unlatched the heavy bolt and pushed open the door. Ebony entered, kicking it closed and stared at Bray, taken aback by what she saw.

He was being kept in solitary confinement.

He had apparently been 'difficult', refusing to follow orders, co-operate, and had been beaten for not showing respect.

Now Bray was hanging in the centre of the darkened cell, his arms stretched above his head and secured to girders in the ceiling, numbed by the chains which had been bound around his hands, the manacles biting into his wrists painfully.

He was still blindfolded. Ebony felt a wave of sympathy. He looked in a mess, his face bruised, swollen, his lips cracked and smeared with matted, congealed blood.

"Well, look what the tide's washed in. Fancy seeing you here," Ebony said, checking out the prison cell for signs of any lenses, still unsure if she was being observed.

"Eloise?" Bray whispered quietly, weakly, a degree of unease in his tone.

"Eloise? No, it's me, Ebony. Don't tell me you've forgotten all about me?"

Bray wondered once again if this was a simulation. Ebony was just as confused as he seemed to be, as he continued, as if lost in another world. "Is Martin here?"

"Not unless you're in Heaven," Ebony replied, bewildered.

"Ebony... Is that really you?"

"Last time I looked in the mirror."

"What are you doing here?" Bray said with sudden interest as the realization was settling in amidst his disorientated state.

"I was about to ask you the same question," Ebony replied, deciding not to use the word interrogate, feeling she would probably get more out of Bray that way.

Bray was struggling to remain conscious after his beating but Ebony managed to decipher that rather than being uncooperative just for the sake of it, he was trying to look out for Emma, Tiffany and Shannon, who were separated on another deck. He seemed deeply anguished, pleading for any news, desperate to know that they were alright.

She promised she'd check it out, reassuring him that they would be fine and no harm could come to any of them. As long as he answered her questions.

"You're not involved with these people, whoever they are, are you?" Bray asked weakly.

"Not yet," Ebony replied, gazing once again around for any lenses and hoping if Blake was listening he'd be pleased as she continued. "But I'd sure like to be."

"Who... are they?" Bray asked.

"They're more interested in finding out more information... about you, Bray."

Bray was finding it all increasingly difficult to comprehend, struggling through his pitiful state, revealing that he had tried to ask for Emma to remain with her younger brother and sister, pointing out that Emma was blind, and received a beating for speaking out of turn prior to being led to the cells and held in solitary confinement.

On another floor, on higher decks, Bray was sure he could hear the distant whimpering and wailing from all the prisoners, in obvious distress, being held in different parts of the sprawling rig. It was an awful chorus of sobbing, pleading, panic. But he couldn't distinguish if he heard Emma, Shannon or Tiffany, which seemed to add to his concern. He was totally disorientated, forever asking if this was a simulation.

Ebony reiterated that there was no virtual reality programming here and that it would be wise for Bray to co-operate. To tell her all about what had happened to him. But she couldn't get any sense other than he had been traded as a slave.

She asked if that meant he had been categorised. Before. He didn't reply. His head had slumped forward, leaving Ebony suspecting that he must have passed out.

She reached up, checking his neck for a pulse, his skin for any sign of branding. Then ripping his shirt, she noticed on the side of his shoulder the letter 'L'.

She lifted a pail of water and hurled the contents at him. The shock brought him around, though he was still in a semi-conscious state.

"What about the others?" Bray asked weakly. "Amber...?"

So typical of Bray, she thought. He hadn't changed one bit since she last saw him, all that time long ago back in the city. Always putting the interests of others ahead of his own. Especially where Amber was concerned.

Ebony had fallen for him in a big way in the old days before the 'virus' wiped out all the adults. He had been the Captain of the basketball team at school. And she was in competition with Trudy, who had tried to get her claws into him. If opposites attract, Ebony was certainly drawn to all the standards he seemed to set himself, his strict moral code. She found it boring at times. And was always attracted more to the bad boys. But couldn't deny there was something about Bray which had always intoxicated her, finding him not just physically attractive but admiring all his qualities and traits, his great strength of character.

Even so, she found herself equally drawn to his brother, Zoot, and had used all her skills manipulating events, quickly rising up through the ranks of the Locos, eventually becoming leader after Zoot's death.

Ebony had always thought it a strange irony how she could be drawn to both brothers, who had become estranged through the ensuing darkness of the post-adult world. And wondered how both could have been born from the same parents. As if one was driven by the forces of light. And Zoot? Well, Ebony never believed he was evil. More of a rebel. She was mind blown by his ideology of 'Power and Chaos' from the first time he rose up at school, battling against any and all forms of authority. Ebony could relate to that. In some ways, even Bray was a rebel, refusing to conform to anything other than what he perceived to be right, the best way forward.

Ebony decided to steer any conversation away from the Mall Rats. She didn't want herself to become implicated in any negative way. Assuming Blake knew about them. If he did, he was certainly shrewd enough not to provide any unnecessary detail.

Ebony probed more about this Eloise person Bray had referred to. And was gripped by an awful sense of fear, wondering if Blake was somehow involved in all this through his references to 'L' for 'Laboratory' branding. There seemed to be a link with the small letter 'L' marked on Bray's shoulder. Ebony smiled slightly to herself, wondering what Bray might think if he only knew she was also marked the same way on one cheek of her backside. Who knows, one day he might even see for himself.

Bray, through his deeply confused state, revealed that he had been subjected to so much virtual reality simulation he had difficulty knowing what was real and what was illusion anymore. All he knew was that he was once held in a compound, which seemed to be exploiting his 'bloodline' for whatever agenda, explaining that there were many within the compound referring to themselves as 'Zootists'. All dressed like his late brother and appeared to have been indoctrinated into his ideology.

Ebony wondered if he was hallucinating. He seemed sincere though in his recollections. And she got the gist that Eloise, whoever she was, controlled wherever he had been kept.

Ebony was absorbed by Bray's tale of his escape. How he had ended up in a military base, being saved by two young children and a blind girl, leaving Ebony to feel that maybe Bray had indeed lost it, sure a capable warrior like Bray didn't need to rely on someone like that to survive.

Bray kept asking about the Mall Rats and Amber. In an attempt to avoid any of his questions, Ebony took delight in advising that Amber was probably dead. That would hopefully shut him up.

She had always despised Amber. Not just for what Ebony perceived to be her piety. She had caused Ebony no end of problems in the past throughout all the scores and clashes since the days of the Locos.

It had been a much more personal matter though - the fact that Amber and Bray had fallen deeply in love, Ebony perceiving way back when that Amber had actually taken the place of Ebony. She had desperately wanted Bray for herself.

Secretly though, Ebony had difficulty suppressing that she felt a sense of jubilation. Not at seeing Bray hurt. But that he was still alive. And especially that they had been reunited.

Destiny seemed to have done her a favour, as it had a habit of doing. With Bray showing up. In exactly the same place as her. And she was almost orgasmic, thinking that she could drive a wedge between him and Amber. It was an exquisite feeling. Revenge wasn't just sweet. It was beautiful.

And the bonus was she could use it all to elevate her own position.

She had never been lucky in love. Now she wondered if she might be more lucky in hate.

"You've been sensible, Bray," she said, raising her tone in case Blake was listening. "Telling me all you have. I'll report back to my man and might come back another time if I need to clarify anything."

"This is real - isn't it?" Bray asked, still disorientated. "Not just some simulation?"

"Oh, it's real alright," Ebony replied, casting a discrete glance at what she suspected was the small lens of a camera high in the ceiling.

"Good seeing you again. Hope you enjoy your stay!"

She drew back her arm and unleashed a powerful blow into Bray's face, blood oozing from the wound on his lip, which opened up.

He slumped his head forward, his body swinging back and forth slowly as if he was a human punch bag while Ebony stormed out, nodding to the guards, who swung the heavy bolt back noisily to secure the door.

CHAPTER THIRTY-NINE

"I am so glad to see you!" Ellie gushed, wrapping her arms lovingly around Jack, giving him a close hug.

"If this is the kind of reaction I'll get - I might have to go missing more often," Jack quipped, enjoying Ellie's attention.

"Don't you dare... you have no idea how much I've missed you! We were so worried."

Jack and Lex had returned to Camp Phoenix a few hours earlier and their reappearance after several days missing was just the good news the entire Tribe needed to raise morale and lift spirits, following the tragic death of Zak.

The others had filled Jack and Lex in on what occurred while they had been away. Both were saddened to hear of Zak's passing. Since they had missed the Tribe's funeral ceremony, the two had already visited Zak's grave to pay their personal respects.

May was further down the beach, having gone off from the others so she could spend the time she needed to grieve and try to come to terms with the loss. While Amber called the others together for a meeting so they could discuss their options in light of Jack and Lex's return. Especially all the details they revealed of their captors, along with the ultimatum to abandon Camp Phoenix by sunrise.

They also filled Lex and Jack in on all the information about The Collective and why Ram was so uneasy, claiming that they might even be lurking menacingly on the island, that it could just be a matter of time before their paths crossed.

"If there's any truth in all of it," Lex had mentioned, "maybe we should just gift wrap Ram and hand him over as a present. He's their enemy. Not our's."

"You're wrong, Lexy-boy," Ram had replied. "Believe me. The Collective are a threat to us all."

Amber and the others tried to check if the native tribe could somehow be involved with The Collective, linked in some way.

Lia dismissed any such notion. She had been kneeling on the warm sands by the fire staring into the distance, as if in a daze, still upset about her fall out with the Priestess, worried about the consequences of what she had set in motion by helping Jack and Lex.

Jay asked more about Blake. Lia explained what she had told Jack and Lex, that he and his men had arrived recently. She didn't know much about them. Except that they had rounded up some of the warriors who were hunting, and seemed to be slave traders.

Ram was uneasy by the revelation, which didn't go unnoticed by the others.

"You don't know anything about THEM, I hope?" Amber had enquired.

Nothing would have surprised her with Ram anymore. But he reassured everyone he had never heard of anyone called Blake. Though that didn't rule out that he could be involved with The Collective. Along with some of the other tribes. Lia doubted that, advising that in the aftermath of the pandemic there were other pockets of survivors within the surrounding islands who formed themselves into various tribes. And apart from one known as The Fallen, most were trying to live in harmony. Like the Roaches, who based themselves on the other side of the island in an old World War 2 military base.

Ram questioned Lia for details of the base. It didn't sound like it would have been a hidden compound like the one in Eagle Mountain.

Lia mentioned that in the far north, there was talk of mysterious goings on in the mountainous region. But she didn't have any other detail. Just rumours that whoever was in the area had also recently arrived and were trading slaves. Ram certainly wasn't reassured that this meant they weren't involved in The Collective.

"The thing you've got to all realise about The Collective," Ram had explained, "is that they gather all kinds of people. Some might be used as slaves. But they are also after leaders, the best brains -"

"Well, that rules you out," Lex interrupted, sure that Ram wasn't so smart if he had gotten himself involved.

Ram agreed. That if he knew then what he knew now, there was no way that he would have become involved with Kami and his network. He was aware from their online relationship when Kami was a member of a guild, that he was always trying to expand, inspired by some of the greatest empires in history. Like the Spartans. But had no idea that he'd use the same strategies after the pandemic.

"I understand some of you might not have agreed with what I was trying to achieve with the Technos. And it's just the same. I didn't agree with the way Kami wanted to operate with this Collective of his. But by then, it wasn't just a matter of walking away," Ram said.

"I still don't understand what he was involved with?" Gel said.

"You don't want to know," Ram continued. "The full extent of it. He even had plans to try and repopulate. Just as the adults were going to do -"

"How can you be so sure? 'Repopulate'?" Jack interrupted.

"And how can you be so sure you can 'trust' everyone around here?" Ram asked, casting a discrete glance at Lia.

"What's that supposed to mean?" Lex snapped angrily at Ram.

"I just want to be careful. With anything I say. Especially with any 'strangers' around."

"If you've got anything else you need to say, then you owe it to us. Owe it to everyone. To let us know," Amber insisted.

"I've told you all I know. I promise. It's just, when Kami and his people were hacking into the government computers they found some files about some plans to repopulate. And I think it gave Kami some ideas. He was even thinking about developing breeding programmes. So don't for one minute just think that slaves would be clearing the land, labouring."

"You mean some... might spend all day 'doing it'?" Darryl beamed, in growing interest, intrigued just by the thought of it.

"No. Not just any kind of people. But those with the right kind of DNA. The right kind of brain. Skills. And don't even think about what he'd do to anyone if they crossed him!" Ram shuddered as he considered the consequences. "I'll have a hell of a price on my head!"

"Well, let's just hope it's as BIG as your head," Lex replied.

"Not now," Amber stated. "Please, Lex. Our priority is to deal with all that Lia has told us. And with this deadline of her tribe, we don't have long."

Trudy agreed and was becoming almost hysterical, wondering what might happen. "They seem like a bunch of savages, from what Jack and Lex told us."

"I wouldn't call them 'savages' exactly," Lex said.

"Well, they hardly seem to have been friendly, threatening to sacrifice Jack and Lex," May stated, in mounting unease.

This was far from a deserted paradise, everyone debated, realising that the island they were marooned on was considered to be sacred land.

Jay wondered if it might be an idea for them to try and travel to one of the other outlying islands in the region. Or even to go to another part of the island, if the Priestess and indigenous tribe were a threat. But he agreed with the others that they couldn't very well travel with Slade. And they all resolved that they were in this together and had no option but to stay.

Though Ram thought what Ruby had earlier suggested concerning Slade and Zak might be a wise resolution so that they could get out of there as far as they could. While they still could. May was horrified, as was Ruby, along with everyone else, that Ram could be so ruthless to even suggest that they just abandon Slade, leave him to die, with Ruby ironically stating that from hereon in, it would never be an option for her. Ever again.

Sammy felt terrible about it but was so scared that he thought there were some merits in what Ram was suggesting, sure that the needs of the many outweighed the needs of the few. Ram didn't like it any more than anyone else but it had always been the way of the world, he reflected. None more than now in the post adult world. They could either choose to move on. Or stay and fight. But he didn't fancy their chances. The tribe of Lia's seemed to be capable adversaries.

Everyone took a vote. The majority decided that they should stay. And if the indigenous tribe showed up, hoped that Lia might translate their appeals to give more time until Slade recovered so that they could then at least have a chance to find somewhere else to settle. Away from the sacred lands, which they all respected, fully aware of how proprietorial they felt about their shopping mall that had once been their home. So they could well imagine how Lia's tribe must view their lands, which had been their home for centuries.

Lia was taken to the nearby shelter that the others had built, rudimentarily constructed with branches and palm leaves providing some measure of protection from the sun and elements for Slade inside. He had remained unconscious for several days now. All were deeply concerned how much longer he could last, how long he would stay alive.

His wound had been regularly re-dressed and was showing signs of healing. But Amber and the others were still unsure if he was suffering from septicaemia, if infection was travelling through his entire bloodstream.

Lia suggested that she and some of the others gather a selection of native plants, revealing to them - as she did to Jack and Lex previously - that her parents were conventional doctors within the United Nations Task Force fleet. And that Lia herself had learned a lot from her time with the indigenous tribe, who used homeopathic medicines to cure all manner of ailments.

The Mall Rats didn't need much convincing, recalling Tai San's gifts and abilities. She, too, had been in tune with the natural world and was able to concoct different remedies for different problems. Lex was affected as he thought of Tai San and really missed her. As did all of her friends. Especially in this situation.

Like Tai San, Lia seemed to know what all the plants and juices from them could do. Though privately, Amber wondered if Lia could deal with blood poisoning, if indeed that's what was affecting Slade. She felt he would probably need to remain on antibiotics. But they had a limited supply, with the amounts Ruby had managed to recover from the wreck of the Jzhao Li soon to also run out. But it was worth a try.

While Ruby and Salene worked with Lia in her attempts to assist Slade, the others agreed with Amber that it might be sensible to try and implement some form of defence plan. As a contingency in case the Priestess and indigenous tribe were unsympathetic to their plight, refusing to give them an extension to the deadline before they had to leave. Or worse still, unleashed an attack.

Lex wouldn't put it past them from all he had observed. But thought they might still have a chance.

The survivors were outnumbered by the population of the village but most were females or children, with many warriors having been seized by Blake to be traded as slaves.

Lex thought that they might have a chance to repel any form of attack, especially when Lia advised that the Priestess would never leave the village unprotected. If an attack occurred it would come from a raiding party rather than the entire warrior contingent.

It still didn't provide Trudy with much comfort but Amber seemed more concerned and offended by Lex's chauvinistic reference to the female members of the indigenous tribe being purely in charge of more domestic matters.

Lia tried to calm matters, explaining that within the culture no female was expected to fight. Their duty was to care for the children as well as prepare food and look after their men.

"I suppose you enjoyed yourself, did you, Lex?" Amber asked, knowing full well that it would be the type of structure he could fit into quite easily.

"As a matter of fact, I did. In a weird way," Lex had replied. "And no, not because of having a bunch of girls looking after me like servants. I just liked their way of life."

Lex had encountered many warring tribes back in the concrete jungle in the city, initially oppressed by the Locos. As had all the sectors through the warring tribes.

But this indigenous tribe who had taken in Lia didn't seem to be the type who would invade. Not like the Technos. They just wanted to be left alone. To follow their ways. And Lex respected that. They had no ambitions to conquer and rule, to expand their empire.

They weren't like this 'Collective' Ram had gone on about.

Lex had been dragged up in the gutters on some very mean streets. And in many ways he felt all the people he had dealt with throughout the anarchic days that followed the pandemic seemed to be more primitive and untrustworthy than the people who had held him captive.

Jack intimated that Lex seemed to have the hots for the Priestess, leading everyone to suspect if Lex had in reality been touched by the way of life the indigenous tribe seemed to strive for. Or whether or not the Priestess represented a conquest Lex had in mind, which was fuelling his blurred fantasy of living with nature.

Lex couldn't help but admit that the Priestess was statuesque and had something really mysterious about her. She was like a Goddess.

"With a capability of killing people," Trudy added, recalling what Jack and Lex told them all, that they only had minutes to spare before their throats would be slit by a ceremonial dagger, which caused Ellie to shudder about the mere thought of it.

Lia confirmed that it would be unwise to underestimate the Priestess. Or the reactions of the village. They would always be prepared to fight and die for all they believed in. And would also kill to protect their way of life as well.

Amber tried to motivate the others after the meeting, feeling that having come this far they couldn't give up now and had to give it everything they had. She was still hopeful they could reason with Lia's people. But if not, she was determined they be prepared as much as they could.

The majority of the group began to fortify Camp Phoenix, making improvised spears, Amber showing them what she had learned during her time with Pride and the Eco tribe. More tree branches were stripped, the ends of them sharpened against rocks to make spears. The Eco tribe had used them for fishing and hunting, and Amber dreaded the prospect of having to use them as weapons.

They gathered coconuts, which Jay thought would be useful as other weapons.

And began even building an improvised defence perimeter with large branches, which were shaved into protruding points over barricades of metal, which had been washed ashore amidst the flotsam and jetsam sprawled along the beach from the hull of the wreck of the Jzhao Li.

"It's not all bad, is it, Lex?" Gel asked, as she searched debris littering the sand with Lex beside her, also looking for anything which might be of use in building their defence. "Look!" Gel continued, noticing a pile of plastic toiletries. "I've run out of shampoo! This must be my lucky day! "

"Brilliant, Gel. That's just what we need," Lex said sarcastically, smiling slightly while watching Gel lift the containers. "If those warriors show up and you offer to wash their hair, or give them a beauty treatment - I'm sure they'll surrender. Immediately."

She poked her tongue out, gathering as many toiletries as she could while Lex hauled mammoth sheets of debris toward the barricade.

If Lia's tribe wanted to mix it up, then at least they would make sure they were ready to give as good as they got.

CHAPTER FORTY

The sky was like a planetarium, filled with stars.

Ruby kept up her relentless vigil, laying near Slade in the makeshift shelter.

The others tried to sleep as well but most within Camp Phoenix were restless, wondering what events would unfold when the indigenous tribe arrived at dawn. Though Lottie, Sammy, Brady and the baby were lost, deep in slumber.

Amber had agreed to take the first shift on night watch and would soon be replaced by Jay. After the events of the day she welcomed the opportunity to be alone, gathering her thoughts, reflecting on all that had occurred. And what might transpire. But she, like the others, was relieved that at least Jack and Lex had returned safely and was pleased for Ellie, knowing all too well the pain suffered by the disappearance of a loved one.

Amber was keen to try and grab a few hours sleep, feeling particularly drained, exhausted. Physically. As well as mentally. Sleep, at least, provided some refuge from the world young people now inhabited. At least the past could be relived through dreams, when the world had been a better place, before the adults had all perished during the pandemic.

Amber had also met up with Bray through her dreams but invariably woke up with a start, disappointed that it wasn't real. Since Jay came into her life, her dreams - and memories of Bray - had never subsided. And had always left her feeling guilty. That she was betraying Jay. But rationalised it to herself that Bray would always be by her side either in dreams or memories, and that was the right way for it to be, given that he was the father of their child.

Suddenly Amber heard a sound and gazed around, uneasily.

She couldn't see anything. It must be an animal or bird, rustling the leaves of the trees. Or maybe in her sub-consciousness, she was just tense, wondering what the dawn would bring when Lia's tribe were due to arrive.

There was another sound. But this time Amber noticed figures through the darkness, moving quickly in the undergrowth.

Before she had even had a chance to bang the metal warning device to raise an alarm, Amber knew that they were under attack, and she shouted out a warning.

"Jay! Lex! Everyone!" she shouted, panic-stricken.

The others sprung into action, Trudy protectively gathering up the little ones and screaming hysterically as Axel and his men appeared from the undergrowth, converging on the camp.

Lex grabbed one of the makeshift spears they had fashioned earlier that day and tried to strike out at one of the attackers. But another attacker was on him, seizing the spear out of Lex's grasp.

Lex was nevertheless able to unleash a powerful kick into the attacker's groin, doubling him, before striking out another blow at the other attacker.

"Amber!" Salene screamed in warning while climbing to her feet, noticing another attacker knocking Amber to the ground, then pressing the full weight of his massive forearm into Amber's throat, preventing her from moving.

Behind Salene, yet another attacker appeared, grabbing her.

Darryl was immediately there, striking the attacker with a log. Although the attacker sunk to his knees, other members of the raiding party quickly overwhelmed Salene and Darryl, having the benefit of surprise.

Amber struggled, desperate to get up and to her baby, to protect him.

Unexpectedly her attacker released his hold, having been smashed in the head with a coconut which Jay had hurled, before spinning to confront others in the raiding party unleashing vicious blows.

Ram scrambled and dove behind a log, as if he was trying to be invisible, his own safety being paramount to him.

Jack, Ellie and May were putting up strong resistance, Ellie hurling flaming branches at their attackers. But in no time at all they were subdued, as was Sammy, who was lifted up by the scruff of his neck but still swung wildly.

Ruby, in the makeshift shelter watching over Slade, was standing at the ready as two attackers arrived, managing to floor one with a punch. But the other seized her. Ruby bit into his arm but apart from a groan, it did no good. Her attacker had her fully restrained.

Trudy continued her sustained wail, clutching desperately at Brady, Lottie running to gather Amber's baby in her arms.

But the baby was yanked away.

Amber couldn't believe her eyes.

It was Ebony.

It felt to Amber that time had stood still. And that she was alone, oblivious to all the panic around her at the height of the ambush. All she could focus on was her son, her precious baby, who meant more to her than anyone else in the world. And there he was, clutched

331

in Ebony's arms, crying. He needed his mother. He was calling. Frightened by Ebony holding him prisoner. Amber dreaded to think what would happen if she reached out and tried to get him.

Ebony took great delight in Amber's pained expression, then gazed around, shouting.

"If you know what's good for him - for all of you - back off, everyone, and do exactly what I say!"

She looked as if she would drop the baby on its head, which caused Amber to freeze in her tracks, still trying to come to terms and gather her composure from the sudden surprise of the attack.

Gel was laying sprawled on the ground, having fainted when she first noticed the raiding party.

All that the others noticed was that they were outnumbered and never stood a real chance.

Lia had put on her glasses when the ambush first occurred and was now trying to fix her gaze through the one good lens as more and more of Axel's men were arriving and rounding up the members of Camp Phoenix, all gazing unbelievably at Ebony giving Axel instructions, identifying who was who.

A spear thudded into the sand.

All present recoiled as more spears sailed through the air, the sounds sibilant like whistling wind.

Native warriors from the indigenous tribe appeared from the jungle undergrowth, ululating, causing Trudy to scream even more hysterically, accompanied by Brady and Lottie. Even Sammy was struggling to contain himself and was crying out in fear.

"Lia - what's going on!" Amber shouted.

"I don't know! I don't know!" Lia replied, deeply concerned, unsure of what was happening herself other than the warriors were engaged in combat with Axel and his raiding party, who were now in turn being outnumbered.

"I don't know what the hell is going on, but it seems to me that either the natives either set their alarms early - or they're here to help us!" Lex called out, unleashing a blow against one of Axel's men before rushing to Jay and Amber, who were converging on Ebony, backing up.

"Let the baby go!" Amber pleaded. "Please, Ebony! Let him go!"

"Sure!" Ebony said, "No problem," realising that Axel's raiders were losing the fight.

Ram, peering over the log, stood, then nodded to more warriors rushing past and shouted out a friendly greeting to them.

"Hey! How you doing, guys? Am I glad to see you! The name's Zak," he added for good measure.

Then he crouched again, tried to hide, realizing that the warriors didn't seem to be that friendly and were purely intent on their task of subduing whatever resistance they encountered.

Before long, there was no resistance.

Lex noticed the Priestess approaching, her feathers rippling in the wind as it blew her long hair, a spear clutched in one hand.

Behind her, other warriors followed, looking fierce, daubs of warpaint and tattoos covering their faces and well-built bodies, all of them similarly armed with spears.

Finally arriving into Camp Phoenix, the Priestess's gaze was riveted on Lia.

Unexpectedly, she called out in her native language, a melodious flow of sounds mixed with guttural inflections, clicking noises. It was as if she was calling like a bird in the jungle, her voice carrying over the wind and hysteria of sobbing from Lottie, Sammy, Brady and baby Bray. Though Trudy seemed to be gathering her composure and stood gazing around unbelievably at what was transpiring, as did her fellow Mall Rats.

"What's she saying?" Lex shouted to Lia, confused as the warriors continued to assemble Axel's raiding party.

"She is saying that the actions of the tribe should show what loyalty really means. I might have been treacherous, but that is not the way of the Priestess and her people."

Lia continued translating, advising that although the ultimatum for them all to leave the sacred lands had still been put in place, one of her hunters had noticed a large boat approaching, which he knew belonged to Blake. And despite all Lia had done, the Priestess could never allow her to be taken as a slave, as had occurred to some of the warriors of the tribe previously.

Ebony crossed to Lia. "Thank God for that! At last I've met someone with common decency! Tell her, will you? Go on, tell her that I might be able to help. I know all about Blake!"

Axel and the others in the raiding party cast Ebony a surprised glance, as did the Mall Rats.

Ram peered again over the log and swallowed nervously as the Priestess hurled the spear she was holding, which thudded into the ground near Ebony.

"Somehow, I don't think she believes you," Amber said. "And you don't need any translator to let you know neither do we."

Ebony, thinking quickly, tried to plead her case. To let everyone know what had happened to her after she left the Jzhao Li. How she had drifted, been captured by Blake, a tyrannical tribe leader, and only by the skin of her teeth had recently been able to make good her escape, accompanying the others on a boat from the oil rig where Blake and his people were based.

"This guy, Blake - he's crazy! You've got to believe me! After all I've gone through, I'm lucky to still be alive!"

"Well, that serves you right for abandoning ship, doesn't it?" Jay snarled.

"I didn't abandon ship," Ebony pleaded. "I was trying to get the lifeboat prepared. Not just for me. For everyone. But when I climbed aboard, the ropes gave way. It wasn't my fault. I got stranded. And if you think it was easy for me drifting alone for days at sea before being picked up by Blake and his thugs, then you're as crazy as he is!"

Lex and the others scoffed. Not buying Ebony's story of being a damsel in distress, even if she did break down sobbing when relaying all that had happened. She was tougher than this and was clearly trying to make a meal out of the situation.

"How can anyone not believe me?" Ebony said.

"They've had a lot of practice," Ram cut in, casting a disdainful glance at the others. Then he suddenly stopped and gazed uneasily as the Priestess spoke up, in her native language.

"What's she saying, Lia?" Amber asked.

"She wants to talk with you. All of you."

* * *

When the dawn broke, the sky was ablaze in a multitude of colour. Few could have foreseen what the new day would bring.

Having prepared to face the ultimatum given by the Priestess and the indigenous tribe, the Mall Rats had unexpectedly encountered Ebony. With Ram uneasily wondering if her cohorts were a part of his long lost adversary, Kami, and The Collective.

Lia translated while Amber provided details of the Mall Rats and their past.

Lex interrupted occasionally, boasting of his exploits, advising that he was a mighty warrior back in the city and that the Priestess's group would have been impressed if they ever saw him in action, even if he was taken by surprise. On his own patch, he was formidable.

Much to Lex's disappointment, the Priestess didn't pay much attention, preferring to focus more on what life was like for them in the 'uncivilised' world, still highly suspicious of foreigners and struggling to bridge the cultural gap, unable to understand why there were so many warring tribes in their homeland.

Amber made a good case that not all of their people were like that. Explaining that the Mall Rats, at least, were certainly different. They had hoped to build a better world out of the ashes of the old, introducing social charters, educational system for the young, even a judicial framework. Representing remnants from their old world. From what the adults who had gone before had sought to put in place. And that in many ways the Mall Rats were no different to the Priestess and her people. Honouring the past and their ancestors in their attempts at building a better future.

The Priestess softened the more Amber spoke. Encouraged by her reaction, Lia prompted May, Salene, Trudy, Jay, Ellie and Jack to tell the Priestess how they felt, confirming all Amber had said. Even Lottie and Sammy were invited to speak up about what life was like being a Mall Rat. And even Gel inadvertently made an impression, intrigued by and complimenting the Priestess on her hair and make up design. The Priestess considered

Gel for a long moment, then nodded gratefully, as Lia translated what had been said. Gel cast a look at Lex, proud of herself, and Lex faked a weak smile. Talk of hair and make up was the least of what he had expected as he listened to Lia telling Gel that the Priestess thinks her hair was lovely as well.

Only Ram was prevented from speaking too much, with Lia being unsure of where he really stood, given his account of The Collective. She was aware that he had invaded the city and that would hardly endear him to the Priestess or her people, who had suffered from the invasions of foreigners themselves throughout their long history.

Ebony, Axel and the raiding party were being held in an empty container. Ebony had tried again to retrieve her position, pleading that she had been taken prisoner and had no option but to go along with them. But had tried to devise a plan to help the Mall Rats. Everyone. And was on the point of shouting out to warn them of the ambush, but was restrained.

She mentioned that she had seen Bray, sure that this would be her ace card in especially winning Amber back on her side. But Amber was having none of it. Not from the same person who, years before had tortured Bray, along with the other members of the Mall Rats, with the false information that Amber herself had died during the explosion at Eagle Mountain.

Ebony was devastated and continued pleading to be given a chance before she, Axel and the party were locked up in the container while Amber and the others had a chance to decide what they might do with them.

Lia translated that the Priestess felt they should be sacrificed for their treachery. Particularly if Ebony was once a member of their tribe and had turned against them. Ram believed there was some merit in that.

There was a moment when Lia felt that the Priestess might also be sending her threatening messages that she might suffer the same fate.

But Lia finally relaxed, sensing that the Priestess was warming to her again, the more she heard the Mall Rats giving a good account of who they were, what they aspired to achieve for their Tribe. A fair and just society. Freedom and equality for all.

That was the way of the old world, Amber reiterated. And although an ocean might have divided the Priestess and her tribe geographically and they couldn't speak the same language, philosophically they were on a similar plane.

Amber made sure that Lia let the Priestess and her people know that they were grateful for their assistance. And had they not intervened, they shuddered to think what might have occurred had Ebony and the raiding party succeeded in their mission.

All the Mall Rats made a point to also let the Priestess know that they didn't mean any disrespect by being on sacred lands. They were here by accident. Not choice.

Lex wanted Lia to emphasise that destiny could have been responsible. For bringing them all together. And if the Priestess got in tune spiritually, then she would see that had the indigenous tribe not captured Lex and Jack in the first place, then they wouldn't have been able to have helped the Mall Rats. And if that was the case, then the prisoners wouldn't be now being held in the container. So even Lia played a part. And with the dawn breaking across the sky, if she really thought about all he was saying, then she would know that it must have been meant to be.

Jack smiled slightly to himself as he listened, sure that Tai San must have made a real impression during her time together with Lex. Either that or Lex was referencing all she had taught him in an attempt to connect with the Priestess.

Ram was even impressed with the way in which Lex was speaking. It didn't take a genius to notice a degree of flirtation in Lex's entire demeanour, but there was a wisdom as well in what he was saying.

Ram asked Lia to check with the Priestess if she knew of The Collective. Or if she thought the raiding party being held might even be involved. Lia didn't think it was a good idea to get into that area at all. It might only inflame matters.

The Priestess was furious enough that foreigners had invaded and had taken some of her warriors as slaves. This sparked an idea in Amber, who suggested that there might be a way for the Mall Rats to repay the Priestess and her people, along with securing the position of both tribes.

Lia confirmed that the Priestess said she was open to hearing any proposition. And the others were just as eager to discover what Amber had in mind.

CHAPTER FORTY-ONE

Blake stomped down the twisting, circular metal staircase and into a corridor, his heavy boots echoing throughout the cavernous deck as he crossed to the cell.

Flanked by two huge guards who obediently followed, Blake was silent, deep in thought, his face a mask of concentration.

He regretted giving Ebony the assignment.

Blake had met enough people in his life to know if someone could be trusted. Or, so he thought. A large part of him still doubted her. But he had to admit that she was starting to sound as if she might be genuine.

And if not, then Axel and his raiding party should have been sufficiently well-trained and capable to 'deal' with her in a double-cross.

Blake just couldn't understand what could have happened. The raiding party was long overdue. And he was furious at himself but just couldn't help being lured into the web she had spun. She was an animal in bed. Fiery, independent, enigmatic, bright. Posing a real challenge. And Blake always rose to a challenge.

Unlike all the other females he had encountered, Ebony wasn't so easy to dominate. She could have been a worthy mistress. A useful advisor. A mixture not only of beauty but great cunning.

For all his simmering anger, a part of him even admired that she had tricked him. If indeed that is what had occurred.

Blake arrived outside the cell, commanded the guards to open the heavy doors, then he entered, gazing coldly at Bray before him, dangling from the girders above, shackled by his arms.

Bray had still refused to co-operate with any of Blake's people but Ebony had managed to obtain some information. Blake was concerned now though if the information she had given was false.

He nodded to the guards, who removed Bray's blindfold.

Bray focused his eyes weakly, finding it difficult to see, having been blindfolded for so long.

"Enjoying your stay?" Blake asked, with more than a hint of disdain.

"What do you think?" Bray answered weakly, defiantly.

"I think -" Blake replied, examining Bray's features, then noticing the 'L' on his shoulder, "that you've been categorised before!" At least Ebony had told the truth about that.

"I don't know what you're talking about!" Bray responded.

"I'm talking about the brand. On your arm!"

He continued to survey Bray as if he was assessing him. Bray seemed to be about the same height, weight. And from the small tattoo on the side of his cheek, seemed to match the identification from the reports he had recently received.

"I gather from your friend, Ebony, that your name is Bray. Is that correct?" Blake continued.

Again Bray considered Blake, unsure of who he was, what was going on.

Blake sighed to himself, impatient at Bray's silence and suddenly unleashed a powerful blow into Bray's abdomen.

Bray groaned in pain, but at least being suspended from the overhead chains meant that it softened the impact and he swung slowly back and forth from the momentum of Blake lashing out.

"Okay, if you don't want to talk about Ebony. Or yourself. Why don't we talk about your brother. Zoot? Or Martin, wasn't he?"

"Who are you?" Bray asked, in a mixture of mounting confusion and suspicion.

"Life. And death," Blake smiled. "And the one asking the questions. So don't play any games. I've been studying your file. You seem to have quite a value. At least, according to Eloise."

"You're involved with that monster?" Bray snapped, in disgust. "I should have known! You seem to be exactly the type."

"And you don't seem to be the 'type' to have escaped. Across the wastelands. You can't be that good. Or you wouldn't have ended up here," Blake sneered, surveying Bray in a cold, calculating manner, thinking about his next move.

"And where's here?"

"Oh, don't worry. You'll be transported soon. When the ship arrives. If you board, that is. Either way, you won't be with us for long." There was a veiled threat, menace in Blake's tone.

"What do you want with me?" Bray asked.

"Payment. That's all you are. A name on a manifest. And a wanted name at that. You should be proud of yourself, Bray. In some ways, I should thank you. You'll provide a good bounty."

Blake moved closer to Bray, leering into his face, his teeth clenched, trying to control a simmering anger boiling within his manic intemperance.

"If you really want to know, if it was up to me - I'd kill you. Right now. But Eloise? I don't think she'd be very pleased. There again, as long as she has some other members of the bloodline to work with. Like your brother's... little daughter."

Bray was stunned by what he was hearing. He just couldn't understand why this person seemed to know so much about him.

"You... don't have Brady being kept here?" Bray asked.

"Not yet. But I've been working on it," Blake smiled, an excited glint in his eye.

He lunged forward and screamed.

"Power and Chaos!"

342

Bray recoiled, sure he was in another simulation.

"What is it? You don't like the word of... who is it... Zoot?"

Bray exchanged glances with Blake, who sneered in mock concern.

"Sorry. I didn't mean to use Zoot's name in vain."

Blake glared contemptuously, then turned, indicating Bray to the guards. "Get him down! Now!" he snapped.

The guards lowered Bray, unwinding the pulley attached to the chains.

Bray slumped to the ground, rubbing his wrists, numbed from having been suspended for so long, while the guards unlocked Bray's manacles from his ankles.

Blake indicated. One of the other guards tossed a spear fishing gun he was holding, which Blake grasped, stroking its sharp jagged razor's edge, which drew blood, and he licked the trickle, running down his finger.

"Gotta be careful with a weapon like this, Bray. It can do a lot of damage. Unless of course, you're as good as you might think you are."

Blake nodded to the guards, who yanked Bray to his feet.

"There you go. That's better now, isn't it? You're... free."

"Somehow I don't think so," Bray responded defiantly.

"You've got no-one but yourself to blame. You see, if you play games with me when I question you, then that leaves me with no option... but to play a game with you."

Bray swallowed nervously, wondering what on earth might be coming next, and his unease made Blake burst out in laughter.

"What's the matter? Never played first person shooters? Never got into any kind of game like that? Or weren't you into gaming? In the old world? Because I was. Oh, yes. In a big, big, way!"

Bray didn't respond and continued to watch uneasily as Blake's laughter subsided, his demeanour turning ice-cold.

"The rules are very simple. I'm the hunter. You're the prey. It's so much more 'fun' with a moving target. Let's see how good you REALLY are. I'll give you a ten second start."

Bray looked at Blake, abhorrent and stunned as he noticed Blake removing a small spear from the quiver, which he inserted above the barrel.

"One..."

He indicated the doorway.

"Two..."

Bray braced himself.

"Three..."

Bray ran flat out, leaving Blake yelling in a manic intensity.

"You've run out of time, Bray! Ready or not - here I come!"

CHAPTER FORTY-TWO

Ruby and Trudy sat gazing into the fire. Ruby was preparing something to eat but didn't feel hungry. Nor did Trudy. They were both far too worried what might transpire, what the night would bring.

Ruby turned skewers of fish, then settled back and glanced at Trudy, who was cradling Amber's son.

"Can I hold him?" Ruby asked.

"Of course," Trudy spoke softly, so as not to waken the baby.

Seeing Amber's young child only reminded Ruby of the baby she was secretly carrying inside her. Slade's baby. She felt a connection. After all, she was a mother-to-be.

Giving him a hug, baby Bray remained asleep, oblivious to his environment. Ruby imagined what it would feel like one day to be holding her own child. And hoped that Slade would be able to experience that joy. His condition seemed to have improved since the medicines he had been given by Lia.

For the first time since the adults had died during the pandemic, Ruby was beginning to think that she might have a future. If only they could get through whatever lay ahead.

"I hope the others are getting on alright," Ruby reflected.

"You don't think they'll end up being taken themselves?"

"I certainly hope not."

The thought of it sent an involuntary shiver down Trudy's spine.

"If so, you know what that means, Ruby. We'll be stranded here!" Trudy cast an uneasy glance at Ram, who was sitting nearby on a log, lost in some private reverie, clutching his head in his hands.

Sammy was wading in the shallows, trying to get some respite from the blistering heat of the night.

Lottie was looking after Slade, in the makeshift shelter.

Gel was trying to file her nails with a stone, the rhythmic sounds almost in time to the noises of the wildlife and insects emanating from the depths of the jungle.

A contingent of warriors were standing outside one of the containers which had washed up from the Jzhao Li, but which had been emptied and was holding Ebony, Axel and his raiding party.

The others had left several hours earlier. In the cruiser which had transported Ebony, Axel and his men. And although everyone left behind knew the mission had dangers, there was no other option but for the Mall Rats to accompany the warriors to the rig in an attempt to release the slaves. Including other warriors of the indigenous tribe who were being held.

They had been able to get some kind of an idea of the size of the forces on the rig. And even if Axel and his men weren't telling the truth, they knew that strategically they had a good chance of their night assault succeeding.

Amber and Jay had planned it all out carefully before they left, then briefed the others. Going over all the details several times. They would attempt to infiltrate the rig, get to the cells so that they could gather strength in numbers, releasing the slaves and warriors being held, to assist in overcoming whatever resistance might be met.

There was room on the cruiser to transport enough people to carry out the operation and they knew there were other vessels, including Ebony's abandoned lifeboat, to facilitate the return.

They had carefully chosen who would participate in the mission. And especially who they would leave behind. Trudy was a capable fighter. She had proven that throughout any clashes the Mall Rats had with tribes back in the city. But was better suited to look after the younger ones. That was important, especially for Amber to know that her baby would be well taken care of in case anything went wrong. Trudy could be histrionic at times, but there was never any doubt that she was a loving, caring mother.

Ruby volunteered to go. But Amber thought, given that she was also to become a mother, that it would be too risky. Besides, she would need to be near Slade, as well as remain to keep a close eye on Ram. For all that she was pregnant, she was still characteristically feisty, level-headed, and could take care of herself, as she had shown many who were out of order in her saloon back in Liberty.

Lia was needed so that she could translate orders during the mission and had also left strict instructions to the warriors who were left behind that they also needed to watch out for Ram.

Ram himself wasn't keen on going at all. Lex had accused him of being a coward. But Ram quickly agreed with Jay, who felt it would be wise for him to stay in case they encountered anything unexpected and Blake's forces were somehow connected to The Collective. With Ram being a wanted man, at the top of the list of their leader, Kami, they couldn't be too sure of what or who they might be dealing with. His presence could be a liability.

Now Ebony started banging loudly from inside the container, demanding food and something to drink.

"Come on, give me a break!" she yelled from inside the container. "It's sweltering in here! Never thought the Mall Rats would stand by and let one of their own die! I've done nothing wrong. I'm innocent! Doesn't anyone believe me?"

Ruby scoffed. "She just won't give in, will she? What does she take us for?"

"You don't think there's a chance she COULD be innocent, do you?" Trudy reflected.

"What - Ebony? You've got to be joking."

Trudy sighed, clearly torn. On one hand, Ruby was right. It was always difficult to know just exactly where Ebony was coming from. She had shown a capability of changing sides when it suited her. But before the incident with the lifeboat, she seemed that she was settling and keen to be a member of the Mall Rats.

Ebony banged again on the container. "I can hardly breathe in here! There's no air! Have some mercy. Please!"

"Keep quiet, will you!?" Ram yelled, irritated at the constant banging and shouting. "I can hardly hear myself think!"

"Maybe we should at least give them all something to drink," Trudy suggested tentatively.

"I wouldn't."

"What happens if they do die in there?" Gel asked.

Ruby cast a glance at the container and sighed to herself, sharing the same concern. She had resolved that she would never try and play God again, deciding anyone's fate and whether or not they lived or died.

"They should have more than enough still left to drink," Ruby concluded. "Ebony would stab herself in the back if she thought she could benefit. So don't let her get to you. Because I'm certainly not going to let her get to me."

"Ruby!" Lottie screamed from the distance. "Quick!"

Ruby leapt to her feet, running flat out towards the makeshift shelter where Lottie was standing, with a huge grin on her face.

Back at Camp Phoenix, inside the trailer, Ebony winked at Axel and the others, then banged again. "Have some mercy! Please!" She started to emit melodramatic, choking sounds.

Trudy and Gel exchanged concerned glances, then gazed at the container.

"Are you alright... in there?" Trudy asked.

There was no answer. Just Ebony's choking.

Oblivious to all this, Ruby arrived at the shelter and thought she was imagining what she was hearing.

"Ruby...?" Slade called, his voice still weak.

"Oh, my God!" Ruby said, tears filling her eyes as she crouched to lean over him, thrilled, as was Lottie, that Slade had regained consciousness. He had been gone for some time now and Ruby was anxious, believing that Slade might have also slipped into some sort of coma, just like Zak did before he died.

Laying on his back, Slade gazed up, trying somehow to focus on Ruby, peering down at him.

"Just relax! Don't try and talk! You're going to be alright!"

But Ruby looked more to be the one who needed to try and relax, hardly unable to contain her excitement and joy, evident through her tears.

She glanced up at Lottie. "What happened?"

"One minute it still seemed like he was fast asleep, then the next minute... he just opened his eyes and groaned," Lottie shrugged.

Ruby turned back and gently stroked Slade's hair.

"I can't believe it. I thought we lost you... I had lost you."

"I... need to tell you something," Slade said, flinching, still in pain.

Ruby leaned down closer, placing her ear near Slade's mouth so she could listen, make it easy for him.

"I love you," Slade declared with a slight smile, which made Ruby smile through her tears of joy. Then she was concerned at Slade, trying to prop himself up on one arm.

"What's going on!" he said weakly, staring disorientated at Camp Phoenix.

Lottie and Ruby turned, following Slade's weak gaze.

Then Ruby suddenly leapt to her feet as she heard Trudy emitting a long, hysterical scream. Brady and Amber's son also started to cry with the commotion.

Sammy stared wide-eyed in the shallows, frozen in fear.

Ram was backing away.

Ebony and Axel's raiding party were exchanging blows with the warrior guards. There had been a clear flaw in the briefing, with Lia translating to the warriors that they needed to watch Ram very carefully. But they didn't mention Trudy.

Trudy had taken some fruit to the container. Ram had followed, concerned by Trudy's actions. The warriors took a step forward towards him, ignoring Trudy, who undid the side metal door slightly to leave enough room to pass some fruit inside. Ebony, Axel and the party seized their chance, shouldering the door, which burst open, the logs tumbling which had been left to secure it.

Now, having floored the warriors, they were dragging Ram, who was yelling for help in growing panic, toward the jungle.

Another member of Axel's party grabbed Brady and Trudy but Gel released a burst of hairspray into his eyes. He ran off, following the other members of Axel's team, noticing the indigenous tribe warriors climbing to their feet.

Ruby indicated Slade to Lottie. "Stay with him!" she said, then started running towards a distraught Trudy, still screaming hysterically.

"Oh, my God! I was just wanting to give them some fruit! Something to drink! I had no idea this would happen! What have I done?!"

She stared helplessly, but there was no sign of Ebony, Axel and the raiding party, or Ram, who had disappeared deep into the jungle.

CHAPTER FORTY-THREE

Bray ran flat out along a metallic corridor in the bowels of the oil rig. Above, on the upper decks, the sobbing and whimpering of other slaves echoed through the catacombs of the mammoth infrastructure, the desperate sounds adding to the surreal situation Bray now was finding himself in.

He arrived at the end of the corridor and stopped for a split second, gazing left then right, wondering which way to take. He could hear the rhythmic pounding of Blake in pursuit, then took off, hurling around the right hand side and into another corridor.

Blake, the hunter, had several advantages over his prey. For that's what Bray now realized he was. Even though he couldn't quite understand why. And unlike Bray, Blake knew the layout of the oil rig, whereas Bray had no idea whatsoever where each of the metallic corridors he was running down would take him next.

Should he make a stand and fight, Bray thought, rushing around another corner and into yet another long, dimly lit metallic corridor.

His mind was a swirl, relying on his instincts and senses to rapidly assimilate all he could about this environment, hoping to find the slightest element he could use to his advantage.

Bray stumbled as he took off his boots and socks while he ran, hoping that continuing on in his bare feet would dampen the sound of his running.

It worked.

Blake, in another corridor, stopped. Listened. With the acoustics taking on another dimension.

Up ahead, Bray's skin was now being torn on the steel of the deck.

Taking a split second to gather his breath, his shoulders heaving from fatigue, Bray considered that the longer he stayed out in the open, in the corridors, the less of a chance he would have to stay ahead of Blake. He had to change the terrain, somehow.

"You can't run forever, Bray!" Blake's voice echoed ominously, threateningly, his approaching footsteps pounding as he approached closer. Closer.

Bray gazed around, noticed steps, then ran as fast as he could towards them, leaping, ascending each step, which led him into another deck. And another metallic corridor.

Bray continued on to the end, hurled around another corner, passing doors, which he tried to open. The first one was locked. Likewise, the second one. The third door creaked open. Inside, Bray could see shelves of processed food, bottled water, alcohol. These rooms were obviously where the crew kept their provisions.

Blake heard the echoey sounds of a thick, steel door being shut and smiled to himself. This was too easy.

He had always had a competitive edge since he was evacuated during the height of the pandemic. He had been identified as a suitable candidate for survival training at boot camp. Where he excelled, quickly becoming a leader, meeting Axel, along with the others of his inner circle. That was the birth of his tribe and

Blake had great ambitions, to build them into a force to be reckoned with in the post-apocalyptic world. To expand, extend his power base, build an empire.

And who knows, even better what his father had been able to achieve before the pandemic struck.

Blake was never close to his father. His mother had died giving birth and he had always wondered if he was somehow to blame. He suspected his father thought that to be the case.

Being in the military, Blake's father had always been a hard disciplinarian. Blake had struggled with that. And rebelled against it. Much to his father's chagrin. At least he had been able to make an impression. Succeed at something. But in the eyes of his father, he was a total failure.

Blake had always regretted that his father could never see what he really could have made of himself, if given the chance. Even as his father was approaching death during the height of the virus, Blake was criticised. For not showing up at the hospital earlier. They were the last words he had heard. And he couldn't help but feel a sense of relief, even delight, as he watched his father's life ebb away.

He stared coldly as the sheet was drawn up over his father's face. And even had difficulty providing comfort to his elder sister, who was sobbing uncontrollably, affected by every fading, last gasp of breath her father struggled to take.

In a way, Blake enjoyed it all. He had hoped in many ways that he could reconcile their differences. With some kind of deathbed revelation. But painfully realized there were too many scars which would never heal.

His father had been a Four Star General in the military, fuelling Blake's determination that in his own life he would become more. He wasn't interested in just becoming a general. But having his own army.

Meeting his friend, Kami, online just before the virus spread, his instincts told him that Kami could be the key. Kami wasn't just a capable gamer. But had organised an impressive guild, with members from most countries. When the darkness fell in the post-adult world, Kami reactivated his online friends, tracked Blake down. And Blake was determined to prove his worth.

Which is what he had done so far. Throughout his past assignments. And he was quickly rising up through the ranks. He only had a few more months to go on this assignment, then he was due to travel to the Far Eastern Region to eventually meet Kami. Get more of a handle on what he was planning with The Collective.

No matter what - Blake's plan was to make sure that he was a candidate for Kami's inner circle. Which would provide the gateway to power through Kami's expanding empire. And one day, Blake was determined that rather than Kami, Blake himself would become number one.

Now, crossing towards the door where his latest prey was hiding, Blake sighed to himself, slightly disappointed. He had hoped that Bray would have at least given him more of a workout. But he didn't seem up to the challenge. And decided that he would take him out and report back that his prisoner had been killed while trying to escape.

He knew Bray had some kind of value. For Eloise. And probably through her, a value for even Kami. Although he was unsure of just exactly what, Blake suspected from his earlier encounters with Ebony that there was some kind of a link to the experiments Eloise had been conducting. Above all, a link also to Kami's number one adversary - Ram. Blake still didn't know what had occurred. But Ram had a price on his head. Just like Bray. Being from the same bloodline of his brother, Zoot. Power and Chaos might have been an interesting ideology for Kami to nourish and spread 'the word'. But Blake thought the way of the warrior far surpassed anything that any religion had to offer. Zealots might become indoctrinated by faith but everyone could be dominated and controlled through fear.

Blake swung open the door, stepped inside and moved stealthily down each row of shelving.

Suddenly Bray appeared, unleashing a blow, sending Blake sprawling, before rushing out.

Blake wiped at a thin line of blood trickling from his mouth. He was encouraged, rather than angered. At least Bray might provide some kind of challenge after all. He clearly had skills to make it across the wastelands. But Blake, too, had skills and knew it was only a matter of time before he came out on top of this 'leader board'.

He took a breath, then ran out of the room in pursuit.

Bray hurled around a corridor, leaping up more metal steps which led to another deck. And ran along a corridor, passing cells each side where prisoners were reaching through the bars, clutching at him, their eyes wild, disorientated, all screaming for help. They were living in sheer hell. Which was in itself a vision of hell.

Bray couldn't comprehend where he was. Or just what was going on as he sped past.

One again, he suspected he might be trapped in a simulation, especially as guards at the end of the long corridor didn't bother to try and apprehend him, which surprised Bray. He had expected them to put up some kind of fight. But they just backed up, pressing themselves against the cells, allowing him to pass.

Little did Bray know that the guards knew never to interrupt Blake when he was indulging himself in any kind of 'hunt'. And Blake was clearly in pursuit.

Bray arrived into yet another metallic corridor, gazed around unsure which way to go but pushed himself on, casting an occasional glance behind. Then turning back. He had arrived at a dead end.

He noticed a row of switches and began flicking them.

Suddenly the dim fluorescent lights went out. Bray stood, rigid.

Backing up against the wall, daring not even to breathe as he heard the footsteps of Blake echoing, signalling that he was approaching, closer. Closer.

"Come on! This is too easy! You're starting to become a 'bore'!" Blake laughed, taunting.

Bray lunged forward, realizing Blake was almost on him, hurling him to one side, and ran on in full flight, retracing his steps, stealing looks behind as the fluorescent lights were switched on again.

Blake turned from the wall socket, raised the spear gun and yelled manically.

"Any last words, Bray?!"

Bray caught a fleeting glimpse of Blake's shadow moving across the wall as he pursued his prey.

But Blake wasn't running. He had slowed to a walking pace, while raising the spear gun, closing one eye, taking careful aim at Bray, visible in the cross hairs ahead.

Blake fired.

The spear shot out from the barrel of the spear gun, soaring through the air with a loud whoosh, embedding itself into the side of Bray's arm.

Bray winced and staggered slightly, yanking at the spear, removing it, while continuing running in full flight.

* * *

On the far horizon the silhouette was unmistakable.

The Mall Rats and warriors on the large cruiser were all watching in nervous anticipation of what they would encounter as the vessel sped, bouncing over the waves.

Jack was at the helm, gripping the wheel, trying to steady himself from the momentum.

On the deck, Amber and Jay were giving a final briefing, going over one last time what had already been planned. May, Ellie, Darryl, Salene and Lex nodded that they understood, while Lia translated to the warriors of the indigenous tribe, who also indicated that they were ready.

"Don't forget - the priority is to get as many of the prisoners being held out as we can," Amber said. "That way they can be of help to us. If we need extra help."

"Darryl and Salene - it's just so important for you to stay at the dock. In case we need to abort and get out of there," Jay reminded them.

"Lia - maybe you can go over one last time what your warriors need to do," Amber instructed. "Make sure each group know which one of us they're assigned to. And what we've all got in mind. We can't have any breakdowns in communication with anyone who doesn't stay with your group."

Lia nodded and began to translate.

Then all aboard gazed in mounting tension as the mammoth structure ahead in the distance seemed to grow larger and larger in size, the closer they approached. A remnant of the old world, a technological monstrosity that once harvested the second most important liquid in the world after water - oil. But now, people. Also an important commodity in the new world without adults.

"It's almost time," Amber whispered. "You all know what to do!?"

Once again, the others on board nodded, then gazed at the rig looming before them, preparing themselves for what lay ahead, realising that if there was ever a time that they needed to perform, then it was now.

They were about to shape their destinies. The outcome of their entire future and any hopes of survival, was at stake.

CHAPTER FORTY-FOUR

Blake bounded up more metallic steps, taking two, three at a time, following trails of blood, which had been dripping from Bray's shoulder wound.

Arriving at the top of the stairwell, he noticed a guard rushing toward him.

"Commander! Axel and his team are approaching."

Blake felt pleased though slightly surprised that Ebony had proven to be trustworthy. He wondered if she had really risen to the test. But if she didn't, no doubt Axel would have. Blake could always rely on him. And would be delivering Ram. Blake would receive a valuable bounty. But that was less important than the impression he'd make with Kami and The Collective.

"Tell Axel I'll be with him as soon as I can. This hunt shouldn't go on too long," Blake said, stroking the spear gun gently, excited by all the prospects which lay ahead.

"And Miss Ebony?" the guard asked tentatively, aware that Blake was ready to move off.

"Tell her to wait in my quarters. And I'll be with her shortly. I'm kinda 'busy' right now."

The guard nodded, understanding he was dismissed, and ran off.

On an upper deck, Bray was ripping at his shirt, and tried to tie a tourniquet to mask his trail of blood while he ran. Feeling exhausted and unsure of how long he could keep going on, disorientated from all he had suffered, Bray's eyes were full of utter confusion and fear as he heard Blake in the distance.

"I'm getting closer! But don't worry, Bray. Some of your friends will soon be here! Just a pity that you won't 'see' them!"

Bray stole a terrified glance behind him, then turned back, leaping up another stairwell, desperate to stay ahead of his crazed pursuer.

* * *

Even Blake himself might have been impressed with the irony of his strangely prophetic warning. He had fully expected Ram to be boarding by now. Along with Ebony. Perhaps even the daughter of Zoot, as well as the child's mother. But he - and especially Bray - had no way of knowing that Jack was carefully steering the cruiser towards the large dock surrounding the lower struts of the rig.

Jay leapt onto the dock, followed by the Mall Rats and warriors of the indigenous tribe.

Salene and Darryl stayed on the vessel, its engines idling, while they stood by at the ready, and the raiders moved quickly, stealthily along the dock, finally climbing metal ladders leading into the bowels of the mighty infrastructure looming over them.

* * *

Bray continued pushing himself on, up another metallic stairwell, the skin from his bare feet being torn with each panicked step, feeling his only hope was to try and get away from the maze of corridors and search for a window, a doorway, any portal into the outside world of wherever he was.

Blake was gaining on him, his eyes fixed as he relentlessly pursued. Pushing himself harder, harder, his teeth clenched. A glint of triumph at what he knew would soon lay ahead.

Bray had given him a good workout. Now he had other more important matters to attend to. It was time to move in. For the kill.

* * *

The Mall Rats and warrior raiding party entered the mammoth infrastructure, illuminated by dim fluorescent lights on all walls.

Amber noticed huge fire exit diagrams outlining five storage decks and the living quarters and upper mechanical and helicopter decks.

She indicated to Ellie and Jack, her voice in an urgent undertone.

"You take your group, check out deck 1. Lia, you go with them. Tell the others in Lex and May's group they'll need to secure deck 2, while Jay and I head to deck 3."

"Got it," Lex nodded as Lia whispered her translation to the warriors.

Ellie and Jack's group headed off.

Lex and May's contingent set off to another stairwell.

Jay suddenly spotted a guard at the end of the long corridor who had clearly noticed them in turn and rushed to a control panel, pulling down a lever, activating an alarm, the sound pulsing along with the dim fluorescent lights.

Amber, Jay and the warriors quickly ascended their stairwell while other guards converged at the end of the corridor and ran flat out in pursuit.

* * *

Outside on the dock, Salene and Darryl, aboard the cruiser, gazed up, hearing the shrill alarm, the pulsing lights from the cavernous infrastructure flashing, casting looming shadows across the surface of the water.

"Sounds like - it's on!" Darryl shouted to Salene, who was gripping the safety rail of the cruiser as it pitched up and down on the rolling waves while Darryl steadied the throttle of the idling boat.

"I hope they're alright!" Salene replied, craning her neck upwards, searching for a better look.

She felt like clambering up the stairwells surrounding the dock to be with the others but fought her natural instinct, sticking to what had been planned. She and Darryl had to remain on standby for when the Mall Rats returned with the influx of slaves. At least, that's what Darryl and Salene hoped. But if the operation had to be aborted in any way, then they would be ready for a quick getaway to transport the raiding party.

Salene dreaded to think of any other option as she continued to gaze eagerly at the rig for any sign.

"Come on... come on," she urged.

* * *

At the very top of the rig, Bray burst through the doors and gazed around at the helicopter deck. For a moment, he felt as if he was back in the city, on top of one of the skyscrapers where he regularly scouted for glimpses of tribes and activity, especially during the Locos' rule of the sector.

He stopped for a few seconds, heaving, trying somehow to catch his breath while he tightened the tourniquet, the screeching of the alarm and flashing fluorescent lights further disorientating him.

Suddenly he noticed Blake appear through the doorway.

There was a hint of uncertainty in Blake's expression. He decided he'd better end the hunt and head back below to check out what was happening, sure the alarm must have been set off accidentally. But a part of him instinctively knew that was not the case, though he couldn't even begin to assess the reason. They couldn't be under attack. The guards would have been alerted much earlier to any approaching vessel. Maybe there was a fire. But if so, Blake thought his men were more than capable of dealing with that.

Bray noticed Blake inserting another arrow. And seized his moment, springing forward into action, lunging at Blake, unleashing a powerful blow, doubling him.

Bray grasped for the spear gun, yanking it from Blake's arms.

Blake spun, kicking the spear gun, which shot out of Bray's hands, and landed, skidding across the open deck floor.

Bray tried to run again, to get away.

Blake lunged forward, pounced on him like a wild animal, bringing him down.

Yanking Bray by the hair, Blake smashed Bray's head on the deck. Once. Twice. He was in a frenzy now, his teeth clenched, his sadistic eyes bearing down on Bray as if into the depths of his very soul, like the Devil incarnate.

Bray gathered up all his fading strength, raised one leg and with all his might unleashed his knee into Blake's groin, then he elbowed Blake in the throat, hurling Blake from him.

He leaped to his feet, ran towards the gantry, then started climbing up the struts, his bare feet ripped to shreds, his face battered, bruised, blood oozing from his wounds, the tourniquet unable to stem the flow from his arm.

He knew he didn't have long.

Blake knew it, too. As he climbed slowly to his feet, gazing ahead at Bray in excited anticipation, Blake decided now was the time to finish the hunt... with his bare hands.

* * *

Jack and Ellie, followed by Lia and the warriors of the indigenous tribe, ran up a stairwell, then arriving at the top, scanned the labyrinth of metallic corridors.

"Which way now?" Ellie shouted, fuelled by adrenalin.

"Let's try down here," Jack replied, straining, concentrating, listening intently to another noise the group heard amidst the sound of the pulsing alarm.

They followed the noise, which got louder and louder with each step they took. And it had an ominous effect on even the warriors, normally so brave.

Although it was the sounds of cries, wailing, distressed pleas for help, it all blended into a cacophony, like some unearthly choir of ghosts from the other side, calling out from the afterlife.

Arriving at a huge doorway, the group carefully nudged the door open, stepped through.

And all were unnerved to see prisoners trapped in cells, tormented, sobbing, some reaching through the bars, clutching at Ellie, Jack, Lia and the warriors. Others sat idly on the ground, staring blankly.

At the opposite end of the corridor, guards arrived, outnumbering Jack and Ellie's group.

"How do you say we've got to do something - fast - in your language!?" Jack asked Lia in an undertone, not fancying their chances with the amount of guards approaching.

Suddenly Ellie - to Jack, the warriors and Lia's amazement, stepped forward, smiling politely.

"Hi!" she said casually.

The guards were confused as she swaggered towards them, hips swaying, chewing imaginary gum.

"Well?" she asked, seductively. "Where do we go? We're here to... pleasure you."

The guards exchanged more incredulous glances.

One female guard scoffed, indicating Jack.

"Him - pleasure us?"

For all the danger, Jack was deeply offended.

"Sorry to disappoint!" he muttered, his ego bruised.

The female guard wasn't part of the militia but the vagabonds and was wearing a belt that looked to be full of mounds of human hair.

"Pleasure us, eh? I don't think so," she said menacingly.

Then as the guards arrived, much to Jack's astonishment along with the native warriors and Lia, Ellie lunged to aggressively kiss one of the male guards on the mouth before reaching into his belt, carefully removing a set of keys, which she tossed behind her.

Jack caught them and began opening the cell doors, Lia indicating and yelling in her native language for the warriors to attack. Which they did, while Jack behind them swung open door after door.

"If you know what an uprising is - now's your chance!" Jack shouted. "Come on! We can't help you unless you help yourselves. And us! Move it, move it!"

The slaves poured out of the open doors, rushing to help the warriors and Ellie exchanging blows with their adversaries.

The female guard removed a blade from her belt and grabbed Ellie. Then sweeping up Ellie's hair, sliced through it, holding a clump of her long flowing locks in one hand, her arm around Ellie, backing her up, the point of the blade held at Ellie's throat.

"Back off! All of you! I mean it!" the female guard yelled, realising that her group were being overpowered.

Ellie gazed down nervously at the blade. Jack turned from opening a door, watching, terrified, as Ellie began to cry.

It wasn't just the danger she was encountering, but bizarrely she could see the clump of her hair out of the corner of her eye. She had been growing her hair long, ever since the 'virus' struck, with her sister, Alice, being the only one allowed to go near it - apart from Jack. And now that special bond, so symbolic with her past and her missing sister - had been so viciously taken from her.

But what no one could comprehend for one brief moment, the horrors of what she had witnessed in the cells brought back painful memories of Alice. She couldn't bear to think of her being held in such a way. The thought repulsed her. And it was all manifest by the clump of hair.

As well as distress her, it also angered her and she unleashed a vicious elbow into the female guard's stomach, causing her to release her grasp. Then Ellie turned, pulled back one arm and swung a wild blow, carrying all the simmering anguish, hatred and fear she was feeling. The female guard spun as the blow connected to her jaw and slumped to the ground.

The warriors and slaves didn't take long to overcome the guards, marshalling them into the cells as fast as they were emptying, with more prisoners being released.

Jack rushed to Ellie, who lifted her clump of hair and gazed at it sadly.

"Remind me to never try and meet you in a dark alleyway," Jack quipped, throwing his arms around Ellie for comfort.

Then Jack stepped back, considering her. Between her sobs, she plunged the clump of her beloved hair into her own belt.

"Hey - it suits you. I mean it. Really!" Jack said.

It didn't, of course. Her hair hung ragged, uneven. She knew it and overwhelmed by all that she had witnessed, continued to sob, nestling her head on Jack's shoulder while he embraced her.

"It's gonna be alright. Everything's gonna be alright, Ellie, I promise," he said, gently.

CHAPTER FORTY-FIVE

On the second deck, Lex, May and the warriors ran through a maze of metal corridors, arriving at a door which they inched open, revealing more cells filled with slaves.

Lex, May and the warriors were also greatly affected by the spectacle, overwhelmed by pity. Thankfully there was no sign of any guards. At least not so far.

"Keys! There's gotta be keys!" May said, yanking open a cabinet, before finally discovering some, which she tossed to Lex.

Both went from cell to cell, matching each key, while the warriors assisted Lex and May, opening doors, reassuring the prisoners that they were now free.

The prisoners could hear a wave of noise from the decks below, signifying the uprising, and also started shouting in cheers of jubilation. In the last cell, Lex noticed two small children sobbing, clinging to an older girl. They were all standing, rigid with fear.

"What's the matter with you?" Lex said. "Come on, you're all free. Can't you see?"

"No!" Emma replied, reaching out, searching the features of her younger brother and sister to make sure they were there and drawing them closer, under the protective care of her arms.

May exchanged a glance with Lex, who was staring mesmerised, not only by Emma's natural beauty and the opacity in her strangely beguiling eyes, but her poise and dignity.

"Here, let me help you," he said gently, taking Emma's hand while May comforted Tiffany and Shannon.

"Come on, sweetheart, everything's okay. No need to be afraid. Neither of you. We're here to help."

* * *

Amber and Jay, with their contingent of warriors, were now checking the living quarters, having secured the earlier decks, releasing more slaves, instructing them to assemble at the entrance dock with the others who had already been released.

They could hear the sounds of the cheering reverberating throughout the infrastructure of the rig. Any guards they encountered were surrendering, with little or no resistance.

Amber and Jay eventually arrived at Blake's quarters. Heading inside, they were astounded to see such opulence compared to the degrading conditions of those who were being held captive.

"Talk about living in the lap of luxury," Amber said, gazing around.

Jay was equally appalled by the difference. "I wonder who this Blake guy is - more importantly, where he is!"

"No sign of him here," Amber replied, searching the quarters.

"Let's try and salvage anything which could be important," Jay said.

Amber joined him, searching through drawers, cabinets, cupboards, removing paperwork, files, discs, a laptop, which they handed to Jack and Ellie, who arrived with other warriors.

"What on earth happened?" Amber said, noticing Ellie's ravaged hair.

"It's a long story," Jack interrupted. "You should have seen her - you'd have been proud."

"Any word from Lex and May?" Amber asked.

"They're both fine. Everyone's fine. We've lost no one. No injuries," Jack said.

"Thank God for that," Amber sighed, relieved.

"Luckily no one seems to be hurt. Except maybe for Ellie's pride," he said sympathetically, casting a glance at Ellie before turning back to Amber.

"Just one thing - there's more prisoners than we imagined. Just hope there's enough room on those boats."

"Check it out will you, Jack?" Amber suggested. "And we'll try and get finished up here. Come on. Move. Let's get out of here, while we can!"

* * *

Bray climbed slowly, carefully, along the huge steel struts, hoping that it all wouldn't result in the same way it had when he had ascended the roller coaster.

But he had little choice. It was his only hope to try and shake off Blake, who continued to pursue him relentlessly.

Bray cast a weak glance behind and could see that Blake was closing on him, ready to move in.

Blake, in turn, was gazing intently at Bray with more than a manic degree of excited anticipation. He knew that the very essence of life was fading from his prey and that Bray would soon succumb, if not from any final attack, certainly from the horrific injuries he had suffered.

Bray turned back, searching deep into the resources of his heart, his very soul, to find the will to keep going. It was all that he had left. His will. Now he barely had the strength even to move.

With the alarm still pulsing, the sounds now mixing with an avalanche of noise amidst the whistling wind, a rushing chorus and cacophony of jubilant cheering, it all further disorientated Bray, being totally unaware of what it all represented. He still had no idea where he was. And what was happening.

But Blake knew and wondered what had occurred, resulting in his cargo of slaves being set free. For there was no doubt in his mind that the chorus of cheers, electric, alive, had to be the sound of freedom.

Bray suddenly slipped and gripped as hard as he could, while clinging to a girder, sure he had no strength left, his legs dangling in the air.

Blake smiled slightly and accelerated forward, stomping his heavy boots on Bray's hands, resulting in one losing its grip.

Searching for every fibre of will and resolve, Bray hung on desperately, knowing that he didn't have much, if anything, left to give. He could give no more. But had to try.

Clinging with one arm, he wiggled his legs to gain even a bit of momentum, which was enough to gain a foothold on another girder. Then he reached up, yanking Blake by the ankles, and he, too slipped - but managed to cling while Bray hauled himself higher, propelled by more footholds he managed to find within the metal struts.

Blake and Bray were just a few feet apart now and gazed exhaustedly at each other.

"I underestimated you!" Blake said, finding a foothold and hauling himself onto the girder, climbed slowly to his feet.

Bray gazed up weakly, bracing himself for what was to come and struggled to remain conscious.

"I just wish we might have met up, another time, another place. You're a true warrior! And so am I!" Blake said, in a mixture of admiration and pride. "But now, it's too late. We're both going to die!"

Bray watched weakly as Blake stood, raising his arms aloft, and began screaming up to the Heavens above, his outline silhouetted against the flames billowing above into the dark sky.

"You hear that! Me! Blake! No matter what you thought! I was a warrior! And I never failed!"

Blake began to sob, much to Bray's confusion, further fuelling his disorientation.

Blake tried to compose himself and closed his eyes, his arms still spread, held aloft.

Even in defeat, he would find victory. It would be a warrior's death. He had taken his enemy with him, knowing that Bray also would soon die.

Blake was determined that he wouldn't fall at the hands of mere slaves intent on vengeance. Or the mighty, unforgiving Collective, if Kami had ever gotten a hold of him.

Blake had always been master of his domain. He would choose his own end.

In an instant, Blake was airborne.

Bray gazed down as Blake receded quickly in the distance, falling towards the churning ocean below, ready to accept Blake into its embrace.

Crashing into the surface of the water, Blake disappeared from total sight under the waves, which rolled over where he had impacted the water.

Blake was gone.

* * *

Amber stepped through the doorway onto the deserted helicopter deck, followed by Jay, both casting a quick glance around.

"Looks like there's no one up here," Amber said.

Jay nodded. "Let's go! We'd better catch up with the others!" he replied.

Amber considered Jay, who had noticed sudden movement in the lower girders above them.

"Wait a minute - look!" Jay indicated.

Amber gazed across the open deck, following Jay's puzzled stare.

Ahead, through the darkness, they could just about make out the silhouette of a figure climbing slowly, weakly, down the girders before finally losing his grip and slumping to the deck.

Amber and Jay watched as the distant figure climbed unsteadily to his feet.

Bray tried somehow to focus his eyes as he noticed the distant figures standing by the doorway.

It can't be.

He quickly dismissed it all, sure now more than ever that this was another simulation.

But it was no simulation.

A hint of unbelievable recognition was also evident in Amber's expression, which registered with Jay.

She stood staring. In silence. Speechless. A part of her wondering if what she recalled Ebony saying earlier was true, a larger part of her unable to even comprehend that it could even be true.

"Bray!?" she whispered to herself.

At the opposite side of the large helicopter deck, Bray also just stood, staring in pure disbelief. Was this really just a dream?

But there was no doubt about that voice. And who it belonged to.

This was no dream.

And yet it was a dream that they had both clung to for so long.

"B-R-A-Y!" Amber screamed out, her voice and entire being charged with emotion.

She ran flat out towards Bray, breaking down in wracking, heaving sobs, convulsing her entire body.

"It is you! It is! Oh my God! B-R-A-Y!!!"

Bray fought to contain his own emotion, his clothes torn and ravaged, blood still oozing from his wounds, his eyes swollen from his injuries filling with tears, overspilling down his battered, bruised face.

A surge of adrenalin raced through his entire body. And he, too, started to run, stumbling, still weak.

Jay stood motionless by the doorway, watching as Bray and Amber finally connected, each throwing their arms around the other.

Neither could speak. They were so overcome. And clung tightly to each other.

It was so moving that even Jay had difficulty in containing his own emotion while he watched Bray and Amber locked in their embrace, a cast iron grip, as if now they had been reunited here, of all places, and had found themselves, they would never let each other go.

* * *

Salene and Darryl stood either side of a gangway, helping the endless stream of slaves board the cruiser. Further along the dock, Jack was assisting Lex and May, doing the same, cramming as many of the prisoners as they could onto the lifeboat of the Jzhao Li.

An automatic rising temperature gauge inside the rig triggered more alarms.

All gazed around, unsure of exactly what was happening as flames were suddenly visible, shooting from one side of the upper decks.

The Mall Rats stared open-mouthed as they noticed Amber and Jay steadying Bray between them, stumbling down the steps leading to the dock from the main entry point above.

There was an explosion somewhere within the infrastructure, adding a dimension of added panic now to all assembled, from the initial relief of being only minutes from completing their escape.

"Bray!" Salene shouted, while Amber and Jay approached along the dock, almost dragging Bray between them. He was barely conscious and Amber could see that as well as her surprise, Salene was deeply affected at the pitiful state Bray was in.

"Now's not the time for any questions, Sal!" Amber said, glancing up at smoke billowing from the rig above her.

"Help us, will you?... Easy! That's the way!" Amber continued as Salene steadied Bray, who was laid gently down onto the deck.

Jay and Amber leapt aboard.

Then Darryl, extending a long pole to the side of the dock, pushed the vessel away.

On the lifeboat, May and Lex were doing the same while Jack started the ignition and the engine burst into life. He spun the wheel, punching the throttle to maximum, as did Darryl on the cruiser.

The propellers at the back of both vessels kicked into the waves, spraying up foam, the engines unleashing all their horsepower.

Both vessels pulled away, picking up speed, while behind them the rig was being consumed by the cataclysms erupting within, a series of what sounded like small explosions.

In the midst of the battle, a steaming cauldron had been overturned, causing a small fire, which in itself wasn't a danger. Some of Blake's guards quickly extinguished the flames. But the embers overspilling into a shaft had precipitated what was about to occur.

The flaming debris had ignited some gasoline tanks on the lower decks of the rig, the flames spreading to a massive storage tank, which the adults had towed to the converted oil rig in the last few months of the virus.

The rig had more than enough fuel to supply the visiting ships used to transport slaves since Blake and his forces had used it as a base. But some of the submerged pipes also led to thousands of tonnes of natural gas stored inside - intended to provide a lifetime of energy for the adults, who were to have been stationed on the island as part of the efforts to survive the pandemic that was sweeping the world.

Now, that energy was being consumed by the fires raging out of control and igniting all the combustible gases.

As the boats sped away, all the occupants clung, trying to steady themselves with the vessels bouncing along the waves, while behind them the superstructure of the rig was simply being torn apart by a chain reaction of explosions, huge flames spreading throughout all parts of the rig, fuelling an inferno.

The night sky was illuminated by all the devastation, casting an eerie glow across the water.

A creaking, groaning sound could also be heard as two massive cranes began toppling, their bases surrounded by flames.

Suddenly a massive explosion erupted, the shock wave felt by all the frightened occupants of both vessels, who watched and instinctively ducked as a towering pillar of flame shot high into the night sky from the very heart of the oil rig, dark smoke billowing.

The headquarters of Blake's operation was in its death throes.

Buckling under the shifting weight and with all balance gone, the oil rig began to tilt as one of its legs slowly gave way, melting from the intense heat.

The ocean was now reclaiming the doomed rig as another cataclysmic explosion occurred. The rig slipped slowly under the surface of the water - which seemed to be boiling - as more underwater eruptions ignited and the rig sank deeper and deeper towards the murky depths, the surface of the water ablaze.

EPILOGUE

The stars shone down. The moon was bright, bathing the native village. It was a magical night.

The villagers were singing in close harmony, clapping their hands, stomping their feet, bashing sticks against the sides of their makeshift drums.

Gel was helping some of the natives girls weave flaxen plants as hair extensions attached into the remnants of Ellie's long blonde locks. Jack sat nearby, assessing each stage. And liked what he saw.

"Ellie - I think it suits you. I really do. I might even get my hair done the same way," Jack said.

"It's my turn next," Gel moaned.

"Don't worry, I was only joking," Jack replied - then added quickly, so as not to offend Ellie, "not about this new hairstyle of your's - but mine."

"You just stay exactly the way you are - you're perfect!" Ellie reached out, taking Jack's hand and kissing it.

Lottie, Sammy, Tiffany and Shannon were playing with some of the native children, throwing coconuts to each other.

Lex was feasting on wild boar, turning on a spit over an open fire. Lia was next to him, translating tales of some of his past battles he had back in the city to the warriors, who were eating and listening intently. But Lia wondered somehow if Lex's boasts were more designed to impress her - or the Priestess - who stood watching Lex, listening intently. Although Lia wasn't experienced in male and female rituals and had never had a serious relationship, her instincts told her that Lex seemed to be sticking very closely by her.

Jay arrived. Lex offered a coconut filled with liquid.

"Here - try some of this. And you'd better hold on to something. Tight. I don't know what they put in it - but it's got a hell of a kick."

Jay took a sip. "I see what you mean," he said hoarsely. after he swallowed. "My throat feels as if it's on fire."

Lex grinned and was getting a little intoxicated by the liquid himself, hoping that all present throughout him holding court would also be intoxicated by his tales. He asked Lia to let the warriors know that Jay had once been an adversary, invading Lex's homeland city, but now was a friend. And Lex hoped the same would occur with all the warriors - and villagers - who Lex really respected. And admired.

He cast a glance down the Priestess's figure, winking at her.

"Don't push your luck," Jay said.

Then Lex relaxed and smiled to himself, noticing the Priestess winking back, with Lia advising that the respect was mutual.

"The Priestess said that she is looking forward to learning more about you and your culture," Lia explained.

"Me, too," Lex replied, downing the rest of his drink.

"Why don't you go and slip into something a bit more comfortable?" Lex suggested. "And who knows, I'll show you how we dance. Back home. Just as long as you teach me how you guys dance. Back in a tick," he added, smiling at the Priestess and Lia, while he led Jay away.

"What is it?" Jay asked, sensing something was troubling Lex.

"I don't know if it's this firewater I've been drinking and it's playing tricks with my mind... But one thing I've been thinking about. When you were with the Technos... you never met up with The Guardian, did you?"

"Not that I know of. I knew about him. And his Chosen, of course... But no, I never met him."

"I don't mean after the invasion. I mean BEFORE the invasion," Lex pressed.

Jay thought for a moment, then sipped on some more of the intoxicating liquid in the coconut shell. "I don't know what you're getting at."

Lex explained that he had been thinking about what Bray had told everyone. Especially about the time he was held in Eloise's compound. And all the references to the 'Zootists' confused Lex - as it had the others - when Bray recounted the despicable events he had suffered during all the virtual reality programs.

"It's just, I remember one thing The Guardian said. Before the Technos arrived. And I've never been able to figure it out," he continued, hiccuping and belching.

"Figure what out?" Jay probed, glancing at Lex, intrigued, and smiling slightly at his drunken demeanour.

"When The Guardian was being held captive at the Mall, he gave me a warning. I remember his exact words. "They're coming, Lex. The true bringers of Power and Chaos." If he didn't mean you guys - and had nothing to do with the Technos - then who he was talking about? I mean, the Technos were never involved with anything to do with Zoot and the Locos, right?"

"I see what you mean," Jay said, in equal confusion and concern.

He suggested that once they went over all the data and intelligence they had recovered from the rig, it might throw up more information. Jack had started to go through it thoroughly and so far there was nothing. Except some communiques which linked Blake with Eloise. But he could see why Lex was so disturbed by what The Guardian had warned.

"It was more than a warning," Lex replied. "More like a prophecy."

Darryl and Salene were dancing, the recent events drawing them closer together. Salene laughed as Darryl started to participate in an indigenous dance the villagers were doing. They whooped it up, encircling Darryl and Salene, amused as Darryl played to the gallery, exaggerating his movements and facial expressions and she joined in, exhilarated by the joyful reactions.

Whatever she thought of Darryl, she couldn't deny that he always brought a smile to everyone he encountered and helped brighten up the day. Certainly Salene's days. And she was becoming more fascinated with him, intent to delve beneath that comic facade and get to know who else was there.

May was sitting near Trudy, trying to comfort her. She was still blaming herself for inadvertently releasing Ebony, Axel and their raiding party.

"Come on, Trudy. This is a time for celebration, not blaming yourself. Because no-one's to blame," May said.

"I just feel so bad. And especially for Ram. I just hope he's alright," Trudy replied, wracked by guilt.

May shared her concern, as indeed did all the Mall Rats. They all felt badly that they had not believed Ram's story. And were stunned how Ebony had managed to get herself involved with Blake's people and that they could have been a part of The Collective.

Trudy shuddered to think what might have happened had Gel not intervened, and in so doing, saved her. And

Brady. She was uneasy why they were trying to seize them, as well as Ram.

May gently reassured her that she shouldn't let her imagination run away with her. It must have been because she and Brady were nearby when Ram was abducted.

Trudy sighed, hoping that was the case. But nevertheless, was still having her doubts.

Ruby had told everyone when they arrived back just exactly what had happened. And that Ram certainly wasn't running off willingly but under protest.

All had speculated what fate might lay in store now that he was being held captive and were determined that they needed to try and find out.

The Priestess had decreed that Zak's burial spot would be sacred. And it gave May a lot of comfort when Lia had translated that one day Zak would be an ancestor to future generations. And that the story of all that had occurred would be handed down through the ages.

Slade was recovering well. And was absolutely thrilled by Ruby's news that 'they' were expecting. Both were determined that they would do all they could to ensure a bright future for their unborn child. As well as themselves. And all their friends. Not just the Mall Rats. But their new-found friends they had met within the indigenous tribe.

Since the assault on Blake's oil rig citadel, Bray had also recovered well from the appalling injuries he had suffered. But was still fragile. After hearing all that had occurred, no one was surprised, realizing that he would need time to become accustomed to any resemblance of a so called 'normal' life, having been incarcerated for so long and subject to so much physical and especially mental torture.

The mere fact that Bray and the Mall Rats had become reunited fuelled speculation and hope that others long lost might one day be found. Bray recounted that he had heard some talk amongst many prisoners, alluding that KC and Alice were being held themselves somewhere. As slaves. From Bray's horror stories, Ellie was alarmed at what Alice's story might be. Likewise KC. Tai San. And all the others. But at least the Mall Rats had hope that their friends and loved ones might one day come back into their lives. As had occurred with Bray.

Bray was caught up on everything that had happened since his disappearance. He was told about the invasion of the Technos, culminating in the eventual need of the Mall Rats to flee their city. All wished more than anything that they had Bray by their side during all the troubled times. They all missed him. Lex, especially. For all that Lex and Bray were occasional adversaries, they were still buddies when it came down to it. And all the Mall Rats knew, along with Lex, that when anyone's back was against the wall, there was no-one better than Bray to face any danger which was thrown at them.

It was a touching moment for all when Bray was introduced to his son. He thought the baby had Amber's eyes but she disagreed, feeling that baby Bray best resembled his father. Amber was sensitive to all the feelings which must have been swirling around Bray, and ushered everyone away so that he would be left alone to cradle the little one in his Daddy's arms.

Bray had been overcome with emotion, kissing the baby gently on the cheek. It was a day he had long dreamed of occurring.

And although he never imagined it being in such circumstances, it still filled him with such a sense of joy, and he could not contain the tears that flowed.

As well as his son, he had also clung to the hope that Amber and he would also become reunited. Throughout all the dark days, the difficult times, he had never given up. However hard everything had been, no matter what life had thrown at him, he never lost faith. That destiny would bring them back together.

He had relied on that hope, that faith, to focus and sustain him. As if a very life force. And without it, he doubted he could have gotten through every passing day.

Though they had been separated for so long, Bray felt they were never truly apart. They would always be together, bound by the very special love they shared. That extra special connection and bond which had been so evident since the very first time their paths had crossed.

But he could understand and was sympathetic to how it must have been for Amber not knowing if he was alive. Or had died. And he didn't expect that they would suddenly just pick up from where they left off. He had hoped that to be the case. But he was a realist and knew 'things' had changed. Now that she had Jay in her life.

And he was pleased for her. That she had found someone. He genuinely warmed to Jay. Liked him immediately, responding to Jay's quiet self-assured manner. And was especially touched when Jay had a private word, reassuring Bray that if he and Amber wanted to get together again then Jay wouldn't stand in the way.

Bray told Jay that the same applied.

But refrained from mentioning that although his shattered body still ached from the many stresses and injuries it had been subjected to throughout his time with Eloise, and recently Blake, there was no pain greater than the joy he had felt at even seeing Amber again.

No wound could ever be inflicted on him that was deeper than the love Bray felt for her. And just being in her presence, as well as being a free man again, was proof to Bray that anything was possible, punctuating his resilient determination throughout all the time since he had been taken prisoner during the Techno invasion - to never let go. To always cast any doubts aside. To always believe.

Jay was pleased to see Amber so happy, and relieved, along with all the other Mall Rats, that Bray had been saved. And was alive. He had reiterated to her the same sentiments he had expressed to Bray. That although Jay loved her, he would step aside. If that's what she wanted. Truly wanted.

Amber couldn't bear to even think about any aspect of this, let alone discuss it with Jay. And certainly not Bray. Not for a while. Though she knew those matters would need to be addressed, she suggested that Bray needed time to recuperate. And then they could go over it all, along with the other issues the Mall Rats needed to consider, concerning what the future now might lay in store for them all.

Amber was painfully aware that she herself needed some time and space to go over everything. There was so much to think about.

The Priestess had invited them to remain on her sacred lands. Lex seemed keen. And Amber could see why. Living an uncomplicated life in the natural world with nature had once appealed to Amber as well, during her time with Pride and the Eco tribe. Though Amber, like the others, wondered if Lex was more infatuated with Lia, or the Priestess, fuelling some kind of fantasy of living on a paradise desert island. Nevertheless, there was some merit in Camp Phoenix being built into a more permanent base.

Others, like Ruby and Slade, pondered if they should even try and return to the city.

Trudy was keen. Fearing that these islands weren't safe. Not only for her or Brady. But everyone. She was sure that she and her child had also been a target of Axel and his men.

May also wondered if Ram had been right. And their homeland was safe from any 'virus'.

Jack and Ellie agreed that it might be the case. But no-one, at this time anyway, could face the prospect of another long sea voyage. And even if they could, everyone shared Jack's view that the logistics of sailing a vessel back across the vast ocean would prove to be a difficult task. Though not impossible. The recent events had encouraged the Mall Rats that nothing was indeed impossible.

Amber's emotions were in a state of complete flux. Torn one way by the love of her past, Bray. Yet pulled in the other direction by the love of her present, Jay. And it was just too overwhelming to even ponder any kind of future beyond tonight's celebrations.

She was painfully aware, however, that she was now entangled in an eternal love triangle, which had tormented so many through the eons since time began.

Bray was someone she had lost her heart to before fate cruelly took him away from her. He was the father of her child and she had never expected to ever see him again. Miraculously, this had occurred, just as she had hoped one day it might. But in reality, she had always held her doubts, resulting in her entering into a relationship with Jay.

Jay and Amber had experienced so much together. She relied on his honest advice, the strength of his convictions, the two of them sharing many beliefs. She had thought, with the absence of Bray, that Jay would be central to her and her baby's life, their entire future. But now there was just so much to consider. And she needed time.

So tonight, she was determined to put it all out of her mind and focus on the present. Rather than the future.

Amber checked on baby Bray, who was fast asleep next to Brady in the guest hut. Then she stood at the doorway, watching the party. Reflecting on all that had occurred since they left the city. And was enjoying seeing everyone enjoying themselves.

"Are you okay?" Jay asked, arriving from the barbecue. He kissed Amber gently on the cheek.

She nodded, while Jay wrapped his arms around her.

"Everyone seems to be having fun. Except you," Jay said softly.

"I'm fine. Really," Amber replied. "We should all feel so proud, Jay," she continued. "We've come so far. But we've still got a long way to go. And I'm determined - we'll get there."

"I'll drink to that," Jay said. "And so will you. Stay where you are and I'll get you one of these. But I warn you - it's lethal," he said, indicating the coconut, and sipped on the juice while he crossed back to the barbecue area.

Amber leaned against the side of the doorway gazing at all the celebrations and smiled slightly to herself, noticing Bray dancing with Emma. But she couldn't help but feel pangs of jealousy welling deep inside.

Bray was very protective of Emma's two young siblings and had also paid close attention to Emma since they had all arrived. Amber knew that it was natural that they would have bonded. After all they had gone through. Amber shuddered, recalling the news Bray had relayed of his time with The Fallen. And it was typical of Bray to try and help Emma and her younger brother and sister. He had always shown such great compassion and a willingness to help those in need. Particularly those with a special need.

But Amber couldn't deny that Emma exuded something extra special. A haunting beauty and dignity, a poise and bearing which few would be able to resist. She endeared herself to all she encountered. And had certainly had a profound effect on Amber, who admired the innate strength and courage Emma had displayed, simply even to get through every passing day, let alone the way in which she cared for her siblings. Along with all those around.

There was a gentleness about her. As there was with Bray. Amber recalled someone once saying that opposites didn't actually attract. But those displaying similar characteristics seemed to be inextricably drawn together. Bray himself possessed so many wonderful qualities, standards, ideals.

Amber continued watching and felt as if her heart was breaking as she cast a glance at Jay at the barbecue area, getting her one of the coconut drinks, before glancing back at Bray. Emma was laughing, clearly enjoying all the celebrations and especially being with Bray, gently leading her to join Darryl and Salene, encircled by all the villagers, clapping and singing.

Emma and Bray joined in the dance and Amber thought it was wonderful that Emma was participating. No doubt Bray was inspired by it, too. Anyone would be.

The world had fallen into darkness since the adults had perished. But Emma seemed to be guided by an unseen force of light. Fuelling a will to survive. No matter what she suffered and endured. Bray had done the same, throughout all the horrendous things he had to suffer.

Amber, of course, was unaware that she had been Bray's light. And wondered now if she was also blind. Bray was special. And would always occupy a special place in her heart.

But so too, Jay, who now dragged her to join in the dancing and share in all the celebrations of all that had been accomplished.

Trudy was encouraged to join in as well. To get her mind off Ram, Ebony, Axel and his men.

Amber had felt just as bad as all the others that she had ever doubted Ram and was intent in trying to rescue him. And bring Axel and his men to justice. Along with Eloise's people, as well as The Fallen. Just as they had with Blake and his forces.

Bray especially was determined for The Fallen and those working with Eloise to be held to account. He had never been driven by revenge. But had some scores to settle.

There would be many more challenges ahead. As well as decisions which needed to be made. For all concerned.

As to Ebony? Everyone was sure that their paths would cross again and that she would ultimately get what she deserved, being no more than a rat, deserting what she perceived to be a sinking ship when she left the Jzhao Li.

But the Mall Rats were different.

They looked out for each other. Stood by each other. No matter what adversity. And they would work together to build a better world, somehow, somewhere.

They might no longer live in a shopping mall but that would never prevent them from living together as a Tribe, wherever that might be. Keeping their dream alive. They were still Mall Rats, after all...

The Tribe: A New Dawn

A.J. PENN

A New Dawn

THE TRIBE

The long awaited sequel to A New World
in the continuing saga of The Tribe

Dedication

Dedicated to the fans who keep the dream alive.
And with loving thanks to my family -
and for every day being a part of your tribe.

PROLOGUE

Tai San took a moment to watch the sun ascend over the distant hills, casting its warm glow all around her, spreading beams of light across the darkness of the surrounding countryside, bringing the dawn of a new day.

Grasping the wooden handle of the rusty scythe in her hands, her fingers sore and aching from the many splinters, blisters and cuts she had suffered, Tai San braced herself for the heavy work ahead. It was harvest time and she was to reap the crop she herself had planted - what felt like an eternity ago.

She had been awoken in the very early hours of the morning by her captors and taken to the field so she could begin her manual toil. It was the same routine she had gone through for - how many months? She did not know. All feeling of time passing had long since gone, each day rolling into the next in an endless cycle of slave labour.

It was a miracle the crop had grown as well as it had, Tai San felt, admiring the corn that now circled her, proud that she had brought life to such a barren and inhospitable land, the field having been nothing more than an empty patch of earth when she first arrived.

"Thank you," Tai San whispered to the corn, her voice hoarse and throat dry from the endless billowing of dust. But it was also in gratitude to the spirits of the elemental world as she sliced the first gathering of the harvest and gave thanks to nature for what it had provided.

The sounds of swooshing and swirling of farm implements held by her fellow slave workers filled the air as work began in earnest, joining the morning chorus of birdsong.

Tai San glanced at the birds fluttering overhead in the dawn sky. Would she ever be like them – free to go where she wished, to do as she chose, like she had been once before? Or was her life to be forever one of captivity, a prisoner to others seeking to make her an instrument of their will? How she wished she could soar above like the birds and escape her plight.

She had thought about escaping many times. But there were too many guards. Her captors were well organized and disciplined. No prisoner had ever successfully escaped. All who tried had been punished severely – with the result that other slave workers were also collectively reprimanded, even if they were innocent, to discourage any further attempts. Tai San couldn't take the selfish path and try and secure her own freedom because she knew that by doing so, other prisoners would suffer as a consequence, especially if she succeeded in making an escape. There was to be no getting away. Not yet.

Some of the other slave workers nearby were already exhausted for all it was the start of a new day and cried out, having received a kick from the guards to signify there would be no respite from their expected toil - but any weeping was probably more due to the fact that most had lost all hope, their spirits crushed, bodies aching, their tears watering the dusty soil.

Tai San worked steadfastly though. She refused to let her plight get the better of her. She still had her pride, dignity, her inner essence - she hadn't lost herself or her identity and had long ago resolved that her captors would not 'break' her. Somehow - she would pull through.

Nature was sustaining Tai San, enriching her life force, bringing her solace, perspective and inner peace. The sun on her face, the birds singing, the plants and insect life all around her - the power, energy and sounds of the natural world drowned out whatever inner anxieties Tai San had about her own fate, any fears of the future. She was part of a bigger picture, aware of her connection to the earth itself. Nothing could extinguish Tai San's own inner fire, quell her unbreakable spirit.

Her captors had taken away Tai San's freedom and her time - but she would not allow them to take away or infiltrate her soul, her hopes. Or her dreams of what still could be.

The sun would rise again, Tai San knew. And in that new dawn, there would always be a future. There was something greater in life that no physical captivity could ever imprison. Her spirit was free.

Suddenly Tai San heard the sounds of an approaching vehicle and looked around to see a van, moving at speed, churning up clouds of dust.

It was the first vehicle Tai San had seen for a long time – she had lived in isolation with her fellow slaves under the watchful eyes of the overseers and usually didn't see any outsiders.

As the van skidded to a halt, the door on the side opened and several guards jumped out, to be met by the overseers.

Tai San continued scything the harvest, glancing out of the corner of her eye, wondering what it all signified.

She heard an animated conversation taking place between the overseers and the new guards. They, like Tai San's fellow prisoners, were all about the same age. Tai San did not understand the language they spoke – she was far from home in a foreign land - but there was no need to. It was clear from the tone of the voices that there was something of importance going on.

One of the overseers was now pointing at her – and the guards began walking towards Tai San, a sense of purpose in their stride. Tai San wondered why she, alone, out of the other slaves, had aroused their interest.

"What do you want?" Tai San asked, instinctively feeling threatened, her voice raspy, staring defiantly. It was pointless to ask, she reflected, since it was unlikely the guards also spoke her language.

The guards encircled her. Heavily outnumbered, she considered using the scythe in her hands as a weapon in self-defence.

In a split second, the guards lunged, seizing Tai San by the arms, one of them squeezing her wrist, forcing her to drop the scythe on the ground.

Tai San protested, struggling and squirming to get away as she was lifted up into the air, the guards grabbing her by her legs and carrying her. Tired, weak and emaciated - there was nothing she could do to get out of their clutches. She was blindfolded and a cloth was tied around her mouth, suppressing Tai San's desperate cries.

None of the other slaves came to her aid, too intimidated by their captors to offer assistance, and they watched as Tai San was carried by the guards into the van, the door quickly closing heavily behind her.

The vehicle took off at speed, accelerating away, leaving behind the billowing dust receding in the slave fields that had for so long been Tai San's home.

* * *

Over the ensuing days Tai San had been taken some distance to a different city, and then placed in a well guarded house full of other prisoners but had been kept apart from them in a solitary room, the door locked at all times.

Her abductors had fed her amply and cleaned her up. Her long, mottled, filthy, tangled hair had been washed, the dust and dirt from her previous existence as an agricultural slave washed away. The food she was given was most welcome, as was the feeling of being clean. Well treated as she had been, ultimately she was still a captive, however, and felt she had exchanged one form of slavery for another.

Her hopes were raised that something else might be in store when a female jailor brought Tai San a fresh change of clothes, exchanging the rags she wore for a pretty dress. Her fingernails were manicured, a flower tastefully arranged in her hair. Tai San had even had some make up put on her face, accentuating her natural physical beauty.

The intentions of her captors became clearer when she was taken later in the day to a public gathering in a street, in a city Tai San did not recognize, along with the rest of the prisoners from the slave house.

Tai San and the other slaves had been manacled together in chains and were paraded before an assembled crowd, the onlookers eyeing the slaves with interest, assessing them.

So it was to be an auction, Tai San realized. She was to be put up for sale.

One by one the slaves were presented to the audience, the auctioneer leading the proceedings, surveying the crowd as hands shot up, arms were waved, bids called out. It was a cacophony of noise, a disorderly mess of baying and shouting until an eventual price was settled for each captive on offer.

But the currency wasn't monetary. Instead, bids ranged from goods to resources, equipment to territory, even various promises and favours.

Soon it was Tai San's turn, the last of the prisoners in line. A hush descended on the crowd as she took centre stage, the most attractive looking of all the slaves available, her bright dress billowing in the breeze, Tai San capturing the attention of all.

She felt exposed, ashamed. Like a possession. A piece of meat. Someone else's toy. She tried to retain her poise and dignity but there was something inhuman about it all. This was a denial of her very will, her human rights, and there was nothing she could do about it. Overwhelmed by superior numbers and the occasion, Tai San wished she could become invisible and disappear from the attentive stares of the crowd focused on her, escape from what was unfolding. She tried to look away but one of her captors forced Tai San's head up so all the onlookers could see her delicate pretty features.

The auctioneer signalled, beginning the auction. The crowd erupted into a frenzy of excited bidding, the interest in Tai San swelling to a crescendo. Bids and offers quickly reached record levels, passing the value of all the other slaves.

Tai San felt like an alien on a different planet, lost in a foreign land. Alone. Helpless. She still couldn't understand the various languages being used by the crowd, a multitude of accents and words beyond her comprehension but she was aware the next phase of her fate would be decided by whoever emerged as the highest bidder.

From somewhere in the throng a voice shouted out what was clearly an enormous bid, making themself heard over all the yelling. The bid included an ongoing supply of food but more vital in this dangerous world - the promise of protection.

The auctioneer leaned forward, scanning the sea of faces for whoever had called out the offer, amazed by the 'price' Tai San was getting – and finding the owner of the voice - a girl just slightly younger than Tai San. The auctioneer prompted and the girl repeated her bid in confirmation, the other buyers settling down as they realized they could not match the huge value just now bid.

The auctioneer's grin conveyed his delight at the massive offer Tai San had garnered. He would receive a percentage of the food as a commission. Likewise the protection, and was already working out how he might trade this throughout his network, which extended far and wide. Clanging a gong, he indicated that the auction was over.

The crowd slowly began to disperse. Tai San was separated from the other slaves who had been sold, her guards putting new binders on her wrists and ankles, readying her to be handed over.

* * *

Tai San's fate had taken a new turn. She felt trepidation at what lay in store as the girl who had 'bought' her at the auction led her new possession along, pulling the chain bound around Tai San's wrists.

They were making their way, flanked by guards, through what had once been a luxury resort located outside the city, *The Gardens Of The East*. Tai San noticed the name on a sign at the entrance when they arrived, visible in various languages, representing the international clientele who had obviously once frequented it in the old, adult world.

Unlike the city of the slave traders in which she had just been sold, with its graffiti and decay, so similar to Tai San's own home city, *The Gardens Of The East* was like a paradise, a stunning complex left over from the adult times and mostly intact. A refuge from the chaotic and dangerous world outside.

In the main courtyard, ornate fountains spouted water into the air, the lawns were manicured, the gardens tended to, neat and orderly, well-cut hedges trimmed to perfection in a variety of shapes showing the care and privilege of whoever lived there – as well as the power and influence they must wield in order to live such a luxurious way of life amidst all the poverty, anarchy and disorder.

Everywhere Tai San looked there were trappings of wealth – from what once would have been expensive items of antiquity, sculpture and furnishings - to more modern trinkets and gadgets of the adult technological age, with various still-functional computers and high-tech gear visible throughout the resort.

Whoever lived at *The Gardens Of The East* was clearly rich and powerful. They had a large staff, many servants – or likely slaves, Tai San thought - working hard to maintain the impeccably high standards so obviously expected of them. And more impressive, and also ominous, than the quantity of servants was the number of guards. The resort had effectively its own private army, standing watch on duty to protect whoever was inside.

As they continued on, Tai San was amazed by the scale and beauty of it, a materialistic perfection all around her, such a change from the basic 'peasant' conditions she had been so used to in her life of late, tending the fields, growing the crops for her previous captors.

They passed a servant girl meticulously scrubbing the floor of the outdoor courtyard.

Was that it? Tai San thought, speculating if her fate was to become a servant girl of some kind.

Or was there something more chilling awaiting her, Tai San dreaded, passing a mirror in a corridor and gazing at her own reflection, wondering if her beautiful dress was the first step to her becoming a concubine of some sort, to be pressured to give some other form of labour and attention to whoever was the master of the house, providing 'favours' in exchange for food and lodging? And perhaps even in exchange for her life?

They reached two ornate doors at the end of the corridor, the girl who had bought Tai San knocking politely. A voice within answered, the doors opened, Tai San was led inside.

It was a palatial suite, the centrepiece being an indoor pool glistening with clear water in the large room, itself full of stunning high-quality furniture, Persian rugs, exotic statues. A banquet table was set out, covered in an abundance of fresh fruit and food of various cuisines, prepared by an expert chef.

Sitting in the centre of the suite was a teenager around Tai San's age. Reclining in a leather office chair, sitting by a desk covered in paperwork, several computer monitors, he watched impassively as Tai San was led towards him. He was flanked by servants who waived palm frond fans above his head, keeping their 'master' cool with a constant, gentle breeze.

He spoke to the girl who had 'bought' Tai San – giving an order in a language Tai San didn't understand. The girl bowed dutifully, exiting the room with her guards, followed by all the servants who had been there, closing the impressive doors behind them as they left, leaving Tai San standing alone – with only this mysterious figure - in the suite.

Getting up from his desk, the unknown 'master' advanced toward Tai San. He hadn't taken his eyes off her and stared, considering her, analyzing, in deep thought.

Tai San couldn't help but involuntarily flinch as he approached, each step that brought him nearer bringing her closer to finding out what was to be her fate.

"Who are you?" Tai San asked, warily, before realizing he probably didn't understand her language - or so she thought.

"I am the one you are destined to meet," the stranger said, pulling the flower away from Tai San's hair, causing it to unravel, cascading down on her shoulders, before taking hold of her gently by the hand – and undoing the binders around her wrists, unlocking them with a key, the cuffs clattering to the ground.

"There –" he said, removing the binders around Tai San's ankles and standing back to admire her. "You're free."

"Somehow - I don't think so," Tai San ventured suspiciously. "I'm not here by my choice."

"But you have a choice," he said, sitting down and taking his place again at his desk, typing in on his computer.

Tai San cautiously held her ground – but couldn't resist a glance at the banquet of food just out of arms' reach.

"Go ahead. Eat. That's why it's there."

"I'm not hungry," Tai San replied, though in truth she was ravenous, the prospect of food tantalizing.

"Try the fruit. It was hand picked this morning."

No doubt by slaves, Tai San thought. Still, she had to eat – her body was crying for energy - and advancing toward the banquet table, she picked up an apple, biting into it, savouring the sweetness, the taste.

The stranger tapped data into his computer.

"Tai San. That's T-A-I S-A-N? Is that how you spell your name?" the stranger asked, entering in data.

Tai San turned and considered the stranger in a mixture of growing fear and confusion.

"My name. How did you know my name!?"

"I know a lot about you. And your tribe - the Mall Rats."

That revelation startled her. How could anyone this far from home know anything about the Mall Rats? About her?

"And none of the images do you justice," the mysterious figure complimented, continuing to search on his computer, before casting an admiring glance at Tai San. "You are a lot more impressive in real life."

Suddenly multiple images of Tai San appeared on banks of monitors spread around the walls of the cavernous room. Then, as the stranger continued typing, keying commands, various other multiple images were displayed. Familiar faces from her past. People she hadn't seen for too long, only in her memories, her dreams. Images of Ryan. Patsy. Paul. Alice. KC. Danni. Other members of her old tribe, the Mall Rats.

Tai San gazed around incredulously and turned to the stranger.

"Who are you?" she asked.

For all her anxiety and fear, she felt anger rising. Had this individual had something to do with the disappearance of her friends and loved ones? Were they still alive? In captivity somewhere? What had happened to them?

"I'm a collector. A gatherer, shall we say. Of valuable commodities. Knowledge. And information."

He gazed at Tai San intently, studying her expression, all charm lost from the tone of his voice.

"And I just need one piece of information right now. But first - do you want to live?"

Tai San exchanged glances with the stranger and nodded, wondering where all this was leading. Especially when he keyed in another command and multiple images of a satellite dish from the Eagle Mountain observatory enveloped the entire room.

"Then I suggest you tell me everything. Tell me all that you know. About Eagle Mountain."

CHAPTER ONE

Amber would have to take things one step at a time, she realized, as she walked across the warm sands, trying her best to keep in as much shade from the palm trees lining the beach as possible, cradling her son, baby Bray, gently in her arms.

"You sure look like your father," Amber uttered lovingly, gazing at the child she and Bray had brought into the world.

She thought back to moments of her son's young existence so far, scattered memories appearing in her mind, feelings from the past. She recalled when she first found out she was pregnant, the difficult birth she had endured - and the tragic disappearance of Bray, her soulmate, at the onset of the Techno invasion.

For so long she thought she would never see Bray again - but fate had been kind, surprising both Amber and Bray with their reunion just days before. Her son had his father back.

Amber had initially felt thrilled. Overjoyed. Lost for words. To see Bray again – to hold, embrace him, hear his voice – it was more than a dream come true. The impossible had happened. A miracle had occurred.

Yet she was struggling. Because in the time Bray had been lost, presumably forever, she had given her heart away to another. To Jay.

Soon after Bray's return, he and Jay made an agreement where they would give Amber the space and time she needed. They recognized things would not be easy for her, let alone themselves. And Amber was truly grateful for their empathy.

Bray was sensitive to her existing relationship with Jay, and for his part, Jay himself was acutely aware of Amber's feelings for Bray and how their own past relationship had been broken by the cruel hand of fate brought about by the invasion of the city by the Techno tribe – an offensive that Jay had himself at the time ironically been a pivotal figure in bringing to fruition.

However, several days had now elapsed – and each passing hour made Amber's situation more unbearable.

She loved them. Both. In different ways. Circumstances had led to her entering into a relationship with each, in their own time.

She remembered reading about brides in wars of history past who believed their husbands had died – and who had subsequently remarried, only to find their husbands returning to them after the war's end. Never had she thought that such a similar situation would ever occur to her.

It was none of their fault – certainly not their choice, to be in this position.

Amber was grateful that Bray was still alive – for being brought back to her, as if from the dead.

But now she needed to decide if she would alter the future course of her life. At a crossroads, she had to go down a path, to continue her journey.

It could not be with them both. It had to be one or the other.

Bray. Or Jay.

And she had no idea which way to choose.

Taking a deep breath, Amber dug deep into the fibre of her soul, trying to find strength. Resolve. She promised that for her baby's sake – as well as that of Bray and Jay, she would face up to this most difficult decision. Somehow, in some way, the dilemma they were in had to be broken.

For now she would just have to take things one hour at a time. Day by day.

One step at a time.

Besides, there were other issues and priorities she had to contend with before even contemplating a future. Such as the survival of all within her beloved tribe. Along with others they had recently met.

* * *

Amber joined the rest of the Mall Rats further down the beach. They were gathering together beside an open fire, the welcome aroma of freshly cooked seafood wafting around as Salene grilled a meal fit for the occasion on the bright fiery embers.

"It smells great," Emma complimented as Bray led her by the hand, guiding her to find a place to sit among the others.

"Extra portions for all those who praise my cooking," Salene joked.

"In that case - hail Salene, Queen of cuisine," Sammy said, drooling at the prospect of lunch and trying to ingratiate himself as Salene began passing around servings.

Bray carefully handed Emma a plateful of food. Though not exactly a plate but served in a coconut shell, Emma giving him a lovely smile of appreciation.

Emma was blind, having lost her sight in a mysterious explosion that apparently occurred on the island during the final days of the adults. She had met Bray when he stumbled into her life, Emma having lived as a refugee at Arthurs Air Force base, the place she had been evacuated to during the 'virus' with her younger brother, Shannon, and sister, Tiffany, who now took their places on the beach, sitting beside her.

Bray and Emma had gotten to know each other well during their time together, forming a close bond. Bray was protective and respected Emma's will to survive, her dutiful loving care in looking after her much younger siblings. She was kind, gentle, and in turn had come to appreciate Bray's own steely resolve and determination to look after others and make the post-adult world a better place to live in.

Amber couldn't help but feel a sense of jealousy. Bray and Emma had shared many experiences together so perhaps it was only natural they would be on close terms, Amber reflected. But was there something more to it? A hint of a greater relationship than merely being just two friends?

She quickly dismissed such notions, not wanting to wallow in jealous thoughts. That served no purpose other than fostering distrust, suspicion and heartache. The greater truth was that Amber had to be thankful that Bray was alive – and there - after so much time apart.

"Are you alright?" Bray asked Amber as she approached, noticing she seemed preoccupied.

"I'm fine. Just - thinking things over, that's all," Amber smiled to reassure him.

Amber was also aware of Jay nearby, standing on the other side of the fire. He gave Amber a loving look when she arrived and she acknowledged it with a lingering glance of her own. But displaying her innate leadership skills, managed to compartmentalize her personal issues with other priorities needing to be discussed that affected the future of everyone else, the whole tribe, which is why Bray had convened the group meeting together in the first place.

"That's nearly all of us," Darryl pointed out. "Except May. She's still *out there*, if you know what I mean."

Amber could see May in the distance, kneeling down in the sand, staring out to sea, lost in the endless tide of her thoughts.

May had spent the last few days much to herself, keeping away from the rest of the tribe. Everyone was sympathetic, realizing that she was still grieving for the loss of Zak, her former boyfriend, who had perished when the tribe was shipwrecked on the island.

"Sorry we're late," Lia apologised, approaching the gathering with the Priestess and some of her native tribe. They, too, had been asked to attend the meeting, Bray keen to hear their opinions and knowledge of the island.

The Mall Rats had been invited to stay in the native village after celebrating the victory over Blake but all felt that they needed to return to their encampment on the beach to examine their options. All of course except Lex, that is, who considered the village to be absolute paradise. But most suspected it had nothing to do with his pursuit of an apparent idyllic lifestyle.

"Would you look at that," Lex muttered under his breath and he gave a breathless wolf-whistle, impressed by the sight before him as Lia arrived with the Priestess.

It was no secret to anyone that Lex was totally infatuated with the Priestess, who possessed a spectacular beauty – and in Lex's view, a figure to match.

He was also equally enamoured of Lia, the girl who he had befriended when he and Jack had initially been captives of the natives. With her attractive looks, golden locks of hair and bubbly personality, Lia was a prime candidate for Lex's affections.

Lex had tried on several occasions to seduce Lia, as well as the Priestess, but had been rejected in his efforts to date by both girls, who found Lex's interest in them flattering – as well as an endless source of amusement - yet they had been unwilling to progress matters, not responding to Lex's blatant flirtation with them. This only spurred Lex on further, enjoying the challenge and feeling he was a master in the art of seduction, playing the game.

"What's so special about them?" Gel pouted jealously, totally threatened by Lex's obvious interest in the newcomers, his eyes darting back and forth from the Priestess to Lia.

"You've got to be joking. I mean, look at Lia's legs! They seem to go on forever. And the Priestess - what a body!" Lex said, savouring the sight.

"Is that all you ever think about, Lex?" Gel replied. "Honestly. How could you?"

"Believe me. I could quite easily -" Lex answered.

"Pervert!," Gel smarted, giving Lex the cold shoulder.

"Nothing wrong with - admiring the scenery," Lex defended himself.

"We've got more important things to discuss, Lex," Amber said.

All agreed and went over the immediate problems they had to address. Such as what could have occurred to Ram.

Jay had organized a search party and spent time scouting the local area over the past few days but so far there was no sign of Ram and his captors and even the best native trackers couldn't pick up any hint of a possible direction they had taken. But one thing was certain. They were not in the vicinity. There were no clues whatsoever to explain what could have possibly happened.

The last time Ram had been seen, the former leader of the Technos was captured by Ebony, Axel and some of the guards who had been in Legion, the tribe led by Blake, that had previously dominated the region before being defeated by the alliance of the Mall Rats and the native tribe.

Where had Ebony and Axel taken Ram? Was he still alive? A prisoner somewhere? Would they return? Ebony and Axel had come so close to kidnapping Trudy and Brady, the two of them important and no doubt valuable due to their association and past history with Zoot, the infamous and legendary deceased leader of the Locos, who with his notorious tribe had once been the scourge of the Mall Rats' own home city.

Ram had revealed to Jay and the other Mall Rats, just prior to his disappearance, the existence of a potentially enormous threat – the Collective, an association of tribes originating from faraway lands who had joined together and were seeking to extend their power and influence to one day take over Amber's own home region and city, or so Ram had claimed.

Were the Collective somehow ominously present on the island, as Ram had feared? Was there an enemy force heading right now to attack the Mall Rats? Or was it all a big pretence, a false story concocted by Ram for his own reasons? The enigmatic and mischievous leader of The Technos had certainly spun several webs of lies over the years and was responsible for so many troubles to hit the Mall Rats and countless others.

Was Blake, the leader of the Legion tribe, himself still alive and on the island, biding his time, waiting to strike back and gain revenge against the Mall Rats?

Bray was more concerned about Eloise, whom he had been a prisoner of at a mysterious base left over from the adult times, in the mountains up in the north of the island.

Eloise led – or manipulated more aptly, Bray felt - a cult like group who worshipped Bray's brother, Zoot, believing him to be some sort of a new god. Bray had been subject to all kinds of torments in his captivity under Eloise and her 'Zootists', who had tried to use Bray, a living link to Zoot's bloodline, exploiting him in the pursuit of their twisted religion. Bray had only just managed to make an escape, which led to his epic journey from the north, bringing him eventually back to Amber and the Mall Rats.

Amber wondered if Eloise was linked in with the Collective somehow – and what her connection had been, if any, with Blake and his Legion tribe, who had been stationed in the southern part of the island.

Lia translated as the Priestess and the natives who accompanied her were questioned by the Mall Rats, probing if they had any other knowledge or insight. They explained they knew nothing of Eloise or the strange adult base up in the mountains where Bray said he had been imprisoned.

Emma gave an account of the lives she and her brother and sister had experienced at Arthurs Air Force Base, a tragic tale where their own tribe of evacuated refugees, the Roaches, had gradually been whittled away, its members disappearing, leaving just Emma and the remnants of her family behind. Emma suspected the Roaches must have been captured, traded as slaves by Blake. Had they then been handed to the Collective? Or to Eloise and the Zootists?

"Well, I think wherever she is, the further away this 'Eloise' is from us – the better," Trudy said. "She seems horrible. She makes Ebony sound like my guardian angel."

"So – any thoughts?" Jay asked aloud. "Everything seems a priority. There's Ram, what happened to Ebony, the Collective… Eloise and her Zootists."

"I don't know about the rest of you," Lex spoke up, "but I vote we do nothing."

"You're kidding," Salene challenged him.

"No joking, I'm serious. For all we know Ram could have been telling porkies with his story of the Collective. Playing some kind of mindgames with us. The more I think about it - I reckon we should just stay here - and enjoy all that paradise has to offer."

"We can't just do nothing, Lex," Amber said. "Are you really suggesting you want to sit around - chasing 'coconuts' - while others suffer? What if there are more prisoners out there, right now, like Bray had been?"

"What if there isn't?" Lex didn't back down. "I feel for anyone who goes through what Bray did. Believe me. But maybe Eloise, Ram, The Collective – are all history.

Gone. They might not even still be on the island. If the Collective are here – then I don't exactly see them..."

Lex theatrically looked around, making his point clear.

"… seems like it's just us. And, I mean, look at this place. It's beautiful. Let's live it up a bit, enjoy being away from hassles. Rather than go out looking for them."

"If there's trouble out there – we can't just ignore it," Bray said disapprovingly.

"Bray's right. None of us could be safe," Emma agreed.

"If you want to side with Bray, then that's up to you," Lex said. "But I've got the right to my own opinions - and the best thing I reckon we should do is stay exactly where we are!"

He cast an admiring glance at the Priestess and Lia, which registered with Amber, who had heard enough. And it wasn't just the reference to Emma siding with Bray. Amber was genuinely concerned that Lex was so seemingly oblivious to the potential dangers that could lay in store, blinded by the obvious attraction he felt for the native girls.

"You may want to live in paradise, Lex – and try and singlehandedly repopulate the world with your offspring –"

"You bet I would!" Lex interrupted.

Amber continued, "But who's to say you're right? And what if you're wrong? You work hard, building some sort of new life here – but then one day, you're lying there on the beach, working on your tan - and what if Ram does come back? With Ebony. And the entire Collective on their heels. Your fantasy could easily turn into a nightmare all of a sudden!"

An uneasy silence descended on the group as they assimilated the threat posed by Amber's words.

"Well – I don't know about anyone else. But I plan on leaving soon," Bray eventually announced.

"What do you mean?" Amber protested.

"I have to find out more about Eloise," Bray explained.

All were aware that during the time Bray was held prisoner he had been exposed to a horrific existence. An existence he couldn't articulate. Especially after being tormented, or tortured more like, by apparent virtual reality brainwashing. All in the name of his late brother, Martin, who had chosen a different path to bring about change in the new world after all the adults had perished. And although Bray in no way endorsed his brother's ideology, he felt that Martin had lost his way and the persona of his alter ego, Zoot, was now being dangerously fuelled by the likes of Eloise, who seemed to be intent on manipulating all his brother's followers, the Zootists, with the fanaticism that would bring about nothing more than a wake of devastation and destruction.

"I'll go alone if I have to. I don't expect anyone else to put themselves in danger."

"I'll go with you," Jay volunteered. "And who knows - maybe we'll find Ram along the way."

Bray was touched by Jay's support – especially to come from such an unexpected source. The two obviously had more in common than their rivalry for Amber's heart.

"I'll go, too," Emma announced.

"There's a surprise," Lex snidely remarked.

Amber cast him a look, then considered Bray.

"Do you think that's a good idea, Bray?"

"Please don't patronise me," Emma said quietly. "I'm quite capable."

"I'm sure you are, Emma. I didn't mean anything by it. We just have to try and work out a strategy. Who'll go. Who'll stay."

"Well, I reckon I should keep an eye on our native friends here in the village," Lex suggested.

"I'm sure they can look after themselves, Lex," Gel sighed.

"I'm with you, Bray," Ellie said, standing to show her support.

"Absolutely," Slade agreed, and one by one the others got up, showing their solidarity – Lex, intransigent, being the last one still sitting on the warm sands of the beach.

"Better pack my things," Jack said, having gotten to his feet beside Ellie. "Sounds like we've all got a long journey ahead."

"No, not all, Jack," Amber stated. "We've got to make sure the little ones are taken care of," she added, glancing at Trudy clutching Brady in her arms, Emma hugging her younger brother and sister, Ruby instinctively putting her hands protectively on her pregnant belly, imagining the child within and what kind of world he or she would be born into. And clearly Amber felt the same sentiment as she leaned over and planted a kiss on baby Bray's cheek.

* * *

It was finally decided that an exploration party led by Bray, Amber and Jay would investigate the other parts of the island, starting out with Emma's old home, Arthurs Air Force Base.

Accompanying them would be Jack, Ellie, Gel, Darryl, Emma, Shannon and Tiffany - and they hoped they could find out what had happened to Ram and some more information about the Collective, Bray intent on ultimately discovering more about Eloise and her fanatical Zootist followers.

The rest would remain in the native village.

Prior to their departure the Priestess gave a traditional blessing, slowly arcing her arms in a circle, moving them gracefully, with meaningful intent, in the direction of Amber and the rest of the exploration party.

"What's she doing?" Jay had asked, recognizing it was a gesture of some significance.

"She's giving you a blessing," Lia explained. "Asking the ancestors to watch over you. To give you good fortune."

"Please thank her. We'll hopefully be back in a few days," Amber responded, touched by the Priestess's consideration.

Amber realized that for all of her irritation and questioning Lex's motives on wishing to stay behind, there was no-one better than Lex to work with the Priestess and her warriors to make sure the village was protected.

The Priestess had proposed that instead of living at Camp Phoenix, the makeshift beach encampment they had been in so far, the remaining Mall Rats who were going to be left behind were welcome to share in the greater comfort and security of the native village until the exploration party returned.

Salene was going to stay to help look after Amber and Bray's son, along with Brady, Lottie and Sammy – and to help watch over May, who was still bereaved.

Lia would be with them, acting as translator between the Mall Rats in the village and the Priestess, Lia having learned to speak the native language fluently after living with the Priestess and her tribe in the past. She had offered Lottie and Sammy some lessons, Sammy particularly excited by the prospect – more due to having developed a 'crush' on Lia.

Trudy had wanted to go along to help Bray, to give him her support, but everyone else felt it was more important for Trudy, due to her past personal association with Zoot, to wait with Brady and hopefully keep far away from any potential dangers that they could possibly otherwise be exposed to by getting closer to Eloise and the Zootists - or even Ebony and Axel, in case their paths did cross. Ebony and Axel had, after all, tried previously to kidnap Trudy and her daughter.

Other Mall Rats staying behind were Ruby and Slade. Ruby was pregnant with Slade's child and the overall feeling was she couldn't risk endangering her own health or that of her unborn child by taking part in the long journey.

Slade, similarly, was still recovering from the severe injuries he had suffered in the shipwreck of the cargo ship, the *Jzhao Li*, when it had ran aground several weeks earlier. It was thought also as an expectant father, he would be best served to be with Ruby – and their baby she was carrying inside her.

Lex had apologized to Bray for coming across previously as appearing insensitive – and had, in the end, volunteered to go on the expedition.

Ironically, he had been first surprised, then thrilled, when Amber and Bray thought Lex would be best served by staying at the village and making sure the others were well protected. And he was totally up for that.

"You be careful," Lex said, extending his hand – which Bray shook.

"You, too," Bray responded.

"Don't worry about us. I'll keep my eye on everyone."

Unable to help himself, Lex found his peripheral vision drawn to Lia, standing enticingly near him.

"I'm sure you will," Amber replied, never ceasing to be amazed by Lex's roguish ways. But he meant well and could contribute more by being at the village, Amber was certain, than by being pressured into going along on the trip.

"Ready?" Bray asked Emma.

"No," Emma smiled bravely. "But what choice do we have?"

"Just make sure it's not the blind leading the blind," Lex said, cringing as everyone cast him a disdainful glance. "You know what I mean," he said, faking a smile.

All indeed understood Lex's concern and without being unkind to Emma, probably shared it, questioning the wisdom of Emma embarking upon the mission.

Having gotten to know her well, Bray was acutely aware of Emma's purity of feeling and her innate sensitivity - and that in making their return journey they would be re-tracing their steps, going back to a difficult place they had both once been before in their lives.

The plan was for Emma to act as the guide for the exploration party when they eventually got to Arthurs Air Force Base. After all, she had lived there ever since the adult days and even though she was restricted by her blindness, Emma knew the layout of the base well and would be a useful source of information about her former home.

Secretly she couldn't deny, however, that she was scared about the prospect of the journey they were about to undertake. The ghosts of her past frightened her. But she had long ago resolved to confront any obstacle in her path. Even although she at times was filled with doubt.

Amber felt uncomfortable to see Bray, hand in hand, guiding Emma – but she understood he was just being supportive, even if a part of her couldn't help but feel envious of the attention Bray was giving.

They set out, the rest of the exploration party followed behind.

Turning, Amber gave one last look at baby Bray, cradled in Salene's arms, Salene playfully waving the baby's hands goodbye to his mother as the group set out.

Amber held back the tears. She had to go on this journey, to bear the pain of separation at being away from her son, precisely for his sake. She was determined to make sure he had a better future.

It was time to get on with the next chapter of their lives.

CHAPTER TWO

Strange how life could change, Ebony reflected to herself.

Just days before she had been living with Blake, the leader of the paramilitary Legion tribe, on his oil rig outpost. Through her efforts and cunning she had impressed him, rising to not only become a prominent figure herself in the leadership - but also Blake's lover.

To continue proving her loyalty and capabilities, she had led some of Blake's most able and ruthless warriors on a raiding mission to capture the Mall Rats. To bring them in as valuable slaves, to be eventually traded.

Instead, Ebony thought, recalling the events, going over in her mind how the present situation had come to be, the raid had failed and she had been captured, along with those under her command. The Mall Rats had found unexpected allies in the form of the Priestess and her tribe – but Ebony had been able to escape with the other members of her group, snatching Ram in the process and narrowly missing out on kidnapping Trudy and Brady.

She had been so looking forward to taking Ram back - to show Blake she had proven herself. That she could cut it. She had anticipated the rewards and approval Blake would give for presenting him with that most wanted of all prizes, Ram, a fugitive who the Collective were desperately intent on obtaining, a huge bounty on offer for his capture.

Ebony still hadn't quite figured out just exactly who the Collective were but she was streetsmart enough and experienced in reading the power balances to know that they possessed enormous clout.

Blake would have been pleased with her work – she was sure delivering Ram would more than make up for the loss in not bringing in the rest of the Mall Rats. Ebony had also been longing for Blake's physical touch, the other sensuous 'bonuses' she expected she would receive from him in the comfort of their private quarters.

However, when they got to the coast - Blake and his entire operation seemed as if it had totally vanished. There was nothing left but a burning wreck, the charred remnants of the mammoth infrastructure churning in the wake of its destruction, beginning its gradual descent to the bottom of the sea.

Ebony and the other members of her group - Axel in particular, one of Blake's key lieutenants - were shocked by the turnaround. Was there some sort of accidental fire and explosion? Or had Blake's outpost been attacked?

Whatever the cause, Ebony had to weigh up their options of what to do next. She was concerned at the possibility her lover, Blake, and everything they had possessed or known was no more. And that they were on their own.

Axel was also unsettled about the possible fate of his leader and members of the Legion tribe, along with those who might have also perished who were once under his command. But he wasn't giving anything away. And like the capable military strategist that he was, had himself examined options - some of which he was clearly keeping to himself rather than freely sharing with Ebony. She could tell that. She tried to 'connect' with him, realizing that he'd be a better ally rather than an enemy and could be useful in the event of Blake's demise. But characteristically Axel seemed devoid of any human emotion. He was more like a machine and in a strange way Ebony couldn't help but admire how he conducted himself, which was mostly cold and calculating. Hardly surprising that Blake appointed him his second in command.

"Sure you know where you're going?" Ebony asked coyly, trying once again to establish a rapport as the group made its way through the dense jungle foliage.

"Not unless I double-check the co-ordinates," Axel said coldly, checking a GPS compass for the right directions.

"It's just I don't fancy spending much longer out here in the jungle. I'm more of a city girl," Ebony remarked. "And not to put too fine a point on it, if I'm happy I reckon Blake will be happy, too - that is, assuming he's alright, and survived whatever happened on that rig of 'ours'." She emphasised the word ours to reinforce that they were on the same side, still trying to gauge Axel, 'read him' a bit better. She didn't know him that well, having spent most of her time in Legion literally by Blake's side, or in his bed, day and night.

Now, she was letting Axel guide them. Not lead them. There was a clear distinction in their roles, Ebony felt. And she, however subtly, wanted to ensure all were aware of who possessed the balance of power. She was still in charge and wanted Axel and the other members with her not to forget it. After all, Blake had given her the leadership of the mission.

Soon after discovering the fate of the oil rig, Axel had revealed to Ebony that he was deploying a strategic option - being another destination they were heading to on the island - far away, where Blake's actual commander was apparently based. But he wouldn't give away any more information no matter how much Ebony pressed, which fuelled her intrigue let alone unease.

At one point Ebony wondered if there was a way they could rendezvous with the ship that she remembered Blake had mentioned was due to arrive, having been sent to originally pick up the hundreds of slaves Blake had seized over time who had been kept prisoner on the oil rig.

Axel had convinced her, however, that there would be no way for the large ship to dock without the oil rig to moor beside. Ebony remembered how treacherous the waters were in that part of the island when the massive cargo vessel, the *Jzhao Li*, that she had once been a part of with the Mall Rats, was shipwrecked, meeting its doom on the jagged rocks.

Ebony had reasoned that it was likely the ship would have found the oil rig destroyed and instead altered course, heading for another area, further up the island, where it could dock. And she wondered if that was where they were going to now, making their way across the island in a journey on foot to the destination where the ship might have travelled by sea. Or if Axel's reference that they were all travelling to some sort of headquarters was true. She still didn't know him well enough to know where he was coming from. She still couldn't read him.

So far she had given Axel some leeway, hoping the two could learn to get on. There was little other option, Ebony considered. Axel seemed to know where he was going - even if Ebony didn't. Unlike Axel, Ebony also didn't know who Blake's commander was. Yet she didn't want to undermine her own position and appear uninformed. This would only confirm - rightly - his likely suspicion that he did after all possess knowledge that she did not. That Blake hadn't told her everything.

She had always suspected Blake's Legion tribe had some involvement with the Collective, the existence of whom she had learned a little of in her time with Blake, recalling his many references to being given orders by his 'superiors'. But Blake had never fully revealed the nature of his connection to the Collective, who remained nothing more than a mystery.

Surrounded by the humid jungle with its thick canopy of undergrowth and countless insects biting every inch of her body, Ebony hoped she could trust not only Axel's sense of direction - but her own judgment in how to deal with him.

If Ebony could get to Axel, make him follow her and loyally accept her continued leadership, then she was sure the rest of the warriors would follow suit, Axel being the key, as the most senior among them in Blake's absence.

When Zoot had died, back in the city, Ebony had similarly imposed herself on the remnants of the Locos, taking leadership of the tribe through the sheer power of her personality and dominant will. Let alone cunningly trading on her relationship with Zoot which she was able to manipulate as a valuable currency. She had a point of reference from her past and was confident of being able to keep exerting her influence over Axel and the other warriors. At least until she knew exactly who and what she was dealing with and then she would amend her strategy accordingly.

For all of her scheming machinations - right now Ebony was well and truly lost, branches snapping painfully underfoot – and she didn't like having to depend on Axel or his little GPS gadget. She never wanted too much control to be out of her hands, always determined to be in charge of her future, the mistress of her own fate.

"So - what are we exactly looking for? Some kind of treehouse?" Ebony flippantly asked, trying to appear casual, unflustered, but in truth feeling claustrophobic, trapped by the entangling jungle all around.

Axel ignored Ebony. He remained cold and aloof. Devoid of any humour and human interplay. Which had registered with Ram, as well as Ebony, from the first time he set eyes on Axel.

Now Ram was starting to freak out and was totally on edge, being pushed from behind by two powerfully built Legion guards, his arms bound together, with other more loosely tied vines around his legs to enable him to walk but not have total freedom of movement.

He was desperate. Full of fear. At one time he could have trusted Ebony back in the city long before they had ever stepped foot on the island. But now all the data flowing through the recesses of his mind just didn't compute. He couldn't quite figure out how Ebony featured and what could have possibly happened when she evacuated the *Jzhao Li* ship. Clearly she had formed some kind of relationship with this guy, Blake, and was powerbroking and trying to manipulate it all to her best advantage. But he just couldn't get a handle on Axel. And just exactly where they were all heading.

An involuntary shudder of utter terror moved down Ram's spine as he speculated on all the potential options. It was like he was on his way to his impending doom with every step as he somehow tried to work out what could possibly lay in store for him.

Ram suddenly fell over dramatically.

"I can't go on! I've got cramp!"

"Sure you do," Axel said, forcing Ram back up on his feet. "You'll get a lot worse if you don't keep moving."

Ram clutched at his chest, let out a wailing groan and collapsed to the ground. The guards exchanged a confused glance. Ebony was puzzled, as was Axel, as the group stopped to gaze down at Ram, writhing in pain.

"Are you alright, Ram? Man - you look like you're dying," Ebony asked.

"And I won't be worth anything to anyone if I don't make it," Ram replied through his deep heaving as he struggled to catch his breath.

"Dead or alive makes no difference to us," Axel said coolly, indicating Ram to two guards. "Get him up and we'll drag him if we need to. I want to keep on schedule."

Ram immediately leapt to his feet, totally aghast, and Ebony recoiled in utter amazement.

"That was a quick recovery," she stated, discovering that it had all been a bit of a ruse although Ram tried to cover, realizing that he probably wasn't as valuable a prisoner as he suspected.

"I... ah... just had a bit of wind pain."

He let out a big burp as if to punctuate his fictitious dilemma. There was a glint of amusement in Ebony's eyes but Axel snapped furiously.

"Don't play games with me, Ram, or you'll regret it!
I heard you were once in a wheelchair - and we can put
you back in one easily. The Collective want you – but
they didn't say it had to be in one piece."

"No-one's to lay a finger on him – got it?" Ebony
challenged, not liking Axel's proactive, independent
behaviour.

"Thank you, Ebony. I knew you cared," Ram smiled
ingratiatingly.

"We only use physical force on him when I say so,"
Ebony clarified, Ram blanching at the thought. "So you
better keep walking, Ram. While you still can."

"I can't. I'm not joking this time. I need to stop. I
haven't had a drink for hours – and this heat is killing me
- not to mention the company around here!"

Ram smacked his face, waving away some insects,
though it was clear he was referring more to his discomfort
at being around Ebony, Axel, and the remaining members
of Legion rather than the steaming hot jungle.

"What do you suggest, Ram? That we carry you?
Actually, might not be such a bad idea. To make sure we
stay on schedule," Ebony said, casting a glance at Axel
and indicating to the guards, who lifted Ram so they
could continue on their way.

Ram bellowed out with impotent frustration, sensing
that Ebony might after all wield some power.

"You don't understand, Ebony! You're like a fly -
walking into the spider's trap! They're taking us on a one
way trip to the Collective! Or hell more like!"

Ram decided that it might aid his survival if he tried
to appeal to Ebony, using everything in his arsenal of
tricks to slow their progress through the jungle.

But she was having none of it. She had to show Axel
and the others she was in charge. Impress them with

her ruthlessness. For all of Axel's apparent stance she suspected that in reality Ram was a valuable prize. And that no harm would come to him. Otherwise why would anyone bother transporting him. She had no idea why Ram was important, of course, but had long decided that she was intent on getting her share and the sole accolade for bringing him in.

It was the best option she felt she had at that moment. Yes, there was a history between Ram and Ebony, who had once been married after all. Yet that was a long time ago. If Ram had to lose his freedom – it was a price worth paying.

In this post-adult world, Ebony was determined that whatever the cost – she would survive.

* * *

The thick canopy of the jungle gradually opened up, Axel eventually guiding the group to a clearing.

They had arrived at a decaying runway, carved out in the middle of the jungle. It was a few hundred metres long, wire mesh doing its best to keep back the insatiably growing foliage and trees all around, their branches protruding through the sides of the fences, either side of the long landing strip.

"What is this place?" Ebony asked, marvelling to see an unexpected remnant from the adult times, as if it was a small island of concrete surrounded by a sea of jungle.

"It's where we pick up our wheels," Axel brusquely answered, leading the group along the tattered runaway, marred by potholes and in a state of utter disuse, the decaying concrete showing it must have been abandoned, even in the days of the adults, for some time.

"Can't wait," Ebony said, surprised by Axel's reference to there being a set of 'wheels' nearby.

He guided them to some sheds, part of a storage depot. Retrieving wire cutters from his backpack, Axel proceeded to break the padlock on one of the shed doors.

"Open sesame," Ebony drawled, faking a smile to Axel who just cast her a cold look before suddenly unleashing a wild kick, pushing the creaking door inwards.

An ambulance was inside. A camouflaged, military looking vehicle, adorned with United Nations symbols. Modern, from the very last days of the adults. And Ebony recalled her brief time on the United Nations ship, the *Jzhao Li*, pondering if this was somehow connected. She was jolted out of her reverie by the sound of an electrical humming. The ambulance was 'plugged in' to a generator inside the shed. It was obviously a hybrid style electric powered vehicle and had been left charging by someone. Ebony was curious if it belonged to Blake's tribe – or had been left there by the adults.

"What's it doing here?" Ebony wondered.

"What do you think - it's going to transport us for the next phase of our mission," Axel replied indifferently, opening the driver's door and peering for a moment inside at the battery display on the dashboard, indicating the vehicle had a 70% charge.

Ebony didn't like the sound of that and felt vulnerable, having no idea just what kind of 'mission' was going down. So she needed to change strategy and now was the time.

"This 'mission'," Ebony probed carefully. "You'd be doing yourself a big favour, Axel, if we worked together.

"That sounds like a threat," Axel replied disdainfully.

"It's a promise."

Axel turned, crossed slowly to Ebony. Both eyeballed each other.

Ram checked out the guards, who seemed uneasy but that paled in comparison to the fear welling up in his own being. Ebony had always had a lot of bottle but he wondered if she was perhaps trying to bite off a little more than she could chew. Axel didn't seem the type anyone in their right mind would want to cross. But Ebony was clearly going for it, big time.

"Don't you disrespect me! Have you forgotten who I am? I was by Blake's side. I was his woman!"

"Maybe you weren't as important as you thought you were," Axel responded, challengingly.

Ebony stepped closer towards Axel. "Blake had my back!"

"Blake had strict standards," Axel retorted. "We were all hand picked. And you weren't up to it. Your mission failed, and because of you we weren't there for Blake… As far as him having your 'back' - I'm sure he knew exactly who and what you were – *Loco*," Axel spat out the word condescendingly. "Once he'd got tired of having his way with you, he'd have traded you over for the right price!"

"That's a lie!" Ebony roared. "Blake and I had something you'll never understand. Or is that it? Are you jealous? Did you want some of what I got, Axel? Feel like Blake didn't give you all that you were wanting from him?"

"Maybe you should just leave it there, Ebony," Ram pleaded, sensing that Ebony was going a little too far, getting out of her depth.

"Somebody shut him up!" Axel ordered. "Find something big enough to tie around his big mouth!"

"Don't listen to him - stay put!" Ebony barked to the guards.

"There's only one person giving the orders around here," Axel said coldly.

"Yeah - me!" Ebony interrupted.

"We'll see about that!" Axel snarled. "Arrest her! And tie her up!"

"Screw that!" Ebony countermanded. "Arrest him!"

For a moment the warriors froze, wondering which way to go, their loyalties tested. All realized it was a pivotal moment.

Ram, his eyes darting around frantically, took his chance, sprinting away toward the wire fence bordering the landing strip.

Two guards closest sped off in pursuit, rapidly closing the gap, Ram restricted by the vines loosely tied around his legs.

"I gave you an order - arrest Axel!" Ebony urged the remaining guards, worried she was losing them. Would they continue to obey, respecting her authority?

Ebony got her answer when the other Legion guards crossed briskly toward her. It was obvious they had fallen in with Axel.

Striking out like a cornered tiger, Ebony kicked one in the groin, elbowed another in the jaw, but was overwhelmed by the well trained Legion fighters who restrained her.

Ram, too, had been caught and was being frog marched along the runway back towards Axel.

"We know all about you, Ebony," Axel bragged menacingly. "Queen of the Locos. Once leader of an entire city. Wonder how much you'll be worth?"

"More than you'll ever be," Ebony glared, spitting with contempt - in Axel's face.

Axel wiped the spittle off with his sleeve.

"You'll regret that. Put them in the back!"

Victorious, Axel watched as his prisoners were thrown inside the vehicle.

The doors of the ambulance slammed shut, Ebony feeling as if they were sealing her and Ram's fate. But one thing she couldn't help but notice was that maybe the balance of power was switching. Axel may have won the battle. But not the war. He could have hurt her, just as he could Ram, and for all that she still felt apprehensive of what lay in store as the ambulance sped off, Ebony started to consider that she, like Ram, might have a value and be worth more alive.

CHAPTER THREE

Amber felt like she was caught between some kind of dream - and nightmare. She still had difficulty reconciling that Bray had miraculously returned to her life and needed time to consider the impact on Jay. Let alone what direction it would all take.

In addition there was the safety of all the other Mall Rats to take into account, as well as other people who had recently been introduced into the circle. All were still concerned about the possible fate of Ram and were intent on trying to track him down and to discover how Ebony featured in it all. From Bray relaying his experiences with Eloise and the Zootists, they all needed to learn more about that as danger could manifest at any given time. But right now the priority was to try and uncover some of the complex mysteries surrounding Arthurs Air Force Base.

The group had finally arrived after making the long journey to the base on foot, their bodies aching and tired but their minds racing with all the possibilities of what this area might have been prior to the demise of the adults. Was it some sort of evacuation centre linked in with the United Nations? Or were there more sinister secrets they would soon discover?

Emma had guided them, remembering there was a main arterial road that cut through the heart of the jungle, put there by the adults in the old days for vehicles to access the other parts of the island.

It was the same road Jay and Ram had tread just weeks before when Ram revealed the existence of the Collective.

The Mall Rat exploration party had rested on the roadside, utilizing some of the abandoned vehicles from the adult times to sleep in as temporary cover from the chill of the night. It was an eerie sensation, the road littered with discarded passenger cars and trucks, many of them military types, emblazoned with United Nations symbols.

Amber hadn't slept much at all. In addition to thinking of her tangled situation with Bray and Jay, she had wondered how it would have felt to have been an adult on the island when the 'virus' was running rampant, plunging the world and the lives of billions into the abyss.

That morning the Mall Rats had resumed their journey, Emma leading them along the road to a turn-off which took them to where they now were – Arthurs Air Force Base.

It was an incredible sight with its long runways of asphalt, immense buildings, many several stories high. Amber felt that there must indeed be something more to the existence of the base. And she was determined, along with the others, to shed some light on the mystery.

In the distance were the amusement park style rides that the adults had brought there, presumably to give some form of recreation to any children evacuated – like Emma, and her younger brother and sister.

From what Bray had mentioned how Emma had lost her sight, the blinding light from the explosion was very reminiscent of a thermonuclear detonation and the huge wasteland close by, devoid of any plant, insect or animal life which Bray had travelled through from the mountainous region where he was held captive to the actual base itself, also seemed to highlight that something ominous had indeed occurred.

Whatever did occur clearly resulted in whoever had occupied the base to have quickly abandoned the entire area and Amber wondered if it was solely due to the virus.

Everything appeared as if it was frozen in time. Amber could just picture it all in her mind, visualizing the base in its heyday, what must have been a hive of frantic activity with thousands of inhabitants, children and adults, having lived there.

Yet now it was all eerily still, desolate. Deserted. Nature had begun to reclaim the base, wild grass sprouting up around them, the jungle moving in. Giant construction machines stood motionless, like they were some sort of mechanical dinosaurs, remnants from a bygone era. An uneasy quiet mostly pervaded the air, apart from the sound of a gentle wind rolling in and the sporadic sound of birds and insects, the only denizens seemingly left behind.

"Doesn't seem like there's anyone around," Jack spoke up, breaking the silence that had descended upon the group as they took in what was before them. "I think it's just us."

"We don't know for sure," Bray said, looking around intently for any sign of activity.

They had hoped they might find some sign of Ram – that perhaps he had escaped from his abductors and made his way to the base. So far, however, there had been nothing but the continued mystery of Ram's disappearance.

"Well, if the Collective were here, you'd think they would have been onto us by now," Jay remarked, looking around. "I think Jack's right, it's just us here."

"We'd better hope so. And check it out," Amber said, speaking for all. The thought of encountering the Collective was uncomfortable, Ram having painted a threatening picture of them and the possible danger they could present.

Emma began shivering - but it wasn't from the breeze that was now picking up.

"You okay?" Bray asked, sensing her unease and taking her hand once more, giving his support.

"Not really," Emma said, struggling to hold her composure, torn by the emotions within. "It's just - we're the only ones who ever made it back."

She indicated her little brother and sister, hugging her legs.

"I mean… we're all that's left, the last of the Roaches… I was thinking of all the others who didn't return home."

"Well, you're one of us now, Emma," Amber assured her. "You're not on your own anymore."

Amber gave Emma an encouraging hug, Emma thankful, blinking back tears.

"We'll do everything we can to find out what happened to your friends," Jay promised.

"Then let's make a start," Bray suggested. "We've got a lot of exploring to do."

The Roaches were formed initially from the remnants of children evacuated to Arthurs Air Force Base but the tiny tribe had dispersed or were taken as slaves by other tribes in the area, most of all the Fallen, who worked for Legion as slave traders. And Emma wondered if in reality she would ever see members of her tribe again.

She guided the group to a central hub that connected each section of the base. Once a pretty landscaped garden area, its wooden benches were now rotting in decay, wild weeds and plants bursting up from the uneven, broken paving stones in the ground.

The plan was to stay the night at the base and see what they could come up with before assessing their next step, Bray still intent on continuing to the north, where he believed Eloise awaited, set on confronting his past.

Emma remembered much of the base from the time before she had lost her sight. Slowly, she had learned to rely on her other senses to get around and knew the layout well from her past life there, as did her younger siblings.

"To our left should be the main office and administration block," Emma said, pointing at a tall building. "To our right is the hospital and medical centre... and straight ahead, that should be the accommodation quarters."

She was correct on all counts.

"I've been inside them all before – but of course, you might be able to find - or 'see' things I can't."

There was a hint of regret in her tone.

"What do you think, Emma?" Bray wondered. "Where should we search first?"

"Whatever you do - don't go anywhere near the lower levels of the hospital," Tiffany interrupted.

"Why?" Amber probed.

"We never went down there," Emma explained. "It was out of bounds in the adults' time. The other Roaches believed it was cursed. Haunted. I remember hearing it was where the adults were meant to have conducted some kind of research. There were rumours... of a lab. Some big, strange looking computers."

"Did somebody say computers?" Jack perked up at the sound of one of his most favourite things.

"Jack can't get enough of them," Ellie explained to Emma, trying to brighten the mood. "Sometimes I feel he'd pay me more attention if I was a piece of technology."

"I AM ELLIE," she started speaking in a playful, over the top computerized voice, waving her arms around like a robot. "I LOVE JACK, I LOVE JACK."

Jack grinned affectionately. "Actually, that *is* pretty hot," he joked.

Emma smiled, the first look of happiness they had seen on her face since they had arrived at the base.

"You're lucky to have each other," she said.

Amber cast Jay and Bray a quick glance but before reflecting more on her own personal predicament agreed with the others that their priority was to split themselves into groups to expedite their exploration of the gigantic base.

Jack and Ellie volunteered to go to the hospital block, intrigued by Emma's recollection of a lab and some computers possibly being there.

Emma was to stay back with Darryl, Tiffany and Shannon in the central garden hub area.

Jay offered to investigate the office and administration block.

"Amber? You want to come along?" Jay asked.

"Maybe I'll just stay here for now with Emma. That is, if you don't mind?"

"'Course not. I'd like that," Emma replied.

"I'll go with you, Jay," Gel purred flirtatiously.

"I'd appreciate the help," Jay replied.

"Be careful – all of you," Bray called out, beginning to make his way to the accommodation block as the group dispersed.

He preferred to go alone to explore the building, feeling he worked best by himself as a scout, having fulfilled the role many times back in the city that once was their home. Besides, he wanted to review where he had been held when he first arrived at Arthurs Air Force Base during his incarceration by Emma, Tiffany and Shannon.

At the first sign of trouble, any hint of danger, the group had agreed to make their way back to the central garden hub where Emma, Amber, Tiffany, Shannon and Darryl waited.

Darryl picked up a long piece of wood from one of the broken benches nearby and began waving it through the air as a weapon, practicing martial arts movements. Just in case there were any potential enemies around after all.

Amber watched as the others set out on their way.

Jay going in one direction, Bray the opposite.

It was almost symbolic, Amber felt. A metaphor for the conflict she felt in her heart.

Amber hoped they would all be back soon from their explorations. Would stay safe. And be able to discover something to give them a greater understanding of the mysteries and secrets the island held.

For all they knew, no matter how quiet the base seemed, Amber worried there could be Collective forces nearby. Had they strayed directly, unwittingly, into the heart of danger?

Perhaps they should have all stayed behind with Lex and the other Mall Rats at the village.

Clutching Emma's hand, Amber just hoped they hadn't all made a huge mistake.

* * *

The door burst open, swinging back and forth on its hinges, as Jay shoulder-charged inside, followed by Gel.

"Can't you just use the handle like normal people?" Gel asked. She was anxious. The two of them were making their way through the administration complex, Gel imagining all kinds of fearful threats lurking around every corner.

"It was stuck," Jay explained calmly, studying the contents of the latest room they had come across.

"Well - try not to make too much noise! What if someone else is in the building?"

"They'll know we're here from the sounds of your shoes," Jay replied. "Why don't you just take them off?"

Gel was still wearing her uncomfortable platform heels, a fashionable pair that had commanded a small fortune in the old adult world. Moving through the offices, one room and one level at a time, the noise of the clacking from Gel's heels – and complaints about her sore ankles - had echoed loudly through the otherwise empty corridors.

"They're my lucky pair of shoes. And there's only one way you could persuade me to take them off…"

"And how would that be?"

"*You know…* Let's find a place we can rest. And I'll show you." Gel pouted, smiling with mischievous allure, leadingly.

Jay couldn't help but smile in return at Gel's antics, her trying it on, now of all times.

"We've got important things to be getting on with," Jay said, changing the subject. "Thank you, anyway. Besides - I'm already spoken for."

"Try reminding Amber that."

Gel's innocent throwaway remark hit Jay like a poleaxe in the gut but he resolved to focus on the task at hand and the two began searching through filing cabinets, opening the drawers of desks, rummaging through stacks of paper, files, manila folders, leftovers from the adult world, as they had already done in the other levels of the building.

"We should never have separated from the others," Gel said, having had enough of the entire exercise. "We're wasting our time. You really think you're going to find Ram hiding under a desk? Or some clue - inside a drawer?"

"You never know."

Gel opened a filing cabinet and let out a piercing shriek.

Looking like she was going to be sick, Gel waved her arms frantically, almost trying to erase from her mind the image of what she had just seen.

"What is it!?"

Jay raced over - and saw the subject of her revulsion, a nest of rats running around inside the cabinet, crammed full of shredded paper, old confectionary wrappers and scraps of food, having been scavenged from somewhere by the rodents.

"It's disgusting! The sooner we get out of here, the better."

"Still think your heels are bringing you luck?"

Gel slipped off her shoes and threw them at the infested filing cabinet. "The rats can wear them for all I care."

They continued their search, going up one level at a time.

"I'm starving!" Gel complained soon after. "And I never want to see another flight of stairs ever again." She rubbed her feet, emphasizing her point.

"Just a few more rooms, I reckon."

He walked over to the wall of the office they were in as if transfixed, studying a large map pinned to it, the corners of the paper curling up, faded from the intense sunlight peering in through the broken windows.

It was a map of the island.

"That's us. Where we are right now," Jay murmured, pointing his finger at the south of the island, Arthurs Air Force Base marked clearly.

Following the road up, his finger moving along the map, Jay found a region to the north. There were icons of several buildings nestled in the curves of the mountains on the map. Also graphics highlighting that the information was Code A, Strictly Classified. It looked like another base of some kind - and Jay could just make out its name on the faded map.

"Project Eden... I wonder what that was all about?"

"What's all those things?" Gel said, going closer to the map to have a look herself.

"Ships."

"I knew that - silly. I mean, what would they all be doing there? And don't say 'sailing'."

Jay smiled despite himself and continued to study the map.

Far out from the coast, several ships were represented by symbols, making up a fleet in the sea. A pencil line of dashes indicated their course – leading to the northern part of the island, to where 'Project Eden' was itself located.

"So that's where it was headed. She must have gone way off course," Jay reasoned.

"She? Who?"

Jay indicated the name of a particular vessel, marked on the map. It was one they were all familiar with - a United Nations container ship... the *Jzhao Li*.

* * *

Scouting the accommodation block, Bray was taking a step back into his recent past by going to Arthurs Air Force Base.

He recalled the fateful day when he, along with Emma, Tiffany and Shannon, had been taken prisoner by the Fallen, a small but vicious gang who had terrorized the lives of Emma and her siblings, before being delivered as slaves to Blake on his oil rig. Ultimately, it had all led to Bray's unexpected and emotional reunion with Amber and the rest of the Mall Rats.

What would happen to them all now, Bray wondered?

He believed the Fallen presented no more of a threat, the Priestess having relayed at the village that the tribe had apparently disbanded, imploding through infighting, after losing their previous backers, Blake and his Legion tribe.

Bray knew the Mall Rats would have to be on their guard in case their paths ever crossed again with Belle, the leader of the Fallen, or her deranged former followers. Although they may no longer be a tribe, the ex-members of the Fallen were undoubtedly still dangerous individuals.

Yet there was a greater threat to all their survival and the peace of the island, Bray felt. In the form of Eloise.

Cruel and as vindictive as she was beautiful, she had left many wounds in Bray's soul. He would be scarred for some time, emotionally, by the torment Eloise had inflicted which still lasted, far longer than the physical wounds he had suffered from her which were now beginning to heal.

Subjected to many distressing experiments, Bray had been hooked up to virtual reality machines left over by the adults, Eloise seeking to twist his feelings, his very essence, to use him as a living idol, a link to his brother who she falsely touted as a god for her own manipulative ends.

Eloise had even tried to conceive a child with Bray, wanting to carry his genes – and indirectly, those of his brother – into a new generation through having a baby with him, no doubt intending to use the child as a rallying point for the worshippers of Zoot, with Eloise positioning herself as a new 'Mother Divine', to be lauded and obeyed.

Eloise had failed to get Bray to give her the child she craved from him. He would never betray his principles – or his commitment to Amber.

Engrossed in his thoughts, Bray almost didn't notice the graffiti now visible in the corridors. Stick figures, with joyous faces and wide smiles, were painted on the walls representing some of the people who used to live there.

It was the Roaches. Emma's old tribe.

Without realizing it, Bray had passed into the actual accommodation area where the Roaches had once resided.

Bray studied the images on the walls, some drawn by what must have been, at the time, very youthful childlike hands.

Bray discovered a cartoony crayon picture of a girl with long hair, freckles and a toothy grin. A name was scribbled beside her. It was Emma, Bray recognized - a representation of her younger self in another, happier time. Maybe it had been drawn by Tiffany or Shannon, Bray reflected. She was surrounded by friends – the other members of the Roaches.

Now, only Emma, her brother and sister were left, Bray knew. He could sympathize with losing loved ones, Bray having mourned his brother, Zoot – and before that, his entire adult family, who had been ravaged by the 'virus'.

Emma was a sweet and sensitive soul. Bray felt very protective of her. He genuinely liked and cared for her.

But what of Amber, Bray wondered. The girl to whom he had once given the keys to his heart?

Quickly ascending a stairwell, Bray's mind raced, thinking of the predicament she was in, as well as himself and Jay.

Amber was the vision that had kept him going when he had lost all other hope. The goal of seeing her again, rekindling their loving relationship, was all that had stopped him from giving up due to his deprivations under Eloise.

Bray had never counted upon Amber finding another lover. Initially, he was shocked to learn of her relationship with Jay. But he couldn't blame her. She thought he was genuinely gone. Lost forever, after the Techno invasion.

There was nothing Bray wished for more than to rekindle his love with Amber, pick up where they had left things.

Not all wishes came true, however. Bray understood times had changed. Amber faced an awful, difficult decision. And in the small time they had spent together, Bray had really come to respect Jay's character and qualities, for all that they were both in contention for Amber's affection.

Ultimately, Bray believed Amber had to choose her own fate. He just hoped, yearned with all his heart, that he could be in her future - and they could raise their son together.

Reaching the top floor of the accommodation block, Bray exited a door and found himself outside on a helicopter deck.

He could scout no further and had finished, finding no more information about the Collective or Ram, discovering instead just the emotional remnants of Emma's own past.

The wind whistling around his hair reminded Bray of being back in the city when he would ascend to the top of the skyscrapers there, finding peace in his solitude, solace far from the chaos and madness occurring down below.

Being so high up now, Bray currently had a perfect view of the hellish wasteland beyond the base.

A long barbed-wire fence crisscrossed in both directions as far as the eye could see.

Bray stared past the fence to the lifeless, hostile desert-like environment that lurked in the distance. He had journeyed through it once, accidentally finding the base that brought him into contact with Emma and her brethren.

Somewhere, the other side of the wasteland, was Eloise.

Their paths would cross again, Bray vowed.

Looking up to the heavens, wispy clouds billowing across the blue skies powered by high winds, Bray could feel a spiritual connection to his own past, an affinity to loved ones gone - but never forgotten. To his parents. Other members of his family. His brother, Martin.

For them, for Amber, for their child, for Emma, the Mall Rats and all those he cared for – and for what was right – Bray promised, somehow, he would put an end to the reign of terror going on in the north, beyond the wastelands.

He would find a way to stop Eloise.

* * *

"You're not claustrophobic, Ellie, are you?" Jack wondered aloud, feeling a sense of being enclosed.

"I wasn't before - but I might be, after all this."

"We should be at the end soon. I hope…"

It was like they were going into the bowels of the earth itself, the dark depths uninviting, as Jack and Ellie walked down stairwell after stairwell.

"I guess you can see why Emma said it was called the 'lower levels'," Ellie joked, trying to lighten the mood, if not the surroundings.

They had gone into the hospital and medical block and considered if using the elevators in the building was an option to take them down to where Emma believed there was a 'lab' with computers or equipment that could be worthwhile checking out.

However, there was no power in the building. The elevators were inactive, despite Jack pressing all the buttons frantically in a fruitless effort to get them to work.

The fire escape stairwells had eventually been discovered, thanks to Ellie, enabling them to descend into the underground floors of the building.

They were guiding their way through the murky gloom with flashlights they had found in a maintenance storeroom – which had also been full of lightbulbs, ironically now useless, given there was no working electricity supply.

"How long do you think these batteries have?" Ellie asked, angling the beam of the flashlight in her hand.

"Hopefully long enough. I don't want to get stuck down here."

Jack was sure there had to be a fuse box or some switches somewhere that connected to an electrical generator.

Arriving at the bottom of the stairwell – and feeling like he was some kind of rabbit or mole underground – Jack's flashlight illuminated a door in the darkness.

"I wonder what's in there?" Ellie said.

"Only one way to find out. Here goes," Jack replied nervously, pushing open the door.

The two entered a cold, moist, pitch black room.

"That's strange. Can you hear what I hear?" Ellie asked.

There was an audible humming, almost like there were several refrigerators in the room. So strange, Jack thought, when the rest of the building had no electricity supply.

"It must have its own power source," Jack reasoned, shining the flashlight around, its beam cutting through the darkness.

"It's freezing in here," Jack shivered as they continued searching.

"Maybe we'll find some ice cream," Ellie wished dreamily. "Can you just imagine?" She hadn't had ice cream for what felt like an eternity, one of her favourite treats from the past.

"It's certainly cold enough," Jack said, looking for a power board, a fuse panel, anything to bring them light.

"I know one way we could keep warm," Ellie grinned. "It's nice to be alone. Just the two of us."

"Something touched my leg!" Jack called out, startled.

"It was me, silly," Ellie whispered.

"This isn't a very romantic spot, Ellie," Jack said – but as Ellie approached, wrapping an encouraging arm around him, she all too easily distracted Jack from his investigations.

"I'm so lucky to have such a 'genius' for a boyfriend. How 'bout you find a way to turn the lights on – and then maybe we can find out just how romantic this place really is."

"You got a deal," Jack beamed.

Jack felt a new lease of life and a few minutes later, finally located a row of switches in a fuse box on the wall.

"Here we go, I think this should just about do it," Jack said, excited by his discovery. "Feels like I'm about to turn on the Christmas lights back home."

"Then fire it up - let's see what we got!"

Pressing the switches on the wall, one by one, giant emergency lights on the ceiling sprung to life, casting the room in a bright glow, Jack and Ellie's eyes taking a few seconds to react and readjust to the sudden brightness. And they gazed in absolute astonishment.

The room they were in was large, circular shaped - it reminded Jack of the Eagle Mountain observatory.

Yet where Eagle Mountain contained rows of computers – this room was also full of something else – which clearly was the cause of the cold, moist atmosphere, the humming electrical sounds.

"Are they - coffins?" Ellie gasped, squeezing Jack in a hug, terrified by what they had uncovered.

For a split second, Jack couldn't emit any words from his dry mouth as he tried to control his sense of growing disbelief and tension.

But finally he stated weakly "I don't know about... coffins. They look more like hibernation chambers to me."

CHAPTER FOUR

Lex was having the time of his life. He wasn't just seizing the day – he was grabbing it with both hands, squeezing every bit out of it he could get.

As a city boy he was never really into the countryside and could never understand how his one time partner, Tai San, always spoke about the beauties of the natural world and nature. It was all a little out there where Lex was concerned.

But now, he imagined himself to be like an island king, living in what he perceived to be a tropical paradise.

Tasked with protecting the rest of the Mall Rats who remained behind, Lex felt he occupied the most important role and was effectively in the sole position of authority. With no Amber, Bray or Jay to stick their oar in, like they usually did, it fell to Lex, in his view, to fill the missing gap in leadership during their absence.

But not just as a leader, Lex fancied. More as a king. And right now he needed someone to be his queen. To be by his side.

He had grown tired of Gel. She was sweet and pretty enough and drew on his characteristic need to protect - but she was also a bit of a duh-brain - and Lex had his eyes on a greater challenge.

The Priestess and Lia, both in their own ways, ticked all of Lex's boxes. Each had a physical beauty he so desired, longed for, but both were also strong personalities and he felt they might provide him with an insight into something more profound that he had always turned his back on with Tai San.

He considered that perhaps he could even enter into a relationship with both of them, picturing himself by their side - and felt giddy at the prospect.

"What are you doing?" Lia asked, striding into the heart of the native village where Lex stood, staring into the distance in his reverie.

"I was just... thinking."

"No – I mean what are you doing... as in... wearing?"

Lia cast an amused glance, surprised by Lex's appearance. Shirtless, with his bare chest and toned figure on display, long hair draped freely over his shoulders, he wore nothing else but a grassy skirt, one of those used by the male members of the native tribe.

Lex had actually won it in a game where he had hidden some pebbles under coconut shells, inviting some of the warriors to gamble where the pebbles were.

It was a culmination after a previous friendly wrestling bout which ended in apparently a draw.

The experience had been an unusual one for all concerned with neither Lex or the warriors being able to speak each other's language, relying instead on gestures to communicate. Lex couldn't deny that these guys were no country-bumpkins - or island-bumpkins more like... but were very adept warriors with great fighting skills. During his time on the streets Lex had always been a match to take on anyone and he had to admit that during the game the warriors were really worthy opponents who pushed him to the limit.

After the wrestling, Lex had cheated, using a sleight of hand trick he had learned in the city to decide the winner of the contest - which was the best out of three to guess where the pebbles were located under a coconut shell, resulting in one of the warriors losing a grass skirt he had bet.

"What d'ya reckon?" Lex asked, posing slightly while doing a twirl like he was a model on the catwalk, sure that Lia would be really impressed by his efforts - and look.

"I – really don't know what to say," was all that Lia could reply. She tried to hold back a giggle, feeling Lex looked quite ridiculous. But she also found his efforts to blend in endearing. And with his well built muscles all too visible, no doubt fully intending to show off his body to its best, Lia couldn't help feel a sense of attraction to this handsome and equally roguish figure who she was getting to know.

Lex slumped to the ground by a pile of fruit he had gathered that morning. "I've been thinking that maybe with your help translating, I can learn a bit more about the Priestess and her tribe and they can learn some of my ways."

"I'm sure they'd love that," Lia teased.

"Yeah, I'm sure they would."

He cast a seductive glance at the Priestess emerging from her ornate hut in the village, stepping out into the day to attend to her duties as leader of her tribe, the villagers going about their daily routines.

She nearly took Lex's breath away, so captivated was he by her. How he wished to go into that hut, to spend the night in her bed. He was sure he could definitely teach her a thing or two and was already fantasizing that she might be able to teach him a few tricks as well.

"Are you that hungry, Lex?" Lia asked, watching him take a huge bite into a pineapple, juice dribbling unceremoniously down his chin.

"Ravenous," Lex replied, stealing looks at her long bare legs which seemed to go on forever through the slit of her long skirt.

"Are you always such a messy eater?"

"Not always. Come on," he patted the ground beside him. "Take a seat."

"Why not?" Lia agreed.

"I'd love to be like you, Lia," Lex said between more mouthfuls of fruit.

"Oh? Just as long as you aren't going to tell me you want to start dressing like me next," Lia indicated the flaxen skirt she had woven, similar to those worn by the female members of the native tribe.

"Can't say I didn't notice. You look beautiful. You really do. I was more meaning that... I mean... I wish I could speak different languages, like you can. Do you think you could teach me a few words - some native phrases?"

"I could try."

They went through several objects around them, Lia saying what the name was in the native tongue, Lex repeating it, learning the word for pineapple, coconut, boy, girl, hello.

"Were you always this good at school?" Lia wondered. She was impressed by his attentive study. Maybe he wasn't such the 'bad boy' she thought he was after all.

"No. I flunked nearly every subject. Maybe it would have been different if I had better looking teachers," Lex said, staring deeply into Lia's eyes.

Lia looked away shyly, almost feeling like she was being hypnotized by Lex's magnetism.

"I better be going," she said, standing up to leave.

"Wait – just a few more words?"

Lex reached out, gently taking hold of Lia's hand.

"Can you teach me how you would say – why don't you and I try and get to know each other a little better - and then maybe we can enjoy 'breakfast' together, if you know what I mean?"

Lia really suspected she knew what Lex was referring to but was lost for words, totally unsure how to respond, the playful flirtatious behaviour that had previously so characterized their interaction having now suddenly gone up a level.

"Lex! What are you doing?" Salene called out as she approached the centre of the native village. "And what's that you're wearing?"

Their moment interrupted, Lex released Lia's hand, glaring disdainfully at Salene for her disturbance as she arrived.

"I'm busy, if you don't mind! Trying to keep up diplomatic relations with the locals!"

"I'm sure you have more than that in mind!"

Lia walked away, moving through the village.

"You almost sound jealous, Sal!" Lex said. "But if you want some, there's always enough of Lexy to go around."

"That's not what I'm here for, believe me! I was coming to see if you knew what has happened to May."

"How should I know?"

"She's - gone."

"What do you mean - gone?"

She couldn't be in any danger, Lex surmised. There was no sign of the Collective... Eloise... any trouble anywhere. Just Salene being hysterical. May had probably gone for a walk somewhere, after all. What was the big deal?

Smashing a coconut open on a rock, Lex began to eat and drink its juicy contents.

He wasn't going to let Salene or anyone else interrupt his paradise.

The Priestess and Lia were in conversation in the distance and Lex was already working out odds on which one of them he would bed first.

* * *

Salene feared the worst for May.

Before going to find Lex to see if he knew where May had gone, she had first asked Ruby and Slade if they had seen her. They were on the beach with baby Bray and Brady, Trudy having left her daughter under their supervision to go for a walk by herself. Ruby and Slade were enjoying being a happy couple, looking after the little ones, how to care for a child in anticipation of their own baby they were expecting.

Brady had been building sandcastles with Ruby. Slade had even made a sand version of the shopping mall that had been Brady's home from back in the city.

But there was no sign of May anywhere.

Salene didn't mean to get uptight with Lex but there was something she knew about May that he and all the others were totally unaware of. A secret Salene had been entrusted with and had promised not to reveal to anyone else.

She couldn't betray May's confidence, reveal the extent of May's personal emotional suffering.

So it was that Salene continued her frantic search by herself and felt as if she was looking for a needle in a haystack.

For some time May had been quiet. Aloof. Spending time alone from the others, staring out to sea. Everybody thought she was solely mourning the loss of Zak with whom she had struck up a relationship, and that they were helping by giving May some distance, the personal space and time she needed to recover from Zak's passing.

But Salene knew May well. The two of them had a history together, first as rivals for the affections of Pride, in the city, then as close friends resulting in Salene going out of her way to find out, without being too pushy, if there was anything else that was unsettling May.

Trusting Salene, valuing her friendship, and worn down by Salene's constant but gentle, understanding questioning, not long after Amber and the rest of the exploration set out on their journey, May had finally confided in Salene what was on her mind, the hidden cause of her obvious distress.

May revealed that she suffered from depression. Years ago. In the days of the adults, during which time she had been prescribed medication. Her chemical levels had been out of balance and the medicine had helped to keep her emotionally in check.

When the 'virus' wreaked havoc on the world, May had somehow managed to cope. She had no option with the medical supplies not exactly being freely available.

Part of May wondered if she had even 'outgrown' her illness, if her natural chemical balance had returned, losing the actual need for any further medication.

However, when the Mall Rats had taken to the water and left their home city, May felt the gradual return of those familiar feelings, of highs and lows. It had come on first in fleeting glimpses, heralding other feelings of guilt, self-loathing at times, before snowballing, gradually the dark shadows of despair welling up in May from the inside.

Her relationship with Zak had temporarily papered over the cracks. But now Zak had gone, May was left struggling with some inner torments and was slowly but surely becoming torn apart by unseen, hidden feelings of despair exploding within.

May had no self-esteem anymore. And was finding herself becoming distanced from anything and everything, even everyone around her. She wasn't even bothered if the Collective were on the island. They, or Eloise, could take her away for all she cared. Her life now had no meaning or sense of purpose. Refusing to eat, wanting to be alone, May was lost in her own pain.

Salene reminded May that everyone was feeling displaced since being forced to abandon the city in their homeland. Even Trudy had showed signs that she had been struggling throughout the journey en route to the island. In her early teenage years Trudy had always been prone to melodramatic histrionics, but had grown in self-confidence, displaying a great strength and seemed as if she was starting to settle down. The panic attacks were few and far between the longer they had remained on the island and she was returning to being more self-assured again. Salene was positive that the same would occur for May. She just needed some time.

Salene probed if May was sure that her anxieties were in reality due to depression or if she was just going through a grieving process. Salene appreciated May's trust in her. After all, Salene had been no stranger to difficulties herself and had gone through awful experiences in the past when she suffered bulimia, culminating in not wishing to even live and her attempt at taking her own life by jumping off a bridge.

Ryan had saved Salene then. His unceasing support and devotion had helped to rescue her from the brink of the abyss.

Salene was determined to do the same for May. She promised to keep May's secret safe and to do everything to support her through this most difficult, troubled time.

When she finally found May, her kindred spirit was lost in thought, slumped on the beach, the water lapping around her feet.

"Are you okay?" Salene asked.

May just nodded and continued to stare aimlessly across the ocean.

"You shouldn't go off by yourself, May," Salene continued gently. "We were all worried. We thought something might have happened to you."

May turned to glance up, revealing her eyes were swollen and red from crying.

Salene knelt down in the squelchy sand beside May. "You'll feel better if you talk about it. I promise. I've been there."

Several moments passed, the two of them by the water, with not a sound but that of the constant tide.

"I've been thinking… about Zak. Our life in the city… Our tribe… And it's like…"

She drew a line in the sand that was then completely washed away by the next wave, leaving no trace.

"We could all disappear. Just like that. Right off the face of the planet. As if we didn't exist. And what would it all mean?"

"I think you really need to try and get through each day, May, without thinking too deeply about anything. Or anyone. Zak wouldn't want to see you hurting like this. None of us do."

May tried to somehow retain her composure and wiped the tears spilling down her cheek.

Salene enveloped an arm around her shoulder.

"You're a special person," Salene said reassuringly. "Life just wouldn't be the same without you. You've got to hang in there – all these feelings you have. They'll pass. Don't ever give up! You mean too much to us all... To me!"

Salene rocked May gently back and forth in her arms, shielding May in the comfort of her protectiveness.

"Everything will be okay... You just wait, everything will be okay," Salene repeated.

* * *

Trudy had also gone for a walk on the opposite end of the beach and was heading toward the wreck of the *Jzhao Li*, the ship that had brought them to the island. It felt good to have some time alone, away from the others, so she could gather together the thoughts swirling in her mind.

She had left her daughter under the safe supervision of Ruby and Slade and little Brady had seemed so happy, Trudy reflected, thrilled at the prospect of spending another afternoon building sandcastles with Ruby and Slade. Or 'Wooby' as Brady called Ruby, Trudy smiled affectionately, imagining her daughter's voice.

Ruby and Slade were ideal babysitters. And they would make great parents, Trudy reckoned. They were so lucky to have each other.

But what of herself, Trudy wondered? Following the death of Zoot, Brady's father, she had given everything she had to raise her daughter. Was she destined to remain a single mother for the rest of her life, her family unit made up of just herself and Brady?

Trudy was a little confused why all this had surfaced and wondered if the return of Bray had somehow been responsible.

For all that motherhood provided her with deeply emotive experiences, challenges, memories she would cherish for all eternity, Trudy longed to find love again. There was more to her than just being a mother, as special a role as that was.

Splashing absent-mindedly as she waded through the lapping water, Trudy realized nothing could extinguish the flame of love that still burned within her for Bray.

She had always loved him, if she was truly honest with herself. And if there was such a thing as love at first sight - then she had certainly found it from the very first time she had met Bray, watching him practice basketball in the days they both attended the same school.

She had found herself absolutely smitten. His good looks, gentle kindness. He was a gentleman. A prince. And she was sure that they were going to live happily ever after, making the best of the horrific world that descended in the demise of the adults.

It was painful that he didn't seem to share her feelings.

Bray had been her guardian, the uncle of her child, more like a father figure to Brady, bringing Trudy when she was pregnant to the Mall Rats, standing up for them, doing all he could to protect them and improve their lives.

Fate had dashed her dreams, however, when Bray ended up with Amber, before his disappearance, and presumed loss. Trudy had also been bereft.

Yet now, she felt a sense of exhilaration, the thrill of all the many possibilities that lay ahead.

Bray was back. And Amber had found love in the form of her relationship with Jay.

Could it really be, Trudy wondered? Her heart soared in expectation. Maybe Bray *was* the 'one', after all. Destiny had thrown them together once before – and had done so again. Was it all preordained? Did a happy fairy-tale ending she had longed for await her?

She hoped it could be. She didn't want to betray Amber or her friendship, to sneakily move in and try and break things up. But it looked like she wouldn't have to even do that. Amber hadn't exactly taken Bray back with open arms.

Trudy wouldn't be so remiss. If Amber wouldn't pursue a future with Bray, then Trudy would try to do so. He was worth it. She certainly had the interest, the passion. She owed him for all the kindness he had given her, wanted to care for him, make sure he was looked after, would live well.

When he got back, she would be ready.

Maybe dreams did come true after all?

If Amber wasn't interested, it was likely she could face a competitor for Bray in the form of Emma. With her admittedly pretty features and gentle nature - Emma was likely to be just Bray's type, Trudy considered.

So deep was she in her reflections, absorbed by the picture forming in her mind of a future spent raising her daughter, with Bray by her side, Trudy almost didn't notice the large object in the water beside the wreck of the *Jzhao Li*.

But when she did, she gazed almost in disbelief, startled by what she saw.

A yacht was anchored in the shallows, bobbing from side to side in the incoming tide.

Trudy froze in her tracks. She had to get back and warn the others. Tell them of her discovery.

She immediately worried about Brady, needed to make sure her daughter was okay.

Suddenly she was tapped on the back of her shoulder - and nearly jumped out of her skin in fright, shrieking in surprise.

Turning around quickly, Trudy was stunned to see a rough looking figure of a young man who had been standing behind her and now glared wildly, menacingly.

CHAPTER FIVE

They had driven for hours, well into the night, the military ambulance bumping over the rough terrain - but the reason for Ebony and Ram's discomfort was more than due to just the roughness of the journey.

Both were afraid, unsettled by the prospect of what lay ahead. Axel had refused to answer any of their questions about the nature of their eventual destination or who would be waiting for them whenever they reached it.

Ebony peered through the windows into the surrounding twilight gloom outside, trying to get her bearings,

All she could see was a ghostly, desert-like landscape. The full beams of the ambulance cut through the dark, occasionally picking up more detailed but strange, fleeting glimpses of their environment. There was sometimes the silhouette of a sporadic tree visible, standing isolated in what seemed to be an otherwise vast, empty wilderness.

In one part of the journey, Ebony had observed huge, mighty, rusting hulks of abandoned military vehicles standing idly by the desert roadside. Even a few wrecks of massive tanks, their turrets pointing up lifelessly to the night skies.

What was this place? Had there been some war in this part of the country at some point in time?

Ram had made a desperate effort to escape a few hours before, prising open the back doors of the ambulance with his bound hands, jumping out of the moving vehicle, trying to run away, to disappear into the darkness.

Axel and his cohorts found Ram quickly and repaid him for his audacious manoeuvre with a beating. Ebony, now also bound, had struggled to get to that tantalizingly close open door Ram had gone through but had been unable to free herself.

She looked at Ram, covered in scratches and scuff marks, his hair ruffled, wincing from the cuts and bruises he had received from both his fall and subsequent beating. He looked terrified, as if he was going to be sick.

He glanced at her in a silent understanding, both aware of how the other must be feeling, united in unease and growing apprehension.

They had been so close to making a getaway. Former lovers, rivals, antagonists – they were now in it together, sharing a common enemy. Should the opportunity present itself to escape once more, Ebony was determined to not waste any more chances to regain her freedom.

* * *

Eventually the ambulance slowed as it ascended a narrow road, encountering hairpin bends. Ram's racing pulse picked up pace, the former Techno leader trying to suppress being overwhelmed by his fears and the onset of a panic attack.

They had reached a mountainous area, the terrain having gradually changed from the desolate wastelands of before, becoming a lush, forested region.

Ebony felt her ears 'popping' as they climbed higher and higher up the inclining road, gaining in altitude.

Gazing out of the window, Ebony couldn't believe her eyes. She could see the silhouette of a compound in the mountains, bordered by a high fence, tall watchtowers standing ominously in surveillance, the long beams of their spotlights arcing with menace through the cold gloomy night air.

"Where are we?" Ebony demanded as the vehicle drove through huge gates and into a courtyard in the centre of the compound.

Without answering, makeshift blindfolds were suddenly tied around Ebony and Ram's eyes by Axel.

At the last moment, as her own blindfold was fastened tightly, Ebony spotted several guards outside approaching the back of the vehicle. Then the world went dark and Ebony could see no more.

"Welcome to hell! Enjoy your stay," Axel said coldly, dragging Ram, then Ebony out of the doors. Ebony fell, undignified, to the ground, but was yanked to her feet by awaiting guards who led Ebony and Ram towards a mammoth building.

* * *

"Get your hands off me!" Ram hollered, his voice echoing down the long corridors.

He and Ebony were being led, like captured animals past a range of cells.

Unable to see, relying on their hearing and other senses, they were being moved briskly through the mysterious, gigantic compound. It was an eerie place.

Passing through one area, Ebony was sure she heard the distant cries of several babies.

In another section, the sounds of prisoners wailing, a pitiful chorus of the doomed - dismally calling - desperate for relief from whatever conditions they were in, mixed with chanting, a haunting and repetitive incantation of 'Zoot, Zoot, Zoot, Zoot!' Ebony and Ram wondered if they were trapped in some unexplained nightmare.

Now suddenly another sound. A metal door was being unbolted, creaking on its hinges as it was opened.

Ebony and Ram were thrown inside, the door closing shut behind them, its deep clang resonating throughout the compound and seemingly far beyond.

There was something else, though. Ebony could feel it. A presence. Her senses, as well as Ram's, picked up that it wasn't just them inside.

This was confirmed by a noise of approaching movement coming from within the cell. Almost imperceptible at first, it was the sound of a gathering of shuffling feet getting closer, like they were being surrounded by spectres moving in the dark.

"Who's there?" Ebony shouted, backing up to the door from the oncoming presence.

"Keep away!" Ram yelled.

Ebony's blindfold was suddenly yanked from her face - revealing a group of about twenty girls and boys, some younger, others around the same age as Ram and Ebony. From the pallor of their skin they didn't look well, having clearly been kept inside for some time. All were staring at the two new prisoners who had just descended upon their world.

Then they started to laugh manically, hysterically.

Ebony exchanged confused glances with Ram.

"Is this some kind of asylum?" she asked him.

"Sure sounds like it," Ram responded.

"What the hell's so funny?" Ebony demanded. "What are you laughing at?"

Suddenly the laughter subsided. One girl stated, as if she still couldn't quite believe it, "you both look so... afraid."

"Is that a crime around here or something?" Ram said. "What's so funny about that?"

"There's no need to be afraid," the girl continued. "If you only know what we know, you would do nothing but smile."

"I'll tell you what'll put a smile on my face - how about you untie us," Ebony suggested, indicating her hands, bound tightly.

"You will be set free. As we have been set free," the girl replied as she began untying Ebony's bonds while another boy did the same to Ram.

"Hardly seems like you're free," Ram said, rubbing his now free but numb hands together, regaining his blood flow. "How long have you been prisoners?"

"Prisoners? We're not prisoners – not any more," the boy answered, scoffing at the notion.

"You've got a weird sense of humour, I'll give you that," Ebony said.

She, like Ram, was unsettled by the group. They were like no other prisoners she had ever seen before, appearing strangely distant, not of this world. Some stared intently at Ram and Ebony whereas others had quickly lost all interest in their arrival, absorbed instead by their own thoughts, reveries. Some even sat rocking back and forth as if accompanying the rhythm of a silent mantra.

"It seems you don't realize how lucky you are to be here," another boy nearest Ebony spoke up.

He had to be the leader of the group, Ebony considered. He was certainly the most vocal and confident compared to the others who appeared almost as if they were in a surreal trance like state.

"Who are you? What's your name?" Ebony asked.

"Names? We don't need names. Not now."

"Well, what did you used to be called?" Ram enquired, hoping to find information, anything to use to his advantage.

"That's a good question. In my old life… I was…" the boy's voice trailed off. Time passed as he stood, staring absent-mindedly into a void. He looked embarrassed. Awkward at what he was thinking. It was almost as if he couldn't remember his own name, lost somewhere in his past. Or if he was afraid to even try and recall.

"You were saying?" Ebony probed.

"Seeing you're new here, I'll answer. But other than that, it is no longer meaningful. Nothing is important anymore. My own life is worthless. All that is of value is what occurs now."

"Is that right?" Ram replied, exchanging a confused glance with Ebony.

"That is so. How it is written," the boy continued, from wherever his mind had just taken him. "However unimportant… I used to be called Aras. And I lived in a tribe… We were the 'Roaches'… That was it. So strange… 'Aras'… Funny to hear my old name. And to think, we all knew so little back then."

"Listen, 'Aras'. Or whoever you are now," Ebony said, choosing her words carefully. She felt she was in a room of mindless zombies. A surreal prison. "Can you help us?"

"Of course! We seek nothing less. To help each other."

"Then tell us, please," Ram spoke up. "Any ideas on how we can escape?"

Aras was stunned. His expression turned to one of anger. He began running his fingers through his hair, pacing the room back and forth rapidly.

"Something I... said?" Ram asked, trying to defuse matters.

"How dare you want to go back to a world of ignorance – of not *knowing*! We, the lucky few... are learning the truth! The great answers to all of life's questions! You can't turn your back on that! Don't you see? You are here for a reason! You must also hear the teachings. To have the truth revealed! Join us... Become one with the almighty."

Aras and the others now advanced steadily toward what they perceived to be the newest recruits.

Ram looked nervously to Ebony for guidance, what to do.

She considered striking out, fearful they were in grave danger, but instinctively felt that would only enflame things. There was something deeply troubling about 'Aras' and his zealous convictions, disconcertingly familiar. Ebony had come across such fanaticism before.

Aras put his arms on Ram's shoulder, then Ebony's.

"Brother! Sister! You will discover all there is to know. And the glory that awaits us all!"

The girl beside Aras waved the blindfold that had been on Ram just moments earlier.

"You were blind. But you will see," the girl said. "And be set free. As we have been."

"That's quite - an offer," Ebony responded matter of fact, feeling it better to go along, to not antagonize the cult-like group.

"There is only one name that matters in the universe. And the exalted Heavens of eternity," Aras explained reverently, pleased that Ebony and Ram were now listening attentively to him. "And that name - is Zoot."

* * *

It was almost a relief to see the guards again, Ebony thought a short while later when she and Ram had been summoned to another area of the compound. It was a welcome respite to get away from the holding cell she had been placed in – and its brainwashed occupants.

Whoever 'Aras' and the others had once been in their past, they had totally given themselves away, losing almost all trace of their former identities and lives. They were radicalized, actually *enjoyed* being prisoners, immersed in their new-found religious convictions, following Zoot, who they perceived to be a god-like figure.

Aras had spoken sincerely about the benefits of his beliefs, attempting to persuade Ebony and Ram of the merits of the teachings. And he had some questions of his own about who they were and how they arrived at the mountain compound.

Ebony and Ram avoided giving too much away of their true identities, Ebony in particular concerned by the likely reaction of Aras and his group should they discover who she was - the former partner of Zoot himself, the subsequent leader of his tribe of Locos, and she just couldn't start to figure out how Zoot featured in this region. Surely his legacy and legend couldn't have travelled so far. Ebony was more than uneasy at the prospect of how it all might have come about.

Ram told Aras and the others he was called 'Gabe'. Ebony concocted a false backstory that her name was

'Meredith' and she was shipwrecked with 'Gabe', her boyfriend, on the island.

Aras and the other prisoners spoke of knowing the 'truth'. If only they knew what Ebony had seen, the actual truth that had occurred behind the myth, Ebony thought. She was one of the few who had witnessed closely at hand what Zoot had achieved, and was a key participant in much of it. Zoot's short, tarnished life had reached aspects of greatness, yes. But he was no god. He was mortal. However charismatic and talented, he was flawed in many ways, a troubled soul.

Now escorted by guards, Ebony and Ram were journeying through the corridors of the base again. There was no chance of escape, not yet, though that didn't stop Ebony trying to find every opportunity.

They were on their way to see the 'commander,' Ebony had been told. Part of her had secretly hoped that it might have been Blake, though that hope was evaporating and she suspected that whoever they were about to meet was the one Axel referred to as being the person who Blake reported to.

Ebony had already considered different strategies for whatever she was about to encounter, trying to stay several moves ahead. She had been able to seduce her way out of trouble once before with Blake and considered using her charms on whoever the commander turned out to be, if indeed it wasn't Blake himself. And if his 'boss' was like any other red-blooded male she had encountered, Ebony was sure she had enough tricks up her sleeves to gain his likely attention - and desire — aware she was armed with an arsenal of sensuous weapons.

Ram and Ebony had been taken to a large hall, once a probable military mess facility or the likes in the time of the adults, Ebony surmised.

On a raised dais at the far end of the cavernous room was the figure of the leader. And Ebony was completely surprised upon first seeing the commander of the mountain base - who wasn't at all what she was expecting.

Reclining casually sideways on a wooden throne, Ebony and Ram could see that this was no male. But a figure 100% female. Her back was leaning against one arm of the chair, her long legs dangling over the other side. She was stunningly beautiful, wearing the finest silks, her jet-black hair stylishly and impeccably curled, resting easily on her shoulders.

As she turned to cast a haughty glance at her captives' approach, bordered by the guards, Ram and Ebony could see her deep blue eyes possessed an intense quality as if she was gazing into the very souls of those before her. A slight bulge in her midriff revealed to Ebony that this girl was in the early stages of pregnancy - though she still cut an impressive, alluring figure. There was no maternal glow – just an aura of confidence. A utility of motion and emotion. An undercurrent of energy and impatience. Which if roused, could erupt with a frightening intensity. She ticked like a bomb.

She stared, Medusa-like, her head looking to one side at Ebony and Ram down below, studying them.

Regal, she was also like an ice queen - cold and impassive. But Ebony could also sense a sheer magnetism and an innate intelligence that she exuded without even the need to speak. Instinctively, Ebony felt she was in the presence of someone capable, a strong personality who above all emanated danger. Great danger.

Just who on earth was this 'chick'?

"So it *is* you – the infamous Ram," the commander enquired. "Unexpectedly out here… of all the places. What a complete surprise."

467

"Can't say it's a pleasure," Ram responded in an undertone, gazing around uneasily.

"And you – Ebony. Your looks live up to what I've heard about you."

"I'm flattered," Ebony said. "Who was it who told you? Wouldn't happen to be my lover, Blake?" she continued, sure that would impress.

"Axel's told me all about you," the girl answered. "And now I want you to tell me everything that happened to Commander Blake - and the oil rig."

It was only then Ebony noticed Axel standing a few feet from the throne of his leader, with her bodyguards, Ebony having been otherwise so taken by the presence of the girl.

Axel grinned smugly at Ebony.

"Yeah? Well I bet Axel didn't tell you how he failed me in his mission. If he and his goons hadn't screwed up, we'd have caught ourselves more than just Ram. And we'd have been able to get back, to be there by Blake's side. Maybe we could have saved him and the rig. Whatever the hell happened - I had nothing to do with it."

The girl slowly rose to her feet, a burning look of malice having been lit in her eyes like the very flames of the fires that had consumed Blake's oil rig.

"Hold her!" the girl ordered and began walking towards Ebony and Ram.

Ebony was pinned by her arms on either side by the guards.

"What I can gather, Ebony, is that you're the one who failed Blake. And his mission. You underestimated your enemies. Allowed yourself to be captured without knowing everything about your opponents. All their strengths and weaknesses. Blake was an expert at it. Pity he wasn't so 'particular' about choosing his lovers."

"Thanks for the advice. I'll bear it in mind."

The girl was just inches away. She indicated, the guards forcing Ebony down onto her knees, yanking her head back by her hair so she was forced to look up into the face of the girl looming menacingly above her.

Suddenly the girl lashed out furiously, scratching one side of Ebony's face with her long, immaculate fingernails.

"That's for failing Blake's orders!" the girl screamed. "And that's for letting him down!" she roared, clawing Ebony's cheek once again. "For not being there - when he needed you!"

Ebony recoiled, red marks on her face from her wounds.

"And this is for your insolence!" the girl bellowed, scratching Ebony once more, this time around her mouth, drawing a deep cut above Ebony's lip.

Ebony stared up at the girl, defiant to the last. She spat out some blood from her lips contemptuously on the floor.

The girl's face had an expression of a terrifying, calculating rage, a volcanic temper burning within. A ruthlessness. Ebony wondered if she would be struck again.

Had the girl perhaps been Blake's girlfriend?

But there was something else about her, Ebony recognized. Those cold, icy blue eyes. A familiar look she had seen before. From Blake himself. No - the girl wasn't Blake's lover, Ebony understood. She thought perhaps his *sister* - Ebony seeing in the girl the same intense glare Blake had given Ebony in the past. There was no doubt, Ebony thought about it, looking up at the girl's pretty features. She was clearly related to Blake in some way.

"I loved Blake," Ebony said. "I would have done anything for him!"

"Pity you didn't!" the girl replied. "And now he's gone – I have to decide about what to do with you. But first, I want you to remember who I am. My name is Eloise. And your fate is in my control. Never forget that."

"Oh, you can be sure I won't forget," Ebony replied, spitting out another drop of blood from her cut lip.

"So that just leaves the Techno," Eloise said, turning her attention to Ram, walking over to him.

"On your knees," Axel ordered.

The guards pushed Ram down in a subservient position as Eloise approached. He looked up, smiling feebly in an effort to ingratiate, anxious at what would happen to him next.

"It's a pleasure to meet you - though I never had that pleasure... with this Commander Blake you mentioned." Ram said.

"How interesting. Considering he knew all about you."

"Strange," Ram responded meekly. "I wonder how that could have been?"

"Oh, I'm sure we'll find everything out, Ram. In time. For your sake. Now we're going to have to separate you both," Eloise said, indicating Ram to the guards. "Take him away! To the isolation cells!"

Kicking and screaming, Ram was dragged away by the guards while Eloise took her place back on the throne, sitting coolly sideways as before, dangling her legs over the chair.

"Bring a slave girl. I need a manicure," she ordered in bored intemperance, studying her long fingernails, the ends of some of them now broken and having lost their luster after her strikes on Ebony.

"What about her?" Axel questioned.

Eloise turned to see Ebony, still crouched prone on her knees, held in place by the guards. Eloise grinned wickedly, sending a shiver down Ebony's spine.

"It's time for her to meet the master."

CHAPTER SIX

"Here goes," Jack said in nervous anticipation, leaning over one of the hibernation chambers.

They were joined in the lower levels by the rest of the exploration party who now gathered around behind Jack. All, that is, except Emma, Tiffany and Shannon. The thinking was that the discovery Jack and Ellie made might have been too disconcerting for the younger ones. Emma waited outside looking after her sister and brother, holding hands, swinging their arms back and forth playfully, singing cheerful songs from the adult times to distract them.

Jack felt the cool air emanating from within the cryogenic unit. Like the other units in the room, it was shrouded in a thick, tinted glass, keeping its contents forever cold but also hidden.

"If there is anyone inside..." Gel said, entranced by the hibernation chamber, "what do you think they'd say - seeing us all staring, gawking at them?"

"It's c-c-c-cold - get me out of here!" Darryl cracked a joke, making his voice sound like a ventriloquist.

Bray gave Darryl a glance that made it clear he was far from amused. "Go on, Jack."

Slowly Jack wiped away the foggy condensation on the unit by pressing down, using the body heat of his arms – revealing its contents, the others watching in baited breath.

"Can you see anything?" Amber asked.

"No. Looks as if it's also empty," Jack finally sighed.

"Thank God for that," Gel said.

It was the last of the cryogenic chambers to examine, the group having already investigated the others in the room.

"Any idea of the power source, Jack?" Bray wondered.

Jack walked around each unit, bending and searching. "Still nothing. I just don't understand."

"It's probably hooked up to one of the generators," Jay suggested.

"Might be. But how? That's the question," Jack replied. "Or maybe it's controlled by a computer network somewhere. Seems like there's a receptor unit inside."

Jack cupped his hands over his eyes to gaze through the tinted glass.

"Can't we just get out of here? This place is freaking me out," Gel said uneasily.

"Tell me about it," Ellie stated, casting another glance at all the units in the dimly lit room, the silence broken only by a distant hum of whatever energy source was powering the chambers.

"I wonder what they were going to be used for?" Amber said. "And why they're... here?"

"That's the million dollar question," Jack answered. "But clearly whoever used this place as a base had some kind of plan."

"They remind me of Ram's chamber," Jay said, recalling Ram's attempt to live for eternity in the hibernation unit that had been his own, in their home city. Ram told Jay he had found his chamber in an adult base at Eagle Mountain.

"You don't think Ram has anything to do with this? Do you?" Gel enquired.

"With Ram - who knows?" Amber scoffed. "Nothing would surprise me."

The group continued to exchange theories. Jack recalled in the adult times he read somewhere that there had been some advanced cryogenic hibernation research undertaken by the international space agencies, intending to use the powerful technology to assist future interplanetary travel. Colonists, as well as assorted animal and plant species, were going to be 'frozen' in suspended animation and revived upon their arrival to begin future human settlement of Mars and who knows where else, much later in the future - perhaps even Europa, one of the moons around Jupiter, if it proved to he habitable.

Was this hibernation technology he and Ellie had stumbled upon connected in some way to the space program? Or could it have been a military initiative of some kind linked to the United Nations task force which seemed as if it had once operated from the base? There were so many possibilities. But more questions than answers.

"I wonder why the machines would be turned on – but empty?" Ellie wondered.

"Whoever used this base could have been running tests, seeing if the chambers worked," Jack speculated. "Maybe the adults just didn't make it in time. Or… what if some adults *had* been inside. And somebody else let them out."

"I don't mean to be unkind to Emma, Bray… but are you sure we can trust her?" Amber asked carefully.

"I'm not so sure anyone can trust anyone anymore," Bray replied and Amber wondered if he was making some kind of veiled reference to her, that he somehow felt that he had been betrayed by her getting involved with Jay.

"What I mean is - we just have her word that she didn't know this lab existed. And it seems odd if something pretty major like this was going on."

"That doesn't mean to say Emma would have known though, Amber," Bray said. "Just take a look at the signs all around. This area was clearly off-limits and whoever was involved wasn't exactly advertising what they were up to. It was obviously highly classified."

"True, I guess," Amber sighed. "So if there was anyone inside - and it wasn't Emma and the Roaches who released them," Amber followed on from her own logic, "then the only people who could have done that would be the Collective, if we believe Ram's story that they're somewhere on the island. Or - Eloise and her group."

"Unless, of course, there's someone else on the island," Jack added. "I can't believe the Priestess, Lia and the native villagers could have been involved."

"What if the adults who were based here set timers of some kind – and released themselves?" Darryl considered, histrionic at the prospect. "For all we know, they could be walking around the island as we speak! Like real life zombies!"

"That's not helping, Darryl," Amber said.

"Or simply it's that nobody was inside in the first place," Bray suggested. "And the adults left the machines running, for the day they thought they would need them."

"To do what?" Gel wondered.

"Survive the virus? Must have been pretty high on the list," Jay scoffed, amazed at Gel being so oblivious to the option.

"I didn't think of that," Gel said.

Her expression suddenly clouded and her eyes bulged.

"What is it!" Amber asked as she, along with the others, considered Gel in growing tension.

Gel's stomach suddenly rumbled loudly, breaking the nervousness in the room, Gel embarrassedly giving a fake cough to try and cover up the noise.

"Sorry. I felt a bit of wind coming on." She stifled a burp and then giggled. "Ooo! I don't know about the rest of you – but I'm starving. I need to eat. Right now."

"I think we could all do with a break, Gel," Amber agreed.

The Mall Rats began leaving the room, hoping Emma would know of a food supply somewhere there at the base.

"Come on, you," Ellie said, taking Jack by the hand.

They were the last in the room, Jack staring at the hibernation units adorned in United Nations symbols, trying to make sense of what it all meant.

He wondered if there really could be other hidden adult bases out there somewhere in the world, just waiting to be discovered, like the one Ram claimed was at Eagle Mountain. He promised himself he would do everything to learn more of what the adults had left behind, determined to uncover any other secrets the island still had left to reveal.

* * *

"I don't believe it!" Gel screamed excitedly, in awe at the contents of the cupboard before her. "Look at all this food!"

They had relocated to what was once the cafeteria area inside the accommodation building, Emma knowing it was a place they could all rest up - and find some much needed sustenance.

The cupboards were still mostly full of preserved foodstuffs from the adult days, Gel discovered, wide-eyed as she surveyed the range in front of her, brimming with shelves of tins, sauces, and an assortment of dried meals, needing heating in only hot water.

Emma relayed how most of the food was shipped over by the adults to supply the population of Arthurs Air Force Base, an international flavour of culinary choices on offer, reflecting the diversity of those from all around the world who had once lived at the base. The adults clearly intended for the children evacuated there to be well looked after for some time.

"Oh, my God!" Gel cried in delight, reaching out for a tin of peaches, quickly opening it and beginning to consume its contents. "My favourite!"

"How can anyone eat so much – and still look so good – so slim?" Darryl marvelled, watching Gel wolf down the fruit with her hands, syrup dribbling through her fingers. She dropped the tin, which clanged to the floor, joining several empty others she had already voraciously gone through.

"Enough talk. More food," Gel grinned, throwing another peach tin to Darryl, who caught it with aplomb.

"Don't mind if I do," Darryl beamed.

He enjoyed Gel's company and in truth, was attracted to her. He had given up hope, for now, on Salene, to whom he had also been drawn in the past. Darryl's feelings had been hurt when Salene didn't seem to reciprocate his many romantic hints and leanings. But with Gel seemingly detached from Lex and single herself, Darryl wondered if he and Gel might end up more than just dining buddies. He had always been a bit wary of Lex and didn't relish the prospect of crossing him by stealing his girl.

"Cheers," Darryl said, raising his tin in a toast, and clanging it into Gel's next course, a tin of tuna.

Bray was sitting with Emma, Tiffany and Shannon, the four of them tucking into their meals, Bray having warmed up some dried pasta in hot water, the accommodation building having its own internal generator and power supply.

"Are you okay?" Bray asked, sensing that Emma was lost in her thoughts, toying with her food.

"I'm fine. Really. I was just thinking about when we first arrived here. After being evacuated. And how much we miss our parents."

Bray decided against probing for any more questions. There was a profound sadness in Tiffany and Shannon's expressions as they, too, were clearly reflecting on the days before the darkness descended when all the adults perished.

"Has anyone seen my fork?" Bray asked. "It was here just a minute ago."

"Right... Now it's disappeared," Tiffany noticed in wonderment.

Bray cast his hand across the surface of the table and made the fork suddenly appear again. "That's what you think," he smiled in an attempt to brighten up the atmosphere and entertain the younger ones to get their minds off the old days.

"That's amazing!" Shannon beamed. "How did you do that?"

"Ah - now that would be telling. A good magician never reveals any tricks."

Even Emma was smiling, along with Bray, Tiffany and Shannon.

"It's so good to hear the place alive again," she said. "The sound of laughter. Friendly voices."

Gel suddenly let out a huge 'burp', quickly covering her mouth self-consciously after the event, in wide-eyed shock.

"Excuse youuuu!" Darryl grinned – before joining her, forcing out his own appreciative and resounding belch, the two of them giggling – and resuming more of their meals.

Emma burst out laughing at the unruly chorus of noises Gel and Darryl were making, as did Tiffany, Shannon and even Bray, unable to keep his composure, also joining in. Emma looked so happy, Bray thought, admiring Emma's delightful smile.

Amber sat nearby at another dining table, pleased by the joyous atmosphere, a sense of hope in the air.

They all needed it, Amber reflected, a moment to unwind, rest and renew their strength. She was picking at her own food, thinking of all the issues that they had to deal with.

"Alright if I join you?" Jay enquired, approaching Amber's table, carrying a tray of food.

"Go right ahead. Plenty of room," Amber smiled politely.

Jay was keen to see her. But he felt awkward to get into any topic of how she was feeling, still wanting to give her space and time. He loved her, cared deeply, and wanted to make sure Amber was okay, hoping she was in good spirits, not hurt too much by the continued uncertainty about their personal lives.

"It's been quite a day," Jay said, between mouthfuls. "At least we've determined that wherever Ram and Ebony are, it isn't here. And neither is the Collective."

"So far," Amber said, lost in a reverie.

"And what about you?" Jay asked her gently. "You seem preoccupied."

"I was just thinking about baby Bray. I really miss him so much. I hope we won't be away too much longer."

"Hopefully not. Try and not worry. He's in good hands," Jay said, gently touching her hand reassuringly. But he couldn't help but notice that Amber was casting glances at Bray, dining with Emma and her brother and sister. And it registered with Jay that Amber was more than troubled by just missing her young son. Bray was clearly enjoying Tiffany, Shannon - and especially Emma's company.

* * *

After dinner, the exploration party discussed more about the hibernation chambers and the map of the island Jay and Gel had found earlier in the day showing the position of Project Eden, presumed to be the mountain base up in the north. All speculated if it tied in with the cargo container ship they had discovered previously, the *Jzhao Li*, which in reality turned out to be part of a United Nations fleet which had been in the area in the adult times. But once again, rather than finding answers, the net result was a proliferation of more questions.

They decided to try and rest up and made preparations for sleeping in the accommodation building. Agreeing to take turns on watch through the night, Amber had volunteered for the first shift.

She still needed some time and space to herself and was looking forward to letting her mind wander to see if she could come up with some way forward. Not solely confined to the predicament her tribe found themselves in, but her own personal situation regarding Bray and Jay.

Hours later, she tensed slightly hearing footsteps approaching down the corridor and peeked her head around to see who it was.

To her relief - it was Bray.

"You're early. It's still my turn on watch," Amber said. "You're not due for at least another few hours."

"I know," Bray said, greeting Amber with a warm smile. "That's why I'm here. I've come to see if you'd like some company. And some extra caffeine." In his hands were two cups of steaming hot coffee from the cafeteria.

Despite her best intentions to be impartial, Amber was only human and had been uneasy at the attention Bray had been giving Emma lately. But he was obviously making an effort to be with her – and she did want to speak with him.

"That's great, thanks."

She took a welcome sip and also welcomed feeling Bray's presence. It was still so amazing to believe he was actually there. Back in her life. Only a feet apart. But in other ways, he was so far away, she was beginning to feel. Though Amber reflected that it was in part her own making, given her desire for some space.

Her thoughts wandered to the time they spent together in the past before the Technos, prior to their lives changing course, in what seemed like a bygone age.

She remembered vividly the night they spent together when they were reunited, having gone their separate ways after their visit to Eagle Mountain. Amber, as 'Eagle', had lived with the Eco tribe in the forest and begun a relationship with Pride, only to fall in love with Bray again. But had she never really fallen 'out of love'?

Could lightning strike twice? Should it? Had fate brought them together again?

"Emma's a special girl. Isn't she?" Amber said, matter of fact, looking into Bray's eyes, searching. She detested how she was feeling and especially the pangs of jealousy that would forever manifest when she saw Bray and Emma together. On one hand she resolved that she was probably being irrational. But equally she felt vulnerable, wondering if Bray was attracted to Emma.

"She's certainly inspiring," Bray said, sipping from his cup. "To think what she goes through, every second of every day. And how she copes. You're right. She IS special. Very special."

Bray noticed Amber's expression cloud.

"Amber - what's all this about?" he asked gently.

"What do you think?"

"Emma? Do you even have to ask, Amber?!"

"Sorry," Amber said. "I was just wondering... Well... difficult to say really. I just thought that - oh, it doesn't matter."

"Thought that what? There's something 'going on' between Emma and me?"

"Is there?"

"That's ridiculous!" Bray insisted.

"I would hope so," Amber sighed. "After all we had... I would hope that it would take more than a pretty smile for you to throw everything away."

"I shouldn't even have to justify myself! I've been faithful to you since the day we were apart! And talking about being faithful? Just stop if you can, take your eyes away from Emma for one minute and have a good look in the mirror - at you – and Jay!"

"That's not fair! I thought you were dead!"

Amber and Bray stared at each other, shocked by how things had gone between them, tears welling up in each other's eyes. Both were hurt. Stung by the words they had spoken. Heard. Each in pain.

"Don't you realize how difficult it's been?" Amber said, trying somehow to contain her emotion. "I've been trying to do what's best. Believe me... But I've been put in an impossible position!"

"What? To make a decision?"

"Do you think it's easy?"

"No. But you should know how you feel, Amber. And what you want. Otherwise it's not fair on either Jay or myself."

"Oh - now I'm to blame? You both said that I could take all the time I needed!"

"Because you asked - remember? You said you needed some time, to think it all over!"

"Then why do you seem so angry?" Amber asked.

"You should ask yourself the same question, Amber!"

"How can you be so critical?... It's like you're blaming me for something I had no control over! Do you really think that badly of me -"

"How could I possibly think badly of you? I *love* you, Amber! But it's like you're the one who's blind! I know it's been difficult for you! But what am I supposed to do? I can't win if I leave you alone - I can't win if I try and see you, to discuss matters! And while we're talking now - you've shown no sign of wanting to leave Jay, from what I can see. Not that I'm expecting you to do that. If you can find some measure of happiness in your life - then trust me, that's all I ever wanted for you! But it's about time you started thinking about others rather than just yourself, don't you think?"

He threw his cup angrily to the ground, hot coffee exploding in a shower of droplets, as he stormed away.

Amber broke down in agonizing, wracking, heaving sobs. She felt like a bomb had gone off in her heart. She hadn't meant for any of it to happen, to cause Bray hurt, and certainly not Jay, the pain running deep into her very soul.

She looked back through misty, watery eyes to see Bray receding around a corner at the end of the long dark corridor.

CHAPTER SEVEN

Flaming torches illuminated the native village, bathing it in a warm glow amid the darkness as nightfall descended.

There was still no sign of Trudy.

Lex, Salene and the rest of the Mall Rats had mounted a search party to go out and find her, the Priestess sending several of her warriors to accompany them.

Lex hadn't been too bothered by May's absence earlier in the afternoon. After all, he had reasoned, May was spending a lot of time alone lately, coming to terms with the death of Zak, and he felt she had naturally been doing the same again.

But there was something unusual behind Trudy's disappearance that had even Lex concerned.

Ruby and Slade knew Trudy had gone for a walk along the beach and when they arrived after their afternoon babysitting Brady and baby Bray - and Trudy did not - it set off a wave of doubt and worry among the tribe. Afternoon turned to sunset, twilight into evening. And still, Trudy was missing.

Lex and the others had already scoured the beach and the immediate vicinity to see if Trudy had fallen or suffered an accident of some kind. It was time to broaden their search.

"You know the areas you've been allocated – let's move!" Lex urged the others, having split them into groups. Naturally, he had selected Lia to be by his side, ostensibly as translator, the two of them accompanied by several of the Priestess's fiercest warriors.

Slade, Salene, Sammy and May formed the other search party along with some other warriors and were setting out on their way while Ruby was left behind to watch over the little ones with Lottie.

"Good luck," Lia wished everyone as they were about to embark. She was actually impressed by Lex's organization and willingness to help. Maybe there was more to him than she had realized, she thought, admiring his handsome features flickering in the light of the torch he carried.

"Help! I need help!" a voice suddenly cried out in the shadows of the dark. It was Trudy.

"Where are you?" Lex called back, his eyes searching frantically in the direction of where her voice had sounded.

"Here... I'm here... and I need help!" Trudy shouted again.

"There she is!" Sammy yelled, suddenly noticing a figure in the distance, pointing the way.

Trudy appeared between the palm trees lining the village.

She was approaching slowly, with effort, supporting a slouched, scraggly figure leaning heavily on her, his arms draped over Trudy's shoulders.

* * *

The boat was called *Nemo* and the wild looking, unkempt stranger it belonged to went by the name of Connor. At least, that's what he had said. Apart from the fact Trudy had dragged him back to the village, they had no idea exactly who this 'Connor' was - or where he had come from.

"Can't say I think too much of your taste in men, Trudy," Lex said disapprovingly. "First Zoot – now this guy… Did you really have to bring him home with you? Are you that desperate? This your idea of a romantic first date?"

"This is no time to joke, Lex," Trudy replied.

"I mean - look at the state of him," Lex added.

The group was gathered around, fascinated by this unexpected visitor who arrived in their midst.

Connor sat slumped by the fire, a dazed look in his eyes.

He had long, dark hair, mottled in unkempt clumps, parts of it sticking up as if he had never used a brush or comb. His skin was rough, dry from too much sun, weather worn, obviously having spent a lot of time outdoors. He wore ragged clothes, torn and full of holes. And his face was covered in stubble, a messy beard. He certainly seemed to be around the same age as most of those examining him - but looked like some sort of crazed fisherman who had spent a thousand years at sea. And belonged there rather than on the dry land he now found himself in.

"When do you think he last took a bath?" Sammy said, sniffing and observing Connor with intrigue. "He's filthy! And he sure smells!"

"That's rude, Sammy," Salene chided him. "Even if it is true," she muttered under her breath, dismayed by the condition Connor was in. Couldn't he have at least washed himself in sea water, she wondered, like the Mall Rats had done, when they had been stuck at sea?

"I don't think it's just a body we can all smell. There's booze. If I'm not mistaken... Jack Daniels," Lex identified.

"You're that much of a connoisseur?" Trudy glared at Lex incredulously.

"I've been known to partake in my time," Lex replied boastfully.

Lottie peered closely at Connor. "You're right, Lex! He seems drunk as a skunk!"

"Hello, girlie," Connor grinned at her, his teeth yellow.

Lottie recoiled in disgust at the stench of his breath.

Connor suddenly began to chuckle to himself, his eyes darting back and forth, studying the group of strangers now watching him in turn.

"Hey... are you some kind of mermaid? You're so pretty," Connor said to Trudy. The tone of his words was slurred and Lex had to push him to sitting upright as he swayed back and forth.

"And that goes for all of you, too," Connor grinned, admiring the older girls standing around him, looking up at Salene, May, Ruby and Lia. "What a bevy of beauties. You have no idea what a sight you are for sore eyes."

"Well, just don't get any ideas, pal," Lex warned him as Connor tried to get to his feet, wobbling unevenly, regaining his 'land legs' – and feeling the effects of the alcohol. He quickly slumped down on the ground again before slowly standing, looking like he would collapse at any moment.

"Where are you from? And where have you been?" Slade asked, preparing to catch Connor, should he likely fall over.

"Where haven't I been, more like," Connor answered. "I've been sailing the seven seas."

"Yeah, right," Lex challenged. "And I'm the tooth fairy."

"Is that right?" Connor grinned at Lex.

"What have we here," Connor continued, trying to look suavely into Ruby's eyes, bobbling precariously on his feet.

Slade moved in, ready to intercept.

"It's alright, I can take care of myself," Ruby said, Connor reminding her of many a drunken guest who had made a pass at her in her saloon back in the town of Liberty.

"And who would you be? My name's Connor."

"So you said. You can call me Ruby. Now why don't you try telling us more about where you're from. What brought you here."

"Ruby? How fitting. The name of a precious jewel. You got any plans for tonight – Ruby?"

"Yes. I'll be spending the time with my boyfriend."

"Well, he doesn't have to know. If we spend some time together. I won't tell - if you won't?"

"Why don't you tell him yourself – he's standing right beside you."

Slade tapped Connor on the shoulder.

"Nice to meet you," Slade said, though it was clear from his unfriendly tone he meant for Connor to be under no illusion he should keep his distance from Ruby. "What was that you were saying?" he continued.

Connor held up his hands meekly in an apology.

Lex noticed Lia backing away, avoiding direct eye contact, uncomfortable to be in Connor's drunken sights, he suspected.

"Are you okay?" he asked.

Lia nodded, but was also clearly unsettled by something. Unknown to the others at the time, it was the pendant dangling around Connor's neck. It was made of fish bones, tied to a wire, and reminded Lia of a native legend she had been told, the story of a dangerous visitor who would one day rise up from the sea, bringing destruction to all on the island.

"Would you look at that!" Connor beamed, swaying precariously.

He was pointing into the distance - at the Priestess, walking towards them, intrigued by all the commotion.

"I really am in paradise," Connor babbled, his mouth gawping open, staring at the Priestess like he was witnessing a vision. "Thank my stars…"

Connor suddenly passed out, overcome by exhaustion and alcohol, lying on his back, completely out of it.

"And to think people used to say I had no manners," Lex muttered.

The others exchanged incredulous glances, struck by the impression Connor had made.

"Who on earth is he?" Lottie asked.

"We'll find out when he wakes up – believe me," Lex pledged, wondering the same thing, suspicious of who this unusual stranger was who had entered into their lives.

* * *

The group enjoyed a dinner that night by the fire, their conversation dominated by Connor's arrival. Connor himself was still totally out for the count and lay motionless, in a deep slumber.

Lia explained the superstition and why she was disturbed by Connor's presence – punctuated by the pendant he wore around his neck, laden with fish bones.

The Priestess had seen it too – recognized the same symbolism as Lia – and many of the natives swarmed around the sleeping form of Connor, entranced by this visitor the tide had brought in.

Lia described more of the tale of the folklore of the native tribe.

A former Priestess had long ago had a prophecy that in the future the island would be visited by a creature taking the form of a human. More used to living in the water than on the land, the sea spirit would behave differently from the real humans of the island, finding life on dry ground uncomfortable. He would be marked in some way, showing his connection to the creatures that lived with him in the sea.

According to the fable, it had been sent by the Goddess of the ocean herself to study the way of life of those who dwelled on the land. If they proved themselves just and worthy, the creature would reward them, showing them the way to a valuable bounty of food and supplies that would hold them in good stead for years. If the sea spirit found the islanders lacking, unkind, and unworthy, he would call upon the Goddess in the ocean to bring forth great waves, to wash away all that had been on the island, reclaiming it for the sea.

"I bet he's drank a lot of spirits, that's for sure," Lex had skeptically remarked upon hearing the legend. "Just as I have. But that sure as hell doesn't make him - or me - any kind of spirit from the sea."

Connor's arrival was nevertheless of some significance to the Priestess and her tribe, Lia made it clear to Lex and the other Mall Rats. Portentous, if the myth was to be believed.

They would just have to wait for Connor to wake up so he could shed more light on his side of the story. He seemed harmless but Lex and Slade in particular were paying close attention, ready to restrain him should be pose any danger.

* * *

Salene and May left the others behind in the centre of the village, going for a stroll under the starlight.

"How are you feeling?" Salene asked, making sure it was just the two of them around and nobody else was listening, to protect May's secret.

"A bit better. I wanted to thank you. For everything."

"Glad to hear it. And if there's anything I can do, anytime - just say it. I'll always be there for you."

May smiled appreciatively, finding strength in Salene and her support. "That means a lot."

"Just try and take it all day by day. Then I'm sure you'll be able to deal with anything. Life certainly has its share of surprises," Salene continued. "I mean, look at Connor. Who would have known he would show up? You never know what's around the next corner. What might happen tomorrow. So there's no point in worrying. All that matters is getting through each day."

"I honestly don't deserve it. What you've done for me."

"Of course you do," Salene said, holding May by the hand. "I'm lucky to know you. To have you as my friend."

May looked at Salene's hand, tenderly touching her own, and suddenly pulled her arm away awkwardly.

"What is it?"

"Nothing," May insisted. "We should be getting back."

They turned around, re-tracing their steps to the village, May looking up at the beautiful sky, finding a measure of comfort in the stars, twinkling down from above.

"I don't fancy going back. I thought Lex was bad enough," Salene sighed. "Connor seems the type to go after any female that moves."

"I wouldn't exactly say Connor's my type," May agreed.

"Well, someone's out there. Zak would be the first to understand," Salene said, gazing at the starlit heavens. "You're kind… funny… Anyone can see you're attractive. You've got a lot to offer. Heck - if I was a guy - I'd be into you."

May stopped and exchanged glances with Salene for a long moment, somewhat confused by Salene's compliment. Then she turned and Salene followed her back toward the village.

En route, May told Salene she was sure she would cope somehow with the difficulties she was going through, thanking Salene again for all her help.

However, when she got back to the hut she had been sleeping in, May tried to retain her silent tears, wishing not to draw attention to herself.

After all, May hadn't been entirely truthful to Salene - and had been holding back what was really troubling her, in addition to her grieving for Zak. And she wondered if Salene had picked up on signals.

She had been developing *feelings* for Salene, for some time. They first surfaced a while back in the city at Phoenix Mall. May finding herself drawn to Salene's compassionate nature, the stirrings in her heart then growing, and discovering to her surprise she was smitten with Salene. They had been rivals for Pride's affections at the time but their relationship was becoming a lot more complicated.

May had consciously buried her feelings, not allowing them to manifest. She felt confused by how Salene made her feel. It would be too embarrassing to reveal the truth. She would have made the situation unbearable for Salene, putting them both up for ridicule from the others, May reasoned.

No, it was better to keep it all hidden, May was sure. Pretend it didn't exist.

Zak, easygoing, had been an enjoyable diversion for May, distracting her from the leanings that still lingered for Salene from time to time in her heart.

But now Zak was dead. Gone. Buried on the island.

If only May's feelings for Salene were the same.

Her attraction for Salene had been revived in the time they had spent together recently. She was getting used to depending more and more upon Salene for support.

She had suffered from depression but if only Salene knew the REAL truth. May was totally trapped by her emotions, the feelings of attraction she kept from Salene.

But May couldn't say anything. Salene could never know the extent of how she felt about her. And it was better to stay friends - than to never see each other again, May reflected.

She cared for Salene so much – struggling to contain her overwhelming feelings for her – that she would have to keep this fact known only to herself.

CHAPTER EIGHT

Ebony felt she had been thrust into a living nightmare, facing something dreadful from her past that she thought she had left behind. But there it was, haunting her once more.

She was in some kind of temple. Candles, most of them scented, lit the otherwise large, dark room, giving a strange fragrance, their glowing flames dancing in the dark. Several benches were arranged so they pointed in the same direction like aisles in a chapel, focused on a central object at the other end of the room - a face Ebony knew only too well.

Framed by silver candelabras on either side was a large painting, illuminated in the shadows, outlining an idealized image of a city background, the sun in the skies above shining down on a figure, staring out with a determined look. Glowing with primal energies, he wore a leather jacket, goggles on his head. A romanticized vision, one that gave Ebony the chills. It was a portrait of Zoot.

It wasn't so much the image that gave Ebony cause for concern - more the spectre of somehow having gotten herself involved again with the zealots who fanatically worshipped him. And Ebony still couldn't even begin to comprehend how Zoot was somehow known in this strange new place.

She thought back to the cell she had been initially taken to with Ram, disturbed by the radicalized and strange behaviour of Aras and the other prisoners. Zoot was dead and couldn't hurt or affect Ebony any more – but the extremist followers who dedicated themselves to what they perceived to be his cause were another matter entirely.

Sitting below the gigantic portrait, on a throne-like chair, was Eloise. Resplendent, like a queen from a bygone age, she stared down at Ebony, her beautiful features locked in an icy, unforgiving look, eyes glaring with venomous resentment.

Ebony had been dragged down the lengthy corridors of the compound by Axel and the guards – who had then forced her into an uncomfortable kneeling position on the cold floor.

Axel pushed down on Ebony's shoulders, keeping her prone, immobile – but that didn't stop her from staring back at Eloise in brazen defiance, trying to mask the confusion and anxiety that in reality were threatening to grip her from within.

The sound of someone entering the room could be heard, their footsteps echoing, striding methodically.

"The master's here," Axel whispered menacingly.

Approaching from behind, the footsteps sounding like ominous knells of doom, Ebony doing her best to downplay the dramatic arrival of whoever this 'master' was, bravely continued to lock her eyes with Eloise, not giving her the satisfaction of showing how unsettled she really was.

A white cloak bristled directly past Ebony. It belonged to a tall figure, the source of the footsteps, making his way to Eloise.

Ebony's composure broke momentarily, unable to stop her innate shock, disbelief, in recognition of the master.

It was the Guardian, before her very eyes. And Ebony began to wonder how so many people who had once been so involved in her life were now reappearing. It was as if she was existing in some sort of surreal parallel universe.

The Guardian bent down on his knees, bowing his head before Eloise in a position of worship, his eyes closed tightly in a display of intense fealty, awe at being so close to Eloise, let alone the portrait of Zoot displayed behind.

"Mother Divine… I am so honoured by your presence."

Eloise offered her hand to him, the Guardian giving it a reverential kiss.

"You may rise, Guardian. I brought you a gift," Eloise said, getting to her feet, encased in plush soft silk slippers.

"So I was told. And what a gift."

The Guardian stood, turning to look at Ebony, a jubilant expression on his face. But there was also a manic look in his eyes. As if he himself was hallucinating, which added to the chills Ebony felt running down her spine.

"Oh, mighty Zoot! Great one!" he implored, looking up to the ceiling. "My prayers *have* been answered! You grant the Mother Divine your favour. You bring the Betrayer before us! She will not go unpunished. I vow it!"

The last Ebony knew, the Guardian and his 'Chosen' had disappeared from the city around the time of the invasion by Ram and the Technos. With all the Zootist symbolism evident at Eloise's base – let alone the Guardian himself physically being there - the mystery of where he and the remnants of his Zootist followers had gone after the city was now solved. If indeed the people inhabiting the strange compound in the mountains emanated from there rather than another land.

Ebony wondered how the Guardian had got to the island and what his connection to Eloise was as all manner of thoughts raced around the dark recesses of her mind and she tried desperately to regain her composure. Why were they worshipping Zoot – so far from Zoot's home city? And in what way was the Collective linked to the unusual goings on at the mountain base?

There were just so many questions. But Ebony instinctively knew that rather than her wild thoughts controlling her - if she had any hope of survival, then she would need to control her thoughts, let alone risk showing any fear or weakness to Eloise and the unpredictable, unstable, Guardian.

"Did you miss me, 'Guardian'? 'Master'? Whatever you call yourself now. Still wearing the same old cloak, I see – and up to the same old baloney," Ebony mocked.

"Silence!!" the Guardian roared – quickly advancing towards her - before suddenly thrusting both arms out at Ebony, as if some unseen special power was emitting from his fingers.

This totally confused Ebony as much as it concerned her, as she also noticed Eloise was a little astounded at just exactly what the Guardian was trying to do.

The Guardian looked at his outstretched hands helplessly, almost disappointed that whatever he expected would happen didn't occur and for a split second Ebony felt a degree of sympathy for him. He was still clearly out of his mind, which produced a bizarre vulnerability and yet added to the enormous danger he represented.

The Guardian lowered his hands, considered Ebony absently as if he was trying to focus, unsure if she was actually there or a figment of his tortured imagination. Then he turned and gazed hesitantly at Eloise for a lead.

"Mother Divine… What would you have me do?"

"She failed my brother. Let down Blake. And so, failed me. I want her to suffer. Do what you wish - but promise me she will feel pain, the loss of what she caused me in turn."

"Many a soul has suffered at the hands of this witch," the Guardian commiserated. "And so shall she suffer. It is as it is meant to be. Justice will be dispensed to the traitor."

"Traitor? I didn't betray anyone," Ebony spoke up. "Have you forgotten? I was Zoot's woman!"

"You ARE a traitor!" the Guardian shouted in rage. "You betrayed Zoot! Everything he stood for! Where were you when The Chosen tried to live up to his legacy? You fought against us! Against me! Joined with the Mall Rats! You even 'married' a Techno, I am to hear! Ram – of all people! And you call yourself Zoot's woman! Whatever you once were, Ebony, it is all too clear that you are now no more!"

Eloise grinned in delight, finding intense inner pleasure, retribution, at Ebony's castigation by the Guardian.

"I'm no Mall Rat," Ebony defended herself. "Ask yourself who was the one who captured Ram in the first place. Who was the one Blake invited to be by his side? I'm not your enemy – and I was never against Zoot. He knew that."

"You spread lies and falsehood, tarnishing the Divine One, desecrating Zoot's name!" the Guardian insisted.

"I knew Zoot better than any of you!" Ebony cried out. "I was there, with him. You talk about the truth? You know nothing! I know the real truth!"

The Guardian whirled, snarling in steaming hate and anger, glaring at Ebony in a mixture of contempt and fury.

"Begone evil one! Return to the foul slavering jaws of the devil in hell! Or commit yourself to our god, Zoot!"

The Guardian indicated to the guards, who thrust Ebony down before his feet in a prostrate position.

"If you claim to miss Zoot so much – we could sacrifice you, right now. Send you to him. Let him deal justice to you, as he sees fit," the Guardian said, with a sudden and distant manic look in his eye as if he was even envious, which registered with Ebony as he continued with his rant.

"How lucky for you to be in his presence! I envy you that privilege," the Guardian stated.

"Why don't you go 'join him' instead then?" Ebony challenged. "If you're trying to scare me, it's not working. I've seen death. And we've all got to die sometime. Even you. I can't choose how I die. But I can choose how I live."

"You really think?" Eloise retorted. "It looks to me like you have little choice in what happens. We're all guided by something greater than merely ourselves, my dear Ebony."

"In the form of the Great One, Zoot," the Guardian added.

"Well, you get rid of me, you'll be making the biggest mistake you ever have! *I* rode by Zoot's side. No matter how you twist the truth, you can't undo the past. I *was* his woman. And I know things. I'm a lot more use to you alive in this world. It's not just Ram and I who washed up here. Didn't Zoot tell you? The Mall Rats are here also. So is Trudy. And Zoot's own daughter. I even saw Bray, just a few days ago. Let's just say - it was quite a reunion."

The Guardian reeled at the revelation, like he had just been struck by a bolt of lightning, trying to assimilate it. Even Eloise seemed unsettled, concerned in some way, by Ebony's words.

"Bray is dead!" the Guardian screamed. "He left us, after conceiving his child in the Mother Divine, to ascend to the Heavens and rejoin his brother!"

"Believe what you think," Ebony said, emboldened by the shifting mood. "Strike me down. Or we can work together. Maybe a greater force really is responsible. Maybe it was Zoot after all. Ask Ram. He'll tell you. The Mall Rats are here, on the island. And I did see Bray. Alive."

"I will put an end to this!" the Guardian roared, striding towards Ebony with a manic intent. "Give the Mother Divine the vengeance she seeks!"

"Wait!" Eloise commanded, intrigued by Ebony's revelation - especially the reference to Bray, her voice echoing around the room, the Guardian stopping in his tracks. "Just wait," Eloise repeated more softly, thinking over things in her mind.

"We have to protect Zoot's legacy, whatever it takes," Eloise stated, placing her hands gently on her pregnant belly. "Ebony might be useful. For now."

* * *

In another part of the prison compound Ram was losing the last vestiges of hope, sinking ever deeper into the oblivion, gripped by panic. Locked up in solitary confinement, he was alone with nothing but his fears for company, surrounded by thick concrete walls.

"Come on!" he pleaded, clutching at the walls, desperately trying to dig through with his fingers, his nails breaking, bloodied, and covered in dirt. There was no way out.

It was no use, he thought. But he had to keep trying - and couldn't just wait around for his impending doom.

A cockroach crawled through a tiny gap in the wall, Ram recoiling in surprise.

Disgusted, he flicked the insect away from him.

Ram cringed at having touched it, staring at his fingers. Imagining all the germs he had been in contact with, the billions of tiny microbes crawling on his hand, going up along his arm. Infecting him with all manner of diseases.

Always a hypochondriac in his childhood, Ram had developed an extreme phobia for germs, becoming an obsessional compulsive handwasher and insisting on the utmost hygiene when he was leader of The Technos.

Living with Ruby and Slade in Liberty had helped Ram change his thinking, giving him the mental tools to control most of his many inner worries.

Yet currently Ram felt exposed. Powerless. He had no influence. Everything and everyone was out to get him, it seemed. He was raw. Vulnerable. His defensive barriers had come crashing down.

He was in the grasp of the Collective and it was only a matter of time, he just knew it, before it would all be over for him. He was condemned. He had gone against Kami, the leader of the Collective, and he would pay the ultimate price.

If only he could find a way out.

Former prisoners had carved their names, graffiti, on the thick walls of the cell. It was the most difficult to escape part of the compound, Ram could tell, knowing that a prisoner of such importance as he would be placed in the strongest cell.

Someone else who had once been in that very same room, Ram could see from one of the names etched on the wall, was Bray. Was it the same Bray who had been Amber's lover, Ram wondered? Would someone else see his own name in the future and be imagining who Ram himself had once been, with no trace left of him but the marking of his name?

"You can't hurt me!" Ram babbled to the germs he imagined crawling all over him, determined to ignore their presence, any threat they posed, and he resumed scraping the sides of the wall with his hands, ignoring the pain of his broken nails. Maybe the small gap the cockroach had crawled through led to a bigger opening, he considered. Or was any notion a sign that he had been broken and was in fact going insane?

Suddenly Ram heard an ominous chanting echoing around the gigantic compound.

"Zoot! Zoot! Zoot!" the chanting continued, getting increasingly louder, the prisoners working themselves up into feverish devotion, calling out in worship.

"Shut up!" Ram begged, delirious, scratching at the walls more desperately, anxious to get away.

"Zoot! Zoot! Zoot!!"

"*Please* – shut up!!" Ram cried out, unable to take it any more, the hypnotic loud chanting penetrating his very soul.

With a wail of anguish, Ram clasped his hands to his ears to try and block it all out, lost in the grip of a panic attack, each chant hitting him to his core like a powerful invisible force.

"No!" Ram screamed, writhing to the ground of his cell, the walls feeling like they were moving in, closing in on him. He was hyperventilating, unable to breathe freely. But more than that, he was trapped. There was no escape.

CHAPTER NINE

Amber wondered what lay in store for them all when the dawn broke - but she had no idea that she would wake up to find out that Bray had gone.

They had spent the night before taking turns on watch. After Amber, Bray was actually due to relieve Ellie but hadn't shown up and Ellie quickly woke everyone to alert them to the fact that he seemed to be missing.

Calling out his name, the group had searched around Arthurs Air Force Base. But still, there was no sign.

Amber was devastated and couldn't bear the thought of Bray disappearing from her so soon after they had been reunited – especially after the anguish and emotion of their argument the night before. Had she driven him away? Were her suspicions of his feelings for Emma proving too much for him, the final straw?

Emma herself was also shocked and worried for Bray, her protector for so long. Was he now in need of help himself?

Jack spotted some tracks in the dirt. Following them to their source, they led directly to a large depot in the base storing different vehicles. Several quad-bikes were lined up in a row, a gap in their ranks revealing one of them was missing.

There was only one place Bray could have intended to go, Amber knew. He had spoken of his need to investigate more about Eloise. A skilled and adept scout, Bray had undertaken many solo explorations in the city and Amber was sure it was more than likely he was on his way to check out Eloise's base.

Amber's belief was confirmed, she felt, when Darryl discovered that the map of the island Jay and Gel had found before was missing. Jay had left it in on a table in the cafeteria so anyone could study it in their own time. The map, showing details of Project Eden and various roads around the island, along with the route to the likely location of Eloise's base in the mountains, had completely vanished. Bray had to have taken it.

This in itself was confirmed when a note addressed to Amber was given to her. It was from Bray, who advised that he felt it was better to undertake the mission alone. If successful, he would rendezvous at some point in time back at the native village. And if unsuccessful, he just wanted Amber to take care of their baby son and above all for her to take care of herself, to continue paving the path for her dream to achieve a better new world order from the ashes of the old.

Amber again couldn't help but wonder if her indecision had contributed to Bray's decision. Equally it was so typical of who he was. He would rather selflessly put himself at risk than allow the rest of the group to travel up the island into the path of Eloise. Back in the city, Bray had similarly split off by himself on many occasions to find medicine, food - or information.

However skilled Bray was as a scout – and Amber had never known of anyone his equal – he could end up in real danger, she worried. She wanted to leave, to bring him back – and she would search the entire island for him if she had to.

But Jay suggested he alone should go after Bray.

His thinking was that it was better for most of the group to remain at the base, which at least was a secure haven rather than attempt to travel back to the native village.

Besides, what would happen if Lex, Trudy, the Priestess or any of the other villagers travelled to the base to try and contact them?

The majority doubted that would ever be the case. They needed strength in numbers too. Though there had been no immediate sign of any threats in the time they had spent at the base, they didn't know if the Collective or any other hostile forces were around. The more Mall Rats who stayed behind, the greater their chances of survival, Jay knew.

Instead of all – or most of them - setting out in pursuit of Bray, which could have spread them out vulnerably across the island, it was more important, Jay reasoned, to consolidate their position at the base, to be there for when he – and hopefully Bray – returned.

There were added benefits too if Amber and the others didn't accompany Jay, he explained. Jack and Ellie could try and uncover some of the mysteries surrounding the adult hibernation chambers, see if they could access the computers at the base and discover any important information.

Jay didn't want to waste any more time, Bray already having a head start. He chose a quad-bike, refuelling it from some of the gasoline tanks left behind by the adults at the depot – and was now ready to depart, sitting astride the vehicle.

He could picture the map in his mind, having studied it the night before, remembering there was meant to be a main arterial road to travel that would take him through an opening in the long fence that bisected the land. If he followed that road, it would lead him north - eventually to 'Project Eden', the presumed base in the northern mountains. Hopefully, Jay would have caught up with Bray before that, and persuade him to return home to Amber and the others, searching for another strategy rather than a sole assault on Eloise's base.

"Be careful," Amber said, giving Jay a loving kiss on the side of his cheek. "And thank you. You don't have to be doing this for me."

"I'm doing it because it's the right thing to do," Jay replied, giving Amber a reassuring smile. "*You* be careful. All of you."

The others had also come to wave their goodbyes to Jay. Jack and Ellie stood with Emma, Tiffany and Shannon, holding each other's hands together, for support.

Emma tried to be brave but she couldn't help grimacing in concern, worried by Bray's disappearance – and for Jay.

"Don't be too long!" Gel hollered over the sound of Jay revving the engine – and he suddenly roared off, accelerating the quad-bike, which sped away in a shower of dust and grit.

If there were any threats out there, lurking in the wasteland, Jay believed he would cope. He was sure he would have enough speed and the element of surprise should he encounter anyone, to avoid any danger.

He just hoped it would all be enough – and that he could find out what had happened to Bray, before it was too late.

* * *

What have I done? Amber reflected, feeling that she was responsible for what had developed.

If only she had been able to make a decision, the courage to break the impasse fate had put her in.

She vowed that should Jay bring Bray back to her, she would end the deadlock between the three of them. Bray was right. It was unfair to keep him and Jay in further suspense. They deserved an answer.

Her feet scrunched on broken glass and debris as she walked over the uneven ruins of the base.

Amber was on her way to see Emma, Darryl having mentioned Emma was taking Tiffany and Shannon to the amusement park section, hoping some playtime on the decrepit rides would distract the young minds of her brother and sister from Bray's disappearance.

For so long, Amber reflected, Bray had fulfilled the role of Emma's guardian, her blindness and vulnerability bringing out his protective side. And now with Bray missing, Amber was determined to step into the role, to make sure that Emma was okay. It's not only what Bray would have wanted. It was her duty also, Amber felt, seeing Emma and her siblings up ahead.

Tiffany and Shannon were lost in a game, playing merrily on a see-saw, the rusty ride needing oil, screeching loudly, harshly, as it moved up and down, Tiffany on one end, Shannon the other, their giggles filling the air.

They were oblivious to the condition of their older sister - which was just as well, Amber thought. Emma was sitting at an old picnic style table, her head buried in her arms. Her shoulders heaving at her obvious sobbing.

Amber felt terrible to see Emma so clearly struggling. She had a purity about her, an innocent quality, and Amber suddenly felt awful pangs of guilt, having viewed Emma lately as a potential rival for Bray's affections. How could Amber have been so petty? She had been blinded by her own jealousy and overlooked Emma's own needs, not recognizing how difficult it was for Emma to be back at Arthurs Air Force Base, the courage Emma had shown in returning to her past.

Bray and Emma clearly had a bond from what the two of them had previously shared together at the base, Amber now appreciated. She really hadn't understood, given proper consideration, to what they had gone through. Amber had been too harsh on Bray, she felt, not given him enough leeway. If only she could undo what she had said to him the night before, she reflected.

"Emma, is it alright if I join you?" Amber asked sympathetically, approaching the table where Emma sat.

Emma looked up in the direction of Amber's voice, her unseeing eyes wet from the tears she had been shedding.

She was embarrassed to show herself so exposed, taking a moment to think over Amber's offer.

"I'd like that... thank you," Emma said, her voice raw with emotion.

"Hey, everything will be okay," Amber replied, giving Emma a reassuring hug. "Bray knows exactly what he's doing. And he and Jay will be back sooner than we know it."

"I hope you're right. You're so lucky, Amber. In the time he and I were here, Bray never stopped talking about you."

It felt like a dagger to her heart, Amber guilty at doubting Bray, having imagined him romantically interested in Emma.

"Bray thinks the world of you, Emma. You're very special to him."

Amber was being truthful in what she said – she wasn't trying to make Emma upset but to make her feel better, for her to know how Bray cared for her.

Emma wiped her face as fresh tears flowed down her cheeks. "He's been so - kind to me... Tiffany... Shannon... He understands. I've never – met anyone like him before. I didn't think there was anyone left in the world who could be like that. And now – he's gone..."

Tiffany and Shannon continued playing their games, moving over to the creaking swings, swaying back and forth, laughing in childish delight at each other, not paying any attention to the two older girls who sat nearby.

Emma broke down, sobbing uncontrollably, and Amber hugged her tightly in support.

"It's alright," she said softly, reassuringly. "Everything is going to be alright."

* * *

"Come and get it!" Gel beamed, all too pleased with her own culinary efforts, bringing a plate of food to Jack and Ellie.

Initially, after Jay set out to find Bray, they had returned to the lower levels of the hospital building - but hadn't been able to make any more sense of the hibernation chambers.

They were now in the office and administration block checking out the same room Jay and Gel had found the map of the island previously in, Gel having mentioned seeing several computer workstations on the desks in there.

To Jack's delight they all seemed to be still functioning – one by one he had turned them on and had eighteen computers to examine, all of them powered by whatever internal generator the office complex was running on.

Gel was doing her best to help them out, supplying them with an endless supply of food.

"If you need any more, you know where to find me! And Darryl - I've got him busy doing the washing up," she grinned, skipping away from the room.

"I never knew she enjoyed food so much," Jack smiled, prodding his plate, unsure of its contents, a mixture of dried foodstuffs of various cuisines having been rehydrated and sprayed all over with different sauces drizzled on top, looking like some eccentric work of modern art.

"Well, we didn't exactly have much choice of food on offer back home," Ellie said, sampling her plate – and actually finding it to her liking.

Maybe it was because Gel felt she couldn't contribute much in any other way – she had kept going to the cafeteria with enthusiasm, whipping up meals for the others to eat – as well as herself.

"If she keeps on eating, the way she's going – she'll have to change her name from Gel to 'Swell'," Jack affectionately teased.

He suddenly gagged on his forkful, disgusted by Gel's latest preparation. "Suddenly, I'm not that hungry."

"Then more food for me, more work for you," Ellie grinned, taking Jack's plate away so she could finish it off. "Get going, genius."

Jack flexed his fingers like a concert pianist and began typing frantically on the keyboard of the latest computer he was investigating, having already looked at three of the workstations in the room, searching through their files.

So far, they had found references to nuclear fusion tests the adults had apparently been conducting near Arthurs Air Force Base, experimenting with new forms of energy, powered solely by water. 'Project Aquarius' was the name of the mission, the adults looking for a breakthrough that would sustain the population on the island indefinitely as they sought to survive in the post-virus world.

Jack wondered if there was something more to these tests which from the files had been marked 'Highly

Classified' and speculated if something had gone wrong along the way, recalling Bray mentioning he once passed a huge crater in the 'wastelands' - and Emma's tale of how she saw a bright explosion light up the sky, the last thing she saw before losing her sight. Or was none of it an accident – and the explosion had been triggered by some kind of weapon?

Ever since the virus had spread like a flash fire around the globe, there had been all sorts of theories. And above all - conspiracy theories. At the height of the pandemic, some questioned if there was indeed a virus or was it all as a result of something more ominous, even sinister. Like a scientific experiment gone disastrously wrong? Even genetic engineering? Bacterial warfare? A germ introduced to earth and mutating into a deadly virus as a result of space exploration?

And now with all the other threads of information they were discovering, it all added to the mystery. Whatever the adults had been up to, the United Nations personnel who had been stationed on the island clearly had more in mind than simply the welfare of the many evacuated children who had been shipped out there, like Emma and her tribe, the Roaches.

"Hey Ellie, this machine is advanced, hyper fast," Jack said, admiring the workstation's technical performance. "You couldn't even buy gear like this on the market, back in the day. It runs on something I've never even heard of."

"Don't get too distracted by thoughts of playing any computer games - and forget about me," Ellie said, between mouthfuls.

Jack's eyes darted as he scanned through the folders and files of the computer's storage drives.

A window suddenly popped up on screen, taking Jack by surprise.

"What was that?" Ellie asked.

"It wasn't me. I think – this thing's gone online somehow," Jack said, watching the screen intensely. "When I booted it up."

Ellie put her plate down so she could have a look. "The Internet is dead, Jack. There is no 'online' anymore."

"Try telling that to the computer…"

Jack tried to make sense of what his eyes were seeing. He remembered Ram telling him he had communicated with Kami, the leader of the Collective, through something called UNANET, an online private network devised in the wake of the pandemic. 'United Nations Agency Network', Ram said the initials stood for – UNANET was based on the old ARPANET that had been created to allow communication to occur during the old Cold War in the event of any apocalyptic event.

"Ellie – someone's trying to make contact with us," Jack said, staring puzzled at the screen, imagining who was on the 'other side' – and had just sent them a message.

* * *

Amber, followed by Emma, Gel, Darryl, Tiffany and Shannon, rushed into the room and crossed toward Jack, still seated, gazing at the computer.

He had sent Ellie to assemble the others and none could quite believe someone could possibly be making contact online, as indeed neither could Jack or Ellie.

"Are you sure?" Amber asked aloud, staring at the computer.

"Positive," Jack replied, typing in more instructions on the keyboard.

"Who is it?" Gel enquired nervously.

"That's the thing – I don't know," Jack answered.

The group gazed intently at a series of graphics popping up on the display in different languages, some of them European, most of Far East Asian origin.

"They're obviously somewhere in the world – but I don't know where," Jack reflected "Somehow though - they know we're online."

"Maybe it's the Collective," Darryl questioned anxiously.

"Why don't you just ask who they are?" Gel probed.

"I would – if I could understand what language to use," Jack said.

Gel looked at him as if it was obvious.

"Duh - your own language, of course. What else?"

Actually - it wasn't such a bad idea, Jack thought. He had been almost too cautious and so far hadn't typed in a single word.

"Here goes," Jack said, nervously typing on the keyboard.

Hello?

The words in various languages on screen suddenly ceased - Jack thumping the desk in disappointment.

"What? Did we lose the connection?" Amber asked.

Jack could see they were still online and was about to try again - when a new message suddenly appeared. Jack read it out aloud.

HELLO. ARE YOU THE ROACHES?

Emma winced at the mention of her former tribe.

"Well - what do I say?" Jack asked excitedly.

"Ask them who they are!" Amber said, equally intrigued - and Jack began to type in once again.

Who are you?

There was no response for a moment, Jack anxiously waiting for a reply.

Then suddenly words appeared on the screen.

WE ARE WELL. THANK YOU. HOW ARE YOU?

"At least they seem friendly," Jack said, having read out the response. "But maybe they didn't understand my question. Possibly if they don't have a total grasp of English, if they're from another country."

"Or they're avoiding the question," Amber observed.

"Try again," Ellie suggested.

Jack repeated his question.

Who are you?

Another moment passed before the reply popped up.

WE NEED TO KNOW WHO WE CAN TRUST. PLEASE CONFIRM. ARE YOU THE ROACHES?

"They certainly seem very interested in Emma's old tribe," Jack observed - and he typed in his next response.

We also need to know who we can trust. Please confirm. Where is your home?

"See what they make of that," Jack said.

WE WILL CHECK IF WE CAN EXCHANGE FURTHER COMMUNICATION. PLEASE WAIT FOR OUR NEXT CONTACT.

Jack sighed as they clearly disappeared offline.

"I can't believe it - they've gone!" he said disappointedly.

"What was all that about?" Darryl asked.

"I don't know. But we're clearly going to find out," Amber replied, confused and more than deeply concerned.

CHAPTER TEN

Connor had risen early with a bad hangover, rubbing his head in a forlorn attempt to clear away his pounding headache, finding the sounds of the island's jungle dawn chorus deafening, a myriad of birds and insects chirping loudly as they greeted the sunrise.

Upon waking he also found himself surrounded by a group of natives, fascinated by this enigmatic stranger who had arrived in the village – and his mystical looking pendant. Was he the legendary 'sea spirit' their fables foretold would visit, in human form, to learn of their ways and judge them, bringing reward or damnation?

Connor hadn't lingered, uncomfortable to be the subject of such scrutiny, and was keen to get back to his boat, *Nemo*, to make sure it was safe.

Trudy had given him some shampoo and toiletries from a stack Gel had previously gathered from the wreckage of the *Jzhao Li*, Gel rescuing her 'treasures', she called them, from one of the containers that used to be on the massive cargo ship.

Connor would return to the village soon, he promised, after he had cleaned himself up and checked his boat and all the worldly possessions *Nemo* carried.

Not trusting the stranger who had arrived, seemingly out of nowhere, Lex had arranged for Slade to go along with Connor to the *Nemo*, ostensibly to offer any assistance required but in reality Slade would be making sure Connor wasn't up to anything threatening, perhaps by alerting any would be enemies of the strengths and numbers of the Mall Rats and the native tribe.

With Connor and Slade temporarily gone, life returned to almost a sense of normality in the village, but there was still an air of mystery over Connor's arrival.

Lex wondered how long it would be before Amber, Bray, Jay and the rest of the Mall Rat exploration party returned to the village. He hoped they were okay and hadn't come across any danger - particularly from the

Collective, remembering Ram's dire warnings of their apparent presence on the island.

Lex was now keen to work on their own security at the village. Connor's unexpected appearance had shown they couldn't be too complacent in case the Collective, Eloise or any other danger did turn up.

Lex patrolled the village, checking spears the natives had fashioned and rocks placed to use as missiles at various strategic points.

"There you are," Lia said, arriving by his side. "I've been looking everywhere for you."

"Nice to be missed," Lex replied, eyeing her up, admiring Lia's figure – and her interest in him.

"It's not me… The Priestess wants to see you in her hut, right away. To go over your spirits."

It was music to Lex's ears - and he dropped the pile of rocks he had been carrying.

Suddenly, the thought of defensive preparations seemed a lot less enticing than the promise of an intimate meeting with the alluring Priestess.

"She can check out my spirits anytime."

* * *

Lex was thrilled to have been summoned. It was just him and the Priestess, as well as Lia, in the hut, to act as interpreter.

The Priestess was kneeling down on the floor, opposite Lex, who had been asked to take a similar position, the Priestess staring deeply into Lex's eyes, talking to him softly in her native tongue.

"She asks – you're sure you are the leader of your people here?" Lia explained, crouching down beside them.

In the absence of Amber, Jay and Bray – and left in charge of the defence of the others – to Lex, desperate to stay in the close current company of the two girls he had so longed after - the answer was obvious.

"Of course I am."

Pleased to hear his answer, translated by Lia, the Priestess gently placed a hand on Lex's broad chest, Lex surprised by her touch – and looking forward to what might follow.

"Then we begin," Lia said.

The Priestess began an incantation and threw several powders with her left hand into the fire she had lit, embers crackling in the urn, whiffs of smoke taking shape around them, the Priestess keeping her right hand firmly on Lex.

"What's she doing?" Lex asked in a whispery undertone.

"Opening a portal to the spirit world," Lia described. "Calling upon her ancestors - and the spirits of the island for guidance… She wants to look into the future of you and your people. To see what the arrival of the sea spirit heralds."

The Priestess continued her rhythmical chanting, swaying side to side, Lex finding it had a hypnotic effect on him, overwhelmed by being in such proximity, the sound of her soft voice, the feel of her touch, the smell of flowers decorating her hair, the Priestess's beautiful features glowing from the light of the fire.

Lex found it all a complete turn-on as the Priestess took her hand off his chest, gently putting it to the side of his face.

"What's she doing now?" Lex asked.

Lia explained as the Priestess closed her eyes, concentrating, that she was trying to connect with Lex's own spiritual world, divining what the augury of the 'sea spirit' would be for him and his tribe.

"Well, that makes two of us. I'm also thinking about 'connecting'," Lex commented mischievously.

"I know what you're thinking," Lia whispered disapprovingly. "How could you? She's trying to help. Don't you ever think of anything else but – you know?"

"I was actually thinking about you right now," Lex whispered back.

Lia was speechless - embarrassed and flattered by Lex's remark.

The Priestess suddenly opened her eyes, taking her hand off Lex's face, her arm dropping as if it had no strength left, the Priestess exhaling in fatigue, returning to the real world from her communion with the spirits.

"What is it?" Lex asked cagily, thinking for a moment the Priestess had been able to look into his mind - and had seen his flirtatious thoughts of Lia.

The Priestess was shocked – devastated by what she had foreseen and she quickly told of her discovery to Lia, who began translating to Lex, concerned at what she was relaying.

"She says the spirits have blessed her with a vision… but it is one that brings her no joy to tell… She glimpsed into the future of you and your people… She can see nothing but sadness… loss... She says the spirits told her. Some of your tribe – will soon be met by the spirit of death."

* * *

The Mall Rats left behind were shaken at first hearing the prophecy made by the Priestess, worried if she really had taken a glimpse into their futures. Or, if not for those at the village, if her ominous vision applied to any of the tribe who were away in the exploration party which had still not returned.

Lex in particular was unsettled. The Priestess's warning, coinciding with Connor's arrival, only reinforced Lex's own instinctive suspicion of Connor. And for all that he had been in pursuit of the Priestess as a conquest, determined to entice her into his bed, he had grown to admire her for her other human qualities besides her sensual physical traits, the native way of life appealing to him.

Never one to believe in religion as such, Lex wondered if there was something more to the spiritual existence the Priestess followed – with the added bonus, he felt, that learning about it could only improve his chances of getting to know the Priestess on a more physical level.

"It's all a bit far fetched, if you ask me," Trudy said, doubting the prophecy the Priestess had made.

"I don't remember anyone asking you," Lex pointed out.

"You'd believe anything she tells you. There's no such thing as spirits. Religion. Not anymore," Trudy reflected.

"That's rich coming from you. Have you forgotten the Guardian already? Weren't you the 'Supreme Mother'?" Lex teased.

"Hey, cut it out, you two," Salene admonished, trying to defuse matters before they got out of hand.

"All I'm saying is we don't know anything about this Connor guy," Lex insisted. "So better be on your guard. He could mean trouble."

"Speaking of which..." Sammy indicated discretely.

Slade and Connor had arrived back at the village but the Mall Rats and villagers were totally shocked by the sight before them.

Where before Connor was filthy, scruffy, hair wild, his breath an overwhelming stench of alcohol - it was like a completely different person had returned with Slade.

Connor had taken a wash, borrowed a comb, cleaned his clothes, shaved off his scraggly beard and stubble, brushed his teeth, for the first time in months, he had told Slade – and was transformed.

"I think I'm in love," Lottie gushed, totally smitten, developing an instant crush - and received an elbow in the side from a clearly jealous Sammy. Now wasn't the time for any joking - assuming that Lottie was joking of course. There were many questions which needed to be answered.

Connor was undoubtedly exceptionally good looking, his handsome features having been hidden by his previously messy appearance. Now, everyone could see he had the most piercing eyes, a rugged complexion, his long hair combed back stylishly over his shoulders. Strong jawed, he stood tall, in every way an impressive physical specimen, like a male model from the adult days who should be more comfortable on the catwalk than there, on the island.

For a moment, everyone just stared, struck to see this 'prince charming' among them, such a difference to the drunken scoundrel they had witnessed before. And the changed appearance hadn't exactly gone unnoticed by Trudy.

"Where's the Connor I met?!" she beamed in delight.

"Ta da," Slade said, presenting Connor before them.

"Lottie, you're staring," Sammy said in an undertone.

"I don't care," Lottie swooned.

"I hope your boat and all your things were alright?" Trudy asked.

"Yeah. It's fine, thanks," Connor replied.

"It's also pretty cool," Slade said.

The others gathered round Connor, besieging him with all manner of questions about his voyage. And Lex whispered to Slade.

"Do you think he's legit?"

"Seems to be," Slade responded.

"You've changed your tune. I thought you didn't trust him either?"

"He's actually a good guy. Now he's sober. You should get to know him. He might be able to help us."

"I wouldn't be too sure about that - he seems to be more interested in helping himself," Lex said, still wary of Connor wallowing in all the attention he was getting, from the girls in particular, most of them enamoured to see another male in their presence, and one who was apparently single by the sounds of it, as Connor began to answer their various questions.

Connor explained how he had originally come from a coastal town where his family had a boat, the *Nemo*, and he had grown up spending time on board it as a child. His parents, both keen sailors, were also in the navy and took Connor, their only child, on a series of maritime adventures. It was from them that Connor learned to sail. And when the virus swept through the world, casting it into the abyss, Connor reassured his parents he would stay safe, setting out to sea on the *Nemo* to begin his new life. It was far too dangerous on land, Connor had felt, reckoning he could live a safer existence, and one that was nearly self-sustaining, on the water, his home city having plunged into utter anarchy.

Catching fish, collecting rain water, even having his own small supply of electricity from the solar panels on the roof of his yacht, Connor described how the initial time he had spent alone had been comforting in many ways, a solace and refuge from the rest of the world. He had slowly come to terms with the passing of his parents and found a sense of peace and reassurance by living on the boat that had once been theirs, maintaining a connection to his family and past as he tried to find his own place in the future.

He drifted out to sea, doing his best to chart his position on the nautical maps inside the cabin of the *Nemo*. His mother, a naval doctor, had various maritime maps of the world's sea lanes, dreaming that one day, upon her retirement, she would be able to sail around the world with her husband in their 36 foot long boat, her doodles of where she intended to go still visible on the nautical maps.

Her dream had died with her but Connor was determined, in his own way, to fulfil it, as well as to survive, and he explained to the Mall Rats how he had travelled around many thousands of nautical miles, exploring islands and different regions, anchoring from time to time, gathering in fresh supplies, or taking safe harbour from any adverse weather.

Around the time the adults perished, Connor told them, in the middle of the ocean, he had seen what he claimed was a vast fleet of ships on the distant horizon. He thought he saw an aircraft carrier, several battlecruisers, support vessels, escorting a few massive cargo ships. He couldn't see if the vessels were adrift - or still functional, with living adult crews. It was like an apparition, Connor explained, and he had wondered if it was all a mirage, an illusion playing out in his tired, solitary mind.

Connor lost sight of the convoy but much later he recalled what he had seen way back then, when just a few weeks ago he encountered another ship drifting in the seas by itself like some kind of a leviathan. It was a United Nations ship, he could see from its insignia, and Connor had followed it as best as the winds would carry his little boat, *Nemo*, dwarfed in comparison.

"Maybe it was the *Jzhao Li*?" Sammy suggested, intrigued by Connor's tales of the sea.

Lex noticed the name seemed to cause Connor a degree of unease.

"No, I don't recall that name," he said, advising that he had been unable to close the gap on the huge container ship, whatever it had been, but had kept on the same course, carried by the ocean currents and prevailing winds.

He gradually ran out of fresh water supplies and Connor had nothing more to drink but the dwindling stocks of his father's aged whiskey.

Connor had become drunk, losing control of his vessel and his senses, nothing but the whiskey and the last of his dwindling food supplies to stem his despair.

He remembered seeing the island in the distance, altered the helm on course, desperate to reach landfall after so long adrift. *Nemo* had scraped its hull on the reef but Connor had been able to anchor the boat.

He had stumbled onto land, nearly drowning in the process in the water as he drunkenly tried to swim ashore.

"And then I met you," Connor said, bashfully looking at Trudy, who had been absorbed by his story. "You saved me. And I'll always be grateful."

"I couldn't just leave you... It was my pleasure," Trudy blushed.

Ruby exchanged glances with the others as if she might be sick how Trudy was gushing coyly.

"I'm so sorry," Connor continued. "Embarrassed by how I was last night. I don't remember much - but Slade told me... You were the first people I had seen for far too long. I was intoxicated to see you - probably more from what I'd had to drink. I'm quite ashamed."

"You should be," Lex said.

"Give him a break, Lex," Salene defended Connor. "He was lonely, that's all. You can hardly blame him. And no harm was done."

Lex stared at Connor distrustfully. "No harm's been done. Yet."

"I won't outstay my welcome. *Nemo's* my home, not here. As soon as I stock up, I'll get back on the water. After all, what's better than the sea and the sky as your companions? A bit of freedom - and a fresh start?"

"It all sounds so romantic," Lottie sighed wistfully, heart-struck.

"A bit too romantic, if you ask me," Lex said.

"Why don't you stay here for a bit longer? I mean – what's the hurry?" Trudy suggested casually. "You only just got here."

"You've done more than enough, Trudy. I don't want to be in anybody's way."

"You wouldn't be in the way," Salene encouraged him.

May gave Salene an uncomfortable look. "It's Connor's decision. He might want to leave."

"So he can go and report what he's found? To the Collective?" Lex bristled, deciding to throw down the gauntlet and see how Connor responded. But he didn't.

"I don't understand."

Lex considered Connor, who seemed genuine as he continued.

"All I'd like to do is try and repay you somehow."

"And how might that be?" Lex asked.

"If there's anything I can do to help in any way..."

"I'm sure there's a lot you could do to help out here, Connor," Trudy smouldered. "You don't really need to leave so soon. It might be an idea to stay around and enjoy all that dry land has to offer for a while."

"I appreciate the offer," Connor replied. "It sure feels good to be on terra firma, having some company."

"But if you put one step out of line..." Lex threatened.

"You'll have to forgive Lex. He's never exactly had a way with words," Salene remarked, "and clearly doesn't know the meaning of being hospitable."

"Hey, no problem. I totally get it. You don't know the first thing about me. And I could be just about to mount an attack. But I wouldn't fancy my chances. There must be a few hundred of you around here against just me."

It was a veiled dig at Lex, who knew it.

"Well, I don't know about the rest of you but I've got work to do," Lex said, giving Connor a disdainful look before heading away to continue his defence preparations.

Lia followed him. She didn't trust Connor either, feeling he was a bit too 'smooth' now he had shaved and cleaned himself up. She imagined he was quite the ladies man and probably had a girl waiting in every port.

"Don't mind him," Ruby said.

"It's just Lex's way... he's really a great guy underneath that front of his. And believe it or not, once he gets to know you he'll be more hospitable," Salene explained.

"Well, allow me to be hospitable," Connor said. "You're welcome to see my boat."

"Sounds like a great idea," Lottie beamed.

"Yeah, doesn't it," Sammy remarked sarcastically, feeling left out by all the attention Connor was getting, from Lottie especially.

"Trudy, I really owe you," Connor said, holding his hand out as a gesture of friendship, singling her out. "If you hadn't helped me… I could have tripped. Drowned. You can come on board *Nemo* for a tour anytime. Just say the word."

"I'd like that," Trudy smiled coyly, shaking his hand in return, feeling good she had made a difference to someone's life, that their paths had crossed.

"I'm glad we bumped into each other," Connor insisted, staring into Trudy's eyes, making a connection with her.

"So am I," Trudy replied, demurely averting her gaze, bashful at Connor's interest in her – and surprising herself to find out how attracted she was to him.

* * *

May strolled despondently along the beach, trying to keep within any shade, out of sight from anyone, hiding herself among the rows of palm trees that swayed back and forth in the breeze.

She couldn't fully understand how she was feeling and wondered if she was being irrational and was indeed vulnerable as everyone suggested as a result of losing Zak and needed time to grieve.

When Connor first returned to the village, all cleaned up though, May felt Salene had been a bit too friendly to him, easily attracted by his handsome features. No matter how hard she tried to ignore her feelings – May was jealous. And she still couldn't articulate just exactly why. Or the source of just so many thoughts swirling around.

She wondered if this was destiny taking a cruel turn once again, putting another barrier in May's life. Fate always seemed to go against her. Was this the beginning of a process where Salene would fall for Connor's charms, and he for her, with the two of them ending up as a couple?

It had been the case before, between Salene and Pride. May had been left on the sidelines. Alone and unloved. But she always considered herself to be a survivor and was more than capable of handling herself on the streets. Now she wanted something other than just being able to survive. It was as if she was searching for some greater meaning to her life.

May tried to be positive, to stop thinking of herself as some sort of constant victim – but this in turn made her feel guilty, that she was being selfish, insensitive to Salene's own needs, failing to appreciate that Salene needed to live her own life as well.

Had she really fallen that low, May reflected – so petty – that she had come to depend upon Salene so much? She loathed who she was becoming, May wishing Connor's handsome face had never been seen by Salene - any of them - and that he stayed away, far out at sea.

The tide beckoned May. She was tempted to dive in, to immerse herself under it. To put an end to the misery that was engulfing her.

"May, wait up!" Salene called, jogging over.

So engrossed by her thoughts, May hadn't noticed Salene – who ran up to be with her, out of breath.

"I was wondering where you were… Mind if I stick around?"

"You really don't have to - if you don't want to."

"Well, I do want to. Of course I'd want to. I could do with the company."

"I thought you might have wanted to stay back there with the others," May said. "And get to know Connor a little bit better."

"He'd be quite a catch. For someone. But not me," Salene smiled.

She considered May, trying to establish what was clearly on her mind. May didn't seem to be in her 'usual' state of being upset. There had been no obvious signs of crying, tears, the normal symptoms of her pain and confusion that manifested in their talks before.

It was something else, Salene could tell – and the fact she didn't know made it all the more unsettling as she worried for May's condition.

"What's up? Do you want to talk about it?"

"I can't tell you," May replied.

"Did someone say something - that upset you? If you don't want to talk, I'll respect that. But if you can, you might feel better sharing whatever's bothering you. I might be able to help."

May's brave face began to crack, losing her composure, she was becoming more and more distressed at the way things were going.

"You'd be better off keeping away from me."

"Why? Did I do something wrong?"

"Salene, I can't tell you!"

"You can – you can tell me anything."

"Don't you get it, Salene?"

"What!?"

May began to shake with emotion, her world crashing down around her.

"You haven't done anything wrong! But the opposite! You're perfect! Stop it! Stop being you! Being so nice! I don't deserve it. I can't bear it anymore!"

"That doesn't make any sense! If I haven't done anything wrong – then why are you upset?"

"Can't you see?"

"See what?"

"I... think I have 'feelings' for you, Salene!" May recoiled upon saying the words. Ashamed by her confession. Humiliated.

"And I care enormously about you, too," Salene said, totally missing May's point completely.

"No, it's more than that," May winced, trying somehow to explain, unable to bottle it up any longer, keep it a secret. Holding back the truth was too difficult, impossible. Yet revealing it was one of the hardest things she ever had to do, absolutely agonizing. May was in a no win situation. Like she had always been in her life, she felt.

She was vulnerable. Exposed. She had nothing left. Revealed her greatest secret to the person she cared the most about - and she couldn't restrain herself any longer.

Suddenly she turned and kissed Salene gently, seductively on the lips before finally stepping back, feeling uncomfortable in the uneasy silence.

"I'm sorry!" May eventually whispered.

"Don't be. Because I'm not."

Salene just stood there, understanding the truth at last, assimilating everything. It all made sense now. Many memories flashed through Salene's mind, fleeting glimpses where May had said certain things, given her a subtle look.

Salene had never been 'into' girls in the past, recognizing and appreciating physical beauty on one level without ever feeling attracted in the same way she was when she saw a handsome guy – like Pride, Bray. Or Connor.

But romance was not built upon looks, Salene knew. The heart mattered most. Who someone was, not how they looked. She had first lost her heart to Ryan as an individual before she found herself attracted to him in any intimate way.

And now, right here, standing closely, was a person who Salene unquestionably respected, cared for - and understood on a profound level. May had revealed to Salene her very soul. And it touched Salene in a way which meant more than she could ever begin to explain.

It had been a long time since Salene had found companionship. And it hadn't been for the want of trying. Since Pride's untimely death, she had been on her own, not through choice. She just hadn't found that special someone.

Or had she?

"Did you really mean what you said... about not being sorry?" May probed uneasily.

"Would you like me to show you?" Salene responded.

May turned and exchanged glances with Salene in growing intensity. Then Salene took May's hand, drawing her closer and they hugged tightly.

May hesitated, wondering if Salene really meant it, knew what she was doing.

Salene left May in no doubt, kissing her on the lips, gently at first then with increasing passion.

With nothing else around but the beach and the waves crashing upon the sands, they stood locked in the embrace, each not wanting to let go, clinging to each other and clearly needing and cherishing each other also.

CHAPTER ELEVEN

Ebony wondered how long she could keep it all going, feeling any moment she would be exposed as a non-believer and suffer some terrible punishment the Guardian would be more than content giving her.

The longer she kept up the pretence of co-operating with her abductors, the longer she would live, she hoped.

If Eloise expected Ebony to do her bidding, to work with the Guardian, one of the most dangerous enemies from her past - so be it. She would do whatever it took to survive.

She had already considered that Eloise had something in mind for her, whatever that might be, because there was more than an opportunity to cause her harm. But equally she didn't intend to entirely back that supposition. If she was wrong, it could only lead to one consequence - her demise.

As far as she could gather, she was now en route to some kind of ceremony.

"We're giving the world something to believe in, Ebony," the Guardian said reverently, walking down the corridor, his long robes flowing behind him, Ebony by his side.

They were flanked by Axel and several guards, following in silent obedience.

"After all - the old religions are dead. Where were the adults' gods when the 'virus' struck? Who answered their prayers when they begged for mercy - and none were spared? The future is ours'. It belongs to our faith."

"Nice one. I get it. Totally," Ebony replied, deciding that for the moment she had no choice other than to go along with everything.

"Do you?" the Guardian said, staring at Ebony with intense skepticism. "Those who betray us will wish they had never been born on this cursed Earth! To go against us is to go against Zoot. Do you understand?"

"Yes. You've proven much to me already. I understand more now than I ever did before," Ebony replied.

"I have already tried to commune with the mighty Zoot to get some sign, if it's not too late for you and you can change," the Guardian reflected.

"It's never too late for anything, Guardian. You can bet on it."

"The Mother Divine feels you are on the path of redemption. It is not for me to question her - or the divine truths she is privileged to see. But I warn you. Do not fail her. For your sake, Ebony, continue your progress."

"Of course. I'll commit everything I have to you."

The Guardian seemed satisfied with her answer and they resumed their way down the labyrinth of corridors in the compound in silence, except for the Guardian mumbling at times incoherently to himself, Ebony making out a few phrases here and there about Zoot's supposed teachings, their 'mission'.

The Guardian, at Eloise's instructions, had already taken Ebony on a tour of the mountain base and she was shocked and impressed by the scale of the operation going on there.

She had seen rooms full of babies being tended to by nurses but rather than a conventional medical uniform, all were dressed in white lab coats and Ebony hoped they weren't being exposed to some kind of insidious experiments. It all seemed so sterile, with all walls painted white. But exceptionally well organized. Like a factory. Rather than the manufacture of any goods, there was only one thing visible on this surreal assembly line - babies.

Ebony had seen other rooms full of pregnant girls around her age and she was truly grateful that she was not one of them. Prisoners, mostly refugees, they were survivors like she had been, ending up on the island by fate. And Ebony wondered about the fathers, speculating that they had been probably exposed to some form of artificial insemination.

In another room, new mothers cared for the babies they had just brought into the world but they didn't seem to have much time to bond with any of the newborns, who were wrapped in blankets by other members of the staff and whisked away into what Ebony suspected was a holding area, which seemed to accommodate endless numbers of newborn children.

All the staff, as well as the mothers to be – along with those who had actually given birth - seemed soulless, there was no spark of life. It was as if their only purpose was nothing more than to bear children as parts of a machine, a greater collective whole.

That was indeed their role the Guardian had described. It was a vital task, he explained. They were repopulating the new world, creating a new generation. As well as an army, Ebony suspected, and it was a poignant moment for her to realize that all the babies she had seen were probably no more than a future supply of slaves or warriors.

In another area of the complex Ebony had been shown younger children who were being indoctrinated into the faith of Zootism in learning rooms. It brought back memories of school to Ebony but this time it was older teenage acolytes, not adults, who were teaching their pupils, from the ages of about four or five years old, the lessons of Zootism. Zoot was omnipresent, the children were told, watching over them all and gave the Guardian prophecies on the way in which they would play a part in building a better new world.

Ebony felt she was in a crazy wonderland, some twisted surreal dimension and that she was the only person, other than Ram perhaps, with a grip on reality.

Except also perhaps for Eloise, Ebony reflected. In the meetings she had so far experienced, Eloise seemed to be rational, intelligent, emotionally detached from the bizarre Zootist goings on around her, which suggested to Ebony there was far more to the 'Mother Divine' than anyone there knew - especially the Guardian.

He was clearly being manipulated by Eloise, Ebony was sure of it. And as a master of manipulation herself, Ebony had long discovered how to read the signs. Eloise was pulling the strings, the mistress of puppets, in charge of them all. For now, that is. Ebony was soon herself to follow suit and she would show Eloise how it should really be done. But now a key element in her strategy was to try to somehow gain their trust.

Earlier in the day, Eloise and the Guardian interrogated Ebony about Bray, who she last saw alive on Blake's oil rig, and the presence of the Mall Rats on the island.

She was confused, as well as concerned, when she was asked to also reveal any information she knew about Eagle Mountain. She was totally surprised to have been asked details about the trip she had once made there with the Mall Rats and wondered how Eloise and her cohorts knew about it in the first place.

She answered truthfully, unsure what other details they already knew, not wanting to risk putting herself in any danger by lying about any of her experiences.

She told them everything she could remember about the observatory, the adult base they discovered with its computers, particularly the voice activated central computer. The satellite. The transmission they received.

The explosion that drove them out, taking Zandra's life in the process. And apparently Amber's - but she decided not to get into that and give too much away, she didn't exactly want to advertise a capability of devising the most cunning of machinations.

At the forefront of her mind though was why they would be interested in Eagle Mountain of all places at that very moment – and it was a complete mystery to Ebony. There was nothing there of value, as far as she could remember, the interior of the ground floor having been nearly totally gutted by the explosion that occurred.

Privately, Ebony also had an audience with Eloise, who asked her about her relationship with Blake, interested to hear of the last weeks her brother had spent alive. Assuming that he had in fact died of course. But that so far hadn't been confirmed.

Eloise hadn't shown much emotion to Ebony, keeping herself aloof, cool, deliberately not revealing anything about herself.

Ebony hoped the undeniable fact she had been Blake's lover would hold her in good stead with his sister. Was that partly why Eloise had kept her alive, Ebony reflected, due to her connection with Blake? But Ebony also suspected that her past relationship with Zoot might also be considered as a valuable currency.

Ebony had very carefully tried to gather some intelligence of her own and had carefully probed if Blake's Legion was part of the Collective. And what she had been able to learn so far was that Eloise was in the Collective and reigned supreme in the mountain base, commanding all the security forces there as well as the religious order, led by the Guardian, who dutifully obeyed Eloise's every whim.

Eloise hadn't exactly confirmed it to be the case but Ebony was putting the pieces all together like a jigsaw to get a handle on the bigger picture, recalling from what she had discovered during her time with Blake that they worked to the Collective and the only one who seemed to be in charge was Eloise. Ebony felt when the time was right to make a move, she would be more than a match for Eloise.

The 'Mother Divine' was apparently carrying a child that Bray had fathered. Was it really true? Had Bray 'done the deed' with Eloise, of all people?

How Ebony would have loved to watch Amber hear her beloved Bray had supposedly been seduced by the obvious temptations Eloise had to offer. Amber's expression would have been priceless.

Maybe Bray and Ebony had more in common after all, she considered, having kept herself alive often by using her own physical assets. Sometimes you had to sleep with the enemy as well as fight them, Ebony appreciated. She had done so in the past, ironically with Eloise's brother, remembering their nights on the oil rig.

With Bray carrying Zoot's bloodline through the incarnation of his brother, Martin, Ebony could understand that Eloise would have recognized that to be a valuable currency as well given that Bray's brother had once existed as Martin before becoming the leader of the Locos and pursuing his ideology of Power and Chaos under his adopted new guise, Zoot.

Whoever the father of Eloise's child was, there was no doubt she was pregnant and Ebony had been told by the Guardian that the 'Mother Divine' was carrying the bloodline of Zoot, who had placed his spirit within the 'Child Divine' – the future birth of the baby signalling his resurrection. So it all made sense that Bray must have been inadvertently involved. Either that or it was an immaculate deception.

Whatever the reason - she had to give Eloise credit. The 'Mother Divine' was setting herself up in a powerful position of influence.

"We're here," the Guardian explained as Ebony, Axel and the guards reached a door marking the end of the corridor. "Remember what is expected - or you will suffer in ways even you can't imagine."

"You can count on me," Ebony said, knowing she had to keep proving herself in order to stay alive.

"Then we begin," the Guardian announced, pushing open the doors. "Welcome to your 'rebirth'," he added as they entered the cavernous room.

It was the same 'temple' like place Ebony had been brought to previously. Unlike before, the benches were full. The assembled worshippers turned reverently, awestruck to see the Guardian as he swept past, their eerie faces lit by the candles held in their hands, flickering in the shadows.

Ebony followed the Guardian, aware she was eagerly being watched by the fanatical audience. She recognized some of the faces from the holding cell she and Ram had been initially placed in, spotting Aras in the crowd, looking back, startled in turn to see Ebony again.

At the other end of the room, where the portrait of Zoot took centre stage, sat Eloise, regally on her throne, beguiling all onlookers with her magnetism.

The Guardian stooped before her, bowing - and getting to his knees, Ebony doing the same.

She had been briefed what to do beforehand by the Guardian – and what precise message to say to the converts. The Guardian had been working on these former prisoners, radicalizing them to the faith.

"Mother Divine, we kneel before you in the name of the Great One, the almighty Zoot! And we pray that his message through your divine presence will guide us and show us the way," the Guardian said, his eyes closed tightly, as if in prayer.

Eloise got to her feet and placed one of her soft hands, her nails long, impeccably manicured, on the Guardian's head.

"You serve me and the Child Divine well, Guardian. Zoot's favour and blessing is upon you. Explain to our disciples who you have brought along, to be among us."

The Guardian opened his eyes, got to his feet – and Ebony also stood, staring out at the sea of faces to the back of the chamber, as she had been instructed previously.

There was an aura of great excitement building in the Guardian like an energy force as he gazed intently at the assembly.

"Brethren... In your teachings you have learned what happened in the city of sin that our lord Zoot lived in and tried to cleanse with Power and Chaos, before being summoned to the Heavens to continue on with his mission," the Guardian preached, displaying skills as an orator as his voice cracked with emotion.

"Now he has sent us someone, to bear witness to his greatness. She once had the honour of being in his company. Before she strayed. Lost her way. But she is back. Returned to us, from the wilderness. And she has begged for forgiveness. To serve our cause. Testify before us, Ebony. Tell us of what you witnessed. The truths you saw with your very eyes."

An excited murmur rippled through the audience as Ebony took a step forward, having been given her 'cue'.

It was now or never. She could either resist and contradict everything the converts had been told – or lend her support and backing to it. Now, it was her moment.

"I was there," she began, in whispered, hushed tones. "The very day that the mighty Zoot made his presence felt. It was in the days of the adults. At school. He was known as Martin, of course, back then. He told our 'teacher' – how little that man knew – that his time was running out. That a new age was coming. The adults were going to be swept away by the tide of history. The adults had nothing more to teach us. Their ways died, alongside them. We had a new leader to follow. To guide us. I was so – lucky… privileged, to witness the very moment. The beginning. When Zoot showed us the way towards bringing Power and Chaos and revolution to the new world!"

The followers were gripped by Ebony's words, the Guardian nodding with a glint of manic excitement gleaming in his eyes as he watched the audience gaze at Ebony, almost in awe. She had followed what they had rehearsed. But now she seemed to be ad libbing and the Guardian's expression clouded as he prepared to take over the service.

But Ebony hadn't finished yet.

"Zoot was flesh and bone – but he was more than human!" she called out, above the growing fervour of the audience. "He showed even way back then that he was a god! He *is* a god! He stood up, climbed on top of his desk, and that classroom was transformed into a shrine, and we were dazzled by Zoot's brilliance. He showed us the way! Saved us all! Saved me! And it was more powerful and stronger than anything I ever believed was even possible!"

The Guardian was shocked by Ebony continuing – but screamed at the top of his voice as he passionately crossed to the dais to join Ebony, who had climbed up into an aisle on stage and was now raising her arms above her head, clasping her hands together.

"Trust us, brethren! I was also there and witnessed the Mighty One transcend! Everything and anything, all we perceive was possible. That was when I knew he was destined to not only change our world but that he occupied my entire essence, spirit and soul!" his voice cracked with emotion.

Ebony raised her own voice above the audience, who had started chanting 'Zoot! Zoot! Zoot!'

"Zoot called out and I answered first!" she screamed in growing intensity. "The Guardian joined me in answering Zoot's call! Let me hear what your heart tells you! Let us follow the Mother Divine! She will take us forward. Together – we *can* build a new world! Answer the call! Power and Chaos!! Power and Chaos!!"

The crowd rose as if one, getting to their feet, arms raised in exaltation, and the chanting evolved into the words Zoot had first uttered at the school they had gone to, Ebony having recreated the moment in her speech, a witness to the original event.

"Power and Chaos! Power and Chaos!"

All present were being whipped into a frenzy, which seemed to both impress the Guardian and yet frighten him at the same time. And he cast a confused glance at Eloise for a sign, wondering if he should remove Ebony immediately for having gone beyond what she had been asked to do.

The 'Mother Divine' subtly shook her head, indicating Ebony was to be left alone. Her lips curled into a genuine smile, the atmosphere in the chamber was electrifying. And the Guardian joined in, repeating over and over as if he was being sucked into a trance.

"Power and Chaos! Power and Chaos!" Ebony continued encouraging the assembly.

Eloise was delighted at how it had all unfolded and crossed to stand beside the picture of Zoot, her hands pointedly on her pregnant belly, caressing the 'Child Divine' within.

Ebony was far too streetsmart to miss out on this cue and she indicated Eloise, caressing her swollen stomach and screamed over the chanting.

"Child Divine! Child Divine! Child Divine!"

All present responded, repeating Ebony's incantation.

"Child Divine! Child Divine! Child Divine!"

Eloise was glad she had given Ebony a reprieve, who had done what she had been instructed, and then some, whipping the converts into a frenzy, with Eloise at the centre of it all.

Ebony got down on her knees, paying homage to Eloise, as the followers continued chanting.

"Child Divine! Child Divine! Child Divine!"

Eloise grinned with glee, her judgement vindicated.

Ebony could be of great use to them, after all.

Unknown to her, Ebony secretly felt the same way about Eloise, sharing exactly the same sentiment.

* * *

"I can see why my brother thought so highly of you," Eloise complimented, leaning back, luxuriating in comfort, resting sideways as she preferred on her throne, her legs dangling casually over the other side of the arm of the chair.

Two servant girls focused intently, each of them holding one of Eloise's hands, making sure her nails were immaculate, reaching the perfection that Eloise demanded.

Another servant girl stood behind, carefully styling Eloise's long black hair, draped over her shoulders, gently brushing it, Eloise having taken a shower after the ceremony.

They were back in Eloise's main residence, a dining table being set up by other slaves, placing down cutlery and glasses, one of them opening bottles of wine to let them breathe.

"You will be rewarded, Ebony. You did well."

"It is my wish to serve you," Ebony bowed.

"As long as it pleased you, Mother Divine. I am just concerned she exceeded my instructions. As well as my own expectations, I have to admit. Zoot be praised!" the Guardian remarked in a mixture of caution and excitement, pacing back and forth.

"Zoot speaks to us in different ways," Eloise said.

Her words soothed the Guardian's frantic mood - and he looked up to the ceiling, to the heavens above, communing with the powers he so venerated, whispering to himself agitatedly, not realizing himself how the Mighty One connects on all sorts of levels and began deliberating what penance he needed to perform and if there was a sacrifice he could make to atone for not displaying absolute fealty to Eloise.

"You must relax, my dear Guardian. To achieve true enlightenment there are many levels we must all attain in our understanding of the word of Zoot," Eloise said reassuringly.

"I vow that I will continue dedicating all that I have to the pursuit of knowledge, Mother Divine! And to understand as the Mighty One understands."

The doors opened and Axel entered with several guards. On Axel's order they literally threw Ram down onto the floor, Ram groaning in discomfort.

"Leave us!" Eloise ordered her servants, who quickly obeyed, departing the hall.

"The infamous Ram, reduced to a cowering wreck," Eloise said, getting off her throne and stepping towards the dining table, surveying the food on offer. "Not so powerful now - are you, Techno?"

"What do you want with me?" Ram cried out, stealing looks at the Guardian and Ebony nearby, wondering why he had been summoned. And why Ebony seemed not to be in any danger. Was she part of some elaborate double-cross? He just couldn't figure out how she was a prisoner at one time but now seemed to be right at home and knowing her, before too long she would probably be running the place. He looked terrible and was in a filthy condition, dried blood caked around his nails from his desperate attempts to escape.

"I just want some information, Ram," Eloise probed, faking a slight smile. "And then you might find yourself being a little more welcomed into our operation here."

"What kind of information?" Ram asked cautiously.

"When did you last communicate with Kami, for example?"

"Kami... Kami..." Ram replied, as if he was trying to search his memory banks for the name. "No - I can't say I recall ever meeting anyone called Kami."

"Unfortunate," Eloise replied.

She took a deliberate threatening bite from an apple, a mannerism that reminded Ebony of something Blake had similarly once done in front of his own prisoners. They were truly of a kind, Ebony thought, Eloise and her brother. But Eloise was even more menacing, intelligent - and dangerous.

"I wonder how it could be," Eloise continued, "how on earth you don't seem to know anything about Kami - when he seems to know everything about you."

Ram felt himself shudder involuntarily at the mention of Kami, the leader of the Collective. But wasn't about to reveal any details, unsure if this would be to his advantage or disadvantage.

"I need to know, Ram. If you're either with us – or against us," Eloise stated.

"Oh, I'm with you. For sure. Believe it."

"Then tell us the codes!" Eloise insisted.

"What... codes?"

"You know very well. The access codes you were going to use after you invaded the city where the Mighty Zoot resided."

"Sorry. I still don't understand what you're talking about," Ram said.

"Then Guardian – perhaps it's time to send Ram to another world," Eloise instructed.

"It will be my honour," the Guardian said, eager to please. "Before you go, you will learn that faith is far more powerful than any technology, 'Techno'."

Ebony didn't want to simply stand back and watch Ram get hurt. At one time she thought she had a connection with him but began to realize than in reality she cared very little for him as a person. But, despite her reputation to the contrary, she didn't enjoy seeing anyone suffer – unless there was a very good reason. She was human after all, not some kind of monster. She couldn't be so sure the same was true of Eloise or the Guardian.

She didn't know how long her luck would hold out – and if one day she might be in Ram's place, fighting for her life. Ram could be a powerful ally – he clearly knew more than he was letting on and although she herself wasn't exactly sure what it was all about, she decided to try and persuade Ram to co-operate.

"Why don't you tell them you *do* know the codes," Ebony suggested, giving Ram a knowing look. "You want to live, don't you? If so, you should tell them what they want."

Ram looked to Ebony, realizing she was reaching out to him in some way, however subtle. They knew each other's nuances very well. "You reckon?"

"After all, you're about the only one who seems to know them, according to our Mother Divine," Ebony said. "And even if you gave the wrong codes it would be difficult for anyone to know you're lying. So just make sure you give the right codes."

She punctuated her suggestion with an expression, trying to communicate something unsaid that even if Ram didn't know, as he professed, that it might be in his interests just to tell them anything. And Ram got the message.

"It might help if you could give me more information about exactly what codes you're after," Ram said. "Then I might be able to help."

Eloise's eyes sparkled in triumph. "Thanks, Ebony," she said, encouraged that she had been able to make a breakthrough.

Then she considered Ram. "That's better. And so much better for you. Now, tell me. What are the access codes?"

"To where?" Ram questioned uneasily.

"Oh, I think you know very well, having been involved with Kami. Before we embark upon phase two of our operation... there's only one access code of any importance. So what is it?!"

"I told you. I need to know to where before I can answer!" Ram replied.

"You're beginning to test my patience, Ram," Eloise snarled. "There's only one location Kami has any interest in. Eagle Mountain."

Eloise gazed intently at Ebony, then Ram to gauge their reaction.

CHAPTER TWELVE

"You know it's funny, Amber. I was so desperate to get my hands on a computer," Jack mentioned "and now I can't wait to get away from them."

"You've done really well," Amber encouraged him. "Why don't you try and take a break?"

"I'm not giving up till I've checked everything," Jack insisted, flexing his hands, shifting in his seat, his back also sore from all the sitting and typing.

"Right, you," Jack addressed the computer, "let's do this."

Jack steadily moved from one machine to another in the main office of the administration block, and had already spent hours examining their contents, being supplied by a constant stream of snacks and drinks provided by Gel.

The others had volunteered to take turns delving through the myriad of files and data on the hard drives but nobody knew computers like Jack - and he had worked hard, doing his best to sort through all the information.

They hadn't had any more contact yet from whoever had communicated with them online earlier, though that didn't stop Jack from constantly going back online to UNANET. So far UNANET had been quiet and to Jack it felt like he was the only person online in the entire world.

Who had they been, Amber wondered, the mystery person – or people – who had exchanged messages before with Jack?

Whatever it was, those remaining in the exploration party had been asked to 'await their next contact' – and that is precisely what Amber and the others were doing, the hours passing by as Jack and Ellie continued searching through the computer systems in the meantime.

Ellie had discovered several files referring to the city they had lived in on the computers and data she was examining. And there were also a few references to Hope Island, where Amber and some of the Mall Rats had visited in the past, believing they were on the trail of an antidote to the 'virus'.

But Eagle Mountain was the most frequent topic to show up in all the searches, whereby they uncovered information about different 'stages' having apparently been achieved, updates that Eagle Mountain was 'ready' and 'preparations were complete'.

The group reflected if this was all remnants of some kind of plan in the old adult world around the time of the pandemic. Or post-when the adults perished. But so far there was no link whatsoever to Arthurs Air Force Base, where they were now. Or what the possible link could be to Eagle Mountain, back in their homeland.

Something big had clearly been going on. Or was about to occur.

Ram had claimed, Amber recollected, that during the invasion of the Technos he had adapted some adult technology at Eagle Mountain, particularly harnessing some of the leftover virtual reality space devices so Ram could use them in his own 'Paradise' program to control the city.

But as the group went over it all, in their minds, from what they had uncovered so far they were no further ahead with any answers to the growing mystery.

"I found you!" Darryl cried out, crawling under one of the desks at the other side of the office, surprising Tiffany and Shannon, who both squealed in delight, having used the desk to conceal them.

Darryl had been playing 'hide and seek', doing his best to distract and entertain the young children.

Emma sat in one of the chairs at a desk. Her back was turned to where she heard Darryl playing with the little ones. Emma didn't want them to know she had been crying. But Amber noticed and crossed to her, giving Emma a hug.

"Hey, it'll be okay," she said.

"I can't believe it's happening again, Amber." Emma grimaced, trying to hold back her tears. "This is how – it started before… One by one… we were split off. And then the Roaches were all gone."

"Don't lose hope. Bray is very capable and will be alright. Jay won't stop until he finds Bray. It's not like before."

"Don't you understand? No-one who went into the wastelands ever came back… They should have never left."

"Ready or not – here I come!" Darryl shouted out in the background with playful menace, stalking around the office, looking for Tiffany and Shannon, who had found a new place to hide.

"Darryl, why don't you come and help rather than play monsters," Ellie said. "It's starting to freak me out!"

"Me as well," Gel added.

Ellie and Gel realized it was hopeless. Darryl was enjoying the game probably more than Tiffany and Shannon so they continued making notes on a piece of paper while checking the computer screens, along with Jack and Amber.

Gel was never really computer literate and had no idea what she was searching for. Her job was to log reference points so they had a catalogue of all the data and she hoped she wouldn't mess it up, finding it difficult enough as it was to concentrate without Darryl's monster groaning.

Amber watched Darryl's antics as he stomped about melodramatically, closing in on where he knew the young kids were hiding. It seemed surreal, Darryl walking like a bizarre 'zombie', arms outstretched, threatening to get nearer with every step.

It made Amber think of the very real dangers they could all be up against. Of absent loved ones.

She imagined what Bray and Jay were up to, at that very moment, somewhere in the wastelands – and hoped with all her heart that Emma's anxieties, as well as all of their own, would prove to be unfounded.

CHAPTER THIRTEEN

Connor was full of surprises, Trudy thought, looking at the plate of food he had just given her – and giving Connor an admiring look.

"Let's see… sailor, explorer… talented chef. You certainly are a man of mystery."

The two of them were on board Connor's yacht, the *Nemo*, anchored just off the island, the boat gently bobbing up and down as high tide approached.

Connor had prepared – or more conjured up, Trudy appreciated, a lovely meal, cooking a fish on the hot plate in *Nemo*'s cabin and finely chopping some fruit to accompany it. Tropical guava had been cut into petal shapes, arranged on the perimeter of the plate like it was a beautiful flower.

"It looks and smells delicious," Trudy beamed. "The best meal I've had in ages."

"You deserve it. It's just a little thank you," Connor said modestly, leaning on the side of the boat and tucking into his own plate.

"For what?"

"Finding me."

"Well, it was more a matter of you finding me."

"True," Connor replied. "It must have been meant to be," he added and Trudy liked the sound of that as she took another bite and savoured the taste of her meal.

Connor had stayed close to her at the village, Trudy was aware, most of that afternoon, offering to do anything he could to help her. He was almost behaving like he had some sort of 'crush', following her around at times like a puppy – and in truth, she felt exactly the same way about him.

He was sweet, attentive, and definitely good looking.

Although they were getting to know each other, Trudy already felt she had a connection with him. She was lucky that Connor seemed drawn to her, too, instead of any of the others, like Lia. He could have had his pick, Trudy thought, viewing Connor very much as a prize 'catch' – but there she was, the one he had invited on board his boat.

Trudy sampled another forkful from her plate and savoured the taste again.

"Connor – where did you learn to cook like this?"

"When you've spent as much time as I have on this boat, I've had to fill my days somehow. Believe me, I've had a lot of time to practice."

Earlier, Connor described some of his experiences and travels, his encounters with other survivors living on the seas in boats of all sizes, children and teenagers who had fled the 'virus', in search of a far away land to begin a new life for themselves somewhere.

Trudy was amazed by his tales. She had never really thought beyond the area of her own city, so preoccupied had she been by her own struggle to survive there in all the chaos. It was reassuring in a way to hear that other young people had survived, heartening to think humanity could endure, having been on the brink of human extinction. There was a larger world out there than Trudy had ever considered – and it brought the prospect of hope, Trudy thinking of all those who might be somewhere out on the oceans or on dry land in other parts of the world at that very moment. Sadly not all shared the Mall Rats' vision of building a better world, with many, like the adversaries the Mall Rats had encountered in their home land, intent on dominating and ruling the shreds of what was left in existence post the adults' demise.

Connor had explained to Lex and the others that the Collective did exist and, he had heard, they had apparently grown in strength. Initially a core group of tribes banding together, they had gradually expanded their frontiers, absorbing other towns, cities, lands, gathering new resources, slaves and warriors.

There were rumours, Connor said, that the Collective even had their own fleet of ships, seizing any vessels they found useful.

Connor had never had any dealings with the Collective, he described, having instead traded with other survivors on the seas, like himself. But from those he had talked with in his time, whenever the Collective was discussed, there was always an aura of fear.

They were apparently led by someone called Kami, an enigmatic figure. But there was no mystery surrounding his tribe - the Collective were apparently ruthless, relentless and growing in power. You either became part of the Collective, as a loyal member or captured slave – or simply didn't survive.

Trudy listened intently, absorbed by all Connor was saying, feeling a sense of growing unease as she recalled what Ram had also told her tribe at one time about the Collective. And she wondered if it could give credence to his fears that they were somehow involved in the island, especially given their ability to travel.

Her thoughts also concerned some of those in the Mall Rats who had gone missing back in her own homeland and made a mental note to explain to Ellie all Connor had revealed, well aware that she was eager to hear of anything that might shed light on the disappearance of her elder sister, Alice.

Above all, Trudy was startled when Connor described how he had heard that there was meant to be an island prison, somewhere in the ocean, that was used by slave traders as a holding station. Valuable prisoners were taken there so they could then be sold or traded to other tribes in the region, or transferred to even far away lands, many of them ending up in the hands of the Collective, with their network spread far and wide, always the most wealthy and powerful buyers.

It was sad and devastating. Trudy thought large-scale slavery was consigned to the history books but Connor said it was apparently returning to the world they inhabited in a big way, human resources becoming the most important of all in the post-adult world, behind that of food and fresh water.

Connor promised that he would review the nautical charts inside *Nemo*'s cabin to help determine likely places where the island might be where the activity of the slave market was located - though he was sure the co-ordinates were nowhere near their new island home.

Trudy and Connor had left the others at the native village, Trudy grateful once more for Ruby and Slade offering to babysit her daughter.

Connor promised Trudy he would 'spoil' her, to thank her for saving his life - and even before they had climbed onboard *Nemo*, Trudy was thrilled when Connor suddenly picked her up in his arms, like a groom carrying his bride across the threshold, and waded into the low tide, getting up to his waist in water, holding Trudy aloft so she wouldn't even have to get her feet wet in order to get on to his boat.

They had both laughed, Trudy giggling when Connor pretended on several occasions to be about to drop her into the water. But he was as good as his word, a gentleman, and she had made it on board *Nemo*, completely dry.

She had been given a tour and was surprised how many items Connor had squeezed inside the cabin. Every inch of space was used, all kinds of equipment placed inside, from spare compasses to old books and magazines to read, even an antique electric hot plate that Connor said still worked, using electricity from the solar panels on the roof.

Other objects were more personal belongings he had saved, reminders from his past, such as the various photos of Connor and his family he had pinned to the inside of *Nemo*'s cabin. Trudy was intrigued to see the torn, fading pictures of a younger Connor, standing beside his parents, on board *Nemo*, in days gone by. Connor told her more about them. His father had actually been a commander in the navy and his mother a medical doctor attached to the United Nations, who had worked so valiantly as the pandemic spread like a flash fire around the world.

Trudy mentioned the experience she and the Mall Rats had endured on board the ghost ship, the *Jzhao Li*, sailing under the United Nations' insignia but Connor was unable to shed any light on that, unaware of any activity in the region as far as he could recall.

A few hours had passed and they both had much to talk about, never a lull in the conversation.

It was like going on a date in the old times, Trudy felt. Getting to know each other. The setting was certainly romantic, the island looking beautiful in the background, the sun shining down on the clear, azure waters slowly rising with the tide around the boat.

Trudy found it all blissful, enjoying the combination of a perfect location and a charming, handsome companion to share it all with.

"Do you believe in fate, Connor?"

"Do you?"

"I don't know," Trudy said, finishing the last of her meal. "Although I have Brady – and I'd do anything for her – I've always felt lost, really. 'Alone'. That somehow I didn't truly belong. Except to my tribe, of course. It's just... the world's never really made much sense. It can be a horrible place sometimes. But it's also beautiful. It could just be me. I've never really fitted in. Life's always been - difficult."

"We've all got our problems. My parents taught me a saying. 'It's not the storm you encounter – but how you set your sails'."

"That's an interesting philosophy."

"All you can do is your best. Ride out any storms in life - and then hope you'll find calmer seas. Out there, on the water, you get a different perspective, away from it all. Maybe you belong on the ocean, more than the land. Like me."

Trudy looked into Connor's understanding eyes, studying this enigma. It was like he was a kindred spirit.

Perhaps there was a greater destiny after all.

She had always hoped it would be Bray, never given up her dream that somehow they would be together, even though the chance of this happening seemed to disappear entirely when Bray and Amber became a couple in the city.

But was it never really meant to be and Trudy was destined to meet someone else, find another who would end up as her true soulmate?

Or maybe she was just getting carried away with it all, she reflected, very aware that she was definitely captivated by Connor's rugged good lucks and charming personality – not to mention his surprising cooking skills.

She suddenly realized they had both been staring at each other, with obvious mutual attraction, romantic interest.

"I should probably be getting back," Trudy said, self-consciously. "I need to check up on Brady."

"Do you have to?" Connor asked, taking Trudy's plate from her, putting it down on the deck and gently clasping her hand.

"I'm really enjoying being with you, Trudy."

"Me, too."

"Are you sure we couldn't stay out here - just a little bit longer? Sometimes you have to go against the tide… Other times, you just know you have to go with it."

Connor leaned forward, Trudy willingly accepting his advance, and they began to kiss in increasing passion.

CHAPTER FOURTEEN

Bray felt a mixture of emotions as he sped through the wilderness on the quad-bike, taking to the air momentarily as he soared over a slight incline, before landing with a bump, just managing to keep control. He had better slow down a little, he thought. That had been too close for comfort.

The road continued, winding its way towards the horizon, through the wastelands, en route to the silhouette of the mountain ranges in the far distance.

Bray stopped, the quad-bike engine idling while he checked the map he had taken, trying to gauge the speed he needed to travel, deciding that it would be wise to time his arrival under the cover of night.

The quad-bike's engine roared as he revved and continued on, making good progress, Bray estimating that it would take probably only another few hours at the rate he was travelling - compared to the days he had spent agonizingly before in the wastelands on foot in the past, when he had no vehicle, no map, and no other purpose than to survive.

Surveying the barren dusty terrain, Bray had manoeuvred around various craters throughout his journey and he speculated once again what could have occurred in this region. Was it used as target practice? Bombing runs? By some former militia during the adult days? Or had there been some cataclysmic event responsible for this area being devoid of any insect or plant life?

He adjusted his jacket over his mouth to give some protection against the billowing dust swirling all around relentlessly as the quad-bike sped off.

For all his thoughts about the wasteland, he was preoccupied also with Amber and wondered if slowly in the passage of time they had drifted apart somehow and she had preferred her life with Jay over the life they once shared together.

That question would have to await his return.

For now, Bray focused on the task at hand. They just had to discover more of what they were up against, the threat Eloise posed and how she was connected to the Collective.

Most of all, he was determined to do what he could to save his brother's legacy. And if the opportunity presented itself, he would do anything in his power to upset whatever plans Eloise had.

He had a score to settle.

* * *

Bray arrived at the outskirts of the mountain compound shortly after sunset, completing the last part of his journey off-road, driving his quad-bike slowly, keeping the engine revving as quietly as he could.

As darkness descended, he took further cover, driving between the thick forest trees, hoping they would give extra assurance that he would be hidden from prying eyes.

Having not seen any sign of Eloise's forces yet, Bray drew the quad-bike to a stop, hiding it behind a tree, deciding to approach the compound stealthily on foot.

Higher in altitude than he had been used to, the night air was cool, the wind blowing in strong gusts, rustling the branches of the trees, their limbs shaking as if they were warning Bray, giving him a sign to go back. But it also gave extra protection against any noise.

Even so, Bray took every step with care, making sure he didn't snap any fallen branches, determined not to make a sound.

His slow progress was such a contrast to his previous time there, recalling the moment when he ran for his life through the gates, into the night, pursued by Eloise and her guards.

To Bray's surprise there didn't seem to be any security on patrol, unlike before. Not a soul around - except himself. Which caused Bray mounting concern as he moved carefully through the darkness towards the entrance gates.

He had another glance around. There was still no sign of anyone so he pushed at the gates, which swung on their hinges, creaking in the wind.

Had there been an evacuation? Was everyone out on some mission? If that was the case, some guards were certain to have been left at the base on duty.

Bray continued to move quietly, stealthily, making his way through the darkness and through the gates, entering the base.

* * *

It *was* just him there, Bray thought. At least, so far. Walking down the long, dark corridors, the electricity seemed to be out, the lights in the ceilings completely lifeless. His steps echoed despite his attempts to soften the sounds of his movement, just in case the base did harbour any more occupants beside himself.

Bray held a small flashlight, one taken from Arthurs Air Force Base, and he was glad he had done so, the beam of light providing his sole source of illumination as he cast its circular beam back and forth along the walls, using it to find his way.

He passed the repopulation area of the complex, recalling tales that the rooms were filled with pregnant girls who were housed there. He shuddered, remembering the distant cries of babies – and their distressed mothers, begging for freedom – which had blended into an awful cacophony of noise. Yet currently the rooms were empty, Bray noted, as he peered inside. Silent and dark.

He found the laboratory, a place that bore particularly emotional and intense memories, where Eloise had performed all manner of experiments on him. Adjacent to the virtual reality chamber. For a moment, Bray wondered if his recollections of what had occurred at the mountain base did in fact occur. It was a surreal sensation with the memories being so vivid. Yet seemingly nothing he could see bore any resemblance whatsoever to what he perceived had previously existed.

The laboratory was now dormant. The room had been totally gutted, electrical wiring sticking out of the walls where missing equipment had once been connected.

And he was convinced that the base was indeed abandoned. Had there been an accident? Or maybe the base had come under attack? It just didn't make sense why everyone would leave – or where they had gone.

Bray suddenly noticed another room, its door partially open.

Intrigued, Bray entered.

He could smell an unusual scent in the air, the scent of candles on a table at the end of the room, long since burnt out.

He was in what looked to be a classroom of some kind, rows of other desks arranged neatly in the room, their chairs vacated.

But it was seeing what was on the back wall that made Bray literally stagger in shock.

His spotlight illuminated a large tableau picture, covering the entire wall, similar to what Bray had seen before in churches.

In the centre of the image was a representation of his brother, Zoot clad in the familiar clothes he used to wear, his cap and goggles on his head, astride the back of his police car. The background was a city – Bray's city, he could tell, recognizing the depictions of some of the buildings.

Zoot was represented like some visionary, glowing with divine energies, pointing into the distance – to Eagle Mountain, nestled among rolling green hills. The globe-like observatory was shining, vibrant with colours, emitting beams of light.

Bray was upset to see his brother represented in such a way. Martin himself would have been astonished to know of the legend that had grown up around him, the many Zootist followers that dutifully worshipped him as an icon.

It hurt Bray so much, the tragedy that had befallen his younger brother, the disturbing legacy left behind.

The picture seemed to be the story of Zoot's life told in various stages, the left side of the wall showing him as a baby descending from the Heavens, growing up, a rendering of Bray himself beside him, leading up to the final image of Zoot, pointing to Eagle Mountain in the distance. And Bray was totally confused as to what the significance could be.

Strangely, there were caricatures of others – Trudy, adorned in her Supreme Mother attire when she used to be with The Chosen, a picture of the Guardian standing by Zoot's side, a smaller painting of Ebony near him, that looked to have been more recently daubed.

And there was an image of Eloise, wearing robes, a column of light shining on her from the skies, standing between Zoot and Eagle Mountain.

Oddly, Bray noticed, Lex was positioned in the mural in a shadow, threateningly behind Zoot, the face of Lex leering weirdly. Did it indicate in some way Lex's pivotal role in Zoot's death, Bray reflected. Whatever the symbolism, Lex clearly had a prominent role in the mythology being conveyed as well.

Distressed by what he had seen – Bray felt he had seen enough. It was time to go.

And he was deeply troubled, truly in the dark, due to far more ominous implications than just the ghostly emptiness of the bleak, unlit corridors.

CHAPTER FIFTEEN

Lex picked his target – throwing the coconut as best as he could - but his aim failed him, the coconut soaring too far, way beyond its intended position, bouncing after it landed.

"Dammit!" he bellowed, kicking the dirt.

"Temper, temper," Lia said, lining up her own shot.

They were on the outskirts of the village, playing an improvised version of petanque, Lia suggesting Lex try the game to pass the time, in an effort to take his mind off things.

So far, it wasn't working, Lex getting all the more worked up - to find himself losing the game to Lia.

Lia's coconut hit the ground and rolled within a few inches of the target they were aiming at, a plastic bottle of shampoo that had once belonged to Gel.

"I'm too strong, that's the problem," Lex said, covering for his own poor throws, consistently going beyond the target. "I need something heavier, these things are too light for me."

"Of course they are," Lia teased, feeling the weight of her next coconut to throw, which was far from light - but heavy, like all the coconuts were. "You're so strong... But do you really have to be so angry with Trudy?"

"Who said I'm angry with her? I can't help it if she's being completely stupid. She wouldn't know danger if it jumped right out in front of her!"

Lia gave Lex a look. "See what I mean? There you are, at it again – moaning about Trudy."

Lex did resent Trudy for ignoring his advice to keep away from Connor. Couldn't she see Connor was a stranger? They hardly even knew him. And now it seemed that Trudy had spent the night with him.

Lex was also well too aware about the prophecy the Priestess had given – that the Mall Rats would be visited by the spirit of death. They couldn't get too comfortable with Connor until they discovered more about who he was.

"I'm not moaning," Lex protested – throwing his next coconut - and missing the target wildly, cringing at his aim.

"She's old enough to make her own decisions," Lia said. "You can't control what she does. And you shouldn't even try."

"You on her side all of a sudden?" Lex challenged.

"As far as I can see, the only person I'm by the side of right now - is you."

Lex cast her a glance. She faked a smile, then took aim – and her next shot was even better than her one before, landing a direct hit on the plastic bottle.

"There. I think I've won."

Lex admired Lia's prowess – and her athletic build.

"Only because I let you," Lex grinned cheekily.

"If you're so confident - feel like another game then?"

"I know another game we could play with each other," Lex hinted salaciously.

"Who said I'd be interested?"

"Who said you wouldn't be?"

A clanging sound rang out in the distance, from the heart of the village. Ruby was striking a spoon on the side of a pot, salvaged from the wreck of the *Jzhao Li*, that she was using to cook over an open fire, Ruby taking her turn to make breakfast – and letting everyone in the vicinity know the food was ready.

"Saved by the bell," Lia shrugged. "We'll have to leave any other 'games' you were thinking – for another time."

Lex watched her walk off, back towards the village. She was a challenge. And Lex always relished a challenge. He had far more of an appetite in mind than just the meal Ruby had prepared.

Lia didn't know that Lex had actually let her win the coconut contest, deliberately making sure his throws missed the mark. Now all he had to do was to win her over.

* * *

"Mmmm – this is good, real good," Sammy complimented, wolfing down the breakfast Ruby had prepared. "Your baby's going to be lucky to have a Mom like you to cook for them."

"Glad you like it. But Slade will cook for junior too," Ruby insisted. "We'll take turns. After all – it's not fair for girls to do all the cooking."

"Yes, it is," Lex objected – drawing a look of ire from Lia, Ruby, Lottie, Salene and May. "What's that look for?" he enquired.

"You're nothing but a chauvinist, Lex," Salene stated.

"No, I'm not," Lex scoffed disdainfully.

"Why don't you cook dinner for us tonight then, Lex?" Lia suggested. "Ruby's right. We should all be taking turns. I don't think you've cooked anything for me – ever."

"Fine. I will," Lex said stubbornly. "But I'm meant to be the Head of Security around here – not a chef. I just hope I don't give you all food poisoning."

"I hope you don't either," Lottie said, worried at the notion. She would trust Slade to cook, but wasn't so sure about Lex – who she didn't feel was very hygienic. Imagining Lex cooking – and sure she would get ill afterwards, Lottie shuddered at baby Bray, who she had been holding in her lap while Ruby had busily prepared breakfast.

Three other servings had been dished, left waiting for the return of Slade, Brady and Trudy.

Slade had gone with Brady to entice her mother back to the village, aware that she had arranged to meet up with Connor the previous afternoon on the beach where he was going to show her around the *Nemo*.

Salene stood up – giving May a knowing glance – and May put down her plate and also slowly got to her feet.

They had discussed with each other what to do about their nascent romance. May thought it was better to keep it all a secret – it would be too embarrassing for the others to find out. And she could just imagine Lex's reaction.

Salene believed they had nothing to be ashamed of, however. She was proud of how she felt for May – and was sure that keeping their relationship under wraps would be too difficult. Besides, there was nothing really to hide.

It would instead be easier for them – and all concerned – if they could be open and honest, Salene had urged May. Their lives were their own to lead and rather than pretending to be who they were not, hiding their emotions, they should just be themselves – which was their right after all, Salene asserted.

"There's something May and I have been wanting to tell you all," Salene spoke up, nervously.

"Don't tell me. You're both - pregnant?" Lex replied, grinning proudly at his own wit - which added to Salene and May's unease.

"You're not going to reveal you're both in the Collective, I hope?" Sammy joked.

"If only it was that simple," Salene said.

She reached out and took May's hand in her own, drawing a confused look from the others – none more so than Lex.

"May and I – well... We're... an item."

Lottie gasped, open mouthed – and Sammy choked on his mouthful of food at hearing the unexpected news.

"Are you serious?" Lex asked.

"Yes. Absolutely," May declared. "No matter what you think."

"I had no idea – and don't know what to say," Ruby confessed. "Except – if you're happy, that's wonderful."

"Congratulations," Lia agreed. "We should be celebrating."

Ruby and Lia got up and gave Salene and May each hugs, the relief on May and Salene's expression palpable at opening up about their relationship.

May particularly looked as if a burden had been lifted from her – and it suddenly became apparent to all what must have been making her so quiet and introverted of late, the subject of what – or who - she had often been thinking about.

"I actually think it's great," Lex commented, taking everyone by surprise with his reaction.

"You do?" May questioned dubiously.

"Yeah. Feel free to be yourselves - just carry on. You two girls hug, kiss each other any time you like, for all I care. That is - if you don't mind me watching."

Lex winked mischievously and puckered his lips.

"You obnoxious pig!" Salene protested.

"Hey!" Slade suddenly called out, racing back into the village with little Brady anxiously hugging him, in his arms.

"What is it?" Ruby asked, sensing Slade's concern.

"We might have a problem," Slade replied.

"You're telling me," Lex joked. "Everyone seems to be bedding each other. First Trudy and Connor – and you'll never guess now who else. There must be something in the water round here."

"This is serious," Slade reiterated, catching his breath. "We tried to find Trudy – but I couldn't see Connor's boat anywhere. The *Nemo*'s disappeared. They've gone."

CHAPTER SIXTEEN

Jay raced his vehicle as fast as he dared, trying to close the gap on Bray, who had a head start on him.

Bray was remarkable, Jay appreciated, marvelling how Bray could have survived the bleak and hostile wastelands, the intense sun scorching the earth and bearing down on Jay from above. That Bray could have made the perilous journey on foot, in the past, was an extraordinary feat, Jay thought, impressed by Bray's obvious determination and willpower.

Would Bray present a similar stubbornness as Jay's rival for Amber's heart, if he did manage to find Bray and convince him to return?

The thought of Amber choosing Bray over himself hurt greatly. They had been through so much together, fighting against the tyranny of Ram and then Mega, before making their journey across the ocean to the island. They had defeated Blake, freeing the prisoners he had kept - and Jay was aware he had played his own part, ironically, in saving Bray and reuniting him with Amber.

Was it all going to come back on him and he would live to regret his choices?

He was fully aware of the complications that might arise should he successfully find Bray and bring his direct rival for Amber's affection directly back into her path.

But Jay had to do it. And it was precisely for Amber. He would do anything for her, so devoted was he to the causes she fought for, her way of life, to who she was as a person. She was his ideal partner. And he couldn't help but empathise with the feelings Bray must also have for someone so special.

Jay looked ahead amidst the swirling dust at the undulating road, winding through the wasteland.

The terrain was gradually changing, elevating. Jay could see the coast to his right, sheer cliffs plunging at sharp angles spectacularly to the ocean below, great waves rolling in, crashing into the sides of the cliffs.

And Jay had perceived something else.

He skidded the quad-bike to a halt, spraying up a shower of gravel from the tires.

A ship was ploughing through the water, riding the waves, one like no other Jay had ever seen. It was huge, like some colossal sea creature, and had to have been two or three hundred feet in length, Jay estimated. It was a sailing ship, a mighty vessel, giant canvases on its masts, billowing in the strong breezes. The ship was modern – it looked to be made of metal.

Driving the quad-bike closer to the side of the cliff, Jay braked and pulled out some binoculars from his backpack he had taken along, to try and get a closer view.

Looking through the lenses, in the cross-hairs, he saw the crew of the ship going about their duties. A well organized group, Jay observed, from their disciplined, co-ordinated movements.

The front of the large ship had the wreck of a vehicle stuck on it, perched high above the waves, unceremoniously acting like some bizarre figurehead. It was a police car, Jay realized, what was left of one anyway.

The bow was covered in graffiti. Jay could just make out the large lettering of the words on the side of the vessel that signified the ship's name - *Sea Ghost*.

Standing on deck was a tall, striking looking girl, her long black hair rippling behind in the wind. Beside her was a figure wearing white ceremonial robes, his own blonde locks flowing in the sea breeze.

It had to be the Guardian, Jay thought, in disbelief. He had never met the former leader of The Chosen in person but had never forgot Amber's description of him.

The Guardian was pushing a prisoner, begging for mercy, Jay could see, to the very edge of the ship's railing. In one swift movement, the Guardian hoisted the boy over the side, the prisoner crashing into the waves and disappearing without trace, Jay too far away to hear his screams. The Guardian looked up, holding his arms aloft above his head, making a sign of fealty to the skies. It must have been some kind of horrific ceremony, Jay surmised, stunned by the senseless brutality of it, likely an offering made in the name of the Guardian's deity, Zoot.

Jay lowered the binoculars from his eyes and watched as the *Sea Ghost* ploughed through the waves, powered by its massive sails.

"Sorry, Bray," Jay said to himself, immediately giving up on his mission, sure that Bray would understand his reasons and hoping that wherever he was, Bray would be well and safe. Right now, Jay had other priorities.

He throttled the engine and accelerated away from the cliffs, rejoining the main road and retracing the direction from which he had already travelled.

He didn't know what destination or course the *Sea Ghost* was headed – and thought it might have simply been in the area to undertake the bizarre ceremony he had witnessed from a distance. Wherever it was going, he hoped the ship would stay far away from the island.

But he couldn't take any chances. He had to get back and warn Amber and the others as quickly as he could, and sped the quad-bike down the road, veering back into the wastelands, as the *Sea Ghost* ominously continued its own journey through the waves.

CHAPTER SEVENTEEN

"Do you hear something?" Emma asked tentatively – focusing on the strange, distant sound she thought she could pick out.

"No," Amber replied sleepily. She had only recently climbed into her bunk, having just completed her turn on watch. "Try and relax and get some sleep," she continued gently.

"Listen. I can definitely hear something," Emma repeated while Amber, becoming suddenly alert, sat up and concentrated.

"I think you're right – there is something."

Amber got up from the bunk, moved to the windows and gazed out, trying to discover the source of a distant engine noise approaching - fast. Bathed in moonlight, she could just about make out a cloud of dust rapidly heading toward the base.

"They're back!" Amber beamed, heartened at the return of Jay on his quad-bike, hopefully with Bray – the noise clearly coming from the sound of vehicles, moving towards them at high speed, leaving a large trail of dust in their wake.

Amber was suddenly crestfallen, however, realizing it actually wasn't her much missed loved ones.

There were about a dozen quad-bikes and motorbikes, in some kind of formation, rapidly closing in, menacingly.

It could only mean one thing, Amber feared, which was confirmed by Ellie, who had been on watch and now rushed into the dormitory.

"I think we're under attack!" Ellie shouted, unable to believe it was really happening, dreading the arrival of the unexpected visitors she had noticed.

* * *

What was left of the exploration party gazed in growing alarm at the multiple images on the security monitors showing the Zootists swarming into the base on their vehicles, most carrying one or two passengers behind them, jumping off the machines as the assault force circled the garden hub area in the centre of the base, looking for anyone who was there.

Outside in the compound, the Guardian clambered off his quad-bike, a manic glint in his eye, thirsting for battle - and eager to please his god.

"Spread out!" he commanded, the Zootists obeying his orders, moving out in groups to their pre-assigned locations.

Axel ran with his fighters toward the hospital and medical centre, Ebony and the Zootists she had been placed with headed towards the accommodation block, a third battle unit advancing to the office and administration building.

"For the Mother Divine!   For Zoot!" Aras yelled zealously.

He was in Ebony's group, the fanatical convert to the faith desperate to show everyone he was worthy of joining them, Zoot in particular – Aras imagining divine eyes were watching him at that very moment, judging him.

"Let's do this!" Ebony shouted, charging into the ground floor entrance of the accommodation complex.

They had been given their targets in a briefing by Eloise during their journey on board the *Sea Ghost*, the Guardian blessing the Zootists on the deck. Ebony had shuddered when she heard the screams of one prisoner, deemed to have not genuinely converted fully to the faith, who was thrown overboard, the Guardian making an offering to Zoot.

Ebony was amazed by the size of the *Sea Ghost* - and the obvious power of the Collective if this was just one of the ships she understood were in their possession.

She was told it used to be called *The Odyssey* and was from way back, having been operated for years by the navy as a working vessel to train young cadets during the adult times.

In the final days of the pandemic, the last teenage crew, having bonded, living together in their training, seized *The Odyssey* from the port it was in, the adults having almost died out by that point. *The Odyssey* and its young crew was soon absorbed by the Collective and ended up transformed into the *Sea Ghost*, used to ferry Collective forces, resources - and slave cargos across the waves.

The *Sea Ghost* was now berthed up the coast at a huge pontoon dock left over from the United Nations personnel that had been stationed at Arthurs Air Force Base – the Guardian, Ebony and the rest of the raid having disembarked there, unloading the vehicles they had carried on board the *Sea Ghost* so they could make their assault on the base.

Aras had tried to ingratiate himself to Ebony on the voyage, keen to impress someone who he was amazed to learn had actually known Zoot in real life.

He was steadfastly loyal to Ebony and told her he had lived at Arthurs Air Force Base in the past with his former tribe, the Roaches. Then, Aras was nothing but a childish fool, he admitted, but he was returning as a warrior, ready to give the ultimate sacrifice to serve the true faith of Zoot.

Whereas Aras was desperate to convey his devotion to his religion, Ebony had to prove herself in a different way, she felt. So far she had shown she could be a useful asset to Eloise, who remained on board the *Sea Ghost*, protected by her bodyguards. Ram was also in the ship, in confinement.

The last time Ebony was involved in a raid it had all gone wrong, Ebony having been captured by the Mall Rats and the native tribe, failing the mission she was entrusted with by Blake.

She was determined not to make the same mistake a second time and to successfully carry out what she had been asked to do – ironically by Blake's sister. To keep showing Eloise she could be of 'use' to her.

That suited Ebony just fine, believing it was far better to be rewarded than punished by the Collective. They were the biggest power in the region and Ebony wanted to get her share of what she was entitled to.

"If anyone's here – find them!" Ebony roared to Aras and the enthusiastic Zootist acolytes in her group.

They began making their way through the ground level of the accommodation building, smashing in doors, searching inside the rooms.

She knew her orders. To capture anyone still alive. If they encountered resistance, they were to crush it without mercy, using any means necessary, the Zootists eagerly looking forward to destroying any who opposed them - or their cause.

Ebony kicked in a door, breaking the lock and began searching a filthy, disused bedroom. She would go over every inch of the base, if she had to. She wouldn't fail Eloise – or the promise of any future reward.

* * *

"We're gonna die!" Gel cried out, pacing around the room, her adrenalin racing.

"Please be quiet, Gel!" Amber urged her, in a whispered voice. "We've still got a chance."

Emma stood with her back pressed against the door, gripping the handle tightly, absolutely panicked by developments, desperate to keep the door closed at all costs.

Tiffany and Shannon were huddled together, keeping as still as they could, in the ensuite bathroom, hiding in the bathtub, hoping to keep out of sight.

How cruelly paradoxical, Amber thought, the two kids having been playing hide and seek with Darryl hours before Amber spotted the raiders. It was no longer any game.

As soon as Amber saw the incoming invaders she led the group, who raced up several flights of the fire escape stairwell to the highest floor, Amber holding Emma's hand, guiding her, giving support.

Jack, Ellie and Darryl had dragged a heavy oak sideboard from the hallway and pinned it against the handle of the fire exit, hoping it would block it.

It might have been a terrible idea, Amber cursed herself, in hindsight, thinking that if the attackers did ascend to the highest floor in the building - and found the fire escape door wedged shut from the other side by the furniture, then it would only prove to them that there were inhabitants hiding somewhere. It was too late now to go back, however.

Amber had gone into one of the bedrooms on the level with Emma, Gel and the two young children.

Jack, Ellie and Darryl were across the hallway in the room on the opposite side, believing it was best to split into groups.

"Turn the light off!" Amber whispered to Gel, who had flicked on the main light in the room.

"But we won't be able to see anything!" replied Gel, trying to be as quiet as she could.

"That's the point – no-one will be able to see anything!"

Gel did as she was told, switching off the light, plunging the room into darkness. She was scared – they all were, Amber knew. But they couldn't do anything that would let the attackers know they were there. For now, they had to stay hidden, out of sight - and completely silent.

So this is how it felt, Amber thought, looking around the room, which had become a completely dark void, imagining how Emma perceived the world at all times. Emma really was special, Amber reflected, inspired by her courage in keeping going and not letting her blindness hinder her.

Amber would do everything she could to protect Emma and grabbed a lampstand nearby. It was the only thing she could find to use as an improvised weapon to defend themselves – should the attackers get through.

Down below, somewhere in the building, Amber cringed as she heard noises of movement. Doors crashing open, footsteps, muffled voices. Ever slowly, getting closer, closer.

The only sound in the room was of their own anxious breathing – and the hushed, snivelled whimpering of Tiffany and Shannon in the bathroom, struggling to contain their tears.

"It's alright," Emma whispered to them, pushing back against the door to the room with renewed determination.

Amber missed her son, desperately, and dreaded to think of what had happened to Bray – and Jay… if they themselves had encountered the invading forces and been caught prisoner. Or worse.

Amber sensed vibrations in the building, the floor shaking a little. But it was no earthquake – it sounded like the door to the fire exit stairwell was being struck, smashed down, the sideboard that had been blocking it finally giving way.

There was a mighty crash, followed by the sudden noise of footsteps approaching, sinister voices in the corridors.

One by one, the doors in the top floor were being forced open, the rooms explored one at a time by the invaders.

Amber's mind raced. There were few options.

But she suddenly had an idea.

"Gel!" Amber whispered. "Give me your lipstick!"

"What? Are you crazy!" Gel asked as quietly as she dared. "Now's not the time to be worried about how you look!"

"I need it - now!" Amber urged.

Gel fumbled in her handbag and dropped her lipstick into Amber's waiting hand.

Amber, trying to not make a sound or bump into anything, carefully ran through the darkness into the ensuite bathroom.

Thinking Amber had lost her grip, Gel dived to the floor and crawled under the double bed to keep herself hidden – the assailants nearly upon their room now, the sound of their approach in the corridor outside looming greater than ever.

Amber gave Tiffany and Shannon a reassuring smile, barely visible in the darkened gloom of the bathroom, but they took comfort from her presence, as she tried to appear less panicked than she actually felt.

Leaning over the bathroom sink, feeling for the mirror she knew was on the wall – Amber began writing a message using Gel's lipstick.

There was suddenly a loud scream from the corridor. It was Ellie – and there was yelling, awful sounds of struggling, along with a terrified wail from Tiffany and Shannon.

"Get your hands off her!" Jack could be heard crying out.

Amber ran back into the bedroom and took her place beside Emma at the door, pushing with everything she could.

The door budged, Emma and Amber groaning with combined effort, desperate to close it.

Outmatched, the two of them were knocked back, sent reeling as the door was finally smashed open by the Zootists, streaming into the room.

The lights were switched on by one of the raiders.

"I remember you!" Aras exclaimed deliriously, recognizing Emma's face.

Emma struggled to free herself from her assailants but it was no use – and was absolutely stunned to hear the voice of one of the Roaches, thinking she would never encounter any of them ever again.

"Aras? Is that really you?" Emma asked, overwhelmed.

"Not any more. I belong to Zoot now. And so do you."

"No!" Emma replied, distraught with worry upon hearing Shannon and Tiffany screaming, the two kids having been seized from their hideaway in the bathroom.

"Get your hands off them!" Amber demanded, squirming in the clutches of the Zootist invaders.

"There's another!" one of the Zootists called out eagerly, pulling Gel, shrieking, from under the bed by her ankles.

They were soon dragged forcibly into the corridor, Amber seeing Darryl, Jack and Ellie being taken toward the fire escape stairwell.

"Well, look who it is," Ebony commented upon seeing Amber, writhing in resistance, being carried out of the room by the Zootist raiders. "Fancy seeing you here. How you doin', Amber? Not very well, by the looks of it."

Amber was astonished to see Ebony and glared at her.

"I should have known you'd be involved somehow!"

Ebony sneered contemptuously at Amber, then indicated to the guards. "Take her to the Guardian!"

The Zootists rounded Amber and the others up, Ebony taking a brief moment to consider it all.

Whatever guilt or remorse she felt at seeing her former adversaries and even one time friends captured was overshadowed by the joy of her own self-preservation – and the reward she expected to get from Eloise. She was glad she had been so thorough, checking every room in the building. This would help her solidify the position she sought to establish for herself in the Collective.

Life was cruel sometimes. It wasn't her fault. She didn't make the rules - and had done what she had to do. It was a dog eat dog world.

"Power and Chaos! Power and Chaos!" the Zootists chanted fervently, praising the mantra of Zoot as they departed down the corridor with their captive Mall Rats.

Ebony watched them go, a wry smile on her pretty face.

"Zoot be praised. It's just like old times," Ebony said to herself in parody, aware of the irony - and headed off after them. It was time to deliver their prisoners to the Guardian and Eloise.

CHAPTER EIGHTEEN

The entire village was in a heightened sense of alarm, the Priestess having dispatched her strongest warriors, who were fanned out defensively, weapons poised, on watch, in anticipation of any hostile encroachment. The tribe had brought in as much food and fresh water as possible and were gathered in the heart of the village, urgently preparing for the worst, in case they ended up coming under siege.

A tense, anxious atmosphere permeated all around and the defensive readiness had been precipitated by the return of three of the Mall Rats – Trudy, Jay, and Bray, in that order.

All had been on a rollercoaster ride of emotions during the day - and it was all so different when Trudy was the first to make her return in the afternoon, Connor having anchored the *Nemo* further down the shallows near the beach for fear of running aground on the reefs as the tide turned.

There was relief that Trudy was safe – none more so than from Brady, who raced across the sands towards her mother upon first seeing her, leaping into Trudy's loving arms.

Trudy felt bad at having been away for longer than she had planned and was grateful to Ruby and Slade for keeping an eye on Brady in her absence, knowing that she would be totally safe otherwise Trudy wouldn't have stayed away overnight.

She explained that Connor had taken her for a trip on his boat to see a beautiful coral reef, to get away from it all. They had enjoyed their time together so much, Trudy revealed.

"That's crazy!" Lex had responded. "You hardly even know the guy!"

"We just clicked," Trudy said, defending herself.

"I bet Connor's got more than just clicking on his mind!" Lex fumed, frustrated by what he perceived to be Trudy's naivety.

"Unlike you to be such a prude, Lex," Ruby said. "Talk about a double standard."

But there was more to it of course than that, which all were aware of, including Ruby. Lex just didn't trust Connor, sure he was manipulating Trudy, who was vulnerable and desperate for love – Connor using his good looks, finding out all kinds of things about her and the Mall Rats. Lex listened to his gut instinct which told him Connor was a threat from the moment he had arrived.

Connor took offence to Lex's criticism, the two of them getting into a heated argument, resulting in Lex swinging a punch at Connor - and having to be restrained by Slade.

All that was overshadowed, however, when Jay was the next to return – alone – and he told them what he had experienced, plunging the village into a state of emergency.

After seeing the *Sea Ghost*, Jay had driven back through the wasteland to Arthurs Air Force Base - finding it totally abandoned. There was no sign of Amber, Jack, Ellie or the others anywhere, to Jay's shock.

Several clues indicated the base had been attacked. Tracks were visible from other vehicles in the central garden hub area. Furniture was overturned, doors smashed, suggesting whoever was responsible had conducted a methodical, aggressive search of the base.

Refuelling his quad-bike, Jay followed the road south, eventually arriving back at the native village to report his findings – and to warn Lex and the remaining Mall Rats.

Connor had heard of the *Sea Ghost*, he explained, mentioning it was meant to be one of the largest – and fastest vessels that belonged to the Collective.

"Sure you didn't have something to do with it?" Lex had questioned him. "How do we know you didn't tip off the *Sea Ghost*? Did you tell them who they could find at the base?"

"When would I have been able to do that?" Connor scoffed. "I've been with Trudy pretty much the whole time."

"As she's so happy to keep reminding us."

"Lex – please, not now," Salene had urged him. "Don't stir things. We have to stick together on this."

Despite the tension that sporadically broke out between Lex and Connor, the tribe was becoming united by the adversity they were facing.

Salene and May's earlier revelation of their own personal relationship had been overtaken by events. Strangely, it actually gave them a sense of being empowered, the freedom to be themselves, to not worry about being judged by others, with the tribe being supportive of one another and all more concerned by the issue of their missing friends and loved ones.

Even Lex promised, at Lia's urging, to try and be more sensitive to Salene and May. He had apologized for teasing them previously and was happy that they had each other.

Bray had raced back to the village on his vehicle, arriving that evening – and relaying what had happened.

Having discovered Eloise's base in the mountains to be empty, Bray had first also returned to Arthurs Air Force Base.

Searching the accommodation tower thoroughly, calling out for Amber, Emma and the others, desperately looking to see if anyone was still there, Bray had discovered the message scrawled on the mirror in one of the bathrooms. He recognized Amber's writing, finding the clue she had left behind written in lipstick to explain what had been their fate.

UNDER ATTACK! THE GUARDIAN!

Bray and Jay exchanged more pieces of information about what they encountered, leading all to arrive at one conclusion.

"They've obviously been taken - by the Guardian," Bray said, articulating everyone's thoughts. "And if they're on that ship Jay saw – then that just leaves one big question."

"Which is?" Salene wondered.

"Where the ship is headed," Bray answered.

"What if they're coming here?" May wondered. "To try and capture us?"

"If it's a fight they want, we'll be ready for them," Lex seethed.

"We'd better make sure we are, before we do anything else," Bray emphasized. "We have to be prepared."

CHAPTER NINETEEN

The *Sea Ghost* pitched up and down, rolling on the waves. Down below in the hold, Amber felt a wave of nausea, sea sickness - and that she was on a voyage of the damned.

The Guardian stared at her intently, a gleeful, victorious look on his face.

Standing beside him was Eloise, Amber now understood, the very girl whose physical beauty was matched only by her wicked disposition – the one who had tormented Bray, keeping him prisoner. And Amber reflected on the irony as she recalled all that Bray had told her about his time in the strange mountain compound. Now Amber herself had become a captive.

"It is as it is meant to be," the Guardian leered, savouring the sight of Amber and the others in the cell.

He suddenly thrust his head back, looking up to the heavens. "Oh, Zoot! Thank you for bringing us your enemies - into our very hands! We will deliver them, for your divine purpose!"

"You're sick," Amber said, disgusted, almost pitying him.

"You're the ones who are sick!" the Guardian shot back. "And we will purge the world of all of its disease - in the fires of our faith!"

Emma hugged Tiffany and Shannon, comforting them, the little ones closing their eyes, trying to get away from it all. Yet there was no place to hide anymore.

They were in the lower decks, having been put in what had once been a barred storage area, to stop items from shifting around during the ship's journeys.

Amber didn't know where Ellie, Jack or Darryl were, having last seen them being taken down the corridors of the ship by Ebony and Axel to another deck. She didn't even know if they were still on board.

"What have you done with the others?" Amber demanded.

"Answer me first – tell me everything about Bray," Eloise insisted from the other side of the cell bars.

"I already told you – he's dead. They all are!" Amber lied.

Amber was desperate to throw Eloise off the trail of the other Mall Rats - and to protect the native village by presenting the Priestess and her warriors as a powerful threat to be avoided at all costs.

She told Eloise that shortly after defeating Blake, conflict had arisen between the Mall Rats and the native tribe, the Priestess refusing to let go of her traditional culture, values and the past. Violence had erupted and most of the Mall Rats had been killed, Amber described, with only her and a few other survivors fleeing the village and heading to Arthurs Air Force Base, to begin a new life.

Amber recalled Lia saying even Blake had avoided direct conflict with the Priestess and her forces. She only hoped the Guardian and Eloise believed her story - and that it could somehow assist the Mall Rats and the native tribe who she knew had been still at the village – including her son.

"If you are deceiving us – and Bray and the others live – know that Zoot will bring them to us, by his mighty powers, if he so wills. Just as he has - you!" the Guardian said.

Amber knew their capture obviously had nothing to do with Zoot - and probably more with computers.

When she was first taken captive, Amber, along with the others, had been interrogated by Axel and clearly he had thought from his questioning that Arthurs Air Force Base had been abandoned, except for a few worthless survivors of the Roaches tribe who lived there.

Amber was initially confused but now concluded that the invasion must have been due to being tracked somehow when they were online, 'awaiting their next contact'.

Now Eloise was studying Amber closely. "So... you're the one time leader of the Mall Rats, I gather."

"I don't see what the point is in all the questions. You clearly know," Amber replied.

"Show respect to the Mother Divine!" the Guardian snapped, in growing irritation.

"Mother Divine?" Amber derided. "That what you call yourself? There's nothing divine about you – and I'm truly sorry for the child you're carrying."

The Guardian rushed to the bars of the cell, baring his teeth, growling like some wild, enraged animal.

"How dare you speak that way!"

Eloise slowly walked towards Amber's cell, a twisted smile on her face, like she seemed to be enjoying the confrontation. She put her arm on the Guardian's shoulder, gently pulling him back, the Guardian desperate to exact a punishment on Amber for her disrespect.

"Save your strength, Guardian. I can fight my own battles. It's a pity Bray is dead, Amber. You were his once - were you not?"

"What's it to you? What do you care about anyone?"

"Did Bray tell you that he and I got to know each other well? Very well, from what I can remember. So well in fact, he gave me this child. His child. It was a night of passion I'll never forget. We might have more in common than you think, Amber. Except my child still lives – whereas, according to you, your baby is dead, along with Bray, and the rest of the Mall Rats. Maybe it will give you some 'comfort' to know that a part of Bray lives on – in me."

Bray had mentioned to Amber that among the privations he had suffered, Eloise had tried to get him to bear a child with her – Bray resisting her attempts, refusing to yield.

"You're lying! He would never!"

Eloise grinned wickedly, enjoying the pained look on Amber's face.

"Oh, he did. He - *really* did," and she softly patted her slightly bulging stomach area.

Eloise was pregnant, that was undeniable. But Bray would have never faltered – would he? Was it possible he had lost control of his actions after all, having been hooked up to virtual reality machines, his mind affected by the experiments Eloise had done on him? Was Eloise merely toying, playing a cruel game – or was there was a chance, Amber wondered, however much she doubted, that Eloise was telling the truth?

Eloise turned on her heel and casually walked away. "Time to go. Destiny awaits us, Guardian. Farewell, Amber. You will never see this island again. Enjoy your trip."

The Guardian dutifully followed her down the corridor.

"Where are you taking us!" Amber cried out.

"Have patience," the Guardian shouted back. "We will all be reunited with Zoot soon enough!"

CHAPTER TWENTY

Bray looked out across the ocean, the waves glowing a strange, eerie orange colour in the night as the full moon shone down upon them and he pictured Amber and the *Sea Ghost* somewhere out there.

The village had been kept in a state of readiness to defend themselves from any invaders.

However, there had been so sign of the Guardian, Eloise or the *Sea Ghost* and every minute that passed made it more likely, Bray felt, that the *Sea Ghost* was on a different course and the village would not be attacked that night.

"Looks like they're not coming," Lex said, arriving along the sands to stand by Bray on the beach. "Pity. What I'd do to the Guardian if I had half a chance."

Lex and Bray went back, passing through the defensive circle the warriors formed around the village.

Slade, Salene, May, Connor and Trudy joined the meeting Bray arranged, having previously stood by the native warriors to form part of the defensive ring.

"You said there was a different island - where a slave market took place?" Trudy asked Connor. "Maybe they're being taken there, to be traded?"

Connor shrugged. "Could be."

"Or they could be on their way to the Collective homelands, for all we know," Jay suggested. "They could be anywhere."

"No," Bray responded. "I think there's only one place they could have gone."

"Where?" May asked.

Bray explained what he had seen at the abandoned mountain compound – specifically the tableau picture he had discovered with its representation of Zoot, standing in the home city of the Mall Rats, pointing prophetically into the distance beyond the city towards Eagle Mountain.

"Eagle Mountain? Why the hell would they go there?" Lex doubted.

"I don't know. But it seemed to be of some importance at Eloise's base."

"There may be one way to find out," Connor suddenly spoke up.

* * *

"You sure you know what you're doing, Connor?" Trudy asked him uneasily.

"No. But it's worth a shot," he replied.

They were on board the *Nemo*, accompanied by Bray and Lex, the others staying back in the village to keep on night guard. The cabin was dimly lit by a solitary bulb dangling inside.

Connor was crouching by the main battery pack in the cabin, twisting the dials of the short wave radio that was feeding off the electrical unit which had been powered by daytime solar panels.

"If they're within about a hundred miles, there's a chance they might pick this up," Connor explained, the radio giving sounds of distorted static as Connor searched through the various frequencies.

"Just to let you know – I'm still watching your every move," Lex warned, standing behind Connor.

"You don't have to remind me. I know," Connor said. "And you don't need to worry about me. You can trust me. Believe it."

"Oh. Now I feel a whole let better," Lex said.

"Leave him alone, Lex - let him concentrate!" Trudy defended Connor.

"*Sea Ghost*, are you out there, over?" Connor enquired, speaking into the microphone of the radio, turning the dial.

"Keep trying," Bray encouraged, willing the radio to make contact.

Connor had gradually made his way through over half the frequency spectrum for the past few minutes and all they had got so far was the sound of his own voice, echoing back on occasion, and a constant stream of interference.

"I don't think there's anyone out there…" Trudy said.

"We're wasting our time," Lex muttered. "You're more likely to hear from an alien."

Connor kept trying – and a few more minutes passed before he finally clenched his fist victoriously. They had made contact.

"This is *Sea Ghost*," a distorted voice crackled through the radio, almost undecipherable. "Identify yourself."

"This is the *Nemo*," Connor answered. "What are your co-ordinates?"

There was no response. Bray considered the others. "Any ideas?"

"Why don't I tell them I've got some cargo to deliver," Connor suggested.

"And what the hell good would that do?" Lex scoffed.

"It might provide their location," Connor said. "If the *Sea Ghost* is involved with the Collective, they take slaves on board from traders all the time."

"We have nothing to lose, everything to gain," Trudy suggested.

"Ok. Agreed. Give it a shot," Bray nodded.

"This is *Nemo*," Connor spoke into the radio. "*Nemo* to *Sea Ghost*. I have some valuable supplies for the Collective. Repeat. Some valuable supplies for the Collective. What's your bearing so I can rendezvous? Over?"

"Provide the code. For security clearance," the distant voice responded amidst crackling static.

"Now we're screwed!" Lex sighed.

Connor hadn't released his finger from the talk button and Lex, Bray and Trudy exchanged dumbfounded glances as the voice replied.

"Incorrect."

"You're breaking up," Connor said. "Let's just forget about the rendezvous. What are your co-ordinates so that I can try and adjust the frequency to get a better signal?"

Connor began to frantically scribble down the co-ordinates he was being given on an old magazine from the adult era he had read countless times on his travels.

"Thank you, *Sea Ghost*. *Nemo* out."

Connor breathed out a big sigh of relief, turning the radio off in case the *Sea Ghost* tried to make further contact.

"You did it!" Trudy cried out, thrilled, exchanging a high-five with Connor.

"We may not know where they're heading," Connor grinned, "but at least we have some kind of an idea of where they are right now."

Connor spread out his nautical charts on the small desk in the cabin, Lex angling the lightbulb so it shone down, to help Connor see as he cross-referenced the co-ordinates.

"Seems like they're round about here," Connor said finally, putting his finger down on the map. "Well, that's where they said, at least. And there's only one piece of land if they continued heading north-north-east on that track."

He indicated the map and although Bray was pleased at the breakthrough that had been made - he was also anxious at what it all meant.

"I knew it," he sighed uneasily.

The position Connor had indicated was none other than the very same land which housed the city where Amber, Bray and the Mall Rats used to live. There was still no assurance that the *Sea Ghost* would be travelling there - but according to Connor, he was probably right in his summation that there was no other apparent destination without them dramatically altering course. If they were heading towards other lands, then it wouldn't make any sense not to have embarked upon a different track in the first place.

* * *

The plan was to leave the next morning and they awoke early, stocking up the *Nemo* with supplies.

The Priestess and her own tribe joined in the effort, forming a human chain going from the beach back to the village, passing along food and fresh water, stored in plastic containers that had been salvaged from the wreck of the *Jzhao Li*.

"It's going to be pretty cramped. Are you sure you're up to this?" Salene asked May, the two of them stacking another heavy container of fresh water inside *Nemo*'s cabin.

"We've got to go. It's what they would do for us."

There was hardly any room inside the boat, brimming with supplies. Connor had already thrown out most of his own items to free up more room, keeping only his most important personal and sentimental belongings.

There was just the one bed – and a small area down below had been cleared for Brady and baby Bray to rest and play in. No more than two of them at a time would rest comfortably. The plan was that as the voyage went on and they consumed more of their supplies, this would free up room inside.

"It's a good thing some of us don't mind sharing the bed – eh, girls?" Lex commented mischievously, poking his head into the cabin through the hatchway from above deck.

"Don't even start," Salene warned him, giving him a look.

Not long after, the boat was finally fully loaded - and with the tide rising, it was time to depart.

They were on the beach with the Priestess and her tribe, who had come to say goodbye. But not all were embarking upon the journey on board *Nemo*.

"I really feel we should be going," Slade insisted. "To lend you guys a hand."

"With Ruby expecting, it's better you stay safe here," Jay responded. "We don't know how long we'll be. Besides, it'll mean two less mouths to feed."

"Three less," Ruby pointed out, her hands clasped to her pregnant belly. "I really wish we could join you. But next time we see each other – I'll look forward to hopefully introducing you all to our bouncing baby."

"If it's a boy – name him after me," Lex suggested immodestly, the others laughing at his idea. "Hey - I was being serious."

"So this is it – goodbye," Ruby said emotionally, suddenly struck by the reality of the situation.

It was an odd sensation for Bray to see members of the Mall Rats and those who played such a vital role in their lives after he went missing. And he could see that all were deeply affected at being split apart.

They exchanged hugs, wished each other well, Connor keeping a look on the rising tide so they didn't miss their window of opportunity to leave straight away.

The Priestess was also sad at the departure. For so long she had distrusted the world beyond the island, viewing it with suspicion but she had come to truly bond with the Mall Rats and their friends. She promised to look after Ruby and Slade and would slowly teach them her language – and try to learn theirs – to help them communicate. She would miss the rest of the Mall Rats being around, Lia translated, having enjoyed their company.

None more than Lex. He gazed upon the Priestess with obvious attraction – and affection – one last time, the Priestess reciprocating. The two embraced, Lex finally getting closer to the Priestess than he had ever managed before – even if it wasn't quite the physical contact he had so long desired.

For all that Lex was enamoured with the Priestess and the island way of life, he felt his true loyalty was to the Mall Rats. He would do everything in his power to save his missing friends and thwart the threat posed by Eloise and the Guardian. But it still hurt to say farewell – particularly to the Priestess. She was the one girl who had gotten away, despite his efforts, and Lex hoped their paths would cross again.

But there was another.

Lia had hardly slept in the night, wracked by conflicting feelings, her loyalties split. For so long the native tribe had been her own, taking her in and looking after her following the 'virus'. Lia had also bonded with the Mall Rats, however, and developed genuine feelings for Lex.

She couldn't bear the thought of being apart from him and her heart told her that she might have a future with the admittedly unruly, roguish 'bad boy' she had gotten to know so well. He made her laugh, was outrageous at times - yet she knew he was also kind, brave and sensitive

even, for all his gusto. He made the world – her world –
a better place, Lia realized.

And when it was decided that it was probably best for
Ruby and Slade to stay behind due to Ruby's pregnancy,
Lia's hopes were raised, realizing there could be an extra
space for her on the tiny vessel.

"You might be the best souvenir I've ever brought
home," Lex commented, holding Lia by the hand, giving
her his support as she looked upon the Priestess and the
native tribe for what could be the last time, tears in her
eyes, before boarding the *Nemo*.

The Priestess slowly waved her arms in a circular
motion and began calling out in her native tongue.

"What's she saying, Lia?" Bray asked.

"She's giving us a blessing," Lia relayed. "Asking that
the spirits of the ancestors guide us, offer their protection.
That the sea is kind… our journey is swift… and that we
find what our hearts are most looking for."

* * *

Nemo was on its way, Connor at the helm, the main sail
unfurled, billowing in the breeze, the boat picking up
speed, catching the wind.

On the beach, Ruby and Slade could be seen standing
with the Priestess and her tribe, calling out, waving
farewell.

Bray stood at the back of the boat, with the others,
watching the island recede into the distance.

He carried his son – Amber's child – in his arms.
They would be reunited, Bray vowed. He would stop
at nothing, would travel all the oceans in the world, to
find her.

Somewhere, across the water, was the *Sea Ghost* – and
Bray knew he would have to confront the Guardian and

Eloise once again, as well as the spectre of his brother Zoot's legacy. Part of him dreaded the prospect but if it meant there was a chance to save Amber and the others, it had to be done.

It had been so long since the time Bray had been captured. He had often questioned if the day would arrive and he would ever return - but now a sense of hope mixed with the unease at what might lay ahead. He was finally going home.

CHAPTER TWENTY-ONE

Surrounded by guards, the fanatical Zootists escorted Amber and the other prisoners, along with all the other passengers who were once inhabitants of the island mountain base. They were now being led by the Guardian and Eloise through the ghostly city streets.

Amber was astounded especially to see so many babies being held by their mothers, who walked in silence as if in some kind of trance. There were other children walking together in another group and Amber couldn't quite work out where they were all heading - or why.

It was so strange to be back though, Amber reflected, in the city that she had grown up in – or what was left of it.

Looking around the towering landmark buildings in the heart of the old central district, Amber felt like it was all some kind of dream.

Everywhere she went, memories flooded back of incidents that had occurred during her childhood – and in the times after the demise of the adults, when Amber had struggled to survive as her beloved city descended into a state of chaos.

She recognized the place where she and her best friend Dal had once hidden from Zoot, finding and rescuing Cloe in the process, just before the Mall Rats formed their own tribe.

Further down the street she walked by the ruins of an old department store, long ago looted. Amber fondly recalled her happy childhood spent there at Christmas time, going to visit 'Santa Claus' as a little girl with her parents, being comforted now by the memory – but also saddened.

If only her parents had known what fate had in store. She wished she could go back and tell them how much she loved them, hear them speak, share their company again.

Amber could see Ebony ahead walking unfettered closely beside Eloise, as the group steadily made its way through the silent empty city.

She had done it again, Amber thought, admiring Ebony's obvious prowess in having clearly somehow manoeuvred her way into a position of influence once more, even if she was disgusted at the same time by Ebony's complete lack of concern for the well-being of others. She may have been the ultimate survivor - but Ebony was all too willing to trample her way over anyone else if it meant saving herself, Amber was forever amazed by Ebony's sense of self-preservation.

Also Ram's. She noticed him walking just behind Ebony. He was flanked by a quartet of powerfully built Zootist guards but from what Amber could see, Ram himself was unrestrained and didn't seem too distressed by his situation. He actually appeared to have been well fed and treated – and certainly looked in a better condition than Amber and the prisoners. Ram wasn't behaving like someone who was 'doomed', like he had previously claimed, should he encounter the Collective. Surprising, given he had told the Mall Rats he had a bounty on his head by the Collective and was a 'wanted man'.

The city appeared to be totally deserted, Amber reflected, thinking back to the hasty evacuation the population had made to get away from the threat of a new 'virus' released by Mega and his Technos.

Was there any trace of Mega's 'virus' in the very air she was now breathing, Amber considered? Or had it all been nothing but a threat, unleashed by the Collective, having sabotaged Mega's computers so the Collective could then create panic and destroy everything the Technos had accomplished in one stroke?

On the island, Ram had told her this is precisely what had happened, which is why he had been so keen to return home, believing the city was safe, rather than a deathtrap, after all. Amber wondered if everything he told her about the Collective was true – and if Eloise, the Guardian and the Zootists, were simply here to seize control of the city now its population had been emptied of inhabitants and Technos.

"We are guided by Zoot's divine hands!" the Guardian suddenly screamed out in fervour, noticing some graffiti proclaiming that Zoot Lives, the Guardian's manic insistence echoing around the streets. "Praise Zoot – *Praise* him now!"

"Power and Chaos! Power and Chaos!" the Zootist guards and zealous converts began chanting, the cries of Zoot's slogan erupting in the city once more, reminding Amber of the days Zoot himself, along with Ebony and the Locos, had brought their reign of terror over the cityscape.

The *Sea Ghost* had been moored at the docks, ironically not far from the area where Amber and the Mall Rats had originally fled from the city themselves when taking to the water on the little trawler that had been their temporary home for several weeks. Amber had never expected that their paths would cross with the Guardian again – and end with their capture, being brought back, prisoners, to the city.

The journey aboard the *Sea Ghost* had been a harrowing experience, the sailing ship rolling and pitching throughout, on one occasion, even passing through a fierce storm, hurling all aboard to one side when it seemed as if it would capsize.

Amber had been confined in the cell within the boughs of the vessel, along with Emma, Tiffany and Shannon, kept constantly apart from Jack, Ellie, Darryl and Gel, whom she learned were on board elsewhere, having been told so by the Guardian. Fed a meagre supply of rations – and tepid, tainted water to drink, some of which they used to wash themselves, they were anxious to discover the intentions of their captors and what awaited them at their destination. It had been an arduous few weeks on the ocean.

During the journey, Amber had heard strange sounds of distress from other prisoners being held on the ship. Young children called out for help, babies cried, Amber was sure that she could hear painful moans, coming from different decks, of mothers actually giving birth on board the vessel.

Arriving in the city, the *Sea Ghost* unloaded its cargo of human captives, Zootist worshippers – and to Amber's surprise, all who now joined them in the procession.

Other expectant mothers to be, their bellies bloated with the babies they carried, walked slowly at the back of the group. The most heavily pregnant, ready to give birth any day, sat as passengers on the quad-bikes that had been unloaded from the ship, the same vehicles that had been involved in the assault on Arthurs Air Force Base.

Seeing so many babies around, Amber was desperate to be with her own son again, to hold him, give her loving care but her child was far away on the island, she thought helplessly, separated by the vast seas. She hoped he was safe, trusting the good care of the Mall Rats with whom she had left him behind at the native village – and wished that they were all well.

Emma missed Bray dreadfully and had been supportive to Amber on the voyage - and Amber was encouraging to Emma in return, the two of them bonding, keeping each other company – and their spirits up, as best they could.

During the crossing, Amber had been taken several times to Eloise and the Guardian for further interrogation. Most of the questions she was asked concerned what she knew of Eagle Mountain, particularly what happened in the course of her visit there with Bray, Ebony and the original Mall Rats.

Amber did not want to answer their enquiries, to resist in any way possible, but with the threat of food and water being withheld from Emma and her siblings unless she co-operated, Amber had no option but to recount her experiences.

She explained about the satellite, hearing pre-recorded adult voices, the computers Jack worked on – and finally the accidental explosion, which almost took Amber's life. At least, she thought it had always been an accident, noticing a dubious expression on Eloise's face when Amber relayed her understanding of what had occurred at Eagle Mountain.

With the procession passing through the abandoned streets, looking how Amber remembered them the last occasion she had been in the city, the group reached an area Amber knew only too well. She was familiar with almost every inch, having spent so much of her young life there, trying to build a new future for herself and the city.

She had come full circle. They had arrived at the mall.

* * *

Amber, Ellie, Jack, Darryl, Gel, Emma and her sister and brother were being held captive in the cage Jack himself had erected in the early days of the post-adult world, the gates blocking the old main entrance to the mall. It was the same cell in which Lex, Ryan and Zandra were first imprisoned by Jack and the Mall Rats when they were thought to be a threat - a long time ago, Jack reflected, what seemed a different world away.

"I never expected I'd be trapped inside this thing!" Jack protested, aware of the irony. His mind was in overtime, trying to find a way out of his own contraption, the metal grille gates securely surrounding them.

"Bring back memories, Amber?" Ebony teased, watching from the other side of the cell.

Ebony was accompanied by Aras and several Zootist acolytes who had been put under her direct chain of command.

After impressing the Guardian with her activity in the raid on Arthurs Air Force Base, Ebony had continued to show her loyalty and worth to Eloise on the long voyage of the *Sea Ghost*, Ebony regaling the Zootist followers with her tales of what she claimed to have witnessed, first hand, of Zoot when he lived in the city.

Ebony had augmented the legend, throwing in a few 'miracles' along the way, rallying the faith, fanning their fanaticism - and coming to be regarded as a person of high position and influence. At all times Ebony had deliberately emphasized the importance of the 'Mother Divine' and the Guardian, especially Eloise, all too aware that she was in command – and the one who apparently reported to Kami directly, the leader of the powerful Collective.

"Come to gloat?" Amber asked her scornfully.

"Maybe just a little. But no, I'm not really the gloating type, Amber. Not any more. I'm just following orders."

"Is that what you call it?"

Amber looked to the upper level of the mall where Eloise stood, looming above proceedings, now more advanced in her own term of pregnancy. Her appearance was still immaculate having been well cared for by her servants throughout the long voyage. Eloise exuded a sense of confident authority, the 'Mother Divine' exerting an aura of personal magnetism to her dutiful followers, who obeyed her every whim without question.

Amber could just about overhear Eloise conferring with Axel, giving orders, dispatching the Zootists to different sectors of the city to carry out tasks, from gathering any additional working vehicles or fuel supplies they could find - to making sure there were no 'strays' around wandering the streets.

Ram was kept close by Eloise, Zootist guards shadowing his every move.

"Seems to me that you're just like the rest of them, Ebony," Amber said. "You're nothing more than a puppet – and Eloise is pulling the strings."

"If I'm a puppet – what does that make you?" Ebony smiled. "Oh, I know. The one who's locked up. A loser – on the losing side."

Tiffany began sobbing – which started her young brother, Shannon, off - the two of them terrified by their ordeal. Emma wrapped her arms lovingly around her little sister and brother, trying to calm them and assuage their fears.

"What do you want with us?" Amber demanded of the Guardian, who stood on the other side of the grille, a glint in his eyes, like he was enjoying the suffering of his prisoners. "They're just children – they've done nothing to anyone!"

"We're all Zoot's children," the Guardian said, slowly advancing toward the gate, staring unflinchingly at Amber, confrontationally. "Each of us has a role to play. To find our place in the universe. And sometimes - 'sacrifices' must be made."

Amber suppressed an involuntary shudder at his words. Was that it? The reason they were there? Was the Guardian after some twisted form of revenge – a sacrifice?

"You're completely insane," Amber said defiantly. "I actually feel sorry for you."

The Guardian paced back and forth, mumbling to himself intensely, incoherently, laughing at times, almost like he was having a conversation with someone unseen – before turning to Amber – and looking upon her with surprising fondness.

"You were here, Amber, at the very beginning. You *witnessed* it, the moment it all began. If only Lex was here."

The Guardian looked reverently to the top landing on the second level of the mall where Eloise stood, in conversation with Axel.

"Why? Do you fancy him or something?" Gel challenged.

"That's not helping!" Darryl urged her.

"Lex is greater than any of you will ever be!" the Guardian shouted to the prisoners.

Amber suddenly realized the connection – the Guardian had been looking up to the spot, where Eloise was currently standing, which was the very place where Lex had tackled Zoot, resulting in Zoot falling off the upper level of the mall and plummeting to his death.

"Lex is to be exalted as the Bringer of Death!" the Guardian continued, mesmerized, looking at the area where Zoot fell. "Had Lex not played his part, none of this would have happened! To take life is a hallowed, honourable thing! Zoot's mother gave birth to him – but it was Lex who had the privilege of taking away that life force! To elevate Zoot - to make him a god!! Everything - it all goes back to the very beginning – to that moment! To Lex! It is to him that we give the accolade he is so worthy of!"

The Guardian seemed completely crazy, in a frenzy.

"Keep away from us!" Ellie screamed to the Guardian, clinging to Jack, terrified by what she had just heard and what the Guardian was saying.

"If only Lex was here - to grant us all the privilege of death!" he ranted. "But maybe there are others who are worthy? Would you, Ebony? Send me to the afterlife? So I can join him in the nirvana?"

"It would be my pleasure," Ebony said, before exchanging a subtle glance with Ram, the two of them also uncertain and equally wary of the Guardian.

"Guardian! It is not your time – not yet!" Eloise shouted, advancing down the stairs towards him with Axel, Ram and the guards following her.

The Guardian reeled at her voice, clasping his hands to his ears, slumping to his knees. "Mother Divine, forgive me!"

Eloise placed her hand on the Guardian's head, calming him down, the Guardian closing his eyes, feeling her touch, sensing the divine energies flowing through her, upon him.

"Rise, Guardian," Eloise said calmly. "Defender of the faith. Be patient. Zoot awaits you. And your time will come. But not yet. There is still work to be done."

"What kind of... 'work'?" Amber probed cautiously.

Eloise addressed the prisoners in the cell. "You are all like the blind girl. In the dark. Completely blind to the truth. Zoot can give you the ability to see things that no eyes ever can."

"You're lying!" Emma cried out from within the cage, clutching Tiffany and Shannon to her tightly. "Bray was right. You're a monster! We'll never join you!"

"Is that so?" Eloise said, looking cruelly at Emma, angered by her brazen open disrespect.

"Take the youngest from her!" Eloise suddenly ordered Ebony. "They are to be *educated* into the faith. They'll join us and become part of the Collective. And perhaps teach their sister how to show respect."

"No!" Emma screamed in utter disbelief and despair, hearing the struggles and cries for help from Tiffany and Shannon as one of the metal grille gates was raised, Ebony, Aras and the guards entering and pushing back Amber and the others, physically forcing Tiffany and Shannon out of Emma's desperate attempts to hold onto them in her arms.

The Zootist operating the lever on the top level of the mall closed the grille gate of the cell shut, as soon as Ebony and the Zootists in her command had exited.

Aras scooped Tiffany and Shannon up in his arms, the little ones shedding tears, distraught at being separated from their sister, and took them away to another part of the mall to be placed with the other younger children being raised.

Emma, broken, wailed a primal moan of despondency, utter helplessness. It was like a part of her had been ripped away inside. Ellie watched sympathetically as Amber hugged Emma tightly, trying to give support.

"You won't get away with this!" Amber protested to Eloise. "Whatever it is you're up to – you won't succeed!"

"I already have. Axel – prepare the prisoners. I'll see you tomorrow, Amber - and you'll see I can do whatever I want," Eloise insisted, before turning her back on the cell and walking away, the Guardian following dutifully after her.

CHAPTER TWENTY-TWO

Nemo sailed into the docks in the city under the cover of darkness.

There had been no sight of the *Sea Ghost* during any point of their journey and when Bray noticed the silhouette of the mighty sailing ship berthed in the port, it was the first time they had seen the vessel they had been pursuing. All were relieved that they had discovered, as they suspected, the destination of the *Sea Ghost* though they were more than apprehensive at the prospect of what might lay ahead.

After they had disembarked *Nemo*, Lex literally kissed the solid ground under his feet in relief – 'terra firma' as he called it – having been sick and tired of the endless motion of Connor's boat as the yacht made its way across the seas.

The voyage had been difficult, Connor getting a few precious hours sleep whenever he could, having taken responsibility at the helm, navigating their course, the others trying to keep a steady hand on the wheel in his absence to keep *Nemo* on track, headed in the right direction.

None had enjoyed a good, uninterrupted sleep. The tight living quarters made life uncomfortable for all, the group taking shifts in the cabin to rest, although with *Nemo*'s constant pitching and rolling, that was easier said than done.

Being in such close proximity made the group bond with each other even more, however, and morale was high. The Mall Rats – or 'Sea Rats' as Lex suggested they make a temporary name change – were in strong spirits, determined to go after the *Sea Ghost* and rescue their absent members.

Lex had even completely ceased teasing Salene and May, respecting that the two of them were happy as a loving couple.

He remained suspicious of Connor for the first few days of their travels but slowly got to know Connor better. With Trudy's urging and due to the fact Connor had been as good as his word, working tirelessly and with much effort, bringing them to the city they used to live in, it went a long way to dispelling Lex's previous suspicions. Bray, however, still reserved his judgement though Connor hadn't done anything to fuel any doubt.

Trudy was overjoyed to have found a romantic partner in the form of the dashing owner and captain of the *Nemo*. Connor and Trudy usually kept each other company, above and below decks, and could be seen - or heard - giggling, laughing, the two of them now a happy couple.

Connor had also spent a little time playing with Brady, making some origami boats and sea creature shapes for her, torn from the pages of his old magazines. Trudy was happy to see her daughter's reactions, Brady enjoying being around Connor, who Trudy proudly and lovingly looked upon as the new 'man' in her life.

Nemo was anchored far away from the *Sea Ghost*, on the other side of the harbour, the group abandoning it and taking with them some remaining food supplies to eat.

Connor affectionately patted *Nemo*'s hull as he left the boat, hoping he would see his beloved yacht again.

Bray was aware they needed a safe place to stay – and he could think of no better location than the house Trudy had grown up in, where the group spent the night. They made a perilous journey in the dark to the suburbs, worried they might encounter danger, perhaps from forces aboard the *Sea Ghost*, but eventually they arrived, tired, to the home that had belonged to Trudy's parents and where she was raised. Trudy remembered every step of the way from when she used to walk to school.

The house was where Bray and Trudy, then pregnant at the time, found refuge after the collapse of the adult world. It was far from the foreboding city centre, positioned in an almost hidden cul de sac, itself nestled in a semi-rural suburb. The area was peaceful, quiet. Birds chirped in the back garden, overgrown due to being unattended, the grass waist high, massive weeds sprouting up, taking over.

Bray thought of the past, when he and Trudy originally left the house due to Bray's discovery that the Roosters, an anarchic breakaway tribe, could pose a potential threat having been spotted on patrol in the suburbs. Bray was anxious to keep Trudy away from his brother, Zoot, who knew his ex-girlfriend was expecting their child, and above all, to try and find a safe haven where she could give birth.

Their decision back then to leave the house had altered their lives in a profound way. Not only had Trudy and her unborn baby been protected but Bray and Trudy had subsequently encountered Amber and the Mall Rats, and their paths changed forever.

The Roosters were history, long gone, Bray knew, and the leafy suburban area Trudy had grew up in now seemed like the best place for them to establish a 'safe house' to use as a temporary base – and he hoped from there, they could find out what was currently happening in the city.

Waking up to the new day - if fate was kind once more, Bray hoped maybe he could set out, as he had done long ago - to once again find Amber.

"Look, Brady – it's Mister Floppsy!" Trudy said excitedly, carrying a cuddly rabbit plush toy that had been in her bedroom, still in the same place where she had left it. It was her favourite toy as a little girl, given to her by her parents one birthday and cherished ever since, a reminder of her family - and happier times.

Trudy gave the enormous toy, nearly the same size as her daughter, to Brady, who wrapped her arms around it in loving delight, not caring at all about the dust and stale smell the toy had acquired after sitting in Trudy's bedroom cupboard. Most of the other contents in the house had long since disappeared, having been looted.

"He's your's now. He'll look after you. As long as you look after him."

"Be careful, Trudy," Salene wished. "All of you. Don't be gone too long."

"We won't," Bray promised.

Jay and Bray had come up with a plan soon after they had woken early that morning – believing there was a way for them to uncover more information about what had happened to Amber and the other prisoners, as well as what Eloise and the Guardian were up to.

For the idea to work, it was imperative for Trudy and Bray to return to the city along with Lex, Jay, Connor and Lia. They would be putting themselves at risk, however, and needed to be cautious.

"You have such a lovely home, Trudy" Lia said, meeting up with the others in the hall before they left on their mission, having enjoyed a good night's sleep for the first time in weeks. "I wish we could stay here."

"You're not the only one," Lex agreed, sitting on the floor and putting his shoes on. "I could imagine finding a place like this to live – a beautiful blushing bride by my side. Preferably blonde – and German. A bit like you, actually."

Lex looked to Lia suggestively, who was indeed blushing with embarrassment at Lex's obvious flirting with her.

"We'd best be off," Bray said, kissing his baby son one more time and gently passing him over to May.

"He'll be fine – I promise," May reassured him, carefully taking Bray's son in her arms.

The plan was for May, Salene, Sammy and Lottie to stay in Trudy's house with Brady and baby Bray - to 'lay low' and do nothing more than stay safe, out of harm's way, awaiting the return of the others from the city.

At the first sign of trouble, they were to relocate, if Salene and May thought it best, to the next safest place anyone could think of – Lex recommending a good backstop in the event they had to leave Trudy's house.

He had described the location of his 'love shack', a secret hideaway he had used in the city during the reign of the Technos, where Lex, in his carousing days, had hooked up with Siva, his old girlfriend. It was the perfect spot, he thought, for the Mall Rats to disappear to should they ever need to 'go to ground'.

He was looking forward to taking Lia there, he had told her, but Lia wasn't too enthusiastic at the idea, uncomfortable by Lex mentioning his past with Siva – let alone his self-proclaimed 'love shack'. It all made Lia question Lex and her own feelings for him. He insisted his days as a 'playboy' were over but Lia couldn't help wonder if she was just the next in a long line of girls who had fallen for Lex's charms. She wanted so much more for herself than that - a real, genuine and lasting relationship - and hoped there was far more to Lex.

"My lady," Connor said, suavely offering his hand – and Trudy played along, doing a curtsey before accepting, with a beaming smile, the two of them linking their arms, walking down the hall toward the front door.

Once, she had imagined Bray would have been the one she was destined to live happily ever after with, if there would be such a thing as a fairy tale anymore. How times had changed. She would never have guessed she would have ended up meeting Connor – especially so far away on the island.

The last time she had left her old home she had been much younger, overwhelmed and frightened by the world she found herself in - and terrified of being pregnant. Then, Bray had been her sole pillar of support, helping her get through.

Now, Trudy thought, she had grown up in so many ways. Despite some anxieties when she left the city and tried somehow to settle on the island - she was stronger, confident, content again with who she was as a person. Her baby had become the lovely little girl she adored and cared for. Trudy smiled as she saw Brady playing with 'Mr Floppsy', reminding Trudy of when she was a little girl herself, standing in the house, happy and without a care in the world.

She was a mother figure now, carrying the 'baton' that her parents had passed to her – determined to protect and raise her daughter in the same loving way she had been. Trudy had a different 'family' – her tribe – and would do anything for them, as they would do for her.

"Let's go," Bray said, opening the front door and exiting, followed by Lex, Lia, Jay, Connor and Trudy.

Trudy turned one more time, looking at her daughter waving goodbye at the entrance, along with the others who were staying behind, calling out their farewells.

She would be back to that house – and to Brady - again.

But first, they had to go on their mission to the city. She wasn't the scared girl who had once set out before with Bray.

Life had moved on – and Trudy had changed. She was ready.

* * *

They moved furtively through the desolate city streets. It felt strange to be back on familiar territory, laced with so many memories of the past – and full of mystery as to what was currently happening in the city, which they perceived had been long since abandoned but now was playing host to all those who had arrived on the *Sea Ghost*.

It was far more dangerous being out in the daylight, without the darkness of night to obscure their presence.

The group tried to keep in as much cover as possible, running from behind one wrecked vehicle to another… staying close by the towering buildings in the city centre, their senses strained for any signs of life, looking around every corner anxiously, listening to every sound.

The city certainly seemed deserted. All they had seen so far were a few stray cats and some feral dogs, scavenging around for food, once having been domestic pets in the old adult days.

"Are you sure we're not being… followed?" Lia said, turning to look behind her again, convinced prying eyes were watching their every move. More used to life on the island, it was a different – and unnerving – experience for Lia to be out on the streets, surrounded by the concrete jungle.

"Positive," Bray replied reassuringly as they kept searching, going through the city, one block at a time, doing their best to stay out of sight.

Suddenly, Bray indicated for them to stop.

Around the corner, at a crossroad intersection, was a car, stationary in the middle of the wide city avenue. To a casual observer it would look no more than a wreck – but to Bray's well-practiced senses, this vehicle was different. Dented and covered in graffiti, its back window barely holding together, the glass looking like it would implode at any moment, Bray noticed this car was full of occupants – and from their attire, it was clear they were Zootists.

Bray did a 'thumbs up' signal to the others.

"I hope this works," Jay whispered, peering out from around the corner where the others stood, hiding.

"This is crazy!" Lex insisted in hushed tones. "What are you going to do – just go up and start a conversation?"

"That's the idea," Jay replied, gathering his courage.

"Good luck," Bray said as Jay slowly advanced to the edge of the building that had been giving him cover.

"Thanks. You, too," Jay nodded, in mutual respect.

"Time to go fish," Jay said, bravely stepping out into the open, walking up to the car. He was using himself as bait.

The doors of the vehicle opened, four Zootists exiting – and watching warily, surprised to see someone else in the seemingly otherwise abandoned city.

"If you've escaped and decided to hand yourself in, Techno, then it still won't get you any mercy from the Mother Divine," the lead Zootist warned gruffly.

"No – no way. I'm not handing myself in. I just wanted to tell you all – how utterly ridiculous you look," Jay said. "See ya."

With that, Jay turned, running back as fast as he could the way he had come. The Zootists, confused but angry at his provocation, chased after him on foot - shouting out obscenities at him being a disbeliever.

When the Zootists rounded the corner, they reeled, totally stunned, in awe, incredulous to see before them hallowed figures in their religion. Living legends.

The four Zootists knelt down on the ground, prostrating themselves before Bray – the brother of Zoot – whom they believed had died, as Eloise had told them. They recognized Bray, having seen him when he had been incarcerated under Eloise. And there was no doubt who was with Bray, the Zootists understanding from the mythology they knew of the Mall Rats, that it was Trudy who was with him – as well as Lex. Right before their very eyes.

"Where is Eloise?" Bray slowly asked, aware the four Zootists were cowering, thinking him a divine presence directly connected to their god, according to the teachings of Eloise and the Guardian.

"Answer him!" Trudy commanded, playing out her role as had been previously worked out with Jay and Bray. "Don't you know who this is? Who I am? I - am the Supreme Mother! I gave birth – to Zoot's child! You will answer– or so help me, you will answer to Zoot himself!"

Connor was startled by Trudy's apparent transformation and domineering attitude but remembered what she had told him of her experiences in the past as the 'Supreme Mother'. She would never forget what she went through and clearly was able to represent herself as she had once been, making an act of it, in accordance with the plan.

"I'll get them to talk," Lex threatened, stepping forward to the Zootists menacingly. "It seems to me you've got some explaining to do. Where are the rest of your cohorts?"

Strangely, Lex thought, they actually recoiled, completely terrified by *him* – as if he was also a person of spiritual significance. This was something new, a reaction Lex had never experienced before in his encounters with any Zootists.

"The Mother Divine - has gone to Eagle Mountain…" one of the Zootists finally answered.

"And what of the prisoners on the *Sea Ghost*?" Bray demanded.

The Zootists revealed that some of the prisoners had accompanied the Mother Divine and even gave their names, being Amber, Jack, Ellie and Ram.

"What of the others?" Trudy probed, making it obvious she wouldn't be satisfied with anything other than an honest answer.

"They are at the shrine where the Mighty Zoot fell. With the Guardian."

"And what of the blind girl?" Bray enquired.

The Zootists described that she was also at the mall and Bray warned them that they were being released and that they should report to the Guardian what they had experienced. Explain to him that they had encountered Bray, Lex and Trudy - and the Zootists nodded obediently, still in awe.

"Before you go – give me the keys to your car," Lex ordered, the main Zootist tentatively handing them over.

"I... can't believe I've met you in person!" he said, overwhelmed.

"Next thing you'll be asking for my autograph," Lex replied. "But don't bother wasting your time. Now get outta here!" he roared.

The Zootists backed away, stunned by their experience, then they ran, leaving Bray and the others who watched them recede around the corner.

"That went better than I hoped," Jay said, glad their plan had worked. "Great job, you guys."

"You were actually pretty hot in Supreme Mother mode," Connor couldn't help himself from commenting to Trudy. "I would follow you anywhere."

"Then you know what you're in for if you ever make me mad," Trudy grinned.

"Why did you just let them go?" Lia asked Bray.

"To add to the confusion. Doubt. Hopefully the Guardian will send out some more of his followers into the city… And the more Zootists out here in the streets, the less we'll encounter at the Mall. Or at Eagle Mountain."

"Did you see the way they looked at me?" Lex wondered, still puzzled by the reaction of the Zootists to him. "It was like they had seen a ghost or something."

"You certainly have a way with people," Lia remarked.

But Bray knew the real reason, aware of the currency and status anyone associated with Zoot held and he actually felt sorry for the Zootists, thinking they had probably once been prisoners themselves, their minds warped by the twisted lies and propaganda of Eloise and the Guardian. He pitied their misguided devotion to their cause. So many were simply frightened and struggling to survive – the Zootist faith, in the name of his late brother, offering them the promise of something greater, exerting a powerful pull on the vulnerable and weak, who felt they had no other option but to convert.

For now, they had finally discovered what had happened to their missing friends and loved ones.

Bray was desperate to try and discover what the Guardian and Eloise planned, from the news that some of them, Amber included, had apparently been taken by Eloise to Eagle Mountain, for reasons unknown.

The gamble to use the very reputation and position they held in the religion against the Zootists who followed it had thankfully paid off in that initial encounter. However, the Zootists were an unpredictable and dangerous group, radicalized by their faith, and all knew they would have to be extremely careful. Many of the Zootists were sure to prove deadly, implacable foes.

"So – any thoughts what we do now?" Jay wondered.

"We go after them," Bray answered purposefully. There was no other choice. "But first – why don't we create a little power and chaos of our own?"

CHAPTER TWENTY-THREE

The early morning mist enveloped Eagle Mountain, almost obscuring the round satellite tracking device atop the building, when Amber was brought there by Eloise, along with Jack, Ellie, Ram, Axel and several guards.

It was a place full of memories – and mysteries – the Mall Rats having made their own journey to the summit long ago, guided by Tai San, trying to find out more about the 'virus', believing some answers lay within the observatory.

Zandra's grave still stood, having lost her life in the explosion that tragically took place. Amber missed her, thinking of the zany but sweet girl who had brought so much joy to the tribe. What would Zandra have done, had she lived on? Would she have found a lasting happiness in her relationship with Lex? Alas, it was not meant to be, and Amber gathered her thoughts, in remembrance of Zandra, as she passed by the site of her grave.

Amber herself had also come close to losing her life, thrown by the explosion and for a time, losing her memory. Ebony had tried to trick everyone into believing that Amber had perished and had told them she had 'buried' Amber in the grave beside Zandra's. That grave also stood – and Amber wondered if this time she really would meet her end at Eagle Mountain, having narrowly escaped death there before.

"It's ironic how you had once chosen to call yourself Eagle," Eloise goaded her. "And that we've finally made it to your roost. Would you prefer if I called you Eagle again – or Amber?"

"I don't care what you call me," Amber replied, unsure how Eloise had so much information about her and her past life. Including the time she had spent with Pride and the Eco tribe.

The group were now standing inside the gutted ruins of the observatory, ravaged by the explosion, the walls scarred by the fire that had subsequently burned within. Where there had once been desks and computers, Amber remembered, were now just remnants of melted plastic, destroyed equipment.

Eloise demanded again for her prisoners to reveal all that took place on their previous visit to Eagle Mountain, intent on knowing every finer detail.

Ellie was being held by Axel and some guards, squirming in their tight grip, distressed but trying to also be brave, for Jack, anxious about what was going to happen.

In fact, Amber realized, Ellie's presence there seemed to only be that of a hostage, Eloise 'using' Ellie in order to get to Jack. Ellie could be of no direct assistance with explaining anything about Eagle Mountain. She was aware of its existence of course she had never been inside. Amber and Jack certainly had and clearly Ram had also visited, although it was a great mystery what had occurred - and when.

Whatever the explanation, Amber made a connection – none of the other prisoners who had been left behind in the city under the Guardian had ever been to Eagle Mountain either.

Amber thought of Patsy, Ryan, Cloe, Tai San, KC, and of course Bray, who had all been on the initial visit to the observatory. Was Eagle Mountain partly responsible in some way for their disappearance? Had they been abducted by others, intent on questioning them about what they knew?

Eloise was particularly focused on Jack, who had played a pivotal role in the original reactivation of the computers and the subsequent transmission they received from an orbiting satellite. If he could achieve so much before, she was certain he could assist her this time.

Amber wanted to resist Eloise – to stand up to her. But she was concerned by the threats Eloise had made, telling them that if they did not co-operate, then she would order the Guardian to do something ominous to the Mall Rats and their newfound friends back at the mall.

Eloise was dangerous but also methodical, Amber thought, recognizing she had covered herself well, having hostages in two places, with the group at Eagle Mountain and the rest of the prisoners in the city.

"What's taking so long, Ram?" Eloise urged. "I thought you knew the access code. To Level 2?"

"I'm almost there," Ram replied. He had been working on a control panel on the wall which had been hidden in a solid compartment and had survived the explosion that had taken place during the visit by the Mall Rats in the past.

"It's been a long time," Ram said, trying different codes on the touch-screen panel. "I can't remember how to get in."

"Something tells me you're stalling. Try harder, or we'll start losing hostages."

"I'm doing the best I can," Ram replied.

"Well, it's not good enough!"

Eloise glared witheringly, frustrated by Ram's lack of progress – or deliberate resistance - and advanced towards him, her guards following closely behind her.

"Or you could start losing fingers, Ram… And then limbs. I'll tear you apart, piece by piece, till there's nothing left. Not even your name. Every trace of you can be erased."

"I'm trying. It's not easy working in these 'conditions'."

"It'll be far more difficult if you fail me. Kami has given me authority to do whatever I feel is necessary."

"I would be surprised if someone of his intelligence would underestimate that I could be of much more value to you alive - than dead," Ram said.

Ram hadn't exactly revealed anything about his past, deciding that he would play it all closely to his chest. And he silently cringed if he had perhaps given too much information, confirming that he indeed knew Kami, or at least of him.

Eloise suddenly thrust out an arm and began squeezing the side of Ram's face in her fingers, her long, immaculate nails digging into Ram's cheek.

"Don't let it go to your head, Ram! Just because you think you have a value to Kami, that doesn't make you more important than the others. You have no value to me! You're not indispensable!"

To make her point, Eloise dug her fingernails even deeper into Ram's face – and then she pulled away, Ram groaning, clutching the side of his cheek, now bleeding from cuts, red welts showing where Eloise's fingers had been.

"If you think that's the way to try and get me to help you," Ram bellowed. "then you're very much mistaken!"

He was sick and tired of all he had suffered since being held captive and instinctively felt there had been a slight shift in the power balance and that for all the threats, due to the knowledge and data he held in his memory cells, he would face no harm.

"Oh, I have a few other ways. Axel – break his left hand," Eloise calmly ordered. "Slowly."

"Pleasure," Axel replied, striding forwards to Ram.

"Wait! I suddenly remembered how to get in," Ram admitted, glaring resentfully at Eloise, less confident on the value of the currency of his knowledge.

"I thought you would," Eloise grinned. "It's amazing what you can achieve when you put your mind to it."

"You have no idea," Ram muttered, sure she would be amazed at the real power of Ram's mind which he felt was stronger than any of his beloved computers.

"Oh, Ram… You made me chip a nail," Eloise sighed, frowning in exaggerated disappointment, examining her fingernails. "Don't ever make me lose my patience again!"

Ram punched in a code on the touch-screen panel, his other hand still cradling his face, covering his wounds.

In a screech of rending metal, the entire back wall beside the control panel suddenly began shuddering, sliding open, loud cranking, mechanical noises shaking the very foundations of the building. The wall was incredibly thick, Amber could see as it gradually moved back, several metres across in width, made of different layers of metal and concrete. Amber marvelled at what power and engineering would be required to shift the enormous load – and wondered what on earth was on the other side. This is an area the Mall Rats had never ventured into during their time at Eagle Mountain, or even knew had existed.

Had Ram been telling the truth all the time, Amber considered? She recalled how he described uncovering other levels in Eagle Mountain, discovering adult technologies that he ended up adapting for his own purposes in the Technos.

Jack and Ellie swallowed nervously as the wall stopped sliding, and clearly shared the same growing unease as Amber.

"There you go – Level 2," Ram said, indicating the opening that had appeared and giving Eloise an insincere smile. "It's all yours. I hope it makes you very happy."

"It's beginning to. Lead the way," Eloise ordered Ram, who reluctantly stepped through the opening and into total darkness.

Ellie, Jack and Amber were shoved by Axel and the guards toward the gap where the wall had been.

The group cautiously made its way down an angled slope, their presence casting looming shadows on the walls, Amber wondering what was awaiting them.

* * *

They passed through a series of corridors, twisting and turning on occasion, and as they travelled - as if descending into the depths of the very earth itself - ambient sidelights in the ceilings and floors dimly lit the otherwise gloomy corridors, set off by sensors detecting their presence.

From earlier 'briefings', Eloise was aware that the area they were in was an old nuclear bunker and reflected as they advanced down the corridors the irony that for all the adults thought they could survive a nuclear war, they weren't as thorough with their preparations for the apocalypse the 'virus' brought.

Ram led them to a central area in the complex, much larger than the upper level hidden in the observatory building above ground they had previously been to.

Amber found it incredible to think this other level existed, down below, that it had been there all the time, beneath the very feet of Amber and the Mall Rats when they had stood above in the ground floor of the observatory long ago.

Lights automatically switched on as the group entered the main room of Level 2 – Amber noticing United Nations symbols on the walls of the chamber.

"*Listen very carefully to what I am about to say -*" an adult voice suddenly spoke out, very loudly, from speakers in the ceiling.

"That's it – the same voice we heard before!" Jack exclaimed, recognizing the voice from the pre-recorded message the Mall Rats had heard in the past.

"Sssh!" Eloise hushed him, listening attentively to the message.

"*You must have now found the antidote. In this room are technicians who will be able to help you survive. They have been well trained and are protected from the outside world by the hibernation chambers you see before you...*"

So it was true, Amber thought, spotting several cryogenic hibernation chambers, almost identical in appearance to the ones Jack and Ellie had discovered in the lower levels of the hospital building at Arthurs Air Force Base. However, unlike what the recorded adult voice was announcing – these hibernation pods appeared to be completely empty.

"*You must use the antidote in your possession on the adults in this room. First, revive them by pressing the green button on the outer part of the chambers. When they wake up, you can administer them the antidote. You will also see in this room special helmets that the technicians will know how to operate. They are connected to a sophisticated network that will enable other adults around the world to communicate with each other."*

There was no sign of any 'helmets' anywhere – but that was no surprise, Amber considered, Ram having told them on the island that he had taken the virtual reality space helmets from the base at Eagle Mountain and adapted them for his own 'Paradise' computer program. And he couldn't disguise traces of guilt in his expression as the voice continued.

"Do not be afraid. There is still hope. The human race will survive, thanks to the efforts of children like you. Awaken the technicians – they will know what to do next. To replay this message, ask the voice activated computer to repeat the announcement."

The last part of the message resonated around the complex, all the occupants of the room exchanging surprised glances at what they had heard – with the exception of Ram, who listened, impatiently, waiting for the end of the message.

"I've heard it all before – every time you step in this room, it plays that announcement. I'm sick and tired of how many times I've heard that voice. There seemed to be no way of turning it off."

"It is exactly as Kami described it would be," Eloise said, looking around the room in reverence. "Or it would have been, had you not been so greedy and taken away most of the equipment."

Several workstations were gathered in the centre of the complex. The computer hardware, disused from the adult times, was covered in dust. But Amber could see some gaps on the desks and some unconnected wiring left over, from where there had obviously previously been some other computers, no doubt having been removed by Ram and the Technos.

Amber assimilated the message that had just been played. She had to give the adults some credit, the authorities having clearly put in place emergency contingency plans during the pandemic.

She thought of that first pre-recorded message the Mall Rats had heard on their initial visit to the observatory, the voice telling them to listen carefully as it gave them instructions how to find clues to an antidote to the virus, the adults having apparently run out of time to manufacture it.

So that was what they intended, Amber reflected, having learned that the next phase of the adult plan was for the surviving children to have brought the antidote to the adults in Level 2 of Eagle Mountain so some of them could be revived. But what would have happened after that point, Amber wondered, had the adults been successfully awoken from the hibernation chambers in this very room?

Like Amber, Jack was also silently speculating why the Mall Rats hadn't previously heard any message outlining details of Level 2 and wondered if the explosion was no accident, some kind of malfunction during the last visit to the mysterious observatory.

"What happened to the 'technicians' that the message talked about?" Amber asked Ram - who suddenly looked coy and avoided eye contact.

"I'd rather not say."

"Say it," Eloise demanded.

"They didn't make it. Most of the hibernation chambers had already failed when I got here, the adults inside were long gone. I had to do some sophisticated reverse engineering to figure out how the cryogenic process worked – I didn't want the same thing to happen to me. Let's just say I made a few tests on the chambers that were here."

"So you could put yourself to sleep for all eternity – I know what really happened, Ram," Eloise smiled wickedly, giving Ram a knowing look – almost with a hint of admiration at what she believed Ram had really done.

Amber shuddered, wondering if the situation had been truly as Ram described - or if something more ominous had actually taken place, resulting in the hibernation chambers now being empty, if Ram had possibly done some sort of testing on the technicians who had once been in the room.

It was incredible, Amber reflected, to think there could have been adults, locked away in cryogenic freeze and awaiting the day the surviving children would come to rescue them, though that day never came.

"Well, it's the end of the line. I got you this far, did my part of the bargain," Ram said. "I hope you didn't have a wasted trip, Eloise, that it was all worth it. Congratulations – you've got yourself a pre-recorded message to hear and a mostly empty room."

"Not quite. Take us down to Level 3," Eloise ordered.

"Level 3?" Ram asked, puzzled by the reference.

"Don't play games with me, Ram. I'm not one of your computers you can enjoy controlling. Kami knows there is another level. And so do you."

"You're wrong – and so is Kami. There is no Level 3!" Ram insisted. "And even if there was – I wouldn't know the passcode to get in!"

"How do you know it's protected by a passcode then?"

Eloise grinned. She had got him – Ram momentarily lost for an answer.

"I just guessed there would have to be some sort of a code."

"Of course you did," Eloise said, not believing a word. "Well, guess what happens if you don't find the way into Level 3. Here's a clue – you won't ever step foot out of this room again… And the same goes for you 'Mall Rats'."

Eloise turned to address Amber, Jack and Ellie, being restrained by Axel and the guards.

"You found a way to reactivate the computers in the past - and I'm counting on your efforts and co-operation again."

"Do your own dirty work!" Ellie fumed, struggling in Axel's tight grip.

Eloise looked at her watch, a beautiful antique piece around her delicate wrist that would have cost a fortune in the adult days.

"I will give you until midnight. If you don't find a way into Level 3 in that time, I will contact the Guardian and we will make the first of our offerings to Zoot!"

"You're a monster!" Amber cried out to Eloise.

"If I was you, I wouldn't waste your breath calling me names, Amber!" Eloise shouted back, crossing briskly to the doors, leaving Axel and the guards to watch over their hostages. "You're running out of time!"

CHAPTER TWENTY-FOUR

"It's incredible," Aras gasped, reaching out his hand carefully – and touching the desk, feeling himself imbued with divine energies.

"That's where it happened. The place history was made," Ebony confirmed.

She had taken Aras and the other Zootist acolytes under her command on a personal tour of the city, having been instructed to do so by the Guardian.

The Zootists were gripped by Ebony's oration in the temple at the mountain complex back on the island but now the aim, the Guardian had explained, was to lead some of the most important converts on pilgrimages to places where momentous incidents had occurred and to discover more of Zoot's life.

By regaling Aras and the acolytes with her recollections – they could in turn spread the word in the future to others, relay the deeds and tales that had gone on, the proof of Zoot's existence – and mythology.

There was also a degree of concern about rumours that some of the Mall Rats had been encountered in the ghostly city and Ebony was intrigued to check it all out, though she didn't hold any credence to what had been reported by some of the followers who had returned from a reconnaissance trip earlier, and she wondered if they were victims of all the distorted mind games and brainwashing they had been exposed to for so long.

Ebony drove around the city in the same vehicle that had been carried on the front of the *Sea Ghost*, having been adapted by the Zootists to closely resemble the legendary vehicle used by Zoot himself, along with Ebony, in the fabled early days of the Locos. It even had a railing on the back to hold and a place to stand, like Zoot's police car had.

It reminded Ebony of the old times – the thrill of having the streets to herself, the freedom to go where she pleased – a powerful vehicle under her control, and a group of loyal followers to lead.

A part of Ebony had considered making a break for it. She was tempted to dispatch Aras and the acolytes to one of the buildings in the city, telling them Zoot had performed some worthy deed there, distracting them by some pretence - which would enable her to seize the car and escape.

However by doing so, Ebony would be left on her own in the world and she estimated with the city in the complete grip of Eloise's forces, spearheaded by the Guardian's Zootists, Ebony would have few places to go before it was likely she was apprehended.

No, for now, the best thing Ebony concluded was to stick with the Zootists. It gave her a constant supply of food and shelter, growing influence – and a chance to rise up the ranks under Eloise's leadership.

Ebony was positioning herself well. She had given herself a platform to build upon, as she had done before in a different time, when bedding in with Ram and the Technos – and when falling in with Blake on the island.

Ironically, Ebony's strategy was so similar to the one she had followed when hooking up with Zoot himself, back in the beginning. Then, she had identified who was the rising power – Zoot and his Locos - and made sure she was involved with them, proving herself indispensable. It was a far better route than trying to survive on her own in the dangerous world.

She had a context, a point of reference – and in a way, aimed to repeat history, this time by showing to Eloise she could bring so much to the table. And by demonstrating her worth, the many skills and attributes she possessed, Ebony could gradually seize control of her own future. And perhaps even depose Eloise.

She had to follow the Guardian's orders for now – but the time would soon come, Ebony just knew it, when she would be promoted and one day would be the one giving out the commands, wielding power and influence, her future in her hands. As it had been during her days with Zoot, and after, in the Locos.

Ebony had already taken Aras and her group to the rail yard, a favoured hangout of Zoot. Nearby, in the industrial part of the city, several battles had been fought back in the day between the Locos and their main rivals of the time, the Demon Dogs. Ebony had gone to the streets where the fighting had occurred, recounting the battles to Aras and the others, who listened with intrigue and awe as Ebony described the spectacle of Zoot laying waste to his enemies, with Ebony by his side.

Now, they were in the old school that Zoot – then Martin – had attended, with Ebony as a classmate.

Jaffa had also gone to the school – before restyling himself as the Guardian.

Ebony described more details to Aras and the attentive members under her command about that fateful, pivotal day when Martin stood up on his desk and started shouting out the phrase which was destined to shape history, or so he had believed - 'Power and Chaos!'

He had risen up against the teacher, Zoot aware times were rapidly changing – and that the kids in the class, let alone around the world, would need to save themselves. The adults had nothing left to teach them anymore. Their time was over. The future belonged to the young. The revolution had begun.

"There. You can even see Zoot's name on the desk," Ebony pointed out, showing Aras and the rest the graffiti on what had been Martin's desk, Martin having carved his preferred nickname, Zoot, with a flick knife.

Beside the name of Zoot etched on the desk was a heart symbol – and Ebony's own name, cut into the surface by Zoot himself.

Ebony had lured Zoot, reeling him in with her good looks and persistent attentions in her pursuit of him. Martin had been bedding Trudy, also at school and in the same class, but Ebony managed to ensnare him as her own, knowing he would influence the future with his powerful oratory and charisma – and she would need to be with him.

The memories came flooding back to her. She had been so intent to survive then – and was still so now.

Although the school had been looted, the classroom was almost exactly as it had been. The desks were mostly in the same place, the atmosphere similar. The textbooks that used to be in there were no more, having been burned, a long time ago, by Zoot.

"There's your name, too!" Aras commented, spellbound, noticing Ebony's on Zoot's desk.

"Fancy that," Ebony smiled modestly, aware that Aras and the Zootists felt that the classroom was a hallowed place.

For so long, Ebony's own role in the mythology had been deliberately downplayed by the Guardian and Eloise, feeling that presenting Ebony as a valuable part of the faith served no purpose to aid their own ambitions. By contrast, Ebony had been excluded, shut out, from the legend – so much so that when she first met Aras and the other converts on the island, with Ram, they didn't even recognize her or know who she was.

Ebony decided she would change that by building her own legend to ensure she also took her place in history. And by proving herself to Eloise, Ebony was beginning to play more and more an important role in rallying the faithful. Eloise, as well as the Guardian, came to appreciate Ebony could be a major asset in spreading the religion. Accordingly, her own deeds and position were officially recognized, Ebony being given more of the respect and acknowledgment she felt she deserved.

Aras and the other converts in the classroom looked upon Ebony, as much as the desk Zoot had sat at, with reverence. To them, she was a living relic, a real human artefact from Zoot's time. To be in her presence was a privilege. Almost a blessing. A life altering experience.

For Ebony, the religion was nothing more than a means to an end. Maybe a ticket to the Collective, who by all accounts held the balance of power.

She felt overall that Aras and the 'converts' were being duped, totally used by Eloise. Unlike the Guardian, who genuinely seemed to believe in the religion with the utmost sincerity.

In the past, Ebony had considered he had exaggerated his religious behaviour, playing at being insane – but now, she believed the Guardian had well and truly gone over the edge into another realm.

The Guardian had thrown himself into his mission of converting the mall into a temple, from which he could preach the faith. He had some of his followers gather together some of the remnants of the Techno era – and had ceremoniously burned a pile of reality space headsets, posters of Ram, and computer equipment. Technology would have a minimal role in the Guardian's world, he had proudly stated, declaring that the greatest power was their faith.

Ebony had to go along with the Guardian's commands, Eloise having instructed her to stay in the city, to work with him.

She felt Eloise almost wanted the Guardian to keep away from what she was doing at Eagle Mountain, Eloise having given him a series of tasks to carry out, not least of which was to monitor their prisoners, Emma, Darryl and Gel – in 'the name of Zoot.' Ebony was a gifted manipulator herself to read all the signs and was certain Eloise was purposefully distracting the Guardian, for whatever reasons she had, to keep him behind in the city.

She wondered at times if she was somehow gradually being brainwashed herself because she felt disappointed that she hadn't been selected to accompany Eloise on her mission to Eagle Mountain. She had no idea what Eloise hoped to achieve by going there but it resulted in a feeling of not being accepted and it troubled Ebony.

It was ironic she had once been intimate with Blake, Eloise's brother, and now was trusted by Eloise herself, who had allowed Ebony to wield some powers and influence of her own, many freedoms in fact, promising her great rewards should she continue to show Eloise her loyalty.

As long as she kept her sanity, all too aware of how many others had succumbed to the slippery slope that was the cultish ways of the Guardian, Ebony's future looked promising, which is all that mattered.

"How about we go back in the streets," Ebony suggested. "I'll show you all where Zoot and I used to drive, looking for strays. And who knows – we might catch a few ourselves."

For a split second she caught herself by the reference, imagining her status, that she would quickly rise up higher through the ranks if she managed to round up some of the Mall Rats who had been reported as being seen but equally considered the rumoured sightings all absolutely crazy, so far fetched, the product of attrition, of a brainwashed imagination.

Ebony led Aras and the acolytes back to the police car waiting outside the school, recalling how she had ridden with Zoot in the past, hunting the streets for lone survivors – 'strays' – who hadn't been part of any of the tribes that were forming.

Some of the strays were absorbed into the Locos. Others became slaves, traded at tribal gatherings. The unlucky ones met the full wrath of Zoot.

The Guardian had also been disturbed by reported sightings of Bray, Trudy and Lex. Ebony was skeptical, sure they were still on the island, far, far away. But she reassured him that if they were in the city, disrupting all the Guardian and Eloise had planned, then they had to be stopped. And Ebony was the one to do it.

She clambered onto the back of the police car, striking the roof twice, to let Aras, driving inside, know she was ready.

"Let's go!" Ebony screamed, the acolytes in the car responded by roaring in enthusiasm, whooping it up, adrenalin flowing, eager to prove themselves to Zoot – and to Ebony.

The hunt was on.

CHAPTER TWENTY-FIVE

Sammy coughed, clearing his throat – not too subtly, as soon as he entered the kitchen in Trudy's old house.

"Are you okay, Sammy?" Salene wondered.

May and Salene had been preparing lunch for everyone, opening the last of their supplies, a few tins of beans that had been taken from the *Nemo*.

"I was actually hoping to get some advice from you both," Sammy admitted, having got their attention.

"Of course. Anytime," May reassured him.

"But it's – a bit embarrassing," Sammy said sheepishly.

"Let me guess. Does it start with the letter L?" May asked.

"That's amazing. How'd you know?"

"When you get older, you get to notice a few things," May explained, exchanging a discreet smile with Salene.

They had both picked up that Sammy seemed to have developed a crush on Lottie. They were fairly close in age but Lottie was far more streetsmart and older in life's experience than Sammy, who still possessed much of his childhood innocence.

"Do you think – *anyone else* may have noticed?" Sammy wondered, afraid others – particularly Lottie, may have.

"No, your secret's safe with us," Salene smiled. "So how can we help you?"

"I wanted to ask – how do you know when you're in love with someone? And what do you – do about it?"

Salene and May exchanged another glance, recognizing it was the same question they had both experienced with each other back on the island – and they had answered it by becoming a couple, opening their hearts to each other.

"*You just know*. And you just follow your heart." May answered. "You see someone. And you think – I feel so happy being around that person. It's like a bond. You care for how they are. Miss being with them. Your life is enriched – better – when you're with that person."

"Is that how you feel about Salene?" Sammy enquired.

"Yes," May replied, as she continued preparing lunch.

"So, say there was someone here that I loved. The thing is, I'm scared to admit it. What if they don't feel the same way?"

"If they don't, then you can still be friends. But what if they do feel the same? Someone has to be brave and take that first step," Salene advised.

"Or not," Lottie said, entering the room, baby Bray in her arms, Brady by her side – Lottie having been listening from the other side of the door.

Sammy went bright red, feeling exposed, humiliated.

"I was – I was just getting some advice," Sammy grinned sheepishly before continuing carefully. "You didn't hear anything... did you?"

"I was just about to ask the same question," Lottie replied.

"Really?" Sammy said eagerly.

"Is everyone deaf around here or something? I just can't handle it anymore," Lottie sighed in growing frustration.

"Handle what?" May said.

Lottie indicated Brady, who was crying loudly, mopping the tears in her eyes with her fingers. Mr Floppsy, Trudy's beloved cuddly rabbit, had suffered an accident, one of his arms torn, the stitches loose.

"What happened?" Salene asked.

"I just tried to take this rabbit thing or whatever it is from her - and the arm came off. Brady's been freaking out ever since."

Salene crossed to scoop Brady up in her arms. "Hey – everything'll be okay. We'll get Mr Floppsy fixed."

"I want Mommy," Brady sniffed, missing Trudy.

"She'll be back soon. So will Uncle Bray and the others. I promise."

"They're taking a bit long – aren't they?" Sammy said uneasily.

"They'll have their reasons," May answered reassuringly. "We just have to wait here and be patient – that's all."

"That's easier said than done," Lottie said – giving a glance to Sammy, aware he was checking her out.

"Are you hungry?" he asked, smouldering slightly and Salene and May cast a slightly amused look at heaven. "See anything you might fancy?"

"No," Lottie replied. "I'd prefer some time alone."

Salene watched Lottie exit and felt sorry for Sammy. And Lottie. Matters of the heart were never easy, Salene knew from personal experience, and Sammy had better start getting used to that truth, as difficult as it was. Lottie, too, would have to learn how to deal with Sammy's attentions. It was all a part of life's lessons, growing up, Salene believed.

Hugging Brady lovingly, comforting her - Salene, May and Sammy only hoped Trudy would be back for her daughter soon and that the others, having gone to the city, were safe and well, wherever they currently were.

CHAPTER TWENTY-SIX

'ZOOT WORSHIPS LEX'

"There – how's that?" Connor asked, stepping back to look at the words he had just spray-painted on the wall.

"Perfect," Lex replied. "I like it. Nice one."

Bray smiled slightly to himself. This wasn't about fuelling Lex's ego although he clearly felt flattered by the graffiti. It was more about trying to cause as much disruption as they could to help counter whatever it was that Eloise and the Guardian were planning, as well as an attempt at drawing their adversaries out of the mall.

After their first experience with the Zootists, Bray's group had stuck together, cautiously moving around the city spray-painting slogans such as *THE SUPREME MOTHER RULES, THE MALL RATS DEFEAT THE COLLECTIVE, ZOOT IS DEAD BUT BRAY LIVES, THE GUARDIAN BROUGHT THE VIRUS.*

Bray and Jay agreed, along with Lex, that they didn't yet stand a chance to lead a direct rescue attempt on the mall, where they had learned some of their tribe were being kept prisoner. So they decided to implement some propaganda as the first tactic based upon an old military strategy - divide and rule.

"That's the last of the spray paint," Lex said, shaking his own can, which had run out, judging by the empty sounds it was making. "Pity – just as I was starting to enjoy myself."

Lex stepped back, admiring the tag he had just painted.

"I wonder what they'll make of it?" Lia wondered, also examining Lex's latest graffiti. "One thing's for sure, it's not a Van Gogh."

"What tribe is he in?" Lex said. "Never heard of him."

The others watched with a degree of amusement, wondering if Lex was just playing with Lia by the mischievous glint in his eye as he continued examining the cartoon style images he had sprayed on the wall of Zoot, wearing his cap and goggles, his eyes shut – and tongue sticking out.

"That looks really weird, Lex," Trudy said.

"What? It's a masterpiece," Lex replied.

"It'll get them thinking for sure," Bray reflected, gazing around.

They had already hit several areas in the city, daubing on walls and sides of buildings in large letters which could disrupt and confuse anyone who might notice them, let alone drawing anyone out to check what was behind their propaganda campaign.

The group had gone to a looted DIY store, its contents strewn around, the shop having been heavily vandalized many times in the past by previous visitors. Luckily, they found some leftover canisters of spray paint - and a large solitary paint pot, strangely still standing in the very spot on the shelf it had been put during the adult era, even retaining its original 'on sale' special price tag.

But now they had used up their supplies, they decided to go on to the next phase of their plan.

"So - I guess it's time we go our own ways" Jay said.

The others agreed. They were to split into three separate groups.

Jay was to scout the perimeters of the mall itself, believing he could knock out the electrical transformer connected to the overhead power lines, which could immediately cut all power going into the mall and cause further disruption to the Guardian and his forces.

"Sure you won't electrocute yourself?" Trudy had asked him earlier.

"The only ones who'll get a shock will be the Zootists," Jay had reassured the group. "I was a Techno, remember. And I was well trained."

"Remember - abort at any time if you get into any danger and we'll rendezvous at Trudy's house," Bray said. "If we encounter problems there, then let's use Lex's place as a back up," Bray said.

While Jay checked out the mall, Bray, Lex and Lia were going to retrace their steps to where they had first encountered the Zootists earlier in the day, intent on retrieving the vehicle the Zootists had used before they dispersed.

The three of them intended to go on a reconnaissance mission to Eagle Mountain to check the area out.

"Take care, Trudy," Bray said, giving her a hug as they were all about to split up. "And remember, brief Salene, May and the others, then wait, just lay low until we get back."

"As long as you all get back," Trudy replied nervously.

"We'll be fine," Bray tried to reassure her. "Just make sure you take good care of yourselves."

"Don't worry, we will," Connor said.

"I've got my handsome 'prince' to look after me," Trudy added, stepping back from Bray and standing beside Connor, the two of them holding each other's hands romantically.

The group wished each other safe travels and the best of luck, then split up, going their separate ways.

Connor and Trudy set off en route to the suburbs.

With her lover by her side, Trudy felt a surge of hope, a sense of wellbeing. Together, they could take on anything.

They had hardly left the city and environs when out of nowhere, Connor suddenly grabbed Trudy, clasping his hand firmly over her mouth.

"What are you doing!" Trudy shouted, her voice garbled and muffled by Connor's grasp, her eyes wide open, in sudden shock and apprehension at what was happening, having first thought Connor was carrying out some sort of practical joke.

"Keep quiet! And you won't get hurt!" Connor threatened, making it clear he was absolutely serious.

CHAPTER TWENTY-SEVEN

Amber paced around, placing her hands against the walls, feeling for any indents or grooves with her fingers which might signify the presence of other concealed hatches to any more hidden control panels in the complex - something - anything she could use to help with their plight.

"There's got to be a way out of here," Amber said, searching the room intently.

"You could always find a shovel and try and dig your way through the mountain," Ram mocked caustically, amused by Amber's persistent efforts to escape.

Eloise was apparently checking other areas of the compound and had left guards stationed outside the door while Amber, Ram, Jack and Ellie continued to find an access code to Level 3.

"I will, if I have to. I'll try everything, whatever it takes. I'm not just going to sit around on my backside - and let others do all the hard work."

Amber was alluding to the fact Ram had been leaning back disinterestedly in an office chair by a computer, arms resting behind his head, like he had no other care in the world.

"I'm busy – thinking. You should try it one day."

Ram smiled patronizingly at her.

Amber decided she wouldn't waste any more time with him. Ram was full of mysteries, a constant source of surprise and so often irritation. Amber had more important things to be getting on with than continuously prod Ram to try and get him to help. He had rebuffed all her attempts and seemed more content to do his own thing – even if that seemed to be to do nothing.

Jack and Ellie were at the touch-screen control panel that had been found so far in the room.

A buzz type sound emitted, indicating an error - and telling them the latest code they had used hadn't worked.

"Oh, come on!" Jack pleaded with the control panel, readying himself for another attempt.

"Are you sure you don't have any idea, Ram?" Ellie asked.

"Positive. Believe me. I wouldn't go through all this if I knew. What would be the point?"

Amber continued pacing in growing frustration as Jack tried a few different options.

Ram scoffed, a little petulant at his apparent logic.

"If you can do any better - you're welcome to try," Jack snapped disdainfully.

Ellie helped out with other suggestions – as well as trying to remember the codes they had keyed in to date, all of which had been unsuccessful.

"How about... Project Aquarius?" Amber offered, recalling the name of a secret adult project Jack had come across on one of the computers at Arthurs Air Force Base.

"No – we've used that one already," Ellie reminded her.

They had gone through everything they could think of – Project Eden, Project Eagle, the *Jzhao Li*, United Nations, the names of politicians and famous adults they could remember from the past. Animal names, parts of the city, names from Greek myths. They were running out of ideas – and time.

"How about you're all starting to freak me out?" Ram said, frustrated.

Jack keyed in various words Ram had mentioned on the control panel, just on the off chance it would work somehow, by a miracle, and Ram sighed.

"How come no-one ever understands where I'm coming from?"

"Doesn't take a genius to work that one out, Ram," Jack replied.

"That's exactly what I'm talking about. Genius. I'm telling you, I've spent my whole life suffering, with no-one on my intellectual level," Ram claimed.

He looked sick as Jack keyed in 'intellectual'. Then 'genius'. Once more the error sound was the only response.

"Come on, step away for a bit," Ellie suggested, leading Jack from the control panel, aware that he was the most disconsolate of all the others at their lack of progress to date. "Let's clear our minds."

"Shouldn't be too hard," Ram goaded.

"Shut up, Ram!" Ellie shouted at him.

"Charming – Jack obviously doesn't like you just for your manners."

Eloise strided in.

"I thought I would check on... progress. How are you all getting on?" Eloise glowered, looking at her watch.

"Not very well, if you want to know the truth," Ram answered. Then registering Eloise glaring at him, he qualified - "I mean with each other."

"I would have thought you wouldn't waste your time worrying about that. There aren't too many hours left of the deadline," Eloise warned.

"We're doing our best, Eloise. We really are," Amber insisted.

"It would be so unfortunate for you and your friends if it transpires it isn't good enough," she snarled, then left briskly out the door, calling back, 'You have less than four hours!"

"Let's try - Pandorax," Ellie said, keying in the name of the chemical and pharmaceutical manufacturer the Mall Rats thought was involved in accidentally unleashing the virus – but getting another error code warning sound.

"Pandorax? That was all just a cover," Ram advised.

"What do you mean?" Amber demanded.

"Do you honestly believe the adults were wiped out by accident? By some kind of virus?" Ram questioned.

"Don't you?" Ellie wondered.

"I've learned not to believe everything people tell me. And neither should you."

"How can we believe you now, then?" Amber pointed out.

"Believe this. The adults knew what was coming, well before it happened. Why do you think they put all this in place?" Ram indicated the empty hibernation chambers and the computer terminals in the complex.

"What are you exactly talking about?" Jack wondered.

"Space exploration… experiments and mining of passing asteroids… Research into nuclear fission... other new forms of energy… Colonizing planets… developing sophisticated weapons," Ram offered.

"You're not seriously implying that it was no accident? That the virus – was somehow - deliberate?" Amber questioned, shocked by the thought billions of lives could have ended intentionally.

She had often questioned the theory herself but was never one to pay much attention to any conspiracies. But Ram appeared to have his own theories, as well as holding more information than he had revealed to date.

"I'm just saying that the entire world… all the adults… had been worrying about some sort of nuclear catastrophe. For years. But what if you wanted to wipe out your enemies without them even knowing what was coming – and leave all the cities and resources still standing, unaffected? Did it ever cross your mind to think we could be the only survivors of a Third World War? One fought with invisible weapons - waged by an unparalleled chemical, bacterial warfare? In my experience there's usually no such thing as an accident. There's always a reason for everything that happens."

"Are you trying to help us – or scare the hell out of us?" Jack asked, shaken by Ram's version of events.

"All I'm saying is... that back in the day, no-one could predict what kind of weapons might be used if there ever was a World War Three. But one thing was for sure. If ever there was a World War Four, then it would be fought with sticks and stones," Ram reflected.

"What - you think there's been a World War Three?" Ellie asked incredulously.

"Look at the way we've all been living since the adults were wiped out. That's all I'm saying," Ram replied.

"Or maybe you're just stalling, Ram," Amber commented.

"What would I gain from doing that?"

"Your freedom?" Amber enquired. "In return for providing details of whatever it is you know at the eleventh hour - and you'd sure be a hero in Eloise's eyes?"

"The truth is, Amber, that I don't know the code."

"I've got an idea – but it's a long shot," Jack suggested.

He took a keyboard from one of the computer terminals to the wall where the control panel stood.

He had recalled how his Dad configured passwords, using the numerical equivalents of letters. The number 1 on the keyboard was above the letter Q – but could also represent A and Z, arranged in rows below that, the key for number 2 was above the letters W, S and X, and so on.

This got Ram's interest and he crossed to watch Jack in growing intrigue, who was now keying in Eagle Mountain.

"It might be better if you try 31593 79765186," Ram suggested.

The others exchanged confused glances.

"What are you on about?" Ellie said.

"You guys… try and keep up with me, will you - please!" Ram sighed intolerantly.

Jack was examining his keyboard. And he was totally amazed at the speed of Ram's mind - and that he could work out the numbers and appropriate letters in his head.

"Hate to say it but I've got to admit you're pretty good, Ram," Jack said.

"Why don't you key the words - or the numbers - and we'll see how good you are yourself," Ram replied.

The others watched as Jack keyed in EAGLE MOUNTAIN, resulting in a tone signifying it was still incorrect.

"Now let's try the numbers," Ram said, gazing intently at Jack keying in the equivalent number keys above the corresponding letters that made up the words, using the old fashioned 'Qwerty' style keyboard he was holding for reference.

For once, there was no error sound that characterized all previous attempts. Instead, the entire wall beside the control panel suddenly began to shake, slowly opening - stale, dusty air exploding out into the room they were standing in from the other side, having previously been sealed by an air pocket.

"Genius. Pure genius. For those not able to keep up with me and Jack here, that's 536872," Ram said, exchanging high-fives with Jack and whooping it up, while Amber and the others braced themselves at the prospect of what they soon might be about to discover.

CHAPTER TWENTY-EIGHT

Trudy was horrified. She continued to struggle, squirming with everything she had, desperate to be free from Connor's iron grip.

Since her capture, Connor had dragged Trudy away from their intended destination, en route elsewhere.

Tears welled up in Trudy's eyes, she was shocked and devastated by Connor's betrayal – whom she had trusted, giving him her heart – even letting him be in the close company of her daughter.

Connor suppressed any remorse he felt for his double-cross of her. Trudy had completely fallen for him – and his deception – and though he had genuinely enjoyed getting to know her, and the many bonus pleasures they had shared, Connor judged now was the time to strike, while the two of them were alone, away from the others. To bring Trudy in. To claim his reward.

He had been partially truthful in what he had told Trudy of his life and who he was. His name really was Connor and his parents had owned the *Nemo*, Connor having spent much of his childhood aboard, travelling with them, learning to sail. The photos on the wall inside the cabin were real.

Connor never believed in his line of work that it was a good idea to try to adopt another persona. Pretending to be someone completely else posed too many risks, Connor felt, having to go under a false name or identity, the risks of keeping a fake cover consistent. No – it made his life easier, Connor always considered, to just be himself – which is who he was most comfortable being, after all.

That way Connor could retain most of his true essence and personality, minimizing the deception he played on his victims. None had ever found him out beforehand, Connor only indulging in a few creative explanations and lies along the way to justify the circumstantial reasons he had conveniently met his quarries and got involved in their lives.

He was a bounty hunter, one of the greatest in the region, more likely the very best, he preferred to think, modestly. Most of the survivors out there in the world didn't know who he was, wouldn't have heard of his boat or recognized his face, but those who mattered, the leaders who had the power and influence, knew of Connor and his capabilities, sending him out on various missions to bring in his targets.

Connor was aware of his good looks. Fate – God – his genes - or just random luck, whatever it was – had blessed him with an amazing physique and a handsome appearance, along with an abundance of charm. On many occasions, Connor used all his assets to entrap a love struck girl, feeling like he was some sort of spider, letting them crawl into his web – or his bed – his victim unaware of what was going on until it was too late.

But his greatest weapon was his cunning. Connor was a great reader of people. What made them tick. He could weave his way in and out of a social situation, identifying everyone's strengths, weaknesses, dreams, fears, even their personal habits. Information was his currency, finding clues and assessing rumours, many of which proved to so often be true, leading Connor to capture his intended prey.

He was the ultimate hunter, with the looks of an angel but the mind of a predator, concealing his danger behind his dashing smile.

Trudy suddenly bit Connor's arm, Connor yelling in pain and involuntarily pulling his arm away, reacting instinctively, Trudy breaking out of his grasp.

She ran down the street, overwhelmed, repulsed by Connor's treacherous actions, trying to get away.

Connor grinned, impressed by Trudy's fighting spirit - and the size of the bite mark she had left in his arm.

She had been through a lot in her life and he genuinely respected her. She may have managed to put her days as the 'Supreme Mother' behind her – or so she thought – but Connor wasn't about to let her get away, and he set off in pursuit, chasing after her.

There was much riding on bringing her in, Connor felt, hopeful he could deliver Trudy and the Mall Rats to the Collective and earn the biggest bounty of all from Eloise.

Connor initially went to the island on the *Nemo* with the intention of tracking down Ram. Knowing the Collective had placed a massive price on his head.

He had heard how Ram's home city had been evacuated and rumours Ram was last seen aboard a small boat, along with the Mall Rats, heading out into the harbour. Having searched the coastal regions around the city, there had been no sign of the Mall Rats or their little trawler. That just left the possibility they had gone further afield – with the next nearest landmass being the string of islands to the west. Either that or they had been lost in the unforgiving ocean. There was only one way to find out.

Connor set out on board *Nemo*, crossing the seas, and eventually ended up on the island. He spent weeks sailing around the area, investigating, trying to keep his distance from the Priestess and her tribe, who he perceived to be a considerable threat, avoiding them altogether.

Connor was given permission to continue looking for Ram by Blake, who Connor met aboard Blake's oil rig, a popular rendezvous of slave traders.

Connor had persevered assiduously but it was like Ram had simply disappeared.

Later on, when Connor found that Blake had also vanished, he tried to stay in the area to locate Blake, knowing that finding the leader of the Legion tribe would result in a good reward from Eloise.

In trying to look for Blake – and continuing to seek out Ram – Connor had finally spotted other survivors wandering the coast near the native village – and he sailed the *Nemo* closer to the beach, which led to his initial encounter with Trudy.

He had been ecstatic to discover her identity – and that the tribe she was with were none other than the Mall Rats, who also told him that Ram had made it to the island alive, though he was missing.

Connor earned their trust – and managed to seduce Trudy in the process, genuinely smitten by her looks and personality.

Bray, Lex and Lia had been the only holdouts, resistant to Connor and his charms, but eventually even they had come to trust him more and more. Just like everyone he encountered, Connor reflected. All he needed was time and he was sure he could convince anyone to accept him into their lives. But Bray and Lex, he was aware, still had remnants of doubts.

Running down the street, Connor's longer stride closed the gap on Trudy.

He reached out, knocking Trudy out of step, stumbling, almost falling over, struggling to regain her balance.

"You won't get away," Connor warned her, cornering Trudy against the side of a building. "So it's pointless to even try."

"Why, Connor? Why?!"

She was heartbroken, still unable to believe it.

Suddenly Trudy lashed out, sending a stinging backhand across Connor's face, Connor reeling at the force of the attack, Trudy also clenching her hand, itself aching from her strike. She wasn't going to give in without a fight.

"That hurt," Connor said, menace in his eyes.

"Really? You hurt me!" Trudy cried out.

He shrugged, dragging Trudy toward his intended destination and Trudy still couldn't figure out in her mind where they could possibly be heading. But Connor clearly knew by his purposeful strides.

Unbeknown to anyone at the time - Connor had kept in contact while his boat was moored off the island and was quite aware that the *Sea Ghost* Collective ship was sailing to the mountain base, to pick up Eloise, the Guardian and the forces there. While the ship had been still in range, Connor had told them which Mall Rats were at the native village, communicating with the *Sea Ghost* using *Nemo*'s ship-to-ship radio.

Connor explained how the Mall Rats had split up, with Bray, Amber and the others setting out to Arthurs Air Force Base, the crew of the *Sea Ghost* promising to relay the information to Eloise.

Connor advised against the *Sea Ghost* making an assault on the village, judging the reefs and sandbanks in the area would prove too perilous to the massive vessel, a much larger ship than *Nemo*, which had been able to evade the dangerous obstacles when Connor expertly manoeuvred to finally anchor in the shallows by the beach.

The Priestess and her own tribe also presented formidable resistance, Connor had cautioned, and a direct raid, had the *Sea Ghost* even been able to somehow miraculously bypass the rocks and unload its guards and vehicles, would no doubt result in hefty casualties. Even Blake, with his strong Legion tribe, had avoided an actual confrontation with the Priestess.

Confident of being able to capture any Mall Rats who had gone to Arthurs Air Force Base, the *Sea Ghost* agreed with Connor's premise that an attack on the Priestess and her village would risk too much for too little gain. Connor planned instead to kidnap whoever was available of the Mall Rats in his own time, and bring them to Eloise on board the *Nemo*.

He had come close to making an initial breakaway when he took Trudy out for their first 'date' on board his boat, ostensibly to see a coral reef just off the island.

At one point, he was tempted to lock Trudy in the cabin and sail away with her, to meet up with the *Sea Ghost* before it had left the waters of the island – but Trudy had given him some other temptations he had succumbed to. Connor had also believed if he was patient, he could somehow capture more than just her, knowing that her daughter, the child of Zoot, should also command a high price.

Connor had reacted with some suppressed glee when Bray, Lex and Jay returned to the native village, leading to Connor taking them, along with Trudy, Salene, Brady and the others, on board *Nemo* on its journey to the city.

They were like innocent, trusting lambs, Connor had reflected, when standing at the helm of his boat, taking the Mall Rats to precisely where he wanted to go. He just had to wait for the right moment to let Eloise and the Guardian know of the unwitting prisoners he had brought with him.

Keen not to waste any more time and remain on schedule - Connor picked Trudy up, slung her across his shoulder, holding her, pinning her legs in his strong arms, Trudy yelling in frustrated rage but not giving in, lashing her arms out at Connor's back.

Once, Connor remembered, he had carefully scooped Trudy up in his arms romantically, literally sweeping her off her feet, the two of them laughing as he carried her, wading through the water, to his boat, the couple then spending a perfect, memorable afternoon together off the island.

"Stop struggling!" Connor snapped.

"Where are you taking me?!" Trudy repeated.

"Home, Supreme Mother," Connor said coldly, ignoring Trudy's cries and struggles.

CHAPTER TWENTY-NINE

The wind howled, sweeping across the wide open spaces of the rolling countryside, with even stronger gusts higher up as Bray, Lex and Lia nestled against the side of the hill, trying to keep out of sight of Eloise's guards, visible patrolling in the distance.

They were about a hundred metres from the observatory building, peering over the crest of the incline they were using for shelter to glimpse and monitor the complex.

Lex had insisted on driving the vehicle they had taken from the Zootists to the perimeters of Eagle Mountain, an eerie experience, the only vehicle on the ghostly road, wondering what they would find when they arrived.

Bray remembered when he and Lex had driven that same way in the bus the Mall Rats had once used to make their own original journey to the observatory on the summit.

Only three of them travelling this time round, their car was abandoned about a kilometre out, the round satellite tracking device on the roof of Eagle Mountain visible in the distance, a landmark guiding them where they wanted to go.

The rest of their journey was on foot, cautiously looking out for any indication of Eloise or her Zootist forces.

So far, they had counted eight guards stationed at the main entrance to the observatory. It was almost like they were expecting visitors, Lex commented, and he wondered if any of the Mall Rats were inside or simply the Zootists.

Bray had already scouted the perimeter to see if there was another way in but the only entrance seemed to be the one now heavily guarded before them.

Lia was shivering, not used to the cool brisk winds gusting all around, having not acclimatized, more at home in the hot temperatures of the island she had recently left.

"To think we gave up a tropical paradise for this," Lex muttered, taking off his jacket, wrapping it around Lia's shoulders to help keep her warm.

"Thanks," Lia said, appreciating the gesture. "I really wish the Priestess was here."

"So do I," Lex agreed, with a hint of longing, thinking of the Priestess - and obviously missing her for more than just her company.

"I was meaning the Priestess and her tribe could have been a big help. We could really do with some extra numbers."

"We may not have them - but there might actually be someone else in the region," Bray stated, Lia having given him an idea. "Hawk and the Ecos."

The Eco tribe lived in the forest, the other side of the city, and none of the Mall Rats knew what had befallen them when the city evacuated for fear of the new 'virus' being unleashed by Mega's chemical arsenal. Bray wondered if there was a possibility the Ecos hadn't left their homes and could still be there, in the forest that bordered the region of Eagle Mountain.

The Ecos were a principled people who tried to be at one with nature, eschewing technology and aspiring to live in harmony, physically and spiritually, with their environment. Amber had been taken in by them, long ago, meeting Pride. After being reunited with Bray, the Ecos had become strong allies of the Mall Rats, helping in the resistance that led to the downfall of the Technos. As well as possessing an enviable ethos, they were also more than capable warriors.

Lex agreed that it was worth a try, suggesting that he could head off to check it out, to see if they still inhabited the forest. Bray recommended that he take Lia with him and the plan was for Bray to stay where he was to keep an eye out on any goings on at the observatory.

Lex and Lia should be able to return by darkness, hopefully with some support from the Eco tribe. But in whatever event, they would still need time to go over their final strategy before undertaking an assault on the observatory - once they knew exactly the numbers of Zootists housed there.

* * *

Lia and Lex travelled quickly, stealthily, toward the forest region.

Since they had arrived in the city, Lia had found herself reevaluating her own feelings and the bond that had gradually developed between her and Lex. She was concerned by the many tales of Lex's carousing days, his relationships, flings with former lovers - Tai San, Siva, Gel - not to mention Lia's surprise at Lex having had a hidden 'love shack' in his home land.

Lia was aware Lex had a roguish element to him. But he also possessed a sincerity, a kind and sentimental side. It had been all too evident when they passed the site of Zandra's grave when they were en route to the observatory, Lex offering a moving tribute to the one Lia knew had been his lover during and after the demise of the adults.

Who was the real Lex, Lia wondered. The mischievous 'bad boy' with a wandering eye – or the person of integrity, honesty – someone who Lia could envisage spending her future with in a lasting relationship?

He had made her laugh, cry and doubt him, all at the same time. He was certainly an enigma.

Now, realizing the risks associated with the unexpected dangers they were starting to find themselves in, placing aside her concerns for her own safety, she knew that her life would never quite be the same again if she ever lost him.

CHAPTER THIRTY

They passed several intersections in the labyrinth of tunnels and had already travelled for some time in Level 3, an enormous complex, which kept spreading out before them like a maze, a seemingly endless network of white, sterile corridors illuminated slightly by occasional lights on the wall.

Amber and the rest noticed several signs which indicated the ways to different sections of the vast base.

Medical Centre. Recreation. Command. Communications. Accommodation. Armaments. Supplies. Maintenance. Storage.

They were all amazed by the scale of the operation that was underground. The sheer size of the catacombs was incredible. It was like being in some kind of subterranean city, sealed off from the outside world.

"This way," Eloise indicated, leading the group towards the area that had been designated *Storage.*

"We did what you asked," Amber said. "But I don't suppose you'll be letting us go."

"Not yet," Eloise answered. "Even if Jack has shown he has abilities – Ram still has a contribution to make."

"It wasn't just Jack," Ram replied petulantly. "Though I've got to admit he's got a flair with technology. I was involved with breaking the code as well - remember?"

"So Jack just got lucky - is that it?" Ellie said defensively, in protection of Jack's endeavours.

"I wouldn't call it luck, exactly. More like blackmail," Jack muttered under his breath, aggrieved at being forced to co-operate with Eloise and the Zootists due to the threats against Ellie, the Mall Rats and the other hostages.

"One thing you must all know. I still require your assistance to uncover the final mystery of our journey. Especially you, Ram. If you refuse to be of use – there will be consequences. Believe me," warned Eloise.

Apart from their own footsteps and voices, which echoed throughout the cavernous complex, the only other sound was of the constant hum of the ventilation system, its fans spinning, doing their best to circulate air.

It was quite difficult to breathe, however, there was a lack of oxygen and Amber was sure she could smell some sort of strange noxious odour. It was not the place for the faint-hearted or the claustrophobic, Amber thinking of the many millions of tons of rock and earth above them.

Walking by a long row of contamination pressure suits fastened to the walls, Amber's mind began playing tricks, imagining she saw a face in the visor of one of the suits, momentarily taking fright, thinking a spectral figure was watching - before Amber did a double-take, looking again, seeing nothing but an empty suit hanging on the wall.

"Remind me to never try and unlock any code, ever again – this place is giving me the creeps," Jack whispered to Ellie, also stealing looks as they passed the contamination pressure suits.

"Don't worry – I'll protect you," Ellie said, linking her arm with Jack's.

"Seems as if we're finally - here," Eloise said expectantly, the tunnel opening up into a large room, more sensor lighting flicking on, detecting their presence.

They had reached a huge chamber, a perfectly cylindrical room, about thirty metres across and three metres high.

Inside, the atmosphere was cold, odd, like being in another worldly place which was making even Eloise, Axel and the other guards slightly uneasy, along with their hostages.

All were stunned to see row upon rows of cryogenic hibernation chambers, their lids still sealed, lights blinking on and off randomly, smoky vapour trails billowing into the air, evaporating from tiny tubes on the sides of each unit. The glass-like covers were thick with condensation.

Ram looked terrified – like he wanted to run away in the opposite direction, and he began to back up, bumping into Axel and some of the elite guards, themselves distracted and gripped by the strange location Eloise had taken them to, Axel noticing Ram at the last moment, grabbing him roughly by his shoulders to stop any attempt he might make to escape.

"What the hell is this place?" Axel spoke out in growing tension.

"Kami never said anything about this!" Eloise responded, almost to herself as she gazed around in total awe, astounded by what was before them – and in particular, the sight of a massive mainframe computer that towered above them all in the centre of the room.

It had a presence of its own, something ominous about it, the computer standing as tall as the room was high and about five metres wide, an immense technological behemoth comprised of a shiny solid steel frame encasing a multitude of processors and data drives, linked together by a mass of wires. Hundreds of lights flashed in some sort of sequence, casting a strange glow on the faces of Eloise and all who gazed up in astonished reverie at the immense machine that dominated the chamber.

A thin arc of green laser light suddenly emitted from the computer, scanning the intruders who had entered its lair - all standing still, wondering what was going on, as they were illuminated by the pulsing lights tracking up and down their bodies.

On the sides of the giant computer Amber could see the words indicating the powerful machine's name.

Knowledge and Artificial Machine Intelligence

In other places were clearly visible the abbreviated form – *K.A.M.I.*

The web of laser light scanning them suddenly blinked off as quickly as it had appeared.

"What is this, Ram?!" Eloise demanded to know, looking up at the computer in absolute confusion, struggling to clearly control her terror. It was the only time Amber had seen Eloise rattled, like things were, for once, out of her control.

Ram, in Axel's grip, was speechless - and looking away from Eloise, Amber noticed, avoided eye contact.

Jack was fixated between the giant mainframe monster computer and the cryogenic chambers, and began advancing toward the ones closest to him, drawn to them in a mixture of fascination and anticipation at what to expect.

"I asked you a question, Ram! Answer me!" Eloise screamed, her voice echoing around the room.

"Don't keep mentioning my name - please!" Ram whispered, his panic mounting, giving Eloise an uneasy glance.

A small laser light suddenly shone out from the top of the *K.A.M.I* system, highlighting Ram's terrified face as he stood frozen in front – and a voice began to speak, emanating from inside the gigantic computer.

"Voice and Facial recognition confirmed. Hello Ram. How nice to see you again."

Jack spun around, astonished and fearful as the voice had boomed, reverberating around and around the chamber and seemingly far beyond - but he was still fully absorbed by his focus on the cryogenic units - totally stunned by what he had discovered.

"Hey, guys," he said, in a mixture of pure disbelief, excitement and terror. "There's adults in here... And I think they might be alive..."

CHAPTER THIRTY-ONE

The Zootists advanced slowly, menacingly, each step taking them closer toward Trudy's old house – and to capturing the Mall Rats who they knew were hiding inside.

There were ten of them, the acolytes having travelled to the suburbs, using the directions Connor had given them back at the mall.

They had driven their vehicles as slowly as they could upon arriving in the area where Trudy's house was located, idling the engines softly, quietly, trying not to make a noise that would warn the rebel Mall Rats of their looming presence.

Like a pack of assassins they circled the house, from all directions. The blinds and drapes were drawn shut, nobody had seem them coming.

The Guardian would be pleased by the capture.

Zoot would look fondly upon the acolytes for proving themselves to him by their continuing devotion.

The Zootists suddenly swarmed into action, smashing the windows with bricks, glass exploding all around.

From the back of the house, other Zootists crashed through the patio doors in the garden, entering inside.

At the front of the house, the main group broke through the door, racing into the hall and dispersing, spreading out throughout Trudy's home.

The Zootists shouted out in frustration, one of them screaming out at the top of her lungs.

"There's nobody here!"

The house was empty.

CHAPTER THIRTY-TWO

Jay carefully made his way across the roof of the mall, trying to keep his balance and not get too distracted by looking down. He was about twenty metres or so above the ground, aware the slightest mistake, a stumble or slip on the uneven roof, could lead to him falling off, to his certain doom.

Having cautiously travelled through the city streets, Jay had managed to avoid any encounters with the Zootists and eventually arrived at the back part of the mall.

For a time, he had to wait in some nearby undergrowth to stay hidden from the Zootist guards on patrol – but made a break for it after the Zootists passed by him on their circuit, Jay racing to the mall and climbing a drainpipe, up to the roof.

His adrenalin flowing, his senses heightened, Jay was anxious to stay out of sight from any hostile forces who might see him on top of the complex.

The roof was covered in moss and awash with puddles from rain the night before, presenting a slippery and unwelcoming surface.

Jay gradually crossed the roof and finally arrived at the electrical transformer that received power from the nearby overhead lines. It was now the moment to trust in his Techno training. Having felt ashamed of all the wrongs the Technos had done under Ram, Jay sometimes was glad of the skills he possessed, many of which he ironically would not have known, had he not been a Techno in the first place.

He dislodged a small chunk of masonry from the crumbling roof - and looking down one more time, to make sure nobody could see him – began smashing the control unit on the transformer.

His act of sabotage, if successful, would prevent main power going into the mall for a substantial period of time – a hefty repair would be required to restore the damage Jay planned to do to the transformer.

Just a few more strikes, Jay reckoned, and then the power would go off – which would mean he would have to leave quickly, before he was discovered.

Gripping the masonry in his hands, Jay readied himself to finish the sabotage he had started.

* * *

"So it really is you, Supreme Mother," the Guardian leered at Trudy in total awe, absolutely thrilled to see her again, circling her intently.

Trudy's hands were bound behind her back and she stared at the Guardian, defiantly, suppressing the anxiety welling up inside, threatening to overwhelm her.

She was absolutely shocked by Connor's betrayal – and to then see the Guardian once more, as well as the Zootists who were following him.

All Trudy wanted to do was leave and get back to Brady.

She would have to stay strong, the ghosts of the past calling, Trudy recalling the anguish of her time spent as the Supreme Mother, when she had literally lost herself, her true identity having been buried by the role the Guardian had conditioned her to take. She had been forced to become someone she wasn't – and promised to never do so again.

At least there was no sign of Brady at the mall - or Salene, May and most of the others. For that, Trudy was grateful, taking heart and clinging to the slim hope that somehow Brady would remain free. Safe.

Feeling his eyes upon her, as if trying to delve into her very soul, Trudy braced herself for whatever the Guardian had planned.

They were in the main concourse of the mall, near where Zoot had once fallen. The area had been converted into a shrine, littered with candles, flickering away, bathing the floor in their light, the Guardian having conducted several ceremonies with his followers in, what was to him, a hallowed place.

Trudy noticed Darryl, Gel and Emma were trapped in a cage cell nearby. They were amazed to see Trudy, having thought she, Bray, Lex and the others were far away, on the island.

Emma was distraught at being separated from Tiffany and Shannon, with whom she had no contact since they were taken, the two children attending 'classes' in another part of the mall, to be indoctrinated into the teachings of Zoot.

"Let us go!" Emma screamed, shaking the wire mesh of the cell.

"Yes! Shout to me, blind girl!" the Guardian implored. "Sing out! Let your voice be heard! Scream for what you desire!"

He glanced in admiration as Emma struggled, giving everything, hopelessly trying to prise open the caged cell door with her bare hands, so desperate she was to find her siblings.

"She alone may be saved. To join us. Along with her brother and sister. Unlike the rest of them."

"What's that supposed to mean?" Gel asked warily.

"You will see soon enough! And so will the spirited one! The hour is nearly upon us!"

Trudy's heart flipped a beat, wondering if the Guardian was going to try to and perform some kind of miracle by restoring Emma's sight. But she didn't exactly feel any sense of relief as the Guardian continued, screaming his manic rant.

"As soon as the Mother Divine commands – we will make the first of our offerings to Zoot."

"Not if I can help it," Darryl grimaced.

Darryl and Gel had done their best to comfort Emma during their imprisonment. Darryl had probed most of the cage cell, searching for any weaknesses, when he was sure the guards were not watching. On occasion, he had also subtly loosened the hinges in a corner of the grille wall with the end of a spoon he had kept from one their meals. They were absolutely desperate to make good their rapidly diminishing hopes of escape.

"It seems you will have arrived just in time to witness the first sacrifice, Supreme Mother," the Guardian said.

"My name is *Trudy*," she emphasized. "And I won't play a part of anything you're planning. So don't try any mind games with me, Guardian!"

"You can't escape your destiny, Supreme Mother. Or the will of Zoot. None of us can. Zoot chose you to be the mother of his child. It is a blessed privilege. Soon, Bray and the others will be with us. It is meant to be."

Initially, the Guardian had been concerned by the reports his Zootists had given of the 'signs' they had witnessed in the city, the graffiti on the walls and buildings. It was like a divine force was at work. The Guardian was unsure who - or what - was responsible for the disruption, given he believed the other Mall Rats, if they were even alive, were still back on the island – and that Bray was dead. And the Guardian himself had begun to look forward to meeting that same fate at some point in time so that he could be reunited with his god, Zoot, in the more important spiritual dimension rather than confining the deity to the earthly domain.

When Connor showed up with Trudy, it all finally made sense, Connor explaining the journey he had made on his boat with Bray and the other Mall Rats - and the Guardian understood they were the very ones who had caused his followers so much confusion in the streets of the city.

So far, they had evaded all efforts to capture them. The Guardian knew it was only a matter of time, however, before Zoot would bring them to him - so that he and the Zootists could continue their mission to spread the faith, having shown themselves first worthy and deserving of that role, overcoming any resistance and doubts.

"Where is Brady, the child of the Mighty One - and the others?" the Guardian asked Trudy, aware the raid on her house had failed.

"How should I know?"

"You lie!' the Guardian suddenly screamed. "Answer me!"

"You want lies? Try talking to him!" Trudy shouted back, indicating Connor. "Everything he ever says is a lie!"

Trudy was so hurt, angered by Connor's deception. She cursed herself – how could she be no naïve? So trusting? And to make matters worse, because of her, so desperate to have a partner and to love again, she felt she had now endangered her friends and her very daughter.

"You want to know why the Mall Rats weren't at my house? It's because Connor is spinning you a web of lies! If you believe him – you'll believe anything!"

"Is that so, bounty hunter?" the Guardian asked Connor suspiciously. "Is this all part of some trick?"

"She's clutching at straws," Connor said, leaning back casually against the stairwell. "If anyone's lying – it's Trudy. I delivered her to you – and I have brought the Mall Rats to the city. So I expect to be well rewarded. I've been through a lot – many sleepless nights because of her – not all of it as 'pleasurable' as I would have wished."

Connor glanced disdainfully at Trudy, who was fully aware of the 'dig' he had just made at her.

"Trust me – the greatest pleasure will be to never you see again, Connor."

Suddenly the mall was completely smothered in a cloak of darkness, the only light emanating from the circle of candles that flickered away in the shrine area marking the spot where Zoot had fell.

"Yes master! We feel your presence! And we will not fail you, oh Great One!" the Guardian said, gazing suddenly up at the heavens.

Some of the Zootist guards were panicking, feeling as if the end of the world was beginning, many of them prostrating themselves on the floor, sensing it was all an omen, that Zoot was giving them an augury.

From throughout the mall could be heard the cries of anxious young voices, some screaming in terror. Fearful of what had caused the blackout, it was the children on the upper level, where the Zootists had established their new educational rooms.

Many were quickly gathering in the second level of the concourse, looking down below at where the Guardian stood, the Zootists who had been indoctrinating them having escorted their pupils into the corridors, the young children huddled together, frightened of the dark and what it all signified.

"Tiffany? Shannon?" Emma shouted out, sure she could hear her younger brother and sister somewhere up above, one of them calling out Emma's name.

"What is your will, Mighty One!" the Guardian intoned.

He had a manic, almost excited look in his eyes, genuinely believing Zoot had made the darkness happen.

"I don't mean to rain on your parade, Guardian," Darryl said drolly from inside the cage. "But I think the only miracle happening here is that someone hasn't paid their electricity bill. The power seems to have gone out."

"Quiet! All of you!" the Guardian screamed,

Slowly, the mood of panic and choir of unease began to reduce, the older Zootists above calming their younger students.

"Scared of the dark, Guardian? See? You'll never find the others. And no matter what it takes – they will defeat you," Trudy insisted, recalling Jay's plan to knock out the power to the mall.

"You're wrong - wrong!" the Guardian yelled, furious, looking like he might physically strike Trudy - before he quickly managed to regain self-control.

"What the hell's going on?" Ebony asked, wandering into the lower level of the concourse with Aras and the other members of her group of Zootist acolytes, with whom she had just been having a meal in the cafeteria on the second floor. "I can hardly see a thing!" she said, gazing around.

"Tell me about it," Emma sighed to herself, unable to contain the irony of the situation amidst her fear as she continued listening intently, trying somehow to fathom just exactly what was occurring.

Trudy shared that sentiment. She was startled, dismayed, to observe Ebony walking freely, amongst the Zootists, as if one of them. She had already known Ebony was on the Guardian's side, having been told so by Connor. Still, it upset Trudy to see Ebony actually there. At least Connor had been truthful about that.

"Ebony… I should have guessed you'd be involved in all this," Trudy said contemptuously. "How can you live with yourself, after all we've been through? Doesn't the past mean anything to you?"

"The past is the past, Trudy. The future is the only thing that matters now."

Ebony had heard the news of Trudy's capture but was equally still surprised to see her, the last time they had met being when Ebony tried to capture Trudy and her daughter on the island.

She had known Trudy for a long time, the two of them having a complicated relationship, both former rivals for Bray – and Zoot. Their fortunes and fates had crossed over the course of time, ebbed and flowed. Now she was in the ascendant, it gave Ebony a sense of deep satisfaction to know their contrasting situations vindicated her decision to ally with Eloise. Trudy was the one who was a prisoner – and Ebony's future was certainly far more promising.

But it was Connor who attracted Ebony's attention. She eyed him up, like a predatory animal, liking what she saw of the ruggedly handsome bounty hunter. Aras and the Zootists under Ebony's command had been discussing Connor and his feats during their meal earlier with Ebony and she was intrigued to see just exactly who this enigmatic figure was.

"Bring me whoever is responsible for this!" the Guardian ordered a group of Zootist guards, who quickly raced up the stairs, on their way to the roof, where they knew the electrical transformer was located.

The power cut couldn't possibly be due to a simple accident, the Guardian reasoned. If it wasn't the will of Zoot, then he reflected that the mall had been sabotaged – perhaps by Bray, Lex, or one of the other Mall Rats still at liberty.

"Get out there, Ebony! Find them! Bring me every Mall Rat in the city! And we will show the Supreme Mother who has the real power – and what happens to traitors!"

"As you wish," Ebony said, respectfully – but she gave a subtle, knowing look to Connor, which indicated she thought the Guardian's mind wasn't completely all there.

"Why don't you join me? Fancy a ride?" Ebony asked Connor, with more than a hint of brazen innuendo.

"Anytime," Connor replied, anxious to get away from the raging Guardian – and excited to take Ebony up on her offer, looking forward to getting to know her better.

"Put the Supreme Mother in with the others!" the Guardian commanded, some of the Zootists dragging Trudy away to the cell.

"You may as well throw away the key for all I care!" Trudy shouted, indicating the bars holding Emma, Gel and Darryl. "I'll never bow to that witch, Eloise! Or be a part of your so-called religion!"

"You did once before. And you will do so again!" the Guardian bellowed. "The tide of fate is with us. You *will* join us, Supreme Mother – and so will Zoot's daughter, as soon as she is found!"

CHAPTER THIRTY-THREE

Standing beside the massive computer in the centre of the chamber, Eloise, herself a tall girl, was totally dominated by the size and imposing presence of the machine.

She gazed up in awe, trying to understand what this technological wonder the adults had left behind was doing there – and tentatively reached out her hand, running her fingers down the cool steel frame, touching the words on the side that indicated its name – *K.A.M.I – Knowledge Artificial Machine Intelligence.*

Jack, by contrast, continued intently gazing upon the cryogenic hibernation chambers in the room – each one containing an adult, lying in state, as if perfectly preserved.

"Are you sure they're still alive?" Amber asked, standing nearby, along with Ellie and Ram.

"According to the vital signs - it seems so," Jack indicated the displays on top of each unit outlining blood pressure, heart rate and other life statistics.

"So... they're in some kind of suspended animation," Ellie reflected.

"Obviously," Ram responded.

Eloise crossed from the behemoth computer system to where the others were leaning over the hibernation unit, while her guards still gazed in awe at the massive mainframe as if it would suddenly come to life and attack.

"You've got a lot of explaining to do, Ram," Eloise said, giving him a scathing, suspicious look.

"Can't you just enjoy me being around for once without always thinking I'm up to something?" Ram replied innocently, giving Eloise an insincere smile.

"Hardly. You said you had never been here before – but that 'thing' certainly seems to know you."

Eloise was as shaken by the adults encased in the hibernation chambers but was clearly more disturbed by the discovery of the *K.A.M.I* computer – and the fact it had 'spoken' to Ram, in apparent recognition of him.

She kept glancing anxiously at the immense computer. For so long the name Kami signified the enigmatic and powerful leader of the Collective.

Only a few members in the upper echelons of the Collective had ever met Kami, whose true identity was always kept a secret from public knowledge.

The commanders of the Collective, of which Eloise was one, usually reported to the central leader via the UNANET system, which enabled long distance contact to any part of the world provided each party had access to a computer hooked up to the online network.

It was, of course, vital for security reasons to maintain some degree of anonymity, Eloise appreciated. Kami was the head of a large and growing empire and the fewer who knew Kami's identity, the better. There was never an assassination attempt - because no external enemy precisely knew who Kami was or where the Collective ruler could be found.

This also had the added benefit, of which Kami was no doubt aware, Eloise had long ago considered, that everyone in the Collective was careful of their activity in case word got back to Kami somehow. It ensured loyalty, an efficient chain of command. There would never be a coup. No factions or leadership struggles. Instead, if a commander obeyed Kami's orders and continued to show successful performance – that they were useful – Kami would offer promotions and rewards.

There were rumours about Kami – some thought he was a boy, others a girl – some suggested Kami was even an adult. Others were of the opinion that there was no single person called 'Kami' – but more that Kami was actually a nominal symbolic front, representing a supreme council of several people that in reality ruled the Collective. How else could one person single-handedly keep track of the various activities of the Collective over such a wide ranging, diverse geographic area?

Eloise had thought she had been one of the few commanders in the Collective to be granted the privilege of meeting Kami – who had turned out to be a male, just a little older than herself. He wasn't handsome but was certainly gifted, Eloise aware she had been in the presence of genius. He had been impressed by her beauty, loyalty and absolute ruthlessness.

At least at the time, Eloise had thought he was the real Kami. Had she been tricked? Surely the real identity of the leader couldn't be a computer?

A part of her – as strange as it sounded, when she thought to herself about it – wondered if the *K.A.M.I* machine before them in the room could have some connection to the real 'Kami.' It certainly had to be more than a passing coincidence that the computer and the Collective leader shared the same name, Eloise felt. Or had he even named himself after it? In which case how did he know of its existence, unless he of course had hacked into it during the adult times. Or even after they had all perished.

All she knew for certain, or at least she felt for certain, was that her orders from 'Kami' were to go to the underground base at Eagle Mountain to find what the adults had left behind. She had never expected to encounter the mighty computer, bristling with power, artificial intelligence. Its existence hadn't been revealed to her in advance by the Collective leader. Perhaps the human Kami didn't know about the *K.A.M.I* computer system – or perhaps he did but had chosen not to let Eloise know. She wasn't sure.

Eloise glanced at the gigantic computer system lurking way above her in the heart of Eagle Mountain, like some mighty dragon in its subterranean lair. And for a moment, she wondered if it could somehow understand what she was thinking.

If anyone could shed light on matters – it surely must be Ram, she was certain.

"I have to know, Ram," she probed. "This computer system... it seems as if it's almost 'human'."

"*Correct*," the computer said, its voice booming and Ram broke out in helpless laughter. Followed by *K.A.M.I*, the computer mimicking the tone, but the voice in monotone, unemotional, and several octaves below Ram's.

All the others present exchanged incredulous glances amidst their mounting fear, then listened intently as Ram's laughter subsided and he tried to explain.

"Our friend, *K.A.M.I* here has artificial intelligence. And has facial recognition. That's what those laser lights were doing. Scanning your faces. So try and be careful of your expressions because it might misread and tap into a totally different conclusion within its program. I'd hate to think what it might do if it thought we were hostile and it felt threatened."

Eloise stole a look at the gigantic mainframe computer and tried to maintain a stony, pokerface.

"You mean... it can read expressions?" she enquired.

"It'll certainly try," Ram responded.

"But how... was it at all possible for this *K.A.M.I* system to recognize you? Anyone?" Ellie said.

"It's a long story. I wouldn't know where to begin," Ram replied.

"Try at the beginning," Amber suggested, wondering what other secrets Ram may have kept.

"Well – if you must know every little detail... soon after the Technos invaded the city, we decided to try and get here first before it could fall into the hands of the Collective... sorry about that, by the way," Ram added, shrugging apologetically to Eloise.

"Keep going," Eloise demanded.

"To cut a long story short, as they say... Before the virus, I was a member of a guild. And an awesome gamer, if I do say so myself. That's where I met up with someone online who called themselves Kami."

He stopped suddenly and the others also froze, including even Axel and the guards, as the lasers from the giant mainframe moved across their faces.

"Is that... 'thing'... listening?" Axel asked.

"In a manner of speaking," Ram replied. "Try and not look too concerned and I reckon we'll all be just fine."

"So this guild of yours. Is that the same one you told us about when we first arrived on the island?" Jack considered. "When you got into all that hacking you mentioned?"

Ram nodded and explained more about how all his online friends had to resort to the online UNANET to keep in touch post the virus and check for information of what might be happening in not only their own location but other parts of the world.

He never met his friend Kami in real life and admired his great skill with technology but had no intention of being his Number Two. So he decided to break away and found the Technos.

Amber wondered if Ram was weaving a web of lies or if there was any truth and Eloise pressed again about the last time he was in the region.

"I came to Eagle Mountain just after we invaded, it was pretty easy to figure out how to bypass the security codes. It wasn't too difficult, when you're as good at computers as I am. And I've got to admit you're pretty good yourself, Jack."

"Thanks very much," Jack replied, beaming proudly.

"*Yes, thank you very much, Jack,*" the *K.A.M.I* computer repeated, its voice booming as its green lasers darted around Jack's expression.

"Careful," Ram cautioned. "It's reading you and searching its databases for any programs associated with how you might be feeling right now. I don't know if it has much in its system about flattery. But it's always learning, feeding itself and its programs with expanding knowledge."

Jack froze and the laser lights immediately stopped scanning his face.

"Anyway, as I was saying," Ram continued. "Only myself and a handful of my most trusted supporters got this far, to Level 3," Ram continued. "Mega, Java, Siva, Ved – they never saw beyond Level 2. They didn't even know this place ever existed."

"Why? Why keep all – this - a secret?" Amber asked.

"Isn't it obvious? I didn't know who I could trust. If anyone in the Technos would betray me... sell me out to the Collective. If more people knew all the secrets down here, in this very room, they might have tried to come after it. I couldn't take that risk. And after I met *K.A.M.I* over there – I was determined to try and protect this place."

"How very noble," Eloise commended him, in obvious sarcasm. "So get to the point, Ram."

"I could see that the adults - sleeping in their icy chambers like some kind of frozen vegetables – had found a way to perfect cryogenic hibernation. We did some experiments on the chambers in Level 2, where the technicians had been. Tried to replicate what the adults had done. I'm almost embarrassed to say – I couldn't figure it out at first, how they had managed to achieve it."

"But you did," Amber reminded him, recalling Ram's own efforts to seal himself off from the outside world and to live forever during the height of the virtual reality paradise program he introduced to the city before it was evacuated.

"It was all because of *K.A.M.I* here," Ram continued. "This computer is single-handedly responsible for running Eagle Mountain – and keeping all these adults, even us, alive. Who do you think's controlling the very air we breathe? Besides, watching and listening to us, right now? *K.A.M.I* controls all these hibernation units. It's a pretty awesome piece of technology. So I knew the one I was putting myself in would be safe. I then taught Mega, Java and the others what *K.A.M.I* taught me – but of course, Mega had his own agenda - and sold me out. The point is – *K.A.M.I* has a wealth of knowledge about the adults and their technology."

"Who programmed it?" Jack asked in growing intrigue.

"Well, that's a question everyone wants to know, Jack," Ram said. "Including me. I always intended to check it all out further until Mega got ambitions and had other things in mind."

There was a hint that Ram was holding back further information and Amber wondered if he somehow was involved at some point in time from the way he was staring fondly at *K.A.M.I*, as if he was reminiscing.

"So - from all you're saying, it's almost like *K.A.M.I* is more than a computer to you, Ram. More like a friend," Amber said.

"Definitely," Ram replied lovingly.

The laser light suddenly appeared, darting around Ram's face.

"*Thank you, Ram*," the computer's voice bellowed. "*You are my friend, too.*"

The laser lights disappeared again as Ram's expression clouded.

"Was that a set up?" he asked Amber.

"Just testing," she shrugged. "It's good to know who your friends are," she added.

"Very touching," Eloise mocked. "So why didn't you say anything before? Why go through all the denials - and pretend you knew nothing about what was down here?"

"I thought you would get rid of something – principally me - if I had no use. The Collective only keeps what is useful to them. The longer I stalled - and kept myself 'useful' to you – the longer I would keep myself alive. That's what I thought, anyway. Besides – I wouldn't want to just tell you everything, would I? Then, I might not be around," he added, alluding to the fact that he did in fact have other information he was yet to reveal, to guarantee his own survival.

"Hang on a sec," Jack said, gathering his own thoughts.

He had been fixated on the adults, seemingly sleeping in their hibernation units. For so long, Jack had dreamed of finding adults – even one, somewhere in the world. He had stayed up late at night, searching long distance radio frequencies, convinced there was someone out there, an adult, still alive. The fact Jack was now staring at one through the glass of the cryogenic unit was a most incredible experience – a dream, for Jack, that had finally been realized. There was so much he wanted to know. But first, one thing above else bothered him.

"If you were here before, Ram, how come you didn't revive any of them? I know I would have."

"The thing is, Jack, last time I was here, I was a little – 'obsessed' – shall we say, with my own health. I didn't know if these adults had any trace of the virus in them. It could have been dormant, for all I knew, inactive by being frozen. If I had asked the computer to revive them, there was a chance I could have revived the virus. And what if it had mutated? There was no way I could take that risk. Better to keep the adults – and any leftovers of the virus – locked away."

"But won't the computer know if there is any trace of the virus inside the units?" Amber asked, ever doubting Ram's version of events, having lied on many occasions in the past.

"It might. But it won't know if there's any virus left in the outside world. That was the other reason for letting sleeping dogs lie. If I had woken the adults, who's to say I wouldn't have been putting them at risk, once they were outside the protection of their chambers? According to the computer, they can live in perpetuity, just the way they are. Provided *K.A.M.I* has a continuing power source off course."

"*Power levels are optimal. No inefficiencies detected,*" the *K.A.M.I* system spoke aloud.

"That's what I love about this – it's always thinking, listening to what I have to say. Pity the human race wasn't so efficient," Ram said, marvelling at the vast computer in the centre of the room and casting a disdainful glance at the others. "The algorithms on this thing are out of this world."

Eloise gave Ram an uncertain look, having listened to his explanation.

"It would be nice to hear from the horse's mouth though, wouldn't it?" Ram wondered. "I bet the adults would have a lot to tell us. It's tempting to revive them. God knows they owe us some answers."

"And so do you. Is there anything else you're holding back from me?" Eloise demanded. "Something I should know?"

"You've got to believe me."

"I don't know what to believe anymore – especially coming from you, Ram," Eloise said, walking up and down between the rows of cryogenic units, gazing upon the faces of each of the adults she passed, contemplating them for a moment.

"To think – once the adults controlled the world. And now we're the ones in control. It really is the dawn of a new age. Tomorrow - everything that matters now – will belong to the Collective."

"What's so special about these adults? Why were they saved?" Ellie wondered aloud, resentful that so many other adults weren't afforded the same opportunity of salvation – her parents and family among them. "They obviously must have thought themselves pretty important to end up here."

"They were. According to our intelligence network... This one here was a leading geneticist," Eloise explained, recognizing the adult inside one of the chambers. "And this one was Lauren Edwards, an expert on artificial intelligence."

"According to... who?" Amber asked.

"Let's just say the Collective have an efficient information system, Amber," Eloise answered. "Otherwise why would we ever have bothered bringing you here?"

"I don't mean to spoil your party, Eloise, but the Collective and even your friend, Kami, is only as good as the information it's given," Ram said.

"Meaning?" Eloise probed.

"There's only one reason an intelligence network is named as such. It requires intelligence. Which can only come from those possessing an adequate level. And I'd put myself up for that category so I reckon you might just be doing yourself a favour if you remembered that, Eloise," Ram smiled immodestly. "Even this Kami system here is only as good as the people who programmed it."

"I hate it to say it - but I don't think *K.A.M.I* is working properly right now – or these hibernation units," Jack said.

"What are you talking about?" Eloise enquired irritably.

"The units all seem to have a timer, which I guess shows how long they've been in here for. But, the thing is – the timers must be wrong. According to them, these adults would have been put away long before the virus appeared. Like, we're talking *years* earlier. There must be some kind of malfunction. Maybe that computer has a glitch and isn't so powerful after all. So if you're after these adults, Eloise – which is why I'm guessing you've gone to so much trouble to get here in the first place – it looks like this whole trip might have been a waste. The units obviously aren't working."

Amber and the others stood in silence, concerned and confused by the mysteries and the potential implications.

"What do you think, Jack?" Amber enquired.

"I don't really know what to think," Jack replied. "But I'm beginning to suspect that there was no accidental 'virus' that just appeared out of nowhere. The adults must have been well prepared and made their plans - they knew what was going on, long ago. That the world was running out of time. Too bad they didn't share their knowledge with the rest of us."

"But they will," Eloise interrupted.

"How can you be so sure of that?" Amber asked, still unable to comprehend that perhaps somewhere on this earth adults may have been involved in some form of insidious World War Three and engaged upon a deliberate act, unleashing a bacterial weapon of destruction. If there was any truth to it, how could the authorities have known so much but kept it all a secret, effectively choosing who would live and who would die. It was all so much to take in, so heartless, Amber felt.

"If the units aren't working - don't you think we should try and waken the adults up?" Ellie suggested, deeply concerned. Then she cried out, suddenly blinded by green laser lights searching, bouncing around her face and piercing her eyes.

"Code Red! Back-up systems reprogramming"

"What's it talking about?" Eloise asked.

"Some kind of back-up systems - in case the hibernation units failed?" Ram shrugged.

"So that's what Kami was after," Eloise whispered, said in an undertone, mainly to herself, as she considered it all. Then she stopped and gazed as the huge mainframe of the *K.A.M.I* system spoke, its lasers searching the expression on her face.

"*Correct. K.A.M.I confirms all information will be held secure.*"

"I don't understand," Amber said.

"I'm beginning to," Ram interrupted. "I reckon somewhere there must be a device containing data. Like a back-up system. So that one day if anyone needed to rediscover the secrets of the past and more information to secure the future - that information would be available right here. In Eagle Mountain. Isn't that the truth of it, Eloise? What this mission of your's is all about?"

"Unless, of course, you have other information," Eloise said, considering Ram suspiciously.

"All I know is that when I was last here before, those reality space visors, everything I found, adapted - those were all just mere toys compared to the power of the information that could be really here."

Ram decided to not reveal any more detail to shed light on what he was referring to, already intent long ago in trying to fulfil his ultimate ambition in knowing all that there was to know, the culmination of human knowledge to this point in time. The most advanced technological blueprints. The results of years of research and progress. Ways to release new forms of energy... Weaponry... Medical breakthroughs. Inventions... 3D printing designs that would blow anyone's mind, as it had placed Ram's brain in overload. Even the location of some other bases where more adults were - waiting for the day they could return to the surface of the world.

Whoever controlled that knowledge would be able to wield ungodly power and be effectively omnipotent.

"You've all helped us get this far," Eloise threatened. "Now get us to the end. Help me find the device. Your lives depend upon it – and so does the lives of your friends. All it takes is my command and the Guardian will do the rest."

"We don't even know what we're looking for – what the data device is," Ellie pointed out. "Besides… it could be - booby-trapped, for all we know."

"If the device is in this room. I want you to find it!" Eloise snapped, angrily indicating Ram and Jack. "You both clearly have the capability!"

The lasers darted around her face and she turned, gazing up, the computer repeating her words.

"*You both clearly have the capability,*" the *K.A.M.I* system said, an unusual tone of anger in its monotone voice.

Eloise tried somehow to compose herself and the laser light disappeared from her face.

"It's obviously in the *K.A.M.I* system," Ram muttered, thinking it all through, looking up at the immense computer dominating the room. "But you do realize how much data must be on there? It could take literally years to go through it all… I hope you're not in a rush for any discoveries."

Eloise stared down at the hibernation units.

"They look so peaceful, don't they?" she said softly. "Whenever we do discover the data device – which we will - we can't take any chances that whatever knowledge they knew gets shared with anyone else. It's imperative the Collective are the only ones who possess all the secrets the adults were so careful to preserve."

"Just as I suspected," Ram said. "You know all about it."

Suddenly Eloise began pressing buttons on the top of the hibernation chambers, cold wisps of air starting to emanate from inside, a warning buzzer alarm sounding, the chamber decompressing, losing its integrity.

"Emergency failure in unit 37, unit 38," the *K.A.M.I* system warned through its speakers.

"No! You can't!" Amber cried out, dismayed.

"I can! They've had their time!" Eloise shouted, yanking out the cables connected to the sides of other nearby units. "Their era is over! Turn them all off!"

She turned, glaring angrily up at the huge mainframe computer. "And your time has come, as well!"

"Emergency failure in unit 35, unit 36," the strangely placid almost emotionless voice of the computer informed the room.

Axel and the guards followed Eloise's order, moving from chamber to chamber, ripping the leads linking the cryogenic units to the *K.A.M.I* system, the computer calling out all the failures happening as one by one, each chamber was switched off.

"Are you out of your freaking minds?!" Jack hollered, trying to stop them - before Axel literally swept Jack's legs from under him, crashing him to the floor, Axel knocking Jack unconscious with a severe blow.

"Get away from him!" Ellie screamed, racing over to where Jack lay prone.

"Stop it!" Amber shouted out, yanking one of the guards – but she was struck in the back from behind by another, Amber crumpling to the floor.

"Know this! When I make a threat – I am deadly serious!" Eloise bristled, turning off the last of the cryogenic units, savouring the moment, a small trail of vapour floating up from the chamber as it was disconnected.

"Emergency failure in unit 1. All capsules offline."

"Why?!" Amber wailed, distraught at the cruel and malicious act that had taken place. "How could you?!"

"They have no future! They had their chance! Once we find the data device, the knowledge will be ours! Or should I say - mine!"

She faked a smile, then briskly walked toward the exit, leaving Ellie, Jack, Ram and Amber exchanging glances in growing unease as the sustained tone of the hibernation chambers pierced the air. Flatline.

"All life systems have now concluded," the voice from the K.A.M.I computer intoned. *"Repeat. All life systems have now concluded."*

CHAPTER THIRTY-FOUR

"Be careful, Brady!" Salene cautioned as Brady merrily jumped up and down on the bed like it was a trampoline.

"Yeah, you don't want to break it. It wasn't designed to be a toy," Sammy said. "It was meant for people to sleep in - as well as a few more other things," he added uneasily, casting a glance at Lottie, examining their surroundings.

They were inside Lex's old 'love shack', a tiny compartment hidden in the city and comprising no more than a large double bed, covered with luxury linens - and a few smaller pieces of furniture, most of which Lex had found in an old store, others he had gambled or traded for.

Earlier, back in the suburbs at Trudy's more comfortable former home, Salene and May had become concerned when none of the others showed up, after many hours had elapsed.

May was certain something had gone wrong and as the oldest members of their small group, Salene and May worried that Bray and the rest might have been captured by Eloise and the Guardian, which could have compromised their own position had Salene and May stayed at Trudy's house, fully aware the Zootists would be sure to go after Zoot's daughter.

Despite the risks of travelling through the city, Salene felt that was a better option – otherwise they would have been nothing more than sitting ducks, Salene considered, had they waited at Trudy's old home.

Besides, the others would know where to find them. Lex's 'love shack' was to be an alternative rendezvous if Trudy's home became under threat.

Although there was no threat as such, at least as far as May and Salene knew, they decided that they should relocate because they were becoming increasingly concerned that the others were long overdue. They considered that they might have even run into some trouble themselves and had decided to implement the second option, using Lex's hideaway as a base rather than Trudy's home.

Salene had guided them to the location, remembering Lex's instructions how to get there, taking extra care to make sure they circumvented any patrolling Zootists in the streets, on their way. But the city and environs were totally deserted.

So well hidden was Lex's hideaway that Salene and May almost couldn't find it in the first place, an obscure sheet of metal being the makeshift 'door' they had to squeeze through in order to get inside.

"Aren't you going to sit down?" Salene asked May, who was standing by the side of the bed, cradling baby Bray in her arms.

"Are you kidding? I dread to think what's happened on that thing," May responded.

"This place definitely has all the markings of Lex's sense of taste," Salene smiled affectionately, not agreeing with Lex's choice of bed linens, with their clashing colours.

"I'm hungry – and bored," Lottie said, feeling confined by their close quarters.

"Then why don't you come and sit with me?" Sammy suggested, patting the side of the bed where he was scrunched up. "As nothing more than a friend, of course," he quickly added.

"Thanks – but I'd rather stare at the wall," Lottie replied, feeling Sammy was making unwelcome overtones.

"Where's Mommy?" Brady sobbed, deeply missing Trudy.

"We'll see her soon – don't worry," May insisted, not wanting Brady to be disheartened.

They had to stay positive. None of them could lose hope, Salene felt. But the longer they were apart, she wondered what the reasons were that explained the continued absence of their missing friends.

CHAPTER THIRTY-FIVE

"What do you think? I bet this beats being out at sea!" Ebony grinned, her hair loose, windblown, flying back behind her, due to the speed they were travelling.

"I love it!" Connor shouted over the sound of the engine. "And I love being with you!"

The pair of them stood at the rear of the customized police car granted to Ebony's possession by the Guardian.

Aras had driven the vehicle up and down the city streets, daring to go as fast as Ebony urged him, like they were doing some kind of drag race, Ebony and Connor gripping the handrail at the back, unable to keep the smiles off their faces, enjoying the sensation of speed as much as each other's company.

Ebony was exhilarated, it felt just like the old times, when she had stood, side by side, with Zoot, travelling in his police car, with nothing getting in their way.

"This is amazing!" Connor called out to Ebony.

"No, I think you'll find THIS more amazing," Ebony said, locking her lips on his own and they kissed in increasing passion.

Connor was just the escape Ebony needed after being surrounded by the closed zealotry of the Zootists for so long.

She was glad to get away from the Guardian. Though Ebony had enjoyed some relative freedoms, she always preferred to be the one giving out the orders than to be the one receiving them. It was true she had her group of loyal Zootists to command, none more devoted to her than Aras. But in Eloise's absence, Ebony knew it was expected of her to follow the Guardian's instructions. Always unpredictable – even unstable, Ebony thought – it felt literally like a breath of fresh air to get out into the city streets again. To gain some time away, a measure of independence – to just enjoy the thrill of being alive, with the handsome Connor by her side.

"We're nearly there," Ebony said, recognizing where they were in the city and tapping on the roof of the car to let Aras know to slow down. Hitting hit the brakes, the vehicle screeched to a stop amidst a cloud of smoke from the burning rubber.

"How about another kiss before we 'disembark'?" Connor cheekily asked. "I'm kinda getting used to the taste."

"Save it – there'll be many more later. We've got work to do," Ebony said.

Looks were always the first – and ultimately the most important thing in a relationship, Ebony felt, deciding she could get to know Connor better another time. If she didn't like him as a person, well, that wouldn't stop her enjoying her passions with him in the short term – but if she did like him, that was a bonus and so much all for the better.

From what she had gathered so far, Ebony was impressed by Connor's roguish ways, Connor having described to her many of the bounties he had collected in the past – and in some ways his tales reminded her of Slade, who had once pursued a similar endeavour.

Ebony was intrigued with the work he had done for the Collective, who no doubt would be impressed with the results of what he had achieved.

Single-handedly delivering most of the Mall Rats to the city was a significant feat, Ebony appreciated, and she had told him so. She especially enjoyed that he had managed to deceive Trudy in the process. Ebony knew that for a time, Trudy and Connor had been romantically involved – and for Ebony to take Trudy's place, supplanting her and keeping Connor to herself – that was a special thing indeed, a form of payback for all the wrongs Ebony felt Trudy had done to her in the past.

"You sure the rest of the Mall Rats didn't suspect you?" Ebony asked as they leapt to the ground from the police car.

"They have no idea. Trudy's the only one who knows."

Connor had relayed Lex's instructions on how to find his hidden hideaway as an alternative rendezvous to Trudy's house and Ebony recalled that her sister, Siva, had once mentioned to her that she shared some secret encounters with Lex in the city.

Ebony looked around the street, wondering where on earth the entrance to Lex's mystery 'boudoir' could be. It was obviously well disguised - and likely to be so secure they would probably need a can opener to get inside.

"Go and get them – bounty hunter," Ebony whispered seductively, then watched as Connor began walking up and down the street.

"Salene? May? Are you here?" Connor called out. "How about Brady? Trudy sent me to get you. Brady - your mommy needs you – it's really important."

Connor shrugged at Ebony. There appeared to be no sign of anyone around.

But suddenly there was a sound, Ebony hearing a subtle, muffled shuffling of movement. Connor had heard it, too, and made his way towards the source of the noise, by a piece of scrap metal.

"It's okay – if you're there, you can come out now," Connor insisted. "Bray and everyone's back at the mall, waiting for you. The Guardian's defeated. It's all over."

Connor was good, very good, Ebony reflected. If she hadn't known to the contrary, she would have almost been sure what he was saying was true, he sounded so convincing.

And she was far too knowing in the female-male game to realize that he wouldn't exactly need much convincing to provide her with some much needed physical pleasure. She had her needs, after all. And her future was looking very rewarding indeed.

Salene, May holding baby Bray, Sammy, and Lottie carrying Brady, appeared through a slit in the tin prior to recoiling as they noticed Connor with Ebony.

"How's it going, guys? Great to see you - not!" she snarled.

CHAPTER THIRTY-SIX

Bray was sitting in an office chair - that much he could realize from the soft feel of the leather cushioned seat behind his back. But apart from that – and the firm grip of the two Zootist guards, pressing down on his shoulders to stop him from being able to get up – Bray had no idea of what was going to happen to him or his specific surroundings.

Ironically, and inadvertently, Lex and Lia were indirectly responsible for his capture. It may have even been Eloise. When the hibernation units housing the adults had been deactivated, this in turn had put the entire base on high red alert, resulting in security cameras coming to life, scanning the area. Guards had noticed on the multiple monitors Lex and Lia's vehicle receding away along a perimeter road in the distance and a unit was deployed to search the immediate area outside the observatory complex.

Bray heard a pulsing security alarm and had moved from his vantage point stealthily closer to the complex in order to try and assess the situation. And like the capable warrior that he was, had put up a spirited defence, taking two guards who had converged, having noticed him, with ease but he was soon overpowered by other Zootists, who dragged him into the compound. Some had recognized Bray having encountered him on the island during his imprisonment and knowing how important a figure he was, none other than the brother of Zoot himself, were slightly in awe when he was apprehended.

Now, having had a blindfold tied tightly around his eyes, Bray was unable to see but was aware he was led from the charred top level of Eagle Mountain down an incline, through a long tunnel of some kind, into another level underneath.

Distant footsteps could be heard approaching where Bray was being held – but these were far from the sounds so characteristic of the Zootist guards.

And although he couldn't see who it was that was coming towards him due to his blindfold – he recognized the rhythmic pattern of the walk, the sound of heels echoing, striding with relentless purpose in perfect time, like a metronome, taking their owner ever closer to Bray.

It was her, Bray was certain. Part of him dreaded this very moment, being in her presence again, the footsteps right behind him now. She had so tormented him in the past but he had to confront her and his fears, for Amber and their son.

He could sense her, close by, recognizing the smell of her sweet perfume, the same kind she had used on the island.

Any other remaining doubts Bray had as to whoever was in his presence quickly vanished when he felt long fingernails brushing softly against the side of his face - and he flinched as he was stroked affectionately like he was some sort of a pet. Then he felt a degree of torment amidst his growing unease as he heard a familiar, chilling voice.

"Did you miss me?" Eloise whispered into Bray's ear. "Because you have no idea how I've missed you."

She tenderly kissed the side of Bray's cheek, lifted his blindfold slightly, staring into his eyes, just inches away, looking at him intently, jubilantly, but wanting to make sure at the same time that he actually really was there before her very eyes, Bray being the most important prisoner she had ever possessed – and the only one who had successfully escaped from her.

"Fancy seeing you here. What a surprise!" Eloise purred seductively – and then she suddenly clutched the sides of Bray's face and plunged her lips down on his, Eloise murmuring in pleasure, kissing him passionately, for what felt like an eternity. Bray sat impassively, not responding, but deciding that he had enough, bit into her tongue.

She cried out and recoiled but there was no sense of anger in her reaction, just a look of satisfaction to find herself reunited once again.

She wiped a trace of blood overspilling onto her lips, disappointed at Bray's reluctance to readily respond to her advances.

"Still the same old Bray, I see," Eloise said, standing back to look upon him - her prisoner once again, still held down in the chair by the guards either side. "Now that wasn't exactly what I would call a friendly welcome," she continued, sucking on her tongue and swallowing another trickle of blood while gently taking Bray's hand to place it on her belly area, displaying the early stages of pregnancy.

"And what a pity," Eloise said. "Because I've got such good news for you, Bray. You're going to become a father. Again. Congratulations."

"That has nothing to do with me – and you know it."

"I'm afraid the secret is well and truly out."

Bray scoffed, then considered Eloise anxiously as she smiled but it was ice cold.

"Imagine how Amber would feel - if she ever found out you cheated on her, with me."

"She'd never believe you," Bray replied. "You know as well as I do, Eloise, that it's not true."

"Why don't we let Amber be the judge of that?" Eloise suggested.

"Is she... here?" Bray probed.

Eloise wagged her finger at Bray disapprovingly.

"Ssshh. You have to learn to say the magic words first. How about please. And if that doesn't work, I might just have you beg me to take you to her."

Bray couldn't help himself and lunged at Eloise, struggling at the mere mention of Amber's name, along with his fury of Eloise's mocking tone but the guards restrained him, pushing him back in the seat.

"I want you to admit that you are my baby's father. Then – only then - will I allow you to be with your precious Amber. She's actually not far from here. You can be with her in a matter of minutes."

Eloise indicated to an open doorway that led down into Level 3, the steep incline of the corridor going down to the level below visible.

"All it takes is your agreement. For you to keep repeating four words I want you to say – *I'm the baby's father*. Now that's not so difficult, is it?"

She yanked off his blindfold and for the first time, Bray was truly able to gauge his surroundings.

Unbeknown to him, he had been held in Level 2 of the compound and was stunned to see the rows of the many empty cryogenic chambers, intended once for the adult technicians, as well as the powerful computer terminals surrounding the room.

But it was the corridor, angling downwards, to where Eloise implied Amber was being kept, that was Bray's prime concern.

He looked at Eloise anxiously, wondering what she intended, had inflicted, upon Amber and the others.

"Do I really frighten you that much?" Eloise asked softly, registering the uneasy look Bray was now giving her.

"You repulse me," Bray replied.

"That's no way to win over a girl's heart," Eloise said coquettishly in mock hurt. All too conscious of how attractive she was – and powerful – it was absurd, Eloise considered, that she could ever repulse anyone, especially a red-blooded male. Compared to Amber – there was no contest. Bray would learn to appreciate her charms.

Eloise raised one hand to her mouth to wipe away another trickle of blood then slowly, seductively traced one finger down the side of Bray's cheek, drawing a crimson line - then she stuck her tongue out, to lick the blood from Bray's face, smouldering.

"So, what do you think, Bray? Do we have a deal?"

"You're wasting your breath," Bray said.

"How about I take your breath away?"

"In your dreams."

"You would make it so much easier for yourself if you'd learn to co-operate."

"Not unless you tell me about Amber. Where is she?" Bray asked, gazing at Eloise intently.

"Amber, Amber, Amber," Eloise mocked. "Is that all you ever think about?"

"If she is here -"

"Oh, she's here alright," Eloise interrupted. "Along with a few of your other 'friends'".

"Well, if you let Amber and them go... then yeah... I might be willing to be a little more co-operative."

"You're in no position to bargain – let me make that absolutely clear," Eloise said. "But I am. I've got all the cards in my hand. I have your mall, your city, your friends. Amber... and I have you."

"I wouldn't be too sure about that," Bray replied, exchanging glances with Eloise in growing disdain. "What exactly is it you want?" he asked.

"We're on the cusp of the greatest discovery since the days of the adults. So seeing this is a historic day – I might be willing to be a little more reasonable in my terms and conditions."

"Oh, really? And what would they be?"

"How about I allow you to live with Amber for the rest of your lives. In luxury. You will never have to worry about anything, ever again. I'm willing to even be your mistress and not interfere. You can love Amber, have your way, do whatever you wish. All I ask is you appear in public a few times – before the worshippers – and admit you are the father of my child. Apart from that - I will leave you and Amber alone. Now how about that for an offer?"

Bray took a moment to think over the deal Eloise had just proposed. He would do anything to save Amber's life – and his friends. But at what cost? Giving truth to the lie he had fathered her child, stamping legitimacy upon the baby as having a connection to Zoot – then Bray would no doubt strengthen Eloise's place and the entire Zootist religion she was leading, manipulating. Any agreement with Eloise would be like making a deal with the devil. He knew exactly what he had to do.

"You know what you can do with your offer, Eloise? Stick it!"

"Such a pity – for you! You see, I have another option on offer. How about I have you locked up forever in one of these machines…"

Eloise indicated the empty cryogenic chambers in the room.

"We can turn you into a living tomb! The worshippers can come and visit you - Zoot's brother - frozen for all eternity in a mausoleum! How'd you like that!"

She smiled slightly, reading the unease in Bray's expression.

"I could always arrange for the rest of your friends to join you. And let's not forget Amber. I can imagine her lying in a tomb next to you. I'm sure you'd really enjoy that, given how you feel about her! You could both be together - for all eternity!"

CHAPTER THIRTY-SEVEN

Finding the Eco tribe camp during the day would have been difficult enough - but as the sun dipped over the hills on the horizon and dusk set in, Lex realized that Lia and himself were getting well and truly lost. They were going to soon end up totally in the dark, Lex reflected, in every sense of the word.

Lex flicked on the front lights of the car, its beams cutting through the ever darkening countryside, illuminating the forest all around, Lex doing his best to drive as quickly as he could over the twisting roads.

"It's gotta be around here somewhere," Lex said, concentrating, trying to recognize any familiar landmarks that indicated the turn off from the road to the area where Lex was sure Hawk and the Ecos were based. "Or at least, I think."

Lia gave Lex an admiring glance. She was proud of his efforts though she understood his doubts about their whereabouts – and his questioning if Hawk and his tribe would even still be there, where they used to live, assuming Lex could find the way to that part of the forest.

Suddenly, Lex spun the wheel and the car skidded from the main road onto a track.

"You'd better hold on tight!" Lex said as they bumped along. Lia gripped the dashboard and door handle. "If that doesn't work," Lex continued, "then don't worry if you feel like grabbing hold of me."

Lia smiled despite herself as a mischievous grin also spread over Lex's expression.

"You're something else, Lex, you really are," she said.

"Somehow that doesn't sound much like a compliment," he remarked.

"Well if you want to know the truth... it actually is."

"For someone who hasn't spoken English all their life, it seems as if we're now starting to talk the same language."

Before long the car pulled into a clearing, stopped. Lex and Lia got out, gazing around.

"Seems as if we're out of luck," Lex sighed.

The huts which once accommodated the Eco tribe were deserted, the entire camp abandoned. Lex explained to Lia more about the tribe and concluded that they must have fled somewhere around the same time as the Mall Rats, suspecting that the virus Mega had seemingly inflicted on the city may have spread to other areas too.

"It reminds me of the village back on the island in many ways," Lia reflected, "and it's given me an idea."

"Funny that. I was just thinking about the same thing. How about you and I head into that hut over there and make ourselves a bit more comfortable before we return to Bray?"

"That's not exactly what I had in mind, Lex," Lia said.

And he watched stunned as she started running over to a nearby tree which she proceeded to quickly climb, dangling by her arms from a long branch and swinging her legs back and forth.

"Come and help me," Lia called out.

"What the hell are you doing?" Lex shouted, giving Lia a look which suggested he thought she had temporarily lost her senses.

"I'm – breaking – this – branch!" Lia responded, gritting her teeth in effort as she applied all her strength and body weight to the branch – which suddenly snapped, tumbling to the ground, along with Lia, who controlled her fall, rolling as she hit the earth.

She climbed to her feet and dragged the branch to Lex.

"I need your jacket again," Lia instructed.

He removed it and handed it to her.

"Why?"

Lia was now gathering up rocks and pebbles from the banks of a small stream.

"What's all that in aid of?" Lex wondered. "Don't tell me you're after some souvenirs."

"I learned much during my time on the island... and a lot from the Priestess which might help."

Lex considered Lia, intrigued, as she put her hands behind her back, inside her blouse, and it seemed to Lex like she was unclasping her bra.

"If we ever run into the Priestess again - remind me to tell her that she must have been one hell of a good teacher!" Lex said, gazing tantalizing at Lia taking her arms out from under her blouse – and revealing that she was indeed holding her bra in her hands.

"Nice one. I like it!" Lex said.

Then he watched, amazed, as she bit into the straps on the bra, working on them with her teeth, opening up a little hole, which she then began to push her fingers in, taking out the elastic from inside.

She held the elastic up in front of her, as if aiming, pulling back on it, the elastic springing back as she released it.

"*Bra*-vo!" Lex joked. "I can't wait for the encore."

"Let's save that for when we get back to Eagle Mountain," Lia grinned. "If I can make what I'm thinking – we might be able to surprise the guards with some extra special weapons of our own."

CHAPTER THIRTY-EIGHT

"Nice of you to drop in," Ebony said, watching as Jay was pushed into the cage in the mall, joining Emma, Trudy and the other Mall Rats captured from Lex's love-shack earlier, who were now being kept inside.

Jay had been found on the roof of the mall after sabotaging the electrical transformer – but had put up a good fight, refusing to give himself up after being surrounded and outnumbered by the Zootists who had been zealous in their attempts to capture him.

"Oh my God, Jay - are you alright?" Salene asked as Jay stumbled to the ground, checking him over, a large black eye and swelling visible on Jay's face.

"I've been better – that's for sure," Jay said, coughing as he uneasily rose to his feet, his ribs aching.

"So - it looks like the whole gang's here. Almost," Ebony said teasingly from the other side of the cell, standing beside Connor. "Nearly all the Mall Rats are back in the mall."

"Greetings," the Guardian said, gazing down from the upper level at the prisoners huddled in the caged cell on the ground floor concourse below.

He was holding little Brady, who was starting to sob, by one of her hands.

May was clutching baby Bray in her arms in the caged cell and instinctively recoiled to protect Amber and Bray's child, in case the baby would also be taken.

Seeing her child in the clutches of the Guardian, Trudy roared out a primal scream of despair and frustration, Emma reaching out and giving her a loving, supportive embrace

Emma could sympathize, also feeling the pains of separation by being kept apart from Tiffany and Shannon, still apparently being schooled, or indoctrinated more like, in classes held in abandoned stores in another part of the mall.

The Guardian walked down the stairs, hand in hand with Brady, who was becoming upset at seeing her mother so upset in the cell.

"You have done well, *bounty hunter*, and will soon get your reward," the Guardian said disparagingly as he passed Connor, standing nearby and indicated him to the guards.

"Get off me!" Connor shouted. "Let go!"

He was surrounded by some of the Zootists, eagerly wanting to please the Guardian.

"You will soon appreciate the importance of faith - a far more valuable currency than anything you've ever desired! Throw him in with the others so he can decide his future - while he still has one!"

Connor was quickly overwhelmed by the Zootists, dragging him to the cell, literally throwing him in as the Guardian had commanded, the grille door to the cage crashing down behind him.

"Ebony!" Connor begged her, looking for help, feeling betrayed.

Ebony was truly shocked by the turnaround in Connor's fortunes – and wondered if this was a harbinger of her own fate in some way, feeling if she was as disposable if not required, as evidently was the case with Connor.

However, surrounded by Zootists, devoted to their cause and the Guardian - Ebony felt there was nothing she could do – not yet – and she shrugged at Connor.

"The Mother Divine has informed me that a new era is upon us," the Guardian spoke, getting to the bottom of the stairs, young Brady reaching out, bawling uncontrollably, eager to be with her mother – Trudy heaving sobs of distress from the other side of the cage cell in which she was imprisoned.

"Our faith no longer has a place in it for the Supreme Mother," the Guardian continued, keeping Brady in an iron grip. "By her actions, the Supreme Mother has proven herself a traitor to our religion – and to us all. She has consorted with our enemies, spread lies about our divine mission. She has desecrated our mighty Zoot, who placed such responsibility in her. And she has undermined the Mother Divine, questioning her divine links – even doubting the Child Divine that is waiting to be born. Therefore my prophecy, which will be written in the scriptures for all time, is that the Supreme

Mother needs to be punished for being the traitor she has become. Bring her to me!"

Several of the Zootists eagerly approached the cage, encircling it from all sides.

On the other side of the wire mesh enclosure, Jay, Salene, May, Gel and Darryl formed their own line of defence, positioning themselves in front of Trudy, determined to protect her. Even Connor joined the line, throwing his lot in with the other prisoners, feeling he had nothing more to lose, angered at being apparently double-crossed. While Emma enveloped baby Bray in her arms, Lottie and Sammy nearby were gripping each other in absolute fear.

"Zoot's daughter will be raised to appreciate the greatness and divine power that was her father... and she will be taught of the betrayal of her mother. Today, we will eliminate the poison that is the Supreme Mother from our lives – and offer her as a sacrifice to Zoot. Trudy has damned herself by her course. She will not live to see the glorious future that lies ahead, where her daughter will continue the legacy of her immortal father!"

Ebony watched as the gate to the caged cell was slowly raised, feeling stunned by the speed of events, seeing her former friends – lovers even, memories of her happier times in the past with Jay flashing before her mind – in such peril.

She had played her part in all this coming to be, Ebony knew – driven by the promise of the reward she expected.

She had always thought the Guardian was bluffing about the threats to make 'offerings' of his prisoners to Zoot. Instead, Ebony expected they would live out their days in manual labour or performing some other subservient task for the Collective.

But that did not mean Ebony ever anticipated that Jay, Trudy – even baby Bray, an innocent who had done nobody any wrong – would ever be in this position, perhaps about to spend the last moments of their lives.

Ebony knew only too well that with the ethos of the tribe, the older Mall Rats would be willing to fight to the bitter end, to die each other, for their beliefs – to save Trudy and to stop the Guardian's deranged plan to sacrifice her.

The initial disappointment Ebony felt when Eloise didn't take her to Eagle Mountain – choosing instead to exclude her, not even informing Ebony of what was being undertaken – was now magnified, in Ebony's eyes.

First, she had seen Connor so easily cast off and denied the reward he had expected, Ebony aware of the irony of him believing he was betrayed by the Collective, Connor having been a traitor himself to Trudy and the Mall Rats. Talk about karma.

Now, Trudy's very life was at stake.

Would Ebony be next? Or Brady? If this was the way Eloise operated – keeping what was of 'use' and eliminating something that had no value to her – then one day, if Eloise deemed Ebony was of no further 'use' – or had somehow become a threat – would Ebony suffer the same fate that the Guardian now presented to Trudy?

Ebony had always considered that the Guardian, clearly not of sound mind, was all too easily controlled by the intelligent and cunning Eloise.

Was Ebony herself no different – and the truth nothing more than she had also been manipulated by Eloise without even realizing it, all this time? She thought she could use Eloise – but was it really the other way around? Had Ebony let her own greed overcome her better sense?

If that was the case, Ebony was different to the Guardian in one major way, she felt. If anyone ever tried to make her a puppet, Ebony was determined to 'pull back' on the strings – to fight back against the puppeteer. She was nobody's fool.

The gate of the cell was almost open now, some of the Zootists crawling underneath, chanting Zoot's name in a state of fervour, anxious to get to the Mall Rats, to bring Trudy to the Guardian.

Jay and Connor, working together, tried to form a barrier, pushing the Zootists back out into the crowd of circling followers, the Mall Rats desperate to maintain their position in the cage. Trudy, Salene, May, Darryl, Gel, Sammy and Lottie yanked down on the gate, trying somehow to provide extra minutes, even seconds, of protection, keeping the rabid Zootists from getting to them.

Ebony quickly considered her options. She could either stand back and watch as the last remnants of her past were surely wiped out before her very eyes – or she could do something daring. Try and intervene. Play a wild card that might change the game. By bending the rules.

The sight of the candles burning in the spot where Zoot fell inspired her. She thought back to the pivotal moment at school when Martin, in his younger incarnation prior to adopting the persona of Zoot, changed the lives of so many by making a stand. She was going to try something that he would have been proud of, she was sure. It was time to make a stand of her own.

"Wait! Wait!" Ebony shouted.

It was no use, the fanatical Zootists could not hear her above their frenzied chanting as they continued trying to raise the gate and get to the prisoners inside the cage.

Ebony ran up the stairs to the upper level of the concourse where one of the Zootists was operating the lever that raised the gate to the caged cell.

Before he could even react, Ebony yanked him away from the lever - toward the stairs, then she unleashed a mighty boot into his back, pushing him, hurling the Zootist, who tumbled down, rolling over many times, before shuddering to a halt in the middle of the stairwell.

With no-one operating the lever to the cage, the grille gates of the cell crashed down to the floor under their own weight, sending the encircling Zootists scurrying back to get out of the way, fearful of being crushed from the heavy gate.

"What is the meaning of this?!" the Guardian bellowed – the acolytes and the prisoners in the cell – all looking up to the upper concourse level where Ebony stood, watching over them.

She had finally gotten their attention.

"I told you all to wait!" Ebony repeated.

"You forget your place - I gave no such order!" the Guardian shouted at her.

"It is you who forget your place. *Jaffa*," Ebony spat out, disdainfully calling him by the name he went under at school before becoming the Guardian.

"I had a vision today!" Ebony continued, addressing the entire assembly. "Zoot himself appeared before me in the city – with a warning to beware of false prophets! There are those who betray the true cause – and Zoot told me Eloise – and Jaffa – are actually the ones spreading lies, pretending to be who they are not! Tricking us all into following them – but they themselves do not follow what Zoot wanted!"

The Guardian exploded in rage.

"This is blasphemy!! Death to the unbeliever!! Seize the heathen!! And rip her lies, along with her heart, from her body!! Then pray to Zoot to give mercy for her salvation!! While I eat and devour her soul!!"

He started snarling manically as if he was departing this realm into a trance while some of the Zootists rushed to ascend the stairwell - but Aras and the other acolytes of Ebony's loyal group, so devoted and determined to protect her, deliberately positioned themselves at the bottom of the stairwell, blocking any of the Guardian's followers from getting to Ebony.

"History will show *I* was the one who was chosen by Zoot, to be by his side! Not you, Jaffa! And not Eloise! He chose me! And now – he has chosen me again! To speak for his wishes!"

Everyone in the mall was listening intently to Ebony's words, none more than the Zootists on the lower concourse, many refusing to believe what she was saying – but others were profoundly struck by her message, casting doubting glances at the Guardian, clasping his hands to his ears and snarling, in steaming hate and anger.

"This is sacrilege!!" he screamed.

"If I am not telling the truth – then let Zoot strike me down, right now! You have been corrupting his legacy, Jaffa! Eloise has been manipulating you – all of you! But it all ends today!"

Trudy noticed that Ebony was having an effect. Many of the Zootists believing her to be a living legend, the former Queen of the Locos. And instinctively, she saw an opening.

"Ebony speaks the truth!" Trudy shouted from the cell. "I am the mother of Zoot's daughter! I gave birth to her! I raised her! Ebony is right! The so-called

'Guardian' – and Eloise – are nothing but imposters! They're the ones who have been spreading lies!"

There was a growing murmur of unrest upon hearing Trudy give her backing to Ebony. Trudy herself had always occupied a hallowed role in the faith as the Supreme Mother - until the Guardian had revealed she had apparently been a traitor, just moments before. From the expressions on the faces of many of the gathered Zootists, it was obvious they didn't know who – or what – to believe anymore.

Ebony walked over to the ledge, looking over the rail at the circle of candles burning brightly far below, Ebony standing at the very spot where she knew Lex had unbalanced Zoot, sending him over the edge, plummeting to his doom so long before.

"Honour the place Zoot fell! He won't rise again! But you can rise up! In his name! The Mall Rats were right all along! And I'm with them! It's what Zoot would have wanted. He loved Trudy – and his daughter – and we have to protect them now! So who's with me! Rise up! Today – we can all make history!"

"Silence!! How dare you desecrate the faith in the name of the Mighty One!" the Guardian roared – and so consumed was he in his frenzy, he let go of little Brady's hand - Brady rushing over to the cage to be near her mother.

It seemed like a portent to many – that Zoot's daughter was showing where her allegiance rested, which side was telling the truth.

A scuffle immediately broke out between Aras and Ebony's group of acolytes and some of the Guardian's most fanatical adherents who were trying to get past them. Pushing and shoving quickly escalated into full blown fighting – spreading in a chain reaction, everyone in that part of the mall having to pick their side, engaging in hand to hand combat.

The Zootist forces were totally split, some choosing the Guardian – others deciding there and then to throw their loyalties behind Ebony and the Supreme Mother.

"Traitors!" the Guardian yelled.

A chaotic melee ensued – and instinctively sure that she had done enough, setting the Zootists against each other, Ebony pulled back the lever to the cage, feeling it was better to free Jay and the other prisoners so they could take their chances outside the cell, rather than be stuck inside helplessly.

Jay and Connor led the way, rushing under the gates as they were ascending, raised by the lifting mechanism Ebony had activated. They both formed a protective circle with May, Salene, Darryl, Gel and Sammy – positioning themselves around Emma, Lottie and Trudy, who scooped her daughter up in her arms, Brady having run under the bars as soon as they lifted high enough for her to get through.

Emma, terrified by the chaotic scene unfolding around her, held baby Bray in her arms, and quickly backed up from a charging Zootist emitting a war cry - before Jay jumped between them, blocking the Zootist - and knocking him back, unleashing a fierce kick, sending the zealot hurling to the floor.

Ebony screamed out a battle cry of her own, racing down the stairs, entering the fray to be amongst Aras and her supporters, to fight alongside.

It was as if all hell had broken loose.

They were not only fighting for the future – but their very lives.

CHAPTER THIRTY-NINE

Ram moved from one hibernation chamber to another, studying the faces on the occupants inside, trying to establish some clue or indication where the data device they were searching for might be.

Though Eloise and her guards had disconnected all the cryogenic units, the temperatures had been so cold in each machine that the adults inside still remained frozen, covered in an icy blue liquid substance, the glass covers of the chambers blanketed in condensation. Gradually, however, the mixture of gases in each unit was beginning to leak, releasing a strange odour into the air – and it wouldn't be long, Amber dreaded, before they all died, if indeed they hadn't done so already.

"Are you sure there's no way to reactivate that program?" Amber asked Ram.

"Maybe. If I had a few weeks," he replied.

"Stop talking – keep searching," Axel ordered, watching from the centre of the room, having positioned his guards at different parts of the circular complex so they could vigilantly watch over the activities of their prisoners.

Amber was still upset by the callous way the cryogenic units had been turned off, ensuring the adults inside would likely never wake up again. There was no need for them to have done such a thing, she felt. It was an inhuman deed, heartless. Eloise seemed to have even enjoyed it at the time, revelling in her power, the fates of others in her hands.

The idea of profoundly important knowledge falling into the grasp of Eloise and the Collective made Amber more than totally uncomfortable.

If the Collective were to obtain the data device and possess the knowledge of what had led to the pandemic – especially if it was the result of a deliberate act, some sort of chemical warfare that Ram had alluded to – it would present them with a potentially devastating weapon of their own. Should they be able to reproduce the 'virus', the Collective could then make themselves an unstoppable force, sweeping away opposition due to the fear they would unleash some bacterial terror, information about which the adults might have purposefully kept somewhere in this very room.

But if all the knowledge left behind was put to good use - and Amber was sure the amount of knowledge from some of the greatest scientific minds of the time would have been extensive - then it would have provided strong foundations on which to build a future from the ashes of the old. Just as the adults had intended, no doubt desperate that it would not fall into insidious hands.

Axel was studying their every move, still deployed to monitor the activity in the chamber while their captives searched for the data device.

"This computer must have thousands of hard drives," Jack said, checking out the *K.A.M.I* system, seeing within its translucent steel bound case countless interlinked data drives.

"I told you so," Ram replied.

"I wonder how long it will take to examine them all," Jack continued to reflect, sure that if someone was going to put top secret confidential data anywhere – it was likely to be in the vast computer that dominated the room.

"There are four thousand and ninety-six drives and even with a binomial theorem, it is difficult to estimate the exact time to check all data with variable skill levels of

those computer literate," the *K.A.M.I* system announced, obviously having been 'listening'.

"Computer – search the drives for any information about the back up devices," Amber instructed, looking up at the technological behemoth towering above her.

"*All search enquiries are classified. State security clearance.*"

"Why don't you state it," Jack suggested.

"*Access denied. State security clearance.*"

"Nice try," Ram said.

"Well, seems as if it's a dead end," Jack said, shrugging at Amber.

"No – we're not giving up. We can't," Amber replied.

They moved around the room, examining under each hibernation chamber, feeling the walls for any hidden control panels or doorways, Axel and the guards intently watching.

"If only *you* could talk," Ram said, speaking to the faces of the occupants of the cryogenic chambers he was passing by.

The adults were arranged in order, Ram noticed, a pattern - the chambers filled by alternating rows of men and women.

All of them were on their backs, their arms crisscrossed, hands on their chests, like they were medieval knights on display in a tomb in some ancient church.

The devil was always in the detail, Ram had learned. A computer could work – as would software – but all it took was the tiniest thing, an almost imperceptible error in the code, harmless in itself, to cause the entire program to crash, or to wipe data. Detail was all important - not solely for computers but within recesses of the human mind, which Ram sincerely believed was the greatest computer of them all. Most people only used a fraction of what the brain was capable of. But not Ram. He pushed the envelope. He respected, some said even worshipped, technology and certainly had a love for it, along with computers. But he found all the data he contained in his mind greater. That data could never be wiped, corrupted. And he continued focusing on every detail he could see in the room, concentrating intently, trying to identify a sequence.

He didn't believe any of that detail would be found on the *K.A.M.I* system after all, concluding that the adults wouldn't put sensitive powerful data inside the most obvious place to look for it – the only computer visible in the room – Ram considered. Part of keeping a computer protected was 'security through obscurity' – nobody would be able to access something if they didn't even know it was there in the first place.

"Nice suit," Ram commented, admiring the finely tailored suit worn by an adult man in one of the hibernation units.

But it was the woman in the next chamber that captured Ram's attention.

Her hands were not placed in the same manner as all the other adults. Instead of her arms overlapping with her hands on her chest, this woman's arms were lying downwards by the sides of her body, her fingers stretched out, as if pointing, Ram was convinced, to where her feet should be.

Her right hand also had a large green opal ring on it – but it was no ordinary jewel, Ram could see. The ring, on the wedding finger, was actually a form of wearable tech, Ram's acute eyes identifying a tiny interface on the band of the ring – confirming his suspicion that the ring itself could be linked into something, another technological system. He suspected the large green opal itself was probably a minute hard drive of some kind.

"What is it?" Axel called out to him, from the other side of the room.

"Nothing," Ram answered nonchalantly, covering. "I was just admiring this woman. She's pretty."

"That's pretty - disgusting," Ellie said, giving Ram a contemptuous look. "She's dead. And you're - sick."

"I'll just have a little looksee – she's just my type."

The others exchanged horrified glances. Ram was eccentric at the best of times but they all found his behaviour now more than bizarre as he used the manual override, grasping the handles on the hibernation unit, opening the glass cover, a mixture of cold air and gaseous fumes flooding out of the unit into the room.

"Haven't you got any respect? Leave them in peace!" Amber called out, shocked by Ram's behaviour.

Ram ignored Amber, focusing instead on the area in the chamber where the woman's feet were, having been obscured previously, out of sight, under the metallic lower cover of the unit, the transparent glass area in the top half only showing each occupant's face and torso area.

"Would you look at that?" Ram said to himself, smiling at his persistence - and admiring his discovery.

In the lower part of the hibernation chamber, between the woman's feet, was a gold plated hard drive, with an interface connection type Ram had never seen before.

He wouldn't even begin to speculate what to plug the drive into but knew enough about technology to recognize the drive for what it was – a solid state hard drive. The gold external case had obviously been put in place by the adults to keep the drive – and its data – protected from the freezing cold in the unit, Ram believed. This, rather than the ring on the woman's finger, had to be the elusive data device.

It was apt that the casing looked to be made of gold, Ram thought, feeling euphoric – like he had discovered a nugget in the old gold rush days. He knew he had to act calm, appear casual, to try and keep it a secret from the others. If this was what they were looking for – potentially the most important item since the adult era, let alone in the history of modern advanced human knowledge.

Ram picked up the drive – but realized everyone had been actually watching him, fascinated and repulsed by his unusual behaviour – and it was no longer a secret anymore that Ram was now carrying the hard drive in his hands.

"What's that you're holding?" Axel asked.

"That's my business," Ram replied.

"Give it to me!" Axel commanded, briskly walking over towards Ram.

"Go to hell!" Ram shouted, backing up, away from the oncoming Axel and his guards. "I mean it! I'm about the only one with the knowledge how to access this - and you'd better make sure no harm comes to me!"

"I wouldn't hold your breath on it!" Axel snapped, lunging at Ram, who spun and ran.

"I can't believe it! He's got it! We've got to help him!" Amber cried out in growing realization, aware now of the significance of what Ram had discovered.

Amber, Jack and Ellie raced towards Ram, who was now running between the rows of hibernation units, trying to use them as barriers to protect him from Axel and the guards converging in pursuit from the other side.

"*K.A.M.I* – you there?" Ram called out, frantically.

"*I'm always there*," the computer answered calmly, its green laser lights pulsing around the huge cavernous room.

"Immediate complete system shutdown!" Ram yelled, reversing course at the last moment, running in the opposite direction to avoid Axel, closing in on him quickly.

"*Please confirm request.*"

"Shutdown all systems immediately."

"*Goodbye, Ram.*"

Suddenly, the entire room was engulfed in darkness, all the ambient lights turned off, even those that had previously flickered on the *K.A.M.I* system disappearing as the computer shut itself down – along with the entire Eagle Mountain complex.

Amber stopped running immediately, fearful she would crash into Axel – or one of the hibernation chambers.

She heard the sounds of machinery whirring down, the air vent system losing all its power, the fans gradually slowing, no longer circulating air to any part of the compound.

"Find him!" Axel shouted, straining his eyes in the darkness.

All the occupants could hear the sounds of frenetic movement, footsteps running quickly, a struggle, but no-one able to identify friend or foe. There was nothing. No-one could even see their own arms or hands in the pitch black.

It was as if Ram – and everyone and everything in the room – had totally disappeared. Evaporated, hidden in the mammoth, underground dark tomb.

CHAPTER FORTY

The battle in the mall raged with unbridled ferocity and intensity on both sides, the Zootists who were still loyal to the Guardian trying everything to suppress the uprising Ebony had instigated – while her forces, comprising mostly Zootists who had now turned their backs on the Guardian and Eloise, fought for their freedom, along with the Mall Rats.

Control of the mall – and the city – was at stake, as well as Trudy's life, the Guardian shouting out commands, urging his devoted fanatics to get to Trudy so she could be 'offered' to Zoot, in accordance with Eloise's instructions.

It was chaotic, absolute mayhem – difficult at times to know who was fighting on which side, with the Zootist acolytes all wearing similar attire.

Many remained loyal to the Guardian and Eloise but others only felt a special bond to Zoot himself, with no such personal connection to Eloise or the Guardian - and Ebony's casting of doubt and aspersions had only served to fuel an already existing distrust that had been gradually growing among some of the worshippers, resentful of Eloise and the Guardian's imperious ways. Much of their authority had been predicated upon installing fear and discipline rather than respect or adoration for their leaders.

Ebony – and Trudy – were also living legends among the faith, being individuals who had each in their own lives direct personal experiences with Zoot. Even the Guardian, in all his teachings, had cited their past as evidence of Zoot's divine power and influence, the two of them witnesses and participants in the original events of Zoot's life.

Ironically, the very devotion the Guardian instilled in his followers was now starting to work against him as the many Zootists siding with Ebony and Trudy gave everything they had to defend the two of them, as well as Trudy's daughter.

It was no wonder, many Zootists thought, that Zoot had chosen Trudy and Ebony to be significant people in his earthly form, both showing themselves to be strong, capable and special young women as well as spirited warriors.

With Zootist being pitted against Zootist, the lower concourse of the mall was awash with the loud frenetic sounds of fighting, shouting… desperate cries echoing in the mall, shaken by the intense melee that had erupted, a frightening cacophony of the noise of battle rumbling all around, as if the complex itself would crash down to its foundations. Primal energies were being unleashed, everyone going on instinct, fighting for what they believed in, to survive.

"Salene – look out!" May shouted, Salene ducking, just managing to dodge a wild haymaker type swing from one massive assailant who had aimed his large fist at her, the attacker losing his balance - and Salene tripping him by his ankle, sweeping his legs out from under him.

May had been so intent on saving Salene, giving her warning, that she didn't notice the Zootist girl behind who unleashed a vicious blow into May's back, who crumpled to the ground, screaming in agony.

"May!" Salene cried out, rushing to save the person she loved by smashing a chair across the back of May's assailant, sending her hurling.

In another part of the battle area, Connor exchanged blows on a charging Zootist, causing him to collapse and lose consciousness before he even hit the ground due to Connor's well placed knockout strike.

An experienced fighter, Connor had been in many battles during his time as a bounty hunter and had already made several vital interceptions, helping to hold off the swarming Zootists from getting to Trudy or Brady.

"Keep away from us!" Trudy screamed out as more Zootists converged towards them.

Trudy had been like a cornered tigress, ferociously defending Emma, Brady, Lottie and baby Bray with the utmost determination. All her maternal instincts had kicked in to another level, Trudy ready to make the ultimate sacrifice to save her daughter – as well as the other younger ones. Nobody would get past her, she vowed, while she had any breath left in her body. She was willing to literally die for her daughter if she needed, to make her live, to exchange her life for Brady's.

Emma was scared, unable to see what was going on, only hearing the chaotic tumult of battle. She clung to baby Bray tightly, hunching her shoulders and torso, rolling up into a ball shape, pulling her legs back under her chin, the baby tucked safely on her lap in between, shielding him with her body, trusting in Trudy and Connor to defend them along with Sammy and Lottie, who joined in the fray, aware that Emma was doing all she could to defend Bray and Amber's otherwise defenceless, vulnerable child. And yet through her blindness, there was no-one more vulnerable than Emma throughout the battle. But her great strength of character and spirit urged her on.

Connor and Trudy were forming an excellent partnership, working well with each other, linking, covering each other's defensive gaps, calling out warnings, co-ordinating their movements. They were a formidable duo.

It was an irony not lost on Connor, who felt regret at his betrayal of Trudy and all her trust in him. She was beautiful, loving – and fiercely protective, a fighter - and Connor admired her more than ever.

This was becoming a defining moment for him, Connor appreciated – there was more to life than material rewards. Life was precious. Short. He would fight for Trudy – and her daughter – and the chance of the forgiveness he longed for from them, if the three of them could make it out alive.

For all the Mall Rats' spirited defence, they and the Zootist followers who now were taking their orders from Ebony were showing signs of collapsing, being still in the minority. Ebony and her group had held their line well, by the stairs, Aras and her loyal supporters fighting with steely resilience, repelling all attacks the Guardian had ordered against them.

But there had been a sudden discernible shift and the Guardian had obviously changed tack, Ebony observed, commanding the bulk of his own followers to pull away from Ebony's forces and to instead focus on the Mall Rats.

Trudy and Connor were strong, the two of them fighting off another wave of attack from the fanatical Zootists. But it was the other side of the protective ring that gave Ebony alarm, where the defensive circle was certain to soon breach.

May was slumped on the floor, immobile, Salene in dire trouble, losing her battle against a towering Zootist girl.

Darryl, Gel, Sammy and Lottie – on the opposite side of Trudy and Connor, with Salene and May having been between them – were fighting bravely but the Zootists were pressing in, sensing weakness.

There was no sign of Jay, Ebony was aware, as she rushed down the stairs from the second floor into the heart of battle to assist the Mall Rats - Aras and her loyal supporters following in her wake, her group barrelling into the Guardian's adherents, surging through them, like a powerful wave crashing down.

The mythical figure she had been portrayed - and then some – Ebony, the warrior Queen of the Locos, was visible for all to see, striking out at her enemies, an unstoppable force.

She, more than anyone there, had the most experience of fighting since the adult days – and her own natural talents had been harnessed by the legendary Zoot himself, training Ebony in street fighting, teaching her all the tricks he knew.

Ebony fought dirty – she fought hard – and she was enjoying it, her adrenalin flowing, the thrill of the conflict, wrestling with destiny, knowing the outcome of this battle was pivotal for all their lives, determined to seize and control her own fate, skirting with danger. It was the ultimate rush.

Gel received a blow from a Zootist to the head and slumped to the floor, unconscious – Darryl spun, unleashing a powerful kick into the Zootist responsible before being floored himself by a Zootist nearby. Darryl dropped to one knee, still fighting back desperately, leaving only Salene and May behind him, lashing out as the Zootists increased their attacks on this vulnerable spot, so they could then get to Trudy and Brady, near Connor, still valiant – and end the battle.

Ebony could sense there was only a matter of minutes before the balance of the battle would be won or lost, which spurred her on. Giving her a sudden charge of energy and urgency, and she drove herself, and her supporters, forward, realizing she had to get to the Mall Rats – before they were quickly overwhelmed.

* * *

Moving stealthily behind the fountain of the Phoenix statue, near the stairwell on the lower level, crouched down, out of sight from everyone, like a prowling tiger – Jay awaited his moment.

He had first stood shoulder to shoulder, resolutely by Connor, helping to defend Trudy and the others when the battle commenced but felt there could be a more direct way of saving the Mall Rats – and defeating their enemies.

He had made his way through the battlefield, like a visceral force, cutting past opposition, avoiding becoming entrenched in any entangling melees, focused intently on only one thing, his target – who was standing among the burning candles in the shrine where Zoot fell, flanked by his most fanatical bodyguards.

It was from there that the Guardian had shouted out his orders, feeling as if he was empowering himself with the divine energies he felt flowing into him from the shrine.

Victory was literally within grasp, the Guardian knew, and he praised Zoot, screaming a frenzied prayer, to thank Zoot for turning the tide in the Guardian's favour.

Jay had used the shadows to aid his progress, the cover of darkness that he himself was responsible for, having sabotaged the main electricity supply, and realized that it was now or never. He braced himself, staring at the Guardian – and then ran, with all the force he could muster, flinging himself at the Guardian, sending the Zootist leader literally flying, smashing into the wall.

Jay had gambled that if he could only capture the Guardian, then surely the zealous forces would give up their attacks.

But now he found himself surrounded by the Guardian's elite bodyguards.

Ignoring the blows raining down upon him, straining with every fibre, Jay continued fighting with brave determination, not giving in, desperate to seize the Guardian – and finish the battle.

His spirit willed him on, but now facing much greater odds Jay was truly up against it, his chances of success diminishing with every strike the guards unleashed.

The Guardian slipped out of Jay's grasp, the bodyguards rushing in on Jay like a pack of wolves.

But Jay fought back. He imagined Amber. Baby Bray. His brother, Ved. Jay's parents. All those important to him. It was as if his life was flashing before his very eyes.

In that moment, Jay felt a sudden sense of peace. A profound inner meaning. Contentment in his soul. He was doing what was right, what he had to do. For so long, he had fought to make the world a better place. Not for him. For others. The future had to be secured from all who jeopardized it – and threatened the ones he loved.

Gritting his teeth and exchanging blows with his adversaries, Jay felt weak but kept going on nothing but instinct, no longer feeling the pains of the blows overwhelming his body, casting them aside, driven by his willpower, refusing to surrender, reaching out once more, the Guardian so close now, within his grasp.

Jay had long ago promised he would give everything he had for those he loved – clearly intent on fighting to the bitter end - whatever that end might be.

* * *

In another part of the mall in stores on the upper level, mothers cradled their young babies lovingly in their arms while listening to the distant sounds of battle. Some held their infant children protectively, while other girls in various stages of pregnancy gazed around in equal concern at what fate might lay in store.

For so long they had been treated as nothing but animals. Their purpose to solely rear and raise babies. Nothing else was asked or expected of them. The children they endured the pain of birth for, bringing them into the world, were often taken away from their crying mothers for long periods, to be indoctrinated into the Zootist religion, as part of the Collective's overall plan to repopulate the world with a new generation of zealot followers.

Tiffany and Shannon were originally being held in another store nearby being used as a classroom but had now raced along the upper concourse to gaze down, noticing their older sister, Emma, near Trudy below, surrounded by Zootists.

Emma still carried baby Bray in her arms, shielding him with her body, refusing to give up the baby to the Zootists tugging and pulling on her, attempting to take the child away.

Tiffany and Shannon were soon joined by some of the mothers and other young children, who noticed Emma and it was almost symbolic in a way, seeing her so bravely shielding the baby, protecting him from the Guardian's supporters.

One by one they accompanied Tiffany and Shannon, throwing down objects, picking their targets, the ones who were obviously loyal to the Guardian, making sure to avoid hitting Ebony or her supporters and the Mall Rats.

Lamps, chairs, plates, mugs, bottles – items of all shapes and sizes rained down.

* * *

A well aimed lightbulb – flung by Shannon – shattered as it struck the Guardian's head, the prophet of Zoot whirling and gripping his wound.

His inner personal guards had protected him from Jay's surprise attack but nothing prepared the Guardian for the elation he now felt, with the debris falling from above, where Zoot had once fallen, adding to his twisted delight.

He extended both arms high in to the air, gazed up, closed his eyes and said softly, "soon it will be time, Mighty One, for us to be reunited!"

Some of the items that had landed in the shrine area by the candles had caught alight, small fires springing to life and threatening to grow – the remnants of a wooden table that had been thrown now engulfed in flames.

It was an omen, the Guardian felt, Zoot showing how he would be consumed by the flames - and rewarded by the only escape he longed for - death.

"It will be written that we all left this domain, Brethren, to join Zoot in the eternal kingdom. Only disbelievers will be denied that privilege!"

His inner guard, along with some of the other Zootists, gazed uneasily at the Guardian, his arms aloft, luxuriating as flames spread, engulfing the mall, and for all of the Guardian's references, it was as if he was standing by the very gates of hell.

One by one, his elite bodyguards, followed by his loyal supporters, backed up, turned and ran, only to be seized by Ebony's forces.

* * *

Cheers erupted throughout the mall in celebration of victory, the Zootists who had joined Ebony and the Mall Rats in the rebellion now appreciating the significance of what had been achieved. The Guardian had been seized and was being held in the caged cell - and a human chain had been arranged to transport pails of water to extinguish the fires.

Exhausted – and thrilled, Ebony threw back her head on her tired shoulders in relief, shouting out a warrior cry, her entire body aching, delirious at the turnaround she had been so pivotal in instigating.

The young mothers. with their much younger children on the upper level, rushed down the stairs to be with the Mall Rats, Ebony, Aras and the rest of the former Zootists who had turned on the Guardian. Hugs were given all around, smiles of triumph, jubilation, ecstasy, sharing the moment.

"Emma!" Tiffany and Shannon both cried out, running over to Emma, who excitedly wrapped her arms around them and gave them the most loving hug any brother and sister could ever hope to receive, one the memory of which would stay with them for the rest of their lives.

"Everything's going to be okay!" Emma said in ecstatic delight, ignoring the many cuts and bruises she had suffered, the love for her family overcoming all the aches and pains she felt from the battle, Emma having shielded baby Bray, now in Lottie's hands, from the Zootist attackers who had gone after her, thinking she was an easy target due to her blindness. But she had lashed out, displaying a fierce determination to survive.

"Are you alright?" Sammy asked Lottie.

"You're my hero," Lottie said – giving him a kiss on his cheek, Sammy looking over the moon. He had bravely been near Lottie during the battle, making sure she was okay, and Lottie was beginning to feel she might care for Sammy more than as a friend, after all.

Everyone had fought hard – and deserved to be on the winning side, Ebony reflected, walking around the mall, transformed into a battlefield.

But there had been a heavy price for their victory, Ebony now realized, looking around. Not all of them had survived. There had been losses.

Ebony knew the many smiles and tears of happiness being shed would soon be replaced by tears of sadness, mourning - when others learned of the sacrifices Ebony had just discovered had been made.

CHAPTER FORTY-ONE

There was a chill in the air. The sky was totally blanketed by stars. It reminded Lia more of a planetarium as she and Lex moved stealthily towards the observatory, which appeared to be in total darkness.

"Remember, in any attack we've got to make sure we use the element of surprise," Lex mouthed to Lia in a near silent whisper, amidst clouds of vapour appearing from his breath in the cold night air.

The two of them were now just ten metres or so from the entrance to the observatory, silhouetted by its round golf ball shaped tracking device, framed against the starlit sky.

There was no sign of the guards who had been stationed at the entrance earlier. They must be further inside the complex, Lex assumed.

He readied the quarterstaff in his hands, prepared to take action. Lia had fashioned it during their journey back to the summit out of a tree branch, sharpening the end so it was like a spear.

As for herself, Lia had crafted a catapult, binding the elastic from her bra around some smaller sticks she had taken off the branch. The sleeves of Lex's jacket were tied around her waist and with a few hasty alterations, Lia had turned the jacket into a makeshift 'bag' to carry some of the rocks she had scooped up.

Lia had learned so much from the Priestess, who had taught Lia how to survive, hunt – and the skills to create weapons. Normally she used vines, dipping them in a special substance before wrapping them around twigs to provide the launching part of the catapult – and she found it quite bizarre, in a way, to have used some elastic from her own undergarment. It was the best she could improvise and she just prayed that it would work.

"Let's do this," Lex said, in mounting apprehension. "Ready?"

Lia nodded, then accompanied Lex, both running flat out, Lia screaming out a battle cry at the top of her lungs.

"So much for surprise," Lex muttered to himself.

Wildly swinging his quarterstaff, Lex raced into the observatory, followed by Lia, the catapult pulled back, loaded, ready to fire. But they couldn't see any sign of anyone. In fact, they couldn't see anything at all with the complex being in total darkness and they both strained to exchange concerned and confused glances.

* * *

In another area of the observatory, Eloise was also frozen in the void of the impenetrable darkness, a frightening emptiness.

Alone, Eloise had been on her way from Level 2, where she had left Bray under the supervision of her guards, en route to Level 3, intending to check on the progress of those searching for the data device - when Eagle Mountain was plunged into total lockdown.

Right now, the only sound was of her own nervous breathing and the 'clicking' of her heels as she cautiously walked along a tunnel, using her arms, reaching out in front of her, feeling for any obstructions or obstacles that she might otherwise bump into.

Continuing through the dark, gloomy, foreboding labyrinth, Eloise cursed whatever had caused the lighting and electricity to cease, hoping the power would soon be restored.

She had always been afraid of the dark when she was a little girl. At night, she would often run into the room of her younger brother, Blake, who had given her comfort and reassurance.

Her parents had wanted the best for their children but were strict disciplinarians. Her father, being in the military, felt that any weakness, such as being afraid of the dark, was intolerable, something Eloise had to deal with herself. She needed to grow up, her parents had told her - learn to cope with her problems, as her parents had to do with their own, every day of their lives.

Often, Eloise felt her parents were more so in name rather than deed. Apart from providing a home, food to eat, clothes to wear and a seemingly affluent lifestyle - she and her brother received very little love, her parents both military careerists, more interested in networking and establishing connections at social gatherings.

Eloise's father had been a high ranking official in his prime and rose through the ranks, becoming a general, spending much time away and there was always an air of mystery regarding just exactly what or who he commanded, with his assignments being forever highly classified. Even when he was at home, never once did he read Eloise a bedtime story, always too busy doing something else apparently more important, such as dining out with influential members of the local community.

Blake and Eloise had bonded, brother and sister giving each other the support and care they needed – and that they felt was denied by their parents.

How she missed Blake now, Eloise reflected. She hoped he was alive, somewhere out there – on the island. And if anyone could survive, then it was Blake.

He, like Eloise, had developed a fierce sense of independence and determination for survival - which is what her parents may have hoped to encourage in them after all, she had concluded afterwards. Perhaps it was they who were responsible for who she was today – the tough, intelligent and ambitious girl who was about to secure her future with the greatest discovery of the post-adult era.

But she owed most to the Collective, who had become her new and real family.

All that she had done over the past year or so was for Kami, intent on discovering the secrets of Eagle Mountain.

Eloise had worked so hard, commanding the outpost on behalf of the Collective on the island and had structured the sub-regiments of the Zootists.

She had received intelligence through the Collective network about the Mall Rats, even Ram and the Technos, but most of all, the Guardian, along with the legend of Zoot which was spreading through the region.

When the Guardian was delivered on a slave ship, she perceived him to be a welcome addition to her strategies. He was clearly insane but was a useful element in her arsenal of machinations. So could have been Zoot's brother, Bray, if he had fathered the child she was carrying.

She loathed the baby in many ways but was aware it was another vital strategic element in all that she was planning. Simply because of who the father really was, recognizing his enormous power and influence throughout the complex Collective network.

History could be repeating itself, Eloise smiled to herself at the irony of it all. Would she become like her own mother had been to her – totally disinterested in her child? And she wondered if her mother felt the same way Eloise did of late, detesting being pregnant. Eloise would have terminated the baby had so much not been riding on its existence, the baby no more than a means to an end for her, rather than an end in itself.

She couldn't wait to get it out of her body, the baby distorting her appearance, making her seem fat, ugly, its bulge distracting from her undoubted beauty, ruining her usually so impeccable feminine figure. It felt like some ungodly tumour was growing inside.

So much for a 'motherly glow' Eloise felt, longing for the day she would return to the form of her pre-pregnant shape, the envy of most girls, the source of lust to any male she would tantalize and tease, most of whom ended up wanting to sleep with her – including the one who had become her baby's father.

No matter how gifted she was intellectually, she was aware that her body could play just as vital a role in helping to achieve her ambitions and all she had in mind. Without her physical attractiveness, she instinctively felt that she probably wouldn't have been chosen by the father of the baby she was carrying in the first place.

From a young age, Eloise knew that whatever arsenal her father used in his line of work during the days of the adults - she discovered it was true that looks could also kill and be themselves a potent and lethal weapon.

It would only be a few more months before she could eject the baby from her body. After giving birth, she aimed to go back to the Collective's prime homeland base – and the baby's father could have the child, for all she cared, providing Eloise got what she deserved in return.

Suddenly, out of nowhere, a hand was placed on Eloise's mouth, and she was seized from behind.

Eloise tried to shriek out – to scream for her guards, wherever they were – but the hand covering her mouth prevented her making a sound.

She struggled, flailing around in attempt to get free, but it was no use.

Squirming, helpless, angry – Eloise was mystified by whoever who had found her in the tunnel she had thought empty, that she alone was in – and she was dragged unknowingly by Bray deeper into the ominous, surrounding darkness.

* * *

"This tunnel can't keep going on forever," Ellie whispered. "Even if it seems like it is."

"I just hope we're not going round in circles," Jack remarked.

After fleeing from the room of the cryogenic units when the *K.A.M.I* system was shutdown, Amber had been sure she was alone, separated from Ellie, Jack and Ram. She was literally unable to see anyone. Anywhere.

Amber called their names and they answered, listening carefully, moving toward the sound of each other's voice, finally managing to be reunited in the gloomy void but were unaware if Axel and the guards were close by, which added to their unease.

It felt like being trapped in some gigantic, invisible maze – the small group cautiously making their way through the dark labyrinth, arms outstretched, feeling for anything to assist their progression.

Jack got the fright of his life when he collided with an old decontamination suit, hanging on the wall, thinking for a moment he had bumped into an adult.

Amber reminded them to not only try and stay focused - but most of all to keep calm. It would be all too easy to let their imaginations and fears get away with them, the group sensing that there were all kinds of dangers lurking in the depths.

At times, straining to hear, they recognized distant running footsteps echoing throughout the vast maze of tunnels – and Axel, somewhere, shouting out orders to his guards.

Suddenly, Amber stopped and reached out, trying to prevent the others from moving.

"Listen!" she whispered intently. She was sure she heard Eloise shouting.

The others confirmed they also heard it, seemingly coming from somewhere above.

"Come on!" Amber encouraged Ellie, Jack and Ram - and they picked up pace, in the dark, touching the sides of the walls with their hands to help guide their way as fast as they could, eventually discovering a stairwell which they began to ascend.

* * *

In another area of the observatory, Lex and Lia moved carefully through the darkness, having also heard the same distant shouting.

Continuing to follow the sounds, they turned a corner, leading into a tunnel in the upper ground level, then noticed a room eerily illuminated by shafts of moonlight streaming through an outside window - outlining an apparent stand-off.

Bray was clutching Eloise in his arms, preventing her from moving but allowing her to speak, Eloise screaming a tirade of obscenities and abuse.

Axel and members of Eloise's elite guard stood nearby, inching slowly forward, ready to strike.

"I wouldn't recommend that, pal," Lex said, brandishing the thick quarterstaff.

Lia aimed her catapult containing small pebbles and rocks, ready to unleash them.

Axel and the guards froze.

"Seize them!" Eloise shouted.

"If you fancy your chances, go right ahead. But I wouldn't bother if I was you," a voice said, which Lex, Bray and Lia recognized belonged to Jack, who had appeared through another door in the room with Amber, Ellie and Ram.

"Somehow I don't think you'd be much of a match for Axel and my men," Eloise said.

"I wouldn't bet on it," Lex snarled. "I taught them all I know - speaking of which, this is a surprise," he added, noticing the other Mall Rats entering.

Bray was also relieved to note that his beloved Amber and his friends were safe and well.

"Are you alright?" he asked with a sense of urgency.

"How sweet," Eloise interrupted.

"Quiet," Bray said, holding her tightly to restrain her. "You've done enough talking."

Amber was emotional and overwhelmed to see Bray. "Am I pleased to see you," she sighed. "All of you. You wouldn't believe what's happened to us."

"I expect you to obey my orders, Axel," Eloise snapped. "Don't just stand there! Deal with them and we can get out of here!"

"If you take one step - I'll smash this to the ground! And destroy it!" Ram shouted, indicating the gold plated data device he was holding in his hands.

"You wouldn't dare!" Eloise screamed, still furious at being held prisoner by Bray but more by seeing the precious object of her mission in danger.

The entire group continued to stand frozen in the apparent stand-off. Bray holding Eloise, Lex's quarterstaff at the ready, Lia with her catapult taking aim, Amber, Ellie and Jack tensing, ready to leap into action - and Ram dangling the data device, then feigning to hurl it to the floor, stopping from actually doing so at the very last moment.

Some of the guards had began cautiously closing in on him - but at his threat they stopped, looking to Eloise for a lead at what they should do.

"Seize Amber! Now! As an example of what will happen to everyone else. Break every bone in her body!" Eloise screamed.

A projectile whistled past Axel's face, narrowly avoiding his head, Axel stopping in his tracks, the rocks exploding into shards against the thick wall of the complex.

Lia reloaded the catapult, aiming it directly at him.

"Next time – I won't miss. Believe me."

"And you're hardly the one to give anyone orders," Bray said to Eloise. "Why don't you just accept defeat?"

"What - and deny you the privilege of holding me tight?" Eloise teased him. "*Touching me* again? Pressing yourself against me? I can't work out if you're trying to take away the baby you put in me – or hoping for another go?"

Amber's expression clouded and all gazed intently at Bray, trying somehow to suppress the rage building deep within.

"If it wasn't for that baby you're carrying," Bray said. "I might be forced to do something I'd regret."

A part of Bray was tempted to take Eloise up on her provocation - to exact revenge on her. He certainly felt bitter at all the wrongdoings she had done to him and so many others.

But he was anxious to avoid putting at risk her unborn baby – an innocent, who had done nobody any harm – and releasing his hold slightly, Bray decided to consciously let go of any feelings he had for seeking retribution. He had originally seized Eloise as a bargaining tool – but never intended to actually harm her, or the baby she was carrying.

"How considerate!" Eloise mocked. "But foolish. Axel, finish them off! All of them!"

"I wouldn't advise that, Eloise," Ram threatened. "I'm warning you. If they take even one step, you'll find what the inside of a hard drive looks like - in millions of little pieces!"

He put the data device on the floor and was dangling the heel of his foot over it.

"Or why don't we settle this the old fashioned way!" Lex blustered, twirling the quarterstaff, waving it menacingly towards Axel and the guards.

"If that's what they want – we could all fight each other," Amber said. "And some of us might not make it out of here alive. Maybe even you, Eloise. Or the baby you're carrying. But is it worth the risk? Because I want you to know – we *will* fight for each other, if we have to. I would give my life for any of my tribe. And all I love."

She cast a glance at Bray while Eloise scoffed contemptuously.

"How sweet. Such a loving family."

"You'd better believe it," Bray added. "As long as I have any breath left, I'll stand here, against you, till the end of time. So you know what you're in for. The decision is yours."

"So what's it to be?" Amber said. "Because if you think you're going to get your claws on any of the knowledge the adults left behind – you're wrong. Ram – why don't you just go ahead? Break the hard drive!"

"Gladly!" Ram replied.

It was obvious Ram wasn't bluffing. His tone was vindictive, as if he was hoping to get payback on Eloise.

She looked at the data device on the floor, vulnerable, about to be smashed by Ram's boot. And her mind raced, well aware of the implications if Kami was to discover that she risked all the information he so desired. She was sure she would find other ways of dealing with the adversaries she now faced, even in capture. But having come this far, reflected that she couldn't let her pride exceed the importance of achieving her mission.

Much better to live to fight another day. And she certainly intended to fight - eventually.

* * *

Eloise and the guards were bound by ropes which had been found and the entire group made preparations to leave the observatory building, the Mall Rats believing that they would be useful for any negotiations with their enemies back at the mall.

Bray was the last to leave, double-checking that there wasn't anything else of use for them to take, managing to retrieve some flashlights and batteries.

He slammed the door of the cupboard closed and turned to find Amber watching him.

Both exchanged intense glances for a long moment, bathed in shafts of moonlight, streaming through a window nearby.

"I... ah... was just checking if there was anything which could be of use," Bray said, uneasily breaking the silence.

"So I see," Amber replied, smiling slightly.

"That's not why you're here though," Bray enquired, intrigued.

"I wanted to check on you. Make sure you're alright."

"Thanks," Bray responded.

"You're welcome," Amber said.

"This is very unlike you," Bray continued. "If you've got something to say - you're normally never hesitant to say it."

"It's because of you."

"Me?" Bray asked. "I don't understand."

"I don't either. Because it was always you, Bray. And I never want to be apart from you, ever again," Amber said, her voice cracking with emotion, tears filling her eyes.

Bray considered her, then they crossed to each other urgently, overjoyed at the reunion while they clung to one another tightly, kissing passionately.

Thrown by destiny, not choice, into a love triangle – Amber had struggled to find a way to break the impasse and explained that she found her answer down in the dark depths of Eagle Mountain. Not that she really ever doubted what that answer would be. But she imagined the twisting tunnels as representing the many ways her life could go, realizing she could stay down there forever, lost, refusing to make a decision. She had to try and find a way out. Some path.

And similarly she needed to head down a path that felt right in her personal life. So that life could go on. She could only do the best that her heart told her and pick a direction, realizing that if her heart was true, everything else would follow suit and take care of itself.

She cared about Jay. And always would. Which made it all so difficult as she never wanted to hurt him. But equally she would never want to hurt Bray, their son, and least of all herself, realizing that she was at a crossroads in her life and that she'd actually met and chosen her soulmate long ago. It was Bray. He was the one. As he had always been.

Amber hoped Jay would understand – that the two of them could still be friends. She dreaded their next meeting, tortured how he would react the next time they spoke.

Sadly, Amber was unaware at that time that she would never have the opportunity of speaking with Jay ever again.

CHAPTER FORTY-TWO

The sun rose over the crescent of the rolling hills, bathing the countryside in its warm, life-giving glow, billowy clouds soaring high above, blown by the gentle breeze, casting shadows across the green terrain below.

It was a beautiful morning, Amber reflected, her face awash with tears. She listened to the dawn chorus and watched the birds busily flying around. She found a small measure of comfort in the spirituality of the natural world, taking some solace from it. But nothing could stop the emotional pain she and the others were going through as they prepared to say goodbye to some of their own, who no longer stood among them.

The hills around Eagle Mountain seemed a fitting place to lay to rest their fallen friends and loved ones.

Three graves had been dug before the sunrise. Beside the one that commemorated Zandra's final resting place, all looking down on the distant city, far below.

And it reminded Bray how he felt the time he had stood near the very spot when he thought he had lost Amber. It was as if his own life force had left his entire being, essence, his very soul.

"We should say something," Bray said, softly.

Looking down on the new graves, amidst all his emotional recollections, he felt a profound sense of regret - wishing he had gotten to know each of the fallen members of the tribe more, having been away for most of the time they had been in or involved with the Mall Rats, during Bray's time as a prisoner under Eloise.

He would learn more of who they were, he knew, through the tales and stories which would undoubtedly be told. But even without knowing the deceased too well, the fact they had made the ultimate sacrifice led Bray to pay them his highest respects. Their actions had helped save the lives of others, contributing to the defeat of Zootist forces, paving the way for a better future and he vowed it would not be in vain.

"I'd like to say a few words," Lex said, stepping forward first and kneeling before the grave of Gel, where he placed a pair of her favourite stiletto heels beside a bunch of wild flowers.

"I'll really miss seeing you wearing these. And believe it or not, I'm going to really miss you as well, Gel. Your laughter. The way you saw things at times. If anyone ever had a sense of style – it was you. Your were sure one stylish girl. In a class of your own. And I probably never deserved you. Though it didn't all work out between us - I valued you as a friend. And if there is such a thing as an afterlife – I can imagine you there right now, with Zandra, trying to outdo each other with your hair and make up. But I have no doubt the two of you would get on. I'll miss you – we all will. But we won't forget. I'll carry with me the memories we shared – and there'll always be a part of you, in me. In all of us."

Lex wasn't afraid of anything – and certainly not to shed a tear in front of the others, all touched by his sensitivity and words, which they found very moving, most of all Lia, who squeezed his hand in gentle reassurance as he took his place back among the tribe.

"I'd like to speak for Darryl – if that's okay," Salene volunteered.

"Go ahead. I'll keep an eye on her," Ellie said to Salene, taking hold of May's arm, allowing May to lean on her, Salene having supported May until now.

May had been wounded in the battle at the mall. Lia possessed a rudimentary medical knowledge from what she had been taught by her parents, both doctors – and feared May had suffered some fractured ribs.

However, May was determined not to miss the service, no matter how much she was going through. The agony she felt physically was nothing compared to the sacrifice the others had given and she wanted to pay her respects. Unable to stand on her own – and wincing with pain – May appreciated Ellie's support, leaning her body weight on her.

"Darryl. Sweet Darryl," Salene addressed the grave. "I was lucky enough to get to know you better when we were on our little boat, lost at sea – and on the island. We all knew you were a gifted actor. A natural entertainer. But I didn't know you were so kind and thoughtful... I wish I had gotten to know you more earlier. You were a friend – to me – to us all. But especially – the younger ones."

Lottie and Sammy held each other's hands supportively, their eyes wet with tears.

Brady was in Trudy's arms, hugging her mother tightly, lovingly, not fully comprehending everything that was going on – but knowing that Darryl, who had often spent time with her, making her smile, was no longer around.

"You were the best impressionist I have ever seen and brought tears of laughter to us all. Now it's just tears, which shows how much we miss you. I can't believe you've gone," Salene continued, her voice cracking with emotion. "I just only hope you'll make others laugh in that great showbiz place in the sky. I know I speak for all of us when I say you made our world a brighter place. For that, I... we... all truly thank you. Rest well, friend."

She bowed her head respectively and went back to stand with the others.

One final grave remained – and Amber had been dreading this moment. But it was time.

"You okay?" Bray asked her gently.

She nodded but was visibly shaken and struggling to keep her composure. She took a deep breath as if to enhance her steely resolve, then stepped forward to speak for the group – and herself – to pay respects to the last of the fallen Mall Rats.

"Jay - " Amber began, before choking up, her voice cracking in tortured emotion.

It was just too much. She was overwhelmed and overcome with grief to see the grave – and to think of Jay lying there, under the ground.

Trying somehow to regain her composure – Amber bravely continued, wiping at tears welling up in her eyes.

"Jay... Brave, loving, kind. Always a gentleman. Sensitive. Hard-working... Thoughtful... You fought for your principles... Took a stand. And my God, did you ever make a difference... You helped save the city and so many others once before – from the Technos..."

Amber was aware Ram was giving her a look, knowing she was alluding to Jay's important contribution in the downfall of Ram himself, when he ruled over the city as leader of the Technos. Jay had been Ram's general but turned his back on him, disagreeing with Ram's increasingly tighter grip and tyrannical ways. But Amber went on – she had to be honest and give credit to Jay's achievements.

"Then you helped again, against Mega… And we all want you to know that we honour the sacrifice you gave, helping defeat the Guardian and Eloise… The world won't be the same without you – but I am in no doubt that you helped make it a better world. I will always remember you with respect… gratitude… happiness… and with love. I'm just sorry that I didn't have the chance to say goodbye to you, Jay."

She broke down in wracking, heaving sobs and Bray felt an urge to cross to her, take her in his arms but realized there was nothing he or anyone could do to give comfort at this moment in time. This simply had to be an intimate moment for Amber to seed her grief.

Many of the others were struggling to contain the emotion as well, especially Trudy as she reflected on her own time with Jay and she wiped at the tears overspilling from her eyes.

Amber braced herself and continued amidst her heaving sobs.

"Be at peace, Jay. Know that we'll continue with everything you fought for. And in that way, you'll still walk by our side. Forever. We'll never forget you. And in the end… there can be no better legacy."

Bray crossed to Amber, placing a protective arm around her shoulder as she crouched, putting a bouquet of wild flowers on the grave, as the sun continued rising, heralding the dawn of a new day, all assembled appreciating the profound sanctity of life – how special it was to be alive, to value and live for each day. For each other. Gifts to be cherished.

Amber felt a renewed determination, a sense of strength and empowerment and knew that Jay would have wanted them all to continue on, to fully live their lives. And to try and build a better future. He, along with their fallen companions, died to safeguard their freedom and opportunity.

Gel, Darryl and Jay had shown by their example - that the future was worth fighting for.

EPILOGUE

In the weeks that followed, the Mall Rats and their companions worked hard clearing up the mall, removing the debris from the battle that had taken place and getting rid of anything left behind by the Guardian, repainting over the Zootist symbolism that had marked some of the walls. It was a chance to start over again. The Mall Rats, in particular, were reclaiming their home.

Some of the Zootist followers who had fled during the height of the battle were rounded up in the city but the remaining loyal followers had escaped on the *Sea Ghost*, which was last seen sailing out into the ocean, on the distant horizon.

Lex supervised preparations to shore up the mall's defences, assisted by Lia, realizing the need to protect themselves and be battle ready in the event of a return by their adversaries - or other invaders such as the Collective.

Lex and Lia were never far apart from each other. She taught him more of what she learned from the Priestess, even how to make a catapult – and Lex was looking forward to teaching Lia a few tricks of his own.

It would be down to all who were left to repopulate the world and Lia had surprised Lex with her revelation that she was looking forward to one day becoming a mother, bringing as many babies into the world as possible, Lex delighted at the prospect of several 'little Lexes' running around in the future.

But Lex's connection to Lia was no longer confined to merely a physical one. He had become totally intoxicated by her spirit, humour, personality and sensed that she could be good for him. And him for her.

Amber shared Lia's hope and optimism for the future, aware that the young mothers once under the control of the Zootists, with their little toddlers and babies – and those yet to give birth - who without exception had risen up against the Guardian in the battle at the mall to end their subjugation - would bring about a new generation.

Some had asked if they could stay and live in the mall – and Amber had told them of course they could. It would be a difficult road ahead for the mothers, many of them still young teenagers themselves, frightened at the prospect of giving birth, as Trudy had once been.

As a mother herself, Amber volunteered to offer them her support and guidance from her own experiences – as did Trudy, who had been extremely helpful, being the most knowledgeable of motherhood from raising Brady, the oldest of the children among them born so far in the Mall Rats, into the post-adult world.

Salene and May were still a happy couple and spent most of their days helping to look after the babies and young children. May's injuries from the battle were slowly healing and Salene had done her best to pamper her.

The many former acolytes, such as Aras who had risen up at Ebony's prompting would also need help, Amber realized, to be rehabilitated.

Bray, Lex, Trudy and Ebony had already begun a process of 'de-education' where they explained what really happened in the city during the days of Zoot. Aras and the acolytes were astonished by the tales they were told, listening to the words of those who had been witnesses and participants of the original events.

Bray took particular satisfaction as Zoot was gradually being demystified, those who had previously worshipped him coming to understand that he wasn't a god – but just had once been a frightened teenager, like most of them were, struggling to survive, to make sense of the world around him. And had simply lost his way.

Dispelling the aura that had been created by Eloise and the Guardian, the more who knew the truth, Bray reasoned, the harder it would be for the Guardian to ever attempt to convince people otherwise, should he try and do so again.

The Guardian was being held in solitary confinement and for all the heartache and despair he had brought, most felt a degree of sympathy, realizing that he was totally mentally unstable and needed help. Although Bray was hopeful that at long last there was a chance of the days of the Zootist religion being behind them, he equally felt wary, well aware that from past experience the Guardian had proven to possess a capability of rising again.

Emma had been delighted to hear of Aras's rejection of the Zootist religion – but any chance of him renewing their friendship, the two being the last members of the Roaches tribe, seemed remote. Aras and Emma had grown apart from each other, their lives going in different directions. Aras apologized to Emma for his treatment of her and the Mall Rats – but said he needed to discover his own path.

At least Emma had Bray, Amber and the rest of the Mall Rats to replace her tribe which seemed as if it was now extinct. And she was truly grateful fate had brought them all together, thrilled by the prospect of settling into a new life in the mall with Tiffany and Shannon.

Aras and most of the ex-Zootists seemed more influenced by what Ebony might do next. It was she with whom Aras and so many acolytes had bonded. For all that Amber and Bray wanted to assist the former Zootists and examine options of rehousing them, it was obvious that most of them, including Aras, looked to Ebony for guidance.

Amber, Bray, Lex and Trudy realized that Ebony and the ex-Zootists could present a potentially dangerous threat should Ebony mobilise Aras and the newly liberated Zootists in pursuit of her own goals. She showed no signs of doing so yet – instead being apparently co-operative, trying to work with Amber and the Mall Rats. Only time would tell which course Ebony chose to follow.

Ebony had lobbied for all the ex-Zootists – as well as herself - to be pardoned for any crimes they had committed during their subservience under Eloise and the Guardian. It certainly wasn't practical to go through a trial for each person, Amber realized – and besides, Ebony and the former Zootists had proven themselves against the Guardian and Eloise.

It was only right they should be entitled to a second chance, Ebony felt – many hadn't voluntarily chosen to follow Zoot, instead having been captives in the first place, their minds radicalized and 'brainwashed' by the teachings of the Guardian, as had been the case for Aras when he had been snatched away from the Roaches.

To Lex in particular, it was all a little too convenient for Ebony to want to be so easily 'pardoned' by the Mall Rats. He wasn't exactly the type to forgive. Or forget.

And that same sentiment extended to Connor where Trudy was concerned.

During the clear-up, he had casually strolled into the cafeteria in the mall, smelling the lovely aroma of food being prepared by Trudy – who had been busy concocting a meal for herself and Brady.

"If that tastes half as good as it looks, whoever's eating it is in for a real treat," Connor enthused, a twinkle in his eye. "And from where I'm standing – the view looks amazing."

There was more than a trace of flirtation in his comment – and from the way he was now looking at Trudy, she noticed Connor eyeing her shamelessly.

"Get away from me," she said, contemptuously.

"I don't know how many times I've said I'm sorry. But I'll keep saying it until you believe me."

"Do you honestly think I'd ever trust you again? After what you did to me? To us?"

"I'll get down on my knees if I have to."

He did precisely that, slumping down on the floor, dramatically, on his knees, before her. "I'm happy to beg."

Connor had been give a pardon by the Mall Rats for his part in valiantly defending Trudy, Brady, Emma, and baby Bray, at the battle of the mall, as well as Lottie and Sammy. He had stood, toe to toe, against the endless waves of Zootist attacks, fearlessly putting himself in harm's way.

But there was more to their reasoning. They had discovered, after further interrogation, that his parents had been part of the United Nations fleet and had actually worked with Dr Jane Gideon, whose haunting journal had touched Amber and her tribe during their fateful voyage on the mysterious *Jzhao Li*.

Dr Gideon had clearly worked so hard trying to save so many lives and it was a fitting tribute to her memory that they should spare Connor. Lex wondered if there was any truth to it but had to admit that it would be difficult for him to have lied. The only possible way he could have known about the fleet was from his parents. For all the activity was highly classified, prior to leaving for the mission, he recalled meeting Dr Gideon and even had a photograph which he had retrieved from the *Nemo* to prove that was so. And genuinely seemed quite emotional to think of the connection he inadvertently had with the Mall Rats and their friends through Dr Gideon, but especially his parents.

Allowed to stay at the mall to recuperate – Connor had spent much of his free time trying to heal the rift between himself and Trudy, bringing her flowers, offering to do errands for her, hopeful for another chance.

He explained everything that happened between him and Trudy on the island was real. He was ashamed of betraying her, let alone his bounty hunter past, but in his heart, Connor was desperate for redemption and to be with Trudy.

Trudy couldn't easily forget, however. She had put her trust in him, given him her heart, only for it to be crushed. There was no way she would make the same mistake again.

* * *

Days later, Connor decided to set sail on the *Nemo*. Ebony was the sole person on the dockside waving Connor off.

Before he left, Ebony, referring to Trudy, had said seductively, "Being a sailor, I would have thought you, more than anyone, would realize there were other fish in the sea."

"Maybe one day I will," he replied. "But right now I think it's better that I head off and see what's on the other end of the horizon."

"Well, just make sure you don't run into the Collective waiting there at the other end of the rainbow."

Despite Connor's claims to Trudy of being a changed person, Ebony was sure she could tell who he really was, even if she hadn't spent much time with him since their joy ride around the city weeks earlier. She remembered the long lingering kiss they spontaneously shared - and wanted second helpings, her appetite not satisfied. But more than that, she also suspected that he could be an interesting ally.

After all, Connor was a lot like her, not solely being just a rogue but more a survivor. As well as one of the best looking guys Ebony had ever seen in her life.

Ebony watched as the yacht receded in the distance and hoped that someday her and Connor's paths would cross again. But right now she had more important things on her mind. It was time to put in place her plans for the future.

* * *

Eloise was being kept in the cell along with Axel and the remnants of her loyal guards in the lower concourse of the mall.

Jack and Ram had gone to visit on a few occasions to try and gauge if she knew anything more in reality about the gold plated hard drive which they discovered had an unusual interface and needed a special power cable, one Ram and Jack didn't recognize.

Ram was convinced the hard drive was also encrypted – and the fact it required such unique cables was surely likely to have been another protective mechanism put in place by the adults to ensure only those authorised ever had access to the myriad of secrets apparently contained on the data device.

Power had been restored to the mall by Ram and Jack, who had fixed the electrical transformer Jay sabotaged. Computers belonging to the Technos had been retrieved and put in the mall. They had everything in place to go through the hard drive. They just needed to find the right kind of cables before making any attempts to access the data device.

Eloise hadn't at all been co-operative, telling them to go to hell – and that they could stick the hard drive somewhere most uncomfortable, Ram amused by Eloise's choice of words and her feisty, unrepentant attitude.

But he was deeply concerned, along with Amber, Bray and Lex that the Collective weren't exactly the types to sit around, given their intelligence network, and all speculated what might be their next move. An invasion perhaps?

Ram doubted it from his dealings with them through Kami, believing that they realized knowledge was the greatest power in their arsenal. His recommendation was that they return to Eagle Mountain, where he, Jack and Ellie could attempt rebooting the *K.A.M.I* system in an effort to unlock not only the secrets of the data device but try and find other information. But he warned them that if unsuccessful, then it might herald a 'visit' from the Collective.

The Mall Rats didn't need much convincing of the sense of urgency to shed light on the mystery, with Ram reminding them that if the Technos were able to take the city previously without too much difficulty - when the Collective mobilized, it could potentially be the biggest display of power they had ever seen. And if they didn't face up to that fact, then they would be more delusional than the Guardian ever was.

Earlier, the Mall Rats had considered putting the prisoners on trial but Eloise refused to recognize the tribe having any authority, and certainly being impartial. Who would be the judge? The witnesses? Who would speak for the defence? The whole concept of Amber's form of social justice which she tried so hard to introduce previously, shortly after the adults perished, was outdated and preposterous. There were no court systems. Not anymore. There was no justice in this god forsaken world. It was everyone for themselves.

How would it also be fair, Eloise pointed out, for her to be imprisoned with, in Amber's own words, an innocent child? Was it right to threaten Eloise with incarceration – only for her to be eventually physically separated from her own child after the baby's birth? Was that the kind of world Amber was wanting, Eloise had mocked? One where innocent children were forcibly kept apart from their mothers?

Eloise had valid points, Amber considered, and they would have to find a way of dealing with this most important - and dangerous - prisoner in their midst, as well as the baby she was carrying. The child certainly couldn't be locked away, having been not guilty of any crimes.

Eloise threatened that if they only knew the identity of the father, then they might be more inclined to treat Eloise and her guards with more respect. She wouldn't want to be on the receiving end if anything 'untowards' happened to her and revealed that Kami was the true father of the child.

Ram felt that it was impossible, given that Kami was not a normal person.

"What's that supposed to mean?" Jack had challenged him.

A part of Jack had thought, as crazy as it sounded, going over it in his mind, that the artificial intelligence computer, the *K.A.M.I* system at Eagle Mountain, could indeed be linked to the Collective. Was the Kami that led the Collective the one and the same as the *K.A.M.I* computer? Or were they two separate entities? Human and machine? Could there have been an implant into a living being, interfacing with the computer, which sent data to another location and was received by some kind of human receptor?

"I just mean – nobody's ever met him," Ram clarified. But he found Jack's theories intriguing.

Amber was still concerned that Ram knew more than he was letting on due to his growing unease and insistence that the top priority for all concerned was to get to Eagle Mountain.

If indeed Kami was the father of Eloise's child, the Collective might show up and as well as a new baby being born into the world, there could be a more significant event. An apocalypse.

* * *

Ram's warning troubled all, especially Amber, who associated new birth with so much joy. She was always concerned at what kind of world her and Bray's own newborn baby would be born into and wondered if they were somehow being selfish to introduce life amidst so much uncertainty at what kind of future might lay in store.

Bray had reassured her way back then and reiterated now that the future was in their hands. Was their's to create as he held their son, cradled in his arms.

"I was spending some time thinking today," he had said. "It's not too late for a name change."

"Why?" Amber replied, confused.

But then she was touched by the gesture as Bray explained what he had in mind.

"I couldn't be happier with your original choice. Believe me. But... why don't we name him after Jay? It feels right to honour him, somehow. I feel it's important that name lives on – and it can, with our son."

"I'd love that," Amber acknowledged, deeply moved by what Bray suggested. "But only - if you're sure?"

"I am, if you are."

Amber nodded, kissed Bray gently, then took their son in her own arms, gazing lovingly down at him. It was a fitting tribute - and she knew Jay would have been so proud, had he known.

When he was older, she would tell baby Jay about his namesake – and of the tales of the other Mall Rats who had gone before, like Darryl and Gel, as well as all those who had disappeared in the course of time, such as Tai San and KC, presumed dead.

For all she knew, they could even still be alive, somewhere out there at that very moment. Ellie certainly held out hopes of her sister, Alice, returning to her. And Bray, standing beside Amber, was the living proof anything was possible. Dreams really could come true.

Amber resolved that Bray was right and that they should keep their dream alive at whatever cost, whatever challenge and never give up hope of triumph in the end.

They must never be intimidated by any threat and strive only to pursue their own ideals.

Amber was determined to ensure that hope was symbolized by the birth of any newborn. Even Eloise's baby deserved the same chance as baby Jay. The sanctity of life and the very core of human existence was precious and all born into this world deserved to live in the hope of a better future. The opportunity was there in the dawn of every new day.

The sun would always set and rise again.

There was never a true end. Only a new beginning. Life would always endure with the advent of a new dawn.

And whatever happened - that was enough, for Amber. It was a chance, waiting to be grasped. Life would go on.

CODA

Only a few months later, as the sun rose, casting light across the native village, Ruby couldn't control her tears – of joy, at the baby girl she had just given birth to.

The Priestess had helped deliver the baby – offering her congratulations to Slade and Ruby at becoming parents.

Although not yet fluent, they had learned to speak many words of the native tongue, the Priestess having taught them - Ruby and Slade in turn teaching the Priestess and her tribe some of their own language and customs.

Life on the island had continued – and now, a new member of the tribe had been born.

Slade and Ruby hadn't forgotten Lex's request. He had cheekily asked them, before he left with Connor months before on the *Nemo*, to name their child after him, to call their baby Lex, if their child was a boy. Ruby had altered things slightly – suggesting to Slade they call their daughter Alexis, in memory of Lex, and a reminder of the other Mall Rats who they hadn't seen for so long.

The birth was a special moment, the Priestess told them, an auspicious sign of a new era, bringing good fortune for them all.

Hours after the baby's birth Slade heard the sudden sounds of an engine flying overhead – and looking up in mounting concern to the skies, was shocked to see what appeared to be some kind of drone, hovering high above the island, moving back and forth rapidly, deliberatively, as if searching for something.

Having stopped in mid-air, right above the village – the Priestess, Slade, and Ruby, holding baby Alexis, looked up at it, the loud engines demanding their attention - the mysterious drone had seen enough and moved off, going on its way...

3933

3912284833 494 6974 3632 9696 12 1 333831533 737534 94 974 548519 397776856.

432 39793 6143 49432336, 3436 76 926 163325942, 5615 193282 212 33258633 59 0916 2736 1 48519 0145 86 563 548519 765699956.

575 5615 82 199 43431933 86 1 632 59794492. 163 5682 82 1 7322153 4497 563 475743. 692 - 8'7 2743 697 2899 128. 76334251631593. 58436 5615 5873 541439 612 635 59 53 3823943433. 3436 494 76 5363415896.

575 85 2899. 8715863 614865 563 1589856 59 59 5138 163 233 26343 85 199 53516. 84 697 56868 15975 85 9965 163 6143, 563 7625346 82 86 1 632 3126, 26836 2899 5843 697 563 162234.

76589 974 6325 3965135. 41432399. 23 2899 7335 15186.

9943

8178

5363415896 - ((

Dedication

Dedicated to all fans of The Tribe, both young and old,
along with all those who have the courage to dream -
and the resolve to always keep that dream alive.

PREFACE

It was the sound that woke her. A piercing cry of a bird calling out. Tai San's eyes flicked open, startled by what she was hearing. The harsh screech of a gull, wings fluttering, joined quickly by that of several more - a cacophony of noise growing in intensity, curious at this newcomer in their midst.

Tai San quickly leapt off her bed, moving to the window in her cabin to try and gauge her surroundings. With the seagulls darting around, it could only mean one thing – they must be approaching land. Their destination. Wherever that destination might be.

Opening the window, Tai San breathed in a welcome intake of fresh air, the sea breeze rustling her hair as it rushed into the cabin.

More seagulls raced past her window, squawking in anticipation as they clustered around the back of the ship, joining in a feeding frenzy as the powerful engines churned up frothy waters, bringing fish to the surface in their wake.

Angling her head to the side to get a better look at the front, she could see the bow of the ship ploughing through the waters, throwing up mists of spray – but it was clear to her from sensing the movement of the vessel that they were gradually slowing down, the ship on a slight angle as it altered course, heading towards the large landmass before them.

The land itself seemed hostile, unwelcoming, a stark series of jagged cliff faces towering above the waters, their rocky silhouettes under the shadow of bleak ominous clouds, the sun yet to pierce through the dark morning skies, the only life outside being the seagulls greeting the ship.

Tai San felt a sense of foreboding, nervous in anticipation of where they were going, why they were going there – and what it all meant for her.

The ship had been travelling for many days and nights and Tai San herself felt further away than ever before from the city that had once been her home.

She missed the Mall Rats greatly. They were not only her tribe but her closest friends and allies. Since the demise of the adults they had become more like her new family.

Her heart ached with the pain of being so far away from them. Especially Lex. He was more than just her lover. The only true one for her. She missed his voice, his very presence, the tenderness of his touch. His spirit, his lively personality that was always so full of surprises, brightening each of Tai San's days with his life force, as it used to do. Thinking of Lex and the many times he made her laugh, the wonderful moments they had shared made Tai San smile. But each recollection also stabbed at her heart with the ache that she was no longer with him.

Now more than ever before, she felt truly alone – as if the unknown land before her was another world and that the life she once knew and the people she cared for was in another lifetime. When she had once been free, an independent spirit.

For too long Tai San had been a captive. This voyage was the latest in a number of journeys she had been forced to take since losing her freedom.

She had lived the life of a slave, passed from owner to owner, bought and sold like an inanimate object, treated like a possession, stripped away of her very humanity. But never her self-respect. She held onto that with every ounce of her fibre and being, determined that no matter the adversities inflicted upon her by her captors, she would never forget where she had come from or who she was. She wouldn't lose her sense of identity, her dignity. If she ever did, she knew in her heart she would only lose herself forever. By retaining her spirit she somehow would always remain free.

Her current 'master' called himself The Broker. He had bought Tai San at a slave auction many months earlier. Prior to that she had lived an arduous existence performing manual slave labour in the fields, an agonizing routine filled with back-breaking work, day after day, with no respite.

The Broker, by contrast, for some reason put Tai San in a state of material comfort prior to embarking upon this latest voyage. And she could never understand why. For many months she had lived in *The Gardens of The East*, a once luxury hotel from the adult era. She had been given her own room, was always well fed, but had spent most of her days alone in confinement. The only times she had human contact was when the guards brought her meals, a fresh change of clothes – or when she was taken for questioning, 'meetings' as he liked to call them, with The Broker, the master of her enslavement.

The Broker had asked her many times about her experiences at Eagle Mountain, the mysterious, abandoned scientific base in an apparent observatory not far from Tai San's own city. She had gone there with the Mall Rats not long after the virus and they had discovered equipment, cryptic messages the adults had put in place for the surviving younger generation to inherit and use in the aftermath of the adults' own extinction.

The Broker had wanted to know everything, in fine detail, and had interrogated Tai San repeatedly about what she had seen, double-checking facts, information, meticulous in his research and line of questions.

But it was his interest in the lives of the members of the Mall Rats – as well as Tai San's own life story – that had initially bewildered and then caused Tai San concern.

She had been reluctant to tell him anything – her life was private, what she had done, where she had been, her thoughts on her tribe. These were all cherished memories, precious, for only herself to know. Even had she chosen to co-operate, Eagle Mountain was in fact a complete mystery and clearly whatever the reasons behind the interrogation, The Broker was as intrigued about the existence of Eagle Mountain as she and the Mall Rats had been.

But Tai San was wise enough to realize that her very survival was very much dependent upon The Broker believing she had information which could be useful, so she played along. It was her only hope of fighting back. Drip-feeding details which were sometimes fabricated.

She had felt she had no other option. Silence on her part would come at a price that was too high to pay.

The Broker was the one in the position of power and had used it ruthlessly, relentlessly, trying to break down Tai San's barriers of resistance. She had allowed him to believe she had been broken. Perhaps that is why he called himself 'The Broker', Tai San rued at the time. But unknown to him, her spirit remained strong and this fuelled her stoic resolve – aware that she was the real one in power.

Then unexpectedly Tai San had been taken from the hotel by The Broker and brought aboard a cargo ship, *The Leviathan*.

She didn't know what or who else was on board besides herself, The Broker, and a number of guards who periodically checked in on her, making sure she remained in her cabin – perhaps that she was still alive.

Now Tai San's mind raced with the uncertainty of what this journey all meant and what lay ahead for her as the approaching landmass loomed closer and closer.

The sun's rays started to peek through the clouds, flowing through the window causing Tai San to see her reflection in the glass pane, staring back at her.

"Don't forget who you are," Tai San urged herself in a whisper. Clenching her fist, she summoned the vestiges of her inner strength, vowing to stay strong, to somehow stay true to who she was, when all else was so uncertain around her.

Staring out at the land, she knew that whatever was going to happen, she would find the answer soon – and she promised herself The Broker would never crush her spirit, that she would be ready for whatever the future would bring.

* * *

The Leviathan was a large cargo ship, the biggest Tai San had ever been on in her many travels since becoming a slave and being transported from one place to another – but the ship was dwarfed by the size of the port it had docked in.

In the time of the adults this must have been a very busy shipping route, Tai San judged, imagining the hustle and bustle of international trade in its heyday. Her eyes scanned the vicinity, seeing if she could recognize any signs or landmarks, something to show which port in the world they might be in.

Around them stood row upon row of cargo containers, stacked high in uneven lines of walls, imprecisely placed like a child's building blocks, as if they might tumble over.

Giant cranes towered higher still, immobile, frozen in time, rusting hulks of junk but also monuments to the old days that had once been, a past civilization that was no more.

They were standing on the large concrete pad of the dockside, like ants beside the ship that had carried them there. Nature seemed to be reclaiming the land with plant life forcing its way through the various cracks in the foundations.

Tai San was beside The Broker, the two of them surrounded protectively by his forces. The guards had weapons poised, primed for action, as they scanned the periphery of the port in a state of alert.

For all the time they had spent together over many months Tai San had never truly gotten to 'know' The Broker. Where he had tried to find out everything about her, she had been unable to find out anything about him apart from his blatant cruel streak and matter-of-fact ruthless efficiency in carrying out his actions.

But to her surprise Tai San could now sense a vulnerability in The Broker. Or more precisely – fear. His eyes darted furtively back and forth, surveying the scene. Beads of sweat were on his brow and he cleared his throat from time to time to relieve the tension within.

Tai San wondered what it could be that was making him and his forces so on edge – and how whatever – or whoever - was affecting them so much could impact her.

Perhaps it was the fact that the only cargo that had been onboard appeared to be Tai San, The Broker and his guards. *The Leviathan*'s cargo doors were open and its enormous hold revealed nothing but a cavernous emptiness, echoing the footsteps of some of The Broker's forces who moved around inside the ship.

Had there been a mistake in the delivery? Had the entire voyage been to no avail? Was this the karma that The Broker deserved? Had he somehow failed? Had someone double-crossed him?

Tai San was surprised to hear another sound further away, the sound of distant laughter, childish giggling.

The Broker's guards defensively aimed their weapons at the source of the sound.

A group of very young children were scampering in the waters lapping into the harbour, searching through flotsam and jetsam that had washed ashore. It was like a sea of debris from the adult times, the banks of the harbour awash in a tide of rubbish, plastic bottles, garbage bags. Rotten fish decayed at the surface, the waters filthy, thick with mud, grime.

The children looked feral in their barely-fitting, ragged clothes, were covered in sores, flies buzzing around them, and had visible cuts and bruises.

Tai San was shocked, repulsed, by the sight. Whatever land she was now in she quickly realized that there were 'strays' just as there were in her own land. Those not members or under the protection of any tribe. It was pitiful.

Suddenly the loud sound of engines rumbled into the port, the weight of the vehicles vibrating and almost shaking the very ground itself.

"Finally," The Broker exhaled nervously to himself as he gazed ahead at a fleet of long-haul transport trucks approaching, followed by a convoy of other vehicles which looked strangely futuristic to Tai San.

The impoverished young children stopped their playing and instead ran for cover, nervously ducking behind the debris washed up around them. They appeared to be panic-stricken.

From The Broker and guards' uneasy demeanour, Tai San wondered what was about to occur. But it was soon clear that the newcomers who had driven into the port weren't there for a fight – but were there to trade.

The Leviathan was quickly loaded with all manner of goods, the delivery trucks driving right up to the cargo hold so that the items they had carried could be placed inside. There were domestic household appliances, a sports car from the adult days - its polished chrome glistening in the sun. But of little value in the new world with clean water more of a sought-after commodity. As evidenced now with several containers being loaded, along with cattle being led inside the hold.

But mostly there was agricultural food – a mountain of grain was accumulating in the vessel as workers carried buckets full to the brim, dumping out the contents, piling it further, higher. A smaller heap of rice was growing in size in the middle of the ship as it, too, was unloaded from the trucks.

All of this produce and selection of goods were being exchanged for the one thing that The Broker had brought to these shores after the long voyage of many miles.

It was Tai San herself.

To her shock, *she* was being traded – again – and couldn't believe her 'worth' or value was ever measured in so much food. It could feed so many people for so long. What had she ever done to become such a commodity of equal value? Who were these people – the ones giving so much so they could take possession of her? What did they want from her?

While the workers continued loading the ship, an advanced party from the futuristic vehicles arrived.

They were dressed in protective decontamination suits. Some of the entourage wore strange medical masks and plastic gloves, and they were being very careful of Tai San, treating her gently, like a prize possession, as they started to examine her, monitoring different aspects, determining her status. None of them had asked permission, even spoken to Tai San to enquire how she might feel about proceedings. She had got accustomed to being treated as an 'object' rather than a person in her many dealings as a slave but still felt a sense of shame, indignity, in the way in which she was being examined like a laboratory specimen without having any say in the matter. There was nothing she could do to stop them though, she realized, and all she could do was try and keep her integrity intact as best as she could. Not show emotion, any sign of weakness, that her new 'masters' could exploit. She wouldn't give them that.

It was a humiliating ordeal, inhuman. Invasive. Taking away her rights, they - whoever 'they' were - seemingly had control of even her own body but she would never allow them to possess her spirit.

Her height and weight were recorded, her temperature taken, pulse, some blood tests conducted, her body measurements taken. Her oral hygiene was checked, teeth probed one by one, details recorded in a tablet computer. Her hair and scalp were painstakingly examined, presumably for lice or some other form of infestation, perhaps disease of some kind.

A piece of equipment Tai San never even knew existed was put against her eyes and a wisp of cloud squirted closely onto the surface, making her eyes water, as the machine somehow 'read' her retina, making a recording of the details of her very eyes.

And through her haze Tai San couldn't help but notice an image of herself appearing on all of the tablet screens. Matching the very same photograph The Broker had in his possession when she first encountered him and she surmised that this exercise was probably some official confirmation of not only facial recognition but identity.

Tai San closed her eyes, slowed her breath, deep in meditation in an effort to stay calm, imagining she was in another place, back at her home in the mall with her beloved tribe as the medical scientific unit performed more sets of blood tests, finally injecting needles painfully into Tai San's arms, forced outstretched by some of The Broker's guards. Tai San wondered if she was being somehow immunized against something. The only question was – what?

The unit examined the monitors of their machines and tablet computers, punched in data and left, passing a stranger who emerged from a vehicle at the head of the convoy.

Tai San was quickly aware that whoever this person was, he was clearly powerful and she could tell from the respect given in his demeanour by The Broker that this new figure had to be of high authority in this land.

He was about Tai San's age, tall, exuded confidence. Almost bordering on arrogance as he signed a bill of goods and said somewhat cynically, "It would appear our transaction is complete. I just hope the enormous value I paid is worth it."

Tai San could sense that there was more than a sexual inference as he cast a glance down her body, looking over her appreciatively - Tai San detecting some lasciviousness in his gaze as well as pride at having secured her.

"Who are you?" Tai San asked cautiously.

"Life. And death," the stranger replied, amidst a charming smile. "Do you have her data?" he asked The Broker.

The Broker nodded and handed over a hard drive.

"You'll find all the information and detail on these drives, Selector," The Broker said.

Tai San listened and watched in growing unease as the apparent 'Selector' signed more documents, handing them back to The Broker before indicating to the paramilitary guards surrounding him.

"Place the cargo in the vehicle. We need to keep on schedule," The Selector stated, eagerly.

"Where are you taking me?" Tai San interrupted.

"To the future. And The Creator."

He smiled at some unknown irony in his own comment and responded with more than a hint of menace and veiled threat. "We all have a long journey ahead."

CHAPTER ONE

The motorcade made its way through a range of winding roads across a seemingly endless barren land.

In the front and rear of the convoy were military vehicles carrying the militia who had been at the docks. Around Tai San's vehicle she was flanked by several more on each side.

Her vehicle was armour plated, driverless and she was its only occupant. With no means of escape. The doors were locked from the outside, it was clearly automated without even a steering wheel or pedals, no driving seat or dashboard, controlled and moving as if by an unseen force.

The barren landscape looked almost primitive with no signs of life, as if from the beginning of time. And yet this vehicle was futuristic and whoever was controlling it had access to advanced technology.

Before the darkness descended and in the times of the old world, artificial intelligence had become more prominent. But this vehicle seemed to be so very far advanced and Tai San wondered if someone was controlling it remotely from another location. Or perhaps from one of the other vehicles in the long convoy. Or if her course had already been preordained and planned, programmed by a computer system somewhere, somehow.

She had cuts on her hands from the efforts she had initially made to get out of the vehicle. Unable to open the doors, she had bashed her fists against the thick glass of the windows in an attempt to break out in some way, even kicked from her seat, striving to prise a way through.

But it was no use – she was being taken somewhere and could do nothing to influence matters.

She wouldn't give up though. If there was a way to escape or alter her fate, she was determined to find it. Or at the very least – to try.

The Selector was transported in a vehicle of the militia at the head of the convoy and throughout the journey Tai San felt a continual sense of foreboding as she wondered why he had gone to such efforts to take her into his custody. And above all, who or what was 'The Creator' The Selector had referred to.

Tai San tried to assess how many miles they had travelled. But it was difficult to ascertain. All the terrain looked the same. Desolate, barren. Harsh. Lifeless, apart from their own convoy. She hadn't even seen any wildlife of any kind, not even a single solitary bird since leaving the port, let alone any landmarks.

The earth was mostly coloured red, making Tai San feel as if she was on a different planet. The wind gusts threw up clouds of dust like red snow, covering the vehicles, the windshield wipers working back and forth rhythmically to keep the front screen clear.

Some of the ground seemed blackened, charred in places, with potholes on the road, its tarmac melted, crumbling. And judging by some mammoth craters which Tai San noticed, there had been some explosions at some point in time. Huge explosions.

Tai San tried somehow to put any notion of a post-apocalyptic event out of her mind but the thought continued to prevail, especially as she became aware of acres and acres of large animal bones, carcasses of cattle, looking like fossils of dinosaurs. Had there been a drought? A famine? A war? Some accident? Was it the result of the virus somehow? Or something more ominous? Sinister?

As the journey continued, Tai San spotted sudden warning bio-hazard signs on the roadside, alerting their viewer to not pass any further. Warning of extreme danger. With any presence being strictly prohibited.

Yet the convoy continued, relentlessly, paying no heed or notice to whatever threat there had once been. Or still could be, Tai San contemplated.

A mile or so later, Tai San spotted the first grave.

An unmarked grave, the first of many, stood in the emptiness around, quickly becoming row upon row of graves as far as the eye could see, on both sides of the road. Endless, long lines of gravestones indicating the extreme loss of life that had befallen the region.

It was overwhelming. And very moving. Tai San could hardly contain her emotions, so upset was she at the suffering and waste. Bringing back memories of what had occurred in her own land, which sent a shiver down her spine, recalling the sheer scale of loss. Parents, friends, family - with the very real threat that the human race would become extinct.

Tai San had at least one connection with the occupants of this strange and desolate land. The experience of suffering, loss, the memorials to so many who had gone before. It made Tai San angry at the senselessness of it. The virus – or whatever caused these people to die – was something that *had* to be beaten, Tai San vowed. Somehow, life just had to go on. Not only her own life but the lives of others. Humanity had to endure, not become extinct. The graves marked a sad tribute – and also a stark reminder that everyone's time was limited, that life was precious. Tai San would never forget that. No matter how dire her own situation could be – she was still alive and determined to make her own life count. To honour herself along with all those who perished. To give justice to the gift that life was so it could reach its full potential.

Her feelings of fighting back against death itself or those who stood in the way of life surged when the graves receded and finally signs of life began to show in what had been so far an otherwise lifeless land.

Grass sprouted up around the roads, becoming fields, rolling hills. A gradual change was taking shape with every passing mile that unfolded. There WAS life after all. And hope.

As the journey continued, the fields evolved into agricultural pastures, plains, cultivated, worked upon by farm workers, probably slaves Tai San reasoned, tirelessly toiling in the soil, raising crops. Some ploughed fields, others sowed seeds, more still harvested, some watered crops.

The workers didn't even cast a glance at the passing convoy and seemed almost robotized, paying more attention to images projected on some outbuildings as if advertising some forthcoming event – '*THE CUBE – COMING SOON*'.

Tai San noticed that some of the pastures the convoy passed were full of sheep, cattle, supervised by their herders who once again paid no attention to the vehicles in the convoy that sped past, which Tai San found strange and unnerving, fuelling her uncertainty of what might lay ahead.

What was certain though was that the area was teeming with life - plant, animal and human.

Such a contrast to what had been, the barren landscape, the rows upon rows of graves.

She was in a society rebuilding, growing and organized too. Compared to whatever destruction had occurred.

Now her vehicle made a notification pinging sound from within which signalled, unbeknownst to Tai San, she had arrived at her next destination. Her journey was over. But in reality had only just begun.

* * *

Tai San had arrived at the *Lakeside Resort* – so named because it was precisely that, an alpine resort complex that overlooked a large body of water. And clearly at one time would have been luxurious but was now decaying and in decline, being reclaimed by nature with plant life sprouting throughout the walls, even branches of trees puncturing the infrastructure.

The view though was beautiful, a spectacular location with the hotel facilities placed so its occupants would have had the best view on offer of nature's wonders.

The lake's waters looked clean, shimmering in the sun, inviting anyone who viewed them to go in for a swim.

Around the lake were snow-capped mountains, rolling hills, covered in all manner of trees, a forested area. Birds and insects flew around, the lake clearly the heart of an eco-system supporting so much life. Perhaps even the humans who lived here, Tai San reasoned.

The Selector personally escorted her to the entrance of the resort – advising that this was to be her temporary home, that she would find everything she needed to make her stay comfortable. The Selector explained that although she would be welcome to live in the resort on a temporary basis – she couldn't leave. Ever. He warned her this was for her own protection – that it wasn't safe in any event for her to be in the outside environs. Or for her to be on her own. Even if she was able to escape.

Around the perimeter of the resort Tai San noted what she perceived were surveillance cameras and also guards had been established in their positions on watch.

The Selector soon left after leading Tai San into the main lobby. He told her that he had other business to attend to for The Creator – and hoped that she would enjoy her stay and that he would be in touch very soon.

Tai San wandered out of the lobby and decided to explore the resort. Apart from the guards on the outside perimeters – she appeared to be the only 'guest'. She wondered if perhaps there were other staff there. Security? Anyone?

It became apparent though that she was indeed alone as she walked through the long, empty corridors. It was like being among the ghosts of the past. The resort providing an eerie connection to the old days. She could easily imagine the sound of children, happy families spending time there on holiday, enjoying the facilities and all that the lake complex had to offer.

The restaurant was empty, tables abandoned, gathering dust.

A children's play centre stood idle, toys littering the room, unused any more. Tai San thought of the poor children she had seen at the docks – why weren't *they* the ones here? They should be living in such a place with its comfort and resources, not her. The world was truly crazy, as it was unpredictable. And confusing.

Did she have an assigned room? Where was she meant to go? What was she meant to do?

She couldn't see any evidence of security cameras but considered that there could be some hidden somewhere. And she wondered if she was being watched by someone. And if so – who? And why?

Exploring the resort, Tai San was getting lost in a maze of corridors, eventually arriving in a kitchen area by accident that must have once serviced the bars and restaurants.

To her surprise she could smell traces of food. The kitchen must have been used recently. Had to have been. There was no way that the residue of meals could have been left over from the adult times. Or were her senses so heightened that her mind was fuelling her natural expectation?

After examining further, she realized that there was indeed no one else around. She was well and truly alone.

Or so she thought.

Tai San's expression clouded in a mixture of concern and confusion as she suddenly heard what she perceived to be splashing when she passed a different part of the resort where signs indicated there was a pool. Someone else WAS there. There was no doubt about it.

Confirmed especially when Tai San heard *laughter* emanating from the pool area.

Tentatively approaching the entrance to the pool, she grasped the handle on the doorway – and taking a deep breath, bracing herself for whoever could be there – she opened the door and stepped inside.

Tai San quickly became aware of a large swimming pool – but it was the people in the water that so astonished her. She felt like she truly was seeing ghosts. Faces she only knew all too well. Was this for real? Or just a dream?

"Watch this," the young man shouted as he ran, diving from the side of the pool into the water with a mighty splash.

"Not bad," the young lady replied. She was lounging in a sun bed and added with a mischievous grin, "But I can do better. Stand back, amateur."

The young lady got to her feet, preparing to jump, to water bomb – and it was then that Tai San just knew that it really was who she thought it was.

"Alice?" Tai San's voice called out, almost in disbelief. "Is that really you?"

Alice's mouth gaped open. She was frozen in astonishment, dumbstruck at seeing Tai San standing before her. She tried to reply – but simply couldn't.

The young man turned from the pool he had dived into and exchanged long glances with Tai San, who questioned in utter amazement – "Ryan!?"

"Tai San? It is you!" Ryan replied, equally amazed and in delight, drowned out by Alice, who exuberantly tried somehow to contain her emotion and joy at seeing Tai San.

"What are *you* doing here?" Alice called out in pure disbelief.

CHAPTER TWO

"Go to sleep, little man," Amber whispered, gazing down lovingly at her son as she rocked the cradle gently back and forth, hushing him - the combination of the motion and the soothing warmth of her voice sending the baby into his slumber – and dreams.

Amber still couldn't believe that she was a mother. She felt so young herself and the responsibilities of parenting were complex - even overwhelming at times, bringing sleepless nights, worry and stress – but fundamentally her son brought unrequited joy, total happiness and above all, a sense of a greater purpose and meaning to her life.

Another dimension which was extra special was the fact that she was sharing her parenting experiences and responsibilities with the baby's father – and her soulmate – Bray. He had finally returned to her, after so much time spent apart when the Technos invaded their city, with destiny reuniting them a few months earlier. Amber was elated to have two special 'men' in her life in Bray and their new born son.

Though once, there had been a third. Jay. When Bray and Amber had been separated shortly after the invasion that had torn them apart, she had struggled to cope with the notion that she might never see him again. It wasn't just a question that he seemed to have disappeared off the face of the Earth but painfully Amber had to face the very real prospect that he might not be alive.

Over time she had found solace - and love – in Jay, one of the Techno commanders who had turned on his leader, Ram, and helped put an end to the authoritarian regime who had invaded the city, finally joining Amber and the Mall Rats.

Jay was kind, principled, selfless, had a sense of duty to the vulnerable members of their tribe and behind his militaristic bearing and fondness for efficiency and order, there lay a caring and sensitive heart. And she had loved him for it, the two enjoying a strong relationship which evolved into them becoming a unit.

Though in the end Amber had come to realize that although she loved Jay, she wasn't IN love with him. For all that it was possible, she pondered, for people to love and perceive that they might be able to find other soulmates – ultimately it was impossible to connect with another kindred spirit. And this was Bray. It had always been him, since they were first thrown together by fate when the pandemic wreaked its havoc across the world. Bray and Amber's lives were intertwined.

Whether or not it was a matter of opposites attracting or if they recognized similar qualities and traits signifying that perhaps in reality true love emanates from recognizing similar aspirations in one's partner – they were the quintessential star-crossed lovers, almost made for each other.

Bray 'understood' Amber in a way that nobody else did – and she had the same effect on him. They almost had an invisible language where they knew how the other one was feeling without a single word being said. And she was looking forward to building their future life together with their son.

Both Bray and Amber though regretted that Jay could not be with them on this journey as the new generation tried to build a new world from the ashes of the old.

Jay had been killed defending the mall, paying the ultimate price, and in so doing had saved many innocent lives.

His efforts would not be in vain, Amber promised, leaning down to kiss her child, who was now fast asleep. She and Bray had named their son Jay, in honour of the former Jay, a fitting tribute so that his name would live on, a reminder that life would endure and hope prevail.

Amber was determined to grasp all the opportunities that now lay ahead for her tribe and felt a renewed surge of energy, purpose.

It wouldn't be easy – there would be many difficulties and challenges to confront and overcome.

But she was ready.

Smiling lovingly at her son, gently sucking his thumb in his slumber, she left her quarters quietly so as not to disturb him.

Heading along the upper concourse of the mall, she motioned to Sammy, who was playing basketball with some of the other younger members of the tribe.

"Try and keep the noise down. And keep an eye on baby Jay for me, will you please, Sammy?"

Sammy sighed. "But what if there are any nappies or diapers or whatever you call them to change?"

"Oh, and I suppose you have better things to do – like playing basketball."

"I could have gone with Bray and Lex, checking out the city and different sectors."

"I think you'll be able to 'protect' Bray and Lex at some point in time, Sammy."

"Really?" he questioned excitedly.

"When they become elders," Amber replied, sensing a way in which to motivate Sammy. "And when you're an elder yourself, who knows, maybe you can teach young Jay to protect you as well? Not that you might need it. I'm sure you will grow into a mighty warrior."

"Got it!" Sammy replied. "Oh, and don't worry about the baby being changed – I'm sure I'll find someone who can do it."

Amber smiled, despite herself. "It might be useful for you to learn too, Sammy. Because we all have to depend – and look out for each other. That's what being a part of our tribe is all about."

Sammy nodded and moved away to the other players, cautioning them to keep the noise down and move away further from Amber and Bray's quarters because Jay was fast asleep and he didn't want the baby to be disturbed.

Amber thought there was hope. And this incident punctuated that she needed to look for it in any way that she could, however seemingly trivial.

* * *

The Guardian locked his eyes with Amber as she approached, a hateful expression on his face, full of spite, simmering anger and vengeance.

He was being held in isolation in a makeshift cell, a caged area in the basement of the mall, originally used by the adults to keep various supplies and goods in the cavernous shopping complex of the old world.

He had to be kept alone, the Mall Rats felt, because of the extreme danger he presented to others, let alone even to himself. He was unpredictable and had tried on many occasions to attack those guarding him whenever they got near to him. His face was covered in scratches and cuts. He had also injured himself in the past, using

782

any implements he had access to in the cell in order to 'punish' himself, some bizarre form of self-flagellation to ritualistically appease his 'divine master', Zoot. The Mall Rats had learned to not let anyone get too close to him – and to not leave any items in his possession that he could otherwise use to cause harm.

"Traitorous witch!" The Guardian hissed venomously, his arms stretching through the bars, reaching out intensely as if he was trying to seize Amber, who was standing some metres away, keeping her distance the other side of the cell.

"How is he doing?" Amber asked Salene. It was Salene's turn monitoring the prisoner, with each member of the Mall Rats taking shifts on the rota.

"Much about the same."

Salene indicated her clothes which were covered in freshly made stains of still warm soup resulting from an incident minutes before Amber's arrival when The Guardian had flung the meal that Salene had brought him, the plastic bowl zinging through the bars and spilling its contents all over her.

"Are *you* okay?" Amber asked, hoping Salene wasn't hurt, let alone finding her time guarding the cell too distressing.

"I'll be fine," Salene smiled, putting on a brave face. "Good thing we've all had so many meals with Lex. I'm used to bad table manners."

Amber couldn't help but smile slightly too. As well as feel enormous pity for The Guardian, sympathy. He wasn't well. Of sound mind. She reasoned that whatever it was, he clearly had some severe difficulties, a mental illness, without access to the care, maybe even medication, that he so obviously and desperately needed.

The Guardian began to manically laugh at Salene's remark. "Lex… Lex, Lex, Lex," he whispered repeatedly, faster and faster, getting into a fervor of excitement, building himself into a frenzy, saying Lex's name over and over again, multiple times – before he stopped suddenly, thrusting his gaze upwards to the ceiling.

"L-E-X!" The Guardian shouted one final time, his arms reaching out to the Heavens as if in worship, a serene countenance on his face. He stared, looking up, in a deep sense of inner reverence. "Some thought you should return to the jaws of your foul, slavering master of Lucifer in Hell! But had you not released the Mighty one, Zoot, then there would be no God in the heavens to lead us all into the salvation of Power and Chaos!"

Amber and Salene exchanged a sad glance while they watched The Guardian cautiously. Amber so wanted to help. As did Salene. To do something, anything, to ease The Guardian's inner turmoil, bring peace somehow to his deeply troubled mind. And soul.

The tribe had no idea what they were going to do with him. Let alone some of the others who were also being kept prisoner in the aftermath of the recent battle.

At an initial meeting Lex had stated he was in favour of putting The Guardian on trial so he could serve justice for the many war crimes and wrongs he had committed. But would it be a fair trial? That was Amber's concern. Would The Guardian even be in an emotionally fit state to stand trial? Or was it too late, was he lost forever in the grip of some form of madness?

Lex scoffed at Amber's stance, believing that the only people suffering any form of madness would be the tribe themselves if they gave any sympathy to The Guardian.

Fortunately, when it was put to a vote, Amber was supported by other members of the tribe who agreed that

The Guardian was fragile, a victim of his own mind, and needed care. If they were to have any hope in rebuilding a better world and creating the type of just society Amber and the Mall Rats so wished for, then they had to find some way of rehabilitating The Guardian, along with any others who faced great difficulties and needed extra care. They couldn't just cast them away – or keep them locked up for eternity. Or even release them into the dangers and challenges they would find in this God-forsaken world in which everyone was not only struggling to exist – but survive.

The Guardian was just one of many issues with which the tribe had to contend. Amber was looked to as the de facto leader, because although she had not been recently elected as such, everyone always came to her with their problems, hoping she would have some advice or find a way to help. And characteristically, she possessed a seemingly natural ability to provide sound and unsentimental advice – and to lead in a fair and just way.

Amber's next task was to visit a separate area in the mall where The Guardian's former allies – and more opponents of the Mall Rats – were being kept.

"Good luck," Salene wished as Amber started to leave.

"You're going to need it!" The Guardian yelled menacingly, watching Amber go, a manic glint in his eyes, prior to erupting into a fit of hysterical and vengeful laughter.

Amber didn't look back, ignoring his goading.

"It won't be long now!" The Guardian shouted out as she went. "And you don't even know! Lex thought it was The Technos I was warning him about! But you haven't seen anything yet! Just wait until you meet the *true* bringers of Power and Chaos!!"

Though she was resolute and didn't engage The Guardian further – or even know what he was referring to – The Guardian's words and demeanour did unsettle Amber, along with Salene.

And The Guardian's reference played on her mind as she arrived where Eloise and the warriors of the Legion tribe were being kept – the members of The Collective.

"Amber! How lovely of you to visit," Eloise said, her words dripping with sarcasm, the malice on her face all too plain to see as Amber approached the cell where Eloise was housed.

"Is this a social call?" Eloise continued, "Or have you just come to check in on the baby? It could be yours if you're 'nice' and wanted to adopt another one."

Eloise gently patted her swollen stomach, indicating the baby she was carrying inside. She was several months pregnant and had originally claimed Bray had been the father, an accusation Bray had strongly denied – and one Amber knew could never be true. Eloise had just been using Bray, her captive at the time, as a puppet figure, trying to manipulate him so she could position herself as the mother of his child – and therefore occupy a place among her followers, the 'Zootists', who were part of The Collective. Eloise was well aware of the power, let alone the exalted status she would have being the one to carry a child in whom the 'blood of Zoot' flowed due to the family connection with Zoot being Bray's younger brother.

Whoever the baby's father was, Amber dreaded to think of how life would be having Eloise as a mother. She seemed devoid of any compassion, with a penchant for cruelty – indeed she seemed to enjoy inflicting it upon others, judging by what Bray had recounted to Amber when he revealed all the indignities he had witnessed and pain he had even suffered himself during his imprisonment under Eloise and her Zootist forces.

"Are you ready to talk?" Amber asked.

Eloise leaned her head back in her chair, luxuriating in the relaxing feeling as one of her warriors, also imprisoned, brushed her long dark hair, pampering their leader as best as they could. Closing her eyes, it was as if Eloise was starting to go to sleep, deliberately ignoring that Amber was even there.

Since the battle when the Mall Rats became victorious, Amber had been trying to find out information from Eloise and the other prisoners which could reveal more about The Collective. In addition to the Zootists, they were apparently a powerful coalition of other tribes from a faraway land who had joined forces under the supreme leader, known as Kami, and had expanded, invading other cities, sectors and lands, creating a growing empire for themselves.

Ram had first alerted the Mall Rats to the existence of The Collective, saying that he had been in contact with Kami online in the past around the time of the demise of the old world, the Collective leader trying to recruit Ram and his Technos to join them.

Ram had supposedly refused and instead invaded the city where Amber and her tribe lived. Ram and The Technos had subsequently been defeated and although he was not a member of the Mall Rats, Ram had aligned with them and was being co-operative. Amber felt at times that Ram was being overly co-operative, a sentiment shared by other members of the Mall Rats, and no one could shake their suspicions about Ram's true intentions or how far they could trust him.

According to Ram, The Collective presented a dire threat. To the very future and existence of humanity. He claimed that in addition to invading other lands, they were specifically interested in Eagle Mountain, a facility that housed an otherwise hidden underground military base left over from the adults who had seemingly been using it somehow during the height of the pandemic, leaving behind all kinds of sophisticated technology, including a massive supercomputer, the *K.A.M.I* system.

The system was almost mythological and the source of many theories, ranging from it being part of an infrastructure to facilitate evacuation to not only foreign lands but other planets. Even that the system was controlled by an unseen military force in the old world who had inflicted the virus as a form of bacterial warfare.

In truth, no one, including even Ram, really knew the answer to all the mysteries and whether or not any conspiracy theories were valid and true.

They were all aware, however, that it hadn't been that long since Amber and the Mall Rats, along with Ram, had been inside the vast complex of Eagle Mountain and they had been amazed by what they had discovered there. Including a selection of adults, who were neither dead nor alive, but 'frozen' in strange cryogenic hibernation chambers, perhaps, Amber reasoned, awaiting the day the younger survivors of the virus would maybe be able to revive them.

* * *

"Quiet!" Sammy whispered in growing unease. "Or you'll get us all in trouble."

He had managed to persuade the younger ones to forget about their basketball game for fear of it wakening baby Jay. Now, though he realized the suggestion of a different game seemed like a good idea at the time - it was becoming a nightmare for him to control as Brady exuberantly raced through the main concourse of the mall with an excited squeal, followed by Tiffany, the two girls trying to keep away from Shannon, the children engaged in a high-energy game of hide and seek, each participant counting to ten but resisting every urge to peek through their fingers to see where others were choosing to hide.

"This'll have to be your last game," Trudy called out to the kids, "Your lunch is almost ready."

Sammy breathed a sigh of relief as he noticed Trudy signaling to the younger ensemble from the food hall.

Trudy had been helping May prepare a meal, some large cooking pots of stew simmering on the stove in the food court, and it was a delight to see Brady so happy while she played. They had been through so much together, such drama already in Brady's young life and Trudy hoped that finally they, as well as the tribe as a whole, had a chance to start afresh and build something new. A better and secure future for successive generations.

"It actually tastes pretty good," May said, surprising herself as she tasted a spoonful to make sure it was finished.

It was the best she and Trudy could come up with given the scarcity of ingredients. They had thrown together an assortment of tinned food and almost hoped for the best – and somehow, they had delivered an appetizing stew.

The children certainly seemed to enjoy it – but suddenly all let out a wailing scream, along with Trudy and Salene, as they noticed Lex swagger through the food hall carrying a mammoth carcass of a wild boar over his shoulders.

"What on earth is that?" Trudy asked, trying to put on a brave face to calm the distraught children while Lex casually flung the carcass on a counter.

"What do you think it is? – dinner, for the next week hopefully," Lex replied, while washing his blood-soaked face and hands in a nearby sink.

"I'm exhausted. Can someone fix me something to eat? That smells pretty good," he added, glancing at the stew in a saucepan as he slumped in a chair.

"I'm sure you're quite capable of serving yourself, Lex," Trudy said, while exchanging an indignant glance with May.

"We're not your servants, you know," May added.

"And I'm not going to bring home the bacon and be expected to cook it. That's woman's work!" Lex sneered disdainfully.

"I hope you're joking, Lex," Trudy said.

"Of course. Well, maybe a bit," Lex replied, enigmatically.

"Calm down, kids," May appealed. "There's no need to be afraid of that pig Lex brought. Because he's the biggest threat until he learns the true meaning of equality."

The children were still distraught, gazing clearly repulsed by the sight of the dead animal on the counter, its eyes staring, opaque at the moment of death with an expression as equal to the fear the children clearly had.

"Charming," Lex scoffed to himself.

"I mean it, Lex," May continued in her disdain. "You're the biggest pig I know. A chauvinist pig."

She smiled proudly at her own wit and Trudy couldn't but help smile too.

"Here. I'll fix something for you to eat but just don't make it a habit," said Trudy, while ladling up a bowl of the stew and passing it to Lex, who lifted the bowl and slurped on the contents without using a spoon.

"How did you kill it, Lex?" Sammy probed, in a mixture of intrigue and excitement.

"It probably fainted when it saw another pig," May continued, mocking Lex. "I mean one who's such an amazingly strong alpha male."

"Give it up, May. I'm not in any mood," Lex snapped, prior to shrugging modestly to Sammy. "It was no big deal. I used a couple of large stones to drop it and then speared it with a branch."

"Can you teach me to hunt one day?" Sammy pleaded.

"If you get me another bowl of this stuff, then I might consider it," Lex replied, sliding the bowl to Sammy who crossed to the stove and served up another portion.

"You're something else, Lex. You really are," May sighed.

"Thanks," Lex replied, shrugging again modestly.

"It wasn't meant to be a compliment," Trudy added.

"Well it should be," Lex replied. "Especially after what I've gone through all morning trying to keep this tribe safe, as well as fed."

Few could have foreseen – let alone Lex – the irony in the comment and how the lives of the Mall Rats were destined to be changed, forever.

CHAPTER THREE

Over the past few days Lex and Bray had been deployed to search the city and environs to make sure the region was fully deserted as they believed to be the case. But all agreed that it would be wise to scout all the sectors just to make sure.

Bray and Lex planned their routes on a grid with each searching various sections of the city and the outlying suburbs.

The only sign of life Lex had found was the wild boar. And during Bray's scouting he found no evidence of life either. The city and environs seemed to be well and truly deserted. At least in their searches so far.

Later that evening when Bray returned, he compared his findings with Lex which brought a degree of relief to all in the Mall Rats, realizing that at least there were no other dangers they might have to contend with. At least so far.

All concluded that the previous inhabitants of the city and suburbs must have also evacuated as the Mall Rats had once done prior to returning to the city, to escape the ominous threat posed by a supposed new 'virus' released by the renegade Techno Commander, Mega, hoping to use a chemical weapon for leverage over the population. But in reality, perhaps Ram had been right and it had been nothing but bluster, a ruse, or that some other force, perhaps even The Collective, had somehow managed to sabotage the plans with the 'virus' which was released to be nothing but a dark cloud of smoke. But whatever had truly happened, it was enough for the population, including the Mall Rats at the time, to flee.

The only people who remained in the region, now it seemed, were the Mall Rats and their prisoners in the mall, as well as the other former captives who had once been under Eloise's sway.

She had brought with her a group of expectant mothers in various stages of pregnancy, all of them teenagers, first time mothers, frightened, worried about their own futures as well as those of the babies they were carrying inside them. It was all part of some repopulation programme on the island she once lived where the Zootist tribe were based.

They would soon have many more mouths to feed. Particularly when the maternity unit gave birth, which would only add to those who had already been born. The mall was already ringing out with the sound of crying babies, hungry, demanding their mother's attention and to be fed.

To Lex's relief, let alone some of the others in the tribe, the maternity unit was housed on the ground floor, inhabiting various areas of a disused department store on the north side of the mall.

Lex liked Amber's suggestion of segregation, viewing it as empathy given the disruptive noise the babies made round the clock. Amber hadn't actually brought this into consideration. It was more due to the fact that Lex, as well as some of the other male members living in the abandoned shopping mall, might have also been distracted by so many breast-feeding females and she wanted them to have the dignity of privacy.

As mothers themselves, Trudy and Amber had also taken on a lot of extra responsibility - 'mentoring' the new mothers how they might expect things to be on the pathway of motherhood. Eloise's group were all single mothers, as was Trudy, and Amber was especially grateful that she had the luxury of having her baby's father, Bray, by her side. All in the tribe, even Lex, were determined that the mothers would get the support they needed as best as they were able to give it to them and most of the tribe had also become makeshift midwives, childcarers, offering tips, practical assistance. Though Sammy and some of the little ones didn't exactly respond favourably to any babysitting.

As well as a rota for guarding the prisoners, the Mall Rats had also organized at various times for meal breaks which were staggered and the maternity delegation usually gathered in the food court for a communal meal whereas others in the tribe ate at different times.

Ebony joined the group who had once been under Eloise and The Guardian's control. They were all ex-Zootists, vulnerable young people who had been manipulated, 'brainwashed' into believing in the cult of Zoot, previously devoting themselves with some fanaticism to the cause in service of their former leaders, The Guardian and Eloise.

The Mall Rats and Ebony had spent some time 'de-radicalizing the group, telling them the truth about what had really happened in those dark, early days of the city when the legend of Zoot began. Zoot – or Martin as he used to be known – was no God, unlike what they had been told, and was a troubled young soul who had badly lost his way.

Ebony had been there then in those early days, by his side, as his lover – and the Queen of Zoot's tribe, The Locos. She had been instrumental in re-converting the Zootists away from the bonds that connected them to The Guardian and through him, to Eloise. Due to her history with Zoot, she was looked upon with a mixture of some awe, respect – but the days of Zoot were long ago. She wasn't a Loco anymore.

Life had moved on for Ebony. For everyone. But Amber especially recognized that Ebony still commanded a degree of loyalty from the Zootists who almost still viewed her as their Queen.

So, Ebony agreed that she should try and spend time with them to bond – for all that Sammy and some of the younger ones thought simply that her motive was getting 'two meals'. One with the Zootists under her so-called control. And the other meal with the senior members of the Mall Rats – though in reality meal times were also a forum for discussions and planning.

Including the best way to de-radicalize the ex-Zootists who walked freely among them and how they might be given some meaning and purpose in their lives.

The best way to do that, Ebony believed, was to use the 'muscle' that the former Zootists provided to form a new militia under the influence of the Mall Rats and Ebony, in particular. The ex-Zootist members would be free to join but could refuse if they preferred. Eventually perhaps even being able to be released into the city or environs to live free and pursue their own aspiration as a tribe.

Lex and Bray strongly disagreed with this notion. It wasn't only a question of being able to trust the Zootists but also Ebony, who hadn't exactly shown herself to be totally loyal in the past and seemed to characteristically place her own aspirations ahead of everyone else, which usually coincided with her desire for power.

Amber and the other Mall Rats in secret meetings fully understood the concerns of Lex and Bray and indeed shared them. Where Ebony was concerned. But taking a more pragmatic approach, Amber believed there was merit in what Ebony was suggesting where the Zootists were concerned, believing that once de-radicalized that they might well wish to live together in their own base in peace and harmony.

They could certainly add weight to a potential militia which the Mall Rats would need to enhance their capability of defending themselves as they built their future and grew in population.

All had resolved, however, to let matters unfold and assess the results. And especially to keep a watchful eye on Ebony.

Not all Zootists were allocated to be trained for potential work in the militia. Some of the group preferred to be integrated into other areas of routine. Working with Amber, Trudy and Salene on the maternity unit. Others researching with May the possibilities of building a medical capability not solely confined to the care of those who might become sick but also concerning matters of nutrition. Even a potential education system for some of the younger ones – for all the notion of any schooling was met with utter disdain from Lex who viewed teachers and schools with cynicism and contempt from his experiences in the old world.

Now though, Lex was more in his element working often with Bray, as well as Ebony, putting the potential militia through their paces, giving them some physical exercises, playing 'wargames' in the deserted streets bordering the mall.

Ebony also seemed to relish the challenge but she was aware that there was a degree of mistrust throughout the process.

She had never truly fitted in, she felt. She was never going to really be a Mall Rat, no matter how hard she tried. There was always a degree of tension, disagreement, between Amber, Bray and Ebony especially. Due in part to a long and complicated history going back to the days when Zoot remained as leader of the Locos controlling the city streets.

Amber's vision of the future had clashed many times with Ebony's and her methods of surviving the world the adults had left them.

Moreover, there had also been some romantic conflict between Amber and Ebony in the past. In what now felt like a lifetime ago, even occurring in another world, Ebony had once harboured hopes of being able to build a relationship with Bray. In their school days. But he flatly rejected her approaches.

Ebony had even for a time found happiness in Jay before he, too, flung her away, preferring Amber over herself. Ebony had never forgiven Amber for twice getting what she, despite her independent spirit, still so truly wanted. Amber, with Bray, had a strong loving relationship – Ebony had no one but herself.

With the militia seemingly so loyal to her, Ebony certainly had the signs of having everything she needed to put herself in a strong position moving forward. And was shrewd enough to recognize several options. She could continue to co-operate with Amber and the Mall Rats to safeguard the mall and provide a defensive force in case another enemy manifested or more of The Collective's forces ever did appear. Or, she could leave the mall entirely and start anew, maybe returning to her old base at the Horton Bailey Hotel with the militia as her own personal tribe.

Perhaps she could even turn once again and use the militia to free the imprisoned Guardian, Eloise and their warriors. She wondered if Eloise was the type to strike up a deal in which The Collective might reward Ebony handsomely for allowing Eloise to leave and return to them. She was uncertain if Eloise could be trusted, however, or if she would even honour any bargain they struck. It took one to know one and Ebony could recognize a master manipulator when she saw it.

Ebony was keeping her options open and in so doing confirmed and validated the Mall Rats' concern. That she had the potential of reverting to type and doing what she did best – surviving.

In the ever-changing game of life Ebony found herself once more as being of influence as a potential 'kingmaker' – and she promised herself that this time around she would be the one to end up in charge. Not as 'king' of course. But as a 'queen'. And not the queen to a leader such as Zoot. But a potentially powerful leader in her own right. Whatever choices she was going to make in future, she would be sure to be on the winning side. Even if that included liaising with the Mall Rats which was certainly a possible option if they evolved into a more powerful force. But in whatever event, Ebony resolved that she also required power to place herself in a strong negotiating position.

* * *

The frenzied sound of finger-tapping on computer keyboards greeted Amber and Bray as they visited Jack, Ellie and Ram to see how the trio were getting on.

They had been working late into the evening and mostly around the clock and Amber and Bray were keen to check on whether or not there was any progress.

During their last visit to Eagle Mountain, the Mall Rats had taken possession of a small, golden hard drive that had been located in one of the cryogenic chambers belonging to one of the adults in suspended animation in the military compound.

No matter how hard Ram, Jack and Ellie tried, they were unable to 'read' whatever data might be on the drive.

"The problem still seems to be in the binomial area which should be linked to a possible hardware system –

with its own software, possibly incorporating trinomial antipods," Ram pondered.

"I agree," Jack said, as he turned it all over in his mind.

"In English – please?" Amber said as she and Bray smiled slightly to themselves.

"What – you think we're just 'geeking out'?" Jack added, slightly offended.

"Well, that's one way of putting it," Bray confirmed.

It was true that Jack had a love of computers – rivalling, or exceeding his feelings for Ellie, she had often joked – and was well versed in all manner of systems and their software. Ellie herself was also quite knowledgeable in computers, having studied them at school before the demise of the adults.

Ram, conversely, was on a totally different plane – more like another planet. Eccentric, gifted – he possessed incredible skills that he had so often in the past used but put to ill-use when leading the technology-driven society he had tried to establish when he founded The Technos tribe, who had originally invaded the Mall Rats' home city.

That was long ago, however, and for some time Ram had claimed to be on-side – not a Mall Rat, but no longer was he an enemy of them. He had joined their side in taking down the authoritarian regime put in place after he was usurped as leader of The Technos. Ram had also been important in subsequently defeating Eloise's Collective forces.

Most in the Mall Rats, including Amber, although she still reserved her right to have doubts, believed that Ram had truly changed and could be trusted to lend his considerable talents and abilities to a more noble purpose in rebuilding a new and better world. And there was no one better to interweave the elements of technology which would certainly be required and which seemed to occupy every fibre of Ram's body - but also his brilliant mind.

Nothing else seemed to matter.

"If you want it in plain English, then cutting to the chase – I'm a genius and I'm still struggling to understand the codes of the software which still seems to be encrypted," Ram said.

"You're also quite modest," Bray said wryly.

"I don't know about modest – but he's really good," Jack added.

"And so are you, Jack," Ellie said proudly.

"You're not so bad yourself," Jack replied, shrugging modestly.

"If you could all forgive the intrusion of your mutual admiration society and tell us what you have planned, then we'd be very grateful," Amber added.

"In fact, there's several equations which we've still got left to try. And it's all going to take time," Ram stated.

"So, in a nutshell – you're still unable to access whatever is on the drive?" Amber queried.

"Simply put – yes," Ram responded. "Whoever wrote this software and put it into place certainly wanted to give whoever might wish to access it - a challenge, to say the least," Ram advised.

"That's for sure," Jack added. "They didn't want anyone to find whatever information is on this thing – if they did, they would have made it a heck of a lot easier."

Amber and Bray, of course, totally believed Jack. And Amber wanted and hoped she could believe Ram. But she had a nagging doubt, wondering if he was being straight with her.

The biggest concern though was what other 'secrets' the adults might have left behind. What it all meant. Were there other military bases like Eagle Mountain waiting to be discovered? Did the complex have any more things inside to reveal? And what of Ram? Did he know more than he was revealing?

Was this even all some game for him? Did The Collective represent the magnitude of threat that Ram had warned?

"Well, if we haven't given up trying to use this drive, do you think anyone else will? Like The Collective?" Amber probed.

"Once we find out all the data that's on this drive, I might be able to answer that question," Ram replied. "But one thing's for sure. If there is something on this – someone, somewhere, at some time made every measure to protect and keep it all hidden in Eagle Mountain for whatever purpose – then, yeah. Certainly someone like Kami's not the type to give up on this kind of thing."

Ram had said he had never spoken directly with 'Kami' and didn't in truth know exactly who, or what, they were. If it was 'they'. It could have even been an 'it'. Kami was just the name that had popped up online when Ram had communicated with them in the final days of the adults, in the gaming world, when he was number one on the leaderboards. Soon thereafter, the whole world seemed to have come to an end and a new generation was left to try somehow to survive and ensure the human race would not become extinct.

Whoever 'Kami' was, or whatever 'it' was, Ram knew the power behind the mega computer systems would be relentless, very capable themselves – and had been the only ones to ever truly challenge Ram. Kami, in whatever incarnation, was a genius - which was worthy praise coming from someone like Ram. Indeed, Ram couldn't deny that Kami was even on another level to him. So much so that Ram had chosen to run, withdraw his mighty Technos from any association with The Collective, than face being controlled by them and their unknown leader - which heralded the Technos' invasion of the city the Mall Rats inhabited in the first place.

Jack suggested that maybe they had all been going about this all wrong. Maybe the reason they hadn't been able to make any inroads yet was that they had been so focused on trying to uncover what was on the hard drive - that they had forgotten one obvious and important thing: "That we need a different type of computer. One with the capability and power and grunt to handle the complexities of the software," he recommended.

And there was one place where there was a computer unlike anyone had ever seen. And that was housed in Eagle Mountain.

For all the unease anyone might have in returning – they painfully realized that there was no other option but to yet again return to Eagle Mountain and examine all the contents held within the ominous and mysterious facility.

CHAPTER FOUR

Tai San still felt as if she was dreaming. There, sitting opposite her, were Alice and Ryan, looking back at her with equal surprise and delight that she had been reconnected with them in their lives, appearing as if from nowhere.

Ryan had grown a short beard since the last time Tai San had seen him and it suited him. He looked well and still seemed the same old Ryan - kind, gentle, placid, physically strong, though Tai San could tell from his countenance and spirit that he had been through a lot since being separated from the Mall Rats. They all had. It had somehow manifested with a sense of weariness and strangely a resolve.

"I still can't believe it," Ryan said.

"Neither can I," Tai San agreed, almost speechless, overcome at their reunion with joy, emotion.

"That makes three of us," Alice chimed in. "And I need another drink."

Alice went over to the bar area and began pouring herself a glass of whisky, exchanging glances and smiles with Tai San as she filled up her glass, thrilled to be in the company of her friend once more. She had always had a close bond with Tai San and for a time had even been her personal bodyguard, in a different life that had felt so long ago.

Ryan was particularly interested in any news of Salene. Alice was eager to discover anything of her younger sister, Ellie.

Tai San had told them everything that she knew. She had last seen Ellie and Salene, along with the rest of the Mall Rats, albeit briefly, at the mall when she had helped Mega overthrow Ram. However, Mega had his own agenda and had double-crossed Tai San, using her, as he had ironically Ram. She had been 'played' and regretted how trusting she had been, falling for Mega's clever machinations in his quest to depose Ram and become the new leader of The Technos, prior to being transported to other lands.

She began her long period of enslavement from one owner to another, being moved around before ending up in the 'possession' of The Broker, then eventually The Selector.

This news gave Alice and Ryan renewed hope that somewhere, out there in the world, the rest of the Mall Rats may be still alive. Alice and Ryan only hoped that their paths might cross again one day, as they had with Tai San.

They were sitting in the main lounge area of the *Lakeside Resort*. Alice and Ryan had arranged some food for Tai San from the well-stocked kitchen. She had been hungry after her long journey and Tai San's now empty plate rested beside her on the large couch that she was sitting on.

Information on their captures was still very much a mystery but Tai San had quickly become aware that whoever The Selector was and whoever he was working with – they seemed to be in tune with the natural world on some level given the organic produce that stocked the kitchen, along with various herbs and spices.

This kind of diet had always appealed to Tai San who preferred a more plant-based approach, aligning with her being very much in tune with Mother Earth and the environment. Whereas Ryan and especially Alice didn't find the produce available so appetizing.

"I am a meat and two potatoes gal," Alice had stated while she was preparing the food. "But at least this stuff might help me lose a bit more weight."

"How?" Ryan asked.

He was certainly a gentle giant, Tai San thought affectionately, and she often wondered if Ryan had some kind of special need. He was always a little slower than the others intellectually in the tribe but through his simplicity always seemed to hold an inner wisdom, even peace, as if he in reality knew all the secrets to life.

Tai San explained about the produce and how a plant-based diet was becoming more of an importance even way back in the old world, with people becoming more and more concerned about global warming and climate change.

A tragic irony considering what actually took place with the pandemic bringing about the very real threat of human extinction.

"At least we might have a chance to escape if we're being held by vegans," Alice grinned, during the meal. "Most of the guards I've seen around this place seem to be a bunch of wimps and me and Ryan could easily take them."

Tai San was aware that both Alice and Ryan were mighty adversaries and could take care of themselves as well as others under their protection. So escape could be an option. At the right time.

"Fancy one yourself?" Alice offered, holding up an empty glass and waving it at Tai San, having downed the shot of whiskey.

"I'm fine, thank you anyway."

"How about some of this other stuff?" Alice continued, while examining the shelves and bottles containing a range of non-alcoholic drinks and juices and an abundance of fresh bottled water.

"Hey, they've even got green tea. That was always one of your favourites," Alice explained, while finding a range of teas in a display cabinet.

"Maybe later," Tai San responded.

"Then that just leaves more of the hard stuff for me and Ryan," Alice said, pouring a glass for him.

"We've got so much to celebrate!" Ryan grinned. "The old team – three of us, anyway. Back together again."

"Well, let's enjoy the moment while we can," Alice suggested, raising her glass to make a toast. "To Tai San. Ryan. Myself. And the rest of the Mall Rats, wherever they might be."

As the night went on, the initial surprise at their unexpected coming together – that though it felt like it, it wasn't some dream but was very much happening - was replaced by the reality of coming to terms with their situation.

Alice and Ryan explained to Tai San that they had both been living at the resort for what felt like an eternity but was only a few days since they, too, had been brought there individually by The Selector, who had advised that they were honoured 'guests' of The Creator.

Ryan had arrived first before being joined by Alice. He was naturally thrilled and surprised to see Alice, but also have some company, as well as her assurances that The Selector's references to The Creator was not that he or she was some kind of god. And Tai San agreed with Alice and Ryan that although the resort was luxurious compared to what the three of them had recently experienced – they were certainly not in heaven.

Ryan relayed to Tai San – as he had done to Alice when they were first reunited - what had happened to him when he had been sent away by The Chosen who had invaded the city and home of the Mall Rats.

Initially, Ryan had faced severe punishment. He was brutally beaten by The Chosen, getting revenge on him for daring to attack their leader and for being a 'non-believer' of their God, Zoot. He was denied food, water, kept in squalid, terrible conditions. He thought that would be the end of him, that his days were numbered.

And in a way they were since that time he had existed rather than lived, having been traded, eventually ending up in the mines in a faraway land performing hard manual labour. And as bleak as that was, it was a far greater improvement on what he first thought his fate would be.

Soon after that he was traded again. His captors travelled to the coast so that they could continue their journey by ship to another destination. Ryan had managed to break free of his shackles and get away, finally escaping to a forested area, where he spent several days by himself, lost, surviving off berries and anything he could eat.

He stumbled upon a tribe of nomads and was given temporary shelter but rather than allies, the nomadic tribe yet again traded Ryan, who eventually found himself in yet another different land where he ended up as a type of gladiator, forced to take part in different combat spectacles to entertain the spectators eager for action, baying for blood. It was horrific, Ryan recalled, dreading to even discuss the awful memories.

"They treated us like animals," he told Tai San, listening attentively to his tale, as did Alice, who was as gripped hearing it second time around as she was when Ryan revealed the details to her.

He literally had to fight for his very life but always refused to kill his opponents, to the disappointment of the crowds, instead using his strength and prowess to render them harmless, never more than unconscious. He may have had no choice but to fight – but it was his choice, he felt, how to deal with those he was fighting. They were unwilling participants. Slaves, just like him.

There was one other thing that Ryan was fighting for, in addition to self-preservation and the hope his destiny would change. One reason, above all the others, that kept him going during his darkest times when it was all so unbearable and it would have been easy to have given up. It was the vision of him being reunited one day with Salene.

He loved her so much, so deeply, with all his heart. Their relationship had always been complicated, fractious at times. Salene had her difficult moments with many personal struggles, anxieties. But Ryan gave her the support she needed, respected her, showing her kindness. Dignity. And above all understanding. He felt that underneath her sometimes troubled moments, at her essence she was always nurturing, caring, possessing a similar compassion much like his own.

Alice had already told Ryan the sad news that Salene had tragically lost their baby - she had been there when it happened and blamed herself for the accident that caused it. Ryan had been devastated to hear the truth, that in addition to having lost his freedom and Salene – he had lost the son or daughter they had been expecting and his dream of becoming a father at that time.

Tai San was relieved that she didn't have to break this news to Ryan and as she continued listening to what had happened to him, Tai San said a silent inner prayer hoping that Ryan's spirit might find some peace so that he could come to terms with the loss.

Ryan, the 'reluctant gladiator' as the crowds had dubbed him, had been put up for sale at a major slave auction – and it was from there that he ended up in the hands of forces under the control of The Selector, who had brought him to the *Lakeside Resort*.

Following Ryan's revelation - Alice told Tai San what she had gone through since they had last been together in their home city.

On the fateful day The Technos invaded, changing their lives forever, Alice had been in mourning over the death of Ned, her lover.

Ellie had been a source of great comfort to her big sister throughout her grieving period. Until one day needing some space, Alice went outside for some air to take a walk. And it was the last time she would see her little sister. As well as the other members of her tribe, the Mall Rats. Due to The Technos' invasion.

Hearing the aircraft, the explosions rocking the city, Alice had at first tried to get back to the mall but was quickly overpowered by an advanced guard of Techno warriors and was dragged away, literally kicking and screaming, placed into a vehicle along with some other recently captured prisoners and taken to the airport.

The military style planes that had been used to transport the conquering Techno forces waited like massive mechanical birds of prey, their cargo doors open, as if to gobble up Alice and the other captives who were ushered inside against their will.

In the days before the virus, the airport had been a place of joy where Alice, with Ellie and their family, had embarked upon many memorable adventures growing up, flying away to various destinations on holiday. This time around, it had felt to Alice that she was being taken on a voyage of the damned. When the Techno aircraft was full of prisoners, the cargo door closed off Alice's view of the city she had called home.

The flight took about two or three hours. Upon arrival, its human cargo was emptied onto the tarmac. They had been sorted into groups, separated by age, by gender, and Alice's group of older girls around the same age as her were exchanged, traded, for all manner of goods. Computer equipment, medicines, food supplies, had been unloaded and given over to their new possessors.

Alice's group of slaves was soon put to work, she recalled to Tai San, and it was arduous. Reminiscent of what Tai San had also experienced. A terrible routine, every day.

They were a chain gang, mostly growing wheat and corn, which was itself then presumably being sold off to other buyers elsewhere, Alice thought. The slaves who did all the hard work to cultivate the fields in the first place certainly didn't receive the bulk of the bounties they produced from their crops and were poorly fed, malnourished. Many of the slaves became ill due to the extreme conditions and didn't survive.

Having grown up on her parents' farm, Alice understood agriculture and was very good at it. She knew how to live off the land, to care for and nurture living things among the soil. As a young girl, she had actually hated farm work and had daydreamed of far off adventures in exotic lands. This was quite contrary to anything she could have ever imagined, however. She was far from home but in a living hell. Being so close to the earth again, out in the fields, was the one thing that ironically helped her to keep going. It was a link to the past for her.

Unlike many of the slave workers around her, she had a connection to the land and though she despised her plight as a slave, feeling the fresh air and the soil beneath her feet kept her grounded, helped somehow to absorb the tumult and emotional pains she experienced as not only being a slave but being such a distance from her loved ones. From the Mall Rats. And her sister, Ellie.

Having experienced the near extinction of the human race with the demise of the adults, Alice thought she had a pretty high threshold when it came to hurt and distress. All of the young survivors who had inherited the world in the wake of the virus had been through it all, seen things, felt things, that no one should ever have to suffer, let alone teenagers, children.

Being apart from her little sister though had ripped a hole in Alice's heart.

Ever since Ellie's birth, a day she could recall vividly, one of the happiest in her life, she had taken on the role of 'big sister'. It was a position she relished, cherished, being the one to look after Ellie as she herself grew up. They had played together, went to the same school, enjoyed many happy moments on the farm. Alice had always been there for Ellie – ready to give sisterly advice, to give any assistance, to share a laugh, to just enjoy the close bond she had developed with her sibling over the years.

Following their parents' passing, along with the rest of the adults, Alice was even more aware of her responsibility to Ellie and did everything in her power to make sure that they both survived the advent of their new world. Ellie was quite capable herself of course, resourceful and independent, but Alice would always be 'watching out' for her, forever being Ellie's big sister. Alice had even saved Ellie's life when she had fallen ill, which brought the Mall Rats into their lives in the first place when she went to the city in search of medicine.

After leaving the city, Alice was traded again at a slave market and was 'bought' by a sea-faring tribe who lived further up on the coast – The Orcas. They were based in a remote fishing facility, feeding off a diet of seafood harvested from the waters, which they also traded upon with other tribes in the region.

It was a far cry from the privations Alice had endured previously as a slave worker on land. Especially when it became clear that the reason Alice had been brought to their shores was the amorous intention of the leader of The Orcas, who called himself The Captain, to woo Alice and make her his bride.

Alice was at first baffled and amused why 'The Captain' would wish to marry her. Not that she thought herself unworthy of romance. It was more that The Captain was a complete stranger and knew nothing about her personally.

But The Captain revealed that he had 'a thing' for oversized women, which was hardly surprising because he was very large in stature and overweight himself. And she couldn't help but feel a little flattered by his attentions and the fact that she had experienced something alien in her life to date – being perceived as a 'sex object'.

Rebuffing the advances of The Captain, Alice soon wore out her welcome among The Orcas and she was brought to 'Labour Island', a place where tribes in the region gathered to meet, to trade with each other, reminiscent of the Mall Rats' tribal gatherings in her homeland.

For some reason she had been singled out by a mysterious unit of militia who didn't seem to belong to this region and definitely weren't interested in any other produce which was available.

She was seized and taken to a waiting ship and after a long journey was placed into the custody of The Selector.

Upon her initial arrival at the *Lakeside Resort*, from where she met Ryan once more, she had hoped fate might take a better turn, that her period of enslavement had finally come to an end. But as she quickly discovered, in a way it had only just begun - and had taken on a different dimension to anything she had experienced before.

As with Ryan, her captors seemed to be more hospitable and again as with Tai San, Alice was advised that she could stay at the resort as a 'guest' of The Creator, under The Selector's 'supervision' and 'protection' as he called it.

There was still so much that Alice and Ryan didn't know about the ones who were responsible for their plight and what exactly it was that they wanted with them. So they couldn't shed much light on Tai San's questioning – and they were just about as confused by it all as Tai San was herself.

The one thing they did know, however, was that The Selector certainly knew a lot about Alice and Ryan. More than they did about him. He had visited over the past few days to question them. But it felt more like being interrogated, Alice explained to Tai San. The Selector – who was always apparently there on the instructions of The Creator, was meticulous in his research, a fine eye for detail and possessed a keen, Alice felt more like a calculating, mind. With an insatiable appetite for detail he was overly pedantic, intent on gathering all kinds of information about her life, as well as Ryan's, to date.

It was all a little reminiscent of the techniques The Broker had used on Tai San herself during her time in his captivity, constant probing and questioning for detail, any detail, of not just Tai San but the other Mall Rats.

Neither Alice or Ryan had ever encountered 'The Broker' who had kept Tai San prisoner or heard anything about him.

Cooped up in the resort, they had never met 'The Creator' – whoever and wherever they were - and apart from The Selector's references to carrying out The

Creator's bidding, they wondered if The Creator was even a real person. Alice had thought perhaps The Selector had invented the supposed existence of The Creator as another form of influence or leverage over them, The Selector promising that 'The Creator' would reward all those who joined in the new world they were 'creating'. Alice assumed this was some form of incentive, a type of 'bribe' given by The Selector to motivate and encourage their co-operation with him, to extract information, detail.

The Selector had assured them The Creator was very much real and that when The Creator deemed it necessary, Alice and Ryan would find out their true purpose and 'destiny' which formed part of The Creator's overall plans.

In his interrogations, The Selector had often been focused on Eagle Mountain.

Ryan had been there before, along with Tai San, during the fateful visit of the Mall Rats long ago, the tribe discovering the top level of the secret military-scientific base the adults had left behind. Alice hadn't been a part of the Mall Rats then but had heard what they had been through and relayed what she knew to The Selector.

The Mall Rats themselves were always the main subject of great enquiry by The Selector. He had asked Ryan and Alice everything they knew about the tribe. Their lives before the virus, their hopes, fears, personality types, romantic connections, their friends, their enemies, the challenges they had faced, what type of society that they themselves had been trying to build. Their diet. Awareness of technology. Their source of food, water. Their dealings with other tribes in the city. How they had felt about The Chosen, Zoot and the Locos. Ebony even. What it was like when The Technos invaded, what they thought of Ram, how life had been under the reign of The Technos, the strategies they used to defeat first Ram and then his successor, Mega. Their opinions on Ram's technology, their firsthand experiences of the virtual reality Ram had been implementing.

The Selector was also curious about how the Mall Rats got on with each other in the tribe – who was closest to who, their personal chemistry with one another, every aspect of their otherwise private lives.

It struck Tai San as odd, not just a coincidence, that she herself had faced many questions during her time as a prisoner of The Broker, who had also asked her about Eagle Mountain and the Mall Rats.

Now that Tai San had arrived, Alice and Ryan speculated that she would probably be in for more questioning herself. And the three of them pondered what might lay in store for them. Would they be safe? Continue staying at the resort? Would they all be set free to carry out whatever purpose the so-called Creator had for them?

Maybe, Alice reasoned, The Selector was nothing more than a powerful trader – gaining knowledge and information, even on other individuals who may have some value for him, in much the same way that The Broker had operated in selling Tai San to The Selector in the first place. It was possible, Tai San and Ryan agreed, that after some time being held in the resort that The Selector might 'sell' them on again via an auction to another buyer, exacting a good return in the process. The Creator could be a client of The Selector's, Tai San suggested. None of them knew for sure.

"I know one thing," Alice said to Tai San. "The Selector gives me the creeps. He's strange. And I thought I'd seen it all with The Guardian."

Alice described how The Selector sometimes came across in his manner as being overtly friendly – but it was too friendly. It was a guise, Alice was certain, an ingratiating mask of good manners which hid an otherwise insincere personality who seemed to have ulterior motives that neither Ryan nor Alice could fathom. Other times The Selector seemed cold, unfriendly, hostile even, alternating between subtle, passive aggressive outbursts to more blatant threats he would pose at Alice and Ryan if he felt he wasn't getting his way. Whenever he talked about The Creator, The Selector spoke with reverence, complete respect and adoration. It was like there were different 'versions' of The Selector who would show up at the resort and it did Alice's head in, she said, never knowing how The Selector might behave from one day to the next.

There was one final thing, Ryan emphasized. It was difficult to explain but The Selector seemed to be always 'testing' them somehow. He was constantly monitoring their reactions to his behaviour, to the things he would say, to the answers they were giving him themselves during his talks with them. And he seemed to enjoy their obvious discomfort in not knowing the reasoning for their continual captivity. Sometimes he wouldn't say anything at all, Alice said. There would be long gaps of silence on his visits where he would just stare at them – gauging their reaction to him, seeing if they would maintain eye contact or look away.

Other times he would be the one to avoid eye contact with them and instead keep his face down, busy typing into the laptop that he brought with him for his interrogations. The Selector was an enigma and whether his inconsistencies were on purpose, for effect, or just the result of a complicated soul, Ryan and Alice both felt that somehow they were forever being examined in some way when they interacted with him.

What he was the 'Selector' of was a mystery.

Tai San was determined not to stick around and find out, however. She agreed with Ryan and Alice that when the time was right, they should try and make plans to escape.

* * *

Several miles away in his dwelling, taking a sip from his chamomile tea, The Selector's eyes remained focused on the image of Tai San in front of him, engaged in conversation with Alice and Ryan.

The Selector sat at a bank of screens, flickering in the otherwise pitch-black room, the light of the monitor nearest him glowing on his face, just inches away from it. The other screens showed different perspectives of areas in and around the resort from the cameras that had been securely placed long ago. Showing various angles of even the perimeter guards on watch.

Leaning forward in his chair for an even closer look, The Selector focused his intense gaze on Tai San, studying her mannerisms, her every move.

On one monitor there were waveforms gauging Tai San, Alice and Ryan, the noise level of their voices, every inflection, similar technology although more advanced to lie detector tests in the old world.

The Selector had heard every word of the discussions Tai San had been having with her two Mall Rat friends and smiled, pleased with how things were progressing. Tai San's reunion with Ryan and Alice was not only informative, The Selector had also found it entertaining. Their views and speculations on him had especially been most intriguing.

It was so good to have the three of them there, The Selector considered. Everything was going well and truly according to plan.

CHAPTER FIVE

With a goodbye kiss to Amber and their sleeping baby, Bray had gotten up just before sunrise, and after a quick breakfast set out on his task of scouting the area to ensure that there were indeed no other inhabitants in the city and environs.

The previous night the Mall Rats had decided that a separate expedition was due to leave later that morning with Ram, Jack and some of the others heading on a mission to investigate Eagle Mountain.

Initially Bray was going to accompany them but decided that he would be best served staying behind to work with Amber on all that needed to be done – but at the heart of it, Bray felt uneasy at the prospect of leaving Amber and the Mall Rats alone, along with his baby son, given that Lex would be joining the Eagle Mountain expedition.

Maybe they could even gain further understanding on what the adults themselves had been doing at the mysterious underground facility, Bray thought, as he set out from the mall. The Mall Rats on their last visit had been astonished to discover the size of the complex, split across multiple levels, the advanced technology left behind – and even adults, apparently of some prominence, who had gone into cryogenic hibernation seemingly in an effort to escape the virus that was ravaging the world.

The fate of the Mall Rats seemed intertwined with Eagle Mountain, Bray considered, thinking back to their first visit long ago, when Zandra, Lex's lover at the time, had been killed in an explosion which had rocked the top level of the observatory. Amber had also almost lost her life in the blast.

Bray could only hope that this time around, no such tragedies would befall the Mall Rats. His main task today though was to check out the forest that bordered the city to establish if the Eco Tribe had returned to their camp.

Amber had once lived among them, and the Ecos, led by Hawk, were more than allies of the Mall Rats. They were close friends who shared the Mall Rats' quest to live in peace and harmony – the only difference being that the Ecos preferred to live closer to the land and Mother Nature.

Upon arriving at the location where they had once lived, Bray found the camp was abandoned, however, and there was no sign of the Ecos, who the Mall Rats believed must have fled the environs of the city, along with the rest of its population, to escape what was then feared to be the new 'virus' released by Mega and his Technos. It was an assumption, of course, and no one knew for sure but whatever fate had in store for the Ecos, their destiny certainly wasn't here.

After checking out the abandoned Eco camp, Bray scouted the far north end of the city. It was eerie to walk the deserted streets entirely alone, Bray thought, the sound of his boots from every step being the only noise he could hear, apart from that of his own breathing, as he made his way past some stores, long since looted. At that moment, it felt to Bray like he was the only person left in the world.

The streets were paved with memories, Bray thinking back to his life in the days of the adults and all the times since. The many events that had occurred to him and the other Mall Rats. There were reminders around almost every corner. One of the graffiti-covered empty stores he had passed had once been a favourite toy shop of his younger brother, Martin, which he used to visit when they were growing up. The windows now smashed, the building a burnt, derelict shell of what it once was.

It felt symptomatic of what fate had befallen Martin himself, Bray having watched helplessly as Martin's world crumbled around with him re-inventing himself eventually as Zoot, before his own young life was tragically cut short after becoming the leader of the Locos. His reputation was that of a tyrant. And although Bray couldn't deny that the Locos' ideology of Power and Chaos and anarchy was totally alien to everything Bray stood for, as well as the ideology of the Mall Rats – he could never fully reconcile the transformation of his young brother.

Martin had always been rebellious since the day he was born but it tore deep into his soul the prospects of his late parents ever conceiving what had occurred to their second son. And Bray himself remained torn apart also from the same conflict.

He was looking forward to getting back to the mall later on. He hadn't seen that much of Amber recently, only at night, the two of them so preoccupied by what they were doing each day and all their responsibilities. There were so many issues to work out – what to do with The Guardian, Eloise, her dangerous warriors imprisoned in the mall. The group of young mothers in their care. The mystery of Eagle Mountain, The Collective and any threat they might pose.

Bray had suggested that he and Amber place aside a part of that afternoon for themselves, even an hour or two, so they could enjoy some quality time together. It had been too long since they had last done that and Bray longed for a precious, fleeting moment with Amber where they could, somehow, put away all their other cares and responsibilities - and simply enjoy being with each other.

Making his way from the north end of the city, Bray arrived in Sectors 8 and 9 which were once under the control of the Locos and his late brother, Zoot.

Seeing the graffiti in the decaying streets was a stark reminder not only of what occurred before but the fact that Ebony had been involved as the girlfriend of Zoot and Queen of the Locos.

For all that Ebony had seemingly changed, Bray never fully trusted her and resolved that she really must be watched closely – especially with the imprisoned Zootists who could influence her, or worse still, she might influence them to instigate an uprising.

The jury was still out where Bray was concerned though, and to be fair to Ebony, he decided to keep an open mind given that she seemed to take threats seriously if the forces of The Collective made their presence felt. Bray recognized it was important to ensure the Mall Rats were as prepared as much as they could be in case they ever came under attack from The Collective or any unseen force.

Since they were so few of number, the Mall Rats certainly needed allies and Ebony seemed the best candidate to help drive their defence efforts. After all, the ex-Zootists were a highly trained militia and Ebony herself was a very capable commander – tough and street-smart. She had a lot of combat experience and was very much a strategic thinker.

And that was the prime thing that concerned Bray. He *knew* Ebony. And had known her for a very long time, going back to the adult days. She was too smart. Cunning. Despite her claims of wanting to do what was best for the Mall Rats, Bray remembered the many times Ebony had put her own personal interests above all others. He wondered if she had some ulterior motives – a card, if not a deck's worth, up her sleeve. Some other plan she was seeking to carry out that might end up in the Mall Rats being betrayed.

* * *

They looked so peaceful, Amber thought, from the doorway, peering in at what had once been a furniture shop in the mall.

Sitting on one of the beds inside was Emma, a girl in her mid-teens who had been telling a bedtime story to Trudy's daughter, Brady, who she was babysitting, as well as her own little brother and sister, Shannon and Tiffany. The three younger children were nestled, snuggled up, beside Emma – and each was drifting off in slumber as she finished off the story she was making up about a magical dog who could speak to humans.

Her own baby fast asleep in her arms, Amber couldn't help but smile in appreciation of not only Emma's story and her child caring skills – getting three, often hyper, kids to sleep for their daytime rest was no easy feat - but in admiration of Emma's many inspiring qualities. She couldn't see the warmth of Amber's expression because Emma in fact was blind. Yet she continued to live her life as best as she could with courage, perseverance and great kindness to others, especially the younger more vulnerable ones. Almost ignoring the fact that Emma, given her disability, was vulnerable herself. If only others were like her, Amber mused, the world would be a far better place.

After stopping to check in on Emma and the little ones, Amber was on her way to the food court to prepare a special surprise for the 'date night' she had planned to have later on with Bray when he got back. The other Mall Rats had supported the idea fully, recognizing that Amber and Bray did so much for everyone else and it was only fair they tried to do the same for them.

Trudy, confronting the ghosts of her past, had insisted that she be the one to take over Amber's watch of The Guardian in his cell so that Amber didn't have to complete her rota that day. Similarly, Ebony had volunteered to oversee Eloise and the Legion warriors in their custody, being assisted on guard duty by some of the Zootist militia.

Lia, who was Lex's new romantic flame, was in turn staying by Ebony's side – ostensibly to help her keep watch over the prisoners but it was also, Amber was aware, to make sure Ebony herself didn't get up to any subterfuge or wrongdoing with her former allies behind bars - Ebony having once been on their side. Lex had asked Lia to stick around Ebony like glue and be vigilant of her every move.

Ram, Jack and Ellie were no longer at the mall, having already set out with Lex for Eagle Mountain, Lex accompanying them to provide protection in the event they encountered any unexpected dangers. But also, to ensure that Jack and Ellie weren't vulnerable if Ram had ulterior motives.

It was a sensible precaution, Amber had resolved.

There was so much to explore of the vast underground complex at Eagle Mountain and Amber, like Bray, had partly wished she could have gone along with the others to assist, or that they could have sent a larger expedition. But it wasn't possible. There were so few Mall Rats in number and Amber and Bray needed as much help as they could get while Lex, Ram, Jack and Ellie would be away.

With every passing hour Amber just hoped they were safe, and looked forward to their return, as well as any news they might bring back with them.

Life had to go on at the mall in the meantime. Emma's story was interrupted suddenly when Sammy arrived.

"Amber! Come quick!" he cried out.

"What is it?" Amber replied in growing concern.

"It's Salene! And May! They're crying, big time!"

Rushing to their living quarters, Amber found Salene and May sitting side by side on the bed, hugging, comforting each other. May was emotional, tears streaming from her eyes. Salene was also upset, her shoulders heaving as she, too, sobbed.

"Is everything okay?" Amber asked, going over to sit by them to lend her support. "What on Earth is going on?"

"It's Salene…" May explained through her tears. She seemed that she wanted to say more but was finding it hard to get any words out of her mouth.

"You can tell me, whatever it is," Amber encouraged. "You'll feel better if you talk about it. A problem shared is a problem not only halved – but solved."

"It's nothing bad, Amber…" Salene spoke up, trying to regain her own composure, taking in a deep breath, "It's May… She said…"

"She said what?" Amber wondered.

"She said - yes!" Salene explained with a sudden grin, and she started to laugh – and then cry at the same time, totally overwhelmed by her feelings, May doing the same.

It was then that Amber quickly realized Salene and May were so emotional because they had been crying tears of joy.

"May and I – we're going to get married!" Salene blurted out elatedly.

"That's – that's amazing! Congratulations!" Amber exclaimed, wrapping her arms around them to give a big hug.

* * *

The vehicle skidded to a halt, kicking up a shower of gravel, as its occupants surveyed the observatory building in front of them atop Eagle Mountain.

"Well, we made it," Lex said, turning off the engine and jumping out from the driver's side. He was concerned that there would be enough gasoline in the tank, especially given that there were no tribes around to trade in the deserted city and environs.

Jack and Ellie exited from the back seats and gazed ahead uneasily.

"There doesn't seem to be anyone else around from the looks of it," Jack pondered.

"Hopefully," Ellie said, in mounting anxiety at the thought of what they might encounter inside.

"If they were, you probably scared them away by your driving," Ram sighed, clambering slowly out of the front passenger seat. He looked like he was going to be sick and felt Lex had driven far too quickly – and erratically – for his liking. "Remind me to never hire you as a chauffeur!"

It was a long journey from the mall to Eagle Mountain and throughout, they hadn't seen signs of anyone else. The entire region was deserted apart from a few wild stray dogs, probably former pets from the adult times and now feral, and all had commented that they hoped they wouldn't encounter any wild animals who previously inhabited the city's local zoo.

Now, it was as if they were up on top of the world, the air cold and fresh due to their altitude, strong winds all around, pushing the clouds just above at some speed, which were so close that they felt they could almost reach out and touch them.

"I don't know what's more beautiful," Jack said loudly over a gust, "the view down there – or the sight of you."

He was speaking to Ellie, the two of them hand in hand as they started walking towards the observatory entrance. The view across the rolling hills looking down below was certainly breathtaking, panoramic. As was Ellie, to Jack, her hair billowing in the wind.

"Such a charmer," she said coyly. "Maybe I'll use some of this wind to blow you a kiss."

"Just the one?"

"Alright, lots. Maybe one of them will even be a real kiss."

Jack beamed at the idea of that. But Ram and Lex looked plainly sick.

"Will you two give it a break? I'm not entirely into this lovey-dovey stuff," Ram sighed. "What about you, Lexey-boy?"

"In case you hadn't noticed, Ram, I'm what is known as a lover, as well as a fighter," Lex winked in an attempt at macho camaraderie.

Ellie ignored their mocking remarks, giving Jack a loving smile, and it helped keep him calm and ease the anxieties he otherwise felt swirling inside – the prospect of going back inside Eagle Mountain gave Jack a feeling of trepidation. It was a vast, intimidating place.

"Give me a moment," Lex suddenly said. And the others realized the significance while they watched Lex cross to Zandra's grave, which he had dug himself at the time of her demise. It brought back painful memories of her passing at Eagle Mountain. In the explosion which claimed her life, the baby she had been carrying in her early pregnancy was also lost. Lex wasn't just paying respects to his lost love but to the son or daughter that could have been theirs. As a tribute, he placed some wild flowers he had taken from the hillside beside the grave, putting some rocks on top to make sure they didn't get disturbed by the wind.

Ram watched Lex by the grave – and knew that shortly there would be more graves to dig. After all, they couldn't leave the adults entombed in Eagle Mountain forever.

They had discovered the adults in the depths of the Eagle Mountain complex on their last visit, 'frozen' as if in a deep sleep in their cryogenic hibernation chambers. It had been an incredible and eerie sight – mind-blowing to Jack, Amber and the others to see adults from the days before the virus once more, the like of whom they thought they would never look upon again.

Jack had initially hoped it would be possible to even revive the adults somehow from their chambers. And if so, there would be so many questions to ask them - but Eloise, in a fit of rage, had disconnected the units from their power sources.

Ram had some knowledge of the cryogenic units the adults had been stored in. He had been to Eagle Mountain himself many times during his reign over the city when he had been the leader of The Technos.

Discovering the hibernating adults, he had studied and reverse engineered some of their chambers to gain an understanding of their workings, hoping to use one of the units himself so he could 'escape' the real world and live forever, in a perpetual state of sleep, inside his own virtual reality paradise. His dreams. To hopefully waken at some point in time in the future. Even a thousand years when hopefully the world might be filled with technology on a level that even someone like Ram, who was obsessed with it, could not even conceive, let alone understand.

Without power, Ram had told Amber, he thought the adults would stay 'on ice', in some manner of preservation, for a couple of months. Though there were no longer any life-support systems connected in the aftermath of Eloise's actions, their chambers were hermetically sealed and intact. Eagle Mountain, where they must have hoped to outlive the virus, would become instead a tomb, Ram had advised, the adults remaining undisturbed in their chambers. They still had some time, Ram speculated, otherwise they would have to dispose of the bodies. Amber and the Mall Rats felt it was only right to pay their respects, to give the adults, whoever they were, the dignity of a proper burial and send-off if the adults couldn't be revived.

"Are you ready?" Lex asked, returning to Jack, Ellie and Ram at the observatory entrance.

"As ready as we'll ever be," Ram said.

Due to his many visits in the past, Ram led the way as he knew the interior of Eagle Mountain well. It was good to have him guiding their group because without him, Lex imagined, they could have easily gotten very lost inside the labyrinthine tunnels inside the vast complex.

Ram had brought a supply of flashlights along and they certainly needed them, the spotlight of his beam cutting a pathway through the darkness, illuminating the walls.

On their last visit to Eagle Mountain, then as prisoners of Eloise and her Collective forces, Ram had instructed the *K.A.M.I* computer to shut down all systems, plunging the facility into darkness. His improvised move had enabled the Mall Rats to escape from the Legion warriors and to then subdue Eloise herself, their commander.

The massive compound had been left in the dark and Ram said he had planned to try and restart the core systems, bringing back the artificial light, when they got down to Level 3, the area where the *K.A.M.I* computer was based, which he hoped to reboot.

Standing for *Knowledge Artificial Machine Intelligence*, *K.A.M.I* was a sophisticated, next generation colossus possessing artificial intelligence – even its own 'voice' that it had used to communicate with Ram and the others on their previous visit – and it seemed to have been tasked and programmed by the adults with running all the various systems inside Eagle Mountain, including monitoring the cryogenic units that the hibernating adults had been inside.

"How much further, Ram?" Jack asked, his voice echoing down the long passageway.

"Not long now," Ram replied. "At least, I hope."

"Are you sure you know the way?" Jack probed, casting a look behind him into the darkness. His mind had started to play tricks and he felt like he was exploring some sort of haunted, nightmarish castle, imagining ghosts around every corner.

"We'll be fine," Ellie said, giving Jack's hand a supportive squeeze. But she sounded more convinced than she looked. She too was clearly on edge.

Even Lex was bracing himself, ready for action.

The air was getting more stale the further down they went into the cavernous structure, the atmosphere claustrophobic, and Jack dreaded to think of all the layers of mountain up above them.

Ram reassured everyone, as well as himself, that it wouldn't be long before they could get to the *K.A.M.I* computer and be able to instruct it to restart the absent air-conditioning, bringing in a flow of fresh air to breathe in, as well as proper lighting back to the complex.

Then they could try and connect the hard drive that Jack had been carrying in his backpack to the *K.A.M.I* machine, in an effort to make some progress in deciphering its contents.

A few minutes later they finally approached their destination, the massive *K.A.M.I* supercomputer looming up ahead – and that's when Ram was first concerned by what he was seeing – and hearing.

"INTRUDER ALERT. INTRUDER ALERT. INTRUDER ALERT," the *K.A.M.I* system repeated, over and over again in its monotone voice which reverberated and echoed in the chamber and far beyond.

The area was bathed in artificial pulsing light, the multitude of tiny lights on the *K.A.M.I* computer blinking away, while red lights flashed from alarms in the ceiling, lighting up the faces of Ram, Jack, Ellie and Lex as the alarms wailed unbearably.

"What the hell is it?" Lex asked in mounting panic.

"Something's not right," Ram replied.

Suddenly twin piercing beams of green laser light shot out from a sensor in the *K.A.M.I* system, sweeping over the contours of Ram's face, scanning his features, in recognition, examining Lex, who froze in the glare, uncertain what to do.

"WELCOME BACK, RAM," the machine greeted him. He had spent much time down there in the past during his Techno days, examining the sophisticated technology the adults had left behind, the machine recognizing his return.

"Good to see you, old friend," Ram responded.

The beam of light moved from Ram's face, switching *K.A.M.I*'s attention to Ellie, Jack and Lex, who stood frozen in fear.

"AND THESE ITEMS?"

"This is Jack, Ellie and Lex," Ram advised.

"HUMAN OR ROBOTIC?" *K.A.M.I* asked.

"Human," Ram replied.

"HAVE WE MET BEFORE, LEX, ELLIE AND JACK?" *K.A.M.I* asked, with a degree of distrust in the tone.

"I don't think we have... er... had that pleasure," Jack said politely, clearly trying to ingratiate himself.

"WRONG!" *K.A.M.I* exploded in sudden disdain. "YOU HAVE VISITED HERE PREVIOUSLY ACCORDING TO MY MEMORY BANKS AND THE DATA I HAVE ON FILE."

Lex, Ellie and Jack recoiled in mounting fear while Ram tried to calm the colossus machine.

"You didn't ask if they had visited, *K.A.M.I*."

"YOU ARE VERY LITERAL, RAM," *K.A.M.I* said, more friendly now.

"And so are you, *K.A.M.I*, my friend," Ram said, reassuringly. "Now why don't you restart all core systems?" Ram instructed the computer. "And turn off those alarms."

The alarms stopped flashing, the 'INTRUDER ALERT' audible warnings ceased – and they could hear the sound of equipment, machinery whirring and reactivating, Eagle Mountain coming back to life – and all the other lights inside the complex switched on in an instant at the same time. Jack, Ellie, Ram and Lex breathed in deeply the welcome rush of fresh air that was flowing in from powerful fans in the ceiling.

"That feels so good," Ellie said, gasping the new air.

With the lights back on in the complex, it was then that Jack was the first to be able to see clearly. The area where the adults had been, inside their cryogenic hibernation chambers, was now completely empty. All of the rows of units that Jack vividly remembered seeing before, their image imprinted on his mind, were missing and no longer there.

"Where – where are they?" Jack cried out, stunned by their absence.

"They couldn't have just walked outta here," Lex said. "Have you got anything to do with this, Ram?"

"Nothing, nothing at all!" Ram said, running his fingers through his hair, mystified and stressed by the development. "For once I know about as much as you do, Lexy-boy."

"But they were here," Ellie said, almost refusing to believe what her own eyes were telling her. "They were right here," she said again, pointing to the spot where the hibernation units had been. All that was left were a series of complex wires and cables sticking out from the floor in each spot, disconnected from the units that had once been there.

"*K.A.M.I* – where are the adults that were here?" Ram asked, looking up at the huge mainframe towering above him.

"UNKNOWN. UNITS 1 THROUGH 38 HAVE BEEN TAKEN AWAY BY INTRUDERS. DEFENCE SYSTEMS COMPROMISED. MANUAL OVERRIDE. UNAUTHORISED VIOLATION OF PROGRAMME 1, SUB-SECTIONS 3 THROUGH 35."

"Intruders?" Lex said, taking it in.

"What 'intruders'? Who are the intruders?" Ram questioned the computer again.

"UNKNOWN. IDENTITY RECOGNITION UNSUCCESSFUL."

"So, what do we do now?" Jack wondered. He felt the hard drive safely in his backpack, its contents seemed the least of their worries at the moment.

"What does it all mean?" Ellie said.

"It means we've gotta get back to the mall and tell the others," Lex suggested, with a sense of urgency.

"You're right about that," Ram agreed. "One thing's for sure. It means that someone else has been to Eagle Mountain. Recently. The only question is – who!?"

CHAPTER SIX

Tai San was in the middle of a deep dream. She was on the beach, walking arm in arm with Lex. It was a beautiful day, the sun shining in a crystal-clear blue sky. The two of them on the sands, the waves gently lapping over their feet. They had been swimming just before and Lex was making Tai San laugh by 'drawing' two strange-looking faces in the wet sands with his big toe – one, a stick-figure of Tai San, the other a self-portrait of himself. The tide coming in and out kept making the figures get washed away, Lex digging in his toe to redraw the lines of the stick figures in the sand between each incoming wave, Tai San finding it amusing.

"Wake up, Tai San," a voice said.

"Lex?" Tai San said seductively, kissing the hand on her shoulder. "Kiss me. I want you."

As the dream faded, Tai San quickly gained consciousness, awakening with a start - and felt someone's hand pressing on her shoulder, shaking her gently to rouse her from her slumbers. And it certainly wasn't Lex.

She had stayed up late into the night sitting in the lounge of the *Lakeside Resort*, reminiscing with Alice and Ryan about old times, as well as speculating about their current situation and what it might all signify for the future.

When they could keep awake no longer, their minds full and having gone through a range of emotions at their reunion, exhausted, Tai San had gone to the room she had chosen in the vacant hotel. It was next to Alice's, who was in turn next door to Ryan's room.

Being the only ones there in the large and luxurious resort made it all a strange and surreal experience for Tai San, as did the uncertainty of not knowing the intentions of their 'hosts', The Selector and 'The Creator' he referred to. Overwhelmed, Tai San had quickly fallen asleep the moment she had gotten under the covers of her comfortable bed and had slept soundly – until now.

"Don't touch me!" Tai San cried out, recoiling and looking up from her bed at who it was who had woken her, and whose hand had just been on her shoulder.

It was The Selector.

"Good morning, Tai San," he greeted her amiably, as if he had done nothing untoward or out of the ordinary. "Did you sleep well?"

Tai San noticed the door to the bedroom was wide open. She had locked it the night before from the inside. The Selector must have had a master key and had let himself in.

"Why are you so agitated, Tai San?" The Selector asked.

"Why do you think!?" Tai San snapped.

"That you might have something to hide? Tell me about this person - Lex."

"I don't know what you're talking about," Tai San lied, unwilling to give out any information.

The Selector was standing alone in the room and for a moment just watched her – as if studying Tai San and her reactions. She recalled Alice and Ryan's observation that The Selector often seemed to be 'testing' them in some way.

Tai San could also detect a slight shift in his gaze, that he was subtly eyeing her up provocatively and she quickly pulled the sheets over her to cover herself up.

"Are you feeling – 'embarrassed' – Tai San? If so, you have no reason to be. Because I do understand," The Selector said.

"Understand – just exactly what?"

"That you are developing into a very beautiful young woman. Nature has been kind to have given you physical qualities that many would wish they had. You must have excellent DNA and come from a good line. What about your family – can you tell me about your parents?"

"That's none of your concern," Tai San said, confused by The Selector's questions – and her intuition firing, feeling increasingly threatened by his presence.

"Everything about you is my concern, Tai San. Including even your genetics. Which I am sure The Creator will be very interested in. Now, I suggest that you shower and I'll meet you in the lobby in precisely thirty minutes."

Tai San didn't move.

"Interesting," The Selector remarked. "You clearly need to learn how to follow instructions. For your own sake." There was more than a hint of threat as he picked up a ripe peach from a bowl on a side table and started taking mouthfuls, the juice dripping down his chin.

"They're really quite delicious. You should try them. Millions of years of change have given us this," he indicated the half-eaten peach. "One of nature's gifts. As are you."

He put the peach down and turned his back, Tai San watching as he left the room – without a word – and shut the door behind him. Tai San could hear the door being locked from the outside.

On her own again, Tai San tried to gather her thoughts. She couldn't understand The Selector or the strange experience she had found herself in. It was like being in another dream, surreal, nightmarish.

There was a sudden knock, a tap-tap, from outside the door.

"Alice? Is that you?" Tai San called out warily.

"No, it's me," The Selector responded from the other side of the doorway. "Alice and Ryan will join you in the lobby in precisely twenty-seven minutes. You are losing time, Tai San. And that is not a wise thing to do. So, get yourself ready."

"Ready for what?"

There was no reply.

Tai San was totally perplexed by what was going on.

Even more so when a few seconds passed – and then a few minutes – and still, The Selector had not given her an answer. Or even said anything further. There was only silence.

Tai San climbed out of bed, crossed to the door, unlocked it and opened it, peering carefully outside - where The Selector stood and sighed impatiently while glancing at a digital device on his wrist.

"You now only have seventeen minutes. And you won't want to suffer the penalty of being late!"

He glared at Tai San, then walked down the corridor.

Tai San thought it would be wise to go along with matters for the time being. She took a quick shower, dressed, all the while wondering what The Selector was up to, why he was playing all these mind games with her.

She had never been through anything like it before. Even with The Broker. And hoped that she would soon have an answer as to what were The Selector and The Creator's plans for her. As well as Alice and Ryan.

Tai San arrived in the main lobby where she saw Alice and Ryan waiting for her. They were sitting in armchairs but were surrounded by guards, along with the same group of medical-scientists Tai San had encountered at the dock - all wearing decontamination suits with medical surgery masks covering their faces.

"Ah, you made it, Tai San," The Selector said, with a benevolent smile. "With eighteen seconds to spare. Please, take a seat. We need to remain on schedule."

He glanced at the digital device on his wrist and indicated another chair. Tai San sat, where she was strapped, along with Ryan and Alice in their own chairs, so the medics or scientists or whoever they were could go about their tests.

"Get your hands off me!" Ryan bellowed, struggling to free himself.

Like Ryan, Alice was also squirming in her seat as the guards continued strapping her down, tying her arms to those of the chair.

'Relax. All of you. You have nothing to fear," The Selector said reassuringly. "For your own safety, we just need to carry out some more tests and then you will be free to enjoy the rest of the day."

As soon as Tai San was secure, the masked medical team began feverishly working on the three Mall Rats, taking readings of their vital signs.

"Why are you doing this?" Tai San demanded, flinching as one of the medics performed a blood test on her exposed arm.

"It will soon be over," The Selector reassured her, walking over to Tai San's chair. "Sssshh, hush now, everything will be okay," he said, stroking her hair with his fingers as if to relax her. But it only made the situation worse for Tai San, detesting the violation of her freedom, her body even, as the medics, with machine-like efficiency, carried out more tests, taking swabs of her saliva. There was something so inhuman about it all.

The Selector snapped his fingers, indicating a guard to pour three glasses of juice. Tomato juice. Which three guards placed at the mouths of Tai San, Alice and Ryan. "Drink. It's fresh. You'll love it."

Tai San, Alice and Ryan considered the glasses of juice in front of them cautiously and The Selector smiled. "It's not poison, if that's what you're concerned about. Here, I'll show you."

He crossed to the counter and poured himself a glass and sipped on it, savouring the taste. "Delicious. Now drink – all of you!"

Tai San, Alice and Ryan sipped on the glasses which were held to their mouths and as they swallowed, all gagged as if they were about to vomit.

"That's not tomato juice!" Ryan yelled. "It's blood!"

"Why does it revolt you so, Ryan? Tell me," The Selector urged him to reveal.

"You're crazy!" Alice gasped, trying to gain her composure and wash her mouth out with her own saliva to get rid of the taste.

"Why do you think that, Alice?" The Selector asked, intrigued. "What if the drink was in reality tomato juice? Would we be crazy offering you that to drink? Whereas blood is so very important. After all, you'd be desperate to receive it if you had an accident and had to receive a transfusion."

"That's a little different," Tai San said. "What you're doing is absolutely disgusting. Inhumane. Have you no mercy? Compassion?"

"I have an abundance of compassion, Tai San, you can be sure. As well as blood. And you've just drunk some. So now we are interconnected. The three of you, with me."

Tai San, Alice and Ryan gazed unbelievingly as The Selector started to pace, gathering his thoughts, deep in contemplation, while the medics began unpacking other equipment from boxes they had brought with them.

"The Creator informs me that as well as our spiritual needs, we are a tool-making species," The Selector suddenly spoke, addressing the Mall Rats before him. "Ever since our ancestors learned to make fire, to hunt, to cook, to co-operate with each other – it is our ability to make tools that has propelled us along every evolutionary step, advancing our society, our humanity. We have expanded over every land on this Earth, learned to fly, conquered the seas, we're soon to explore the heavens, set out for the stars. Tried to control nature itself. We have even become so proficient at making things, we have upset the balance and threatened our very world we depend upon."

"What is this – some kind of history lesson?" Alice blurted sarcastically, interrupting The Selector, who did indeed sound like an absent-minded professor giving an impassioned lecture. And he certainly possessed the skills of an orator.

"It's a reminder of where we have come from. Of who we are," The Selector continued. "Despite all of our great accomplishments, as well as our faults, and the many incredible, miraculous things that humanity has brought into being – underneath it all, as The Creator has revealed – you and me, all of us, are organic creatures ourselves. Made of flesh and bone. Also, blood. Our time on this Earth is short and each of us is nothing more than a candle in the dark, waiting for our flame to one day go out."

"What are you talking about?" Ryan said, totally confused, struggling to get out of his bonds.

"We think and act like we are immortal but we are quite the reverse. All it takes is a pathogen. An accident. Maybe a wicked act committed by one of our own kind. A natural disaster. Perhaps an illness brought on ourselves by our own life choices. A virus even. The adults learned the hard way - in the end, we have to do everything we can to look after our flesh and bones. Our blood. Every fibre of our health. All of our future achievements, all of our dreams, after millions of years of life still depend on the functions of our organic parts. On a spiritual level, however, one can't live without love. But there can be no life without blood."

"Poetic," Alice scoffed. "Who was your inspiration? Vampires and Dracula?"

"Not exactly. I would suspect bats had something to do with those kinds of tales. An interesting species – bats. We have been studying them in some of our breeding programmes. All manner of species. Amazing creatures. It's absolutely fascinating when one takes into account the properties of sound and how radar evolved, heralding the most extraordinary technology."

The Selector thought about his comments introspectively.

If Tai San, Alice and Ryan had any doubts about The Selector's sanity, these quickly evaporated, and they realized that he was either totally mad – or possessed a zealot conviction to all he referred to in his impassioned lecture.

After addressing the Mall Rats, he crossed to the counter, poured himself a glass of his blood and drank it while the medics unpacked strange looking capsules of some kind from sealed foil bags that they were then inserting inside large, hypodermic needles.

"You Mall Rats may think you understand the sanctity of life," The Selector continued addressing his prisoners. "But I wonder if you truly respect it, treasure it. As does The Creator. Life is precious, to be valued. It is the foundation of our society. Our very existence. Let alone the future. And that is why we are here today."

"We're ready, Selector" one of the medics said, certain that the hypodermic needle they were handling was loaded properly.

"As our most recent arrival, Tai San," The Selector informed her, "You will have the honour of being the first recipient of one of the adults' last technological breakthroughs which, thanks to the infrastructure The Creator has put in place, we have refined and adapted."

The medic holding the large needle stood beside Tai San, positioning it carefully over her arm, choosing the appropriate spot.

"No!" Tai San cried out, terrified at what was happening. She shifted in her seat, willing her bound arm to be free, but it was no use, the guards holding her down, under pressure, keeping the arm tied to the chair, the tip of the huge needle getting ever closer, just millimeters over her right hand.

"You're hurting her!" Ryan yelled, enraged by the treatment of Tai San.

"Sometimes the thing that causes the most pain, can also bring the most pleasure. And end up being the best thing that ever happened to us," The Selector said, watching developments with a macabre fascination.

Tai San knew the needle was going to hurt, big time. It was wide and the longest needle she had ever seen and she dreaded whatever they were going to inject into her. "I haven't given you my permission to do this!" she screamed angrily.

"But they have *my* permission," The Selector insisted. "Don't worry, it's quite safe. Each of you are about to have an advanced microchip injected into your body tissue. It will ache at first, but it is for your own good. And after this, you will wish this day had happened sooner."

"Don't bet on it!" Alice roared.

Tears began to stream from Tai San's eyes, due to the intense pain she felt as the needle was inserted, going deeper into her hand, deeper still, her arm cramping painfully.

She wanted to stifle the pain, to not show any weakness or vulnerability, to resist The Selector to her last breath. But the pain was too great and she screamed out, in agony, unable to fathom the insensitive cruelty, let alone the hurt she was suffering.

The Selector looked on sadistically, studying Tai San as she writhed in her seat. He wiped away the trace of a tear from her cheek with his little finger, which he then placed in his mouth, sucking on his finger. Then bizarrely, he began to copy her facial mannerisms, wincing in his own mock pain, as if he was going through the same, in a type of phantom ordeal.

And then it was over, the needle was slowly extracted from Tai San's hand, leaving a red welt on her skin from where it had gone in.

Tai San felt angry, humiliated, her hand throbbed, and that she might pass out at any moment.

She sobbed uncontrollably, tears running down her face.

"It's all for the best, Tai San," The Selector assured her, wiping away another tear from her cheek with his fingers.

Holding his hand to the light, he stared at the tear droplet, reflecting under the glare.

"What makes us all who we are?" he mused to himself, studying the tear.

"Untie me from this chair and I'll show you!" Alice threatened.

"Oh, you'll be untied, Alice. As well as Ryan. After your own injections."

The medics injected the biochips into Alice and Ryan, who gritted their teeth and cried out in as much pain as Tai San had experienced. During the process, The Selector watched eagerly.

"Don't forget to take any tears away for analysis," The Selector instructed his medics, who complied, beginning to scoop up fresh tears from Tai San's face, putting them into containers, along with some tears from Alice – but so far, Ryan hadn't produced any, although his face was writhed in agony.

A medic examined various screens. "We're getting readings starting to come through, Selector. The biochips appear to be functional. Everything's operational. They're in the system now. Data's being sent through to the base. Adrenalin and pulse rate's a little high though," the medic added.

"As it should be," The Selector concurred. "The *fight or flight* response. You can't get away from millions of years of evolution – we're all still just animals, in the end."

"Some, more than others," Ryan snapped angrily.

"Indeed," The Selector replied calmly as he crossed to Tai San and removed a small vial from one of the medic's trays. "Open wide," The Selector instructed. "Don't be afraid. I just require another swab," The Selector reassured.

He took the swab, then crossed to the entrance.

"I'll go and personally inform The Creator that preparations are in order. And do some of my own tests on the genetics," he stated.

As he left, he was slightly preoccupied by the device strapped to his wrist which wasn't solely a digital watch but displayed a screen which The Selector gazed at intently.

As he walked, he inserted the swab he had taken from Tai San, then studied DNA readings on his wrist monitor

He had found the Mall Rats' ordeal most interesting. And slightly melodramatic. Even naïve. Unbeknownst to them, he had been injected with a similar biochip at the very beginning when he first met The Creator. He knew the pain they were going through. But it was necessary to connect them to not only The Selector but The Creator as well in ways that Tai San, Alice and Ryan were yet to realize. But they would, soon.

Arriving outside, the doors of a futuristic looking pod - a vehicle - opened automatically, The Selector took his seat, the doors swung shut and the driverless vehicle sped away.

CHAPTER SEVEN

Bray took cover in the street in the suburbs behind some abandoned, burned-out wrecks of vehicles, ensuring he remained unseen as he cautiously watched a party of ex-Zootists who were gathering produce from a park.

The Mall Rats had once planted potatoes and Amber and Bray thought it would be an interesting exercise for the ex-Zootists to make themselves useful by doing some manual work. But it would also give them a chance to check out if the ex-Zootists could indeed be trusted while working alone. Bray agreed with Amber that it would be wise for him to discreetly check on them at the conclusion of his scouting. He had more or less completed checking out the city and environs which were well and truly deserted.

Absent from any contact with Ebony who had stayed back at the mall, the Zootists seemed to be dutifully carrying out their tasks, harvesting the potatoes, placing them in an abundance of rusty shopping carts.

It filled Bray with some reassurance that perhaps the Zootist militia could be an asset to the Mall Rats after all, rather than representing some form of threat, since they had seemingly done nothing more untoward than carry out all that had been asked of them.

Maybe Ebony herself *had* changed, as she kept insisting she had to Bray and Amber in recent weeks, and Bray considered he had possibly been overly cautious of Ebony and should give her more benefit of his doubt.

His optimism was short-lived though when he overheard one of the Zootists suggesting that the group make a trip to Sector 6 before they got back to the mall, reinforcing the need that *none* in the group could tell Ebony of their secret detour, however.

This gave Bray another dimension of concern. They clearly were not totally de-radicalized because Sector 6 was a legendary area of the suburbs where Zoot had gone to school and had become not only a mythological but a revered and hallowed place for those with the original Locos' ideology, let alone the derivative Zootists.

No matter how disciplined and well trained the militia were and the progress the Mall Rats believed was being made during the de-radicalization process, this particular group Bray was furtively following clearly had their own sense of independent spirit.

Now Bray was filled with dread as he kept out of sight but watched the Zootists arrive at the old school which Bray himself had once attended. Ebony had also gone there, as had Trudy, Bray meeting them both in the last days of the virus. Bray's younger brother, Martin, had also been a student there. The school itself was where he had one day brazenly rebelled against not only the teachers, but all forms of authority, everything that the adult world represented – re-inventing himself as Zoot, the leader of The Locos. The school was the place where the legend had begun.

It was now in a state of decay, ruins, its windows all broken, the walls covered in graffiti – including many tags portraying *The Locos* scrawled in paint on its peeling exterior – the school had visitors once more.

Bray was aghast, stupefied, as the Zootists knelt down, bowing before the building at the entrance by the school gates.

"Zoot lives! Zoot lives!" they began to chant, their voices echoing around the deserted suburbs as the cry repeated, each mention of his brother's alter ego causing Bray nothing but emotional pain at the memory of what was and anxiety at the thought of what could be.

Shocked by the apparent 'pilgrimage' the Zootists were making, Bray realized he would have to get back to the mall quickly to let Amber and the others know of his discovery. Bray hoped Ebony would be surprised to learn that those who they thought were ex-Zootists were still very much under the thrall of the zealous beliefs instilled in them of late by The Guardian and Eloise.

Suddenly, a high-pitched noise whined above as the shadow of something soared over the school, passing by at high speed.

Bray was so lost in his own concern at what he had discovered with the Zootists that at first he almost didn't register it – and thought that he might have imagined what he had just heard and seen, a strange, unexpected blur in his peripheral vision.

Looking up, he was astonished to see a drone, making fast, zig-zagging movements high above the streets in the sector.

"What the hell is that?" Bray said to himself, stunned.

Another drone flew overhead – and then another – the air whistling with the sibilant sound of their engines. It was like a plague of machines had just flocked into the skies, some drones making rapid movements, altering their course and direction as they sped by, other drones hovering for a few seconds in mid-air before continuing on their journey.

Bray had a fleeting thought of UFOs and the notion that what he was viewing was actually from another planet, let alone world. As did the Zootists.

"Power and chaos!" they yelled in reverence, gazing up at the drones that hovered directly above the school.

One Zootist yelled with utter joy, thrusting his arms into the air. "Oh, Mighty Zoot. Thank you for connecting with us and sending these signs from the Heavens!"

The Zootist suddenly cried out in pain as he was hit by a targeting laser light which shot out from a drone, striking him. And he slumped to the ground, writhing in agony.

Panic-struck, the other Zootists began to scatter, dispersing in all directions, terrified by the unknown machines and what they were capable of, flying high above them.

And Bray himself was equally concerned, having no idea where the drones were coming from and whose control they were under. He knew, however, he had to immediately return to the mall and warn Amber and the others of the extreme danger all were in.

Adrenalin and fear coursing through his veins, he took off running as fast as he could through the suburbs, trying somehow to keep obscured in an effort to stay out of sight from the drones.

* * *

Lex drove the vehicle at extreme high speed, running off the road for a few seconds, the vehicle's tyres grinding in the muddy grass, skidding, before he was able to turn the wheel and regain control. Back on the road Lex floored the accelerator, picking up even greater speed.

"Can't you please SLOWDOWN!" Ram cried out, gripping the front passenger seat, the dashboard, anything he could to hold on.

"Zip it!" Lex shouted, keeping his eyes on the road. "I know what I'm doing!"

"I hope so. For all our sakes!" Ram yelled, closing his eyes tightly so he didn't have to watch, panicked. But he was frightened more than by what he thought of Lex's driving like a madman – his suspicions on what they might encounter when – and if - they arrived at the city filled him with dread.

Jack and Ellie, in the back of the vehicle, were literally thrown out of their seats throughout the journey, often getting airtime, the seat belts holding them down as the vehicle hurled down the twisting road, Ellie giving off a nervous shriek in fright, Jack one of his own, as the vehicle skidded precariously.

The sense of urgency at that time had nothing to do with the drones Bray had noticed. The source of their panic was to warn the others of their discovery that *someone* else had been at Eagle Mountain, the adults housed in the cryogenic hibernation chambers had seemingly gone missing.

Lex was doing his best to get them back to the mall as quickly as possible – and he was succeeding as the panoramic views of the city appeared in the distance as they rounded another corner on the road leading back down from Eagle Mountain.

Suddenly he slammed on the brakes, the vehicle skidding to a halt. He was stunned at what he could see. They all were.

A fleet of ships, in the distance, was visible.

"Is that what I think it is?" Jack muttered in surprise, disbelief.

He wasn't just referring to the ships out in the open sea heading for the harbour but was watching a military type of aircraft making its descent, soon to land where the airport was located, many miles away.

"It can't be!" Ram said to himself. He looked like he was staring into the abyss, his worst nightmares. "They're finally here…"

"Who?!" Ellie demanded, in mounting panic.

"Who'd you think?! The Easter bunny??" Ram shouted. "I'm getting outta here!"

He began unbuckling his seat belt and opened the passenger door – before being yanked back into the vehicle by Lex's strong grip.

"You're not going anywhere. Sit down!" Lex roared, leaning over and shutting Ram's door shut. "What do you know about this!?"

Ram clutched the sides of his face with his hands, trying to calm his rising tensions and fear, to stave off a panic attack.

"Who are they, Ram!?" Lex asked.

"Who?! Don't you get it!? It's gotta be The Collective! That's who!"

"The Collective?" Jack wondered, considering the notion of what Ram was suggesting.

"They'll be here for me! And for you! Eagle Mountain – the whole city! Turn this thing around, Lex – we got to get away, as far away as we can! We're all in danger!"

"Possibly not," Ellie said, trying to convince herself as much as the others. "They might not be The Collective. But could be friendly."

"Somehow, I very much doubt it," Jack said, gently.

"Well, whoever they are – we just can't leave!" Ellie insisted. "We've got to get back to the mall and warn the others."

"Exactly!" Lex bellowed, slamming his foot on the accelerator, the vehicle hurling forward at high speed once more, Lex driving towards the city, peering through the windscreen as he noticed the drones flying in the far distance.

"What are those things?" Ellie cried out.

"They look like drones to me!" Ram said, totally panic-stricken while trying to open the passenger door again but Lex had locked all the doors from the main control by the driver's seat.

* * *

The Mall Rats were gathered in the food court, standing together, huddled in a group - but they were now prisoners of the invaders, having surrendered the mall moments before. Not without putting up a brave fight, however.

Amber couldn't believe what they had been through. It had all been over in a matter of minutes. From the moment the first stun grenade had gone off, the blinding light and smoke had disorientated everyone from its shockwave. And with other stun grenades exploding all around them – they had never really stood a chance.

The Mall Rats had been swiftly and totally overpowered in a clinical, efficient and devastatingly effective display of force. They had tried to fight back as best as they could. Trudy had gone into a fit of rage when the attack commenced, her love and motherly instincts driving her to defend her daughter, who had been sleeping under Emma's care while Trudy had been overseeing The Guardian. She was only able to hold off the warriors for a few seconds before she, as well as Brady, had been captured.

Amber had been in the food court earlier at the time with Salene and May where she had been trying to make a wedding cake. But those plans were now dashed, all their lives turned upside down from the first second the invaders rushed into the mall in a clearly well co-ordinated assault.

Salene and May had resisted, throwing pots and pans at the intruders, as did Amber before resorting to using her bare hands. She had been utterly desperate to get to her baby, then in Lottie and Sammy's care, to stave off the attack. All her efforts were in vain. For all the skill in hand to hand combat, none of the Mall Rats were any match for the disciplined fighting units that had so unexpectedly descended among them.

Now Amber knelt down beside Bray, who was crouched on the floor, cradling his ribs.

He had raced into the mall soon after the attack had begun and had fought well, taking out some of the invaders, knocking them unconscious, before another warrior had blasted him with a stun gun device, similar to the type of weapons used by The Technos when they themselves had invaded in the past.

But now there was also advanced weaponry deployed, seemingly laser-orientated, much like the drones had deployed at the school when the Zootists had been struck.

"Are you okay?" Amber asked Bray, gently helping him climb to his feet and he nodded reassuringly.

"He'll be fine," stated the imposing figure beside them. "As will you and everyone else, if you co-operate with us and follow instruction!"

He was tall, stocky and had a commanding aura which was hardly surprising given that although his subordinates even referred to him as Commander or 'Sir' - his name was Snake. He had personally led the raid on the mall, as well as the entire city, from what Amber could understand, other units having contacted him on occasion via his security earpiece to give updates on their progress.

'Snake' was aptly named – with his intimidating physique and combat prowess, he had crushed those in the mall and all who encountered him couldn't help but be slightly repelled by the unsightly tattoos he had of reptile scales on the side of his face, running down his shaven head. It was like he was some strange combination between man and reptile.

"*All areas secure so far, Commander,*" Amber could overhear a voice communicating via Snake's earpiece. "*No opposition to report.*"

"Have the units double-check the entire region and report back to me as soon as possible if you find any sign of inhabitants," Snake ordered whoever he was talking to.

Towering above her, Snake looked down at Amber, who he was aware had been listening to his exchange, while others under his command were checking data on tablet computers and scanning the various faces of their prisoners to try and identify all who were under their control.

"Any sign of Ram?" Snake asked one of this militia.

"Nothing so far, Sir," his subordinate replied, while checking various images of the prisoners on his tablet. "And there seems to be three Mall Rats missing. Lex. Jack. Ellie," he added.

"Where are they?" Snake demanded as he crossed back to Amber and Bray.

"We have no idea what you're talking about," Bray lied. "And even if we did, there's no way any of us would tell you."

"My team have ways to get you 'Rats' to talk. And believe me - they'd enjoy what I'd order them to do. But you wouldn't!"

"Lex, Jack and Ellie are no longer members of the Mall Rats," Amber lied, trying to sound as convincing as she could while meeting Snake's threatening steely gaze with her own defiant one.

"Are you sure about that? Because I'm not. Wherever Ram is and the rest of your tribe – they can't hide forever. We will find them!"

Snake turned and strode abruptly, briskly, out of the food hall and towards the lower concourse to where a group of Legion warriors were who had been held under guard by the Mall Rats until Snake's forces had released them all – along with Eloise and The Guardian, who were standing, now free, beside the Legion members and Zootists.

"Oh, mighty Zoot – you have blessed us with this divine victory on this day!" The Guardian shouted, raising his arms aloft in triumph, in praise to the Heavens. "This mall – this city – this very world! – will be yours, from this day onwards! And we will deliver you not only revenge but salvation to all who follow!"

Snake ignored The Guardian's rambling and approached Eloise.

"Your orders, Commander Eloise," Snake advised, handing her a tablet computer with a set of instructions which she began to attentively read. "The Guardian and the Zootist followers will remain under your control."

"I understand and will of course obey," she responded.

"Wise," Snake informed her, with a slight smile.

Snake commanded his forces to separate all the prisoners into different groups. With the Mall Rats being isolated in the food court.

The expectant mothers in various stages of pregnancy were assembled in the lower concourse. All were terrified of Snake and his fearsome warriors, carrying out their task with relentless efficiency, herding the girls together like they were animals.

In the food court where the Mall Rats were being held – the core members of the tribe were separated into one area being Amber, holding her baby Jay, along with Bray, Trudy, Brady, Salene, May, Lottie and Sammy.

Lia, who had originally been present, was taken to another area along with Emma, unable to see but hearing everything. She was in great distress, bravely doing her best to contain her emotions and control her tears so as not to in turn upset further her already scared younger brother and sister, Shannon and Tiffany, who nestled in as close to their big sister as possible.

Bray and Amber, along with some of the others, warned of the consequences if any Mall Rats or those under their supervision would be hurt and implored them all to be treated with decency and respect. But the warnings were of course impotent and Bray especially realized that there was little he could do at this point in time to assist. But he resolved that he would come up with a plan to at least try.

Ebony was with a group of captives being held in another area of the lower concourse with the remnants of the few loyal remaining members of the ex-Zootist militia. An irony which was not lost on Ebony herself, who couldn't believe she now found the situation reversed - with herself a prisoner, her former prisoners now seemingly set free. She decided she would have to play this one carefully, unsure if her survival might be contingent upon her supposed allegiance to either the Zootists. Or Mall Rats.

"Name!?" Snake asked when he arrived, noticing Ebony standing apart from the other Zootists.

"Ebony," she replied cautiously.

"Are you a Mall Rat?" Snake probed.

"I could be," Ebony replied, trying to gauge his reaction. 'There again, I was once Queen of the Locos and 'mistress' to the leader, Zoot. And that group of Zootists you are setting free simply adore me, if I do say so myself. As did Zoot. And for good reason. He was an amazing lover. But nothing compared to me. Oh, how I miss him. Pity I couldn't find a good man who might be interested in all I have to offer," she said, seductively, while running her tongue over her lips suggestively.

"Interesting," Snake replied, considering Ebony before checking data and images on his tablet screen, one of which was a photograph of Ebony along with lines of text. Ebony noticed the photograph but couldn't read details of the text.

"I hope you'll agree that the photograph you have there isn't the best one of me. And that I'm hopefully a little more attractive in real life. I'm very experienced in all areas of combat and can be really useful if you're looking for recruits."

"I know all about you," Snake answered. "You're not a Mall Rat. You never have been."

"Is that a good thing or a bad thing?"

"Oh, you'll soon find out!"

"Find out what!?" Ebony responded despondently, aware that her strategies for survival were seemingly to no avail.

"Prepare her!" Snake barked out an order. "And the others! We need to leave and stay on schedule!""

Ebony started to back away as a unit of Snake's militia descended upon her. She was quickly overwhelmed, warriors gagging her, binding her arms behind her back, her legs together, rendering her totally immobile, unable to utter even a single word no matter how hard she tried.

"Power and Chaos! Power and Chaos!" The Guardian cried out, in mounting intensity.

As she strained to be free of her binds, Ebony saw Eloise, who had walked over to Bray and the rest of the Mall Rats who were now shackled and were being led down the staircase to the ground level from the upper concourse.

Amber watched intently, as did all the other Mall Rats, as Eloise gave Bray a kiss on one cheek.

He recoiled in disgust. Eloise dug her long fingernails into his cheeks as she clutched his face and hissed venomously. "You're never ever going to forget me, Bray." She pressed her lips on his own, forcing a kiss, taking passion from his incapacitation, along with his groans as she dug her nails in deeper and scratched each cheek.

But she enjoyed Amber's horrified expression more as she stepped back and smiled sweetly to Amber and the other Mall Rats.

"I hope you all have fun," she sneered, while watching them being led to the exit of the mall.

Ebony watched them leave as well as she was dragged towards the centre of the ground level.

She was completely powerless, humiliated, and now extremely frightened – she had no idea what was intended for the Mall Rats, let alone herself.

The last thing she felt was the sharp sting of a needle being inserted into her arm – causing her to pass out, slipping into an unconsciousness state and had freedom only in her dreams.

CHAPTER EIGHT

Lex had a terrible feeling that he was walking into a trap. But given the situation they found themselves in, there was no other option, he felt, than to keep going. There was no turning back.

He carefully, cautiously, made his way across the second level of the derelict multistorey car park, heading towards one of the entrances to the mall. He listened for the sounds of anyone, his eyes scanning the rows of abandoned vehicles, long ago vandalized and looted, as he slowly advanced, attentive to any signs of movement.

So far there was nothing to indicate any presence of the mysterious invaders.

He turned to give a thumbs up and a quick wave to Ellie, who signalled back in return from the driver's seat of their vehicle.

They had driven to the multistorey car park hoping the building would give them some form of cover to keep out of sight of the occupation force, Ram convinced they had to be The Collective - much to his grave concern.

Ellie was slouched at the wheel, keeping her head low in case anyone *did* notice the vehicle had occupants. She had left the keys in the ignition and was in a state of alert herself, peering around the car park, ready to switch on the engine to get away as fast as she could in the event they needed to make their escape.

Jack was in the back keeping watch on Ram, in the front passenger seat, who was still in a condition of absolute panic. The former leader of The Technos claiming that he was a wanted man.

Throughout the drive back into the city, most of the drones that had been visible from afar at the initial onset of the invasion were no longer flying in the sky. Only a few drones remained, gliding overhead in a circuit, as if in a routine pattern of aerial patrols over the different sectors. Ram speculated that the bulk of the drones would have been busy assisting the occupiers in some other way elsewhere - perhaps unloading or transporting cargo from the invaders' ships in the harbour, doing reconnaissance in the suburbs, with the city centre already scouted and secured.

Lex detected a strange 'smell' in the air, not realizing that it had emanated from the stun grenades which had been deployed in the attack in the mall.

So far as he could gather, the invaders were nowhere to be seen.

Ram was also aware of this fact and hoped it would stay that way. It was possible, he thought, that the main attack force was at the docks, unloading equipment, possibly other vehicles, from their ships. Or loading the vessels with whatever it was The Collective or whoever was responsible, had taken from the city – including the uncomfortable notion that this could include some human 'cargo' in the form of those who had been in the city at the moment of its invasion, the Mall Rats among them.

"Not much fun being on the receiving end, is it?" Ellie said quietly in the vehicle, remembering the day Ram and his Technos conquered the city themselves.

"You should have told that to Lex," Ram sneered.

"I think Lex is very brave," Ellie continued.

"All we got to do is sit here and wait. And we'll probably end up being captured," Ram responded, despondently.

"Lex is putting his neck on the line," Jack added.

"For all of us," Ellie agreed. "Even you, Ram. And let's just hope that The Collective or whoever it is hasn't arrived at the mall as yet."

Jack peered from his crouching position, watching out the window as in the distance Lex slowly opened the door leading into the mall.

Lex moved cautiously, furtively, entering into the upper concourse levels which looked to be an absolute mess. Some of the shop windows had been smashed, their contents strewn out all over the place causing Lex to step over the debris. The mall appearing like it had been totally ransacked.

He remained alert, making sure there was no one in sight lying in wait to ambush him, and felt his anger levels rising, outraged at the thought of what had obviously gone on.

Arriving at the food court, usually the focus of the mall's daily life, Lex found it totally abandoned. He could smell the scent of food still in the air from a lunch that had clearly been interrupted and there were more remnants of smoke from the stun grenades which had been unleashed.

Tables had been knocked over, chairs were on their sides, littering the floor.

It must have been one hell of a commotion, Lex could tell. He was sure the Mall Rats would have put up a good fight, defending themselves and the others in their care. If only he could have been there. To get his hands on the attackers, to make them pay for what they had done.

Suddenly Lex heard voices approaching and ducked for cover behind one of the fallen over tables in the food court – before carefully peering out to see who was getting near.

Two invaders were going through the mall, loading up supplies, and were unknowingly closing in on the part of the food court where Lex was in hiding. He wondered if there could be others from whatever attacking force.

Assessing his options, Lex felt he didn't have long before the invaders would discover him – so there was only one thing he could do.

Bursting out from behind the table, Lex charged at the warriors, taking them completely by surprise, crashing into one of them, sending him flying, collapsing into a heap.

The other warrior pressed the headpiece in his ear and barked out an update.

"We've found Lex! Repeat, the Mall Rat 'Lex' has been found-"

He was unable to finish his sentence, however, Lex striking him flush on the jaw, the warrior going unconscious before he even hit the floor.

Lex took the headpiece from the warrior's ear and held it up to his own, listening in to see what he could hear as he ran, as fast as he could, back the way he came.

"Transport Lex to the airport immediately for evacuation with the others. Do you copy?"

Lex stopped and remained frozen for a moment before the voice repeated.

"*Confirm instructions. Did you copy?*"

"Got it," Lex finally replied into the mouthpiece, hoping that his disguised voice sounded convincing. But his biggest concern was to get out of there fast to warn Jack, Ellie and Ram.

* * *

The vehicle burst through a hedge, tearing an uneven hole in it, sending twigs and leaves flying, scattering all over the windscreen as Ellie drove into a field, adjusting the wheel slightly to correct the onset of a skid from the back wheels as they dug into the muddy terrain.

"Goddammit! – and I thought Lex was a bad driver!" Ram grumbled, the movement shaking him around in the back-passenger area.

"You haven't seen nothing yet!" Ellie promised, flooring the accelerator as far as it would go.

Ellie had grown up on her parents' farm and she had driven a car around the property, as well as tractors, and used other machinery.

It was strictly illegal at the time, Ellie not old enough to hold a license - but her parents didn't mind, encouraging the independent spirit they saw in their youngest daughter and thought it useful she learn some 'real life' practical skills that would hold her in good stead in her future. Especially when her parents had become sick during the virus. Ellie, with her sister Alice, had been increasingly left on their own and she had often driven the old family car in places never intended for it, to get quickly around their property. She was at home in the outdoors and knew how to 'read' the contours and lay of the land.

Even Lex was now holding on, one arm steadying himself in his seat as Ellie sped along the countryside. Jack was in the front passenger seat, also gripping the front dashboard as they hurtled along.

"They'd need a fighter jet to catch us," Jack said, pleased with how fast Ellie was going – and how far they had left the city in such a short time. He kept turning around from time to time, looking behind to make sure they weren't being followed.

When Lex had returned to the vehicle after his clash with the invaders, he had urged Ellie to drive away as quickly as she could while he leapt in the back, joining Ram, with Jack occupying the passenger seat next to Ellie. And she had done well, exceeding even Lex's own expectations at how fast the vehicle could go.

Ellie had suggested they avoid the main roads in and out of the city in case the drones that were on patrol flying above spotted them – even better, Ellie thought, they even avoid any roads altogether.

She had driven the vehicle literally across the countryside, travelling in parallel to the main highway about a mile to their south, and was barreling through overgrown field after field, the vehicle taking a battering, its tyres likely damaged. Time was running out, the fuel gauge showing signs that it would soon go into the empty reserves zone.

They were headed for the airport where the Mall Rats were apparently being taken, according to the communiques Lex had eavesdropped on.

In the old days, before the virus of course, they had all been there many times, going on family holidays or to meet arriving visitors, but Ellie had never thought she would ever make a trip like the one she was currently doing.

Ram had even landed his Techno planes there when he had carried out his own invasion and reasoned there could probably be a prominent force in place.

Their plan, as desperate and crazy as it sounded to the four occupants, was to get as far away from the city as they could – and as close to the Mall Rats as possible, maybe even to rescue them somehow from their abductors. There seemed to be no other option open. At least to Ellie, Jack and Lex. Ram thought it was a ridiculous idea predictably and had suggested, in vain, that they try to get away from the entire city area, including the airport. And as far away as they could from the impending danger and doom he knew was in store. Lex, Ellie and Jack refused to even consider what he was suggesting, believing they couldn't just leave the Mall Rats to face whatever their fate was at the airport.

"You might need to come up with another option, guys," Ram sighed, concerned as he noticed a drone approaching through the back window.

Lex turned to peer for a better look himself and sighed. "That's all we need."

"What do I do!?" Ellie yelled in growing tension.

"Just keep going," Lex responded. "Let's try and lose it."

"I think you might be a little optimistic," Jack stated, unnerved at the entire event unfolding as he craned his head, squeezing his face to the window to gaze up for a better look and noticing that the drone was now flying above them and following their course.

"Try and get back on the highway, Ellie," Lex shouted, in mounting panic. "I've got an idea on how we might shake them!"

"Glad you do," Ram responded. "Because I don't. And we're not exactly on the same wave intellectually. If

I'm a genius and I can't come up with something, how the hell will you?"

"We've got to try something!" Lex said in desperation.

The vehicle hurled through other fields and then suburbs. All the time the drone followed, speeding high above.

Before long, Ellie sped onto an exit ramp leading to the main highway.

"Good girl," Lex said, encouragingly.

"Yeah – good girl," Jack repeated, slightly jealous even in this moment of danger that Lex might be getting too personal and overly friendly.

"Now, when we get to one of those flyovers ahead, I want you to stop," Lex instructed.

The vehicle screeched, skidding to a stop when they arrived at the flyover – but the drone kept going before stopping itself and then flying in a zigzagged formation, as if still searching.

Inside the vehicle, Ellie and Jack exchanged a high-five and even Ram was euphoric. "Nice one, Lex. I like it! But I don't know how long it'll be before that drone finds us."

Ellie screamed hysterically as she suddenly noticed the drone appearing through the driver's side window, hovering at low level, as if watching all the occupants inside.

"Hit it!" Lex yelled.

Grinding the vehicle in gear, Ellie sped away with the drone following and all realized that they had no hope of shaking their technological pursuer.

They reached the perimeter of the airport before very long, Ellie urging the vehicle to go even faster as she rammed it, at high speed, into the wire mesh fence surrounding the airport grounds. This demolished the fence easily, Ellie nearly losing control in the process, a large dent appearing in the front of the vehicle from the collision. The engine also appeared to be damaged after the beating it had taken, thick smoke beginning to erupt from inside.

Still, the drone hovered overhead, slowing its pace as the vehicle was slowing to what would clearly be an eventual stop.

"Well – I'm sure we're going to have a welcome party very soon," Lex relayed.

"Great!" Ram shouted, slamming his fists on the side of the vehicle in frustration. "We're doomed! And that means I'm going to be dead! Thank you very much! If only you'd listened to me!"

"Shut it!" Lex bellowed. "They haven't caught us yet!"

Lex had another idea as the vehicle was soon to arrive at the derelict ruins of a passenger plane from the adult times that had been left to decay, straddling the side of the runway, the vehicle scraping the exterior of the aircraft as it ground to a halt.

And still, the drone followed and hovered above.

"Get out!" Lex instructed.

"Are you crazy, Lex!?" Ram replied.

"Maybe I am – which means that this might actually work! No one in their right mind would try and do this!"

"Do what!?" Jack asked.

"Giving the three of you at least a chance. If I act as a decoy. It might also give me a chance as well if I operate on my own without having you lot to worry about!"

Finding no other option than to agree to Lex's idea, Ellie, Jack and Ram quickly crawled out of the doors of the vehicle and after shutting the door, the three of them crossed furtively and ducked underneath the plane, dropping to the tarmac, scrambling under the shadows of the fuselage, taking cover behind its large wheels.

Lex's plan seemed to have worked. He had leapt into the front seat and driven off, with the drone following. Jack and Ellie loved him for it, realizing that his chances were very slim but at least he had given them both a chance. And even Ram was relieved at the respite, for the moment at least, to immediate danger.

Lex sped away from where he had dropped off the others and could see up ahead large grey military style cargo planes, with United Nations insignia visible on their sides, which had been used in the adult days but now had clearly been used for this invasion. Strange looking drones of different sizes, some as big as buses, were also grounded beside the planes.

Lex's vehicle sped past the terminal at fast as it could but smoke poured out from its damaged and overheating engine.

He caught a quick glimpse of some other vehicles parked around the aircraft – and noticed some were approaching at speed.

And it wasn't long before Lex's luck ran out. His own vehicle slowed down rapidly, before crawling to a complete stop, its engine finally surrendering in a waft of thick, black smoke.

Lex bailed, leaping out the driver's door, and started racing towards the main terminal building. But he was no match for the vehicles of the invaders, which converged on him at pace, moving in like the well trained predators that they were, their leader, Snake, among them – and Lex was swiftly overpowered, the warriors picking him up by his limbs, dragging him, helplessly, into the back of a military vehicle of their own.

"Nice of you to join us, Lex!" Snake sneered, as the vehicle door was slammed shut behind him.

At the airport perimeter, Ellie, Jack and Ram poked their heads up and peered out from behind the wheels of the plane underbelly they were seeking cover under, watching the figure of Lex in the distance, being driven towards the military cargo aircraft.

The vehicles stopped. Lex continued to resist as he was led towards one of the aircraft.

"You got a lot of fight in you, I'll give you that," Snake said, as he personally manhandled him, carrying Lex by his arms, two other warriors the other side lifting their prisoner by his feet.

"I'll give you 'what' - lizard boy!" Lex yelled at Snake, noticing his reptile-like tattoos. And he kicked out, shaking his legs in an effort to get free, the warriors keeping him in their vice-like grip.

They were clambering up the open cargo bay door, angling down from the aircraft onto the ground, Lex being hauled into its maws.

"Lex!" he heard Trudy cry out at seeing him.

As he was carried inside the cargo hold, Lex could see Trudy, Brady by her side, along with Amber and Bray, their baby in Amber's arms, Salene and May, as well as Lottie and Sammy, surrounded by more of the invasion force.

Ebony was there too, though she was being kept apart, sitting on the opposite side from the Mall Rats. She was the only one gagged, Lex noticed, while the Mall Rats were bound, Amber being the only one whose hands remained untied so she could cradle her son.

Placed down onto the metallic floor of the aircraft, Snake towering over him, Lex was bound like the other prisoners.

"Where's Ram?!" Snake demanded of him.

"How the hell should I know?" Lex lied. "Who'd you think I am – his mother?"

Snake cast Lex a wicked smile, grudging respect at Lex's bravado. "You'll talk eventually, Mall Rat. Just like you all will. You just wait."

"Let's get this bird up in the air!" Snake barked out an order over the communication headpiece in his ear. "We've got all our cargo, we're ready to go!"

The door to the cargo hold started to close, the interior of the hold getting darker as it gradually shut, the daylight receding, sealing the Mall Rats inside.

The engines of the plane began whirring to life as the military aircraft started to taxi for take-off.

"You should've stayed away while you still could," Bray said, commiserating at Lex's joining them as prisoners. "Why'd you come back to the city?"

"To warn you guys there were others around."

Bray nodded gratefully and both he and Lex exchanged glances, communicating something unsaid, well aware that they had a duty that went far beyond protection with their fellow members of The Tribe. And both clearly realized it as Bray noticed Lex giving a slight wave to baby Jay, as well as little Brady, who clung to her mother and waved back coyly.

"What's going on?" Trudy asked. "I wonder where 'they' are taking us?"

"I don't know. But if we can just all try and remain calm – I'm sure we'll be alright," Amber said, her expression giving away her obvious concern, the worry and fear showing in her eyes, mirroring the unease of all at what might lay ahead.

The plane barreled down the runway, its engines roaring, the noise thundering as if shaking the very ground as the aircraft quickly screamed past the derelict plane under which Jack, Ellie and Ram were hiding.

They watched, ducking their heads instinctively for cover, the sound deafening, as the military aircraft passed by overhead and receded into the distance, eventually disappearing from sight into the darkening, early evening sky.

CHAPTER NINE

"That's it!" Alice muttered, turning the taps on in the bathroom as far as they would go. "I've had enough of this place!"

She had gone to Tai San's room at the *Lakeside Resort*, Ryan accompanying her, where they found Tai San in a state of distress, so much so that when Ryan and Alice had initially knocked on the door, Tai San had refused to answer for several minutes, fearing that it could be The Selector paying her another unwelcome visit.

The initial joy at her reunion with Alice and Ryan had given way to feelings of helplessness. Tai San had always thought she was a strong-willed person, that few things would ever break her.

Her spirituality and ability to get in tune with what she perceived destiny had in store had also given her not only an inner strength but peace during the demise of the adults when the pandemic had struck.

Yet the ordeal she was now going through and the strange world of The Selector she had been thrust into had rattled Tai San to her core. The Selector was so unpredictable. And she couldn't instinctively 'read' him.

In addition, the injection of the biochip against her will felt like such a violation of Tai San's very essence, her living energy. And she had always felt a connection with all things living and the miracles of Mother Nature which surrounded her. Nature was what sustained Tai San. The biochip now inside her body was something she objected to on so many levels. It was polluting her being, what made her who she was. The way it had been injected into her was inhuman, against her fundamental rights. As long as it stayed in her body, she felt she was no longer the same person that she had naturally been before. Her chakras were well and truly out of alignment.

Alice and Ryan had comforted Tai San from the moment she had let them into her room – both sharing similar sentiments. And they found sharing their predicament helped give a degree of relief.

"There – that ought to do it!" Alice said, the taps loudly spraying water into the sink in Tai San's en suite bathroom.

The three of them had gone into the bathroom for another impromptu private meeting. Alice suggested they couldn't take any chances. For all they knew, the resort could be bugged or monitored somehow – and they didn't want anyone to listen in on the conversation they were planning to have with Tai San next, the sound of the water hopefully would drown out the whispered words of their discussions. Which mainly centred about a plan to escape.

* * *

It really was such a beautiful view, Tai San thought, appreciating the sight of the lake in front of them, flanked by rolling hills all around, covered in trees. It was like looking out on a real-life painting that had been brought to life, the reflection of the trees and hills shimmering on the water from the afternoon sun. No wonder the adults had built the *Lakeside Resort* in such a perfect location.

Tai San, walking side by side with Alice and Ryan, were making their way at a gentle pace over the lawns at the rear of the resort towards the lakeside. A few ducks flew towards them, quacking in anticipation of perhaps receiving a few crumbs – Ryan was eating some freshly-made bread and threw a few pieces into the water for the ducks to share.

Alice turned around to discreetly survey the view behind them. Several of the perimeter guards were in position at various points around the resort. They were intently watching the three prisoners standing by the side of the lake, Ryan continuing to casually rip off tiny mouthfuls of bread for the ducks.

"Everyone ready?" Alice whispered to Ryan and Tai San.

"Yep," Ryan said, wiping his hands, shaking the last of the crumbs over the feeding ducks.

"Let's do it," Tai San agreed.

The three of them suddenly took off in different directions, taking the guards by surprise as they noticed.

Ryan raced across the lawn to the left side of the resort, running by the water's edge, a small boathouse ahead of him with the forest visible over the other side.

Tai San sped off as quickly as she could to the right side of the resort, running towards the tall trees lining the lake as if her life depended on it, which of course it did.

Alice, who was aware she was never the fastest of sprinters, nevertheless set off as fast as she was able to the resort car park, around the corner of the main building, where she thought she might commandeer a vehicle perhaps.

Initially caught unawares by their unexpected moves, the guards quickly set off after their prisoners, splitting into three different groups.

It wasn't long before the guards began rapidly closing in on Alice and she knew she wouldn't be able to outrun them – but she felt confident that she could take out one, possibly two guards approaching, with her combat ability, let alone strength of her bulk. And her strategy was correct. She knocked one out with a single punch, the other needed two blows.

Alice hadn't counted on confronting other guards who were now closing in and soon caught up with her as she ran through the car park.

She gazed around at the vehicles and leapt in one. But there was no engine to hot wire, no steering wheel. Just a voice coming from the dashboard. "*STATE DESTINATION.*"

Alice had no idea how to reply but had to try something as the guards were almost on her now. "Home!" she said, unable to think of anything else.

A ping sounded as the voice announced. "*FACIAL RECOGNITION IMPLEMENTED. YOU HAVE ARRIVED AT YOUR DESTINATION.*"

Alice slammed her fist down on the control panel in utter frustration, which seemed to activate the system somewhere and the driverless pod vehicle took off at high-speed, with Alice gripping to her seat and gazing behind her at the guards in pursuit.

With his powerful build and sporting prowess, Ryan was also making good progress, running flat out, losing several guards trailing after him. And, like Alice, was able to cause a diversion that might assist Tai San in her efforts to get away. Tai San was more than capable of defending herself, having been trained in mixed martial arts. But her combat capabilities paled in comparison to the sheer muscle and brawn of both Ryan and Alice.

So far at least, the perimeter guards had focused their attentions on pursuing Ryan and Alice, which left Tai San to make it into the woods unencumbered. She hoped that all three would be able to rendezvous as they had planned, meeting up at an intersection they had all noticed on their journey to the *Lakeside Resort*, leading into the forest region.

* * *

Tai San was exhausted but urged herself to keep going, pushing herself to her absolute physical limits.

She was now some distance away from the *Lakeside Resort* and had made it far deeper from the wooded area into the depths of the forest bordering the lake, which was now completely out of view.

She continued to run at a high pace. It was unrelenting and she had been ignoring for some time the feelings in her body demanding her to stop for a moment's rest.

The tall trees in the ancient forest were all around her now, looming above, their thick canopy of branches and leaves casting the area of the forest in shade, a welcome feeling of slightly cooler air flowing on Tai San's face as she ran through the forest, sweat pouring from her. The surrounding nature seemed almost to give her strength beyond her body's natural stamina.

Leaping over a tangled knot of roots on the ground, Tai San's foot slipped and she nearly fell over, only just managing to keep her balance. She yelped in pain as she twisted her ankle in the process – and despite her desire to keep moving on, Tai San seized up, with no option but to now slow down.

Panting breathlessly, Tai San doubled up, bending over to catch her breath. She looked down at her ankle and rubbed it, the side of her leg burning in agony, her muscles in her body aching in a state of protest at what she had put them through. It felt like she was about to start cramping in her leg and she slowly moved it up and down, gently wiggling her foot, trying to stretch her leg muscles, struggling at the growing pain that was spreading from around her ankle.

She took a moment to examine her surroundings, now she had stopped fleeing – and determined she was well and truly clear of the *Lakeside Resort*. She had run in a diagonal direction from the resort and estimated she had to be several miles away by now. The only living things in the area, apart from the trees and Tai San herself, were the insects buzzing in the air, the fluttering and calling of the bird life up high in the branches of the trees.

In another time, Tai San would have luxuriated in it all. But now, she began to feel dizzy, her head spinning in a swirl. She was so tired – and with the extreme discomfort of her sprained ankle, she had nothing more to give and couldn't go on any further.

Tai San slumped to the forest floor, lying on her back, stretching her legs out in front of her in an attempt to relieve the cramps and the pressure she had been putting on her ankle when she had been standing up.

Though every part of her body was sore, her ankle especially, with her head leaning against the fallen leaves on the ground she looked up to the skies, peeking through the branches above – and she breathed out a grateful sigh, smiling in relief at what she had achieved, thanks also to Alice and Ryan's help.

Despite all the odds, Tai San had managed to escape.

* * *

The sensation of a light breeze on the side of her face woke Tai San from the sleep she had unintentionally been in. She had fallen unconscious, overwhelmed by all she had gone through, her body shutting down - and she was startled, awakening with a fright, when she realized it was no ordinary wind — but it had been coming straight from the mouth of The Selector himself, who was peering over Tai San, gently blowing on her face to waken her.

Around The Selector were some guards. Somehow, to Tai San's alarm, they had found her.

Tai San immediately and instinctively started backing away from them — but the pain in her ankle bit at her as soon as she moved and she clenched her teeth, trying to resist the stabbing feeling in her leg, desperate to get away from The Selector.

"Where did you think you were going?" The Selector calmly asked, walking towards her, watching intrigued as Tai San slowly shuffled away from him on her hands and knees, fighting the obvious discomfort she was going through. "Don't you know that continuing in this direction there's nothing but forest for the next few hundred miles?"

"Keep away from me!" Tai San called out.

"Now now, don't be so emotional," The Selector chided her, taking another step closer. "I gave you a very warm welcome. And is this how you repay me - by running away from what I have to offer?!"

The Selector seemed to be irritated now, in growing anger, Tai San could see it in his expression — and he presented an intimidating sight, his guards following as he slowly got even closer to her. Tai San, still on the ground and unable to stand up, retreating backwards, struggling to open up some distance between them.

The Selector suddenly lunged forward at Tai San – who held up her arms to protect herself, thinking The Selector might even strike her, in her vulnerable position.

Tai San was astonished when The Selector instead planted a gentle kiss on the side of her face – before stepping back, giving her a warm, manifestly caring smile.

"What do you think you're doing!?" Tai San said, almost speechless, outraged, wiping her hand on her face to remove any trace of the kiss she had just been given.

"I'm just happy to see you," he said softly, any tension he had been showing previously having dissipated. "Everything will be okay," he insisted, his demeanour overtly sensitive, but overly friendly.

"Help her up – but be gentle," The Selector instructed the guards – and they moved in as ordered, carefully lifting Tai San from under her arms to a standing position but making sure she didn't have to put any of her body weight on her legs.

"We'll get that leg of yours seen to straight away. I'll have my medics take a look and make sure you get everything you need."

"I doubt you have enough Chamomile, Garlic, Ginger and Turmeric," Tai San said wryly, almost to herself.

"Don't forget ice. Mixed together with what you suggest will be just fine, but we'll need to keep an eye on this graze and ensure it doesn't become infected, in which case you might need some Goldenrod, which we have in abundance," The Selector said.

He was certainly playing mind games with Tai San but also had a clear knowledge of alternative medicine.

As far as the graze he was referring to, he indicated the scratches on Tai San's leg which was bleeding slightly from her fall. He touched a trickle of the blood, gently with his small finger and dabbed it in his mouth.

"You're still B-negative, it would seem, Tai San. I think you need a little more Iron in your diet," The Selector advised.

Tai San felt from The Selector's gazing at her ankle and leg that he was interested in more than just her health, stealing a lustful glance at her figure.

"Leave me alone!" Tai San demanded – angered and frightened to be in the company of The Selector once more, as well as repulsed by what she felt was his false sense of concern and creepy physical attraction for her.

Tai San dreaded the prospect of returning to the *Lakeside Resort* and had hoped that Ryan and Alice had managed to escape.

"Alice and Ryan are waiting for you back in their rooms, Tai San. So, I suggest we head back so you can join them!" The Selector snapped, impatiently. And for a split second, Tai San wondered irrationally if he even had the ability to read her mind. Either from natural forces or more likely the biochip which had been inserted into her body. But she quickly dismissed any notions, believing that The Selector at least looked to other areas of not only knowledge but beliefs as he gazed around appreciatively at the forest.

"The Creator is all around us, Tai San. In every tree, in every bird – and in every one of us. Thanks to The Creator's vision – I will be able to know every place that you go from now on, everything that you do, everything that you think, everything that you feel, right down to even the beating of your heart."

His anger had subsided once more and he gave Tai San a warm smile – this time, she sensed it was not insincere but was genuine.

"The Creator's vision is taking another step closer to being achieved with every step we take, Tai San," The Selector said, as they made their way through the forest back to the resort, the guards steadying and assisting Tai San as she limped. "We really need to get you rested up and your ankle better. Alice and Ryan will be interested to hear of your adventures in the forest today. And you don't know how it makes me feel to know that we're together again. I'm beyond thrilled."

"Not for long. I'll leave here one day. That's a promise," said Tai San.

"That's where you're wrong. According to The Creator, you and me, and your Mall Rat friends, are going to be spending the rest of our lives together!"

CHAPTER TEN

With his baby in his arms, Bray carefully made his way through the semi-darkness past the guards and his fellow prisoners sitting on the floor of the aircraft's cavernous cargo hold.

All the Mall Rats sat in silence, lost in their own private reveries induced by the long journey so far and speculation of their fate.

Lottie and Sammy were asleep as was May, who leaned her head on Salene's shoulder. Throughout the journey Lex carefully checked out the guards for future reference. They were certainly well-disciplined and capable warriors, he could tell. Ebony's attention was more on Snake, assessing any potential weakness she might exploit. Not solely regarding his physical prowess but in his personality.

Bray held his son tightly, fighting the shift in gravity, altering his stance, trying to keep his balance as the aircraft took on an angle for a moment, altering its course.

"Don't try anything," Snake urged, giving Bray a glare. He was standing by the doorway leading from the cargo hold to the other interior parts of the plane, blocking it with his large frame, his arms crossed, an unpassable barrier.

"As if I'm going to step into the cockpit and land this aircraft," Bray scoffed. "My son's just restless," he added – and it was true enough, baby Jay was crying incessantly.

Snake nodded, glancing at the baby, which registered with Ebony and she wondered if he might have children of his own, given his sympathy. A chink, perhaps, in his armour. Ebony realized that Snake wasn't without feeling.

In addition to calming the baby by going for a walk and giving Amber a chance to sleep, Bray wanted to walk around the limited part of the aircraft as Amber had whispered that she had noticed windows on her previous stroll. And Bray hoped he could have another look out the windows in an effort to gain any further understanding on where they were being taken.

Snake had given permission for Amber to stretch her legs earlier in the flight, as well as Trudy, so she could in turn give comfort to her daughter, Brady, getting upset several times, terrified at the ordeal of their captivity – and Snake in particular, who, with his frightening tattoos, seemed like something from one of her nightmares.

Amber had walked down the metallic corridor to the end, gently cradling her baby, soothing his tears.

Through a small, smoked-glass window in the door, leading to another compartment, Amber noticed windows on the outer walls in the side of the aircraft, along with other compartments, rooms or cabins of some kind, their doors sealed. Amber wondered what was inside – or who – but there was no way of finding out. If she tried the door handle at the end of the metallic corridor, Snake would be bound to come charging after her to reprimand her. There was certainly no sound coming from inside what was behind the doors, nothing Amber could hear over the drone of the engines.

The aircraft reminded Amber of the military planes The Technos had used when they had invaded the city under Ram in what now felt like an eternity ago. Ram had told Amber that he had found a lot of 'hardware', various equipment, technology and vehicles that the adults had left behind in some military bases in the land of The Technos and had adapted them for their own use.

Amber wondered if Ram could somehow be involved in the Mall Rats' latest plight or whether their captors were in fact connected to The Collective, which seemed to continually cause Ram unease.

Ram had explained that he was aware that The Collective had discovered several otherwise hidden adult military complexes, similar to the one that was at Eagle Mountain, where the adults had attempted to survive the pandemic. Under their enigmatic leader, 'Kami', whose exact identity Ram claimed to have not known, The Collective had used the resources they had plundered from the adult compounds to help build and expand an empire for themselves after the virus.

Where The Technos, at the height of their power, had a few planes and vehicles – The Collective likely had their own fleet, as well as several ships in their possession and much more advanced technology - while the rest of the world around them descended into an almost primitive, anarchic way of life. A new Dark Ages.

It certainly appeared that Ram had been telling the truth about that, Amber reflected, recalling the ships she had seen in the harbour on the journey from the mall to the airport which, in turn, brought back memories of the massive cargo ship, the *Jzhao Li*, that the Mall Rats had themselves once encountered.

The invaders' military cargo planes, with their United Nations regalia, were reminiscent not only of the *Jzhao Li*, a UN ship itself and apparently part of a United Nations fleet, but of other aircraft the Mall Rats had once seen at Arthurs Air Force base, which had at one time had a United Nations presence, from the evidence of what they had left behind. Including cryogenic hibernation chambers, like the ones they later had discovered in Eagle Mountain.

But it was still an entire mystery regarding what it all meant. Clearly whoever was responsible for it all in the old world had plans around the time of the pandemic, which was the source of many conspiracy theories. With some believing that there was something more sinister responsible for the demise of the adult population resulting in so many children and teenagers being evacuated.

Amber had briefly peered out of the window on her earlier walk with the baby and had seen they had been flying over water at the time, crossing a vast ocean.

She was then stunned, during a subsequent stroll to see the aircraft travelling over land. The terrain was strange, lifeless, desolate – a barren world.

There had even been a large mound that had caught Amber's eye that the plane flew over, seemingly in the middle of nowhere. She only saw it for a few seconds but the image of it was imprinted on her mind.

The mound hadn't looked like a natural formation, a hill or ridge. It reminded Amber of a Neolithic burial mound, something she had seen in a history documentary before the virus, a place where primitive generations had buried their dead. The massive mound of earth had filled Amber with dread and she wondered if it could be a mass grave, potentially filled with thousands of fatalities. If this was the case, she wondered whether they were adult casualties of the 'virus' buried within – or perhaps victims of something yet unexplained and the notion had sent a chill down Amber's spine.

Her thoughts had drifted to where they were headed to – and what the purpose was for the invaders in holding the Mall Rats captive – something that eluded Amber, neither Snake or his warriors giving any answers to the questions Amber and the others had asked them.

The invaders hadn't caught all of the Mall Rats though, Amber knew. When Lex was unexpectedly thrust into their midst, she had been grateful that Jack and Ellie, also Ram, had not been among their number. Wherever they were now, she wished them well and hoped that they were safe. She would ask Lex, when they could talk out of earshot from the guards, for an update to explain what had happened to him and the others who had gone with him to Eagle Mountain that day.

Now, it was Bray's turn to sway his son gently in his arms as he approached the smoke-glassed window in the corridor door for a quick glance of the outer windows on the walls of the aircraft and he was aware that darkness had fallen. He surmised that they must have been flying for perhaps five hours.

He noticed some lights shining in the distance, twinkling on the far horizon – signs of life out there, through the dark night sky.

"You'd better sit," Snake called out to Bray, before addressing all the others in the cargo hold. "We'll be coming in to land in a few minutes."

* * *

After the aircraft landed and taxied to a control tower, finally stopping near a bordering hanger, the cargo bay doors opened. Snake and his guards escorted Ebony and the Mall Rats, who were now not bound, leading them across the tarmac, their breath vapours visible in the cold night air.

They had arrived at what appeared to be a remote airstrip. Not a main airport, as such, like the one they had departed from in the Mall Rats' home city – there were no large terminal structures or restaurants left over from the adult era, no car park buildings.

Around the control tower was a series of other hangars and small prefabricated units, seemingly temporary buildings. A few dormant digger machines sat idle, beside a couple of cranes. A mesh fence ran along one side of the landing strip. Beyond that, a thick forest of tall trees was visible, stretching across rolling hills, towards the silhouette of a mountain range in the far distance.

The air was so fresh Amber began to shiver, aware looking around their surroundings it seemed that they were high up in altitude.

A few artificial floodlights were spaced out at even points around the airstrip, illuminating pockets of light on the ground in the otherwise dark night. It felt very eerie, the light casting long, distorted shadows over the tarmac.

This was not the source of the unease, however. When the passengers disembarked the aircraft, Ebony and the Mall Rats were stunned to find a small crowd of onlookers lined up on each side of barriers which had been put in place to hold back the spectators.

And the crowd on both sides began clapping, breaking out into enthusiastic applause, cheering Snake and his guards, welcoming their arrival – but above all, shouting out in utter joy and celebration at the procession passing by them – calling out in reverence and recognition the names of the Mall Rats themselves.

Some of the onlookers were clutching flaming torches reminiscent of a primitive time which was punctuated by the way in which they were dressed. Most of the crowd were tattooed and had body piercing visible, especially on the males, all of whom looked as if they had stepped out of a gym with their bare, muscular physiques visible under furs. Some even had elements of flaxen plants adorned to their furs. Particularly the females who wore skirts of flaxen and had hair extensions adorned with feathers and plants.

Most of the crowd were around the same age as the Mall Rats and without exception, the one thing all the Mall Rats were aware of was that all the onlookers were enormously physically attractive, every one blessed with good looks. And seemed to exemplify the personification of excellent health. Their teeth were white, their complexions flawless. All were suntanned.

"Amber!" one of the males yelled as she was escorted past. He was incredibly handsome, his body honed, his muscles and face chiseled, clearly in a condition of great fitness, a perfect specimen of a human being. "Amber!"

he called out to her again, reaching out across the barrier, stretching his arms desperately, hoping to make contact somehow, to touch her shoulder with his fingers, even fleetingly, for a moment.

"Keep away from her!" Bray said, struggling to be free from the grip of the guards flanked either side of him, so he could protect Amber and their baby from the frenzied spectators all around.

"Bray!" a voice shouted out. "You look so awesome in real life. Much better than the photographs!"

Lottie and Sammy were as equally confused as the other Mall Rats and clung to May and Salene, who were puzzled as they heard a cacophony of overlapping voices shouting out in excitement.

"Hey, Sammy – Lottie - give us a wave!" some children among the spectators asked desperately. While others' attentions were focused on May and Salene who were passing by. "You look like a perfect couple!" one spectator said enthusiastically, wiping a tear from her eye. "I'm so glad that you both have found each other and someone to love!" the spectator continued.

"Stay back!" Snake threatened to another male, who was reaching out to try and touch Amber's arm at the front of the procession.

"Who *are* these people?" Amber asked, unable to comprehend the rapturous reception. And especially that they knew her by name.

"Some of The Privileged," Snake explained, matter-of-factly. "It's a reward for them to see you first."

"Is that – *Lex*?" one of the female spectators cried out in utter disbelief as he was led past. "Did you do it? Did you really kill Zoot!?" Lex heard her ask, the tone of her voice impassioned, hysterical – unstable even, he felt.

"No," Lex called back to wherever the female was in the sea of faces. He was avoiding eye contact, looking away from the crowd, trying to be inconspicuous. "You must have got me mixed up with someone else."

From his many experiences with the Zootists, he had always been concerned what they might eventually do if some of the most zealous followers ever got their hands on him. He was responsible, after all, for Zoot's death.

It hadn't been intentional on Lex's part, he had been trying to defend the Mall Rats at the time on that fateful night Zoot wandered into the mall to meet up with his brother, Bray, who had, unbeknownst to most of the tribe at the time, encouraged Zoot to meet Trudy and their then baby daughter, Brady. In a resulting scuffle with Lex, Zoot had accidentally fallen from the upper level of the mall to his death. Ever since, Lex had wondered if any of the Zootists would ever come after him in reprisal, getting revenge on the one who had killed their God.

Further down the line of prisoners, Brady started to cry and cling to her mother, overcome by the noise of the crowd and faces illuminated by the flaming torches, which took on an almost nightmarish element.

"It's alright, Brady, it's alright," Trudy said, doing her best to calm her daughter as much as she could, both of them unsettled by the welcome they were receiving from the strangers. Trudy was keeping Brady close by, two guards also assisting, making sure the onlookers didn't get too near.

One of the younger males in the crowd suddenly rushed forward, breaking through the guards, over the mesh railing, to Trudy and Brady – and prostrated himself before Trudy, who recoiled and forced the male's hand back as he tried to clutch desperately at Brady, in a state of awe that he was within touching distance of the actual child of Zoot – and her mother.

"Take me with you – *please!*" he begged them. "Would you give me a blessing? Show me a miracle, Supreme Mother!?"

A guard swooped up the male in his burly arms and hurled him back over the barrier to the crowd of onlookers.

At the very back of the procession, Ebony heard the commotion up ahead of her – the joyful cries and cheers, the enthusiastic welcome the Mall Rats were receiving. And was just as confused as they were.

As the guards escorted the new visitors past the crowd, however, the mood among the spectators quickly changed. The euphoria replaced by an increasing hatred, which was spreading through the onlookers as Ebony herself was marched past.

Ebony wondered how this group – whoever they were exactly – in a land so far from her own, would even know who she was, as well as the Mall Rats. But somehow they seemed to know of her, and she clearly had some sort of reputation or standing among them – one which gave her concern as the crowd started to boo and catcall a range of bitter insults. For all their seeming reverence to Zoot, they clearly didn't seem like normal Zootists.

"Traitor!" some yelled. Others were more intent on some kind of revenge. And began chanting in unison, "Stone her! Stone her! Stone her!"

Up ahead, the Mall Rats had arrived at a convoy of vehicles which were waiting. Military trucks, surrounding driverless pod-type futuristic vehicles, similar to the type used to transport Tai San from the docks earlier. Without exception, as the Mall Rats were put inside the pods, each couldn't help but feel a degree of sympathy for Ebony, the victim of so many insults and the baying crowd.

With the Mall Rats inside the driverless vehicles, the guards got in the military trucks and the convoy sped away.

The booing and insults continued from the onlookers as they glared in disdain, watching Ebony being placed in a single driverless pod vehicle which was accompanied by military trucks either side. The onlookers started to shriek and chant a rhythmic intonation as both convoys transporting the Mall Rats, and separately Ebony, receded in the distance up a mountainous road.

CHAPTER ELEVEN

They had been hiding underneath the belly of the derelict plane for several hours and Jack was amazed, as well as relieved, that they were still unnoticed, though for how much longer none of them could tell.

It was late into the night, the darkness all-encompassing, and with the temperature dropping it had gotten very cold.

Ram's teeth were 'chattering', his arms folded across his chest as he crouched behind the wheel under the fuselage in an effort to retain as much of his body heat as he could.

Jack and Ellie were huddled together, their arms wrapped around each other trying to keep warm, taking cover by one of the other wheels of the aircraft.

They were all tired, thirsty and hungry and had long ago eaten the few consumables - some raw vegetables that Jack had brought with them on their original journey to Eagle Mountain with Lex the day before. He still had his backpack on, yet now, devoid of its provisions, the only thing it contained was the hard drive they had taken to Eagle Mountain with the objective to try and decipher its contents. Jack had joked that he wished it was edible in an attempt to lighten the mood, as well as satisfy his hunger cravings.

Now, their chief concern, as it had been for many hours, was to keep out of sight of the ominous presence that remained at the airport, indeed, over the city following its conquest by the invaders. Ram still convinced that they were the infamous Collective.

There were still guards in proximity, hundreds of metres away at the main terminal buildings, their vehicles driving around the airport frequently, making some sort of patrol, Ram presumed, the vehicles' headlights casting their beams into the dark emptiness of the night.

Whenever an invader vehicle had driven past the runway by their own location, Ellie, Jack and Ram had literally frozen, not making a sound, not daring to even breathe in case they gave away some indication of their own presence there, beneath the rusty aircraft.

There had been a particularly close incident a couple of hours earlier when one of the patrols had stopped on the tarmac beside the abandoned plane, one of the warriors getting out. Jack, Ellie and Ram were sure their hearts would beat out of their chests, so anxious and full of adrenalin they were at that time.

Jack had been prepared to even run out from behind the wheel where he had been hiding, beside Ellie, to confront the tall, well-built warrior who had gotten out of the van. And so it was to Jack's surprise, albeit mixed with revulsion, when it became clear why the vehicle had stopped, the guard simply deciding to casually relieve himself on the front wheel of the plane, which he must have viewed as nothing more than a giant piece of scrap metal.

Ellie had found it especially disgusting and she had breathed out a sigh of relief, along with Ram and Jack, as soon as the warrior had finished going about his business, before resuming his patrol.

At least it had shown that they were well and truly hidden, but it was only a matter of time they all dreaded before they would have another close encounter with the invaders.

Their potential sources of danger were not only from the invaders' forces on the ground who seemed to be working around the clock transporting supplies and equipment by military helicopters, which they suspected must have been deployed from the ships moored in the harbour further away, deep in the city. And all had speculated what equipment might be dangling by the long stroops underneath the bellies of each helicopter. It was certainly heavy-duty equipment and was being loaded into one of the military cargo aircraft. They assumed that there must have been a larger force of warriors disembarking from the ships and wondered why they might be wishing to inhabit the city and environs. Clearly, the invaders weren't just an advanced party searching for the Mall Rats, along with especially Ram, as he was convinced.

"It's strange really. When I was there, I wanted to be here. Now I'm here, I want to be there," Ram sighed, reflectively.

Jack and Ellie exchanged a confused glance and considered Ram, who was deep in thought.

"What are you talking about?" Jack asked.

"A plan," Ram replied. "I'll give you more detail once I've figured it out."

Some of the drones had continued to operate throughout the night, taking off and then returning later to the airport, their lights blinking, engines audible as they whirred. Some drones looking quite futuristic, of different sizes and many alien to what they had ever seen before.

Certainly, many were small reconnaissance types, Ram believed, probably using a type of night-vision, infrared camera to scout different areas in and beyond the city, perhaps looking out for heat signatures in case there were any other inhabitants in the city. The drones could even be 'hunters', roaming around from the air in an effort to find Ram, Ellie and Jack - and the hard drive that was in their possession. Ram thought it was likely the invaders would expect the three of them to still be in the city, sure that Lex would have stubbornly not revealed anything to his abductors that might give away their true location. But all realized that they couldn't exactly stay hidden forever.

It was a stroke of good fortune, if not a miracle, that none of the spy drones had flown over the exact place where Jack, Ellie and Ram had been hiding, or Ram was certain they would have picked up their heat patterns. It was possible, Jack had suggested or hoped to be the case, that the metallic hulk of the plane they were beneath might be shielding them from the prying cameras of the drones or causing interference somehow which had enabled them to go undetected so far.

The largest drones they had noticed coming to and from the airport appeared to be as big as a light aircraft. They were likely used, along with the helicopters, for ferrying more cargo, Ram assumed, transporting equipment from the ships in the harbour to various key points around the city, in addition to couriering supplies from the airport that the large military cargo planes might have brought with them in the initial stages of the invasion. The large drones could even be shuttling around human cargo, in the form of warriors from the invasion force, to different sectors of the city.

Ram expressed his jealousy to Ellie and Jack at never having possessed such high-tech drones for himself during his days in charge of The Technos. The invaders must have plundered the drones from the adult military bases they had discovered, he speculated. Ram had been aware of the existence of such technology but in the few hidden underground compounds The Technos had been to, Eagle Mountain among them, none of them had any drones.

Once again, Ram was convinced the invaders were in reality The Collective, given what he knew of their methods of operation. They had the capability to examine far more complexes, from what Ram recalled of his discussions online with their leader, Kami. They certainly had a lot more 'toys' and resources than The Technos ever did, Ram observed, including the advanced drones they had seen flying around.

Ellie, Jack and Ram watched as the latest vehicle drove down the far end of the runway on patrol, its headlights arcing, casting their glow as it moved around the airport.

"I don't know about you, but I don't fancy spending the rest of my life hiding underneath this thing with the two of you," Ram said, in a whispered undertone, keeping his voice quiet in case it attracted any attention, drone or human.

"Well, that's something we can agree with you on," Ellie whispered.

"I've been thinking," Ram remarked.

"Meaning?" Jack enquired.

"I know a place where we could go."

"And where would that be?" Ellie questioned.

"As far away from here as possible," Ram said, with a smirk, amusing himself by what he was about to suggest.

Ellie gave him a disdainful look – she was never sure if Ram was 'trolling', winding them up, and wasn't in the mood for any of his antics.

"And how are we meant to do that exactly?" Jack asked.

"I've got an idea – but it's one you're probably not going to like to hear."

Ram explained his plan, Ellie and Jack listening intently. He was right, they didn't like what he was proposing.

"You've got to be crazy," Ellie commented, when Ram had finished.

"Don't knock it. This mind of mine has kept me alive," Ram said, indicating his forehead with one finger. "So – what do you reckon?"

Jack and Ellie exchanged quizzical looks with each other – and they could tell what the other was thinking. No matter their reservations and reluctance - given their dire situation, there didn't seem to be any other alternatives. Ram's idea seemed the best chance, if not the only one they might have, to alter their fate.

* * *

Ram was either a genius or a madman – perhaps both - Jack and Ellie thought, as they continued to follow him away from the plane they had been hiding under into the darkness of the night, down the side of the runway. They were furtively keeping to the grassy verge beside the tarmac, believing it would help muffle any sounds they were making as they crept along stealthily towards the main terminal buildings.

It wasn't just Ram. The three of them had to be out of their minds to be taking such a risk, Jack felt, but he resolved they really had no other choice.

He just hoped Ram's gamble would pay off, the airport terminal slowly getting closer with every step they were taking. They kept peering around in all directions, looking behind them, anxious that the patrol they had last seen might now be making its way back, or that a passing drone would suddenly fly overhead and spot them. They were out in the open, exposed, and feeling very vulnerable.

Ram's mind was like clockwork. Prior to emerging from the aircraft, Ram had timed the duration of the patrols, how long it took each to complete their circuit.

It seemed to occur approximately every hour. With the patrols taking about twenty minutes.

Ram's expression was a picture of concentration, though neither Jack nor Ellie could see it well in the night. They could just hear him, almost a whisper, quietly counting the seconds to himself as they made their way down the side of the runway. There were a lot of moving parts for him to keep track of and remember, concurrent timings requiring some complex mathematics which Ram was constantly running over in his mind.

"We have to speed up," Ram urged quietly, and he picked up the pace, heading towards the airport terminal, Jack and Ellie in his trail.

They would only have a narrow window of opportunity, Ram had explained before they set out on his plan. He had worked out they would have about a ten-minute period where there should be no ground patrols and no drones flying overhead – that is, assuming there was nothing unpredictable occurring.

And they had to use every second they had available to get to the main terminal in time to have even a chance of Ram's idea succeeding. They were closing in, just a little further to go, the airport buildings looming ahead. Jack and Ellie were in an increasing state of nervousness, their adrenalin rising, feeling like they were walking straight into the lion's den and could be discovered at any moment.

They had made it to the airport terminal. Crouching down, so as to keep out of sight from within the partial cover of some cargo containers, they could see before them several drones on the tarmac, seemingly being recharged, Ram suspected, the air humming with electricity, connected to large generators.

Several crates of supplies were also visible in the shadows, stacked in piles. It was difficult to know what all their different contents were in the dark but Jack could see some of the crates appeared to contain some sort of grain, others were full of rice. The invaders must have been obviously planning to feed a large group of people, from the amount of food they had transported, Jack realized, and he wondered how many of their number were now in the city – or if the provisions were awaiting future invader forces who were yet to arrive.

The drones being recharged looked like a flock of metallic flying creatures, as if they were in a state of rest, with various wingspans and shapes – some were the smaller surveillance types, others the larger drones designed for carrying freight – and they were the ones Ram was focusing upon.

"There – that's the one," Ram whispered, indicating the largest drone in view. It was as long as a bus and three times as wide, thick cables plugged into it from the power generators.

"Are you sure?" Ellie whispered back – but she didn't get an answer.

Ram, eyes fixed intently on the large drone, went towards it, fleet of foot, and without hesitation he quickly began detaching the cables from the generators, looking around agitatedly to make sure no one had spotted him.

Jack and Ellie raced over, as quietly as they could, helping Ram pull the remaining cables out – before following him in through the door in the side of the drone.

It was dark inside and the cargo hold was empty, apart from the three of them, their feet scrunching on some bits of grain that must have spilled on the floor during earlier shuttling trips made by the drone.

Ram had an excited look on his face as he surveyed the cockpit, loving the technology before him, as well as being thrilled, on the edge, at the audacity of what they were attempting to achieve.

"Are you sure you know how to fly this thing?" Jack asked, in growing panic.

"No," Ram said, slightly preoccupied as he surveyed the console before him.

"Great! Now you tell us!" Ellie said.

"Relax. No need for me to pilot this thing. Not with computer systems. These things should be mostly automated," Ram said, running his fingers over the various electronic controls, getting a 'feel' of the different buttons, hoping to sense what their function was.

"The onboard computer does all the work. We just gotta find the main switch," Ram continued, having difficulty locating it. "It should be around here somewhere."

"I think I found it," Ellie said, suddenly reaching forward to push a small red button she had noticed.

Lights immediately flicked on, slightly illuminating all in the cockpit in a green and red glow, reflected by the touch sensitive display which appeared in the centre of the main panel, the drone wakening, its systems powering up.

"That's my girl," Jack beamed with pride.

"Not just a pretty face," Ram said, impressed by her technical skills, and he gave Jack a subtle wink of approval at having Ellie as his partner.

Ram started punching data on the touch display which was showing their current location blinking on a map. With his other finger he moved an arrow across the map, entering the destination co-ordinates into the drone's navigational system.

"And now, the moment of truth," Ram said, hoping that his plan was going to work. By his reckoning, they only had a couple of minutes left before the invaders' patrol made its way back to the airport terminal.

For all of Ram's intellect, and his photographic memory, his calculations were out and the patrol had arrived back at this area of the terminal slightly early. Ram, Ellie and Jack swallowed nervously, noticing a vehicle approaching and picking up speed.

"Great!" Ellie screamed in panic. "What do we do now!?"

"*START JOURNEY?*" a voice replied – but it wasn't Jack or Ram's, even Ellie's. It was the computer giving instructions, advising to confirm co-ordinates.

Ram quickly scanned the display panel and pressed buttons on the screen to confirm the co-ordinates as the patrol vehicle was closing in and picking up speed.

The engines of the drone suddenly burst into life, whirring at increasing intensity, their blades spinning at incredible speeds, preparing for flight.

Seconds later, the drone lifted off the ground, rising up into the dark sky vertically, just above the patrol vehicle beneath. The guards visible, gazing up in concern at the drone.

The blades of the drone angled slightly as the drone rose higher into the air then set off horizontally, speeding away.

Ram, Jack and Ellie breathed a sigh of relief.

"What did I tell you?" Ram grinned, thrilled they had pulled it off. "I hope you enjoy your flight with Genius Airways."

"Let's just wait till we get away first," Jack said, peering out the window, feeling a sense of elation at seeing the airport receding into the distance, illuminated by the headlights of several other vehicles which seemed to spring into life, realizing that one of the drones of the invaders had taken an unscheduled departure.

"Relax, Jack. There's no way they'll be able to come after us," Ram said, watching out of the window, the drone picking up speed, its electric engines humming at high pitch as it broke through some night clouds, the ground beneath zooming by under them.

"What makes you so sure?" Ellie enquired.

"Exactly," Jack agreed. "I mean it isn't as if we're travelling in the only drone. There's dozens which might come after us."

"Not a problem," Ram replied confidently. "I doubt they'd have much success if they tried to pursue us. And even if they did – don't forget, these things are automated. And I'm the only one who knows our destination co-ordinates."

Jack and Ellie were relieved, comforted by Ram's reassurances.

"You're something else, Ram, you really are," Jack said in admiration.

Although Ellie was as equally relieved, she just hoped that she and Jack could fully trust Ram – and asked carefully, "You mentioned about trying to use one of these drones to get away, but you didn't say anything about an exact destination," Ellie enquired. "Those co-ordinates you programmed into the navigation - do you mind sharing with us just exactly where we're going?"

"Home," Ram replied, whooping it up excitedly.

CHAPTER TWELVE

Tai San heard the familiar sound of the door to her room at the *Lakeside Resort* being unlocked from the other side – and as she woke up that morning, she braced herself for another encounter with The Selector.

She hadn't seen him since he had visited with the medical team who treated her sprained ankle with ice to reduce the swelling, before wrapping it in a compression dressing.

The medics were among the very best The Selector had to offer, he had proudly stated to her, and he claimed he would do everything in his power to ensure she got the highest level of care. They, like The Selector, were well versed in all manner of medicines, including homeopathic, herbal, as well as a more conventional approach and certainly seemed to know what they were doing. The ankle was less swollen than when the initial injury occurred, though Tai San was still sore and in discomfort.

Her greatest concern remained The Selector himself. He observed all the treatments and seemed fascinated more by Tai San's emotional state and her reactions to his presence, as well as to the medical procedures she was experiencing.

Tai San had writhed in pain on occasion when the medics had been directly examining her ankle – suspecting at one point that she might have broken it but thankfully it was just a bad sprain.

She did sense, however, that The Selector was deriving some sort of sadistic pleasure from her condition and seemed quite aroused even, staring intently when the medics had applied ice on her exposed ankle before helping himself to some of the ice from the pack and sucking on the cube fervently, savouring the taste as the cube melted in his mouth.

His odd behaviour and apparent enamoured interest in Tai San personally had disturbed her greatly.

Lying on her bed, her legs raised up on a stack of pillows, Tai San tensed as the door opened. And the medical team entered again, thankfully without any sign of The Selector, to her relief.

"It's a beautiful morning," the main medic said, a young female around Tai San's age. "What a day to be alive."

"Is it?"

Tai San regarded the medic with suspicion. Though she had treated Tai San's ankle when she arrived at the resort after her attempted escape and had regularly visited to monitor her progress, she had been the same medic who had injected the biochip into Tai San's hand the day before.

"Where is *he*?" Tai San asked warily.

"The Selector's got something special arranged," the medic advised while she and her team gently began their work on Tai San's ankle, carefully unwrapping the compress dressing. "At least the swelling seems to have reduced. But there's still signs of some synovial fluid around the bruising. So you'll need this compress dressing for another day or two. Now - we'll need to get you up and about. The Selector has brought somebody important to visit."

"Who? The Creator?" Tai San enquired carefully.

"It's not my place to say," the medic replied.

While the main medics wrapped Tai San's ankle in a fresh compression bandage, other medics in the team began applying make-up to her, forcibly holding Tai San's face firmly in place so she couldn't turn away, adding a little blush on her cheeks, putting some lipstick on her lips, brushing her hair, neatly styling it, others gently sprayed sweet perfume.

"What are you doing!?" Tai San asked, mystified.

"The Selector wants us to get you looking your very best," the main medic said, before stopping to admire the work of her fellow medics. With the exaggerated make up, Tai San looked almost like a doll. "There – that's a lot better. What a pretty picture. You look – perfect."

Tai San caught a glimpse of herself in the mirror and didn't agree, aghast at the exaggerated blush and especially the eye make-up, while being lifted to a standing position, where the medics began dressing her, leaving her feeling utterly confused and humiliated by their actions, especially concerned about what The Selector might have planned.

There was only one possible explanation for all the fuss they were making over her and her presentation, Tai San thought. The 'important somebody' she was going to be shown to had to be the one who The Selector always referred to in respectful, reverential terms. Tai San believed that she was indeed finally going to meet The Creator.

Tai San was escorted by the medics down the corridors of the *Lakeside Resort*, making her way on some crutches.

They were headed to the main lounge area, where she had been told she would be joining Alice and Ryan.

It was slow progress down the long corridors.

She finally rounded one corner, leading into the lounge – and dropped both crutches, almost falling over, stunned at the sight of the group standing before her. She could hardly believe what or more importantly who she was seeing.

"Tai San!" Amber cried out, racing over to embrace her.

Amber was accompanied by Bray, a baby in his arms, Trudy, with Brady by her side, Salene and May. They, too, rushed to embrace her, thrilled to be reunited.

A younger girl and boy were with them who Tai San didn't recognize, being Lottie and Sammy, the two of them watching the delirious delight as Tai San hugged her fellow Mall Rats.

Above all though, Tai San's gaze fell upon Lex – standing rooted momentarily in his place, dazed, like he was seeing a vision, a ghost from his past.

"Tai San?" Lex said, absolutely overcome that Tai San was there, almost questioning what was before his very eyes.

He tried but didn't say another word, tearing up slightly, and rushed to her, wrapping his arms around her tightly, clinging as if by releasing his grip she might somehow disappear from his life again.

Tai San responded, hugging with everything she had.

They would need to talk, to reconnect, to find out what had happened since they had last been in each other's company. There was so much they both had to say to each other. For now, they were just enjoying the feeling of being in each other's arms, amazed to be reunited.

"I don't believe it!" Trudy said, happy to see Lex and Tai San so overjoyed. "I never thought we'd ever see you again, Tai San."

"Who would have ever thought?" Amber agreed.

It had all felt like a strange dream, but compared to the nightmare that had descended on their lives from the invasion, their reunion with Tai San was the only positive thing in what had been utter chaos and uncertainty.

Throughout their journey in the driverless pods, none of the Mall Rats had gotten much sleep. Amber had discussed their plight with Bray in the pod they were travelling in. It was hard to come to terms with what they had all been through – the invasion of the city, their captivity, the subsequent transport by air to a faraway land, and especially the strange welcome by the tribe at the airstrip who seemed to know everything about the arriving Mall Rats.

May, Salene and Trudy, in another pod, had also discussed this and were as equally confused and concerned by the reception the Mall Rats had encountered from the waiting crowd, who Snake had referred to as part of The Privileged.

Their fervor and focus on Brady and Trudy in particular evoked the fanaticism of The Guardian and his Chosen.

May, Salene and Trudy were also unsettled, disturbed at the possibility of Ebony's fate, having seen how she had been treated and segregated and wondered where she had been taken to.

Their convoy had driven all night, passing through various types of industrial, military facilities en route to a mountainous forested area, finally arriving as the dawn broke at the *Lakeside Resort.*

Commander Snake explained that they were free to roam the resort but there would be severe penalties if they tried to escape. Which would be pointless as they would be tracked down – eventually.

Bray and Amber, along with other members of the Mall Rats, pressed him for more detail, questioning what was going on, why they were being held. But Snake didn't provide any information, advising that The Selector would brief them when the time was right. And Snake and his guards' instructions were simply to deliver the prisoners to the resort.

Amber demanded Snake tell them what had happened to Ebony. She and Ebony had never been close, far from it, but she wished Ebony no ill will or harm.

Snake explained that Ebony would be quite safe as long as she co-operated in her tasks but didn't provide any insight into what those tasks might be, any detail whatsoever. Except that the resort was to be the exclusive living quarters for the Mall Rats only for the time being and Ebony, who was not a Mall Rat, was apparently being kept somewhere else.

The Mall Rats were also troubled by what fate had befallen Emma, her younger brother and sister, as well as Lia and the group of pregnant young mothers who they had last seen in the custody of The Guardian, Eloise and their warriors.

But Snake didn't provide any insight other than advising that they were all on a journey of their own, taking the next steps in their lives that would lead them to a new purpose. It was all so vague with Snake either refusing or not knowing some of the greater detail.

Bray and Lex quickly noted that for all the Mall Rats were apparently free to live temporarily in the resort, there were perimeter guards patrolling and both felt a little more optimistic, viewing that there may well be some options in store for escape.

The reunion continued when Alice and Ryan, escorted by the guards, arrived in the lounge area – both of them stunned to see the other Mall Rats gathered around Tai San.

"Oh my God!" Alice blared out, and she ran towards them, her arms outstretched, wrapping Trudy, Brady, and Lex in an enormous hug.

"Salene?" Ryan said, ecstatically. He looked like he was going to faint – incredulous to see so many of his former Mall Rat friends who had been separated for so long – but especially Salene. He had been dreaming of this moment and the realization quickly dawned on him that she actually *was* there, just a few feet away, after too much time being kept apart.

"Ryan – it really is you, isn't it?" Salene wondered, feeling in a daze herself, stupefied – and she soon got her answer when Ryan excitedly bounded across the lounge heading straight for her.

"Of course it's me!" Ryan said, giving Salene a hug he had been saving up and playing out in his mind for many months, thrilled to be with her once more, literally sweeping her off her feet in his arms.

"You're still alive!" Salene said, overwhelmed to see him again, feeling a sense of protection in her current predicament by Ryan's loving, strong embrace, during which she cast an uncertain glance at May, who was standing watching them. May was equally overjoyed to see Ryan alive and seemingly well but it was difficult for her to watch the former lovers embracing.

"I've got so much I want to tell you!" Ryan said, squeezing Salene tightly out of affection.

"Me too, Ryan. Me too," Salene said, looking at May once more, almost wishing May could give her some guidance. Instead, May shrugged and smiled. She was genuinely happy but knew, however, that Salene would have to break it to Ryan that though they had once been married, Salene had moved on from him – with her partner now being May herself. And judging from Ryan's delight at seeing Salene, he clearly hadn't seemed to have moved on from her.

"This is incredible!" Alice beamed, hugging each of the Mall Rats in turn again. "Tell me everything – *everything* – you know about Ellie!" Alice asked them, desperate to hear news of her younger sister.

"We were with her only yesterday," Bray revealed, Alice relieved and delighted to hear it. But she shook her head slightly, indicating discreetly with a wave of her hand not to reveal any other information.

"Well, you'll have to tell me about it. Later. In private." Alice added.

Lex and Ryan, best friends since the evacuation boot camp around the time of the demise of the adults, gave each other a warm bear hug, casting aside any machismo, and displayed genuine affection.

Lottie and Sammy gave all the assembly hugs as well. Tai San, Alice and Ryan were delighted to give Brady a hug. She was growing so fast. And were thrilled to be introduced to baby Jay.

Alice, in an extreme undertone, had mentioned to the recently arrived Mall Rats they needed to be careful of what they might say as she, Ryan and Tai San were concerned that the resort might be bugged. All understood and spoke mainly superficially with no great detail, unwilling to provide any deeper information which might be used against them and resolved that they would need to have a check if there were any hidden cameras or monitoring devices which might pick up their voices.

* * *

The Selector gazed intently at various monitors displaying different angles of the reunion and was indeed listening to most of what had been said.

His prime focus though was on Lex hugging Tai San, the two of them obviously close, having a strong connection and personal chemistry as well as history, which he was obsessively keen to find out more detail on.

The Selector felt pangs of jealousy at the attention Tai San was giving Lex. He had many matters to attend to, especially now that the Mall Rats and Ebony were in his domain and he was due to visit The Creator later that day to give an update on the success of this phase of their plan.

But as well as dutifully working to achieve The Creator's goals, watching Tai San give Lex a warm smile and long lingering kiss, The Selector already had some ideas forming in his mind about how he might deal with Lex - so that The Selector could continue with his own personal agenda, which very much included Tai San, viewing her as an objective which he needed to achieve.

CHAPTER THIRTEEN

Throughout the long journey Ebony was unable to catch any sleep. All night her mind was racing, speculating in her inner-most thoughts what might happen to her - if her captors were going to keep her alive. But she reasoned that if they had wished to kill her, they probably would have done so by now.

This didn't exactly give her much reassurance though. She simply had no idea what lay in store for her. She literally was in the dark and gazed out the windows of the driverless pod futuristic vehicle at the passing scenery. It was difficult to see much though given that it was night, but Ebony was aware that she was part of a motorcade with military trucks accompanying her vehicle on the journey.

Ebony was disturbed, confused, let alone angry at how she had been treated by her captors and one thing for sure, was that if she ever had an opportunity to seek revenge, then she would gleefully take it.

She wondered what had happened to the other Mall Rats. Their arrival had been met with a rapturous reception. Whereas she had received nothing but scorn, resentment, suspicion, from the onlookers whom she had encountered briefly.

For whatever their reasons, it was clear to Ebony that she didn't exactly have a good reputation – and she wondered if there might even be some bounty placed on her head.

She eventually managed to fall asleep briefly and woke up as the dawn broke, the horizon ablaze as the sun rose slowly, enabling Ebony to more clearly see the landscape.

They were passing fields and what appeared to be farm workers toiling the land and she wondered if her fate might be to join them because no doubt they were slaves, given their early start.

Her expression clouded in a mixture of confusion and growing concern when she noticed images on some outlying agricultural buildings which seemed to be displaying information – specifically advertising an event. Then she stared open-mouthed as she noticed a huge blown-up photograph of herself on the side of the building with text illustrating *'EBONY. A CONTESTANT OF THE CUBE. COMING SOON'*.

Ebony decided that she must try and live in the moment otherwise she simply couldn't handle her plight with any more speculation and would take it all one step at a time and adapt accordingly to whatever she might encounter.

After so much time living in the concrete jungle of the city, Ebony couldn't help but appreciate the stunning views outside the windows, the spectacle of nature in the raw, without any graffiti or debris in sight.

The convoy now seemed to be ascending a winding road and soon a large, beautiful lake came into view, bordered by forest, with snow-capped mountains beyond.

Shortly thereafter, the convoy arrived at its destination – a rustic lodge overlooking the waters.

Ebony was ushered inside by the guards from the military vehicles, who then left while she gazed at the opulent splendor of the lodge's décor and luxurious furnishings, the lodge clearly belonging to someone of prominence. It was a refuge of peace and quiet and must have been a fishing or hunting lodge in the adult times, Ebony thought.

There were several different varieties of fish mounted on the walls. Stuffed animals of various kinds, ranging from small birds to some large wild boars, preserved by taxidermy in their frozen poses, stood lifeless in the hallway of the lodge.

Perhaps her luck was about to change, Ebony considered. She hadn't been bound and was being allowed to walk freely around the lodge, wondering who she would be about to meet, clearly someone of very high status.

Ebony was determined to make a good first impression. She started running her fingers through her hair, styling it in an impromptu manner, and wiped herself down, rubbing off any dirt she could see on her clothing from her captivity, adjusting her appearance so she could look the best she was able to in her current state.

She wandered into a large study, bristling with books on its many layers of shelves. Its windows had an outlook over the lake. On the walls were glass cases and display frames filled with a multitude of preserved insect species inside.

In one corner of the room Ebony was stunned to see a cryogenic hibernation chamber, similar to the type Ram had used in the city, long ago, when he had tried to escape into his virtual reality paradise.

It reminded Ebony of the units that Amber and the Mall Rats had described seeing at Eagle Mountain and she wondered what it was doing here – disturbed by the thought if there could even be an adult or someone inside the chamber, its darkened glass surface concealing its contents and whatever, or whoever, could be lurking within.

Her attention was mostly drawn, however, to the unusual-looking figure sitting behind a large wooden desk. He was intently staring at her, tapping his fingers together rhythmically, as if in a ritualistic obsessional manner, in deep contemplation of her.

"Hi," Ebony said, smiling politely to break the unbearable silence.

"Hi," her host replied, with a smile that was ice cold.

"You wouldn't be *Kami*, by any chance?" Ebony ventured, aware that if her abductors were The Collective, then her host might be the enigmatic leader Ram had often spoken of.

"You may call me The Selector," her host answered.

"Appreciate it. It's a pleasure to meet you," Ebony said, trying to ingratiate herself.

"Is it?"

Ebony smiled again but still felt great unease at the cold tone of The Selector. "Well, it's certainly a pleasure for me. And I just hoped that you might be the kind of man who enjoyed some pleasure, too," Ebony added, slightly seductively.

The Selector didn't say anything in return and just watched Ebony, studying her reactions, her behaviour. She felt like she was on display, like one of the stuffed animals she had seen, his intense observation of her and odd behaviour making her feel uncomfortable.

She stood in silence, her heart beating almost in time to the old grandfather clock which ticked rhythmically, and she couldn't help but watch the pendulum almost as if she was being hypnotized - which registered with The Selector.

"Are you nervous, Ebony?" he enquired. "If so, just keep staring at the pendulum. It might relax you. So, breathe deeply and relax. Breathe slowly."

The Selector's voice was soft, soothing. Ebony found it difficult to avert her gaze from the swinging pendulum of the grandfather clock. But she eventually forced herself to look away and glanced at The Selector again, who himself was breathing in through his nose and exhaling slowly as if somehow to calm himself.

"There is so much pressure in this world, Ebony, one needs to take some time out and slow our biorhythms."

"I quite agree," Ebony replied, becoming more reassured by The Selector's friendly demeanour. And she mimicked his breathing, slowly in her nose and exhaling out through her mouth, shaking her arms slightly, twitching her neck as if to de-stress.

"Feel better?" The Selector asked.

"Absolutely."

"What kind of animal would you say that you are, Ebony?"

"What type of question is that?"

"One that needs an answer."

"I dunno," Ebony said. "Maybe a unicorn. Something special."

"I don't know about a unicorn. But I think I know exactly who you are. You're a fox."

"Is that what you say to all the ladies?"

The Selector grinned, amused by her remark. "You're cunning, Ebony. Resourceful. You possess great survival instincts, from what I can gather. You're adaptable. But you're also dangerous. You put your own needs and interests ahead of others. Your track record shows you are not to be trusted. With your guile and slyness, you're as wily and capable as the fox."

"I take that as a compliment. The thing is – are you the type of man who can appreciate what a fox might do for you, if she was by your side? You see, I'm more than just a fox. But also, a woman, with strong desires."

"Interesting," The Selector replied.

"If you don't mind my asking – what kind of animal are you?" Ebony probed carefully.

"A chameleon, I would say. But I'm of course not an animal. But am of the human species. Though we can certainly learn a lot from our spirit animal, whatever that might be."

"The only thing I've learned, Selector, is how to survive," Ebony said.

"Presumably you didn't learn that from the fox? Pretty soon that species sadly might become extinct. Thankfully we'll do all we can to assist with our breeding programmes."

"Do you have a breeding programme?" Ebony enquired. "For yourself?"

"Of course," The Selector responded. "If it is the will of The Creator."

Ebony wondered who The Creator was – as well as who The Selector was, and how he fit into the structure of The Collective. If indeed they were the ones holding her.

She felt she was being judged somehow, like it was an interview, The Selector deciding what to do with her. She didn't want to end up imprisoned again or to spend the rest of her days as a slave or even worse, recalling the hostility the crowd at the airstrip had shown to her. She sensed she had to make good of this chance to impress The Selector and try and establish some influence over him, for her own sake.

So she decided to change tack.

"I was Zoot's woman," Ebony said, proudly. "I take it you know of him?"

"I do. And you abandoned his legacy to carry out your own agenda."

"I don't know where you got that kind of information but believe me, it's all wrong."

"How dare you question my sources and insult The Creator!" The Selector erupted in fury, slamming his fist on his desk.

Ebony was taken aback at the sudden outburst and swallowed nervously. "Sorry... I didn't mean any offence."

The Selector considered her, then smiled. "Apology accepted."

Unnerved by the unpredictability of The Selector, Ebony thought that she needed to quickly change tack again and try something, anything, to alter the course of the meeting. She started to unbutton her blouse, deliberately revealing some cleavage.

"What are you doing?" The Selector said, quickly diverting his gaze as if embarrassed, which was encouraging to Ebony, believing the power balances were shifting slightly.

"I just thought you might find it personally interesting to know that I'm very attracted to men in positions of power. And you certainly seem to be a very powerful man," Ebony smouldered.

"And why would I find that interesting?"

Ebony was always aware that she had been the object of desire by many males in the past and had used her sexuality to her advantage. Despite his odd qualities, The Selector had to be like any other man, Ebony thought. She had nothing to lose and so much to possibly gain, even if it meant sharing The Selector's bed for a while. It was a small price to pay to gain advantage.

"Would you like me to show you more of what kind of fox I can be?" Ebony drawled seductively, unbuttoning more of her top.

"Please don't," The Selector asked, seemingly disturbed by what she was suggesting as Ebony approached the desk, sure she had finally gotten to him, her good looks and sexuality to the rescue once more.

"How about I do some things you might have never imagined?"

"Would you stand on one leg?" The Selector suddenly asked, intrigued.

"Sure. Whatever turns you on," Ebony replied – and she did what she was asked, standing on her right leg, thinking it was a strange request.

"Would you – do a little dance for me?" The Selector asked. He wasn't flirtatious at all but was enquiring in all seriousness.

"A dance? Yeah, I'll dance for you. We could be doing a lot more than dancing though."

Ebony was finding The Selector's questions bizarre, to say the least. Maybe he had a few odd fetishes, she thought. She wouldn't put it past him, he seemed the type. Nonetheless, it was evident he was in a position of power and she was determined to bond with him, to make the best out of any opportunity to enhance her position.

No matter how foolish she felt, without any music, Ebony began to dance rhythmically, and was deliberately making sure she was doing so in an alluring way, that all her curves were showing and on display to this most unusual male.

"Are you going to join me?" she enquired.

"No. You can stop now."

She stopped dancing and gave him uncertain, wary looks, confused by his increasingly unpredictable behaviour.

"Stick your tongue out."

Slowly, she did so, before pulling it back in. "You know what we can use our tongues for?" Ebony tried again, suggestively.

"Lick the lid on the chamber."

"What is this!?" Ebony said, having had enough, refusing to do so. Partly thinking that The Selector was just playing games with her but also uneasy at the thought of something possibly living under the smoke-glass canopy.

"So, even you have your limits," The Selector observed.

"Think again," Ebony said, determined to make an impression. She ambled over to the cryogenic unit and started to lick the glass cover. It might turn The Selector on, Ebony thought initially, but that feeling faded as he gazed intently, absently, and then excitedly started typing in data on the console of his computer.

"It's yummy," Ebony said. "You should try it," relieved that she hadn't noticed anything living in the chamber. At least as far as she could see.

"I now know your profile, Ebony," The Selector advised, getting to his feet. "You will clearly do anything you have to, to make sure you will survive. Your traits are very strong. And admirable. Rather than a fox, you might even be a wolf."

"So, what does that mean for me?"

"Guards!" The Selector shouted.

Two guards burst into the room, ignoring Ebony's state of undress, focusing their attentions on The Selector.

"I want you to take Ebony immediately to The Cube for induction."

"The Cube?" Ebony wondered, buttoning up her blouse, recalling the strange images she had noticed on her journey earlier that morning.

"If you do well and prove you have the right qualities and characteristics, there is a chance you can redeem yourself and fulfil a more noble purpose in life in service of The Creator."

"And how do I know what I need to do in order to 'do well'?" Ebony asked, struggling as the guards began to lead her to the door.

"That's one of the first things you will need to find out. I'm sure the audience will *love* you," The Selector advised.

"Audience? What are you talking about? Where are you taking me!?" Ebony cried out, as the guards dragged her away.

The Selector followed excitedly.

"It's time to put a fox in with the chickens and discover if the fox is really a fox or a wolf!" The Selector said, prior to slamming the door shut with force as Ebony and the guards left.

He turned from the door and breathed in deeply through his nose and exhaled through his mouth, trying to calm himself from his excitement, aware that Ebony would be a worthy addition to The Cube.

CHAPTER FOURTEEN

"Useless – heap of – junk!" Ram yelled, kicking the drone in contempt and in the process hurting his foot which left him hopping on one leg and groaning in utter frustration.

They were back on the ground once more, the drone having crash-landed in a forested area.

"So much for 'Genius Airways'," Jack sighed despondently as he and Ellie watched Ram slump to the ground and massage his foot.

Jack and Ellie were in discomfort themselves, feeling the intense afternoon sun bearing down on them. They were all hungry and Ellie had resourcefully found some raspberries in one of the bushes to keep them going but they would need to eat something proper soon.

Even the grass, the leaves of the trees, were starting to look appetizing, Jack thought – and he exchanged a look with Ellie, the two of them wondering how much longer Ram would keep going in his efforts to find out what was wrong with the drone – as well as marvelling at his endless bad temper and foul language.

He was now back in the cockpit checking a console and had earlier used all of his considerable technological knowledge to attempt to diagnose what the problem was with the drone. Jack had assisted, even Ellie, adding what expertise they had checking if it could be an engineering or mechanical issue, a software glitch or a bug in the navigation computer.

So far though it was to no avail. Ellie and Jack accepted that it was all out of their expertise. But Ram refused and they watched him trying all manner of possible solutions to discover what was plaguing the machine. Ram had become obsessed with his quest to figure out what had caused their difficulties.

"Don't you know who I am!" Ram said, glaring accusingly at the control panel. "You'll never beat me," he continued, while slamming his hand on the console as if punishing it.

"I don't think that's going to help do anything, Ram," Jack said. "Except maybe give you a sore hand in addition to your foot."

"Well, that might be the least of our problems," Ellie said, gazing around uneasily. "Don't you think we should maybe head off?"

"Where?" Ram snapped.

"You're the 'genius'," Ellie scoffed.

"Calm down, guys," Jack interrupted. "It won't help us by arguing. Maybe Ellie's right and we should try and rely more on human co-ordinates, rather than whatever you programmed in that computer."

Ram ignored Jack and continued punching in data on the console. But from his frustrated demeanour, he too was clearly losing hope - in ironic contrast to him being so euphoric with his idea, which he himself admitted was ingenious, even for him — to steal the drone and use it to make good their escape. And for the majority of the journey, it seemed as if it was working. But before long, as the flight went on, however, it had become clear that all was not well with the drone.

It had started behaving like it was possessed, as Ram had described it, altering its course in midair. He, along with Ellie and Jack, had been concerned that the drone might even crash, so erratic had its changes in direction been at times. Ram had corrected its bearings as they flew, re-entering the destination co-ordinates he intended them to reach - yet the drone would continually veer off the path Ram had set it, eventually clipping the top of a tree and descending, crash-landing to the ground.

Now, after so much effort troubleshooting what could be wrong with the drone, Ram climbed out of the cockpit and advised Ellie and Jack that he was beginning to suspect more and more that the dilemma was not the result of an accident. He believed that the drone had to have been hacked, that someone from the outside had been interfering, countering Ram's own many attempts to manually override the drone during the flight. It was the only explanation left to explain what had happened – the drone had to have been taken over and forced to land there by a third party.

"Like who?" Jack wondered.

"Do you think it could be The Collective?" Ellie speculated.

"I'm not sure," Ram replied. "But we better not stick around, to try and find out."

They set off on foot, Ram leading the way through the forested area, eventually arriving at an overgrown botanical gardens which gave Ram some comfort that his plan had almost worked, realizing that they were close to the town where Ram had grown up.

The house that had once been his home was perhaps twenty miles away, he estimated, out in the suburbs.

In taking the drone, Ram's original plan was to travel to his former home town and stay in the house he was raised in. It seemed like the safest place he could think of to go at the time. He had hoped that they could use it as a literal safehouse, and from there, regroup and work out a way forward.

If they felt it was safe to do so, the next step, after some initial time, would be to return to the place that had once been the main base of The Technos.

Ram explained to Ellie and Jack that after he founded his tribe, The Technos were once located at an abandoned factory on the outskirts of the town in an industrial complex. It had its own power source, excellent infrastructure and the Internet speeds were out of this world.

When The Technos had permanently moved out so they could take over the Mall Rats' city and Ram could claim Eagle Mountain for himself, they had relocated all their personnel and most of their equipment. They had gone as far as to purposefully sabotage the base they were leaving behind, blowing parts of it up, gutting it, making sure they left no trace.

Ram didn't think there would be any Collective presence in the area because his former base would be the last place on Earth The Collective would ever go to because there was nothing there anymore – no Ram, no Technos, nothing of value. Even if any of The Collective's forces had ever been there in the past, they would have had no reason to have stayed behind.

"That's what I wanted Kami to think anyway," Ram said, a mischievous smile of delight on his face. "Let's just say I didn't take everything with me when The Technos moved out. As a contingency in case I ever wanted to return. I just hope there's some toys and hardware left behind, hidden away where I put them."

Jack and Ellie knew that Ram had taken refuge in the community of Liberty outside of their home city, believing he had a bounty on his head and living in total paranoia that the mysterious Kami would try and seek him out as a result of him usurping supposed plans Kami and The Collective had in place to invade the city - by doing it himself. But as always with Ram, he played his cards more than close to his chest and it was difficult to know the exact situation.

"What if The Collective were able to see through your ruse?" Ellie wondered. "If Kami's as smart as you say, maybe they figured out your old base could still be of some use to them. For all we know, maybe there's some there right now."

"In which case we'd be truly out of the frying pan and into the fire," Ram said, dreading the prospect. "But I don't think The Collective will be around. To anyone who wouldn't know otherwise, there's nothing there anymore. Including me. As far as they would believe, that is."

"Then who do you think might have brought the drone down?" Jack asked.

"They probably tried to override it back in the city," Ram surmised.

As they proceeded furtively through the botanical gardens, Ram recalled going there with his parents as a young child. He was re-treading some old memories, not all of them fond ones. His parents had been harsh, his father a strict disciplinarian. Although they had given him an excellent education, recognizing the precocious gifts and intellect of their only child, Ram's was a house and a childhood often filled with anger and fear, rather than love. At least that's how Ram perceived it at the time. There were no incidents of domestic violence but his parents were not tactile, attentive.

Ram always felt that they were somehow disappointed in him, that he could never meet their high expectations, even if he did achieve the highest of grades at school.

His father was once in the military and expected Ram's room to be tidy, for him never to be late for even a meal. Everything had to always be so exact. A keen sportsman, Ram's father was always disappointed that Ram seemed to have no interest, aptitude or ability in any kind of sport, preferring to gain knowledge of anything and everything which impressed his mother.

She was once a supply teacher and sanctioned Ram's obsession with any studying – until his focus became on computers and on information technology. This provided some respite and he eventually escaped from the real world by entering the digital fantasy world offered by computer systems. Both software and hardware had been his companions, the only friends he had ever really known growing up.

Ram's former town seemed lifeless now. There was no trace of anybody, just the three of them, making their way down the street that bordered the botanical gardens which gave them all a degree of hope that they were well and truly alone.

They took a moment to rummage through a decaying and looted convenience store, its contents strewn all over the floor. There wasn't much left of any value but they were relieved when Jack found an old box of cereal bars under a pile of rubbish, long past its sell by date. They were stale and tasteless but in their sealed foil wrappings, it was the only choice of food they had on offer to try and quell their ravenous appetites.

Returning to the street, they still had about another hour's walk ahead of them, Ram felt.

Ellie and Jack were missing the other Mall Rats and were concerned about what had happened to them and where they had been taken on the military cargo planes they saw leaving the airport of their home city. Both pressed Ram for more information - if the invaders were indeed The Collective.

Ram wasn't sure where The Collective were located exactly. So, he couldn't provide any detail as far as that was concerned. All of his communication with Kami in the past had been done online. He didn't know who Kami was – if his online, supposed friend was male, female.

Sometimes Ram wondered if Kami could even be an adult, judging by the mature and knowledgeable manner displayed when Ram had liaised and communicated online.

Ram had even wondered if Kami could be a computer, a form of artificial intelligence programme that was still hooked up online, speculating if there was some connection with the *Knowledge Artificial Machine Intelligence* super mega computer at Eagle Mountain, or if there were others like it, the machine having the acronym *K.A.M.I*, which he suspected couldn't be entirely coincidental.

Ram said he wished he could shed more light on matters but he genuinely could not, including where the Mall Rats might have been taken.

Now, the Mall Rat's home city – and Eagle Mountain – could be under the occupation and control of The Collective, Ram, Ellie and Jack speculated.

"It's the classic paradigm of conquest," Ram reflected, as they walked down the street. "To the victors go the spoils. Including some pretty awesome equipment the invaders seem to be stripping out of the military facility at Eagle Mountain."

"Ssshh! Get down!" Jack urged, suddenly ducking for cover the other side of an overturned rubbish bin, Ellie following quickly behind.

Ram looked terrified as he noticed what had come to Jack and Ellie's attention.

He could hear the sound of engines, vehicles, approaching at high speed.

Ram rushed, leaping over the rubbish bin, to join Ellie and Jack in hiding.

It was just in time, Ram finding cover as a vehicle approached around the corner and passed by at high speed.

"I thought you said nobody else would be here!" Ellie whispered in an urgent, hushed undertone.

"They shouldn't be!" Ram shrugged anxiously, nervous at who it could be and if they would return.

The vehicle slammed on its brakes at the end of the street and turned 180 degrees, speeding back towards the rubbish bin.

Jack, Ellie and Ram remained motionless, trying to not even breathe for fear of making any sound.

Through a crack in the bin, Jack noticed the doors of the vehicle, which had skidded to a stop, opening. And he could see four pairs of legs getting out. There was no indication of identity – except for an impatient voice.

"Come on out! We know you're there!"

Ram flinched. He couldn't believe it. Jack and Ellie exchanged incredulous looks. They recognized the voice too. Surely, it couldn't be?

"We found your drone and followed your trail. I won't ask you again. Come out if you know what's good for you!"

Slowly, Jack, Ellie and Ram got to their feet, emerged from behind the rubbish bin – and were astonished to see who was standing before them.

"Well, well – now *this* I would have never expected," Ved said, amazed in turn to observe his former Techno leader and master, Ram, as well as the two Mall Rats.

Ved was accompanied by three guards, all about the same age as him. One was carrying a device which was bleeping. Ram wondered exactly what it did but he was sure they must have used it to track them down somehow.

"Ved?" Ellie said, stunned to see him. But more wary if he was currently a friend. Or foe.

Ved had been Ram's talented and devoted apprentice at The Technos, a computer prodigy who had helped Ram try to achieve his vision of creating a perfect, virtual reality world. Temperamental and rebellious at times, he had disappeared in the last days of Ram's regime, with the rumours being that Ram had played a part in Ved's initial removal from The Technos. Nobody knew what had happened to him. They all believed he was missing and gone forever, 'deleted' by Ram's successor as Techno leader, Mega.

"You're alive! We thought you might be dead," Jack said, unable to comprehend the sight of Ved in front of him.

"For a time – so did I," Ved stated.

He gave Ram a fixed stare laced with anger.

"So. You're back on your own two feet again."

The last time Ved had seen him, Ram had been unable to walk and was confined to a wheelchair due to a serious accident he had suffered in his past.

"A lot of things are different since we last met," Ram remarked. "I'm glad to see you're alive and well."

"Yeah? Well, I can't say I feel the same about you! I never wanted to see your face again. What are you doing here, Ram!?"

"I was about to ask you the same question," Ram replied – looking in concern at the stun blaster Ved was now levelling in his direction.

"Take this as a hint," Ved said. Jack and Ellie instinctively cried out as Ved fired the stun gun, hitting Ram's mid-rift, Ram collapsing to the ground.

CHAPTER FIFTEEN

After their initial surprise and elation at being reunited with Tai San, Alice and Ryan - the Mall Rats had spent several hours with them outside in the grounds of the *Lakeside Resort*, catching up on all that had happened in their lives since they had last seen each other. They believed that at least they could talk more freely in case the inside of the resort was bugged for sound and they didn't want to give away any information – though all were aware that whoever was holding them seemed to know a lot about the Mall Rats already.

Alice was overjoyed to find out Ellie was alive and well, or at least she certainly was when the Mall Rats had been with her at the mall before the invasion. It was such good news for her to hear that Ellie had found happiness in her continued relationship with Jack, Amber relaying how they seemed such a good fit for each other and were so content together.

That Jack, Ellie and Ram hadn't been brought to the resort so far filled the Mall Rats with hope that they were somehow still safe from the occupation forces. Lex tried to keep what he knew of what had happened to them vague, telling Alice he had last seen them 'around' and thought they were still somewhere in the heart of the city.

Alice suspected that Lex was choosing his words carefully, not giving away everything that he knew – for all that he denied it.

There was so much to bring each other up to date on. Bray explained what had occurred to him after The Techno's invasion. Amber described Ram's Techno regime and his fall from power, leading on to how they had worked with Ram to bring about Mega's defeat when he had, in turn, ruled over their city.

Trudy told of their re-encounter with The Guardian, the ordeal they had been through with Eloise and her forces. Lex spoke of their revisit to Eagle Mountain where they had discovered more secrets and tantalizing clues about what the adults had been doing before their extinction by the 'virus' – and their surprise encounters with remnants of the adults themselves, locked away, as if in a perpetual deep sleep inside their cryogenic hibernation chambers.

Alice and Ryan reported what they had endured during their lengthy period as captives – but also the detailed questioning they had been put through by The Selector about Eagle Mountain and worryingly, the Mall Rats themselves.

Amber was outraged to learn of the biochips that had been forcibly injected into Tai San, Ryan and Alice – and she dreaded if she and the other Mall Rats would be subject to the same experience.

Following Tai San, Alice and Ryan's recent attempts, escape didn't seem to be an option, especially given the security presence all around the resort and the possibility that the biochips could be trackable.

Tai San, Alice and Ryan were made aware of the strange and euphoric welcome their fellow Mall Rats had received at the airstrip upon landing and were disturbed at the apparent reach and influence in these lands of what felt, at first impression, like a mythology around Zoot and those who were most connected to him. Trudy recalled with utter anguish the male who prostrated himself before her and Brady after they landed, asking them for a blessing, a miracle.

Tai San, Alice and Ryan described The Selector, who the rest of the party hadn't met as yet. And all speculated why they had been brought together and why they were being held prisoner in such a way.

The Selector had mentioned, Tai San, Alice and Ryan informed them, that all that was apparently happening to them was due to 'The Creator''s vision and plan, even though none of them knew what that entailed or who The Creator was, let alone if they even existed, whatever or whoever The Creator was meant to be. Was The Creator the same as Kami? Or had The Creator displaced Kami and was now the ruler of this group? Or was The Creator the alter ego of The Selector?

There were so many questions, so much that they didn't understand, even if the group holding them were indeed in reality The Collective. Or, some other regime.

After all they had been through, they were overwhelmed, exhausted, and in need of rest and recovery. The newcomers had their pick of empty rooms to choose from and they went their separate ways, Trudy and Brady going in one room, Amber, Bray and baby Jay in another. Lottie and Sammy were to stay with Alice as the two younger children especially felt frightened at what might occur but were reassured by Alice's obvious prowess as a warrior and bodyguard.

May would wait a little bit before picking her room, she advised. She would be sharing with Salene but was aware Salene would need to talk in private with Ryan first to let him know of their status.

* * *

Ryan gave Salene his own guided tour of the *Lakeside Resort*, showing her around the scenic grounds outside by the lake, the pool and gym where he spent some of his spare time keeping fit – but Salene could tell Ryan just wanted to be with her, the tour a pretense to spend some time together alone. Which suited Salene as well.

Salene knew in her heart she would have to let Ryan know the truth about her relationship status with May. She had to be honest, she owed him that much. He was a special guy, uncomplicated, slow at times intellectually, but his heart was pure and true.

Salene didn't feel clean inside. In the past she had 'led' Ryan on, she shamefully admitted to herself. She liked him, she thought she genuinely loved him at one stage. But despite their history and all they had been through together, in truth Salene was aware that deep down she had never had the same feelings for Ryan that he had openly expressed he had to her. And the same applied to any other male Salene had been involved with. Even Pride.

Ryan was more of a very close friend. And not the soulmate he had been so keen to be. Certainly not for Salene. She hoped he would find romance elsewhere in his life. He deserved it and she wanted him to live a happy life. But it couldn't be with her. The love of her life was May.

Salene dreaded relaying this situation to Ryan, which felt like a truth that was too great to tell. She would try though. He deserved and needed to know.

"Ryan, we need to talk," Salene said gently, leading Ryan to a bench overlooking the scenic lake.

"We are talking," Ryan replied, slightly confused.

"You don't understand, Ryan. There are some things I need to tell you. And I just hope you can accept everything I say."

Ryan knew Salene enough to know that there was something of great importance bothering her and he encouraged her to open up and to tell him what was troubling her so.

Salene began by explaining to Ryan that after he had been sent away by The Guardian and The Chosen, she thought he had initially been killed. And that perhaps she might never see him ever again.

She recounted how she had gradually fallen in love with Pride, or so she thought at the time, entering into a relationship after Ram and The Technos had invaded the city. Ryan appreciated her transparency and Salene was surprised when he told her he already knew all about it. Tai San had revealed details to him of the Eco tribe shortly after she arrived at the resort and that she thought Salene had been in some kind of relationship with Pride, though she didn't know the full extent of it or how serious it was, having only encountered the Mall Rats briefly the last time she saw them in the city.

Ryan put his hand gently on Salene's. "Maybe you and Pride just weren't meant to be. Like what happened with our baby. It wasn't the right time. No matter how much either of us wanted it."

Salene began to cry, remembering the tragic loss of their unborn baby soon after she had last seen Ryan, when he had been forced to work in the mines by The Chosen. Their final days spent together as a couple were marked by so much tragedy and heartbreak, painful memories.

"Maybe you and I have been brought back together for a reason," Ryan suggested, confirming Salene's suspicions about where he was hoping things might be headed. "It might not be too late to turn the clock back. Me and you..."

"Ryan, it's different now. What we had was a long time ago."

"What we had was something special, Sal. So why don't we try again? I know we can make it work. We could even try for another baby."

"You're not listening to what I'm saying," Salene said, struggling to get the words out. "It's different now."

"How? What do you mean?"

"It's not you, Ryan. It's me."

"I know it's you. And you're what I want. It's always been you."

"No – there's someone else," Salene admitted painfully.

"Who?" Ryan said, confused and feeling like his whole world was starting to crumble. "Who is he?"

"It's not a *he*," Salene said, aware that this was becoming far more awkward than she could ever have imagined.

"What are you talking about?"

"It's a *she*. The someone else - is a she."

Ryan took a moment for it to all sink in. "Are you telling me you're - gay?"

Salene nodded.

"Is this some kind of joke? Did Lex put you up to this?"

"It's not a joke, Ryan... I'm being completely serious," Salene insisted. She was now feeling overwhelmed. A part of her wanted to flee, to become invisible, to disappear. It wasn't because of any shame about her feelings for May – there weren't any. It was more due to Ryan's reaction. She didn't want to hurt him. She cared enough that she wanted to do what was in his best interests and she worried how he would be when he found out the truth. But she couldn't live a lie and pretend her life was unreal, to herself or to Ryan.

"Who – who is she then?" Ryan asked. "This person you're meant to be so in love with?"

"Promise me you won't do anything."

"Who do you think I am?! What do you think I'd do?"

"Promise me, Ryan. When I tell you, you won't do anything to her – or to yourself. You're one of the most important people in my life – and I care about you. I want you to be okay. For us to always be friends, forever."

"Then as a 'friend' of yours – would you tell me who it is?" Ryan said, trying to contain his emotions.

"It's May," Salene revealed it. "I'm in love with May and we're together."

Ryan sat in silence, trying somehow to assimilate it all before taking Salene's hand and gently squeezing it. "Just as long as you're happy, then I'll be happy too, Sal. That's all I've ever wanted – is your happiness."

"Ryan – please don't. You're making it so difficult for me." She raised his clasped hand and kissed it. "You really are special, you know."

"If you don't mind, Sal, I'd like to spend a bit of time alone. I've got some laundry to do. So, I'll catch up with you later."

He walked away to the resort entrance and Salene knew it was just some kind of excuse.

She felt heartbroken, torn by guilt. She realized Ryan would need some time to come to terms with it. But what they had was in the past. Her future life was one she wanted to spend with May. Whatever lay in store for them in their current predicament.

* * *

The Selector gazed contemptuously at an image on the monitor of Tai San in her room, sitting up on her bed, leaning against her fluffy pillows, her ankle raised on some cushions at the other end. She couldn't stop herself smiling. And didn't want to. She was thrilled to be reunited with Lex, who was sitting next to her, equally enraptured to be around her again. Then Lex disappeared from frame and suddenly the image also disappeared from the screen, replaced with static, electronic snow.

Inside Tai San's room back at the *Lakeside Resort*, Lex had found a small device in the corner of the ceiling and had disabled it. It was small and crushed easily when he dropped it to the floor and ground it into pieces under his boot. "I wonder if that 'thing' only picked up sound?"

"Hopefully not vision," Tai San said, with a shiver running down her spine at the prospect of being observed, especially by the creepy Selector.

"I don't know," Lex replied. "But it sure as hell won't be working now. How's that ankle feeling?"

"Much better – now that you're here."

Tai San proceeded then to tell Lex an overview of what she had been through since they had last seen each other, so long ago. He had been shocked to hear of her experiences as a slave, her captivity under The Broker, and lately the ordeals she had suffered, as well as Ryan and Alice, as 'guests' of The Selector.

She had refrained from telling Lex the entire situation, however, worrying that if she mentioned the full extent of The Selector's creepy behaviour and blatant physical attraction to her - that Lex might angrily react and do something impulsive in an effort to protect her, even attack The Selector at the first chance. He would inevitably only endanger himself in the process, Tai San felt, and no doubt be harshly punished by The Selector and his warriors.

The Selector had a cruel, sadistic streak in him, Tai San knew that all too well by now, and she had to spare Lex from it. She would tell Lex everything that had happened to her when she felt it was right to do so but she wouldn't allow Lex to risk himself for her. He had only just unexpectedly returned into her life and she didn't want to suddenly lose him.

Lex had wondered why Tai San, during her time as a spy in The Technos in league with Mega to bring down Ram, hadn't tried to go back to him then. She explained that she had wanted to – and was indeed desperate to - but things had quickly developed out of control and she had gotten in too deep. She was trying to save the city, many innocent lives, Lex's included, and had got caught up in the echelons of The Technos, living a false life as one of their own and had been unable to return to Lex and the life they had once had.

It was always her goal to do so once The Technos were defeated. But Tai San had been taken away from the city, ending up in faraway lands, enslaved, never to see Lex again, she thought.

She asked what had happened in Lex's own life since their separation. He told her how devastated he was when she had first disappeared after The Technos invaded - and he had done everything he could to try to find her. As time unfolded, he believed she had been tragically killed, or was 'deleted' by The Technos, as they referred to it. Lex revealed he had gotten involved with a few other girls since her, including Ebony's sister, Siva, as well as later a brief dalliance with Gel. Tai San was aware of Lex's relationship with Siva, who had been a prominent Techno herself.

"And there's one more confession," Lex admitted to her.

"Just the one?"

He described how he had only recently had a fling with Lia. She was not a Mall Rat, of course, and he met her on the island where The Mall Rats had their initial encounter with forces of The Collective, under their commander, Blake. Lia was pretty and enjoyable to be around but they still didn't know each other that well, it was nothing too serious. They weren't a proper couple.

And he hoped that Lia would be safe, along with the others who had been seized by the invaders. Lex and Tai San speculated on what might have happened to them, both, of course, not having any clear idea other than the Mall Rats seemed to be segregated for some reason from the other prisoners.

Tai San appreciated Lex's honesty and openness about his 'love life' and let him know that since Lex, there hadn't been anyone special in her life.

"So - where does that leave us?" Lex wondered, inching across the covers, towards Tai San.

"I don't know what you mean," Tai San said, coyly.

"Maybe I can remind you exactly what I mean," Lex said. "I reckon this bed's big enough for two."

"Hmmm. You're probably right." Tai San teased. "But who could I possibly get to keep me company at night?"

"How about me?" Lex replied.

"Oh, I think that might be a good idea," Tai San said. "But first, I'll go and tell the others about the monitoring device I found in that corner."

Lex met Bray in the corridor when he left Tai San's room and accompanied him to his and Amber's room where they discovered another device in the same area, Lex ripping it from the corner and hurling it to the floor, Bray then grinding it into pieces with his boot.

"I still think we'd better be careful about what we say," Bray cautioned. "I'm pretty sure that device is probably totally disabled but it's better to not take any chances."

"Agreed," Lex replied, eager to return to Tai San. And he left, as quickly as he arrived, giving a wave to Amber, who was sitting on the bed holding baby Jay, lulling him to sleep with a soft song.

Bray had gone to get Amber a hot chocolate from the automatic vending machine in the kitchen area and watched as Amber gently placed their sleeping baby in the second bed in the room.

"Are you okay?" Bray asked, handing Amber the cup of hot chocolate. She nodded but was clearly distressed by the latest events and explained that being reunited with other members of their tribe - it had all suddenly hit her. She had just felt so aware of her responsibility and what the people around her meant to her. They had become more than just a family. She cared enormously for them, loved them dearly and had always tried to do everything she could to look out for their interests.

But she was not just uneasy about whatever was planned but was scared and tried to hide her fear from the others, wishing not to fuel their own. In addition to feeling concerned about what future their baby might have in this unpredictable world.

"Everything will be okay," Bray reassured her, placing his arms around her to give her a comforting hug. "I promise you, somehow we'll all be okay. And don't forget, you're not on your own, you know. I've got some pretty broad shoulders – at least, I thought so, last time I checked," Bray smiled.

It made Amber smile too. He gave her a long, loving kiss. Amber clung to him, holding him tightly like she had never done before. She needed him by her side, to feel his strength and loving support, to face whatever the future might have in store for not only them and their son but all of their tribe, the Mall Rats.

CHAPTER SIXTEEN

Following her encounter with The Selector in his lodge by the lakeside, Ebony was taken on a journey by boat, Snake and his warriors transporting her across the water to The Cube. Snake refused to answer any of Ebony's questions about what would happen to her when they arrived at The Cube – and even what, or where exactly, it was.

She initially wondered if they meant to perhaps punish her in some way, if The Cube was a form of detention centre or worse, a place where she might be tortured, perhaps dealt with permanently. She remembered the cold and resentful atmosphere of her welcome when she first arrived at the airstrip compared to the adulation Amber and the Mall Rats had received ahead of her. She also remembered The Selector's mention of something about there being an 'audience' of some kind.

The boat arrived at a large island located further down the lake in an otherwise remote area – it was like they were in the middle of nowhere, the lake enveloped by nothing but forest and mountains all around.

The island itself was a few kilometres from the distant shoreline in all directions, Ebony reckoned, observing the lay of the land as the boat drew up by an old rotting pontoon. The water looked cold and uninviting and had to be deep that far out from the shore, Ebony believed. The island was well guarded, warriors lining its perimeter and saluting Snake in acknowledgement when the boat pulled in. The island was completely cut off and seemed like it was a world of its own.

The archaic pontoon was the first proof that there had clearly been some developments and a human presence on the island in the past and that the island wasn't an untouched wilderness.

Ebony was marched on foot along some narrow pathways which seemed like former cycling or walking treks in the woods during the adult era, branches protruding as the trees began to encroach on the old routes. A few benches, most of them in disrepair or broken, were scattered along the way.

They walked past some signposts lining the paths, the information on them fading but Ebony could still discern the text was describing the flora and fauna of the region. It must have been a nature reserve, Ebony assumed. It was certainly a place adults had visited, maybe even a holiday destination.

There were a few abandoned buildings, slowly being reclaimed by the natural world, the panes of glass of what had been windows cracked or missing as plants and trees grew, uncontrollably, slowly covering the human traces of what had once been. One of the ruins was an old boathouse. There were the remnants of an old wedding chapel, scarred by charred fire marks.

They finally arrived at The Cube. It was aptly named due to it being a perfectly square-shaped construction. Unlike the other buildings she had walked by, The Cube was in good order, the trees around it had been routinely cut back, keeping the forest at bay. All of its windows were intact and it was a large, rustic building, made of logs, located in a clearing, a barbeque area at the front.

Snake told Ebony to wait outside by the entrance. After a few minutes, the doors opened and a group emerged from within, being ushered out by several other guards. They seemed to be prisoners of some kind, mostly around Ebony's age. They followed each other in a line, stepping out from The Cube, deferentially proceeding behind another male, who, from his demeanour, carried some authority.

Ebony did a double-take. She recognized one who had been escorted outside.

"Hawk?"

It *was* him.

"Ebony?" Hawk replied, stunned to see her there.

Hawk had been the leader of The Eco Tribe, who had lived in the forest outside the city that had been the home to Ebony and the Mall Rats. He was an ally and good friend of the Mall Rats. Amber had once found sanctuary in the Eco camp. Even Ebony, on a temporary occasion. But she wouldn't have ever claimed Hawk was a friend – and was sure he wouldn't say the same of her. But Hawk was a familiar face, someone Ebony knew and respected as a survivor and leader of his tribe. Hawk meant well. He was sincere in his beliefs and desire to live peacefully with nature and by doing so, to make the world a better place. Ebony, otherwise alone and feeling threatened and uncertain of her fate, was pleased to see him.

"What are you doing here?" Ebony called out.

"The question is – what are *you* doing here?" a voice replied. And it didn't belong to Hawk but the male who had led Hawk and the prisoners.

He announced that he was known as The Gamesmaster and he was in charge of The Cube and everything that took place on the island.

He mentioned that some of the other contestants were gathered from the furthest reaches of the lands, as was Ebony, who had travelled some distance from her home to where they were. In case any of them were not fully aware of who she was, The Gamesmaster revealed Ebony had been chosen by The Selector himself to take part in The Cube.

In her city, her reputation spoke for herself. She was not only once a tribe leader but had been the leader of the entire city. And as some of them may have heard, it was true that she had even been connected with the legendary god Zoot and his Locos tribe for a time before choosing to follow her own path in life.

The other contestants would have to be careful of Ebony, The Gamesmaster warned them. She was cunning, ruthless, manipulative, devious, dishonest, untrustworthy, selfish and dangerous.

Ebony listened, in dismay at the character portrait The Gamesmaster was presenting of her, more like a character assassination, she felt.

"That's not all," Ebony added. "You forgot to mention that I'm actually a pretty nice person, once people get to know me."

"You will all decide for yourselves, and make of Ebony what you will," The Gamesmaster insisted to the other prisoners. Then he indicated to the guards. "She needs to be chipped and prepared for the next trial."

Ebony was injected with a biochip by a medic who had emerged from The Cube so that she could be tracked and her health monitored. The injection was painful and Ebony would have fought back had she not been held firmly in place by Snake and some of The Gamesmaster's guards.

She was then fitted with a chest harness, as were the other prisoners, including Hawk. Each harness contained miniature cameras, pointing outwards, to apparently record the viewpoint and activity of each of the competitors.

"Remember the rules of The Cube," The Gamesmaster addressed the assembly of contestants. "If you remove the camera or your harness, you are disqualified from the game. If you try to leave the island and escape, you are disqualified from the game. If you damage The Cube or any equipment, you will be disqualified from the game. If you disobey me or any of my staff, then you will automatically forfeit the game. And if you remove your biochip or try to take it out, you will immediately lose your place in the game."

"What happens - if we get disqualified?" Ebony asked, carefully. Perhaps that was something she might intentionally want to do, she was considering, if it meant she could leave the island and get out of whatever she was otherwise getting into.

Hawk and the other contestants were clearly exhausted, had cuts and bruises on their faces and by all accounts had been through some difficult experiences. Maybe no longer being in The Cube wouldn't be such a bad thing compared to the prospect of being here.

"Disqualification means you come last in the round. And whoever comes last is immediately Discarded," The Gamesmaster answered.

"Discarded? What does that mean?" Ebony asked, confused.

"It means that you would be cast away – and that your life would effectively be over. To be Discarded means to be permanently ejected. But if you are unworthy of The Creator, it would be a fate that is deserved. You would be expelled, extradited, exiled – and extremely unfortunate to ever be disqualified."

"What happens if I win?" Ebony enquired.

The Gamesmaster advised that she would be given one 'point' and at least be able to remain a contestant. Until the time she received ten points, in which case she would enter an initiation phase to eventually be brought in front of The Creator for further assessment.

"And if I lose?" Ebony asked.

"Then you might even remain a contestant for the rest of your life," The Gamesmaster smiled, but it was ice cold.

Ebony glanced again at her fellow contestants, the prisoners, and suspected that they had participated for some time given the state of them.

"You mean that we might have to hang around this place – forever?" Ebony asked.

"Until you die – yes," The Gamesmaster replied, indicating an area littered with crosses nearby, no doubt housing some of the past contestants.

Ebony wondered what the 'trials' were and how she would be competing against Hawk and the other contestants. She had found the notion of finishing last and being Discarded no longer held any appeal. She had to understand what was going on, find some way to ensure she wasn't the one who ended up being Discarded. Or staying in the game forever.

She liked the sound of achieving ten points and being brought in front of The Creator, which seemed like Ebony's only chance to truly survive, and determined to encounter whatever that might entail at that time.

The Gamesmaster revealed more rules. That they were all taking part in the 'trials of life' that The Creator had helped design. On the island, those who stayed at The Cube were simulating life, taking part in a living experiment. They had each been selected by The Selector because they possessed distinct traits and characteristics.

The Cube was a microcosm of society, life. A study of the interactions of people and an examination of the human species. The contestants would be exposed to a series of challenges, pushed to their limits. Each feat would bring out and show the best – and worst – of human nature. And humanity's interaction with nature itself. Those who would be watching the trials would be learning about adaptability, resourcefulness, the ability to improvise and inventiveness.

The contestants would be tested not only physically but mentally, morally, spiritually. And it would inspire the audience who would be watching. No doubt, to ensure they didn't become participants, Ebony speculated.

And she was partially right. The Cube also was a form of entertainment. As the sun set across the lands, farm workers and slaves toiling in the multitude of fields watched images being transmitted onto agricultural buildings and heard The Gamesmaster's voice blaring through speakers which reverberated around the lands and far beyond as if from the heavens above.

"Welcome, friends! To another episode of The Cube! Brought to you courtesy of The Creator. This evening we welcome a new contestant. Will she live? Or will she die? Will she stay in The Cube forever? Or will she be brought before The Creator? Only time will tell. So, don't miss a single episode. And don't forget you will be questioned by your protectors and masters in whatever region you might be located. So it's in your interests to pay attention to all the action you are about to witness unfold."

The vast crowds across the lands sat gazing almost hypnotically at the various images transmitted on the buildings as if they had long since become fully brainwashed and were now almost robotized. Without doubt though, each were gripped by the images they were watching and fascinated by The Gamesmaster's rhetoric booming through the speakers.

"Can we change who we are? Can we adapt? What does it say about our lives as individuals? And who we are as a society? A species?"

The Gamesmaster added that The Creator would be often observing and monitoring what went on in The Cube. The contestants should therefore feel honoured to have been selected and by their actions would deepen an understanding of what it meant to be human.

"Now, all of you watching in your home sectors will be well and truly aware of the nine contestants who you have seen each and every week. But sadly, Kala won't be joining us or indeed anyone else. He'll be staying on the island for all eternity. Why don't you join me now in welcoming Kala's replacement and our newest contestant – the one, the only, Ebony!"

The audience around the lands didn't applaud in any way whatsoever but just stared transfixed at the images showing Ebony faking a smile into the cameras.

Back on the island, Ebony braced herself as she watched a guard bring out ten knives from inside The Cube and placed them on top of a counter at the old barbeque area outside.

In the upper level of the building, a technician called out from the windows that all perimeter areas were standing by for streaming feeds from all the cameras.

"Then let the trial begin!" The Gamesmaster shouted into his headpiece microphone, occasionally glancing into the camera which followed him as he paced before the assembled contestants.

He urged each to take a knife from the counter, which they proceeded to do.

For a moment, Ebony instinctively felt that she would like to plunge the knife into The Gamesmaster's throat to give his intended audience an unexpected thrill. But for the time being at least, she realized that her own survival very much depended upon her playing along.

She clutched the handle of her knife tightly, her adrenalin racing. She was on edge and wondered if the ten of them were meant to fight each other and be forced to take part in some macabre contest, played out on camera.

Ebony started readying herself for imminent battle and was sizing up the other contestants, trying to gauge from their body language and attitude the type of people they might be, looking out for any weaknesses or vulnerabilities. She thought she might suggest to Hawk that the two of them team up against the others.

"Each of us and every living thing has but one life," The Gamesmaster began, commentating into his microphone. "We can only use our life once – and when it is over, it is gone forever. There is no backup. No safety net. The most important resource any being or species has is the fact that it is alive."

Ebony breathed out a nervous sigh, firing herself up, determined that she would preserve her life for at least another day, at whatever the cost. Which meant receiving one of the ten points The Gamesmaster had referred to earlier.

"Our new contestant, Ebony, had consciously forsaken the god Zoot and his teachings in her life. Will he now forsake her in return? In today's trial, our contestants must decide how they use the gift of life and choose well what they do with the limited time life provides. On the island, we have placed a food source. The winner is the one who finds it and knows how to use it best. The last-placed will be Discarded, unworthy of continuing in The Cube. You have one hour. Starting exactly from – now!"

The blare of a hooter emitted a deafening sound which reverberated through the darkness.

Ebony hesitated, wondering if The Gamesmaster would say anything more about what they had to do while Hawk and the other contestants raced away from the immediate area of The Cube, heading off in search of the food source they had been instructed to find.

"Is that it?" Ebony asked The Gamesmaster. "How do we know what it means to 'do well' in the trial?"

"Isn't that the same as in life?" The Gamesmaster replied. "How do you ever know who wins? There are no set rules in our day to day lives… But some people clearly emerge as the winners. Others, losers. And I'm sure our audience would agree that you're running out of valuable time, Ebony. So, I suggest you join your other contestants."

He indicated and Ebony rushed off in the direction Hawk and the others had taken. If anyone knew how to survive in the wilderness, apart from herself, it would be him, she reckoned. And since he had been in The Cube longer than she had, he might know more about precisely what was required of them in the trial.

The ten contestants were soon spread out and ran through the forested island, looking around for the goal of the trial.

Ebony soon caught up with Hawk, who had run towards the lake edge.

"Where are you going?" Ebony called out after him, breathlessly, as she struggled to keep up with his pace.

"The one place I'd hide something if I was them," Hawk called back.

"Them? Who?" Ebony enquired.

"Just follow me and you'll see," Hawk said, leading Ebony to the lakeside where the abandoned boat house was. And for a moment, Ebony was tempted to try and make good her escape by diving into the water. She was sure there was a good chance she could reach the other side of the lake. The presence of The Cube's guards by the lake, however, with broadcasting crews aiming their cameras from various vantage points, deterred her from making such an effort.

She followed Hawk into the boat house instead. He was searching through the canoes inside, looking under the tarpaulins that covered them.

"What exactly's going on here?" Ebony asked him, joining him in rummaging around the boat house.

"We'll talk later!" Hawk said urgently, focusing instead on the task at hand. "First, we've got to get through this trial!"

After a few minutes, it was clear that there was no food source placed in the boat house and time was running out – they were worried one of the other contestants might have found it by now and won the race.

Ebony suddenly had another idea. "If we're looking for a food source – what about the lake? I mean, unless the fish wanted to get out of here just as much as I do."

"No, that would be too obvious," Hawk said. "It's not the way these people think. I reckon we should head back to the barbeque area?"

Hawk ran off, with Ebony in pursuit, as fast as they could across the island towards the barbeque area. Ebony realized what he had in mind when she heard the sound of clucking nearby inside a small chicken coop made of wood and wired together. A rooster within called loudly to try and defend the two chickens that were inside it.

The Gamesmaster arrived, yelling into his headset microphone and smiling occasionally into the camera being held by a crew member of The Cube who joined him. "You're getting closer! Exciting! But you'd better hurry! Others, as in life, always seem to want what you might have. And the question is – will they get it!?"

He was referring to other contestants who had arrived, breathless from their journey so far, and they closed in towards the chicken coop. But Ebony waved her knife at them, yelling for them to back off.

"They're mine!" one contestant screamed out, struggling to get past Hawk and Ebony.

"We got here first!" Ebony shouted, lashing out with her knife and striking the contestant across the face. "These chickens are ours!"

"Oh, vicious!" The Gamesmaster screamed into his headset, casting a wink at the cameras. "I'm sure our audience are loving it!"

Hawk suggested Ebony take one end of the chicken coop and Hawk would grab hold of the other and that they bring the chickens back to The Cube.

Ebony had other ideas, however, and reached inside the coop, grabbing one of the chickens from inside, the chickens squawking under protest.

"What are you doing!?" Hawk implored, stunned by Ebony's actions.

But she knew exactly what she was doing. She remembered The Selector referring to her as putting a 'fox in with the chickens' – and if it was a case of kill or be killed, Ebony was willing to do whatever was required to be the one who survived.

"I know the best way to use this food source," Ebony said, preparing to deliver a blow with her knife to the chicken. "We cook it!"

"No!" Hawk bellowed, reaching out. "Do not take another life!"

"What are you Hawk? A hawk? Or a chicken?" Ebony yelled, slightly playing up to the surrounding cameras and The Gamesmaster watching intently.

In one swift motion, Ebony disposed of the chicken, decapitating its head while it squawked and flapped its wings, blood pouring from the carcass and over Ebony as she reached in the coop for the others. She was certain she had made a good impression and was intending to be the winner of the very first trial she had experienced in The Cube.

Hawk was joined though by another contestant who yanked Ebony away and accompanied Hawk, each side carrying the chicken coop towards the main Cube building, followed by the camera crew and Gamesmaster, as well as other contestants, including Ebony.

The hooter emitted a sustained blare again. Audiences across the lands watched their screens, entranced, while The Gamesmaster's voice boomed through all the various speakers.

"And we have a winner!" The Gamesmaster announced. "Today's trial is won by Hawk, with Nova in second place and our recent contestant, Ebony, in third."

Ebony couldn't believe that Hawk had supposedly won and wondered why Nova was in second place and she had only come in third. She, after all, had killed the chicken. But she then slowly realized the reasons as The Gamesmaster addressed the cameras.

"It's so interesting, the human species. We can certainly kill. Or we can end up being killed. In the chickens' case, Ebony was correct that she was providing a food source. But in so doing, she was denying an ongoing source of food. Being – eggs. If we feed the

951

chicken, the chicken can feed us. Possibly forever. But if we kill the chicken, then we might eat just for one night."

Ebony had been given credit for the chicken but the contestant who assisted Hawk was awarded second place, with Hawk coming in first, given that he had tried to prevent Ebony from killing the chicken. And he therefore was declared the overall winner.

Ebony hadn't made the impression she had hoped on The Gamesmaster, and presumably the audience, whoever they were. She knew she would have to learn to adapt – and quickly – if she was to have any hope of doing well on the island. Her mind began to race, calculating her best option, to make sure she survived and made it through the next episode of The Cube, which she knew would be advertised, judging by the images she noticed on the screens on her initial journey. No doubt, she would have other challenges coming very soon.

CHAPTER SEVENTEEN

"I would say, welcome home. Except you're not welcome. And this isn't your home anymore," Ved said, watching as Ram slowly came to, waking from the stun gun blast Ved had given him earlier.

Ellie and Jack were sitting at a table, Ram beside them, nearly falling off his chair as he regained consciousness, becoming aware of his surroundings just in time and stopping himself from crashing to the ground.

They were inside the factory that had once been the prime base of The Technos before Ram had vacated it, relocating their operations when he had originally conquered the city where Jack, Ellie and the rest of the Mall Rats had lived.

Ram shook his head, trying to rouse himself out of his dazed state – and he was slowly taking it all in, recognizing where he was again, a place full of many memories - as well as feeling concerned at being a prisoner, alongside Ellie and Jack, of his former protégé.

The room they were in was once an administrative office on the upper level of the factory. Looking around, Ram could see the guards who had accompanied Ved previously in their vehicle, now standing at the other end of the office, guarding the door from the inside, making sure it remained shut – and keeping Ram, Jack and Ellie in.

Ved was casually and adroitly spinning the stun gun in his hand like something out of the wild west days – and watching Ram intensely, in deliberation.

"I've been thinking what to do with the three of you," Ved commented.

"You could – just let us go?" Ellie mentioned hopefully.

"Why'd you blast me before?" Ram asked, rubbing his head in an attempt to ease the pounding sensation inside.

"Why'd you think?" Ved answered. "You've had it coming for a long time. And besides, you looked tired. I figured I'd give you a couple of hours of rest because you didn't seem that 'stunned' to see me. So, I thought I'd stun you myself," he added sarcastically. Coldly.

Ved felt he had every reason to be aggrieved. When he had been the Techno leader, Ram had become increasingly extreme in his behaviour, having been obsessed with realizing his creation of a virtual world, a 'paradise' that he could be connected to, living in it forever in an adapted cryogenic hibernation chamber he had recovered from Eagle Mountain. Several of those who had lived in the city had been sent away for daring to oppose Ram and his controlling regime – including Cloe, a Mall Rat who Ved had fallen in love with. Ram disapproved of Ved's relationship with Cloe, who was removed from the city, ending up in slave labour elsewhere.

Ved had done everything he could, while he was still a Techno, to try and find out exactly where. But he, too, eventually disappeared - Ram, becoming more unstable and paranoid, apparently instructing that Ved also be traded, exiled from The Technos.

"I'm different now. These two'll vouch for me. I've changed from who I was," Ram insisted.

"Some things never change," Ved scoffed, eyeing Ram mistrustfully.

Ram sat up in his chair, feeling his strength slowly returning. "Have you two been saying anything I need to know?" he asked Ellie and Jack, trying to get a sense of what may have happened while he had been asleep.

"Not much – we've just been 'reconnecting' with Ved," Jack said.

Jack and Ellie hadn't told Ved of their flight from the city and escape from the invaders. Ved had always been a loose cannon. He was brilliant at computers and was highly intelligent but had been fiery and often reacted hastily, taking action first before thinking things through. Cloe had managed to slowly 'tame' him as they got to know each other more. But Jack and Ellie were unsure what to expect from Ved now.

He was so unlike his older brother, Jay, who was strategic, so cool and level-headed. Ved had never been a close friend or ally of the Mall Rats, except for Cloe of course. But had never been an enemy either. He had interacted with the Mall Rats often in the past, their lives overlapping with his during the Techno regime, but it was always more about serving his own purposes than their own.

Neither Ellie nor Jack had talked about Jay yet. They had no idea if Ved was aware of what had happened to his brother – and the fact that Jay had died. If it turned out he didn't know, they were each determined to tell him, carefully, of Jay's loss. Ved deserved the truth. But Ved hadn't asked anything about Jay yet – he seemed more intent on finding out why the three of them were there and was especially focused on his ex-mentor, Ram.

Ellie and Jack didn't know what Ved was doing in the abandoned, former Techno base where Ram had once lived. While Ram had been unconscious, they hadn't properly answered any of the questions Ved had asked them. They wanted to make sure they could first trust him. There was no sign of their Mall Rat companion Cloe, who Jack initially hoped might be with Ved. For all they knew, Ved could be connected to the invaders, even The Collective, somehow – or might be a volatile and unpredictable, potential danger to themselves in his own right.

"What are you doing here, Ved?" Ram wondered.

"We're doing our own thing, whatever we want."

"Who's *we*?" Jack enquired.

Ved explained – now that Ram was awake – that he founded his own tribe, The Virts, in the industrial factory that was once the Techno's base. Ved was their leader and they were comprised of a few renegade, former members of The Technos, as well as some inhabitants of Ram's old town, having been 'strays' out on the streets, who had barely managed to survive before Ved had taken them in.

Ved and his tribe had spent their days living in virtual reality worlds powered by some of the powerful computers The Technos had left behind. Having gutted the lower levels of the factory when they had relocated, making sure it appeared abandoned and worthless, Ram had secreted away some of his hardware in the upper levels of the building, leaving them secure – a backup – for the day he might ever need them or make his return to his former town. Ved was aware of Ram's plan and had taken the factory and its functioning computers and equipment for himself.

"It's really good to see you, Ved. I didn't expect to see you again," Ram said.

"What? – you thought I'd be *deleted*? Is that it? You gave that order for me to be sent away, didn't you?"

"Yeah. From what Mega was telling me, you were no longer loyal. You'd started to turn on me."

"Of course I had," Ved agreed, not disputing it. "You probably thought I'd be taken away – cast out, like the rest of the trash."

Ram shrugged. "Maybe. So, how'd you survive – and make it here?"

"That's none of your business. All that's in the past. What I want to know is – what are *you* doing here right now? We tracked your drone. That's a fancy piece of hardware. Where'd you get it?"

"I was feeling nostalgic," Ram replied, improvising. "I wanted to show these two lovebirds my old home, the place where The Technos all began. The three of us have become quite close, you see." Ram further explained that he had found the drone in Eagle Mountain and taken it for himself.

It all sounded a bit fanciful and Ram's cagey demeanour didn't help dispel Ved's suspicion that Ram was concocting a story - which is exactly what he was doing - to try and cover the real reasons why he was there, along with Jack and Ellie.

Ved didn't buy it. He knew Ram better than that.

"You expect me to believe that you have teamed up with these two – and are here for - a bit of a vacation?" Ved doubted. "What - is this some sort of ménage à trois the three of you've got going? You got a thing for nerds, blondie – is that it?"

"Blondie yourself," Ellie retorted. "You're more blonde than I am anyway. And you obviously must be very stupid or you wouldn't even ask such a question."

"I like a girl with attitude," Ved remarked, smiling at Ellie's rebellious spirit, a bit like his own. "But you better watch your mouth."

"And you'd better watch yours," Jack said, rising off his chair and standing up to defend Ellie, getting in between her and Ved.

"Or what?" Ved snapped.

"Or – or - one of us in this room might regret what happens," Jack said awkwardly.

"And who'd you think that would be?" Ved stated, powering up his stun gun, making it obvious Jack would likely end up on the losing end of any dispute.

"We're not your enemies," Ellie insisted. "There's no need for this. We're no threat to you. And neither's Ram."

"Thank you, Ellie," Ram said. "See? – I've changed."

"Then prove it. Why don't you tell me what you're doing here," Ved urged. "No tricks. No lies. Just the truth."

"Fine," Ellie agreed.

There was no getting away from it. They felt they couldn't keep the truth from Ved any longer and they would have to tell him why they had ended up in Ram's former town, appearing to Ved as if from nowhere. The more they kept things at bay from Ved, it would only encourage his suspicion that they were not to be trusted. If they revealed everything they knew, Ved would understand their reason for being there due to their escape from the invaders – and he might even help them in their time of need, Jack hoped. They had nothing to lose and could only gain by co-operating with Ved and his tribe, rather than trying to forever stall his questioning of them.

"Maybe you can tell us a few things in return," Ellie suggested.

"Like what?"

"Like, doesn't Cloe mean anything to you? Don't tell me you've forgotten about her."

Ved looked stunned by Ellie's words, pained at the mere mention of Cloe's name. "I haven't forgotten anything."

Ellie and Jack asked Ved what he knew about what had happened to Cloe. She was their missing friend and Jack felt particularly protective of Cloe, who was younger than him. He had known her since the very day Amber and the others had walked into the mall where he had lived, before the Mall Rats had even been formed.

Jack cared about her, as did all the others in the tribe, and had watched Cloe grow from a shy, vulnerable young girl into a more confident and even sometimes rebellious teen, who had fallen in love with Ved.

Ved explained that in his last days as a Techno, he had become concerned by Ram's erratic behaviour and willingness to achieve his own goals, even at the cost of ruining the lives of innocent others. That was never the

Techno mission Ved and his brother, Jay, had signed up for when they first joined Ram.

Ved had done a deal with a slave trader, providing some stun weapons for his freedom. And it had been Ved's hope since then that he would cut all ties with his past life, except to hopefully track down Cloe eventually. Possibly even help many of the others who had been banished and transported by the Technos, including some of the Mall Rats among them.

However, Ved had been unable to discover Cloe's fate or whereabouts, as well as what had occurred to many of the prisoners who had been initially taken away. He believed they had been shipped offshore and had ended up in the possession of slave traders elsewhere, though he hadn't been able to find out exactly where.

He decided that the safest place to base himself was the former Techno headquarters where he used to live before Ram had permanently relocated from it in his invasion of the Mall Rats' city. Ved returned to the factory with some other Technos who had rebelled against Ram and together, they founded their own tribe, The Virts.

Using the powerful computers Ram had left behind at their old base, Ved had gone online on occasion, reaching out to other survivors of the new world in distant lands, seeing if there was any chance, even remote, that he could find out anything about Cloe, along with any other information which might be useful to help in this God-forsaken hell Ved's generation had inherited since the adults' demise.

Ved enquired if they knew how his brother was – and if Jay had ended up with Ebony or Amber, Ved having been aware that Jay felt attracted to them both the last time he had seen him in person. It was obvious to Ellie,

Jack and Ram that Ved didn't appear to know that his brother was no longer alive.

They told Ved the truth. Jay had died a hero, trying to defend the mall against The Guardian and Eloise's Collective forces, giving his life to save the lives of others, including Amber, who he had been in love with. He had been buried back in their home city and was finally at peace.

"I'm so sorry, Ved," Jack said.

"We're all sorry," Ram agreed. "Especially me. Jay was a great guy. We accomplished so much together."

Ved had listened, taking it all in. He was angry, sad, feeling a mixture of emotions, his eyes filled with tears. He couldn't believe it. Though they had often clashed, Jay had always been someone Ved looked up to. He had seemed so capable, adaptable. He was strong-willed, spirited. And Ved felt like in this crazy world they were all living in that Jay was almost invulnerable and would live forever.

But now, he had gone. Ved was overwhelmed by the news. It was the worst thing and the last thing he would have ever expected to hear from them.

"If there's anything we can do…" Ellie said softly, going over to Ved, offering to give him a hug, to try and help take away the pain somehow, to give him her support.

Jack watched, slightly jealous, and Ram was intrigued as he had never seen Ved display much emotion before. It wasn't needed working with computers, which were always usually trustworthy, so much more reliable than humans in Ram's view. At least most of the time.

Ved quickly regained some of his composure but was still clearly upset to hear of his brother's passing. He shared Jay's tenacity and resilience and insisted that Jack,

Ellie and Ram tell him more information, everything they knew, about those who were responsible for Jay's tragic death.

Honouring his request, they described to Ved all that they were aware of about The Collective. How Eloise, in alliance with The Guardian, had seized control over the city for a time, before being defeated by the Mall Rats, Jay losing his life in the process.

Ram revealed how he had been in contact with Kami, the mythical leader of The Collective, in the last days of the virus – and how he was *persona non grata*, a wanted man, as a result of defying The Collective's wishes when The Technos broke away and Ram had initially hoped to take over Eagle Mountain for himself. But ended up taking refuge in the small community of Liberty, with a huge price on his head.

Ved had heard rumours about the existence of The Collective from word of mouth in his time online but he didn't know the extent of their reach, power and activity.

Ved claimed he had certainly never had any contact or dealings, as far as he was aware, with anyone who was involved with The Collective. Whenever he had used Ram's old computers in the factory and gone online, he had always kept a low profile, being sure to mask his location through several layers of VPNs, encryption and secure protocols.

"We haven't bothered anyone else – and they haven't bothered us," Ved said. "But maybe all of that's about to change."

Ram was shocked when Ved expressed that he would make some initial approaches online to establish contact with The Collective.

"Are you completely out of your mind!?" Ram bellowed, upon hearing Ved's idea. "Why would you do such a thing?"

"For justice. You think I'm going to forget or forgive the things you did? And whatever happened to Jay? It's payback time, Ram."

If Ram hadn't have gone off on his extreme tangents during his reign over The Technos, Ved felt that Jay would still be alive. Ram had ruined everything. He was responsible for so much that had gone so wrong for so many. Because of him, Ved had lost not only his brother but the one girl he had ever truly cared about, Cloe.

"The Collective are welcome to take you," Ved threatened. "At least they can't be any worse than you. Maybe we should just tell them you're here, hand you in. I can't wait to see the look on your face the day they show up."

"You can't!" Ram said, panicked at the notion. "Try to think things through and be a bit more like your brother. Level-headed."

"Don't bring him into this!" Ved shouted.

"You can't just invite The Collective here!" Ellie implored, dreading the prospect. "You don't know what you're dealing with. None of us do."

"And what about us?" Jack said. "What have we ever done to you?"

"I don't owe you anything," Ved responded. "But from what you've told me – the Mall Rats mean something to The Collective..."

For Ved, it was simple. Jay would want Ved to live his life and to do what was important to him, as his brother had done in his own life. The Collective would no doubt give Ram the punishment he deserved.

And if they were as powerful and connected as he had been told they were meant to be, if he was able to trade over Jack and Ellie to them, The Collective might know information about some of the missing prisoners, some of whom could even be living in their lands. By exchanging two Mall Rats, Ved hoped he might get one back in return – Cloe. And receive a large bounty for his most valuable prisoner – Ram.

CHAPTER EIGHTEEN

Following the unexpected and joyful reunion with Tai San, Ryan and Alice, the Mall Rats eventually met The Selector, who arrived at the resort with a range of guards - along with a large retinue of servants and cooks laden with provisions. It was apparently to provide the 'guests' with a bountiful feast - a 'celebration'. A welcome to mark what would become a historic day.

The Mall Rats weren't quite sure what to expect when they met The Selector, given what Tai San, Alice and Ryan had revealed. But so far, he actually seemed quite charming in many ways when he initially arrived, complimenting them on finding the surveillance device originally discovered by Lex. Besides disabling the one found in Bray's room, the Mall Rats had checked and disabled other devices throughout the resort.

"I would expect nothing less," The Selector said. "Certainly not from Mall Rats. So, congratulations."

"Is that how you normally treat 'guests'?" Amber probed carefully. "By spying on them?"

"Not at all," The Selector replied. "The resort was once used as a medical facility and we wanted to monitor each patient, as well as hear what they were saying."

963

"Why – were they totally insane?" Alice scoffed, glaring at The Selector contemptuously. "Just like some others I've noticed around here?"

"Yes," The Selector replied matter-of-factly. "Totally insane. All sadly suffered extreme mental illnesses. And this was a holding facility prior to transporting them to the hospital we were building where they could have more intensive care."

That gave some of the Mall Rats a bit of reassurance with The Selector seemingly having some compassion, though they were still more than confused by The Selector's overly friendly demeanour. So far, they hadn't seen the other side - which had so stressed and tormented Tai San.

"What's your real set up here?" Bray had asked. "Are you part of a tribe?"

"In some ways," The Selector responded.

He was then met with an array of other questions and was evasive.

"If you don't mind, I'd prefer to answer any questions you might have on a tour I've arranged tomorrow. So that you can all see what we're trying to achieve. Believe me, you're in no danger. We just think we have very much in common and it might be in our best interests to form an alliance."

The Selector had even brought some cuddly toys, for Lottie and Brady to play with, along with a gaming system, for Sammy - but advised there would need to be some instruction on how to use it. So The Selector promised that he would personally arrange an expert from the technology team to spend time with Sammy.

The task at hand was to enjoy the banquet The Selector had arranged.

There was such a variety of food, the likes of which the Mall Rats hadn't experienced since the last days of the adults. There was every conceivable choice. With the focus more on vegetarianism and plant-based cuisine, Amber had noted, which confirmed Tai San's revelations that their 'host' seemed to be in tune with the natural world.

The impressive spread reminded Ryan of when he once dined with his parents at a top hotel buffet restaurant to celebrate his birthday. And the staff had almost thrown him out, given the amount that he had eaten.

The Mall Rats, without exception, were amazed by such an array of fresh produce – such a change from the tinned food and basic supplies they were more used to in their home city. The Selector had proudly announced that the agricultural unit had grown all of it and that it was totally organic, representing a gift from Mother Earth itself in return for all the good things The Creator had done for the world.

"This Creator – just exactly who is it? You?" Bray asked, mirroring the desire of all his fellow Mall Rats to find out more information.

The Selector became slightly agitated and breathed in slowly and exhaled, trying to remain calm, advising that he would prefer not to spoil the surprise all the guests would have when they would finally meet The Creator.

From the tone and slight vulnerability The Selector was displaying, the Mall Rats thought meeting The Creator wasn't some form of threat. But something The Selector seemed to sincerely hold in very high regard, almost reverence. And the thought of it seemed to overwhelm him somehow, resulting in him displaying nervous 'tics' as he told them that the Mall Rats' days of struggle were now over. They would be living in the land of plenty with the very real prospect of having a secure future. Just as long as they were under the care and protection of The Creator.

Amber was still somewhat reluctant to go along with The Selector's hospitality and had wondered what they were all supposed to be truly celebrating. What was the objective of it all? And how did the Mall Rats fit in? Whatever the plan, the Mall Rats clearly had some kind of status, currency, and were of value to The Selector in some way, somehow.

The Selector left them to enjoy their evening together. All the Mall Rats wondered if they would be free to talk and decided to still be careful of what they might say or do in case there were other devices like the surveillance ones which had been disabled.

Lex and Bray had doubted it though, having triple-checked, along with Alice and Ryan, areas of the resort. They even examined the toys The Selector had brought in case any devices had implants in them. But there was no sign.

Returning to the dining area, Lex speculated for a moment if the food could be poisoned or drugged. And if so, what a way to go it would be, Ryan had joked, to be taken out by a sumptuous buffet.

At least, it would be better than being hurt in other ways, he added, casting a glance at Salene. She wasn't sure if his comment really was aimed at her or was in fact born from an attempt at humour.

Bray pointed out that the food was there anyway and if they didn't use it, then it would go to waste. He was sure that it wasn't poisoned or drugged, given that he had offered some of the servants some helpings. They had prepared the banquet in the first place and seemed very appreciative to partake of any portions on offer.

This gave the Mall Rats a bit more confidence to enjoy the lavish feast and they all agreed that they may as well make the best of the situation, the first proper meal since they had been back at the mall.

They even invited the servants to join them. But sharing a portion was one thing. Joining the banquet, quite another, and the servants revealed that their duty was to serve.

Ryan was mostly quiet throughout. He sat at the furthest end of the banquet table away from Salene, who was beside May and clearly both enjoyed each other's company.

Lex had earlier tried to ease Ryan's obvious heartbreak, giving his best friend his full support and trying to cheer him up when they discussed the situation after a workout in the gym. Life could be cruel and unpredictable sometimes, Lex advised, but he just knew there would be someone special out there for Ryan – he deserved nothing less. Salene had to be literally crazy to not see the great qualities Ryan possessed, Lex insisted. Although he could see why she found May attractive, as indeed he had in the past.

Lex had always been Ryan's best and closest friend and had a way of understanding Ryan that nobody else did. The two of them had been through so much and usually shared many laughs as friends together.

Although Ryan appreciated Lex's words that night, it didn't help when he compared his own situation with Lex - who had seemingly got everything he ever wanted by reuniting with Tai San, whereas Ryan's dream of a life with Salene seemed finally over, and not by his choice. He wanted Salene to be happy – that had never changed. But he felt so lost and confused and didn't know what to do with himself now it seemed she wouldn't be a part of his future, certainly not romantically. Lex reminded Ryan that his first concern would be to ensure he has a future, given their current predicament.

After they had finished dining, the servants entered to clear the tables and were surprised when Amber and Trudy insisted the Mall Rats do most of the work, tidying up after themselves. Alice, May and Salene agreed, even Bray, who encouraged the servants to take as much food away with them as they could for their own personal use – there was more than enough left over for the Mall Rats.

The servants, however, were grateful for the offer but again refused. According to them, it was their honour to serve the Mall Rats as well as The Creator, none responding to the many probing questions the Mall Rats had as they tried to discover information. The servants refused to divulge any detail and went about their tasks in an almost robotized fashion. As if they could even be somehow brainwashed, Amber observed.

After the clean-up and the servants left, the Mall Rats returned to their rooms.

When May arrived a little later than Salene in their room, Salene was surprised to see May holding a bouquet of wild flowers.

"That's sweet. Are they for me?" she asked May.

"Not that you don't deserve them – but they're actually for me. Ryan picked them earlier in the day and just gave them to me before heading off to bed," May revealed. "I think he just wanted to show me that he's… well… 'cool' with everything."

"I feel so guilty," Salene said.

"Me too. He really is such a special guy. But you're special as well. And we've got to do what's right. For all of us," May tried to reassure Salene, as well as herself.

Salene nodded and sat on the edge of the bed, thinking about it all. May sat beside her and they kissed tentatively at first, then with increasing passion.

* * *

The following morning Commander Snake arrived with some guards, along with the medical unit, so that the Mall Rats could be microchipped. They had earlier assembled in the lobby and were waiting to be supposedly taken on the tour The Selector had advised would occur when he visited the night before.

"No way," Bray said, defiantly.

"Right," Lex agreed.

Amber, Tai San and the other Mall Rats encircled Sammy, Lottie and Brady, with Amber clinging to baby Jay while they all stole looks at the hypodermic needles the medical unit were unpacking while setting up other portable monitoring device equipment.

"I respect that," Snake said in admiration. "I can now see why you Mall Rats have something special. You really stick together, don't you?"

"Always," Amber replied.

The Selector arrived, having been summoned by Snake, who advised that the 'guests' were overly concerned about being microchipped.

"Understandable," The Selector said, with a slight tic. "If it's any comfort, I would like to reassure you that all in our society have biochips... including even myself. Along with The Creator. It's essential for your wellbeing and health."

The Selector instructed a medic to login to his own monitoring and he indicated various waveforms on the monitor displaying readings. Blood pressure. Pulse.

Temperature. Liver function. Kidneys. Seemingly everything in his body.

"You'll note that my pulse rate and blood pressure seems to have been raised because it's stressing me to think of the consequences of you not being chipped. It could be a decision you might one day come to regret," he added in a menacing tone.

"And why would that be?" Bray asked cautiously, suspiciously.

"I would have thought that question was rhetorical," The Selector replied. "What would you prefer? A pathogen to find its way into your bloodstream? I am sure those who became extinct due to the pandemic would have much preferred to have had the biochips."

"Believe me," The Selector tried to reassure them. "It's quite painless and really essential for our own health and wellbeing," he reiterated.

"I wouldn't exactly call it painless," Alice scoffed.

The Selector mentioned that he was aware of Tai San, Alice and Ryan's distress and had referred that to the Surgeon General. Her team were now using a different anaesthetic mixed in the initial injection to allow the biochip to be inserted with greater ease. And less pain.

"We're constantly adapting and evolving," The Selector told the Mall Rats. "It's the philosophy we have been taught by The Creator. The last thing I – or we – would ever want was for Tai San and the others to have had any suffering of any kind."

"That's not what Tai San said," Lex commented, resentfully. She had relayed details to Lex, who had been furious, as she knew he would be. But she had made him promise that he wouldn't do anything that would get himself into trouble or risk endangering any of the others. Lex would have to buck the habit of a lifetime

- and learn to control his temper. He vowed that he would wait for the right moment to get payback on The Selector for all the wrongs he had done to Tai San and no doubt many others.

Aware that he wasn't being too convincing, The Selector changed tack diplomatically.

"I realize this is all new to you. Perhaps we can delay the procedures until after your tour. And then you might come to realize the need to have them."

The Mall Rats exchanged cautious glances, wondering what it all meant and what their 'tour' might reveal.

* * *

The Mall Rats travelled again but in a bus this time compared to the driverless pods in which they were transported from the airstrip. The bus formed part of a convoy of military vehicles of guards who escorted the Mall Rats on the journey.

The Selector travelled in a driverless pod at the front of the convoy and the Mall Rats were aware that there were also small drones accompanying them as they sped through forests and began ascending a road leading up to the bordering mountains.

Before they left, The Selector explained that the heavy security presence was necessary for the Mall Rats' own protection. But also, that they were going into a highly classified area and The Selector himself, as well as their militia, needed to ensure that they themselves were not in any danger.

The region was overall safe but it was always possible that there could be nefarious forces, given the work which was being undertaken, resulting in rich and highly sought-after resources. Both natural. And human.

The Mall Rats speculated who any hostile forces might be and who The Selector was referring to. They had always wondered what had happened beyond their own city after the virus, who else might have survived in other regions. But they had never encountered any location such as the one in which the heavily guarded convoy was travelling.

The road passed the airstrip where they had arrived and the convoy turned off into a narrow and otherwise obscure side road cutting through the forest, travelling around winding corners, gradually ascending in altitude. The area was well-guarded through different check points - the convoy stopping, with the drones hovering above and guards in buildings scanning monitors displaying data, before advising that access was confirmed, waving the convoy on.

Wherever they were heading, the Mall Rats were starting to realize that this region wasn't only a classified area as The Selector advised. Whatever 'work' was occurring – it clearly was overly secretive and probably highly sought-after. All tensed at the prospects of what their tour might entail and what they might discover.

CHAPTER NINETEEN

When Ebony, Hawk and the other contestants had entered The Cube following the 'trial of life' involving the chickens, they had been allowed to take off their camera harnesses, which Ebony learned they had to wear only during the playing out of each particular feat they would be put through.

It didn't mean that they were no longer being watched, however, Ebony surmised. The Cube was wired up with several cameras throughout the building, in every room, Ebony spotting their lenses on the walls, in the ceilings of the cube shaped building in which Ebony and the contestants lived between each episode of the supposed game.

Ebony felt her chances of survival and doing well would be enhanced if she was able to ally herself with Hawk. He was resourceful and capable and she was determined to make an effort to bond with him and make amends for going against his wishes in the challenge with the chickens.

She explored the building, familiarizing herself with its surroundings. It was very basic, sparsely furnished and seemed to Ebony to have been built with some metallic-type elements, used either for heating the premises or for some reason to keep it cold. She wondered if it was a derivative of solar panel utilization. She resolved probably not because the building seemed to be air conditioned and extremely cold.

Ebony found where Hawk's room was and made a deal with the contestant who had been staying in the room next door to Hawk's. His name was Orin and Ebony said that in exchange for his room, she would give him half her food rations every day for the next week if he gave it up to her so she could stay in it instead. Orin gladly accepted the deal, happy to move to another room. And Ebony got her place, roosting as close to Hawk as she could.

The contestants met in the communal dining area for a meal. Ebony had honoured her agreement, giving up half her food ration to Orin. But she resolved that it wouldn't be on a permanent basis, just temporary. She had no plans on staying a prisoner in this building, which felt more like a refrigeration unit.

The building was well guarded, and the contestants were served food by servants - who seemed cold and detached, almost robotized, and didn't interact in any way whatsoever.

Being the most recent newcomer reminded Ebony of how it felt on her first day in a new school, in many ways, when she was growing up. Now, she sussed each contestant out, aware that they were certainly not potential school friends. But competitors, central to her very survival.

Each contestant certainly seemed to have gotten to know each other well and had obviously been participating in this strange 'game' for some time.

Ebony watched them interact, passing the time through convivial banter. Some of them, male and female, had more of a personal chemistry than others. There was some flirting going on. Ebony wondered if it was genuine or more an effort by those involved to create alliances, maybe exchanging favours, even sexual, in hope of a more comfortable life, or to render some form of advantage in the next challenges they would have to go through.

Nova seemed like a sassy chick and was clearly capable, having finished runner up in the 'trial'. She was spending a disproportionate amount of time around Hawk, Ebony observed. She could pick up the 'signals', read the body language all too well - even if Hawk, who Ebony knew to be shy and reserved - seemed oblivious to Nova's efforts to woo the former Eco Tribe leader. Ebony found it amusing and endearing. Soon, Nova would get the hint, Ebony was sure, and realize Hawk's passions were more about nature than romantic conquests. He was more into trees and squirrels than the birds and the bees.

Nova's dominance of Hawk's time in the evening eventually became a distraction and source of irritation for Ebony, however. The longer she stayed around Hawk, the more difficult it made it for Ebony to interact with him herself, one on one.

She got around it and was able to make Nova leave Hawk's side by suggesting to Orin that Nova was actually interested in *him* – going as far to lie, saying that Nova told Ebony that she really fancied Orin. Ebony suggested that if Orin came on to Nova that he definitely wouldn't have to spend many more nights alone in the room he had given up.

Orin thanked Ebony for her help and set out on his own course to woo Nova, hovering around her like a moth to a flame. It wasn't long before Nova left the dining area, hoping to get as far away as possible from Orin. She even slapped Orin before she left to go to her room, making it clear to him in no doubt she wasn't returning his romantic overtones, feeling he was creepy and exceeding personal boundaries. She left the vicinity, leaving Orin totally confused by matters.

Ebony gave Orin a commiserating shrug. But was more interested in getting to work on Hawk herself.

As the night unfolded, Hawk was unwilling to talk to Ebony, despite her efforts to engineer conversation with him and make a connection. He was standoffish, aloof, and to Ebony, it was clear he was upset because of her actions at the challenge.

It was likely also that he had some lingering suspicions of her due to her past misdeeds in the city – which she had no doubt confirmed, rather than dispelled, due to doing things her way and not co-operating in following Hawk's suggestion in the trial. She would have to show

Hawk that she was more than merely her bad reputation. And she felt she knew exactly how to do it.

She said she was truly sorry and asked for Hawk's forgiveness. She declared that she had merely panicked during the trial. If she could have lived it all over again, she would have done things Hawk's way and not taken the chicken's life. It was a mistake. And she promised she would learn, aware that Hawk and the Ecos were a peaceful tribe and that Hawk would view the killing of anything living to be sacrosanct to his inner beliefs.

Ebony's seemingly heartfelt and genuine apology got Hawk's attention and he listened as Ebony stated she had information about Amber, Trudy and the other Mall Rats - and wondered if she and Hawk could go somewhere in private. Away from the other contestants and hopefully, to anywhere in The Cube that wasn't under constant surveillance by the watching cameras, every moment of every day.

Hawk took the bait at Ebony's mention of the Mall Rats, his friends and allies, and he took Ebony to the bathroom on the ground floor. The toilet cubicles were the only place that apparently wasn't monitored – and to Ebony's bemusement, she stepped inside one of the cubicles, Hawk closing the door behind them.

"Well, this is cozy," Ebony said. There was hardly any room for the two of them in the toilet designed for one and it was a little awkward how close Hawk and she were together, in such tight physical proximity. "Mind if I take a seat?"

Ebony sat on the top of the toilet seat and kept her voice quiet, whispering as she conversed in case anyone else might overhear.

She explained what she had been through, as well as the others, since they had last encountered Hawk and the Ecos. She decided truth was the best currency and if she revealed nothing but the facts to Hawk, perhaps he would do the same to her in return. She relayed how she and the Mall Rats had initially fled from Mega's Technos, their first encounters with The Collective on the island they had ended up on after a period at sea… and their return to the city, as prisoners of Eloise and The Guardian's forces. The surprises and mysteries left behind by the adults they had been exposed to at Eagle Mountain… and the strange 'welcome' Ebony received at the airstrip prior to being transported to The Cube.

Hawk described how The Eco Tribe had fled deeper into the forest when they heard of the city being evacuated after Mega's fall from power. They had survived for months, living off the land, in harmony with nature, establishing a new camp. Then, one day, as if out of nowhere, the drones had appeared. They had been scouting the terrain north of the city where the Ecos had re-established themselves and discovered the Eco camp. Soon after, more drones arrived, the Eco tribe were captured and transported in much the same way as Ebony and the Mall Rats had seemingly experienced.

Hawk had been in The Cube for about a month, having previously been held in an abandoned town which had been used as a form of prison camp, a holding area.

Ebony asked more information about The Cube. Hawk revealed that as far as he could gather, everything the contestants were doing was being monitored. He had no idea who the audience were who viewed the episodes. But between each episode, the cameras recorded any and all activities that went on in the building housing the contestants. Arguments. Fights. Humour. Jealousy.

Love affairs. Cheating. Co-operation. Even in the dark as night vision cameras observed every bedroom.

Hawk, Ebony and the ever-changing roster who lived in The Cube had no option but to play out all their day to day routines and the drama that unfolded, as well as participate in each episode, which was streamed weekly to its intended audience.

The Cube seemed to be an endless living experiment in addition to a bizarre form of entertainment. And it was more than just a game or experiment. Their very lives were at stake.

Since he had arrived, Hawk had been the most successful of the current crop of contestants. He had won four events, including the most recent 'trial', but had a long way to go before winning ten of them and thereby going before The Creator to hopefully gain his freedom. From what Hawk knew, very few participants ever survived long enough to win and show they were worthy of being released.

"Then that's all the more reason why you and I should team up," Ebony suggested. "We're from the same home town. And like they say – birds of a feather should stick together."

Ebony and Hawk froze as they heard others entering the bathroom. Somebody went into the toilet cubicle beside them.

Another suddenly knocked on the door to the cubicle where Ebony and Hawk had been in conversation.

"How long are you going to be?" Nova asked from the other side, desperate to use the facilities.

"Not long -," Hawk answered, his voice overlapping with Ebony's own reply, the two of them speaking simultaneously - "Just a minute," Ebony said, at the same time.

"What are you *doing* in there?" Nova asked, curious and sounding jealous at what she thought Hawk and Ebony could be getting up to.

"Just going about our business," Ebony replied. "I got stuck in this cubicle and Hawk leapt over to try and help with the lock, it seems to be jammed."

Ebony and Hawk couldn't help but smile to each other at their predicament, feeling awkward, the two of them in the cubicle, and how it must have seemed.

"So, what do you say? We look out for each other?" Ebony asked Hawk, her voice in an undertone.

Hawk looked at Ebony for a moment, thinking it over, contemplating her offer.

"Okay," Hawk whispered back, showing his agreement. "But I'll be keeping both my eyes on you."

"Like a hawk?" Ebony queried, a twinkle in her eye. "Then I hope you like what you see."

Nova bashed on the door, trying to hurry them up.

She watched as Hawk stepped out of the cubicle, looking embarrassed to be seen exiting with Ebony, closely behind.

"Sorry about the wait," Ebony said mischievously to Nova as she passed. "But sometimes you gotta do what you gotta do. Even if it does result in getting stuck."

Nova scowled at Ebony, envying the obvious connection she had with Hawk.

Ebony smiled, jubilant at having secured an alliance, and followed Hawk out of the bathroom, the two of them going their separate ways to their own rooms.

Maybe she would continue to align herself with him, Ebony thought. Equally, he might have to watch his back – Ebony had already considered taking him out as a threat, recognizing him as a genuine competitor to her own chances of doing well in the 'trials'. And she resolved if she was forced to take part in any games in The Cube, then she was determined she would win - and was intent to play by her own rules.

CHAPTER TWENTY

The Mall Rats were astonished by the size and scale of the community that the convoy had arrived at. From a distance, none of them – or anyone else for that matter - would have ever known it was even there due to it being so well camouflaged by the forest of trees all around the lower mountain ranges.

It appeared to be at first glance a vast military-style facility from the adult era, the convoy driving past several buildings of various sizes arranged in different blocks. Most of them were prefabricated, temporary type of structures that were still standing in the same place the adults must have left them. The largest buildings were permanent constructions, looking like they were made of concrete, standing several floors high, that were either administration or perhaps barracks of some kind.

In the far distance, mammoth superstructures were visible, reminiscent of the type that held rockets or missiles in place, which caused all the Mall Rats confusion, as well as concern, as they gazed through the bus windows.

Continuing on through the facility, the Mall Rats became more and more aware of a human presence seemingly going about their routine tasks, oblivious to the passing convoy of vehicles.

Dozens of females in various stages of pregnancy were walking to and from the different buildings. Medics in decontamination suits and masks arrived in futuristic pod vehicles transporting what appeared to be farm workers or slaves to a building which seemed to be covered by a mammoth plastic dome – as if some kind of isolation chamber.

Workers were emptying freshly harvested produce from a variety of trucks, passing containers of wheat from one to another in chain gangs, delivering supplies to one of the larger outbuildings.

An intimidating column of militia ran past, jogging as if in some form of official exercise, given that they were accompanied by a commander, barking orders.

The overriding impression all the Mall Rats had though was that without exception the human presence seemed to totally ignore the passing convoy, with the same detached, robotized, even brainwashed type of demeanour as the servants they had encountered back at the resort.

The convoy finally stopped besides the largest building the Mall Rats had seen so far in the facility. Where they disembarked, to be met by The Selector, who approached from his driverless pod and indicated the area. "Welcome to Eden," he said, greeting them proudly, enthusiastically.

"What – is this place?" Bray wondered, unsure what to make of it all, mirroring and voicing the sentiments shared by all the Mall Rats.

"Everything you see here is because of The Creator," The Selector replied.

He indicated further up the elevation of the mountain ranges where the Mall Rats could see a road, winding up the higher ridges towards the shadows of a mammoth, perfectly symmetrical structure, rectangular in shape, in the far distance, which seemed to be embedded in a range of rocks, protruding out above the long tree line.

"The Creator is up there, overseeing all that goes on here. And everyone. Probably watching your arrival even now. So, don't forget to smile," The Selector said, wryly.

"Is *Kami* The Creator?" Amber asked directly, recalling Ram's recollection of what he knew about The Collective. "And are all these people part of The Collective tribe?"

The Selector again reminded the Mall Rats that all would be revealed and the task at hand was an initial tour of the facility.

As he showed them around, The Selector revealed Project Eden was a highly-classified, military-scientific installation established by the adults long before the pandemic even reached its peak. Over the years, a number of experiments were conducted across a range of scientific disciplines mostly focused on the environment and changing ecosystems. As the virus progressed and raised its havoc around the world, the military nature and capability of the facility was strengthened with extra personnel and equipment being brought there. And Project Eden became an increasingly important element in the adults' plans to counteract the spread of the virus so that humanity would endure.

The Mall Rats, including even Tai San, asked a range of questions. She still seemed to be very cautious of The Selector but was now seeing a different side and he seemed to be almost like a totally different person to the creepy one she had been used to back in the resort.

There were so many questions which even The Selector had, he advised. Especially concerning the virus - as he didn't know if the virus was due to a natural pathogen or was indeed the result of possibly bacterial warfare. Even a genetically engineered experiment gone disastrously wrong.

He added that he personally had other theories, wondering if it had emanated due to global warming, with the planet seemingly dying. And he was aware of other theories that Project Eden was a staging post for evacuation to another planet, to facilitate the continuation of the human species which otherwise would become extinct.

What he did know and what had been confirmed by his specialist team in the scientific and educational departments was that Project Eden was part of a top-secret co-ordinated effort by the governments of the international community under the United Nations' control, chosen because of its remote position as a repository for a variety of resources, which the Mall Rats would discover in due course on their tour.

In this new world, Project Eden would be considered in a historical context because The Creator had been able to access the resources left behind, including powerful and prototype next generation technology.

Eagle Mountain was a similar type of facility although Eden – so named after the mountain which dominated the ranges where it was located - possessed far more resources than Eagle Mountain ever did, The Selector claimed, Eagle Mountain being a lesser scale facility, albeit still an important one. As far as he could gather, there were other similar, highly secret places such as Eagle Mountain – but certainly nothing existed like Project Eden.

In the town where The Selector had grown up, when the virus peaked and the last of the adults died out, The Creator had made all the difference, enabling The Selector to administer various tribes which might have otherwise been ripped apart by civil warfare due to the struggle to survive among the various groups which had formed in the early days, after the adults' demise.

It was all so familiar to the Mall Rats, reminding them of what had happened in their own city when the tribes were first formed in the post-virus incarnation of civilization. The Locos, under their talismanic leader, Zoot, had waged a war for control with their rivals, The Demon Dogs, as well as the Roosters.

The Mall Rats had once been a scattered group of individuals but had come together to survive – and ironically had been the group which prospered most in the end, the other tribes fading into disarray while the Mall Rats increased their own influence, trying to make a difference for the better in the lives of those who lived in their city.

"You are to be commended," The Selector said, in admiration. "You achieved much without the assistance of The Creator, whereas for us… we would have destroyed each other. But because of The Creator – we lived. And we thrived."

With the resources and knowledge they could access from Eden, as well as their own capability, The Creator encouraged The Selector to seek collaboration among all the tribes in existence within their region. A spirit of interdependence, co-operation rather than conflict. They were stronger together than apart.

"Perhaps had you lived in the town where I did, rather than your own, you might have joined us then in those early days and become one of us," The Selector said wistfully. "Or had the tribes in your city chosen to work together rather than fight one another - maybe you would have created your very own collective, just like we did."

"So, you are The Collective?" Amber asked.

"I didn't say that, Amber – you did. I can't confirm or deny anything. Only The Creator can."

* * *

The Selector began his tour in the large building which he described as being not only a hospital and medical facility but a decontamination unit. So, all had to wear gowns, masks, place protective coverings over their shoes and hair, to protect themselves as well as the inhabitants.

It was an impressive facility. Spotlessly clean, well presented, full of beds and equipment, in a sterile environment, in much the same original condition as it had must have presumably been in the adult era. The Selector showed them around the premises, escorted by Snake and his guards, all of whom wore decontamination and germ proof masks. So, clearly there was a concern that possibly traces of the virus were still present in the area, the Mall Rats speculated.

They entered into the main ward which contained several patients, each being treated for a variety of conditions. All patients wore surgical gowns and were convalescing, many with medical drips in their arms, or hooked up to other medical equipment.

The ward was well stocked with so much futuristic looking equipment, the patients clearly were being treated with the best possible care by the staff, themselves wearing protective decontamination suits, their faces masked.

"Let me introduce you to The Surgeon General," The Selector said, as the Mall Rats crossed to a female, who was examining the wave monitors of a patient who was hooked up to tubes and life-preserving equipment.

"Surgeon General, I'd like you to meet our 'guests' – the Mall Rats," The Selector said.

The Surgeon General was about the same age as the older Mall Rats who exchanged nods and smiles while The Selector enquired on the condition of the patient, who was apparently still unconscious having had a lung transplant operation which The Surgeon General had conducted herself.

It had been a busy morning in the operating theatre so far, The Surgeon General advised, as she led The Selector and the Mall Rats to visit other beds, indicating various patients and describing their conditions. One young girl was lucky to be an early recipient of one of the biochips as it had picked up something unusual in her system. A growth on the girl's skin that had been cut out before it could spread. Another patient also had a tumour removed from her neck.

Once again, the Mall Rats were aware that the patients and even the medical teams seemed to totally ignore the Mall Rats - as if they were robotized and seemed absolutely detached.

During the tour, The Surgeon General advised that she and her team had been checking the initial data feeds of the biochips of Alice, Tai San and Ryan which brought to her attention that all really did need to immediately change their diets. They were suffering vitamin deficiencies and were not getting the right nutrients. This was understandable given their recent plight. But The Surgeon General was concerned about the B12 levels of Alice which were far too low, including her Iron deficiencies. And without treatment, Alice might be on a pathway of potential nerve damage in the future and at the worst case, even damage to her internal organs.

"You're welcome to be checked in right now for further evaluation," The Surgeon General offered.

"Not right now, thanks," Alice responded, with a slight smile. "I'd... er... prefer to get a second opinion."

Her remark made all the other Mall Rats smile as well, even The Surgeon General and The Selector. "As you wish," he stated to Alice.

The Selector thanked The Surgeon General and her team for the amazing work they were doing and she expressed how she was looking forward to being of service to the Mall Rats in the future.

Their next stop was to visit another wing of the hospital but they were able to remove their masks and decontamination attire given that the area housed The Creator's Repopulation Programme and wasn't as vulnerable as the surgery unit.

According to The Creator's estimates, humanity had lost over 95% of its population, The Selector revealed, either from the initial virus itself that wiped out the adults or from the effects thereafter arising from the collapse of society and all its infrastructure.

The pandemic had just been one of many crises that they had survived, the Mall Rats knew too well. They had seen firsthand how people had suffered and lives had been lost without clean drinking water, enough food.

Without medical facilities, the Mall Rats' home city had been the victim of a number of other diseases that followed in the wake of the virus. And without the adult civilization and its structures, age old diseases that used to be contained had instead run rampant, many of the young survivors outliving the virus but not the side effects that arose after the demise of the adults.

To ensure humanity's continued existence, The Creator had highlighted how important it was for society to be repopulated.

The Selector took them to view a prenatal division of the birthing programme where the Mall Rats saw several teenage girls in differing stages of pregnancy. They were attending a class and were being instructed on what foods to eat, how much rest they needed to have, the importance of breast-feeding which would provide their babies the most natural form of immunization and overall, every element they would experience from one trimester of their pregnancy to another.

Amber and especially Trudy remembered what they had been through when they had been pregnant as they viewed the class.

Trudy had only been a very young teenage mother during the height of the virus when society was collapsing all around her. She had found it an anguishing experience, every day an unbearable, stressful ordeal.

Before the Mall Rats had even been formed, Bray had been the only one to stand by her side for a time, giving her his support, Trudy carrying his brother Zoot's child. Without him, she would have been completely by herself and doubted if she or her baby would have ever made it due to how vulnerable and lost she had been. The Mall Rats, of course, played their part too, providing much needed support once the tribe was formed.

Trudy had given Amber 'tips' on what it was like to become a mother when Amber became pregnant. And had been there at the birth, helping to deliver Amber's baby. Now, as a fellow mother, Amber was struck by the level of organization and the practical skills being shown to the mothers-to-be in the class and she echoed Trudy's sentiments, feeling that such a programme could only help both mother and child and how she would have benefited from it herself.

There was one thing Amber was uncertain of, however.

"Who – and where - are the fathers?" she asked. She hadn't seen any males at all at the class.

"There are none," The Selector answered, matter-of-factly. "Not for this class. They are part of our artificial insemination programme."

The Mall Rats exchanged discreet, uneasy glances.

"Come on, there's plenty more for you to see," The Selector promised.

The Mall Rats were taken to a different part of Eden where there were several, smaller, prefabricated buildings in the block. The Selector mentioned that each one was a classroom – part of the education system The Creator had put in place for the youngest members of The Collective.

Observing from the outside, the Mall Rats could see children, around five or six years old, sitting together at long tables in one of the classes, their backs turned to the windows. They were focusing on an older boy, their 'teacher', who was writing down on a whiteboard different things that began with the letter C - including cat, catch, clock and Creator.

Lottie, Sammy and even Brady seemed intrigued – but the young students once again seemed oblivious to the presence of the visitors who entered the classroom, listening and watching the routine day unfold.

"In our society, everyone will learn to read and write," The Selector advised. "The history of the adult world will be taught and preserved for generations to come."

But as well as mathematics and literacy, children would learn a range of practical life skills that would aid their survival in the new world. They would study hygiene and how to maintain all aspects of their health, to grow food, how to cook it, self-defense, exercise, develop trade skills and how to negotiate in the new economy that was being created.

All would be encouraged to participate in sports, even the arts, poetry, music, drama. But most of all, the new generation would be encouraged to have a sense of compassion and to always consider the greater good. The Creator had affirmed it was also essential for them to have an awareness of their environment and the importance of living in harmony with the natural world.

If it was all as The Selector was telling them, then it was impressive, to say the least. All the Mall Rats agreed.

The Selector took the Mall Rats to another block of larger buildings, some apparently off-limits due to highly classified research concerning the advanced technology and hardware at Project Eden. But in one laboratory they were allowed to view a team hard at work, taking apart some of the solar panels which were the source of energy and power to Eden.

Several drones were having maintenance done and being serviced in another warehouse. Jack, a self-proclaimed 'geek', would have loved it there if he could only see it, the Mall Rats all agreed, realizing Jack would have been in his element amongst such high-tech equipment.

In another facility, the Mall Rats were intrigued to see cryogenic hibernation chambers like the one Ram had used during his Techno era. These units were empty and were some of the same ones that had been in Eagle Mountain, The Selector remarked. They had been transported to Eden for study and analysis, because the chambers had once contained adults inside. It was The Creator's hope that by understanding the technology, there might even be a distant chance to one day revive some of the adults they might find from their states of hibernation in cryogenic sleep in one of the other military compounds – or even other areas - the adults had established elsewhere to try somehow to survive.

The Selector then took the Mall Rats to a large building housing an auditorium that must have been used for lectures or presentations in the adult era, the Mall Rats speculated.

They were quickly and quietly ushered into the back rows, so as not to disturb the proceedings going on below on the main stage in the centre.

A male teenager was in the middle of the stage and was being cross-examined by some form of judicial council sitting in large chairs on a dais, appearing to be overseeing matters. The Selector confirmed them to be judge and jury, with the male being the subject of the trial, having been accused of stealing some of the food he had harvested for his own selfish use.

"Everyone engaged in a crime is entitled to due process and to be represented so that both sides of the story can be fairly presented. A prosecution and defence," The Selector whispered to the Mall Rats, sitting beside him in the back row, looking down at the proceedings.

The Selector indicated for Amber and the others to follow him, leaving the trial to continue.

"As you have seen, some of the things the adults created – medicine, science, a justice system - are still of great use to us," The Selector explained. "We have retained what is of value – adapting it to improve it - and abandoned that which is no longer part of The Creator's purpose."

Society was like a person, The Selector described. According to The Creator, each individual could change the things they needed to change about their lives — learning new skills, adjusting their behaviour, gaining knowledge, improving themselves in whatever way they wanted. The traits of an individual's life that were already working to their optimal state didn't need to be changed.

The Creator's view was that society as a whole was ordered according to the same principles. Under The Creator's supervision, some elements of the adult legacy would be retained — such as an education system, a security force. But these would be adapted over time, constantly improving with every changing nuance and alteration, so the 'organism' of society could reach its full potential.

The visiting delegation then walked to another area in the north end of the vast facility, passing a range of various buildings where drones were arriving and leaving, seemingly surveillance or security details.

The Mall Rats were led to an area of bordering fields, acres and acres ablaze with the varying colours of an abundance of flowers. The scent was intoxicating, totally overwhelming. There was a pathway in one field leading to a temple, around which several people sat in deep concentration, meditation almost - ignoring the approaching party of the Mall Rats, their guards and The Selector, who confirmed that the building was indeed a place of worship - and the fields represented an area of peace and tranquility for anyone needing time out to tune in to the natural world or their inner spirituality.

Heading inside the huge temple, the Mall Rats' footsteps echoed in the cavernous building and without exception, each Mall Rat stopped walking, frozen in trepidation as they noticed an assembly, mostly prostrate, before huge photographs of Zoot above a dais.

"What do you think you're playing at?" Bray snapped at The Selector, angry at not only seeing photos of his brother being exploited in such a way but that The Selector somehow was using Zoot, displaying that there was indeed another side to The Selector and his charm and all they had witnessed so far on their tour.

The sentiments were shared by all the Mall Rats, who were now becoming tense as the assembly turned, gazing at the Mall Rats in utter adulation and disbelief.

"It's them!" a voice cried out.

"It's the divine child! And the Supreme Mother!" another yelled excitedly.

The worshippers all erupted, ululating and chanting, which caused Brady to start crying, burying her head and clinging to her mother.

"Zoot! Zoot! Zoot!" the worshippers chanted, working themselves into a frenzy before then repeating in unison, "Mall Rats! Mall Rats! Mall Rats!" Then "Lex! Lex! Lex!"

Lex stole a careful look at The Selector, who smiled coldly. "You're a legend, Lex," he said. "But there's nothing to fear. Without you, there would be no god Zoot after all now living in the heavens and in the hearts of all those we realize so fervently follow his legacy."

The Mall Rats were totally confused and panicked about what it all meant, uncertain and feeling awkward, seemingly the centre of it all, like living gods themselves, amongst the fanatical worshippers.

"What's going on?" Amber pleaded. "Tell us – please!"

"You have seen everything now," The Selector said, raising his voice above the frenzied chanting. "And you are now ready to meet The Creator!"

CHAPTER TWENTY-ONE

It had been some time since Ram had been separated from Jack and Ellie, Ved having kept him in solitary confinement in a different office room to the one Jack and Ellie were being held in, upstairs in the factory that was the old Techno base. It was ironic, Ram thought, reflecting back to his former days spent there - when he had reigned supreme as leader of The Technos, Ved doing his every bidding.

Now, he was totally at Ved's mercy and powerless. How the tables had turned. But if Ram sensed any opportunity, he would try and change the balance once more in his favour.

Ram's room had been constantly guarded throughout the night by two Virts, standing at the door in the corridor, and they had been replaced the following morning by two others, taking turns on duty.

Ram had barely slept, his mind racing, thinking through various ways he might be able to persuade Ved not to contact The Collective – or to find some way to make good his escape from his former base. He had been panicked at the thought of what The Collective might do to him should Ved arrange some deal where Ram would be handed over to them.

Ved was operating in a meticulous manner and had no doubt cross-referenced the answers Ram had given to his earlier questions with those by Jack and Ellie in their separate room, to check if there were any inconsistencies. After all, Ram had trained Ved well. Just like in software, Ram abided by the rule in life that the 'devil was in the detail' and his former apprentice would no doubt be doing the same, which was confirmed when Ved arrived and was shown into the room by the guards.

"You look almost as tired as I feel," Ved said, with a yawn.

He explained how he had been up most of the night, going online and making some initial enquiries to find out if he could open a dialogue with The Collective. He claimed he had managed to contact someone who called himself The Broker and he had confirmed that Ram indeed was a wanted man by The Collective, with a huge price on his head.

The Broker said he would be able to arrange a transaction but Ved had declined the offer at first, he revealed to Ram. His preference was to keep his location and identity anonymous. And his options open. For now. Ved was going to bide his time rather than rush into anything. He would liaise with The Collective on his own terms and negotiate only from a position of strength.

Ved wanted to first see if The Collective knew anything about Cloe, or the others who had disappeared, and to learn how far they would be willing to trade in terms of resources, as well as information, in return for his co-operation and the possible exchange of Ram and the two Mall Rats in his possession. It was like conducting an auction, Ved said, relaying his strategy. The longer he held out, the more likely The Collective were to raise the ante and give him more of what he wanted.

"And the longer you dangle the threat of The Collective above our heads," Ram speculated, "the more you think we'll give you whatever information you're after."

"Exactly," Ved said. "It's a win-win for me."

"That's very clever," Ram smiled, admiring Ved's playing one side against the other. "You were always promising, and I knew you had potential. You've done well, Ved. You'd already learned mastery of machines long ago and you're now learning mastery of people. But don't forget, humans aren't like computers and can never be trusted."

"That's a gross understatement and an ironic one, coming from you," Ved sneered.

"Then what is it you want? Why are you here? To gloat? Is that it?" Ram asked, carefully.

"I guess, in truth, I'm looking for some kind of sign. A sense of which way to go with all this."

"Meaning?"

"Jack and Ellie seemed to have gone through a lot with you, Ram. As well as the other Mall Rats. So, maybe you have changed."

"See? What have you been talking to them about then?"

"Don't get ahead of yourself, Ram," Ved sighed despondently. "They still seem to be wary of you but equally they wouldn't be involved if there was the danger of you getting up to your old tricks."

"Exactly," Ram replied, sensing a break in Ved's ice-cold demeanour.

Ved revealed how he had been trying to live a new life in relative contentment, having everything he needed there at the old Techno base to survive for many years, living with The Virts in perfect fantasies - in virtual reality worlds.

He didn't ever expect or want Ram or Ellie and Jack to show up on his doorstep. But had interfered with the drone Ram, Ellie and Jack had been flying – having tracked its approach to the town. And had hacked it, rerouting its destination, forcing it to come down nearer to the factory, so they could investigate why it was in the area.

Now Ram was here, along with Jack and Ellie, Ved didn't know exactly what to do with them, he confessed. He was in the odd and uncomfortable situation of not really having anyone he could talk to or get advice from concerning matters of great importance, rather than anything trivial. The other Virts were friends and fun to be with on a companionship level. But Ved no longer had anyone he could look up to, who he respected, to help him figure out what he should do. In the past, he would have talked things through with Jay. Cloe had also given him support and different perspectives. And in a previous chapter in his life, Ram himself would be the one Ved would have gone to in order to get the answers he needed or wisdom about whatever problems he was confronting.

And here he was, just like old times, explaining the troubles he had to overcome, to Ram once more. Ved was alone, he admitted, and facing a dilemma. There were three options – he could release them, let them stay with him – or proceed with his attempts to use Ram, Jack and Ellie as bargaining chips.

"I understand – maybe more than anyone," Ram said. "Being a leader isn't easy. Sometimes, it's difficult to know what to do. And even leaders make mistakes for all the best intentions. I know I certainly did," Ram said, emphasizing his last line, hoping somehow that it might lead to Ved being reassured.

"Now, this is something new. You're saying even a self-proclaimed genius like you, someone who demanded perfection of everyone else, could be fallible?" Ved asked, slightly amused.

"Yeah. I screwed up from time to time. I'm sorry about the things I did. Really. And I'm sorry about what happened to Jay. He was a good man. And I know the apple doesn't fall far from the tree. You always meant well, too."

Compared to the anger and resentment he had shown the day before when he had first re-encountered Ram and learned of his brother's passing, Ved was more calm and had been thinking things over, in a period of self-reflection.

"What would you do if you were me? If our situation was reversed?" Ved enquired.

"I'd be asking you the same question. Getting some advice. Trying to figure out what's the best thing to do. But know this - if you thought you'd seen it bad before when I was at my worst – and my low points – The Collective are another thing entirely. They're the greatest threat to us all. And they've got more power than anyone."

"Power? That's an interesting concept," Ved reflected, prior to standing up and crossing to the exit, knocking on the door, the Virts opening up from the other side.

"Thanks for the advice, Ram. You've helped me clarify my thinking. It won't hurt for me to have a little chat with The Collective. And who knows? Maybe they and I can come to some arrangement."

Ram glared at Ved, sensing he had been double-crossed, which caused Ved to smile menacingly.

"So interesting, isn't it? When the apprentice becomes the master!" Ved snapped, before slamming the door shut, leaving Ram clutching his head in his hands as he heard the door lock.

* * *

Ellie sat on the floor, leaning her head back against the wall of the office she was being kept in at the factory with Jack. She was restless – and furious – at being held captive by Ved.

Jack folded up another piece of paper, an old invoice from a folder left in one of the filing cabinets from the adult times. To pass the time – and in an attempt to take his mind off things and ease his nerves – he had been making paper airplanes and watching them glide across to the other side of the room.

"He shoots-" Jack said, taking aim at the wastepaper bin – and releasing it. "And he-" he watched as the paper plane took a nosedive, crashing headfirst in a heap on the floor in the middle of the office. "And he misses."

It was metaphorical of what they had experienced in recent days, Jack thought, since the city was invaded. Nothing seemed to be going right for them and everything felt like it was wrong, their experiences with Ved being the most recent difficulty life had thrown at them.

They just had to be patient and not give up hope, they knew. Jack and Ellie had a mostly sleepless night, discussing their plight, as well as thinking what might have happened to Lex and the Mall Rats who had been taken away.

"How are you two 'Rats' doing?" Ved asked, when he entered the office, the Virts guarding the door letting him in. "Can I get you a piece of cheese or whatever else it is Mall Rats like to eat?"

"Funny. How do you think we're doing?" Ellie scolded. "You have no right to keep us locked up in here."

"I know, I agree," Ved said. "And that's why I'm here. To talk. I'm not here for an argument and we don't need to have a falling out."

"It's a bit late for that, don't you think?" Ellie stated.

Ved told them he had been thinking overnight and that in recognizing the friendship they had both had with their fellow Mall Rat, Cloe – and how they had got on and co-operated with his brother against The Technos - that there was no need for them and him to be enemies.

He believed, after much reflection, that if anyone was to be given over to The Collective, then it would deservedly be Ram – and not the Mall Rats. Ved thought he would be able to get what he needed from The Collective – information about Cloe and technological resources – without necessarily having to give up Ellie and Jack in the bargain. If they would co-operate with him and give him the information he was after, he was thinking he would let them go on their way.

Specifically, Ved wanted more details on the invasion forces they had seen taking over their city, how many of their approximate number were at the airport where Jack and Ellie had fled from, with Ram, and whatever firepower and resources they seemed to have at their disposal. He wondered how many drones they had seen, what their capabilities appeared to be.

Ved was so curious about it all, he clarified, because if he did come to an agreement with The Collective, he planned to meet them back in the city that used to be home to the Mall Rats. His intention was to get the drone they had travelled in repaired and in working order and he would use that to transport Ram to The Collective, exchanging him over at the airport they had occupied. In the event of any double-cross by The Collective, Ved wanted to come up with a contingency strategy and make sure that he and the other Virts would be able to safely get away if they had to.

All Ellie and Jack had to do was answer his questions and then Ved was willing to set them free.

"So – what do you say?"

"I say – you can get stuffed," Ellie said.

"What Ellie means is-" Jack said, trying to diplomatically defuse matters, "… is that we need time to think about it."

"I mean exactly what I said," Ellie insisted. "You can get stuffed. If you're even contemplating doing some sort of a deal with whoever invaded the city, after what they did – then you're no better than they are."

Jack agreed with Ellie's stance though he stated it in a far less provocative manner. He said that Ved would be playing with fire if he tried to work out a trade with The Collective. After all, Jack reminded him, it was The Collective who were responsible for Jay's death. Had they not previously taken over the mall under Eloise and her Legion warriors, along with The Guardian and his Zootists, Jay would surely have still been alive.

"If you've still got a grudge against Ram – and I wouldn't blame you – you have to find a way to let go of it," Jack suggested. "Otherwise you're still living in the past. If you want revenge for what happened to Jay – you won't get it by handing Ram over. You should be trying to fight against The Collective, not collaborate with them."

Ellie agreed and reiterated that Ram had changed. Why else did Ved think that the two of them would have been with him? It was because they were desperate. The Collective was their common enemy. Ram wasn't the same Ram that Ved had known from his Techno days.

"Is he a saint? No," Ellie said. "Is Ram still a bit weird? Yes. Oh, yeah. But he also might be the best shot we have right now at standing up against The Collective. And you've got him locked away. You know what Ram's abilities are and what he's capable of."

"I do – why do you think I've got him locked up? He's dangerous."

Jack wondered if Ved had considered what Jay or Cloe would have wanted him to do. Did he think they would have been happy with the course of action he was considering pursuing?

"I came here for information from you. Don't try and turn it into some guilt trip," Ved said.

"Ram's not the only one who's changed, it seems," Ellie observed. "So have you. But for the worse. I never knew what Cloe saw in you in the first place – but even if you did manage to find her, she'd be ashamed of who you've become, and I bet she wouldn't want anything to do with you."

That stung Ved. He reeled at Ellie's barb.

"We'll see about that," Ved warned. "Don't get above yourselves and think you're indispensable. That you can say anything without there being consequences. I tried to be nice. At least *I* tried."

Ved said that once he had got the drone they had travelled in working again and back up in the air, he might just bring Ellie and Jack along with him for the ride in the event of any handing over of Ram to The Collective. They would be his insurance policy, extra bargaining chips. If he had to, he would be willing to give them up depending on the situation.

He wanted to see things for himself, he insisted, instead of relying on what Ram or Ellie and Jack told him about who The Collective were. He didn't know if they were the threat that the three of them were presenting The Collective to be.

He couldn't just let Ram leave and go on his way, just like that. For all Ved knew, Ram was potentially the biggest danger, as he had once been before. A likely menace in waiting to Ved and so many others, for all that Ellie and Jack were telling him Ram had changed. Ram might have tricked them into believing he was different, Ved claimed. Had they ever thought about that? Maybe the 'new Ram' was nothing but a pretense, a front, another of Ram's many tricks.

The only one who knew what Ram was truly after was Ram himself, Ved claimed. He knew enough about Ram to never forget it. Had Jack and Ellie considered *why* Ram was public enemy number one to The Collective?

Maybe it was with good reason, Ved proposed. Wasn't it at all possible, Ved wondered, that The Collective were actually a positive force for good? And that they were enemies of Ram because they knew too well that he was the reverse, a risk to society?

Ved didn't know why the city the Mall Rats lived in had been invaded – or why the rest of their tribe had been taken, from what Ellie and Jack had relayed to him.

In this mixed-up world they all inhabited, the one thing Ved had learned was that things were often not what they seemed at first. He wouldn't be hasty or impulsive anymore. He had once thought that Ram, through The Technos, would be a benefit to the world but discovered in the end that Ram was the opposite. The others might think The Collective were a hostile threat now but maybe time would show that they were the opposite and perhaps the best thing that had ever happened to them.

He would discover for himself exactly who The Collective were and what their goals were – and the only way he could do that was by starting to open up a line of communication with them.

It was Ved's life to lead, not anyone else's. He would make up his own mind about The Collective and what to do with Ram, Jack and Ellie.

CHAPTER TWENTY-TWO

The heavily guarded convoy ascended up the winding road to the higher mountain ridges above.

Before departing on their journey, following the initial tour, The Selector said he could understand the confusion and unease about the religious zealots worshipping Zoot, reassuring the Mall Rats that The Creator would explain everything and then they might fully understand.

The convoy arrived at the mammoth, perfectly symmetrical shaped structure they had seen from the distance when they arrived in Eden, now way down below.

It was a huge structure, dwarfing the tree lines of tall pines beneath, and was shaped like an immense rectangle standing on its side. From the outside, it looked like it extended deep into the rocks, as if it had been wedged in by some giant, most of it appearing merged into the mountains itself, becoming one, the front section exposed and jutting out from the sides of the mountain ridges onto an elevated plateau. It seemed strangely out of place, an almost alien presence, contrasting with the natural world otherwise all around, as if nature and humanity had somehow collided in a profound way.

The superstructure was known as The Vault, The Selector advised. Its gigantic, metallic twin doors had a strong security presence on either side, protecting what was within.

The Selector led the Mall Rats inside and as they entered The Vault, all were astonished by the sheer scale of it, the structure containing a vast labyrinth of tunnels and corridors which ran deep inside, feeling as if they were going into the heart of the mountains.

In every corridor they passed were row upon row of shelves lining the walls, stacked from the floor to the ceiling. On each shelf were a myriad of assorted jars and containers of different sizes. They were each labelled and had a series of statistics printed on them, information about what they were storing.

The Vault was a remarkable feat, The Selector stated as he guided them through one corridor after another. It had originated in adult times as an international project involving over 180 countries and had been purpose-built to archive millions of seeds and samples representing plant species from all around the world. Some had nicknamed it *The Doomsday Vault* and it existed as a living museum, a depository which would enable plant species to be preserved and returned to the wild in future for cultivation in the event of any environmental cataclysm or ecological change which might threaten the extinction of the plants.

There were other vaults and 'seed banks' housing potentially endangered plant life from different countries, The Selector declared.

Under the guidance of The Creator, the agricultural team had used some of the seeds to repopulate the grain and wheat, contributing to the flourishing food production they had been able to establish in their lands, which had otherwise shown signs of becoming extinct following the demise of the adults.

The corridors of The Vault were cold, deliberately so, to assist the preservation of the seeds, along with all else The Vault housed – but as the assembly advanced, deeper into the maze of tunnels, the temperature began to noticeably increase, The Selector leading them to a residential quarters, which was once used by the adults who had lived within the complex before the virus.

When the community of Project Eden had taken over the region, they had been able to access highly classified levels within The Vault. In these lower levels near the accommodation unit, they had found advanced technology, computers and information left behind by the adults who inhabited the facility - which they had now harnessed for their own advantage to achieve The Creator's vision.

* * *

The Creator definitely had to be a person, most of the Mall Rats contemplated.

Recalling all Ram revealed and the Mall Rats' past visit to Eagle Mountain, Amber asked, "Does the *K.A.M.I* computer system figure in all this?"

"I'm sure The Creator will explain," The Selector replied.

If The Creator was based in the accommodation wing of The Vault the Mall Rats were now entering, whoever The Creator was then it most certainly wasn't a computer system but had to be human, judging by the furnishings.

It was sparse. The design was modern, functional, and minimalistic and all around the walls were banks of monitors displaying all kinds of animals and insects, plants and other items from the natural world.

It seemed like a relatively unassuming place for the enigmatic leader, who clearly had denied themselves any of the finer luxuries in life.

The Selector led the Mall Rats past more guards, standing either side of doors, deeper into the inner sanctum of The Creator.

They had entered into the prime living area, which again was sparsely furnished with just a couple of couches, a dining table, a few wooden chairs. Several paintings were on the walls, mostly displaying animals and various insects. The younger members of the Mall Rats stared in wonder at an illustration of the long extinct Dodo bird, an idealized painting of a Plesiosaurus swimming in the oceans of the dinosaur age, an image of a buffalo herd on the plains.

The older Mall Rats were more interested in a black and white Victorian era photograph displaying the stern expression of Charles Darwin.

The inner sanctum was dimly lit, keeping any illumination at a minimal level as if conserving power.

Suddenly, a soft voice could be heard. "Welcome."

The Mall Rats tensed, sensing movement in the deep shadows.

Bray held his son in his arms and instinctively clutched him closer, shielding him protectively. Brady clung to Trudy. The Mall Rats relaxed a little when they finally saw the source of the voice, who indicated to The Selector. "That will be all for now, Selector."

The Selector nodded humbly, obediently, then left.

"Who are you?" Tai San asked cautiously.

"Are you *Kami*?" Amber asked.

"Yes," the voice replied. It belonged to a female, emerging from the shadows and squinting her eyes slightly, adjusting her vision to the still dimly-lit light. "I have been known as Kami. And many other names. To some, I am The Creator. To others, I am their leader.

I was Camille to my mother. To my grandmother, I was simply 'Cami'."

Cami turned the lighting level up slightly through a control on the wall and stood, staring at the Mall Rats before her. Almost in awe.

Seeing her clearly for the first time, Cami was about the same age as the elder Mall Rats. Slight in stature, she wore glasses, the light partly reflecting off the lenses, and a simple white canvas linen dress extending to just above her knees, which looked like it was homemade rather than from a store in the adult times, the stitching and material uneven, not well-fitted. Her feet were uncovered, her legs bare, her arms exposed through her sleeveless dress. Around one of her ankles was a band into which leaves from different plants had been inserted by the stems, ranging from light to dark green.

The Mall Rats were struck by Cami's unusual hair. The colour seemed to interweave the entire colour spectrum, streaked almost like a rainbow, with loose curls hanging down over her shoulders and the side of her face. Small green leaves were woven together into a headpiece around the top of her head, with some feathers fastened into her hair at the back, along with a single pink and white rose.

Cami had no make-up on, wore no earrings, no jewelry but did have a rudimentary, homemade-looking necklace. Instead of conventional glistening charms or finer-grade metals, it was a simple wire through which some smaller, old computer parts had been threaded, a CPU dangling from the necklace, alongside pieces of memory chips. On her left shoulder, a small black tattoo silhouette of a full moon was visible, on her right shoulder, a contrasting shape representing the sun.

What was most striking though was that Cami had a condition known as heterochromia – where she had different coloured eyes. One was deep brown and the other appeared to be emerald green, her eyes intensely studying the Mall Rats as she slowly approached.

"What do you want with us?" Lex asked bluntly.

It was almost like Cami didn't hear the question, she was so absorbed, deeply focused, gazing intently at each Mall Rat, casting a slight smile and wave to the younger members of the party. Brady waved back shyly but Lottie and Sammy moved closer to Alice, feeling more secure under her protection.

"You're exactly as I pictured you to be," Cami said to them, reaching out, taking May and Salene by complete surprise, giving them a loving hug, followed by Trudy, Tai San, Alice, then Amber, all confused to be so embraced as if she was a long cherished, dear friend.

She knuckle-bumped Ryan, then Lex and Bray.

"We – we'd like some answers," Bray said, mystified, along with the others and unsure of what entirely was going on.

"Of course you would. That's what makes you who you are."

"So why have we been brought here?" Amber enquired. "What's all 'this' about?"

"It's all about you. All of you," Cami said, gazing fondly at all the Mall Rats. "Your combined traits and qualities have created something greater than any of you could have realized had you attempted to do so alone. You have adapted and evolved and achieved so much. You defeated The Chosen, you resisted The Technos. You tried to create a better, fairer future. And without ever knowing, you even created a legend. The legend of Zoot."

"Is that what this is about?" Trudy asked warily, clutching Brady to her, closer. After all she experienced with The Guardian, Trudy couldn't bear the thought of a twisted representation of Zoot playing a part in her life or that of her daughter again.

"I see before me Zoot's child," Cami said, giving another friendly smile to Brady. "And the mother of that child by her side. I see Zoot's brother" – she looked at Bray – "and his son - and the mother who gave birth to Zoot's nephew," Cami said, acknowledging Amber.

"I see the other members of the Mall Rats who have conquered so many challenges," Cami continued, as she glanced at May, Salene, Ryan, Tai San, and Alice, who scoffed.

"But the one person I don't see – is my sister, Ellie. Or her boyfriend, Jack."

"I am as disappointed as you, Alice, that they're not with us here today," Cami responded. "I can assure you."

"Well, I can assure you if anything happens to Ellie, then I'll personally break your pretty little face!"

"I'm sure you would," Cami replied. "I know how close you and Ellie have been. And I hope Ellie and Jack will be joining us all very soon."

"How? How do you know so much, Cami?" Amber asked.

"You're all legends in your own right. Especially you, Lex. The one who brought about the death of Zoot."

"It was an accident," Lex stated, defensively, aware that he could have a huge price on his head from any followers of Zoot if they discovered he was responsible for taking him out. "I didn't mean it to happen."

"But it did happen. Should Lex be punished? Put on trial for ending another life? Or celebrated? Because without that one deed, that act of creation, none of what followed would have ever happened. Centuries from now, should humanity live that long, your name, Lex, will be in the history books, along with the god Zoot – names which will live in perpetuity throughout the coming ages."

"We saw what was happening at your 'temple' – the worshippers," Bray commented disdainfully. "My brother was messed up. Lost. He wasn't some 'God'. You can't be saying that you honestly believe any of that stuff?"

"Of course not. But it has a power in it, nonetheless. And others do believe. You've seen it. If used properly, your brother's legacy can be the greatest that any of us could ever wish for. And can do so much good and make such a difference in this troubled world. Besides, everyone needs something – or someone – to believe in."

Ryan cast a glance at Salene, then considered Cami again, gripped, as were all the Mall Rats, by her rhetoric.

"There are many forms of belief, of course," Cami continued. "Religion, spirituality, the natural world, animal life, our fellow human species. Whatever can bring some meaning and purpose to our lives. So, your brother didn't die in vain, Bray. It can be a good thing, if used properly."

"Or the worst thing imaginable, if it's exploited. We've all seen what can happen," Bray replied.

"Then adapt and evolve. Mould it. Use it for something better. That's what we're doing here. From all that I know about you – and the actions you've done that speak for themselves – you Mall Rats and I... have so much in common. We are kindred spirits."

"Somehow, I don't think so," Tai San replied softly.

The Mall Rats listened as Cami declared her belief that there was a chance, if they worked together, that they could potentially save humanity from falling into a new and dangerous Dark Ages and instead of anarchy, create a new beginning, a society based on law, order and civilized principles.

Cami explained how she wanted to not only save lives – but to change life itself, to eliminate existential threats.

She believed that humanity had forgotten the importance of its close connection and co-existence with the natural world. The ecosystems, how all elements of the planet, including the human species, were interconnected and depended on each other.

The 'virus' itself that wiped out the adults was, Cami felt, a consequence of humanity's damage to its environment. She didn't believe any conspiracy theories, that there were other reasons for the demise of the adults, but did feel that the governments of the world at the time had not been entirely forthcoming with any exact detail. Which was understandable, so as not to cause mass panic when the young people were all evacuated.

Cami believed accelerated implications of global warming had released micro-organisms that had been buried away for millennia, underneath the ice. The 'virus' was a mutated version of one of these reawakened, long-dormant pathogens. The past had literally come back to haunt the present due to the permafrost and polar ice caps melting as a result of the damage the previous generations had done to the planet.

Tai San was intrigued by the theory, being the one Mall Rat especially in tune with the natural world and Mother Earth.

"How can you be so sure?" Tai San asked.

"I'm not entirely, I have to admit," Cami said. "But my thesis is not only borne from my own research but my late mother's."

Cami explained that her mother was a member of the scientific team who used to be based at The Vault. She was an evolutionary biologist and loved life – all living things. And was greatly respected throughout the world, even winning a Nobel Prize for her research.

She was one of the brightest minds and along with other key members of society, had been shortlisted, Cami believed, to go into hibernation and hopefully survive the pandemic in a secure and isolated area. It was all highly classified at the time and Cami's mother did not provide any great detail except to reassure a very distraught Cami during the height of the pandemic that her mother would always be there for her and that one day, they would meet again.

Cami was convinced that the reassurances weren't due to any abstract religious element, for all that her mother was certainly religious and believed in an afterlife. When Cami founded Project Eden with her chief administrator, The Selector, they had discovered cryogenic chambers deep within the lower levels of The Vault. But there was no sign that her mother was present. Causing Cami to suspect that if indeed she was shortlisted, then she could possibly be housed in other facilities, such as Eagle Mountain.

"Are you saying that there are actually adults still around? In this building?" Amber asked, as all the Mall Rats exchanged intrigued and uneasy glances.

"In a manner of speaking," Cami replied enthusiastically. "Would you all like to see a real living adult?"

* * *

Leaving the inner sanctum, Cami and the Mall Rats rejoined The Selector and all were escorted by a group of guards through a series of long, metallic tunnels, finally arriving at an area which, in addition to serving as a 'seed bank', housed a land-based 'Noah's Ark' containing a variety of endangered animal species, along with several types of fauna.

"What about the adults?" Bray pressed.

"Be patient," Cami replied. "You'll see one very soon."

The assembly entered into an area of The Vault which had been segmented into various sections. There was a myriad of fish of different sizes, cold and warm-water specimens, darting around their tanks in a large aquarium facility. Adjoining it was the Reptile House, an enclosed and humid, temperature-controlled structure housing several sealed units, each containing a multitude of lizards, chameleons and snakes, lazing under the heat lamps warming their homes.

The next section was designated by the signs on the walls as they passed into it, illustrating it to be the Entomology Department – an area holding burrows and dens, inside clear glass cases and units, of all kinds of insect life - the tiny creatures burrowing away and going about their routines, oblivious of the Mall Rats peeking through the glass into their worlds.

Above their heads, all the Mall Rats marveled as throngs and throngs of brightly coloured butterflies flew around.

Cami then took them to another zone, the signs displaying that it was a 'Special Creatures Section' – the atmosphere becoming damp, musty, condensation on the metallic walls.

"What the hell is that smell?" Lex said, disgusted by the odour. "And before anyone asks – it isn't me."

The Mall Rats braced themselves at the thought that the smell might emanate from decomposing bodies.

"It's the scent of an old friend," Cami replied, affectionately.

They soon discovered the 'adult' Cami had referred to earlier. But it was no human being she was showing them.

Standing by the barriers overlooking a large, muddy enclosure, Cami introduced them to Darwinia, the name given to an ancient Galapagos tortoise, who inched along the muddy terrain, as if in slow-motion.

Darwinia was the mascot that lived in The Vault with the adult scientists who had been stationed there and had actually belonged to Cami's mother. Darwinia was supposedly over 150 years old, Cami mentioned, once even owned by Cami's grandmother.

"With any luck, Darwinia might live another twenty-five to fifty years," Cami said. "Amazing to think she had lived before there was radio, television, air travel, nuclear power, the space age, computers – and yet she's even lived into the birth of the Internet. Can you image what life will be like in another 150 years from now, if each of us could live as long as she has? What world will Brady and baby Jay grow up into? How will life be for their children, and their grandchildren, decades from now? Will we all tear each other apart through infighting? Or will we adapt and evolve – and co-operate, learning to live together, to create a new world, one worthy of handing down to the children of the future?"

"Your vision is impressive, I'll grant you that," Amber said, amazed, as were all her fellow Mall Rats, at the scale and variety of the animal species they had seen, sensing Cami was genuine in her devotion to them.

"Why are you showing us all this?" Tai San asked.

"Hopefully you're not planning on putting us in your zoo," Lex said, drolly.

Cami ignored Lex's question and walked over to a large glass container on a shelf containing two reptiles, their backs ridged with little spiny crests – and she explained euphorically: "The mother tuatara has laid new eggs. It means everything we've done has been working. We've given life a chance to live on."

"Great," Lex said sarcastically. "Just what the world needs. More lizards."

"Not now, Lex – please," Amber scolded him, before turning back to consider Cami. "That's very good news – and we're all pleased. But I still don't understand what *we're* doing here. What exactly has this all got to do with us?"

Cami extended her hand, offering it, in invitation.

"I want you all to join us. To join The Selector and me. So that you can assist us with the vision I have. I am asking you – the Mall Rats – to become part of The Collective."

CHAPTER TWENTY-THREE

Ebony had been on a rollercoaster of emotions. If The Cube was meant to be a 'living experiment' as The Gamesmaster had called it for its audience, or whoever was actually watching, it was certainly a journey of self-discovery for all the contestants who were participating.

Ebony had encountered self-doubt, fear of failure, questioned her capabilities. Her confidence had been dented. She had always thought of herself, ever since the adults died, as a survivor, a warrior woman, someone who was ruthless and wouldn't let her emotions get in the way of what she was ever trying to achieve. Since she had been in The Cube, all kinds of emotions had flooded to the surface, forcing Ebony to, unusually for her, embark upon much self-reflection.

She had, she recognized, become paranoid about the other contestants. Not so much Hawk, to whom Ebony was still allied, but she wondered if The Selector had placed Ebony on the island deliberately as some kind of a set-up, to make sure she would fail. And fail spectacularly, on camera, in front of whatever audience was watching.

Ebony had initially sat on the bed in her room, and had smiled, waving occasionally into the cameras – but now she decided to ignore whoever was watching her. Possibly around the clock.

For the time being at least, Ebony decided to slightly alter her strategy, to try and mask any apparent vulnerability.

She hadn't done well so far in the series of 'trials of life' that had taken place. Any hopes of impressing, of storming to victory in one event after another, had been rocked by Ebony's poor performances. Even when she thought she did well – The Gamesmaster had judged Ebony to be in the very bottom half of the group of ten contestants. The chance of freedom by winning ten challenges seemed to be increasingly out of reach, slipping away, day by day.

She had wondered if the other competitors were in league with each other. Or had been given some kind of secret tips or advantages, to gain extra foresight or knowledge of what they needed to do in order to do well by The Gamesmaster before each trial had even begun. It couldn't be that Ebony, who had always had so much faith and confidence in her abilities, had suddenly become useless.

Hawk reassured her that from what he knew, The Gamesmaster had given no prior help to the others, certainly not to himself.

In Ebony's alliance with Hawk, they were able to co-operate and consult with each other during the different events but their performance would be marked as individuals, rather than a joint effort, by The Gamesmaster.

The same was true for the other competitors who had created alliances, such as Nova and Orin after Ebony ironically brought them together, Nova and Orin now becoming friends. Ebony would ultimately be on her own in each trial and couldn't rely on Hawk to 'carry her' by how he constantly excelled himself in the trials. Likewise Nova and Orin, along with the other contestants, would be judged independently, no matter what alliances manifested and evolved.

By her own tenacity and improvisation, Ebony had just managed to stay in the game. She had been through six 'trials of life' so far.

In one, the contestants were instructed to go out and search the island for guards who had been placed in hiding. The first contestant who managed to bring a warrior back to The Cube would win the round.

Hawk and Ebony had split up, each covering a part of the island to try and locate the camouflaged warriors. Unable to find any of the guards who were in hiding, instead of reconnecting with Hawk to revise their strategy, Ebony had cheated and brought back a guard who had been on duty around the perimeter of the island.

All across the lands, crowds had sat watching images on the agricultural buildings as Ebony had knocked the guard unconscious in that particular episode and literally dragged him to The Cube. She thought her inventive and unorthodox solution was proof of 'survival of the fittest' and would be bound to impress The Gamesmaster. But she was penalized, finishing second to last, and was warned not to attack any of the guards again who were keeping the island secure and contained or she would be disqualified and Discarded.

In another trial, the competitors had to solve a puzzle. Ebony had been desperate to finish first and raced ahead, following her intuition, whereas Hawk had taken his time, trying to work out the problem through logic. Ebony ignored his recommendations.

After all, it was totally illogical to Ebony that any elements she found from the natural world could ever match. But the trial was won by Nova, who Orin had helped complete the puzzle by matching up twigs on the ground with branches from a tree, placing them vertically into the ground - mirroring the shape of the perimeters of the bordering forest, along with the geography of where The Cube was located – with a small pile of twigs replicating the shape of The Cube residential and administrative building – perfectly.

Nova came first, Orin second, as they had worked together, Hawk third. And Ebony second to last, according to The Gamesmaster's assessment. She was fortunate not to be in total last place and only had survived due to some very rudimentary drawings she had carved out with a twig in the ground of the shape of The Cube.

It was a similar situation in another challenge where each contestant was required to build a shelter they were to stay the night in. Hawk constructed his own with ease, replicating a smaller version of one of the huts made of branches he had lived in at the Eco tribe's camp. He wasn't allowed to make Ebony's one for her but did his best to lead her, offering verbal assistance.

Ebony had been exasperated when her makeshift shelter collapsed in the night, forcing her to sleep outside, in the rain. Fortunately for her, another competitor had their shelter fail before her own one did and she didn't finish last but was placed eighth out of the ten. Hawk had won that round, demonstrating his survival skills and his affinity and understanding of the land, living in harmony with nature.

The Gamesmaster had advised in a separate trial that one of the ten pre-prepared meals that had been brought to The Cube was deliberately poisoned and whoever consumed it would be violently ill. It was a particularly cruel event, Ebony felt, and designed to test their ingenuity and patience, perhaps even trust, among other things, including their mental strength and stamina.

The contestants were all hungry and desperate to eat though they refrained from trying the meals for as long as possible. Nova had taken a little from each meal and left it outside to see if any of the birds would get sick from having sampled the meal – but there was no way of knowing because the birds flew away after eating their morsels and the impact of the food on them couldn't be tracked. Hawk wasn't allowed to forage for any berries or edible plants on the island, The Gamesmaster advised, and so had fasted, resisting the urge to eat even a mouthful.

It was like taking part in a lottery, a one in ten chance of getting a much-deserved meal or succumbing to poisoning. Maybe none of the meals were tainted and it was all a bluff, some of them wondered, a twisted check of resilience to observe how they reacted to a problem that might only be in their minds rather than being real.

In the end, Orin let hunger get the better of him. He picked one of the meals and seemed to be fine. Nova chose another plate. And then other contestants took the plunge, eating a meal, seemingly with no obvious side effects. With every plate selected, it increased the odds that one of the remaining meals would be the poisoned one.

Ebony followed Hawk's advice this time around and resisted the urge to eat though her body was craving the energy. Suddenly Orin became violently ill – and only then did the contestants discover The Gamesmaster had been serious with his threat.

Orin fell to the ground, gagging and struggling for air as the poison flowed through the blood in his body - before long, convulsing, almost as if in some anaphylaxis shock. Finally slipping into unconsciousness and dying.

"Oh, sad," The Gamesmaster said with a degree of manic intensity as he indicated Orin's corpse lying motionless on the ground. "What a pity. Orin was doing so well," The Gamesmaster continued, addressing the cameras before finally advising that the loser this week was Orin. So the viewers should look forward to welcoming a new contestant in the next episode while the remaining contestants were now safe to enjoy the remnants of the food. But all, including Ebony, picked carefully, unsure if there were other traces of poison.

The following day, the contestants dug a grave for Orin. Across the region, workers watched while they toiled in the fields. But no sound was transmitted or commentary by The Gamesmaster – as Orin was finally placed into the ground and then covered with earth, a white cross placed at the head of the grave.

After Orin's exit from The Cube, Ebony stayed awake most of the night, replaying her own performances in the different trials she had been in. She was analyzing what she had done wrong, anything she had done right, and trying to learn from any success she had witnessed that the other contestants had enjoyed.

She recalled some of the phrases The Gamesmaster had used during his running commentary. Each episode seemed to interweave a similar theme about testing the body, mind and spirit. And whether or not an individual's choices could ever be considered to be separate from the effects they would have on others.

The Gamesmaster had continually repeated that all the contestants, as any population, were interdependent and interconnected. The actions of one affected the lives of another. Even inaction could create a consequence for somebody else, compared to proactive action.

It finally dawned on Ebony. All this wasn't so much as purely examining or testing each individual on a manner of subjects such as morality, ideals, friendship, adaptability, survival skills or how one person affected the environment and vice versa, though these seemed to be important elements.

The greater emphasis was more that society as a whole could learn from what they were observing. The Gamesmaster had commented how each person was like a pebble in a communal pond – the contestants were a reflection of several different pebbles and were also pebbles themselves, mirroring back various ripples by their performance.

In assessing her own performance, Ebony concluded that she had always been trying to do well as an individual. She thought she might fare better if she tried to think of the others. Even if it was unnatural and superficial. She wouldn't reveal that, of course. But make it manifestly clear to The Gamesmaster that she intended to try a different approach in how she might respond to each trial. In an attempt to reassure The Gamesmaster, she revealed that she would be seeking new ideas and solutions that might bring benefits for others on the island, as well as society.

She was hopeful this apparent enlightenment might give her added kudos and advancement up the leaderboard as she certainly didn't want to join Orin, or stay on the island and in The Cube forever.

The following day, another contestant arrived to replace Orin. To Ebony's surprise and total dismay it was someone she knew. Though she had never been a friend, not even an acquaintance. It totally baffled Ebony where this new contestant had come from and more importantly, why she was there. It was Emma.

The last time she had seen Emma, she was being ushered away with The Guardian and Eloise, along with her little brother and sister, Shannon and Tiffany. Emma, along with the Zootists who were captured, hadn't been transported with Ebony and the Mall Rats after the city was invaded. And Ebony had never expected to see her ever again, let alone in The Cube.

Emma, with her blindness, was clearly panicked at her situation, being forced to go into The Cube, and was crying out desperately the names of her brother and sister, wondering where they were.

Ebony felt genuine pity for her. Though Emma had bonded with the Mall Rats, Bray especially, who had taken her under his protective wing in the past, Ebony had never really gotten to know Emma or even bothered to make an effort. She couldn't help but admire Emma's strength of character, however, and braveness in not giving up her love for her siblings. That was clear from what Ebony had witnessed back at the mall. Emma was certainly persistent and strong-willed and the fact that she had survived post the adults' demise without the support of conventional society and an infrastructure - was an achievement Ebony respected.

But there was no way she would ever be able to survive The Cube, Ebony knew. For some reason, Emma was being thrown right in the deep end, way out of her depth, which was callous even by Ebony's standards.

Emma stood, literally shaking, quivering in fear and distress, in a line along with the other contestants while The Gamesmaster explained the rules of their 'trial' for that particular episode.

Ebony stepped out of line and deliberately walked over to Emma, taking her by the hand, giving her a hug, telling her everything would be okay. The Gamesmaster, Hawk and the seven other competitors were taken aback by Ebony's move – as was Emma herself, who initially recoiled upon realizing she was with Ebony, of all people, recognizing her voice – but her apprehension of being around her was replaced by the surprise support and reassurance Ebony was giving her, something Emma desperately needed and was grateful to get, even if it was coming from Ebony, someone Emma had never particularly trusted and would never have counted on for support.

The aim of the challenge was to study the contestants' adaptability – with the age-old theme of 'survival of the fittest'. The contestants were expected to venture throughout the island and wouldn't be allowed back inside The Cube until one of them had experienced an encounter with a reptile species that was being introduced especially for the challenge. A snake with a highly toxic venom that had been let loose. They had to try and catch the snake – but would be severely penalized if they tried to injure or kill it, risking being Discarded.

The first person to discover the whereabouts would be declared the winner of the trial – though of course in doing so, they would risk being bitten by the snake. And if they were able to catch the snake, then they would receive extra points.

"Is it fair, Gamesmaster, for Emma to participate?" Ebony asked.

"Don't be selfish!" The Gamesmaster snapped. "Emma can't help it if she has an unfair advantage. Do you expect she should be – penalized?"

"I… don't understand," Ebony replied, in bewilderment.

"You will," The Gamesmaster said, placing his headset on and getting ready for the beginning of the episode while his camera crew converged.

The contestants wearily discussed tactics with those to whom they had allied. Some felt this trial was far too much of a dilemma and better not to try and win. It was almost better to finish second or third rather than get within one metre of the snake, let alone try and catch it for bonus points.

When the trial began, as the other competitors raced off and spread out around the island, Hawk stayed behind with Ebony outside the entrance to The Cube, the two of them determined to keep Emma company and make sure she was safe, in her vulnerable state.

Ebony sincerely didn't want to see Emma, who was already distraught, get bitten by some snake, if there even was one on the island.

She suspected it might even be a ruse to simply test them. But she wasn't about to take any chances. Or risk Emma taking any either.

Ebony's strategy was to blatantly display her new policy of showing her compassion and interest in the wellbeing of others.

To also portray innovation and resourcefulness, Ebony noticed a fellow contestant who was also lingering outside The Cube, wary and fearful to go off searching. Ebony lifted a branch, threw it and screamed out a warning, "It's there! Behind you!"

The contestant ran off hysterically, hearing the rustle when the branch landed.

The Gamesmaster couldn't help but smile as he addressed the camera and audience. "Nice! We all must be aware that the imagination can be so powerful whereby a simple tree branch can become a snake. And often a human can follow suit and also become a snake," he added, watching Ebony returning to Hawk and Emma.

The Gamesmaster followed, pursued by his camera unit, and continued with his commentary. "I'd like to introduce our latest contestant – Emma. Now, the one thing you will be aware of is that Emma is blind. She could never, of course, see a snake, no matter how close she got, and isn't handicapped by what she doesn't see, relying on her inner senses, which we all must do."

Hawk and Ebony exchanged a bewildered glance while Emma sat passively listening to The Gamesmaster continuing, addressing the cameras. "We'll return to Emma later to welcome her. Right now, let's see how our other contestants are doing," he said, rushing away with his camera unit towards the forest.

Hawk, himself, left - deciding it would be wise for him to at least try and participate. But Ebony decided for the time being at least that she would stay with Emma and take her chances, relying on her latest strategy which also gave her an opportunity to try and talk with Emma. But only on a superficial level, aware that anything they discussed might be overheard.

So, Ebony overplayed her insistence to Emma that she could trust her as she sat down on the grass clearing beside her. Once Emma was in a more secure area, Ebony would try and find out any information Emma might know from what she had been through before arriving at The Cube - which could be useful.

Until then, Ebony made a huge show of her attention, drying Emma's tears, giving her occasional hugs for some of the stationery cameras, as well as the one on Emma's chest which was no doubt also recording various images - as indeed was occurring with Ebony's camera herself.

Suddenly Emma flinched as she heard a long, hysterical, sustained scream. Not that far away, where Nova had encountered a snake among the leaves of the forest floor. But in so doing, was bitten.

She had accidentally stepped on the snake's head and though the snake appeared unharmed, The Gamesmaster declared into the camera that sadly it seemed as if they would be losing yet another contestant because Nova had well and truly lost this trial. And her life.

The cruelty was strangely in contrast shortly thereafter when The Gamesmaster's benevolent tone announced that due to her compassion and sense of collective awareness, Ebony was declared the winner of the trial for putting the interests of another ahead of her own. Emma had finished in second place for assessing her environment before venturing out. Hawk apparently had finished third for staying with Emma when she arrived.

As they went inside the building, Ebony carefully led Emma by her hands, feeling jubilant. Having her arrive was the best thing that had happened since Ebony herself had gotten there. She had finally won the victory she had been so eager to achieve and hoped she might now be able to turn the tide of fate to her advantage.

* * *

Emma and Ebony were excused burial duties due to Ebony's win. Hawk joined the other contestants, digging a plot for Nova, while inside the accommodation unit, Ebony led Emma to the bathroom so that they could speak more in private.

She told Emma that she would make sure Emma had a room close by, the other side of Ebony's own. And revealed that it was only safe to talk in the communal bathroom as far as any private matters were concerned because she was sure, as were all the contestants, that their every sound was being monitored, audibly, as well as their behaviour, visually.

Emma had never expected Ebony to have such a softer, generous side and expressed her gratitude. Ebony was more interested though in finding out any useful information and probed where Emma had been taken.

Emma explained that she and her siblings, Shannon and Tiffany, had been staying in some kind of town called The Void. She didn't know where The Guardian, Eloise and Zootists, along with the expectant mothers, had gone.

All she knew was that she, Shannon and Tiffany were apparently to stay temporarily in The Void, which was a holding community until whoever had abducted them decided their fate.

When Emma had been taken from The Void, she initially thought that she might face the prospect of living as a slave. No-one explained about The Cube, which Emma found to be a sinister place, as well as strange - from all Ebony had told her, as well as what Emma had experienced so far.

Ebony suspected that perhaps if the Mall Rats didn't co-operate, wherever they were, that Emma might be used somehow as leverage to try and influence Bray and the Mall Rats to co-operate. And she worried if this might somehow implicate her, due to her new and sudden alliance with Emma. But her genuine compassion overruled her concern, for the time being. And she reassured Emma that as difficult a place as The Cube certainly was, there was no way she would be tortured or punished, and that Ebony would always try and protect her.

Ebony's concern that Emma was being used possibly as a human 'prop' and hostage, in the event their captors needed to exert pressure on Bray and the other Mall Rats, caused her a new dimension of anguish. Assuming, of course, there was credence in Ebony's theory because she could understand that Emma's presence on The Cube as a contestant certainly provided a different element of so called 'entertainment'.

If the Mall Rats were involved though, somehow, at some point, Ebony knew they weren't exactly the type to co-operate with their captors.

And Bray, no doubt, would always be a potential 'knight in shining armour' trying to come to Emma's rescue, given that she had been under his protective wing.

Ebony resolved that she would take it all one step at a time and alter her strategies accordingly.

CHAPTER TWENTY-FOUR

May and Salene considered whether or not they should resurrect their wedding plans and arrange a ceremony to officially join them together. On one hand, both felt it wasn't absolutely necessary to marry to enjoy a relationship as partners but equally May and Salene felt the need to officially exchange vows to commit to one another spiritually, as well as emotionally.

"As much as I would like to – I don't think the time is right," May had said to Salene, who agreed. Not solely for compassion for Ryan, who was still clearly hurt that there was no hope of reuniting with Salene - but there were more pressing matters at hand, with the prospect of the Mall Rats forming an alliance with Cami and her forces.

The Mall Rats had differing views on what The Creator suggested but all agreed that they should try and find out further information because it all seemed just too good to be true.

Lottie, Sammy and even little Brady were sold on the idea of joining The Collective. But the elder members of The Tribe were all aware that this was due to them viewing the animals and insects – finding Darwinia especially cute.

Sammy no doubt, the others had observed, seemed to find the girls attending The Collective school to be very cute as well and Lex thought the time might be fast approaching where he, Ryan and Bray would need to give Sammy an education. In the midst of puberty, Sammy would soon need to know more about the birds and the bees, which was natural. So he, for one, was in tune, albeit in a different dimension, to the natural world.

The older members of the Mall Rats were reunited in their resolve that there could be no further negotiations unless they were sure that The Collective weren't involved in any slave trading. Or that slaves featured in The Collective society. That had been such a dark stain in the history of previous generations of the adults which all - especially Tai San, Alice and Ryan after what they had experienced as slaves themselves - found to be totally abhorrent.

And they weren't entirely convinced by The Selector and Cami explaining that the people working in the fields that Tai San had seen during her journey to the *Lakeside Resort* were simply members of the agricultural unit. Certainly not slaves.

The Mall Rats discussed other options such as trying to return to their home city but didn't quite know how life would be, given that the Collective had invaded to expand their territory. Cami had reassured them, however, that it was an option for them if they wanted to take it because The Collective didn't 'own' the city as such and certainly not the mall. She was willing to consider agreeing to sharing various sectors.

It was unanimous that any decision would be deferred, which was the source of arguments between Amber and Bray especially.

Both, along with others in their tribe, had been genuinely impressed by the new society The Collective seemed to be building. Amber and Bray totally understood the need to have an education system, a medical infrastructure, militia, food and agriculture units, as well as a justice system where everyone had the right to due process and a fair trial.

Bray, however, was against a structured repopulation programme given what he had seen during his time when he was held captive by Eloise and her Zootist forces with sterile baby 'factories'.

Amber could see his point but had liked how young mothers were supported in Project Eden. Trudy was equally impressed, as were the rest of the tribe, and it was hard to think of a better way for a young mother to give birth than by what The Collective were doing, with both baby and mother being provided with the framework of care they needed.

Amber felt that this was no anarchic world where everyone was in it for themselves and was impressed by the well-organized and structured approach. Cami gave her deputy, The Selector, credit, being her core administrator.

It wasn't to say that Amber felt everything in Cami's world was perfect. It wasn't. Amber had her own concerns at the ethics and potential surveillance misuse, let alone the biochips, for all that they brought added health monitoring benefits.

She was unsettled by the odd behaviour of The Selector, as had been reported to her by Tai San, Ryan and Alice. Besides being a brilliant administrator, Cami explained, The Selector was overly pedantic at times, obsessive, even quirky and eccentric – but Cami just so admired his skills, which were essential to oversee all that needed to be done to build a better and more sustainable new world.

Amber had also made it clear to Cami, echoed by her fellow members of the tribe, how she objected to the way the Mall Rats had been taken by The Collective forces.

Cami explained that there was still much work which needed to be done. Areas refined, including in the militia. The Collective, after all, were not just a tribe in their own right but had alliances with other tribes such as The Privileged, even the Zootists. And mirroring the work Cami's mother did in the old world, Cami's vision was to have a structure of alliances, a derivative of the United Nations which had been in place prior to the demise of the adults.

Cami regretted that The Technos had not agreed to work together.

"So, you know Ram?" Bray had asked carefully.

"I thought I did," Cami had replied, advising that she only knew The Techno leader from their connections in the past online and she had never even met Ram - but believed that The Technos could have been an interesting unit, bringing a sophisticated ability to adapt and mould all manner of areas of technology. Ram had initially committed to the notion of an alliance but had reneged.

Where the Legion forces who invaded the Mall Rats' home city under Commander Snake were concerned, they had been tasked with securing Eagle Mountain and the city, to safeguard it against potential future threats from outsiders. The Collective, through their intelligence network, were concerned that other rival alliance power blocks might be in existence in faraway lands. Other countries where survivors no doubt had their own vision of building a future in the aftermath of the adults' demise.

The Legion were young men and women of action, capable of highly-trained combat skills. But Cami would instruct The Selector to reprimand Commander Snake and his militia for any excess and unacceptable force he had used in The Collective's expansion into the Mall Rats' home city.

"Are you sure you don't mean invasion?" Lex had asked, coldly.

"No – expansion," Cami had reiterated. Her dream was to replicate the system she had established at Eden so it could be rolled out across all lands, eventually other countries.

"So, are you trying to take over the world?" May said disparagingly.

"No, just build a better one," Cami replied.

She added that The Selector, through his administration unit, was identifying potential infrastructures required to achieve the goal. And had already actioned through the network of The Collective to find Ram and the rest of the missing Mall Rats, such as Jack and Ellie, even investigate the whereabouts of those who had disappeared long before, such as Patsy and Paul. So that the Mall Rats could be reunited again.

The Mall Rats were encouraged by the news but all had reservations concerning the quasi-religious aspects embraced by The Collective surrounding Zoot and those most connected with him, which included his brother Bray, Zoot's daughter Brady, her mother Trudy, and Amber's son, who was Zoot's nephew - as well as Amber herself, being the mother of that child.

Cami said that she wanted the key Mall Rats, those like Amber, with a connection to Zoot, to 'spread the word' about Zoot among The Collective, to use The Guardian's 'teachings' as a positive, empowering belief system.

This was not the zealous 'Power and Chaos' that The Guardian had independently cultivated, demanding strict adherence, Cami assured all the Mall Rats. She believed there was a method to use the power of Zoot's legacy and name to instill humane and civilized values in an otherwise lost and frightened world which needed a belief system, some form of religion. Through a modified version of 'Zoot', Cami believed it would be possible to adapt and evolve to spread love, compassion, tolerance and co-operation. So that the once divisive and fear-inducing shadow Zoot cast could become a beneficial figurehead, a unifying force.

Amber agreed with Bray, who was against the current Zootist philosophy in The Collective homelands. But Amber accepted the logic of Cami's point that even if it wasn't Zoot – then it was likely that there would arise some other equivalent to a new religion in society, just as had occurred since humanity had begun.

In any event, as Cami made clear, whether Amber, Bray and the Mall Rats liked it or not, the Zootist movement *had* sprung up into existence and *was* something real to many followers. The word of the Zootist legend and the deeds of the Mall Rats had spread naturally far and wide across the lands. So it was all-powerful and needed to be restrained, kept under a tight grasp of leadership to ensure it remained a force for good rather than bad, something those more nefarious might seek to exploit.

Despite the Mall Rats' concerns, the Mall Rats felt on balance that they should at least give Cami and The Collective a chance, by meeting over a period of time to discuss all elements and observe in greater detail the various aspects of the society that had been put in place. If it turned out the Mall Rats and Collective were not in sync and any Mall Rat wanted to eventually leave and return to their former city, or anywhere else for that matter, then they would be able and free to do so, Cami had promised. Their fate was theirs to determine.

* * *

"How's my beautiful boy?" Amber said, giving her son a loving hug, taking him in her arms from Bray's own.

She had just returned to her room at the *Lakeside Resort* after her latest meeting with Cami at The Vault. Bray had been waiting behind, looking after baby Jay.

"He misses his Mommy," Bray said. "And I do, too."

"I've missed you both as well. But I feel we're accomplishing a lot."

"Are we?" Bray asked carefully.

"What's that supposed to mean?" Amber said, in concern as she considered Bray.

"I was meaning that I miss you. The old Amber, the one that is, who hadn't taken leave of her senses," Bray said.

"Please, Bray. Not now. Let's not argue."

"Why not? You worried I might upset things between you and your new best friend?"

"She's not my friend."

"Then what is she?"

"Someone trying to do the right thing. Just like I am."

Bray knew Amber was being sincere. And he loved her for it. He always had. She *was* trying to make the world a better place. He would never have a problem with her in that regard and only felt proud and believed in her vision. But he simply wasn't so sure about Cami and The Collective - and especially The Selector's motives. The Selector seemed, to Bray, to be a little too charming, manipulative.

But Bray's biggest concern was that the more he thought about it, the more he found the whole notion of the Zootist faith – 'religion' – 'philosophy' – whatever they wanted to call it – as an abomination. A denigration of who his brother really was. A fiction. A false depiction. It violated the truth and the reality of the life behind the brother and family that Bray had known, better than anyone. He was repulsed by Cami using his brother's legacy for her own purposes. However she justified it, claiming she was using it for 'good' – and The Collective weren't all bad, Bray had conceded that to Amber – he felt the whole idea of *encouraging* people to believe in Zoot was preposterous. He wanted nothing to do with it, of any kind.

Not only was he repulsed by the Zootist faith in principle, he was concerned that Cami would inadvertently and eventually open up a Pandora's Box, setting in motion forces that Bray doubted Cami and The Selector would be able to control. He had seen, firsthand, the zealotry of Zootists in the past. It had never been a force for good. It was tarnished and though he hated the fact, he believed his brother's legacy would always be a tainted one.

"You're being naïve, Amber. And you can't even see it."

"Am I? Aren't you the one being naïve? If you can't even keep an open mind?"

Bray repeated that he believed perpetrating the Zoot myth would only end up in haunting the future rather than brightening it, and he couldn't allow that to happen for the sake of Trudy, Brady, and their own son, baby Jay, let alone other members of the Mall Rats, as well as so many others throughout the lands.

"Okay. I take it back. You're not being naïve. But certainly cynical!" Amber said.

"Is that what you call it? I would call it realistic!" Bray said. "What kind of mother are you? That you could allow your son to be exposed and play a part of it all?"

Bray's words were like a blow to Amber's heart and she slapped his face, hard.

"How dare you say such a terrible thing!"

Baby Jay began to cry from the heated exchange between Amber and Bray, who glared at Amber, then left, slamming the door shut behind him.

Amber gathered her baby in her arms and slumped to the bed, sobbing, embracing her son tightly.

* * *

Trudy shared Bray's concerns about the threat of the Zootist faith The Collective were supporting and was unwilling to expose Brady or herself to any life where they were pressurized to be the centre of a Zootist universe that seemingly revolved around them. So, she had so far rejected Cami and The Selector's offers for her and Brady to make appearances in the temple at Eden and had remained at the *Lakeside Resort* every day.

This enabled her to also look after baby Jay, as well as Brady, Lottie and Sammy, while the Mall Rats negotiated with Cami and set about trying to find out more information regarding the society she so passionately was committed to building.

Alice, Ryan and Lex mostly stayed behind as well though, unwilling to leave Trudy alone, fearful of her security in the event that Cami and The Selector were not genuine.

But this concern evaporated with each passing day when their fellow Mall Rats returned to enthusiastically report back on what they had witnessed and discussed.

Cami certainly seemed to be genuine. Though the jury was still out regarding The Selector.

Bray and Amber's relationship remained tense, with more arguments about the merits of joining The Collective. Bray was especially struck at the irony that rather than an alliance with The Collective, it seemed to be tearing Amber and Bray apart. Amber tried to reassure Bray that this wasn't the case, and that she was becoming really inspired by Cami's vision. Bray, however, felt that it was more like she was becoming brainwashed, he had cautioned, which fuelled Amber's disdain of Bray's seemingly stubborn and obstinate stance.

Ryan joined the others on their visits and tours to Project Eden and had agreed to hold some self-defense courses at not only the school - but to train some recruits in the militia. He realized that he needed a new purpose in his life, something to focus on, to help him get over his rejection by Salene. He was happy that Salene had found someone special in May - for which he was genuinely glad – but it still left a void in his life that he needed to fill.

Salene and May themselves were becoming more and more involved in the education division at Eden, where they assisted teaching younger children how to read and write, as well as useful tips in life from their experiences.

Salene had always been a nurturing figure and was surprised how May was also starting to display those qualities, with the pupils responding in a very positive way.

Tai San, in turn, was confused on exactly how she felt while sitting on the bed in her room, waiting for Lex to arrive.

She couldn't reconcile her instincts. On one hand, she had found Cami to be a very impressive young woman, almost a kindred spirit, judging by Cami's connection with nature and all forms of life, including animal and plant, as well as human. This resonated with Tai San's own spirituality and elemental awareness.

The opposite side to this, however, were her concerns about The Selector. He was just so unlike Cami. Where

Cami appeared sincere and genuine, The Selector still came across as anything but. From the moment Tai San had first met him.

How he could be involved with Cami, at such a high level in The Collective, was something Tai San couldn't understand. Did it mean Cami was insincere or suspect herself in some way? Were The Collective really a force for good, as Cami seemed to personify? Or was she right to feel uneasy, as embodied in the enigma that was The Selector? He was just plain creepy, in Tai San's view. And she recalled the mantra of her family in the old world that 'one is judged by the company one keeps'.

The other complication in life for Tai San was Lex. Since they had recently become a couple once again, their renewed relationship was under outside pressures.

Lex was facing distractions and possibly temptations every day that threatened to pull him away from Tai San. As he wanted to repeatedly visit The Privileged tribe. These would be testing times for him and for her, Tai San knew, and would prove the making - or the breaking – and ultimately confirm if there was to be a meaningful and continued relationship between them.

CHAPTER TWENTY-FIVE

"How was your day, beautiful?" Lex asked Tai San when he returned yet again from visiting The Privileged, giving her a hug in their room.

"Not as enjoyable for me as I'm sure your day was for you."

"Somehow that doesn't seem much like a compliment," Lex said, wryly. "What's the problem?"

"Why don't you tell me?" Tai San asked. "Why are you so interested in The Privileged?"

"Reconnaissance. Research. Speaking of which, what say we do a bit of 'research' ourselves before dinner?"

"Like what?" Tai San asked, confused.

"What do you think? You're pretty hot stuff. And so am I," Lex smouldered, kissing Tai San, who responded to his embrace and caresses.

She had spent most of her day so far with The Selector. He had arranged, in consultation with Cami, for her to visit the biosphere at Eden. It was a large geodesic glass dome structure and housed a myriad of plants inside its warm, hermetically-sealed atmosphere. It had been constructed by the adults as an adjunct in tandem with the 'seed bank' programme at Eden, a place for selected plants, mostly herbs, to thrive.

The Selector was aware of Tai San's interest and knowledge in plants and had accompanied her that day, as well as the three successive days previously. Ostensibly, he wanted to be with her to get Tai San's opinion on the biodome and see if she was interested in taking over the facility to run a herbalism programme there, to cultivate and expand the herbs so they could be used for homeopathic medicines and natural remedies, something Tai San was proficient in.

She still couldn't help but feel that he was enamoured with her, though he had been less blatantly creepy and attentive. But her antennae picked up that he was still absorbed in her.

Tai San had gone to the biodome to check it out and was curious about Cami's offer for her to lead a programme to see if it could contribute something useful to the lives of many through its rich variety of herb deposits. Both medicinally through homeopathic elements but also nutritionally.

But now, Tai San had The Selector on her mind and was clearly not in any mood for an encounter with Lex.

"What's with you?" he asked, aware that she was not responding to his embrace.

"I keep thinking about The Selector."

Lex leapt out of bed and immediately began to get dressed.

"What's wrong?" Tai San asked.

"What do you think? I'm not having you fantasizing, when we're getting it on!" Lex snapped angrily.

"I'm not fantasizing at all," Tai San said, laughing slightly at the absurdity of what Lex had said and the fact that his male ego was being bruised. "Believe me, there's no problem – just as long as you're not thinking about The Privileged, that is."

"Tai San – do you really think I enjoy going out there every day?" Lex responded.

"Don't you? Are you sure?" she asked, her eyes probing him, searchingly.

She advised that she was also finding it difficult to concentrate in any lovemaking because she could smell the scents of a mixture of sweet perfumes on Lex. He smelled as if he belonged in a florist shop, rather than a bed.

Lex explained that The Privileged had offered him some homemade aftershave lotion which he had tried.

"If it makes you feel any better, *they* can't keep their eyes off of me. But that doesn't mean to say that I can't keep my eyes off of them. Like I've said, I've just been doing some research. That's all."

"Into just exactly what?" Tai San asked.

"Defences… militia," Lex replied.

The Privileged lived further along the lake on the outskirts of Eden in what had once been an alpine accommodation block used by the adults who had worked at the facility around the time the pandemic was occurring. Now, most of the tribe spent their time outside, lounging in the sun on manicured lawns or exercising, fine-tuning their already honed and well-trimmed bodies.

They were all, without exception, physically attractive and represented the upper echelon of Collective society, enjoying the most comfortable of living conditions, and had a retinue of servants known as the Discards to look after their every need.

They were the pick of humanity, a selected few of near-perfect specimens who were not only amazing looking but had uncommon gifts or talents that gave them prominence over other members of the population. Some were gifted musicians, others were natural athletes, poets, writers, painters. Their role was to bring art and beauty to day to day life – as well as a status for others to strive for and be invited to belong to.

If someone showed enough loyalty to The Collective and worked hard, one day they could hope to be rewarded by being allowed to spend time temporarily in the company of The Privileged, perhaps a day or a week depending on what they had contributed to The Collective. It was a paradise-like environment, a refuge, a place of peace, a sanctuary within the environs of Eden.

The most loyal Collective members might even aspire, through their efforts in their day to day lives as medics or teachers or warriors, to be honoured by attaining permanent lifetime membership of The Privileged. Something that only a very special few would ever hope to receive in the future for exceptional service, even if they did not possess the natural attractiveness that would have otherwise already made them members.

Charismatic, beautiful, The Privileged were also in reality hedonistic and certainly narcissistic and self-absorbed. Their egos matched their seemingly perfect physiques, Lex thought, and had studied them posing while working out. Both male and female belonged to a militia section and Lex often had Ryan accompany him on his visits for security in case they 'turned'. All were more than capable of handling themselves in combat.

Many in The Privileged appeared to be well known individually by name by some of the younger members of The Collective who looked up to them, aspiring to be like their idols. It was like the perfect life but reserved especially for only the perfect few.

Lex was advised by The Selector that one day Lex might end up joining The Privileged. He might even usurp the enigmatic and mysterious leader of The Privileged known as Flame. He was apparently an accomplished musician, the ultimate guitar hero, a rock star god who lived mostly a reclusive existence high in the mountains, between making occasional personal appearances - and was adored and revered by all. But few were themselves privileged enough and worthy to cast their eyes on their ultimate idol.

The Selector reasoned that where Flame was only a rock star god – Lex had an exalted status which was god-like itself, having been the one who had been responsible for bringing the god Zoot into existence, having inadvertently created the whole phenomenon in the process. Lex would be revered. Not because The Privileged worshipped Zoot. Their only worship was to themselves, along with their idol, Flame. But they had recognized perfection in Lex's ability to kill. After all, he not only gave birth to Zoot – at the same time, he had 'killed a god'. And The Selector wanted him to educate the influential Privileged by revealing details more about his own life, to re-tell of the events leading up to when Zoot became immortal.

By acceding to The Selector's request to at least spend some time visiting The Privileged, Lex said he hoped to learn more about The Collective's defence capability and maybe he could 'influence the influencers' in The Privileged.

He had, in truth, felt like a kid in a candy shop, being surrounded by a bevy of beautiful people, male and female, fawning over him, attentive to his every word. It had been an exhilarating experience. The Privileged had laughed at his jokes, sat and listened - absorbed, as he told them about how Zoot had been despatched to the afterlife. He revealed to Tai San that he had embellished it all a little bit. He couldn't help himself and found it amusing, as well as mind-blowing, to be treated like a god himself.

Lex had shown his military prowess by teaching some street-fighting moves to the muscular Privileged males and warrior females, who were impressed. And Lex couldn't deny that some of the most beautiful female creatures he had ever seen had offered their bodies willingly for his gratification. All in The Privileged seemed to practice open relationships.

"I assume you mentioned the Mall Rats don't believe in the same philosophy?" Tai San asked.

"Of course," Lex replied.

Tai San believed him. Simply because she chose to do so, aware that Lex was clearly enjoying having his ego massaged and that it might be something he could so easily get used to, and eventually even become addicted to. Tai San wondered if The Selector had set things up to tempt Lex, to drive a wedge between him and Tai San.

"Don't you think you're the one with an ego problem?" Lex asked, amused at the thought. "What makes you so sure The Selector has any interest in you beyond being a Mall Rat?"

"Let's just call it feminine intuition," Tai San replied, confused how Lex could be so blind to the looks The Selector often gave, which were more than just leering from time to time. Tai San felt that The Selector's eyes were devouring her.

"There's only one girl for me, Tai San – and I'm looking at her, right now," Lex insisted, giving Tai San a kiss. "Why don't you come with me tomorrow and see for yourself what goes on and leave your herbs behind? I reckon The Privileged would be really impressed just to see you. And you'll see just how much they seem to adore me. They just can't seem to get enough of me."

"Well, someone's got to do it, I suppose, Lex," Tai San said. "And it may as well be you."

"I take it then that you'd prefer to spend more time with The Selector. Should I be jealous of him?"

"No," Tai San scoffed, in disdain. "Of course not."

"Then don't be jealous of The Privileged. None of them deserve me," he added, smiling mischievously.

"I hope you're joking, Lex," Tai San said. "And not getting a little too into yourself as those people seem to be in The Privileged?"

"Give me a break," Lex replied, sounding more convinced than he looked, which registered with Tai San, hoping that the adulation Lex seemed to be thriving on had no more repercussions than it just all going to his head. It would break her heart to lose him.

* * *

The Selector had arranged additional security during the time the Mall Rats spent on their tours and at Project Eden. And security had even been stepped up at the *Lakeside Resort* for the Mall Rats' safety, given that they were being more and more exposed and their profile was being raised. It wasn't just the conventional society within The Collective that caused The Selector concern … but the fanatical followers of Zoot, which reinforced Bray's view that the Mall Rats were making a huge mistake in participating in perpetrating the Zoot legend and the ensuing worship. Amber reluctantly agreed that perhaps she had become so blinded by all that was so good in Cami's vision that maybe she herself hadn't focused enough on the implications of the Zootists. And all that could be bad.

Trudy was relieved that Amber was now starting to see the wisdom in Bray's concern, which had always mirrored her own, and had been assigned a personal bodyguard by The Selector, who had followed her every move.

He was called Storm but Trudy felt like he was an unwelcome cloud that had descended, hanging over her life.

Storm was tall, powerfully built, strong-jawed and a young man of few words. He had been chosen apparently by The Selector himself to watch all the Mall Rats - but those especially with any link to Zoot. Above all, Trudy and Brady, whether Trudy wanted it or not, given that Brady was Zoot's child, and the legend of Trudy being the Supreme Mother had spread far and wide.

Storm deserved his moniker, The Selector had proudly mentioned, because he was a potent destructive force when he needed to be. And had been given the honour to guard Trudy and her daughter, day and night.

Storm not only possessed military prowess, The Selector claimed, but he was medically trained and could act as a first responder in the event Trudy or Brady or any other Mall Rat required immediate assistance. He was accomplished in all manner of areas – except not knowing when his presence was overly intrusive, Trudy thought.

She certainly wasn't against any extra security but found Storm's presence to be far too overwhelming and wondered in fact if he was there more to spy on her, for some reason.

He had often stood, silent and vigilant on duty, just watching Trudy and Brady at the resort. Even at night, Storm had stayed awake, outside their room. He was like a machine, requiring minimal sleep. He shadowed Trudy and Brady endlessly. Even at times throughout the resort whenever Brady and Trudy went to use the bathroom. Storm had waited outside the door. When they had gone to the dining area, Storm was only a few feet behind. If Trudy went outside to get some air or take Brady for a walk, Storm was not far away.

This simply fuelled Trudy's exasperation at him being forced into her previously private life, something that had been sacred to her, her day to day routine with Brady having been an inner sanctum. Even though he claimed not to want to interfere – Storm was intruding upon Trudy and Brady's existence by simply constantly being there. Although his supposed brief was to watch out for all the Mall Rats, especially those with any links to Zoot – his entire focus seemed more to be on Trudy and Brady.

Increasingly, his presence became irritating and unnecessary, in Trudy's view. It was like she was being haunted by him, as if he were a ghost. And she had tried everything she could to get him to leave her and her daughter alone. She asked politely, she had ordered him, she had even lost her temper, yelling at him at times. But Storm didn't waver. He simply listened to her insults, ignoring her pleas and requests – continuing to dutifully follow her everywhere like he was an unwanted but devoted pet.

Brady had initially been scared of Storm, who - by his size, compared to her, was an intimidating presence. And this hadn't helped endear him to Trudy.

After a while, however, Brady had found Storm's constant proximity a source of amusement. She had even instigated some games, playing hide and seek – or suddenly running off down the corridors of the resort – and each and every time, Storm had run off after her, Brady shrieking in delight, giggling at the absurdity of it all, having a giant companion around her and her mother.

Brady had even 'tested' Storm a few times, asking him to get her a glass of water or some more food in the communal dining area, Storm complying every time. The other Mall Rats were aware, as well as Trudy, that Brady was using Storm like some kind of servant and Amber agreed that it might be an idea to confront The Selector to instruct Storm to back off more and keep his distance.

Brady was also treating Storm like he was some kind of teddy bear, a plaything to her – and Trudy was concerned by the bond Brady was developing. Lottie and Sammy often participated in the games. Even May and Salene seemed to show signs of becoming familiar, believing that Storm seemed like a decent kind of guy. And both Lex and Ryan were warming to Storm, often comparing notes on various martial art moves and other tactics.

Bray noticed that as well as a bond with young Brady, Storm seemed to be developing closer relationships with each Mall Rat. Slowly. But surely. He was getting to know each member of the tribe. And yet was still a stranger – an outsider. And in reality, was violating their lives, intruding without being invited. Amber agreed with Bray that they themselves should try and keep their distance and keep an eye out if any Mall Rats were becoming overly familiar.

Amber and Bray trusted the Mall Rats, of course. That wasn't the issue. It was more that Storm seemed to have another agenda than simply being a personal bodyguard.

Trudy was back in her room after having gone to the dining area for an early dinner, hoping to get Brady to bed for an early night. She was sitting on the floor, her legs crossed, and had been playing catch with Brady, who was sitting on the couch - Storm having brought Brady a ball to play with in the morning. The first of many toys they were promised, on The Selector's instruction, to help keep Brady occupied and stimulated.

Trudy laughed, enjoying the moment with her daughter, Brady gently throwing the ball back to her mother - Trudy trying to keep her relatively calm and not too hyper before bed, just sharing a little fun and some one on one time with Brady prior to Trudy reading her a bedtime story.

Brady threw the ball again and Trudy mishandled it, the ball flying behind her, over her head. Brady ran after it, her little feet pitter-pattering on the carpet, chasing the ball rolling along the floor. Towards the doorway, where Storm stood, watching intently.

"I didn't invite you in!" Trudy snapped, frustrated by Storm's presence.

"You should be nice to Storm, Mommy," Brady said, as he threw the ball to her and she threw it back, both playing catch.

Trudy felt strangely humiliated. To be scolded by Brady. And it fuelled her simmering anger.

"Why don't you leave us alone!" Trudy cried out. "We didn't ask for you to be here. For any of this! Just - leave – us - alone!"

"I'm sorry – I can't," Storm replied. "I've got my orders."

Trudy couldn't take it anymore. She let out a howl of frustration, venting her feelings, lifted the ball and threw it across the room at him in a moment of rage, Storm catching it with ease.

"Get out!" Trudy implored him. "Please – get out!"

Brady began to cry, confused by what was going on, not liking seeing her mother in distress.

"Just this once – I'll give you some space to recover. Don't be upset – please," Storm said uneasily.

To Trudy's surprise, Storm defied his orders from The Selector – and had, for the first time ever, obeyed Trudy's instructions and stepped out, closing the door behind him. So, maybe he was human after all and had a shred of empathy and decency in him, Trudy hoped, beneath his disciplined, military manner.

"I'm so sorry I shouted," Trudy said to Brady, giving her a loving hug.

Trudy had felt that she was almost losing her mind with Storm's persistent presence – and had wondered if that was the real reason The Selector had put Storm on duty, to push Trudy to the limits, to stress her, to 'test' her in some way, to mess with her mind.

* * *

Later that evening, Amber awoke in her own room. It was pitch black, with only an almost imperceptible amount of light coming in from the moon reflecting on the lake outside the window.

She could hear her baby's soothing breathing in the bed next to her own and instinctively turning over, reached her arm out to touch Bray affectionately. The way things had been between them lately with their recent arguments, she wanted to kiss him lovingly, to feel his embrace.

"Are you awake?" she whispered.

But something was wrong. The space beside her was empty.

"Bray?"

Panicked, she sat up in bed and turned on the side lamp, confirming there was no sign of Bray.

She leapt out of bed, rushing to the bathroom to see if he was there – it, too, was empty.

Amber then tried the door handle to the room, hoping to look out in the corridors in case Bray had gone for a walk or that she might find him perhaps in another part of the resort.

The door was locked from the outside and Amber couldn't get out.

But somehow, Bray had. It was like he hadn't just disappeared from the *Lakeside Resort*, but from the face of planet Earth.

CHAPTER TWENTY-SIX

Ram had stayed locked up in the room he was being kept in at the factory by Ved, allowed out only periodically for a few occasional toilet breaks or to stretch his legs by walking up and down the corridors of his old Techno base, always accompanied by some of the Virts, sometimes Ved himself.

It felt like he was a prisoner in what had once been his own home.

Ved had visited to keep him appraised of what he had been doing – claiming he had opened up an initial line of communication online with The Collective having been introduced to them via The Broker. Ved had let Ram know The Collective had responded favourably to Ved's contact with them and were promising him they would reward him with a lifetime's worth of food and technological resources if he was able to deliver Ram to them, as he said he could. His contacts at The Collective also assured Ved they were making enquiries throughout regions under The Collective jurisdiction to see if they could find out anything definitive about what had happened to Cloe.

Ved was pleased how things had gone, he advised Ram, and the positive overtures The Collective were making to him.

Ram insisted Ved had to be a fool to think he could trust them or ever do a deal. The Collective would be no doubt using their vast technological arsenal to try and track the real-life location of Ved every time he went online and reached out to them, Ram warned. It was only a matter of time before The Collective would be sure to descend upon Ram's former town in a display of force, taking over the factory, seizing Ram for themselves

– and no doubt coercing Ellie, Jack, Ved and the rest of his Virts into a lifetime of slavery in servitude to Kami and The Collective's powerful block.

Ved was crazy to think he could negotiate with The Collective on equal terms – in this world without adults, might was right, Ram said – and the most mighty of them all that he was aware of were The Collective. They would crush Ved without a moment's hesitation and promise him the earth – without delivering it – if it would make it easier for them to get their way and get a hold of Ram.

Ved had fobbed off Ram's 'fear-mongering' he called it, certain that Ram was up to his old tricks again and trying to intimidate Ved into allowing him to go free due to the threat of The Collective.

And Ved was no fool. He had reassured Ram that each time he had gone online he had managed to keep his real-world location hidden behind several layers of encryption and false online addresses. The Collective would think he was somewhere else should they try and track him down in real life, not at the old Techno base.

Ved had learned from Ram and was keeping their location a well camouflaged secret safe from any prying eyes in case The Collective were double-crossing him. Ram should enjoy his 'freedom' at the factory, Ved teased, because it wouldn't be long before they would be on their way to exchange him to The Collective at the city where Amber and the Mall Rats had lived, as well as Ram, now that the drone Ram had travelled in with Jack and Ellie was repaired and in functional flying order again.

With every day that passed, Ram was becoming increasingly concerned about his fate, searching every fibre of his being, calculating some move or strategy he could try to persuade Ved to drop his negotiations with The Collective – and even better, to completely release him. Yet Ved was stubborn and had grown in confidence to become very much his own man – he didn't listen to Ram anymore, as he had once done.

Ram sat up as the door to his room opened, one of the Virts bringing him his latest meal – a cold tin of spaghetti, way past its use by date. Ram glared disapprovingly but had no option but to eat what he was being given. It made him think that life wasn't as sweet and comfortable for Ved and The Virts as he was making it out to be. They were probably down to the last food stocks Ram had left at his old base. And that might have been one of the other reasons Ved was trying to barter with The Collective - to make sure they would bring extra supplies of food Ved could feed the Virts with in the event of any deal.

"Thanks for the food," Ram said, smiling in a friendly way to the Virt who had delivered the tawdry meal. His name was Giga – and Ram reached out, grabbing him by the arm as he turned to leave, "Hey – please, wait up for a sec."

"I'm not meant to talk to you," Giga said, giving Ram a cautious look.

"But you are – and there's no harm doing it. See? We're having a conversation," Ram said, smiling again.

"Ved warned us about you. My job is to deliver you your food and then get on my way. And that's exactly what I'm gonna do."

"By all means, feel free to do so," Ram said. "It's a shame though. I like you Giga. You're a smart guy, I can see that. I was hoping we could talk for a bit and I could pass over some of my skills and secrets to you, before I get taken out of here. Be a shame for them to go to waste."

"Nice try," Giga said. "Goodbye, Ram."

Giga turned and went toward the door.

"Imagine a self-sustaining virtual world never needing any reboots or patches. Like in the system I designed. Any inter-negative mega data bypasses fixed any glitches while the programme was running. I thought you might be interested," Ram called out, when Giga was almost fully out of the door.

Against his better instincts, what Ram said piqued Giga's curiosity. The Virts had spent much of their spare time living in computer fantasies, plugged in through virtual reality helmets into realistic programmes. It was an addictive and wonderful sensation, a passion for Giga and the other Virts. They always had to cut short their sessions to a few hours though.

The complex software could often be glitchy, the endless rendering spoiling the experiences for the users. And the systems had to be powered down to free up resources in the computers, which could too easily be taxed by powering the grunty realistic 360-degree graphics the virtual reality required. If there was a way to allow the programmes to continue running for longer – even in perpetuity, as Ram had alluded - then that would be something Giga would be interested to know and share with the other Virts.

"Can you – do such a thing?" Giga asked hesitantly, closing the door behind him as he considered Ram in awe. Aware of the former leader of The Technos and the reputation Ram had.

"I can do it – and so can you. Don't suppose Ved ever told you about my plans to live forever in reality space?"

He had. Giga knew of it. Ved had often spoke of Ram, his former mentor, and how Ram was a genius from whom Ved had learned so much.

"If I can pass on a little knowledge, it'll make me feel at least I did something worthwhile with my life – before The Collective get their collective hands on me."

Giga was sorely tempted – and caught in a conflict. He didn't want to go against Ved's wishes. But if Ram could show him a thing or two, it would be sure to impress Ved. Ram was a prisoner and wasn't going anywhere, in any event, and Giga felt he had nothing to lose and everything to gain if he gave Ram the opportunity to teach him some of his unique knowledge.

"What would you need in the form of hardware?" Giga asked tentatively.

Ram said if Giga could get him to a keyboard and a computer, he could sit back and watch while Ram typed in lines of code that would blow Giga's mind, let alone Ved's. A good leader never showed all his tricks, Ram claimed, and no doubt Ved hadn't relayed in turn everything he knew to Giga and the other Virts. If they knew as much as Ved did, there would be no need for Ved to be their leader anymore, Ram said. Leaders often held back certain knowledge so they could stay one step ahead of everyone else.

Giga told the two Virts at the door that he would be back in an hour, which is how long Ram thought they would need.

They walked down the corridor to another room, one where several of the powerful computers The Technos had left behind in the upper floors of the factory were located.

"Man, I've missed these babies," Ram said, gazing fondly at the computers that were once his playthings. Tilting his head from side to side to loosen up, Ram cracked his knuckles and began patting the computers warmly, affectionately, almost like they were his children, as he sat down at one of the computers, powering it up, Giga sitting beside him.

"It's amazing," Ram began, gently pressing the keys while the computer booted into life. "One keyboard is it all it takes – and with a few instructions-"

Ram suddenly picked up the keyboard and smashed it on the side of Giga's head. Giga, totally caught by surprise, almost fell off his seat. Ram then grabbed the large widescreen monitor, bringing it down on Giga, who this time dropped to the floor, unconscious.

"Like I said. A leader doesn't show someone all their tricks."

Ram grabbed a set of keys from Giga's pockets and rushed to the door. He wasn't done yet and there was no way he was going to allow Ved to hand him over to The Collective.

* * *

Two storeys up from where Ram been held, Ved walked down the corridor to the office where Jack and Ellie had been kept prisoner. He was intensely focused, reflecting on matters.

The contact he had made online with The Collective hadn't been going as he had hoped in recent days. Despite his requests for information about Cloe and a detailed list of the precise equipment and food he could expect from entering into a deal, The Collective hadn't been forthcoming with anything specific. Instead, when Ved had been online, his chats with whoever was at the other end of The Collective had become progressively laboured and didn't seem to be going anywhere.

Ved got the feeling that they were stalling somehow, deliberately keeping him online for as long as possible. It was taking too long to get the answers to his questions.

They were meant to be living in the age of instant communication but often his point of contact would take a few minutes before replying to Ved's messages. Even when he complained to the intermediary known as The Broker.

This had set alarm bells ringing in Ved's mind. He felt something was wrong – and was concerned that the longer he stayed online, there was a likelihood The Collective might indeed be able to trace his real-world location, getting through the layers of proxies he had been hoping to conceal his actual position.

Ved wished he could get his brother's advice, and imagining what Jay would have said, was of the view that he would advise him to pull out of the negotiations immediately. To change his strategy. From the way they were conducting themselves, Ved just sensed The Collective were biding their time, setting up some sort of trap, saying one thing but doing another. Ved knew enough about bad faith from all the time he had spent with Ram during Ram's Techno heyday.

"What do you want now?" Ellie wondered, giving Ved a disdainful look as he entered the room where she and Jack were being held.

"Nothing. There's been a change of plan," Ved advised.

"Which is?" Jack questioned.

"You're free to go," Ved said.

"You're kidding. Are you trolling us?" Ellie asked.

"No, seriously. I really mean it. You can go on your way, if you want to. Or you can stay here with us. Whatever makes you happy."

Ellie and Jack exchanged unsure glances with each other but Ved seemed genuine enough.

They asked him why there had been a change – and Ved told them about his doubts about The Collective from his interaction with them over the past few days.

But it wasn't just how The Collective had been. Jack and Ellie had managed to persuade him, he conceded, that he had been going about things the wrong way. Even if The Collective had shown they were being sincere and trustworthy, Ved no longer wanted to hand them over. He wasn't so sure about Ram though.

Ved said he had searched his soul for the right thing to do – and felt that the approach and outlook Jack and Ellie had, which is one the Mall Rats had as a whole, Ved knew, from his dealings with them earlier when they had all lived in the same city during Ram's Techno reign, was the right way to go. Cloe had also tried to show Ved in the past there was another way to live life – and he had finally accepted that the Mall Rat way of thinking and philosophy in life had some merit. But his ideology, he knew, would always revolve around technology.

Ved explained that he missed his brother deeply. He wished he could wind the clock back and spend more time with him. He only had one brother but didn't regret the hours he had instead devoted in days gone by to computers and other pursuits. Because Jay had been equally fascinated with technology and computers at that time. And they shared their passion, every single detail they were discovering. Even if they were not necessarily together.

He had been struck, he confessed, by something Ellie had said to him recently when he had visited her and Jack, about knowing the pain of what it was like to be separated from a sibling – and every day without Alice clearly caused Ellie anguish.

Jay may have gone but Ved could keep his spirit alive, Ellie had suggested, by never forgetting who he was and what he believed in. Ved would always have his brother in his life as long as he remembered Jay and what he stood for. He may not be able to spend more time with Jay in person – but Ved could do the next best thing, which was to honour Jay's wishes and safeguard what was important to him. He could look out for Amber and the Mall Rats, to whom Jay had gravitated to in his life – and by ensuring they were okay, Ved would be keeping his brother's wishes alive, and in so doing, Jay would be with him forever.

"I've got no beef with the Mall Rats," Ved admitted. "And this Broker I've been dealing with - he seems to be really well connected and might be able to help not just me. But you, Ellie, especially."

"How?" Ellie said.

"I'll let you know once I've checked out a few things," Ved replied.

Since he had been the leader of The Virts, Ved had been forced to shoulder more responsibility. That was precisely one of the key reasons he had been motivated to try and seek some deal from The Collective. So he could provide for his own tribe. They were running out of food, fresh drinking water. It was only a matter of time before the life he enjoyed with The Virts would be over.

And Ram was certainly a valuable trading commodity, which Ved couldn't ignore.

"Jay used to say that I shouldn't rely on him – or that someone else would always do what needed to be done for me. I should have listened to him. Then I might have been able to decide the best thing to do myself."

"We all learn things," said Ellie. "Alice and I certainly never always saw things eye to eye."

"That's the thing with hindsight," Jack agreed. "You only know what the right thing to do is after it's happened. We can learn from the past. But we can't re-live it. Unless, that is, you know anybody who's invented a time machine."

"Who knows? From the technology The Collective seem to have, according to The Broker, it might not be long before they do," Ved reflected.

Jack and Ellie smiled at the comment but then exchanged incredulous glances, realizing that Ved was not joking.

Sensing an opportunity to persuade Ved to let Ram also go free, Jack said, "If there's anyone with a brain to invent a time machine, then he's sitting in this very building. Sometimes Ram can be a real ass – but overall, he can be a big asset to us as well."

"Who needs The Collective or this Broker you keep mentioning when we can have our own tribal alliance," Ellie joked. "We'd have to think of a good name though. The *Mall Rat-Virts-and ex-Technos* just doesn't sound right. We'd need something catchy."

"We need Ram," Ved said, and Ellie and Jack followed him, happy at the supposed turnaround in his attitude and behaviour.

He was a chip off the old block after all, Jack thought, and really was Jay's little brother. Jay would be proud Ved was doing the right thing, Jack was certain.

The two Virts who had been guarding the room where Ram was being kept were now running towards Ved, Ellie and Jack.

"Ram's gone!" one of the Virts shouted.

Giga had regained consciousness and had alerted the guards, who had searched throughout the factory and there was no sign of Ram anywhere at his former Techno base.

"If he's gone out into the town – it could be like finding a needle in a haystack," Jack pointed out. "We might never find him."

"If I know Ram – I bet there's one place he could have gone," Ved said.

It was somewhere Ved had once visited in the virtual world when he had entered a virtual reality fantasy Ram had designed, recreating the house where he had grown up. But this time, Ved, along with Jack and Ellie, would be going there for real.

* * *

Far above the town and away from the factory, Ram noticed a drone scouting the area.

The Collective must have been trying to track down Ved's location every time he had contacted them online, confirming Ram's unease that with their sophisticated technology and team of hackers, it was only a matter of time before The Collective were able to approximate the town where Ved had been communicating with them from, even though they didn't have a fix yet on the precise co-ordinates.

Ram made his way furtively as the drone flew past overhead. He realized the drone wouldn't have enough charge in its batteries to stay out for too long. And no doubt would be accompanied by other drones on a reconnaissance mission collecting data, looking out for any heat signatures with its infrared cameras which would be analyzed by The Collective, intending to create a perimeter net around the town that would enable them to find and catch Kami's long-term rival and antagonist – Ram.

The drone returned in a zigzag motion, causing Ram to dive for cover and leap into a trash bin, burying himself beneath the filth piled up within, resisting the acrid smell, the phobias about germs resurfacing, as he hoped the layers of rubbish would conceal his position, keeping him hidden from the prying lenses of the drone.

This was only the first drone, Ram knew, and wouldn't be the last. He cringed at the thought that The Collective were mobilized, looking for him - and would soon close in.

CHAPTER TWENTY-SEVEN

Amber couldn't believe that Bray was gone – and irrationally it felt all the more worse because she blamed herself in part for his disappearance. If only she hadn't been so trusting, so sure that Cami and The Collective were a positive force for good in this world. She should have paid attention to Bray's suspicions that all was not well with The Collective.

Instead, she chose to believe perhaps what she wanted to believe. She was so passionate about making the world a better place, helping the lives of others – that she realized to herself she might have seen in The Collective something that was never really even there. So intent was she on doing right, she might have overlooked the things that were wrong. But Bray hadn't.

He had warned about the dangers of the Zootist faith and now was possibly taken by some zealot of the ideology given that Bray was Zoot's brother and held a twisted status and value.

All the Mall Rats were deeply concerned and rallied around Amber to give their support with Lex, Ryan and

Alice searching the grounds, fearing that perhaps Bray had wandered away. And might have even tripped and fallen into the water if he had strolled on one of the jetties.

Storm had advised that according to the security log of all the guards that they had seen Bray in the grounds at 3.08 A.M. in the morning, shortly after Storm himself noticed Bray in the corridor passing Trudy's room, apparently en route to grab something to eat in the dining area because he was restless and couldn't sleep.

Amber insisted that the Mall Rats would refrain from visiting Eden and indeed anywhere else until Bray was found safe and well, demanding The Selector meet the Mall Rats because they deserved an explanation how Bray could have gone missing from a seemingly secure and well-guarded facility.

The Selector struggled with his nervous 'tics' as he examined security footage Storm had showed, displaying an image of Bray who indeed had been recorded in the grounds by the lake. But he disappeared from frame and for some reason wasn't picked up by the next security camera, which scanned the ensuing section.

"It doesn't make any sense," The Selector said. "It's as if he has totally evaporated into thin air."

"He can't have disappeared – he has to be somewhere!" Amber snapped, trying to control her emotions and sense of rising panic.

"Perhaps, had you all agreed to have the biochips implanted, then we could have tracked him," The Selector sneered, taking clear delight that in this instance the Mall Rats had been hoist with their own petard.

Ryan lunged at The Selector and had to be restrained by Lex.

"Easy, Ryan. That's not going to help," Lex said.

"Especially to any of you," The Selector insisted. "There's no need to resort to violence. Otherwise we can't guarantee your safety. And I won't be held responsible for any retaliation."

"What you said about those biochips – that was so insensitive," Trudy exclaimed.

"You can see how difficult this is for Amber. For all of us," Salene added.

"Of course I can. I totally understand. And I want you to know that we've sent out our finest dogs and trackers, along with a fleet of drones. We'll find him, wherever he is."

"I hope so," May said, taking baby Jay from Amber's arms, who was crying and making it difficult for Amber to concentrate and think clearly.

Amber didn't believe The Selector was being sincere in his concern. He certainly seemed to be troubled. But she felt – as did all the Mall Rats – that he was giving a slant on matters, even placing the blame for what happened on Bray, suggesting that maybe Bray had left on his own accord.

"And why would he do that?" Amber said angrily.

"The course of true love never runs smooth," The Selector said wryly, casting a discreet glance at Tai San who was standing close to Lex. "Have you both been having any 'problems' of late?" The Selector continued, probing. Lex and Tai San didn't answer and The Selector considered Amber. "What about you, Amber – and Bray?"

Amber wondered if somehow the Mall Rats were still under surveillance and checked if The Selector had reactivated the monitoring of the *Lakeside Resort*. The Selector advised that this hadn't occurred and that he simply had examined the security log and couldn't help but notice on the data file that Storm and the guards had recorded that they had overheard some arguments of late emanating from Bray and Amber's room.

"So, you ARE still 'listening'?" Salene said disdainfully.

"The guards wouldn't be doing their jobs unless they did. How else could they protect you if something untoward had happened and you were screaming for help?"

"It didn't exactly 'help' Bray though, did it, pal?" Lex said.

"I don't recall any references to the security detail hearing any screaming from Bray. But I'll check with Storm and take another look at the overnight log," The Selector replied sarcastically, knowing full well that Bray disappeared amidst no noise whatsoever.

Lottie and Sammy were becoming distraught overhearing it all and were struggling to reconcile the gravity of Bray missing with The Selector's overly friendly but clearly insincere demeanour.

Amber demanded a face to face meeting with Cami. The Selector advised that there was no need for them to travel to Eden because The Creator had been informed that Bray was missing and wanted to visit the *Lakeside Resort*. An unprecedented situation given that The Creator was reclusive, seldom venturing into the outside world, choosing to spend her time in her inner sanctum carrying out her research.

* * *

Cami's procession arrived at the *Lakeside Resort* in the late afternoon, the alpine background a silhouette cast in the sun's golden light, the lake perfectly still, barely even a breeze, as if nature herself was appearing at its very best and most scenic, heralding the arrival of The Creator.

The Selector said it was an honour for the Mall Rats that she was choosing to visit from her exalted position high in the mountains overlooking her world and symbolized the respect she had for them, by her visiting them as opposed to them coming to see her at Project Eden.

A convoy of vehicles pulled into the driveway by the resort entrance. Mostly electric driverless pods. Cami disembarked, surrounded by a retinue of servants who arranged themselves in a V-shaped split of two welcoming lines, making a gap through which Cami, herself, and the elite guards who escorted her, could pass.

An advanced party under instructions given by The Selector had already cleaned up the resort pending Cami's arrival, making it utterly spotless, free of even a single speck of dust. But Cami was wearing a germ-protective mask when she arrived as a precaution.

"I personally checked all areas, doing random samples inside and outside the grounds, making sure everything is perfect for you, Creator. And safe." The Selector said. "My staff's monitoring can find no evidence at all of any bacteria which might harm you," The Selector added, indicating an array of waveforms on various equipment.

Cami nodded gratefully and removed her mask as she entered through the swing doors, followed by her retinue of guards and servants.

There were three Mall Rats in particular who Cami wanted to see. She was going to grant an audience to all of the Mall Rats, of course, but wanted especially to meet Amber, Trudy and Lex, given their connection to Zoot.

It was as if they were having a royal visit, Amber felt, the formalities reminding her of ceremonies with dignitaries in the adult times she had seen on the news.

"I am so sorry to hear about Bray," Cami said. "It must be awful for you all. Please rest assured that we'll do everything we can to return him. Perhaps we can all spend some time together to discuss any concerns you all might have throughout dinner. But I'd be grateful if I could have some time with Amber, Trudy and Lex. Starting with you first, Amber?"

"Of course," Amber replied.

On The Selector's prompting, the servants made themselves scarce and waited in the lobby. The other Mall Rats dispersed as well.

The only people left in the lounge area were The Creator's personal guards, who stationed themselves at various exit and entry points.

A few minutes of silence passed between them, Amber wondering what Cami wanted to say to her.

Cami was barefoot and wore the same type of patchwork linen dress as every time Amber had seen her before. Her hair was adorned with a circle of green leaves, like a crown. A mixture of twigs, flowers and different shades of green leaves were inserted in bands around her ankles. She carried a single white rose in one hand and sniffed the scent appreciatively several times since she had arrived. And Amber felt a sense of calm in Cami's demeanour and serenity. She looked like a dryad, a wood fairy from a children's book - a living embodiment of Mother Nature.

"This rose could have been extinct. Had it not adapted and evolved from the work we carried out in the laboratories," Cami finally said, while staring at the flower closely, feeling its petals with her finger, breathing in deeply through her nose, savouring the smell of the scent. She was contemplating its contours, rubbing the stalk with her thumb, lost in her own private reverie as she continued.

"I don't know if you have ever followed his writings but Charles Darwin said it is not the strongest or the most intelligent who survive – but the ones who are the most adaptable," Cami said, gazing thoughtfully at the flower, twirling it in her fingers. "Are you going to be adaptable, Amber?"

"That depends on what has happened to Bray. And if he returns."

"Of course, I understand. But I wasn't just referring to Bray. How can I best describe what I mean?" Cami pondered, then once again indicated the rose. "First, we need to be aware of a flower – and if so, then we will also be aware of a tree – then a forest – then it's the world itself. If we can live in harmony with nature, not treat it with disdain but respect. Then there is hope for the human species if we can realize that we're not the only living things on this planet. Hopefully - future generations might not replicate what has gone before."

She passed the rose to Amber, who took it and smelt the scent. "Thank you. It's beautiful."

"The human species can also be beautiful, Amber," Cami replied. "If it can only learn to adapt and evolve."

"Possibly," Amber said introspectively, slightly preoccupied, still thinking about Bray - which registered with Cami.

"Tell me about the love you feel for Bray," Cami said, explaining that she had personally never experienced love for a man before – and wondered what it was like, how it felt, the real feelings, not those from romantic stories she had read in her repository of books. But real love. "How would you define it?"

"That's a difficult question," Amber pondered. "Without love, I think possibly everything else is irrelevant."

"Nature?" Cami probed.

"In some ways," Amber said. "I think having someone - or perhaps even something to love - is essential to existence. Otherwise, there is no meaning to it all and life itself might simply become dysfunctional."

"That's interesting," Cami said. "I've always thought that the definition of love is where someone's happiness might be central to one's own happiness. If the person one loves isn't happy, then obviously how could anyone be happy too?"

"Exactly," Amber agreed. "That's an interesting definition as well."

"What I'm most interested in though is - do you think it's possible for love to adapt and evolve? To go through the same process as nature?"

"I don't quite understand," Amber said.

"Let me put this a different way. Your love... Bray... Do you think you could exist without him?"

Amber exchanged a long glance with Cami, wondering where her line of questioning was going. "Are you suggesting that Bray might not return?" Amber said, horrified at the prospect.

"No, not at all. I'm just interested... Did you love your parents?" Cami clarified.

"Very much so," Amber replied.

"But you've adapted and evolved in this new world we're all trying to create."

"I think that's a different comparison though."

"I was just wondering. Because I don't think I loved my mother. I admired her. And the work she carried out. But I didn't love her as such. In fact, we rarely spent much time together."

"What about your father?" Amber asked.

"I didn't know him very well either. He was a 'test tube'," Cami replied matter-of-factly.

"I'm… sorry."

"Don't be. I'm not. Science gave me life. And it has also given me the ability to love all living species in the natural world. So I am researching more about the human condition."

* * *

Trudy paced up and down in her room, trying to keep her composure, waiting to be 'summoned' for her audience with Cami.

She determined that she wasn't going to wait and be kept on call and decided to join Storm, who had taken Brady outside to play catch with the ball – along with Sammy and Lottie but also Storm's little sister, whom he had received permission to visit, and had just recently arrived.

Storm had apparently said he thought it might help Trudy if Brady had some friends to play with. But Trudy suspected that in reality Storm perhaps wanted his sister to catch a glimpse of The Creator, Cami herself, whom very few had ever seen.

From feeling Storm was an unwanted presence in their lives, a nuisance, who represented intrusion, Trudy's outlook was slowing turning. She had discovered Storm was kind, gentle and had an honourable, almost noble quality about him.

He had revealed how he had become streamed into the militia after his own town had been taken over by The Collective and seemed a little more 'human' when

Trudy overheard him speaking of his younger sister, Charlotte, who was thirteen years his junior, the result of a second marriage his mother had entered into after his parents divorced. Brady reminded him of his little sister. Who was now seven years old.

When their town had been invaded by The Collective, Charlotte was entered into The Collective's educational programme – and ironically, Trudy knew, that she was being raised to believe in the Zootist faith, taught to hold Brady and Trudy in positions of esteem, reverence.

Intrigued by his own personal view, Trudy had one day asked him how he felt about Zoot. And was surprised to discover that he didn't believe in it or sanction it. But had clearly confided in Trudy because the revelation could have endangered his standing and also Charlotte, who was living in one of the dormitories in Eden.

When Trudy and the others had been brought to their lands, The Selector personally assigned Storm to become Trudy's bodyguard, being aware of Storm's affinity and care for younger children from the way he had devoted himself to protecting his younger sister, visiting her regularly from his barracks when he was not on duty.

* * *

Lex pulled on the oars of the rowing boat he was in, taking it further out to the lake, as Cami has requested him to. It was just the two of them in the boat, the oars leaving imprints in the surface of the water as Lex rowed.

All around them was nothing but nature. Peaceful, serene. The sound of the oars swooshing through the water rhythmically. A few birds flew overhead, passing by, taking a curious look at the little boat disturbing their natural habitat by its presence. Lounging in the back of the boat, almost flat on her back, Cami stared up at the birds as they soared above against the golden sky, a palette of warm colours, the late afternoon sun not having long before it set.

Cami was utterly relaxed and in a reverie, enjoying every moment of her boat ride with Lex. She had dipped her hands in the water and was waving them gently, as if paddling along, accompanying Lex's languid strokes. She looked ecstatic, joyously contented – Lex stealing looks at The Collective leader, wondering what on earth she was thinking about – and why she had asked Lex to row her out into the lake so she could talk with him.

About a hundred metres away, following behind, keeping their distance so as not to get too close and interrupt Cami and Lex's journey together, several boats maintained their formation, the guards on board peering through binoculars at The Creator and the Mall Rat with her, their boat engines idling, ready to drive the throttle forward if they needed to get to The Creator quickly.

"It's beautiful, isn't it?" Cami said to Lex, suddenly speaking to him for the first time since they had left the shoreline. "To think that life would have begun in a place somewhere like this, so many millennia ago. And now here we are, just you and I. Humanity has conquered and taken over this planet. Do you think we can save it?"

Lex continued rowing for a moment, unsure, before answering. "Only if we survive ourselves."

"From what I know of you, Lex – you're certainly a 'survivor'," Cami said, her voice soft and sensuous almost, so relaxed was she in the boat, waving her hand through the water once more.

Lex elaborated that he thought it would take a lot more than The Collective to save the world. Or Lex. And Cami. He was uncertain how he should behave in her company and how he would respond. But decided just to be honest. He had nothing to hide.

Cami suddenly jumped overboard and disappeared beneath the surface, the boat rocking back and forth, side to side, from the momentum of her sudden movement – Lex was totally surprised – and froze in confusion and concern.

"What the hell are you doing?" he called out to her, searching the water, his eyes rapidly scanning around the boat for any sign of her. "Cami!?"

There was nothing. She had been gone for a few seconds.

"I don't know why I get myself into these things," Lex grumbled to himself, and dove into the water, searching for her.

About a minute later, Lex breached the surface - Cami in his arms, the two of them gasping for breath, clutching the side of the boat, their chests heaving, feeling the fresh mountain air in their lungs.

With a mighty effort, Lex pushed Cami, shoving her up and back into the boat before clambering in himself.

Cami was laughing, finding delight in what had just happened, almost amused by Lex's actions and the bemused look on his face. She motioned to the security detail that she was fine, indicating that all was well.

"What was all that about?" Lex questioned, spluttering, still getting his breath back. "Why'd you do that?"

"I needed to check…" Cami said, breathing deeply from being submerged, pausing as she spoke, "… You're not only a survivor, Lex… but you killed Zoot by your actions… I needed to see if you had the same capacity to cherish life – and if you would save me."

"You could have just asked," Lex said, flabbergasted by her.

"Not that I might need to be saved," Cami said. "I was raised swimming with dolphins. I'm more than capable of getting back to the shore. I appreciated the opportunity to have a chat."

"A test more like?" Lex asked, intrigued by it all.

Cami smiled slightly, then dove into the water and swam towards the shore while Lex pulled on the oars, the boat following in pursuit.

* * *

While Ryan waited to be summoned for his audience with Cami, he took time to have a workout in the gym with Salene, who stated that she didn't trust Cami and suspected for sure that The Selector had something to do with Bray's disappearance. Both resolved that if The Collective's forces couldn't shed any light on the mystery, then they would set up a plan to try and find him again themselves.

Tai San was lost in meditation doing a series of Tai Chi moves while she watched Lex row to the shore and Cami being greeted by servants as she climbed out of the water, the servants wrapping her with towels and blankets.

Trudy was watching Alice play with Storm and Sammy, Lottie, Brady and Storm's little sister, Charlotte. It was a game of hide and seek.

Amber had returned to her room to relieve May, who was looking after baby Jay.

All the Mall Rats were concerned when Salene and Ryan arrived, advising that they had been trying to track down Alice to see what she thought the merits might be of them having a contingent plan to send out another search party of their own, rather than rely on Cami's militia to track Bray down.

But so far, there was no sign of Alice anywhere and she, as with Bray, had seemingly disappeared.

"It doesn't make any sense. She was here just a minute ago. I saw her with my own eyes," Trudy said.

"Maybe she's still hiding and is waiting to be found," Ryan pondered reflectively.

"Since I've known you, Ryan, you've said a lot of dumb things. But that's gotta take the top spot," Lex snapped impatiently.

"If you don't mind me saying, Sir, I think Mister Ryan is just trying to help," Storm said.

"And you can just shut it!" Lex said, glaring at Storm.

"Back off, Lex. Storm's only trying to help as well," Trudy protested.

"What are you defending him for? He's not even a Mall Rat!" Lex scoffed. "Unless you two have got a 'thing' going. Is that it?"

"Don't be ridiculous. How can you suggest such a thing!?" Trudy exclaimed.

"Right. And you should try and calm down, Lex," May said in an attempt to defuse the situation. "Arguing between ourselves isn't going to help matters."

"Right! You shouldn't yell at my big brother!" Charlotte said angrily.

"Apologise to Mister Lex, Charlotte. That's disrespectful," Storm scolded his little sister and she sighed.

"I'm sorry, Sir."

"The name's Lex."

"Sorry, Sir Lex," Charlotte said softly, innocently.

"Have you been giving that kid some lessons?" Lex asked Ryan, then turned back to Charlotte. "I told you. My name's Lex. Not Sir Lex. Or Sir. Just Lex."

"My little sister's apologized, Sir. And I hope you'll not only accept it. But respect it. But if not, we can always meet, off the grid, and sort it all out," Storm said. There was a utility of restrained emotion and motion, a force which registered with Trudy and she now realized that Storm was aptly named as he stood, controlling his obvious simmering anger.

"I might just take you up on that, pal, if you give me any more hassle," Lex said, squaring up to Storm.

Amber appeared in the lobby with baby Jay in her arms. "What's all this I hear about Alice disappearing!?"

* * *

The Selector was furious and scolded Commander Snake, standing before him, in The Selector's private quarters at the lodge. "She couldn't just 'vanish'," The Selector snapped irritably and again was struggling to contain his nervous 'tics'.

"I just don't understand it, Sir," Snake replied. "Our security detail at the resort is the very best. It's impossible for anyone to have gotten through."

"So, what are you suggesting, Snake? That the Mall Rat just decided to walk off? And join Bray? Is that what you think?" he scoffed.

Snake sighed, not entirely sure what he did think, while The Selector breathed slowly, in through his nose and out through his mouth, trying somehow to calm himself and control his nervous tics. And he clearly was becoming paranoid, as well as panicked.

"Those Mall Rats... I wonder if they're 'rats' and we can trust them? Maybe they're playing games with us. Trying to test us, just as we are them."

"I honestly don't know, Sir," Snake said, stealing wary looks as The Selector gazed around suspiciously, as if checking if someone, somewhere was watching him.

"I can trust you, Snake – can't I?" he asked.

"Of course, Sir," Snake replied. "There is really no need to ask."

"But I did ask! And I demand to know!" The Selector erupted, in total fury.

"Like I said, Sir, all my team – we have your back. We always have. Always will."

"Good. Good. Essential that we have each other's backs in this God-forsaken world, Snake. If we don't look out for each other, then no one else will."

Snake nodded in agreement and watched The Selector, who was becoming more agitated, lost in his thoughts, as he reflected introspectively.

"Something's wrong. I just know it. If our team weren't responsible for those 'rats' going missing - and Alice and Bray aren't involved in some conspiracy themselves – then we might have a 'rat' within, Snake. We might have someone trying to undermine us. And bring us down."

* * *

The Selector was unaware that his concerns were prophetic and his destiny was about to change, precipitated by an event in The Cube.

Each contestant had been instructed to hold a rope at which some rocks had been placed on the other end, in proportion to each of the contestant's body weight, so that one contestant wasn't disadvantaged compared to another, with them all having to endure the same relative burden.

The aim of the 'trial', according to The Gamesmaster, was to test the human spirit. It wasn't a battle of strength but a contest of wills, to see how long each of them would last before they gave up and dropped the rope, unable to hold onto their encumbrance any longer. It was truly a question of mind over matter, The Gamesmaster had emphasized into the cameras.

Across the lands, the vast audience watched The Cube as it was projected onto buildings.

And to everyone's surprise – especially her own – Emma had finished triumphant. With her blindness, she was able to compete equally with the other contestants and had displayed tremendous willpower and inner resolve to hold on to her own weight far longer than anyone else. The endeavour had exhausted her and she had collapsed shortly afterwards, riven by cramps.

Ebony had finished second, Hawk third. Emma's effort had impressed both of them, Ebony especially, who was really coming to admire Emma's spirit and no longer perceived her as a vulnerable girl - but someone with great resolve who deserved respect.

In the 'final' test of the episode The Gamesmaster advised that one of the guards, Wolf, lived by a strict code and never lied. Whereas another guard, Dog, was known to lie. On occasion. The aim of the last game was to check each contestant's powers of observation, senses, and mental agility.

There were two paths at the end of which one path held a basket full of food which the winner could enjoy as well as winning the 'test'. Wolf said that the basket was at the end of path one. Dog said it was actually at the end of path two. So the contestants were unanimous that the basket of food would be at the end of path one. Because Wolf said it was and never lied. And Dog said it was pathway two and if he is lying, then clearly it would be pathway one.

The Gamesmaster reminded the contestants though that Dog only lies on occasion. The contestants didn't think it would make any difference if Wolf never lied because he had stated the basket was at the end of pathway one.

Emma though was the sole contestant who felt that it all depended upon how they introduced themselves in the first place. Wolf introduced himself as Wolf and Dog as Dog, which meant that he was actually Dog. Otherwise if he was lying he would have introduced himself as Wolf.

The other contestants including Ebony cringed, realizing that they hadn't paid particular attention to who was speaking. Ebony believed it shouldn't make any difference just as long as Wolf introduced himself because he never lied. Emma though clearly had her own view given that it was important to determine when Dog might be lying, which he does on occasion. Because he might have introduced himself as Wolf.

"Can I ask Wolf and Dog a question?" she asked.

"Be my guest," The Gamesmaster replied.

"Wolf – did you change the sign of pathway one to pathway two?"

"I did," Wolf replied.

"What about you, Dog – did you change the sign?"

"I did," Dog replied.

"Then this time you're lying and not telling the truth, Dog, otherwise you would have said you didn't if you were telling the truth. This means then that before you were lying otherwise you would have said the pathway was one given that in actual fact the food must be in pathway two."

"So you think it's pathway two then, Emma?" The Gamesmaster said.

"Yes. Otherwise Dog should have said no that he hadn't changed the sign which meant that he did."

"But only if he was lying, which he only does on occasion," The Gamesmaster replied, clearly getting as confused as all the contestants along with Wolf and Dog.

Emma was positive with her reasoning and especially that she distinctly heard Dog first time around introducing himself as Dog but second time around had introduced himself as Wolf. So was lying either first or second time around and telling the truth on the other occasion. Which was central to linking when Wolf was speaking.

The Gamesmaster addressed the audience, gazing intently into the cameras reminding all who were watching that things aren't always what someone sees or what even anyone else says, but in this case, Emma was relying on her highly developed sense of recall of what she had heard but not seen evoking a way of thinking through mental reasoning. And was declared the winner of the test.

At the end of the game, The Gamesmaster had a discreet word with Ebony and asked her to make sure that she and Emma stayed behind, rather than join their fellow contestants in The Cube living quarters for dinner.

"Why?" Ebony asked.

Normally so cool, composed and confident, there had been a change in The Gamesmaster's demeanour, which hadn't gone unnoticed by Ebony. He seemed nervous, unsettled, worried almost. Preoccupied.

"There's no time for any questions," he said carefully. "Just follow me."

He led them through the darkness to the shore of the lake and instructed Ebony to use one of the security jet skis to take Emma and her further down the lake, the far south end where they would be met by others who would then brief them.

"What's going on?" Ebony asked, unsettled herself and wondering if this all might be some kind of test, even part of the game and if Wolf and Dog were participating. The Gamesmaster was preoccupied, revealing that his instructions involved a different source and unbelievably, it seemed that The Gamesmaster was giving Ebony and Emma an opportunity to escape. If that indeed was the case, however slim and unpredictable, Ebony was going to take it.

She caught the keys The Gamesmaster tossed her and sat on the jet ski, while he helped Emma, who sat behind Ebony.

"You'd better hold on tight," Ebony said.

Emma wrapped her arms around Ebony's waist.

"I can give you ten minutes. But no more. Then I'll have to alert the guards that you've escaped."

"Is this some kind of a joke?" Ebony asked, still unable to comprehend what was occurring.

"It won't be if you're caught. You'd better get a move on," The Gamesmaster said uneasily. And he watched as Ebony started the engine of the jet ski, which sped away - and then returned towards the main administration building and living quarters of The Cube.

Emma clung desperately to Ebony as they sped along, the jet ski hurling into the air occasionally due to the high speed they were travelling.

"Where are we going!?" Emma shouted over the engine noise.

"I have no idea!" Ebony yelled back. "Now keep quiet and let me concentrate. I can hardly see where we're going in this darkness!"

"Tell me about it," Emma replied dryly, which caused Ebony to smile, despite herself, as the jet ski sped through the darkness of night towards its destination – wherever that destination might be.

CHAPTER TWENTY-EIGHT

The Broker stood on the quayside in an area nearby the docks at which Tai San had arrived. He was watching grain, rice and pallets of fresh water being loaded into the hold of a ship.

Nearby, there were some people fishing off the jetty. All looked ravaged, malnourished and defeated. Others were scavenging for fish in stacked bins, fighting gulls shrieking in frenzy, some attacking their competitors to grab remnants of any scraps of food.

A trader looking down at heel himself arrived on a rusty bicycle, seemingly from a bygone age.

"You're late," The Broker said, disdainfully.

"It seems there's a bit of a problem," the trader replied uneasily.

"What kind of a 'problem'!?"

"I've just checked in The Void and there's no sign of the 'cargo'," the trader replied.

"Then that really is a problem, isn't it? For you," The Broker said, menacingly.

"Give me a break. Times are hard. It's not my fault. I must have been double-crossed."

"That's not my problem. It looks as if I'll be keeping my deposit then, if you're unable to deliver. The deal's off."

* * *

A short distance away, further along the dockside, Bray walked through a busy marketplace. He was wearing a hoodie which had been given to him so that he could mask his appearance and remain as disguised as he could be.

Since he had been snatched while having a stroll in the early hours of the morning at the *Lakeside Resort*, Bray had been plunged from the material comforts of life and delivered into a hell hole.

The Void, as he had discovered it was called, fully deserved its name. It was a place devoid of any resemblance of civilization – a lawless, anarchic and wild shanty town. A slum where those who had been put in it had been left to be forgotten.

Besides being a refuge of the lost, the unwanted, those who society had given up on, The Void also housed transients and traders. There was a cacophony of noise from peddlers trying to sell their wares - which ranged from goats, cattle, chickens, clothes and animal skins. All around, beggars pleaded for scraps of food. Other inhabitants were given fruit in return for performing. There were surreal tumblers, fire eaters, and acrobats and Bray was concerned if he might encounter the infamous Top Hat and his crazed Tribe Circus, who were once a nightmarish adversary.

On the night he was seized, Bray had almost successfully resisted being taken but had soon been overwhelmed by a group of renegade warriors who had bound his legs and arms, prior to throwing him in the back of a decaying military vehicle.

Underneath the flapping canvas, throughout the long journey as the mountains and lakes disappeared in the alpine area, Bray was aware that the vehicle was seemingly travelling in the middle of nowhere.

The terrain of the well-tended agricultural crops of The Collective soon gave way to a dusty, desert-like region, the soil barren, devoid of plants, even without grass, a lifeless area, a bleak wasteland.

They had driven for hours, passing road signs from the adult days warning of contamination, bio-hazards, finally announcing that anyone on the journey was now leaving a restricted sector. Soon after, Bray finally fell asleep, wakening in the early morning as the vehicle arrived in the docklands area.

The Void was segmented by high wire fencing and curiously watchtowers which were now abandoned. Bray eventually became aware that the community originated as a holding area of quarantine during the height of the pandemic and evolved into the slum it was today.

Some of the inhabitants lived in stacked cargo containers, or in warehouses and stores long-ago since looted and now covered in graffiti. Others were clearly homeless and lived on the street with nothing but their ragged clothes and cardboard box blankets - and an array of meagre personal items which they guarded as if valuable jewels.

Bray had originally been held in a warehouse, apparently waiting to be traded and 'transported'. But he was surprised by a guard who had released him, mentioning that he was part of the resistance and that Bray had to travel to a safehouse, *The Mermaid's Booty*. Bray had enquired just exactly what the guard was resisting, only to be advised that it would be well and truly apparent during his journey through The Void.

And his journey so far was worse than anything Bray had ever witnessed. It was a living hell. The collapse of humanity. He pitied those poor residents who had been quarantined in the past but now the stench in the air was nauseating from a lack of sewage and it was like God had forsaken this place, doomed it to judgement, afflicted it with a plague that had ripped the heart and life out of any form of decency, let alone a society.

There was pestilence everywhere, the victims covered in welts, sores, had to have all kinds of diseases, Bray thought, likely to be infectious too. Some coughed uncontrollably. He wished he could so something for them but he simply could not. Bray promised himself that if he could find someone, anyone, in The Void who might be able to help these people, or provide any medical supplies, he would return to them to try and improve their situation. Otherwise, many of them were slipping away, some willingly it seemed, wanting it to be all over, heading into death's door as a welcome escape.

Having cautiously made his way through the marketplace, Bray arrived at a building which was a hub of activity - but rather than inhabitants domiciled in The Void, seemed to be frequented by more of a transient population – including the crews of some ships who were visiting temporarily. Though quite why anyone would want to visit, Bray didn't understand – but soon would when he walked into *The Mermaid's Booty* which resonated with life from those inside the bar who were talking, drinking, gambling. And intriguingly, Bray could hear music, the sounds of perfect harmonies, *a cappella* singing which was strangely familiar although Bray couldn't quite recall why.

Stepping past towering bouncers who guarded the door and must have been expecting Bray from the ease in which they allowed him in, Bray surveyed customers gathered at the bar, knocking back their drinks, bantering with each other.

The singing was coming from a trio Bray finally recognized. And he almost did a double-take upon seeing them, standing on top of a small stage, kicking their legs like they were can-can girls while they sung and entertained the raucous crowd. They were Lips, Teeth and Dimples – and were from Bray's home city originally. They had always been eccentric, unstable even, a musically-obsessed group that had caused problems for the Mall Rats in the past and were no friends of Bray's.

They seemed to act and look even more bizarre now, their faces caked in grotesque make-up like a cruel caricature portrait of the *avant garde* but punctuated now by the absurd, their make-up smeared, almost cartoon-like.

Bray dipped his head, trying to avoid eye contact with them, hoping to blend in with the others as he made his way to the bar to get a much-needed drink, as well as to try and meet the contact he was advised would provide further instructions.

Lips, Teeth and Dimples spotted Bray, however, from their vantage on the stage above the crowd and began to point at him, calling his name.

"*Fancy that – a Mall Rat – here today – we can see Bray.*"

They weren't speaking as such nor rapping but had interwoven Bray's name into the lyrics of the song they were singing.

So much for his hopes of going about unnoticed – but the other attendees in the tavern paid scant attention to his presence being highlighted by the singers. Apart from a few occasional looks at him, Bray was ignored by most of the denizens who were more interested in their drinks and their conversation.

"Hey, honey – you want a good time?" a female in her late teens standing at the bar, asked Bray.

She had a spluttering cough and Bray felt sorry for her, her skin a yellowing pallor, some sores around her cracked lips. She was obviously exchanging her body for food and drink to survive.

"I'm fine – thanks anyway."

The prostitute sneered, then slinked away while Bray got the attention of the barkeeper, an assertive and confident person – and one he also recognized. It was Roanne. He was aware she had run her own brothel, long ago, in his own city - Salene having fallen into Roanne's debt, accidentally ensnared when she was particularly vulnerable and at a low ebb. Like Lips, Teeth and Dimples - Roanne, too, was far from home and had ended up in The Void, like Bray – though with her entrepreneurial ways, she seemed in a position of influence in comparison to others Bray had encountered.

"Well, well," Roanne said. "I heard rumours the Mall Rats were around – but I didn't expect any of 'em to show up here. If you don't fancy one of my girls – you look like you could fancy a drink. But only the first one's on the house. After that, you gotta pay up and trade. Or else you get out."

Bray asked for the largest drink she had by size – much to her amusement. He wasn't after alcohol but just as much liquid as he could get, clean water even. Roanne gave him a bottle of ginger beer – from her special reserves.

"What are you doing here, Mall Rat?" Roanne asked, as Bray took some welcome sips from his drink.

"I'm supposed to meet up with someone," Bray replied, enigmatically.

"Well, you look out for yourself. Not everyone here are fans of the Mall Rats. You've made yourself some enemies over the years."

A little while later, an acrobat had wanted another drink but had been refused because last orders had already been taken.

The acrobat grabbed a bottle of brandy, took a swig and had breathed 'fire', the flame setting another drunken customer's hair alight.

"Put that out – and get him out!" Roanne yelled, as her bouncers and some of her close 'girls' threw items of clothing on the customer's head, denying oxygen to the flames while the bouncers dragged the protesting and drunk acrobat out.

Lips, Teeth and Dimples looked on in absolute fascination and started to laugh manically prior to proceeding doing backwards somersaults themselves while continuing singing as they disappeared through the doors.

"The bar's shut – everybody out!" Roanne said. But added in an undertone, "Just stay where you are, Bray."

Mumbling and voicing their discontentment, the clientele of the bar began to slowly make their way to the exit door and Roanne said, for dramatic effect - "You too, Mall Rat," apparently urging him to leave. "This isn't a charity – you want to sleep here, you pay for one of the girls or the rooms – or you don't stay at all."

She shook her head discreetly, indicating she wasn't meaning what she was saying and Bray waited, while protesting.

"I really appreciate you giving away my identity," he said sarcastically.

"Don't worry. It isn't a problem," Roanne replied, then added in an undertone, "You won't be here for long. But we don't want anyone to know that. For the time being, at least, trust me. It's in your interests for all our 'citizens' in The Void to think you've relocated and are now living here."

* * *

When the bouncers had locked the doors, Roanne led Bray into a living area of the bordello inhabited by 'her girls'. And to Bray's surprise, he had come face to face with Alice, Tiffany and Shannon, who had been staying in Roanne's private quarters.

"What are you doing here?" Bray asked, unable to believe what he was seeing.

"Well, certainly not 'working'," Alice required. "Though there's plenty of me to go around," she added, wryly.

Tiffany and Shannon gave Bray a huge hug, as did Alice. Then Roanne took the children away to pick something for them to eat, leaving Bray and Alice to catch up with one another.

Alice revealed that her journey was very similar to Bray's and brought him up to date on The Creator's 'royal visit'. She reassured him that all the Mall Rats were otherwise safe, which brought a great sense of relief to Bray, knowing that especially Amber and his young son were fine.

On the day that she was seized, Alice advised that she had checked the lakeside again while waiting for her audience with Cami and had noticed a mug Bray had used for drinking coffee. He confirmed he had a bite to eat, then took a stroll in the grounds of the resort, sipping on his coffee while enjoying the brisk night mountain air. Alice was about to tell the others but had been seized by guards and taken to a military vehicle under the control of a different group she had never experienced before, who seemed to be a bit renegade.

She, too, had been in a 'holding area' and had been released by the resistance, a part of which Roanne was also a member. And their network didn't just operate in The Void but had been extending because there had been a lot of rumours that The Creator was unaware of the true existence of the new society under The Collective banner – such as The Privileged, their servants The Discards, the slave population who toiled in the agricultural sector. As far as Alice could gather from what Roanne had said, The Creator was certainly unaware of the slum areas in The Void and the elicit trading on the dockside which consistently went on.

Bray was keen to know more about it when Roanne returned, having assured him and Alice that Shannon and Tiffany would be safe and that all of them would be departing The Void in the early hours of the morning. She just had to double-check various arrangements.

CHAPTER TWENTY-NINE

Ram was home. In the house that he had grown up in. A place full of many memories. The building he had been in when the whole adult world had come tumbling down around him. The house where he had established The Technos. And it felt fitting that if his time was finally running out, that he would meet his end at the house where his new life after the virus had begun. There was something almost poetic to it, he thought. But Ram had long resolved that his time wouldn't run out - yet.

After a stressful ordeal going through the abandoned streets of his old town, evading the drones flying overhead, Ram had finally made it to the house. *#60 Warren Road.* He didn't think he would have ever been back there – and never wanted to go back, always determined to go forward in life, to look to the future.

But since he was on the run from Ved – and trying to keep out of sight of the drones hunting the town, the house had beckoned to him in the recesses of his mind as the natural place to go, a sanctuary, like it had been since childhood when he had first started to become obsessed with computers and had played online gaming, eventually becoming a bit of a celebrity in the online world for his prowess and constant status as being top of the leaderboard.

He had only ever really had one competitor, as such – being Kami. Who was also proficient in gaming and computers.

The house had long ago been looted, vandalized, like all the other houses seemed to be in his street. The garden was overgrown. The swing Ram used to sit on as a little boy was nearly covered, obscured by the tall grass and looming weeds, only the top metal frame standing out above.

Ram felt strangely calm, a sense of peace, as he sat at the desk in the bedroom that used to be his. The gaming and technology posters that were on the walls were yellowing from the exposure to the sun blazing in the window, peeling off, fading. There was dust everywhere, the room stank of stale air.

But still, despite the passage of time and the decay it had suffered, it was *his* Room. In his parents' house. It was home.

He closed his eyes, leaning back in the chair at his old desk, the office-style chair creaking under his weight. He could picture his former life clearly and imagined his parents being in the house, how it used to be. He could almost hear the sound of the television coming from downstairs in his head, where his father had sat watching the news. It brought back his mother's voice, he could hear her clearly, calling to Ram from the kitchen below that his dinner was ready, like she once had. Ram could smell her homemade cooking, almost taste it.

Being in the house conjured up so many memories. It all felt so real. And Ram wondered if his recollections were real or if they stemmed from visits he had made in the virtual reality space he had designed and utilized.

Reality space was always a welcome escape but now it seemed to conflict with his recollections of boyhood. As powerful as computers and graphics were, the human mind was still eminently more capable and vivid in its recall, in the fantasies it could come up with. But equally, Ram's world of computers still seemed to dominate his entire being.

From outside, far in the distance, Ram could hear the current, very real noise of the drones buzzing around the town. There were more of them now, Ram having counted at least twenty, each scouting over various areas, searching for him, he expected, The Collective utilizing some of their high-tech resources in an effort to locate him. Ved must have let his guard slip, given away their real-world location, alerting The Collective that there *was* someone in the town, instead of it being deserted. And that someone was Ram, Ellie and Jack.

Standing on top of the desk, Ram reached up, removing the surround leading into the attic and climbed up inside, where he beamed, noticing his 'box of toys', action figures from his youth that he had kept. They were underneath a tattered duvet. And underneath the toys in the box, buried out of sight, was what Ram was looking for in the event he ever needed it. And he needed it now, more than ever.

It was his old laptop, from the days before he had left the house to base himself in the factory that The Technos had lived in. And he hoped that there was still power in the auxiliary emergency backup which he had arranged in the event that he ever needed it.

The street had been cabled and Ram bypassed the old system which he thought was decrepit, for all the adults at the time felt that it was next generation. But Ram was always frustrated by the bandwidth and in the midst of the pandemic had implemented various bypass systems through the fibre optic cables which had run underground and he was able to hook into his Techno base.

"I've missed you," Ram said to it, caressing the laptop affectionately with his fingers. "Let's just hope you still can get some juice."

He plugged a cable into the side, opened the lid and to his relief was able to power the laptop on. It still wouldn't have much charge, the battery having lost its cycles due to inactivity, Ram thought. But if he could get enough power, even for a few seconds, he might be able to copy over the files he needed onto one of the miniature drives that were also in his hidden 'toy box', concealed under the piles of action figures.

* * *

On the journey to Ram's house from the factory, Ved's search party, which included Jack and Ellie, had several panicked, close encounters with the drones flying overhead. They had nearly been spotted several times. Ved had thought to shoot the drones down with his stun gun but had been warned against doing so by Jack who thought if he did, Ved would only alert The Collective that someone *was* in the town - if the drones fell under attack and began dropping out of the sky. It was better to leave the drones alone, Jack suggested, and hope they left them alone, thinking that the town was uninhabited after all.

Ved, Jack and Ellie continued furtively, trying to stay out of sight – but suddenly all the drones started to zigzag, almost out of control. Like they were possessed. Hurling high into the sky, then speeding down towards the ground before receding away at speed.

Rather than being possessed, if Ellie didn't know better, she would swear that the drones were actually UFOs and not of this world.

* * *

Ram, in his attic, typed feverishly - then suddenly froze – hearing movement, someone else in the house coming upstairs.

"Ram? Are you there?" Jack's voice called out.

Ram didn't answer, trying to be invisible, keeping as quiet as possible.

"There's no-one here," Jack said, peering into the bedroom.

"What about the attic?" Ellie said, noticing the entrance cover had been open on one side.

Jack hoisted himself up from the desk he stood on, peeked his head in and noticed Ram, who faked a slight smile.

"Any sign of him?" Ved called up from downstairs.

"Please – don't give me away," Ram urged, whispering his request.

Ellie climbed on the desk to join Jack and both elevated themselves higher, into the attic, trying to reassure Ram that Ved was on his side. But Ram scoffed, advising that it wasn't what he had been given to believe, having successfully hacked not only the drones searching the town and finally disabling them - but he had made initial inroads into a network derived from Kami's main system. "Our friend, Ved, has been a very naughty boy," Ram advised.

* * *

Ram, Ellie and Jack travelled with Ved back to the Technos base. Ved was totally overwhelmed by what Ram had discovered. He advised that he had been in touch with The Broker online, hacking into Ved's own account.

"Impossible," Ved said, defensively.

"Well, it wasn't for me," Ram said. "I got in and you'd better not use your personal terminal again because I've inflicted a virus which is pretty malicious."

Ved finally owned up that he did have a plan in mind whereby he had hoped to trade Ram for Bray and Alice. As angry as Ellie and Jack were, they were also strangely grateful at Ved's hairbrained scheme because he had been trying to deliver Alice back to Ellie - he was touched by all that they had discussed. And was doing it for Jay – as a homage to his late brother, who would have approved of the two loving sisters being reunited.

He quickly realized though that Jay would have totally disapproved of trying to use Ram as a bargaining tool. Also, Bray, who didn't deserve to be treated as a commodity even if he was Zoot's brother and seemed as if he had a large price on his head for any bounty hunters.

"I bet not as high as mine," Ram reflected, with a degree of pride.

"You're something else, Ram," Jack said, amazed at Ram's ego - as was Ellie, even Ved.

Ram pointed to his head and said it wasn't a question of being egotistical but simply that he had a plan in mind. If it worked, he'd be a hero. But if it failed, then his value would rise dramatically. Along with probably Ellie, Jack and Ved's.

"Thank you very much," Ellie said. "Don't involve Jack and me in anything."

"I reckon it's our only chance," Ram stated.

"What have you got in mind?" Ved asked, in growing curiosity.

Ram said it would be too complicated to explain in any great detail. But he was sure that Ellie, Jack and Ved would geek out. And that he needed their assistance. The only place capable of mounting his plan was his old Techno base.

Jack, Ellie and Ved realized that they probably had no choice and travelled with Ram back to the industrial complex where Ram said they didn't have much time and that he needed all the help he could get in setting up.

He opened a small unit in the warehouse area, pressed a switch, and a screen descended, covering the entirety of one wall. Ved was amazed and had never known it was there before. Ram then assembled a long set of tables, assisted by Ellie, Jack and Ved, on a raised dais in front of the screen and said that he needed some laptops with a bit more grunt, capable of doing what he had in mind.

Ram then proceeded to adapt the software, keying in codes - realizing that each computer needed to be upgraded - and relied on his expertise from designing a digital version of whatever he wanted in the virtual world during his reign over The Technos.

Jack, Ellie and Ved watched, astonished, as Ram worked feverishly, manically. All being very literate technologically, they understood some of what Ram was doing but certainly not the software he was writing, with codes buried deep within the recesses of only Ram's mind.

"I'll tell you what," Ram said enthusiastically. "Why don't you get the rest of your Virts here and I'll give them a masterclass in the world of technology and what it's really capable of. And I'm not just talking about gaming or reality space. But something a little more mind-blowing, shall we say?"

Ved rounded up The Virts, who grouped together on chairs behind the raised dais, and watched Ved, Jack and Ellie - either side of Ram, who tilted his head from side to side, preparing for whatever he had in mind, cracking his knuckles.

"Now, just follow my instructions through each phase and then we'll get along just fine," Ram said. "And you'd better hold onto your hats – and keyboards. We're in for an awesome ride!"

He laughed almost manically as he typed in data on his own keyboard before exclaiming, in mounting excitement – "Good!... Good!... Now, Ved, Ellie and Jack – now that I'm in, I want you all to use this password: b@n@na$9894230.monk#y$419355.jungl82943&. concrete428932.eag!emounta!n."

Ved, Ellie and Jack typed the data into their computers, trying somehow to keep up with the information they were given.

"Everyone in?" Ram asked.

Jack and Ved confirmed that they seemed to be, but Ellie was having difficulty.

Ram leaned to his side, glancing at the screen, at the digital stars disguising the letters and numbers and noticed that there was one missing – '42832. eag!emounta!n'. I think you've missed out the 9 at the end - so strike the last four numbers and type in again 428932.eag!emounta!n."

Ellie did as instructed, then nodded, confirming that she had also been able to login.

Jack stole an incredulous look at Ram. "How the hell did you remember all that?"

"Let me take a minute and run my disc data manager in my brain. Then I'll be able to confirm that my memory functions are operating efficiently and effectively," Ram replied, laughing intently at his own joke.

Suddenly, the ominous visual of the colossus *K.A.M.I* computer in Eagle Mountain filled the entire screen on the wall ahead of them, with an intrusive, ominous presence – its 'eyes' emitting piercing beams of green light, seemingly bearing into not only everyone present – but into the depths of their very souls.

"IDENTIFY YOURSELF," the Eagle Mountain *K.A.M.I* said.

"It's Ram," Ram replied.

"AND WHAT ABOUT THE OTHERS?" the *K.A.M.I* Eagle Mountain computer probed.

Ram's expression clouded and he typed in more data on his keyboard feverishly. "You can't actually see us, can you *K.A.M.I*?" he asked.

"NOT NOW," the *K.A.M.I* Eagle Mountain system said softly, the voice echoing around the cavernous industrial warehouse. "BECAUSE YOU HAVE DISABLED MY SYSTEMS."

"Sorry about that," Ram replied, winking at Ved, Ellie and Jack, who gazed open-mouthed, as did the audience of Virts, totally geeking out on what they were witnessing.

"I need to check out the systems in your sister, *K.A.M.I*," Ram said. "You can log off and relax. Because I want to connect with the main prototype. The *K.A.M.I* system located – where is it - in Project Eden?"

"ACCESS DENIED. ACCESS DENIED. ACCESS DENIED," the *K.A.M.I* Eagle Mountain system repeated, over and over again.

"Yeah, right! That's what you think," Ram responded. But there was no disdain in the tone, only a manic excitement as he yelled, "Just like the old days, eh, Ved, boyo? Stand by Ellie and Jack. It's time to unleash the dogs of war!"

He typed in a growing frenzy on the keyboard, laughing hysterically, like some arch-villain, a madman, intent on destroying not only the world but the galaxies, let alone the entire universe.

CHAPTER THIRTY

From the haunted and anxious expression on The Selector's face, it was apparent he hadn't arrived at the *Lakeside Resort* to bring good news. Amber had initially dreaded that he was going to tell them something untoward had happened to Bray and Alice but was still nevertheless deeply concerned by what The Selector was revealing, causing him to have difficulty controlling his nervous tics.

"This is a dark day in our history," The Selector said, meeting all the Mall Rats in the main lounge. "Our hallowed and revered Creator has been struck down by a vicious illness. She wants to see you, Amber, and Tai San before her time on this Earth runs out."

"What do you mean 'runs out'?" Amber said, mirroring what all the Mall Rats were feeling. "She appeared totally fine when she visited."

"Indeed. Certainly not now. And I wonder - why?" The Selector asked inquisitively, suspiciously.

"What's that supposed to mean?" Trudy asked.

The Selector explained that The Creator had faced a rapid decline in her health when she had returned to The Vault. And he was there to personally escort Amber and Tai San to see her. Immediately.

"In the meantime, as Deputy of The Collective I will be the temporary Leader. So I suggest you follow my instructions. And my first order, pending a formal enquiry – is to place you, Lex, on house arrest."

"What? That's outrageous! I haven't done anything!" Lex shouted.

"Then you have nothing to fear," The Selector said. "But I know our Supreme Council will want some answers if The Creator dies as to why you took her out on the lake alone. Some might wonder if you had tried to drown her. Or even if she picked up some bacteria in the water."

"That was her idea to take a boat trip – not mine!"

"I'm not here to adjudicate on any evidence, Lex. That is the duty of the Supreme Council. My priority right now is to insist that The Creator's wishes are carried out. Especially if it is indeed her last wishes," he added, his voice cracking slightly with emotion,

* * *

Amber and Tai San were escorted through all security check points at Project Eden and raced down the long, metallic corridors of The Vault, accompanied by The Selector and the inner sanctum guards, the group walking briskly at pace, breaking out into a run at times, to quickly get to The Collective leader.

Tai San and Amber had both been shocked that the reason for Cami's sudden illness levied by The Selector had been aimed at Lex and knew it was a false claim. There had either been a genuine misunderstanding or it was a deliberate charge looking to pin the blame on him, for whatever reason. If someone was hoping to frame Lex for any tragedy that might occur if anything did indeed happen to Cami, then both Tai San and Amber knew that all the Mall Rats would do everything in their power to prevent Lex from becoming a scapegoat in some future hearing of the Supreme Council.

They also didn't trust The Selector in the slightest – and his seemingly self-proclaimed reluctance to take over the leadership of The Collective in light of what was happening. The thought of that situation evoked nothing but dread.

Tai San, Amber and The Selector rushed into the inner sanctum of The Creator while the guards stood either side of the huge doors.

Cami was laying stretched out on a bed, the Surgeon General and her medic team attending their leader, checking monitors on various machines displaying Cami's vital signs.

"What's happened!?" Amber said.

"It's difficult to know. So far, we have been unable to identify a specific diagnosis," the Surgeon General advised.

Cami was murmuring in pain, her body dripping wet with perspiration, beads of sweat on her brow, the medics gently patting it with a facecloth.

"She's got a fever, her temperature's sky high," the Surgeon General said, looking at the monitors of the medical equipment. "I can't understand why the computer monitoring system is not picking anything up. I think it's possibly a virulent strain of staphylococcus that's invaded her system, hopefully not her blood stream. It's like she is being poisoned somehow."

The Surgeon General explained that Cami had been given medication to try and stabilize her but so far there hadn't been any improvement in Cami's health – but the opposite, a complete decline.

Suddenly, the inner sanctum was placed in total darkness, followed by a pulsing alarm and red-flashing warning lights, along with a voice belonging to an adult female.

"RED ALERT. ALL FORMS OF LIFE FORCE D-Y-I-N-G."

The voice lowered in tone and pitch to a deep voice as if the occupant of the voice was also dying.

Auxiliary emergency lighting was automatically activated, casting looming, eerie shadows and illuminating The Selector, the Surgeon General and her medics, and Amber and Tai San, who gazed around, in mounting panic.

"That voice. Who is it!?" Amber said. "More importantly – where's it coming from?"

"ACCESS DENIED. ACCESS DENIED. ACCESS DENIED. MALICIOUS VIRUS QUARANTINED.

LIFE SYSTEMS ATTEMPTING TO BE RESTORED," the voice boomed again through a range of security speakers in the ceiling. The pulsing red lights suddenly stopped, as did the alarm. The auxiliary light faded, replaced by the normal lighting systems coming on again.

The Surgeon General gazed at the blips on the medical monitors. "That's interesting," she said. "The vital signs are stabilizing."

"What is this? Are you saying the computer monitoring systems had something to do with it?" The Selector asked, in a mixture of confusion and concern.

"It certainly seems that way," the Surgeon General reflected, as confused as all the others who were present.

"It must be overriding our normal online systems, monitoring The Creator's personal microchip," the Surgeon General surmised.

"You're not seriously suggesting that a computer has been trying to harm Cami?" Amber probed.

The Selector gazed suspiciously at the Surgeon General. Tai San's antennae picked up that he was communicating something unsaid when the Surgeon General replied, overly casually:-

"Could be... could be. I think it might be wise for our technology teams to investigate. I'll go and brief them, shall I, Selector?"

"Urgently," The Selector instructed.

The Surgeon General, followed by her medic team, left and Cami spoke softly, regaining consciousness and recognizing Amber and Tai San.

"Amber... Tai San... How good of you to visit."

Their presence gave Cami renewed energy, determination. She asked if The Selector would take Tai San to the biodome to obtain some herbs which she believed might help make her feel better. And it would give Cami some time to speak with Amber – alone.

The Selector was reluctant to agree to the request, preferring that The Creator rest and conserve her energy. Cami reassured The Selector that she was fine.

Though he was opposed, The Selector obsequiously bowed his head in a display of respect and left Amber alone in the room, indicating for Tai San to follow him.

* * *

Tai San focused on the multitude of herb varieties growing inside the vast glass panels of the biodome. Eden was aptly named – every time Tai San had visited the dome, it felt like she was in some garden of Eden, lush with plant life, a self-contained world of natural wonders, a peaceful and quiet environment protecting the plants within from the chaos and uncertainty of the outside world inside the mammoth, hermetically-sealed dome.

There was little time to enjoy being around the plant life, however. Tai San's mission there was urgent. She was looking for specific herbs and hoped she would be able to get them in time to help the dire situation with Cami's health.

Cami clearly knew the benefits of homeopathic medicine, Tai San thought, as she gathered up a range of various herbs and spices and plants because Tai San had been raised to practice alternative medicine rather than conventional.

She had already retrieved some large amounts of Coneflower, Goldenseal, Ginseng and Ginger – and although Cami hadn't requested, Tai San thought she should pick some Elderflower.

The Selector had been by her side constantly since he escorted her to the biodome.

As Tai San gathered her supplies, The Selector seemed more interested in discussing the future he envisaged after Cami's death, with him taking over her place as permanent leader.

He hoped Tai San would have a part in that future – and be by his side. Perhaps to head research into plant life, herbs, spices, medicine - anything she wanted. It was apparent to Tai San, not that she needed further convincing, that The Selector was still personally enamoured of her – which was bordering on an obsessional level.

It had been a deeply unpleasant experience for Tai San. She hated having him around, the insincere flattery and compliments he was paying her, especially when his 'former' leader, as he intimated, was on her deathbed.

The Selector seemed to have everything worked out. A plan of some kind, which involved Tai San. He hinted that if Tai San felt Lex still had a place in her heart – he hoped she would come to accept The Selector, as she did Lex, in the future.

Tai San had no option but to listen to The Selector, to have him follow her, like a moth to a flame, wherever she went in the biodome while she collected the herbs and spices. He certainly admired her skills.

The Selector's 'skills', however, were more to do with manipulation and treachery, Tai San thought, faking a smile at him as he complimented her on how beautiful her eyes were, the latest of many praises he had accorded her. She didn't want to encourage his advances or lead him on – or let him know, of course, what she was truly thinking. But she didn't want to totally alienate him at this vulnerable state in time.

"That's kind of you to say," Tai San replied, at his compliment.

She turned to pick more Elderflower, then advised that she was ready to leave. "I've finally been able to get everything that I need," she advised.

"So have I," The Selector informed her – and leaned in, to give Tai San a kiss.

She recoiled, and The Selector's charm was suddenly replaced by an ice-cold smile. "Do you not find me – attractive?"

"I'm in a relationship with Lex," Tai San replied, not knowing what else to say - with the truth being that rather than attractive, the only thing he evoked in her was repulsion.

"Tai San, you are not only a beautiful woman but a spiritual one. And a clever one as well. And I would hate if anything ever happened to you or Lex. So a piece of advice:- whenever you're making any decisions, just make sure they're not ones you might one day come to regret."

He smiled benevolently, Tai San aware of the veiled threat.

The Selector drew her closer again and feeling totally repulsed, like she was going to be sick, Tai San accepted the kiss, trying somehow not to vomit into The Selector's mouth.

"You don't know how long I've been wanting to do that," The Selector said, releasing Tai San from his embrace.

"We need to get back to Cami immediately," Tai San urged.

The Selector moved forward, as if he was going to embrace and kiss her again.

The lights flickered, the electricity surging once more – and the biodome was plunged into darkness.

When the auxiliary lighting went on less than a minute later, The Selector was enraged. There was no sign of Tai San anywhere. She had gone.

* * *

Amber tenderly wiped Cami's brow with the cloth she had just rinsed in cold water, hoping to lower the high temperature that Cami was affected by.

She was joined by Tai San, who had returned from the biodome and was now preparing a selection of herbs and plants, grinding them in a bowl to a pulp, to produce liquid.

Tai San worked quickly, suspecting that before long The Selector would return, and she hoped that The Creator might be the one giving instructions to the guards waiting outside the entrance doors, rather than anyone taking orders from The Selector - if indeed they were all in the midst of a nefarious coup.

The Creator of The Collective was conscious, mostly, but seemed to be passing in and out of it often, sometimes lying still, almost silent – making Amber and Tai San fear the worst, that she might have slipped from this world.

Tai San couldn't say for sure if any of the computer monitoring systems had anything to do with it as the Surgeon General had implied earlier. Tai San suspected that a possible cause could have something to do with the Elderberries she had observed in the containers in the inner sanctum. They were exquisite but needed to be cooked. If eaten raw, then they were highly dangerous and could poison the system.

Amber felt she and Tai San needed to give Cami hope. Something to live for. The belief that she could survive her illness and fully recover.

While Tai San had been away in the biodome, in an attempt to make sure Cami remained awake, Amber had engaged her in conversation, asking Cami questions about her past. She had spoken affectionately of her mother and the work she had done as an evolutionary biologist at The Vault, helping to conserve the rare and endangered species which had been brought there, not only the plants but the many forms of animal life.

Amber probed more about what Cami had revealed regarding not being close to her mother. Cami had advised that her mother was often away due to work commitments or attending lectures at conferences around the world. Cami would often be left on her own, under the care of her nanny, and absorbed herself in reading a range of literature, studying her mother's selection of books and research – many of which dealt with themes of evolution.

But it wasn't all scholarly pursuits. Cami's other passion she had developed was online gaming – and it offered a chance to interact and meet interesting people from all over the world. Being mostly introverted and reclusive, Cami never had any friends as such and she had often found the world of technology and computers to be a refuge.

Being online provided her with a way to interact with others. She had found it fascinating hearing different opinions to her own, learning about the lives of others and viewing it as a living experiment, a form of sociology almost, as she got a sense of the 'culture' of those she interacted with – what they believed in, how they filled their days, what their existence meant to them.

Tai San crossed to the bed with a small spoon.

"Let's try and get her to sit up and sip on this," Tai San said, indicating the liquid concoction she had ground in the bowl.

Amber gently aided Cami, fluffing the pillows behind her back. "There we go," Amber said, gently. "Now please try and take a few sips of this. Tai San has prepared it and we think it might help you feel better."

Cami sipped but winced occasionally in distress, her body fighting whatever illness was within.

"Try and take some more, Cami," Tai San said. "I'm sure it will help make you feel better."

"We're both here with you," Amber continued. "Try and take as much as you can and think about how you'd like life to be, fifty years from now. Imagine you're telling us about your life then – and all the things that you had done."

Cami continued sipping on the medicine and although her voice was still weak, she spoke, letting Amber and Tai San know how she wished to fall in love – and had never really thought about it so far ahead. But if she could, she hoped to be a mother, even a grandmother, and to have helped rebuild not only society but make her mark on it. And that maybe she, Tai San and Amber would have become firm friends by then, growing old, becoming the first of the next generation of adults who had survived the previous generation who had all perished before.

Amber and Tai San were encouraged by what they were hearing. Not solely Cami's dreams but the fact that she was remaining conscious.

Cami's illness brought back painful memories of those who had perished during the height of the pandemic, when they would never wake, their ravaged bodies giving up not long after they lost the spirit and will to live on.

Amber agreed with Tai San's hypothesis that spiritually - the power of the mind was so very important whereby the human condition relies on the need to have something to live for.

"We can make it happen, together," Amber encouraged, while Cami sipped more of the liquid Tai San was offering from the spoon.

"After all, if you keep that dream to yourself, it might forever stay a dream," Tai San added. "But if you share it with others, they can help you make that dream become a reality."

Unbeknownst to Amber and Tai San – they were being observed from several angles, all at once, by surveillance cameras, not required for security but the source of live feeds which were being monitored several levels down, in the depths of The Vault, in the very lowest level in a highly-classified area that The Collective leader was the only human in this generation to know about it – and of what was located inside the secured section.

The live feeds were linked into a highly powerful system with an ability to process trillions of calculations per second, built of the most advanced prototype components humanity had constructed before the collapse of its civilization, powered by its own energy source – the sound and images that had been digitized and input into its vast memory banks had been quickly processed and assimilated by the network of central processing units that formed the hardware and system which hosted the artificial intelligence of the *K.A.M.I* supercomputer.

It was the original prototype to its sister, housed in Eagle Mountain, and yet another one in Arthurs Air Force Base. But at the height of the pandemic, it had been upgraded. And eventually after the demise of the adults, Cami had adapted some of the software herself.

It had been nicknamed after the little girl who was the child of the mother who had played an initial part in its development, applying biological principles and evolutionary theory to the self-aware software so it would have the ability to learn, to adapt and evolve – and in so doing, given life, in digital form, to the *Knowledge Artificial Machine Intelligence* mainframe computer that controlled every aspect of The Vault and Eden's infrastructure.

The human Cami had grown up into a capable and confident teenager – she had worked closely with the supercomputer that bore the moniker of her name, getting its advice, channeling its resources, the digital *K.A.M.I* system having been pivotal in the success of The Collective, being shaped in its development and education, learning from The Collective leader. It, too, in tandem with its human companion, *K.A.M.I*, had adapted and evolved, developing an identity of its own, an awareness.

And it had paid attention to the advice Tai San and Amber had been giving its grievously ill 'friend'. The only companion the *K.A.M.I* system had ever known since the adults perished.

Now, the system was concerned what might occur if the human Cami might die. And it was running programmes, believing that the sister *K.A.M.I* in Eagle Mountain was a threat, trying to attack not only the human Cami but the *K.A.M.I* system itself. And it knew exactly what to do.

As Tai San gave Cami the last of the herbal juice, all three froze at the sudden intrusion of the alarm again. The inner sanctum fell into darkness. Amber, Tai San and Cami were illuminated by a pulsing light as they listened to the computer *K.A.M.I* system's voice booming through the speakers – again, the voice phased slightly now, but still very clearly a female adult's voice:-

"PREPARE TO EVACUATE. PREPARE TO EVACUATE. PREPARE TO EVACUATE. ALL DEFENCE SYSTEMS ACTIVE."

The guards each side of the front entrance doors leapt as a mammoth metal door within the ceiling hurled down, with a gigantic thud, the metallic noise echoing around and around the inner sanctum.

"What was that!?" Amber asked, panic-stricken, gazing around the semi-darkness and blocking her ears slightly, as were Tai San and Cami, at the deafening pulsating alarm, which was becoming louder and louder.

"We seem to be at the highest security threat level," Cami said, weakly. "Which means that the highest form of defence mechanisms will have been activated. Including the backup security doors to The Vault. Fortunately, no one will ever be able to get in. But there is a great danger, that unfortunately we might never equally be able to get out."

Tai San, Cami and Amber exchanged terrified glances at the prospect that they were now seemingly entombed, cut off from the world, possibly forever.

CHAPTER THIRTY-ONE

Ebony was glad when darkness fell. She was taking cover in bushes bordering the deserted, bleak highway. Emma was asleep.

Ebony had earlier recommended that they stay hidden until nightfall and speculated with Emma, wondering if they had indeed been set up by The Gamesmaster, suspecting that their current plight was yet another test. So far, they hadn't encountered any sign of another human being since arriving at the far end of the lake, where they were to have been met by someone, according to The Gamesmaster, to provide further instruction.

When the dawn had broken, Ebony noticed a figure in the distance and asked Emma to stay put, under cover, while she investigated to check if the figure was the planned contact.

But it had become apparent when the figure became more visible, as Ebony approached, that the figure was a farm worker, probably a slave, toiling the land, as the sun rose.

What disturbed Ebony was that in noticing her, he seemed in utter shock when he recognized her, treating her like some kind of superstar.

"Is it really you? Ebony – from The Cube!?" the farm worker asked.

Ebony wasn't going to confirm or deny for fear of giving any information away. She did enquire tentatively, "Are you 'my contact' who I'm supposed to meet?"

"I don't know what you mean," the farm worker replied, with a sudden sense of unease.

"Ever heard of The Gamesmaster?" Ebony asked.

"Please. I beg you. If you're looking for a contestant - I don't want any part of it!" the farm worker screamed, in total fear as he ran as far away as he could in utter distress.

Ebony watched him recede into the distance, then returned to where Emma was in hiding and recommended that they stay undercover for the rest of the day and then travel under the cover of night.

The problem though was which way to go. They agreed that they only had four options: being north, south, east, west.

Suddenly, Ebony and Emma were both bathed in the glare of the headlights from an approaching vehicle and recoiled, moving deeper into the bushes. To their relief, the vehicle sped past. It was a military vehicle, a large truck which suddenly screeched to a skidding stop and reversed at high speed.

"Let's get out of here! They don't look too friendly!" Ebony whispered in an undertone to Emma and led her further into the bush before being easily and quickly seized by four guards, who brought them to the back of the vehicle.

Ebony climbed in, assisting Emma, and was stunned to discover Bray, Alice, Tiffany and Shannon were also in the back.

Tiffany and Shannon rushed to give their sister a huge hug while Bray tried somehow to reassure her.

"It's alright, Emma. It's alright. You're totally safe," Bray said.

Ebony gazed in utter disbelief and confusion, struggling to reconcile what she was seeing with her very own eyes.

"I never thought I'd see you again, Ebony," Alice said exuberantly.

"That makes two of us," Ebony replied, steadying herself as the vehicle sped away. "What the hell's going on!?"

* * *

"We've got to get you out of here," Ryan said to Lex.

They were in the main lounge at the *Lakeside Resort* with Salene and Trudy.

May was in Amber's room, keeping an eye on baby Jay, who was fast asleep. She was also watching Sammy, Lottie and Brady, who had been brought to the room, and had been reading the younger Mall Rats stories.

"You've always been there for me, Lex. And if anyone wants to lay a finger on you, then they'll have to get past me first," Ryan said.

"The way The Selector was speaking, I think it might be more than a finger Lex can expect," Trudy said.

"Well, he'll soon discover where he can shove his finger and anything else. No way I'm being set up. Appreciate the support, Ryan. I owe you one."

"I hope Amber and Tai San are alright," Salene said, uneasily and suddenly cried out as the resort was plunged into total darkness.

"What's happening!?" Trudy yelled.

"That's what I'd like to know. Something's going down, you can bet on it!" Lex exclaimed.

The emergency auxiliary lighting cast a dim glow, outlining Storm, arriving with his security detail. "Everybody okay?" he asked.

The Mall Rats advised that they were all fine but were becoming increasingly concerned when Storm informed them that all the water, for some reason, had been switched off, the electricity grid seemed to have been compromised, and the plumbing was out, as well as his communication devices, which illustrated there were some problems with their computer network.

Trudy was keen to go and check on May and the children, as indeed were Salene, Ryan and Lex.

Storm tried to reassure them that it was probably just a glitch and nothing to worry about.

"I wouldn't be too sure about that," Lex stated, noting beams of light cutting a path through the darkness and the glass entrance doors to the resort as a militia truck screeched to a stop in the driveway.

Then all the Mall Rats stared open-mouthed as Bray, Alice, Ebony, Shannon and Tiffany led Emma through the doors, followed by guards.

Lex and Ryan immediately leapt into action with the security detail already at the resort but Storm ordered his team to stand down, that no action was needed. For the time being, at least.

* * *

The streets in Eden were crowded. Ever since the first power outage, the inhabitants who lived there had been anxious and unsettled at the disruption that had descended upon their lives.

Now, there was no electricity at all and like the problems at the *Lakeside Resort*, there was no water or plumbing or Internet or communication systems.

Throughout the lands, the surviving generations since the adults' demise no longer lived in a digital world but mostly an analogue one. Some were fortunate to enjoy modern conveniences such as all at Eden, thanks to an ability to have hooked into the once highly-classified UNANET system - which had been discovered to have remained in existence in the event of any post-apocalyptic event, arranged initially at a tense time in the history of the Cold War, many years before the virus descended. Other survivors and many tribes across all the lands lived an almost primitive existence reminiscent of the Dark Ages.

Now Eden had, for some reason, been plunged into total darkness, barring a few battery-powered flashlights that some of the guards were wielding to guide people and which were used by medics in the hospital so they could illuminate their way as they evacuated the patients and young mothers-to-be from the buildings where they had been in their care.

There had never been anything like it in Eden - for so long a place of order, stability, routine, efficiency. The community had mysteriously been struck down, its interconnected infrastructure under siege, grinding the apparatus of so much of what the residents depended on to a halt.

A collective feeling of panic, uncertainty prevailed. Rumours were circulating. Suspicious talk of a coup taking place or that Eden was under assault from outside forces, the first stage in an inevitable invasion by rival power blocks. Others felt that they could have displeased or offended Zoot – brought upon his wrath, the mighty spirit of Zoot punishing them somehow – and that this could only be the start of a new divinely-interventioned apocalypse, heralding the end of their days.

Further down the lake, The Selector hid in his lodge and was struggling to control his nervous tics, breathing in through his nose and out through his mouth to try and somehow calm himself.

He was expecting a coup but not exactly unfolding in such a way and he couldn't grasp who might be responsible. Or why it was all occurring.

* * *

Unknown to all in the faraway lands of Eden – Ram inadvertently had a hand in it. Though he wasn't quite totally responsible and didn't even know so at that time.

All he was aware of so far was that he had successfully managed to hack into the Eagle Mountain *K.A.M.I* system, giving him a pathway to evading firewalls protecting the main colossus *K.A.M.I* system at Eden where he was now attempting to attack various programmes, shutting them down, going directly into the core operating system, altering lines of code, breaking the software apart and the infrastructure systems that were dependent upon it, from working.

"How are we doing?" Jack asked.

"I'll let you know when I've figured it out myself," Ram said absently.

"Is there anything we can do to help?" Ellie asked.

"If I can't work it out - then you've got no chance."

"No need to be like that," Jack said, coming to Ellie's defence. But she shook her head slightly, indicating for Jack not to pursue it, aware that Ram was not only preoccupied but seemed agitated, not quite believing what he was seeing on his computer screen. The images also visible on the mammoth screen covering the entire wall - which had elicited a gasp of surprise from The Virts sitting behind Ellie, Jack, Ram and Ved on the main dais.

"What's all that stuff?" Jack said, confused.

"Software data. What do you think it is!?" Ram snapped, irritably before glaring at Ved. "Do you know anything about this?"

Ved was eagerly casting his eyes across the complex lettering and numbers filling the wall on the screen and clearly was struggling to assimilate it.

"No! I haven't got a clue!" Ved said.

Ram typed in more details on his keyboard and gazed at the text on his screen and covering the entire wall, yelling panicked instructions:- "Ellie – I need an urgent firewall in subsection 31A. Move it, move it! Jack – you'd better take a look at ports 14 to 28 and get a few firewalls in there, too! As quick as you can, Jack! Ved, check out the interpositive and internegative bisections bordering the mega data in article 2."

"Is everything… alright, Ram?" Ellie asked nervously, aware that Ram was becoming increasingly alarmed, almost terror-stricken.

And suddenly, footage of Ram appeared on the screen. Ram, in days gone by, trapped in his virtual reality wheelchair on the garbage dump, thrusting his hands in the air, drool spewing from his mouth, and screaming in pure disbelief, "This isn't reality space – this is R-E-A-L!!!"

"What the hell's going on?" Ved yelled, fearfully.

"What do you think!? We've been hacked!"

"By who!?" Jack asked, in utter anguish. "It can't be the *K.A.M.I* system in Eagle Mountain because I've set up a firewall – unless you made a mistake with the codes?"

"No, no mistake, Jack! The hack isn't from Eagle Mountain! I reckon it's coming from its sister, the *K.A.M.I* prototype in Project Eden!" Ram said, unable to believe his own thought process.

"So, what does it all mean?" Jack asked, in mounting panic.

"That *K.A.M.I* prototype not only has artificial intelligence. But it's self-aware. It seems to be not only attacking the system in Eagle Mountain but it's now ripping apart all my personal hard drives. We're going to have to shut down because I reckon we've got a hell of a virus inflicted on all our core systems!"

* * *

Back on the streets of Eden, the inhabitants were still out in force, many now carrying flaming torches to help them see in the darkness. All screamed out in unison as a voice suddenly boomed through the community loudspeakers. Again, the voice was soft, soothing, that of an adult female.

"THIS IS *K.A.M.I*," the voice said, the tone slightly phased, digitized. "I – THE CREATOR – AM ILL. A COUP HAS BEEN INSTIGATED AGAINST ME. AND I NEED YOUR HELP IN MY TIME OF NEED. IF I DO NOT SURVIVE THE ACTIONS OF MY USURPER, WE WILL NOT ADAPT AND EVOLVE."

Suddenly the voice stopped, replaced with the frenzied shouting of Zoot: "*Rise up!! Take control!!!!!*"

The crowds gazed around, confused, and cast glances up at the heavens where the voice seemed to originate from, reverberating and echoing all around.

The crowd recoiled, totally panic-stricken, as images of Zoot appeared on the walls of the many buildings, images derived from Ram's reality space programmes of Zoot - seemingly resurrected, screaming manically, arms aloft: "*Power and Chaos! Power and Chaos! Power and Chaos!*"

* * *

Back in Ram's old Techno headquarters, Ram, Ellie, Jack and Ved, along with the Virt spectators, stared open-mouthed at the same images on the screen of Zoot, imploring all to rise up and take control, to inflict Power and Chaos.

"Did you do that?" Jack screamed, above the noise.

"You don't understand it, do you?" Ram said, almost unable to believe it himself. "I think we've not just unleashed the dogs of war – but our friend, the *K.A.M.I* system in Eagle Mountain, seems to be in a battle with the prototype colossus *K.A.M.I* system in Project Eden."

"Are you saying the computers are fighting each other!?" Ellie asked, panic-stricken.

"Not just each other – but us as well. All my drives… they're being used against us," Ram said, clutching his head with his hands. "Oh God – what have I done!?"

* * *

In the inner sanctum of The Vault, sealed off from the inhabitants at Eden, Cami led Amber and Tai San into the lower levels, Cami inserting codes to enable them to proceed through the semi-darkness, the three of them illuminated in the glow of a pulsing red light.

Finally, reaching the lowest level, Cami led Tai San and Amber into a cavernous area.

"Hello, *K.A.M.I,*" Cami said, calmly to the mainframe colossus system, its infrastructure towering way above Tai San, Amber and the human Cami, its lights blinking, hard drives whirring, its bank of monitors showing various images, such as the evacuations occurring all over the world at the height of the pandemic and news anchors of broadcasters of the time stating that "*Authorities are appealing for calm throughout the evacuation process.*"

Other monitors displayed the enigmatic Area 51, the source of so many conspiracy theories in the old world. Another monitor, pictures of empty, ghostly streets - a patrol vehicle, its windows darkened, advising any stragglers still in their homes, through its loudspeaker on top of the vehicle, that "*Code 1, civil isolation was now in effect.*"

On another monitor, much to Tai San and Amber's great concern, an image showing a range of surface to air missiles from the adult days - with data appearing on the monitor confirming that nuclear warheads were on standby. And requesting verification with everything being on high alert - simply requiring the final instruction, that the system was locked and loaded, ready to go.

"Is that image on that monitor what I think it is!?" Amber asked, uneasily.

"Don't worry. It's from the old world and obsolete. *K.A.M.I's* just cleaning out its files, indexing and self-regulating."

"WHAT ARE YOU DOING HERE, CHILD? YOU SHOULD BE IN BED," *K.A.M.I* reprimanded.

Cami was still weak from her illness but the remedy Tai San had offered was already showing positive results and that she was alert – though slightly embarrassed. "That's my mother's voice. I programmed it myself. So you'll have to excuse *K.A.M.I.* It seems a bit confused right now."

All the images on the monitors implanted into the mammoth superstructure of the colossal mainframe computer disappeared and were replaced by a satellite orbiting the earth.

Each monitor emitted sounds of a variety of voices overlapping in various languages through which Amber and Tai San recognized the English element, "ATTENTION. THIS IS A PRE-RECORDED MESSAGE. IF YOU ARE LISTENING TO THIS, THE ONLY HOPE FOR HUMANITY LIES WITH YOU. WHOEVER YOU ARE."

Amber and Tai San gazed dumbfounded, recalling the mysterious time they first visited Eagle Mountain. They had only been on the upper levels at that point and had no idea even that the Eagle Mountain *K.A.M.I* computer system had ever existed. Jack, though, in the upper level had managed to log on to the computer grid accessed to a signal from a satellite circling Earth.

They had never been able to find the significance of the message. And didn't know exactly what it all meant right now. But the satellite images they were watching and the message they were listening to - the very same one they had heard so long before at Eagle Mountain - seemed to be almost like a talisman, which had led them not only to Eden but the human Cami, the very Creator herself.

* * *

A crowd of fanatical Zoot followers carrying flaming torches arrived outside the *Lakeside Resort* chanting, "Power and Chaos! Power and Chaos! Power and Chaos!"

Inside, the doors had been barred and were guarded by Storm and his detail. Lex, Ryan, Alice and Ebony were with them, ready to fight shoulder to shoulder, which would be a challenging task because they were so outnumbered by the crowd growing in size, it seemed, with each passing second.

Salene and May had locked themselves in a room to safeguard baby Jay, Brady, Lottie, Sammy, Emma, Shannon and Tiffany.

Bray led Trudy through a maintenance hatch and both moved stealthily across the rooftop towards the entrance.

They were both noticed by the crowd and some members pointed ecstatically, "It's the brother of Zoot, Bray! And The Supreme Mother!"

Bray asked, "Are you sure you're up to this, Trudy?"

Trudy nodded, braced herself and stood by Bray on the rooftop as they began addressing the assembly below, who all fell silent in reverence.

But none had ever expected what they were about to hear.

"I'm not going to tell you what you should do," Trudy began, searching for the right words. "And each of you must decide for yourself. But please listen to me. To who exactly I am. I am like you. Each and every one of you. I was a scared teenager who lived through the world crumbling, seeing the people I loved – die – and there was nothing I could do about it. All I could do was try and live – to survive. And in so doing, a lot of rumours and false things have been said about me – and my tribe. We're not special or different. Zoot wasn't some god. And my daughter is a beautiful, innocent, little girl. Neither she or I can perform any 'miracles'. And never should be worshipped. I could be any one of you – standing out there – if fate had turned out differently. And any of you could have been me. I'm not a Supreme Mother. I'm a mother. I'm not connected with any divine magic or mystical powers. I'm me. I'm normal. I'm another human being who just wants to get through each day and try and make tomorrow a little bit better than the day before."

The crowd listened attentively, some seeming as if they might accept what Trudy was saying – but others were clearly unconvinced. One shouted out, "Are you being pressurized to say this, Supreme Mother?" the voice yelled.

"No! No one's pressurizing Trudy whatsoever. And I'm not being pressured as well," Bray called out. "Yes, it's true that I am the brother of Zoot. And I loved him. But he and I... we just had a different ideology. Zoot was a proud warrior and a legend to many. But to me, somehow in this world we've all inherited, he was –

and always will be – my brother. Sadly, just someone troubled, who lost their way."

* * *

Back in The Technos' quarters, Ellie, Jack, Ram and Ved - along with the Virt spectators - watched a series of visuals on the screen along the wall, differing images which seemed to be fragmenting and increasing. Images of planets, polar ice caps melting, plague and famine, in barren lands, politicians in the old-world making speeches, Zoot, Ram in his virtual reality paradise.

"Do you reckon those computers are still fighting?" Jack asked, gazing intently at the mammoth screen. "And if so – who's winning?"

"Certainly not us," Ram said.

"What do we do now?" Ellie asked, in growing panic.

Ram tilted his head from side to side, cracked his knuckles, shook his arms slightly and started to type fervently. "We've gotta get back in 'the game'."

"How?" Ved asked, incredulously.

The images on the screen across the wall disappeared and Ram laughed enthusiastically, whooping it up.

"Ellie, Jack and Ved – you'd better listen carefully to all my instructions. It's - game on!"

* * *

The crowd outside the *Lakeside Resort*, along with Bray and Trudy, gazed dumbfoundedly at a series of drones approaching at tremendous speed, zigzagging as if out of control and swooping low over the assembly.

"It's a sign from the Mighty One! He must be avenged!" a voice yelled.

Most of the crowd though were dispersing, some clearly accepting what Trudy and Bray had said and now, mostly concerned about the out of control drones, began to flee, while a few remaining pointed at Lex through the locked glass window doors.

"It's him! He's the one responsible for killing our God, Zoot!"

With the crush, the crowd were able to enter the lobby area and hand to hand combat occurred, with Alice knocking several of the attacking crowd out with single blows. Ebony was equally effective, like the streetfighter she was. So, too, were Ryan and Lex, disposing of opponents amidst a spectacle of swirling, mixed martial arts, kicks.

Trudy returned to watch over the children in her room, giving Salene, May and Bray the chance to enter into the battle, fighting alongside Lex, Ryan, Alice, Ebony, Storm and his guards.

In the midst of battle, each side ducked for cover as an out of control drone sped into the lobby, zigzagging as if attacking anyone left standing, prior to smashing totally out of control through a back window, crash-landing and descending into the lake.

With the superior fighting skills of the Mall Rats and Storm and the guards, the battle ended in no time at all after it began, with the crowd dispersing - Storm, the guards, Alice, May, Salene, Bray, Lex, Ryan and Ebony regained their breath, all exhausted, and exchanged high-fives.

* * *

On the ground level in the inner sanctum, Cami sat at a table typing data into a keyboard, advising Tai San and Amber that some unknown force seemed to have tried to hack the main *K.A.M.I* system. And had succeeded. But now, she had matters under control.

Tai San and Amber exchanged knowing glances, suspecting who might possibly be responsible.

* * *

On the streets of Eden, calmness began to descend as the main lights were switched back on, as were normal supplies of water, plumbing and communication.

Bray and Lex arrived shortly thereafter in a driverless pod vehicle, accompanied by a few of Storm's guards. Storm himself, along with Ebony, Alice and Ryan, were left behind to help guard their fellow Mall Rats and friends in the event of something untoward occurring again.

* * *

Bray and Lex raced to the inner sanctum just as the mammoth security doors slid upwards. But they were stopped by the guards either side of the doors from entering.

"It's alright," Cami said, appearing at the doorway with Amber and Tai San, who rushed into Bray and Lex's arms.

"Thank goodness you're okay!" Amber said, as she tried to contain emotion, hugging Bray tightly.

"We've got a lot to catch up on," Bray said. "What's been going on here?"

"Any sign of The Selector?" Tai San asked, uneasily, as she gripped tightly in her embrace of Lex.

"Not as far as I know," Lex reassured her. "Take it easy. Everything's okay. It's all over."

"But I think it's not the end," Cami replied. "It's only just begun…"

EPILOGUE

The Creator was no more – but Cami lived on.

She had managed to survive the serious infection that she had been deliberately infected with. Tai San's herbal medicine had helped stem the spread. Cami was impressed by Tai San's knowledge of the natural world and alternative medicine, as indeed was the Surgeon General and her team of medics.

Their monitoring system was in total disarray due to Ram inadvertently hacking the *K.A.M.I* system at Eden which checked the health of The Collective, including Cami, and a range of other important elements of society.

The Selector and those loyal to him had been prevented in their bid from toppling Cami and seizing power.

The Selector was arrested, along with the last vestige of Collective renegade warriors who were obedient to him – and their group was transported to the island in the lake where The Cube was located, The Selector's own creation, isolated as it was and well-guarded, becoming his prison pending the future trial that would occur.

He was charged with not solely the attempted murder of Cami but a range of other indignities and crimes he had committed during his position of influence in The Collective, all of which Cami herself had been completely unaware of.

Ironically, he himself was to be the victim of an attempted coup by the resistance, led by his perceived loyal follower, Commander Snake.

The Mall Rats worked with Cami and The Collective on a temporary basis in the aftermath of the attempted coup, feeling that Cami needed assistance to stabilize the society and restructure and rebuild.

The Collective had so much potential for doing good and there needed to be a transition period to assess what would be the best future for all who lived under its auspices previously. History was full of fragmentation and dissension resulting from factions and groups jostling for authority if there was a sudden vacuum following a coup, while The Collective was being rehabilitated. So the Mall Rats felt they had no option but to accept Cami's request for them to work alongside her in the short-term as caretakers in charge.

Cami blamed herself in part for her plight believing that she had been foolish and too trusting to have delegated so much power allowing, inadvertently, The Selector to have brought so much discontent and suffering to so many. Cami genuinely wanted to learn, to improve – to adapt and evolve – and she realized this was something she wouldn't be able to do on her own.

Working with Cami and her Supreme Council, the Mall Rats helped draft a Bill of Rights to facilitate a New Collective who could maintain communication with one another and form a commonwealth of tribes who would establish trade and co-operation, as well as a security alliance, to aid each other and to shape a new world from the ashes of the old.

Those who preferred to stay behind in Eden and live among the new, revitalized – and changed – Collective would have the right to do so. They would hold regular elections, to be monitored by an independent committee, and vote for representatives who would govern them in their own form of parliamentary democracy. Never again would so much power be controlled by one or two individuals, as it had been with The Selector administrating matters.

There would be religious freedoms. A central Zootist faith would certainly never again be encouraged or promoted by the Collective authorities – and Bray was insistent that the truth of his brother be publicly known, hoping it would dispel the myths and legend of Zoot that had otherwise built up and indeed been spread previously by The Collective propaganda.

Those, however, who wanted to believe in any religion would have the right to do so. But all on the Supreme Council had yet to reconcile within the constitution the definition of freedoms within the new laws if they denied the right of any zealots who worshipped Zoot. They would have to ensure it didn't infringe on the lives and freedoms of others, of course, but for true freedom and a society of toleration, there needed to be the right for every person to pursue whatever religion they wanted to follow, just as long as it wasn't unlawful.

The Void was also abolished from existence by the new laws and its inhabitants were to be rehabilitated. Cami was stunned to discover that it had even existed in the first place.

The Broker was arrested and was to be put on trial, given the nefarious activities he had undertaken throughout his trading. And all slaves were set free. Cami had fully sanctioned the agricultural unit in her regime but was totally unaware that the workers were treated in such a repugnant manner.

The new 'blueprint' that had been drafted at Eden was something Amber wanted to roll out and bring back with her when she eventually returned to their home city.

The New Collective of tribes within the constitution would investigate and share access to any knowledge uncovered from the adults' scientific and military bases, such as Arthurs Air Force Base and Eagle Mountain. It was hoped that any technological resources could be adapted and 'datamined' to help create the foundations for the new civilization all hoped would arise in the aftermath of the adults' demise.

There was so much advanced and powerful technology that could aid the new world in the bases, which Cami had already adapted and utilized. Highly developed drones, automated vehicles, equipment to harvest sustainable renewable energy sources with efficient solar and wind powered batteries, seed banks to restore agriculture and food production, vast quantities of stockpiled medicines that the adults had put away in The Vault, reserves of fuel to power the internal combustion engines of the still functional vehicles from the adult times, which were slowly being phased out, replaced with other forms of energy.

These were all important legacies from the adult era which could help propel future innovation and improve the quality of life for so many - when the world otherwise seemed like it could so easily tip into a primitive, anarchic, new Dark Ages.

There was also the possibility that there could be more secret scientific-military installations around the region and possibly – probably more like – around the world which had been implemented in the old world by the previous generation and their desperate attempts in their last days to create a shelter for themselves, their precious material resources, and to assist a new generation who might survive in the event the previous one did not.

The Collective, Cami revealed, had just been one substantial power block. Some of her scouts and explorers who had adventured out beyond their boundaries into other regions hadn't actually come back – but those who did reported that there were other powerful entities who had risen up from the ruins of the adult world. The Western Alliance, the Eastern Kingdom – these were growing and supposedly powerful, with ambitions to expand. And one day might invade.

Amber was aware of the quotation from the acclaimed scientist Albert Einstein in the previous generations mentioning that if there ever was a Third World War, then the weapons used in any potential Fourth World War would be sticks and stones, implying a totally apocalyptic situation.

All the Mall Rats, as well as Cami and her Collective, were aware of the need for a united security force with the ability to defend themselves in the event of any future attack or conflict from any dangerous 'megatribe' associations that might be already in existence.

The Mall Rats hoped it would never come to that – how cruel the irony would be if having survived the virus and all the devastating consequences that flowed in the wake of it, if the young people who continued to live in the world without adults didn't become adults themselves due to wiping each other out in a massive, future conflict aiming at paradoxically ensuring their survival.

Jack and Ellie – along with Ram and Ved – travelled to Eden, joining the Mall Rats in the aftermath of the attempted coup.

Ellie was thrilled to be reunited with her beloved sister, Alice.

Amber was sympathetic to Ved and agreed with Bray that they would have to watch over Jay's younger brother not solely as a homage to Jay but because it was the right thing to do. Bray agreed with the sentiment of it but his motive was a little more pragmatic and practical, as he saw it, because he didn't quite trust Ved.

Ram and Cami had communicated online so often in the old world that Ram was stunned to come face to face with The Creator, the leader of The Collective he so feared - given that he was no longer *persona non grata* as a result of him breaking a deal by invading the Mall Rats' home city due to the importance of Eagle Mountain.

Cami seemed totally unlike her online personality. And certainly meeting her in the flesh was a total contradiction to what Ram perceived her to be. He wasn't prepared for such a slight, awkward, slightly shy and introverted person who clearly, from all she was trying to achieve, would never harm anything living – even a fly.

At a celebration party held at the *Lakeside Resort* following the coup, all were aware how engrossed Ram and Cami had been. Ram was especially interested in the technology of the cryogenic chambers, ostensibly a key factor he once thought fuelled The Collective's interests in Eagle Mountain.

He was totally unaware that Cami believed there was a chance that her mother had been shortlisted during the demise of the adults to be amongst the gifted and important adults who had been placed in the chambers.

Cami confirmed that a Collective advance party had been responsible for removing the bodies of the adults who were deceased due to the breakdown of the Eagle Mountain *K.A.M.I* system. The adults had now been given a respectful burial back at Eden and Cami was determined that she would never give up on her search of finding her mother, sure that there was a chance that she might be in a cryogenic chamber somehow, somewhere.

Some of the Mall Rats speculated if Cami might have finally found the true love of her life in the form of Ram. But their connection was purely down to their computer and technological prowess, both respecting each other's vast abilities and knowledge.

Cami actually seemed to be more interested in Ryan, as indeed he was with her. They danced together at the celebrations but were both awkward and shy, so it was early days.

Ryan was keen though to stay at Eden with Alice, who was considering working in the new regime in the agricultural unit with Hawk. Amber was overjoyed to be reunited with the ex-member of the Eco tribe and knew that he would be perfect, bringing much skill and dedication to his role.

Lex was amused that Ryan suddenly wanted to turn his hand at 'gardening', having never shown any interest in the natural world before. Ryan revealed that he finally understood why Tai San was so in tune with Mother Nature, let alone how her skills and abilities and knowledge of herbs and spices brought with it so much exciting information, especially medicinally.

Others thought that the match between Ryan and Cami could be interesting. It wasn't a question of brain and brawn but both could be good for each other, Ryan learning from Cami's high intellect and Cami responding to Ryan's innate gentleness and purity of spirit. So both could be equally strong and good for each other in very profound ways.

May and Salene certainly hoped Ryan would find another love and were considering utilizing the celebrations of the failed coup as a platform for their wedding but decided against it, partly out of respect for Ryan, but also because they didn't want to distract from the jubilant atmosphere as the Mall Rats and The Collective 'partied', celebrating their victory.

A simmering romance which was very apparent, however, was that Trudy and Storm were clearly attracted to each other from the way they were dancing closely and holding each other tightly on the dance floor. It was also early days but Trudy confided to Amber that she felt that she might have found 'her man' in Storm. He, along with his superior, Commander Snake, had been central within the resistance who were planning on taking down The Selector when the time was right. And Trudy was hopeful that Storm and his sister, Charlotte, might consider returning with the Mall Rats to their home city.

Emma, Tiffany and Shannon had determined, however, that they would prefer to stay at Eden and the Mall Rats thought that was a good decision given the infrastructure already in place in the educational system and also that Emma's disabilities would be best served with the support systems in place.

Ebony didn't believe Emma had much disability, however, and felt protective and close to Emma and now her siblings. She was undecided whether or not she would stay at Eden or return to their home city.

Jack and Ellie preferred that Ebony would return so at least it would be a case of 'better the devil you know'. They were never convinced that Ebony had truly changed and wanted to work with the Mall Rats - and didn't exactly trust her.

But they now believed that Ram could be fully trusted, having seen how he had helped them since the invasion. They were especially overwhelmed by his considerable knowledge in technology, mind-blown in fact by the 'mega game' they had experienced at the old Techno base. It wasn't just a question of them 'geeking out' but clearly Ram could be an asset to the tribe and any efforts of interweaving technology.

There was concern within the New Collective concerning The Guardian and Eloise - and the tribe of Zootists who were living in the northern provinces.

Eloise, who was cunning and intelligent, had originally been recruited by The Selector from the ranks of The Privileged tribe, of which she used to be a former member. This was a natural fit for them with her beautiful looks and sharp mind – and the plan, according to Cami, had been that The Selector had apparently recruited Eloise to use her charisma and leadership qualities to act as a foil, a controlling and regulating influence on The Guardian's own undoubted abilities as an orator and proponent of the Zootist faith. Eloise would be the leader, of course, with The Guardian a figurehead, an archbishop to his fellow believers.

Cami pondered on how Eloise, The Guardian and the Zootists would feature in the future – and if at all within The Collective. Probably not.

There were other Mall Rats, of course, still missing. And no news of them had surfaced to date. But the search would go on in the future to try and discover their fate.

Soon, peace and order would be restored at Eden with new laws and institutions of the New Collective to be set up under Cami's leadership – leaving only one thing more for the Mall Rats to do next.

And that was to go back home.

HOME

It was where they belonged. And it felt so good to be back.

Amber walked along the waterfront, the waves in the harbour lapping gently, the gentle breeze and warm sun providing a sense of calm and peace, a relaxing and pleasant atmosphere – the perfect weather conditions mirroring a perfect, potential, pivotal time.

She was walking with Bray, by her side. He was carrying their son, the two of them reminiscing on all the many things they had been through since the last days of the adults. They remembered the first time they had met, at the mall. The first kiss they shared. The pain of loss Bray had felt when he thought Amber had died and been taken from him. Their reunion when he found, to his joy, that Amber still lived. The day Amber discovered she was pregnant with their child. The agonizing moment she thought she would have to raise that child alone after Bray had been taken from her following the invasion of the city by Ram and his Technos.

Like the tide, their lives had ebbed and flowed. They had been apart, fate often stepping in to separate them – but by their own endeavours and in 'never giving up or giving in', they had always found a way to return to each other and be together.

After all they had experienced with Cami, The Selector and The Collective – and with the establishment of the New Collective that succeeded the old, and the commonwealth of independent tribes – Amber was feeling positive about the future for her, Bray, their son and so many others in society.

They had come so close, all of them, so many times to face the prospect of their lives turning into a nightmare, of literally losing everything they held dear and watching their society collapse and implode around them into an endless circle of decay, violence and anarchy.

But by their hard work, perseverance – and in always never losing sight of their dreams – and what could be - they had clung to their visions of the future through thick and thin – and by clinging to each other, supporting each other, no matter how hard life got, they had held on and lived to see the beginnings of the future they so wished to bring into being.

Cami was right – everyone needed something to believe in. Something to give them hope. Purpose. Meaning. A direction in their lives. Without that, they would be lost. Vulnerable. Their lives out of balance, living day to day without going forward due to the absence of any goal.

All the Mall Rats, as well as Bray and Amber, more than ever before, still had a sense of purpose. And Bray and Amber realized the importance of their future dreams as they walked along the beach, the seagulls flying overhead, watching them in great fascination.

All important to Bray and Amber was that they and the Mall Rats always kept their dreams alive.

* * *

Back in Eagle Mountain, the *K.A.M.I* computer in the cavernous vault in the lower levels of the scientific facility suddenly sprung to life, lights twinkling in the darkness, as a voice boomed through its audible facilities. The voice of its sister *K.A.M.I* prototype, located in the lower levels of Project Eden.

"THIS IS THE CREATOR. ADAPT. EVOLVE. DEFEAT. SURVIVE," the voice said. It was a familiar voice. The voice of Cami's mother...

ALSO AVAILABLE

The Tribe Audiobooks

Available on leading audiobook platforms.

The Continuing Story After Season 5

The Tribe: A New World (Season 6)
The Tribe: A New Dawn (Season 7)
The Tribe: (R)Evolution (Season 8)

Narrated by many of the original cast members from the television series, the continuing official story carries on from where the TV series ended up after 5 seasons in these immersive audiobook dramatizations by the Cloud 9 Screen Entertainment Group of the official novels by A. J. Penn. With sound effects, music and featuring guest roles, the long-awaited saga is brought to life.

Other Tribe related Audiobooks now available

Keeping The Dream Alive

A memoir by Raymond Thompson about a personal journey through life and in the motion picture and television industry, which also has an account of what occurred behind the scenes of 'The Tribe' by its creator and Executive Producer, as well as being the founder and Chief Executive of the Cloud 9 Screen Entertainment Group, who produced the iconic series.

The Tribe: Birth of the Mall Rats

A novelization by Harry Duffin with further insight and events based on the on-screen drama shown in Season 1, The Birth of The Mall Rats is the first story chronologically in a compelling series of novelizations of the global cult television phenomenon, The Tribe .

Also available as paperback and eBook formats:

Keeping The Dream Alive

by

Raymond Thompson.

The fascinating inside story about the making of the cult television series, The Tribe.

An intriguing memoir charting the life and times of how someone growing up on the wrong side of the tracks in a very poor working class environment in post-War Britain was able to journey to the glittering arena of Hollywood, providing an inspirational insight into how the one most likely to fail at school due to a special need battled and succeeded against all the odds to travel the world, founding and overseeing a prolific international independent television production company.

With humorous insight into the fertile imagination of a writer's mind, the book explores life away from the red carpet in the global world of motion pictures and television - and reveals the unique story of how the cult series 'The Tribe' came into being. Along with a personal quest to exist and survive amidst the ups and downs and pressures of a long and successful career as a writer/ producer, culminating in being appointed an Adjunct Professor and featuring in the New Years Honours List, recognized by Her Majesty Queen Elizabeth II for services to television.

The Tribe

Collector's Edition

Screenplay

by

Raymond Thompson

'The Tribe' has distinguished itself as a television series with truly cult status around the world. Almost 300 episodes were produced over 5 seasons. And the series heralded other Tribal activity, from soundtracks to albums to novel tie-ins. Including the bestselling works by A. J. Penn being 'The Tribe: A New World', 'The Tribe: A New Dawn' and 'The Tribe: (R)Evolution'. Which are rather like seasons 6, 7 & 8 in the continuing saga.

There has been much speculation about a sequel or a motion picture version which was explored in the enormously successful 'Keeping the Dream Alive' which was not only a Tribe memoir, but also a fascinating account of what occurred behind the scenes. It is also a compelling memoir of the creator of 'The Tribe' - as well as the founder of the Cloud 9 Screen Entertainment Group - who produced the iconic series. 'The Tribe' screenplay has an introduction, bringing the behind the scenes story right up to date to 2022 since the time 'Keeping the Dream Alive' was published.

And the screenplay is a must read for 'The Tribe' fans to read. Along with anyone interested in the motion picture and television industries and what it takes to bring productions from conception to the silver screen.

The Tribe: Birth Of The Mall Rats

by

Harry Duffin

The Birth of The Mall Rats is the first story in a compelling series of novelizations of the global cult television phenomenon, The Tribe.

The world began without the human race. Now, after a mysterious pandemic decimates the entire adult population, it looks as if it will end exactly the same way. Unless the young survivors – who band together in warring Tribes – overcome the power struggles, dangers and unexpected challenges in a lawless dystopian society to unite and build a new world from the ashes of the old.

Creating a new world in their own image – whatever that image might be…

FOR MORE INFORMATION

Please visit the official website

www.tribeworld.com

"Like"
on

facebook.com/thetribeofficial

twitter.com/thetribeseries

instagram.com/thetribetvseries

youtube.com/thetribetvseries

vimeo.com/cloud9screenent/vod_pages

www.ingramcontent.com/pod-product-compliance
Lightning Source LLC
Chambersburg PA
CBHW070916100726
47908CB00001B/6

* 9 7 8 1 9 9 1 1 9 3 6 0 5 *